SELF-C

Mary Brunton was ~~~~~ e
Orkneys, and was edu~~~~~
tuition she became a p~~~~~ ~~~~ French
and Italian scholar.

She married Alexande~ ~runton at the age of 20 and moved to
Bolton and then Edinburgh where she formed a close friendship
with Mrs Izett who encouraged her literary endeavours. *Self-Control*
was published in 1810/11 and was highly praised by Jane Austen
who said that she doubted if she could ever reach such a standard.
In 1815, Mary Brunton's second novel, *Discipline*, was published,
which also influenced Jane Austen. Her third novel, *Emmeline*, was
published posthumously in 1819.

Mary Brunton died tragically in childbirth in 1818, yet her slender
literary output is a central part of women's literary tradition.
Pandora is reprinting *Self-Control* and *Discipline* in the *Mothers of the
Novel* reprint series.

Sara Maitland is a feminist writer. She was born in London in
1950 and grew up there and in South West Scotland. Her
publications include with Zoe Fairbairns, Valerie Miner, Michele
Roberts and Michelene Wandor, *Tales I Tell My Mother* (1978); two
novels, a book of feminist theology, a collection of short stories, and
a study of Vesta Tilley. She is author, with Michelene Wandor, of
Arky Types, forthcoming from Pandora.

MOTHERS OF THE NOVEL

Reprint fiction from Pandora Press

Pandora is reprinting eighteenth and nineteenth century novels written by women, reintroduced to readers today and published in paperback editions. The 1986 selection is to be:

The History of Miss Betsy Thoughtless by Eliza Haywood (1751)
Introduced by Dale Spender

The Female Quixote by Charlotte Lennox (1752)
Introduced by Sandra Shulman

Emma Courtney by Mary Hays (1796)

Belinda by Maria Edgeworth (1801)
Introduced by Eva Figes

Adeline Mowbray by Amelia Opie (1804)
Introduced by Jeanette Winterson

The Wild Irish Girl by Lady Morgan (1806)
Introduced by Brigid Brophy

Self-Control by Mary Brunton (1810/11)
Introduced by Sara Maitland

Patronage by Maria Edgeworth (1814)
Introduced by Eva Figes

Discipline by Mary Brunton (1814)
Introduced by Fay Weldon

Helen by Maria Edgeworth (1834)

The companion of this exciting series is:

MOTHERS OF THE NOVEL
100 Good Women Writers Before Jane Austen
by Dale Spender

While Jane Austen was one of many women writers in her own day, she has since been cast in the role of instigator rather than inheritor of a rich and diverse tradition of women's writing.

In this wonderfully comprehensive and readable survey, Dale Spender reclaims the many women writers who made a significant contribution to the literary tradition. She describes the interconnections among the women writers, their approach and the public response to their work. She also outlines the way in which the records have since been rewritten so that women's contribution to the novel has been largely ignored.

SELF-CONTROL

A Novel by

MARY BRUNTON

Introduced by Sara Maitland

His warfare is within. – There unfatigued
His fervent spirit labours. – There he fights,
And there obtains fresh triumphs o'er himself,
And never-withering wreaths, compared with which
The laurels that a Caesar reaps are weeds

Cowper

London and New York

This edition first published in 1986
by Pandora Press (Routledge & Kegan Paul plc)

11 New Fetter Lane, London EC4P 4EE

Published in the USA by
Pandora Press (Routledge & Kegan Paul Inc.)
in association with Methuen Inc.
29 West 35th Street, New York, NY10001

Set in Ehrhardt 10 on 11½
by Columns of Reading
and printed in Great Britain
by The Guernsey Press Co Ltd,
Guernsey, Channel Islands.

Library of Congress Cataloging in Publication Data

Brunton, Mary, 1778-1818.

Self-control.
I. Title.
PR4250.B73S45 1986   823'.7   85-21777

British Library CIP Data also available

ISBN 0-86358-084-X

TO

MISS JOANNA BAILLIE

MADAM,

You would smile to hear the insect of a day pay the tribute of its praise to the lasting oak which aided its first feeble soaring – Smile then; – for a person whom nature, fortune, and inclination, alike, have marked for obscurity, one whose very name may never reach your ear, offers this tribute of respect to the author of PLAYS on the PASSIONS.

The pleasure of expressing heart-felt admiration is not, however, my only motive for inscribing this tale to you. Unknown to the world both as an individual and as an author, I own myself desirous of giving a pledge of spotless intention in my work, by adorning it with the name of one whose writings force every unvitiated heart to glow with a warmer love of virtue. On one solitary point I claim equality with you: – In purity of intention I yield not even to JOANNA BAILLIE.

May I venture to avow another feeling which has prompted this intrusion? What point so small that vanity cannot build on it a resting-place! Will you believe that this trifle claims affinity with the Plays on the Passions? – Your portraitures of the progress and of the consequences of passion, – portraitures whose exquisite truth gives them the force of living examples, – are powerful warnings to watch the first risings of the insidious rebel. No guard but one is equal to the task. The regulation of the passions is the province, it is the triumph of RELIGION. In the character of Laura Montreville the religious principle is exhibited as rejecting the bribes of ambition; bestowing fortitude in want and sorrow; as restraining just dis-pleasure; overcoming constitutional timidity; conquering misplaced affection; and triumphing over the fear of death and of disgrace.

This little tale was begun at first merely for my own amusement. It is published that I may reconcile my conscience to the time which it has employed, by making it in some degree useful. Let not the term so implied provoke a smile! If my book is read, its uses to the author are obvious. Nor is a work of fiction necessarily unprofitable to the readers. When the vitiated appetite refuses its proper food, the alternative may be administered in a sweetmeat. It may be imprudent to confess the presence of the medicine, lest the sickly palate, thus warned, turn from it in loathing. But I rely in this instance on the world of the philosopher, who avers that 'young ladies never read prefaces'; and I am not without hope, that with you, and with all who form exceptions to this rule, the avowal of a useful purpose may be an inducement to tolerate what otherwise might be thought unworthy of regard.

Perhaps in an age whose lax morality, declining the glorious toils of virtue, is poorly 'content to dwell in decencies for ever', emulation may be repressed by the eminence which the character of Laura claims over the ordinary standard of the times. A virtue which, though essentially Christian, is certainly not very popular in this Christian country, may be stigmatized as romantic; a chilling term of reproach, which has blighted many a fair blossom of goodness ere it ripened into fruit. Perhaps some of my fair countrywomen, finding it difficult to trace in the delineation of Self-Control any striking feature of their own minds, may pronounce my picture unnatural. It might be enough to reply, that I do not ascribe any of the virtues of Laura to nature, and, least of all, the one whose office is to regulate and control nature. But if my principal figure want the air, and vivacity of life, the blame lies in the painter, not in the subject. Laura is indebted to fancy for her drapery and attitudes alone. I have had the happiness of witnessing, in real life, a self-command operating with as much force, permanence, and uniformity, as that which is depicted in the following volumes. To you, Madam, I should perhaps further apologize for having left in my model some traces of human imperfection; while, for the generality of my readers, I breathe a fervent wish, that these pages may assist in enabling their own hearts to furnish proof that the character of Laura, however unnatural, is yet not unattainable.

I have the honour to be,
   with great respect,
    Madam,
     Your obedient Servant,
      The AUTHOR   January 1811.

CONTENTS

———●———

INTRODUCTION

In 1810 Mary Brunton (1778–1818), the daughter of an army officer and the wife of a Church of Scotland Minister, published a novel, *Self-Control* which comes right out of the heart of the literary tradition of moral etiquette novels begun by Fanny Burney in 1778 with *Evelina*. It is not surprising that it does, she was in some ways writing in her thirties for her own younger self. She was born and brought up on the socially isolated island of Barra in the Orkneys, her education was totally neglected by her parents and she taught herself to read and survived on a diet of poetry and novels. In 1798 she was lucky enough to marry a man who she was later to describe as 'my companion and instructor' – if this sounds grim it is clear that she did not find it so. In the first years of their marriage he had a rural pastorate and seems to have given a great deal of time to the serious education of his wife. He was a widely learned man who, in 1803, was appointed Professor of Oriental Languages at Edinburgh University in addition to taking on an urban parish ministry. He seems to have given his wife genuine support and affection, both intellectually and creatively. She started writing after the move to Edinburgh because she was bored by the imposed idleness of town life. After the great success of *Self-Control* she wrote a second novel *Discipline* which was also well received, made her first visit to London and decided to write a sequence of fictions about domestic life – before she had time to produce these she died of puerperal infection after giving birth to a still-born child at the age of forty. It was probably not an interesting life but out of it came an extremely interesting novel.

Her expressed intentions for *Self-Control* were highly moralistic. She intended to show the power of religious principle in bestowing self command, and to bear testimony against the maxim, as immoral as indelicate, that a reformed rake makes the best husband.

In her dedicatory preface – addressed to the author of *Plays on the Passions*, a fellow Scot, Joanna Baillie – she defended her own, and by extension all novels, by claiming

Nor is a work of fiction necessarily unprofitable to the readers. When the vitiated appetite refuses its proper food, the alternative may be administered in a sweetmeat.

Like Jane Austen in Northanger Abbey (Austen was a great admirer of *Self-Control*, and her first published work, *Sense and Sensibility*, which deals with much the same theme, appeared only a year later) Mary Brunton defends the moral worth of the novel within her own fictional text, when Laura, the heroine, and the inane Julia Dawkins debate male morality as represented in the heroes of popular contemporary novels. (Laura's ideal, incidentally, is Thaddeus of Warsaw from an 1803 early historical novel by Jane Porter – and all her preferences are for the heroes of novels written by women; as opposed to Julia's love for Tom Jones.)

Having justified both the principles and the form itself Mary Brunton charges into her enormously long work, with rather more enthusiasm than self-control. Despite its length (which reflects more on the leisure of her putative readers than on anything else) it is a fascinating book: the plot, whose outcome is inevitable and whose working out is improbable, is none the less compelling – a very more-ish sweetmeat indeed. But more important is the personality of the heroine Laura, whom Brunton openly presents as an ideal of womanhood. Most commentators on the book have stressed the conventional aspects of Laura, usually in terms derogatory to Brunton: the depth of her Christian commitment; her 'good' birth and 'natural' dignity in contrast to new-moneyed vulgarity; her selfless self-sacrifice (subtly in contrast to the outrageous demands put on her by men of all degrees); the moral superiority of country life (nature) over a city upbringing (artifice and pretension); her patience, modesty, purity, piety and passivity. But I think they overlook some important details: Brunton firmly defends women's financial independence and right to hard creative work, by making Laura not simply a painter, but one who risks public opprobrium and personal assault by going out into the streets to sell her work, *and* one who holds out rigorously for a decent price.

Laura usually extracts herself from her difficulties, sometimes by gruelling physical exertion – no male knights on white horses for a passive heroine here. But perhaps most interestingly of all Brunton is not embarrassed to make clear that Laura needs all the self-control she can muster precisely because she does love her would-be seducer, loves him passionately and physically. What Austen, for instance, suppresses by means of irony and evasion, Brunton lays on the line: women have physical desires and they are imperatives of a powerful sort. In his final letter the wicked and depraved Hargrave writes 'me alone she loved with passion', and it is true. Brunton is a rigorous anti-romantic: while marriage is a woman's destiny, a good woman must serve her own interests and not get beguiled into self-sacrificial notions about redeeming a weak and fallen man – and moreover God will stand on her side, against her father and her lover if she is strong minded and clear. There is nothing passive about Laura's commitment to her own well being: she is dominated neither by the man in her life nor by her own sexual desires, but these latter do indeed exist and require attention.

Self-Control is not in modern terms a great novel – it is too long, its moralism is too easy, and the author cannot finally resist the lure of melodrama, despite her desire to present social realism – but it is still a great deal more than a literary curio. It is an intriguing and complex illustration of the aspirations of the 'hidden women' of history, and shows especially one of the principal ways in which fairly conventional ordinary middle-class women developed the intellectual concepts and emotional self-awareness that were to lead the next generation, later in the nineteenth century, to demand and achieve real social changes in their unjust and unequal condition.

Sara Maitland

Note: for some of the ideas in this introduction I am indebted to a conversation I had with Dale Spender on a barge in Milton Keynes in the summer of 1985.

CHAPTER I

IT was on a still evening in June, that Laura Montreville left her father's cottage, in the little village of Glenalbert, to begin a solitary ramble. Her countenance was mournful, and her step languid; for her health had suffered from long confinement, and her spirits were exhausted by long attendance on the deathbed of her mother. That labour of duty had been lessened by no extrinsic circumstance; for Lady Harriet Montreville was a peevish and refractory patient; her disorder had been tedious as well as hopeless; and the humble establishment of a half-pay officer furnished no one who could lighten to Laura the burden of constant attendance. But Laura had in herself that which softens all difficulty, and beguiles all fatigue – an active mind, a strong sense of duty, and the habit of meeting and of overcoming adverse circumstances.

Captain Montreville was of a family ancient and respectable, but so far from affluent, that, at the death of his father, he found his wealth, as a younger son, to consist only of £500, besides the emoluments arising from a lieutenancy in a regiment of foot. Nature had given him a fine person and a pleasing address; and to the national opinions of a Scotish mother, he was indebted for an education, of which the liberality suited better with his birth than with his fortunes. He was in London negotiating for the purchase of a company, when he accidentally met with Lady Harriet Bircham. Her person was shewy, and her manners had the glare, even more than the polish of high life. She had a lively imagination, and some wit; had read a little, and knew how to shew that little to advantage. The fine person of Montreville soon awakened the only sort of sensibility of which Lady Harriet was possessed; and her preference was sufficiently visible in every step of its progress. To be distinguished by a lady of such rank and attractions, raised in Montreville all the vanity of three-and-twenty; and, seen through that medium, Lady Harriet's charms were magnified to perfections. Montreville soon was, or fancied himself, desperately in love. He sued, and was accepted with a frankness, to which some stiff advocates for female decorum might give the harsh name of forwardness. Montreville was in love, and he was pleased to call it the candour of a noble mind.

As his regiment was at this time under orders for the West Indies, Lady Harriet prevailed on him to exchange to half-pay; and her fortune being no more than £5000, economy, no less than the fondness for solitude natural in young men in love, induced him to retire to the country with his bride, who had reasons of her own for wishing to quit London. He had been educated in Scotland, and he remembered its wild scenery with the enthusiasm of a man of taste, and a painter. He settled therefore in the village of Glenalbert, near Perth; and to relieve his conscience from the load of utter idleness at twenty-three, began the superintendence of a little farm. Here the ease and vivacity of Lady Harriet made her for a while the delight of her new acquaintance. She understood all the arts of courtesey; and, happy herself, was for a while content to practise them. The store of anecdote, which she had accumulated in her intercourse with the great, passed with her country neighbours for knowledge of the world. To Scotish ears, the accent of the higher ranks of English conveys an idea of smartness, as well as of gentility; and Lady Harriet became an universal favourite.

Those who succeed best in amusing strangers, are not, it has been remarked, the most pleasing in domestic life: they are not even always the most entertaining. Lady Harriet's spirits had ebbs, which commonly took place during her tête-à-têtes with Captain Montreville. Outward attractions, real or imaginary, are the natural food of passion: but sound principles must win confidence, and kindness of heart engage affection. Poor Montreville soon gave a mournful assent to these truths; for Lady Harriet had no principles, and her heart was a mere 'pulsation on the left side.' Her passion for her husband soon declined; and her more permanent appetite for admiration finding but scanty food in a solitary village, her days passed in secret discontent or open murmurings. The narrowness of their finances made her feel the necessity of economy, though it could not immediately instruct her in the art of it; and Montreville, driven from domestic habits by the turmoil of a household, bustling without usefulness, and parsimonious without frugality, was on the point of returning to his profession, or of seeking relief in such dissipation as he had the means of obtaining, when the birth of a daughter gave a new turn to all his hopes and wishes.

'I should not wish the girl to be a beauty,' said he to his friend, the village pastor. 'A pretty face is of no use, but to blind a lover'; – and he sighed, as he recollected his own blindness. Yet he was delighted to see that Laura grew every day more lovely. 'Wit only makes women troublesome,' said he; – but before Laura was old enough to shew the uncommon acuteness of her understanding, he had quite forgotten that he ever applied the remark to her. To amuse her infancy became his chosen recreation; to instruct her youth was afterwards his favourite employment. Lady Harriet, too, early began to seek food for her vanity in the superior endowments of her child, and she forthwith determined that Laura should be a paragon. To perfect her on Nature's plan, never entered the head of this judicious matron; she preferred a plan of her own, and scorned to be indebted to the assistance of nature, even for any part of the perfect structure which she resolved to rear. The temper of Laura, uniformly calm and placid, was by nature slightly inclined to obstinacy. Lady Harriet had predetermined that her daughter should be a model of yielding softness. Laura's spirits were inexhaustible; Lady Harriet thought nothing so interesting as a pensive beauty. Laura was both a reasonable and a reasoning creature: her mother chose that she should use the latter faculty in every instance, except where maternal authority or opinion was concerned. Innumerable difficulties, therefore, opposed Lady Harriet's system; and as violent measures ever occur first to those who are destitute of other resources, she had recourse to so many blows, disgraces, and deprivations, as must have effectually ruined the temper and dispositions of her pupil, if Laura had not soon learnt to look upon the ungoverned anger of her mother as a disease, to which she owed pity and concealment. This lesson was taught her partly by the example of her father, partly by the admonitions of Mrs Douglas, wife to the clergyman of the parish.

This lady was in every respect Lady Harriet's opposite. Of sound sense, rather than of brilliant abilities; reserved in her manners, gentle in her temper, pious, humble, and upright; she spent her life in the diligent and unostentatious discharge of Christian and feminine duty; beloved without effort to engage the love, respected without care to secure the praise of man. She had always treated the little Laura with more than common tenderness; and the child, unused to the fascinations of feminine kindness, repaid her attention with the utmost enthusiasm of love and veneration. With her she passed every moment allowed her for recreation; to her she applied in every little difficulty; from her she solicited every childish indulgence. The influence of this excellent woman increased with Laura's age, till her approbation became essential to the peace of her young friend, who instinctively sought to read, in the expressive countenance of Mrs Douglas, an opinion of all her words and actions. Mrs Douglas, ever watchful for the good of all who approached her, used every effort to render this attachment as useful as it was delightful, and gradually laid the foundation of the most valuable qualities in the mind of Laura. By degrees she taught her to know and to love the Author of her being, to adore him as the bestower of all her innocent pleasures, to seek his favour, or to tremble at his disapprobation in every hour of her life. Lady Harriet had been educated among those who despised or neglected the peculiar tenets of the Christian faith; she never thought of them, therefore, but as an affair that gave scope to lively argument. On Mrs Douglas's own mind they had their proper effect; and she convinced Laura that they were not subjects for cavil, but for humble and thankful acceptation.

In as far as the religious character can be traced to causes merely natural, it may be formed by those who obtain over a mind of sensibility and reflection the influence which affection bestows, provided that they are themselves duly impressed with the importance, the harmony, the excellence of what they teach. Laura early saw the Christian doctrines, precepts and promises, warm the heart, and guide the conduct, and animate the hopes of her whom she loved best. Sympathy and imitation, the strongest tendencies of infancy, first formed the disposition which reason afterwards strengthened into principle, and Laura grew up a pious Christian.

It is the fashion of the age to account for every striking feature of a character from education or external circumstance. Those who are fond of such speculations may trace, if they can, the self-denying habits of Laura, to the eagerness with which her enthusiastic mind imbibed the stories of self-devoting patriots and martyrs, and may find, in one lesson of her preceptress, the tint which coloured her future days. The child had been reading a narrative of the triumphant death of one of the first reformers, and, full of the emulation which the tale of heroic virtue inspires, exclaimed, her eyes flashing through their tears, her little form erect with noble daring, – 'Let them persecute me and I will be a martyr.' 'You may be so now, to-day, every day,' returned Mrs Douglas. 'It was not at the stake that these holy men began their self-denial. They had before taken up their cross daily; and whenever, from a regard to duty, you resign any thing that is pleasing or valuable to you, you are for the time a little martyr.'

In a solitary village, remote from her equals in age and rank, Laura necessarily lived much alone, and in solitude she acquired a grave and contemplative turn of mind. Far from the scenes of dissipation and frivolity, conversant with the grand and the sublime in nature, her sentiments assumed a corresponding elevation. She had heard that there was vice in the world: she knew that there was virtue in it; and, little acquainted with other minds, deeply studious of her own, she concluded that all mankind were, like herself, engaged in a constant endeavour after excellence; that success in this struggle was at once virtue and happiness, while failure included misery as well as guilt. The habit of self-examination, early formed, and steadily maintained, made even venial trespass appear the worst of evils; – while, in the labours of duty and the pleasures of devotion, she found joys which sometimes rose to rapture.

The capricious unkindness of her mother gave constant exercise to her fortitude and forbearance, while the principle of charity, no less than the feelings of benevolence, led to frequent efforts of self-denial. The latter virtue became daily more necessary, for misman-agement had now brought her mother's fortune almost to a close; and Captain Montreville, while he felt that she was injuring his child, could not prevail on himself to withhold from Lady Harriet the control of what he considered her own, especially as her health was such as to afford a plea for indulgence.

Laura had reached her sixteenth year, when Mr Douglas was induced, by a larger benefice, to remove to a parish almost twenty miles distant from Glenalbert; and parting with her early friend, was the severest sorrow that Laura had ever yet known. Captain Montreville promised, however, that his daughter should often visit the new parsonage; but Lady Harriet's increasing illness long prevented the performance of his promise. After a confinement of many months she died, and was lamented by her husband, with that sort of sorrow which it usually costs a man to part with an object which he is accustomed to see, when he knows that he shall see it no more.

It was on the third evening after her mother's funeral, that Captain Montreville prevailed on his daughter to take a solitary walk. Slowly she ascended the hill that overlooked the village, and, stopping near its brow, looked back towards the churchyard, to observe a brown hillock that marked the spot where her mother slept. Tears filled her eyes, as, passing over long intervals of unkindness, she recollected some casual proof of maternal love; and they fell fast as she remembered, that for that love she could now make no return. She turned to proceed; – and the moist eye sparkled with pleasure, the faded cheek glowed with more than the flush of health, when, springing towards her, she beheld the elegant, the accomplished, Colonel Hargrave. Forgotten was languor; forgotten was sorrow; for Laura was just seventeen, and Colonel Hargrave was the most ardent, the most favoured of lovers. His person was symmetry itself; his manners had all the fascination that vivacity and intelligence, joined to the highest polish, can bestow. His love for Laura suited with the impetuosity of his character, and for more than a year he had laboured with assiduity and success to inspire a passion corresponding to his own. Yet it was not Hargrave whom Laura loved; for the being on whom she doated had no resemblance to him, but in externals. It was a creature of her own imagination, pure as her own heart, yet impassioned as the wildest dreams of fiction, – intensely susceptible of pleasure, and keenly alive to pain, yet ever ready to sacrifice the one and to despise the other. This ideal being, clothed with the fine form, and adorned with the insinuating manners, and animated with the infectious love of Hargrave, what heart of woman could resist? Laura's was completely captivated.

Hargrave, charmed with her consummate loveliness, pleased with her cheerful good sense, and fascinated with her matchless simplicity, at first sought her society without thought but of present gratification, till he was no longer master of himself. He possessed an ample fortune, besides the near prospect of a title; and nothing was farther from his thoughts, than to make the poor unknown Laura a sharer in these advantages. But Hargrave was not yet a villain, and he shuddered at the thought of seduction. 'I will see her only *once* more', said he, 'and then tear myself from her for ever.' – 'Only this once,' said he, while day after day he continued to visit her, – to watch with delight, and to cherish with eager solicitude, the tenderness which, amidst her daily increasing reserve, his practised eye could distinguish. The passion which we do not conquer, will in time reconcile us to any means that can aid its gratification. 'To leave her now would be dishonourable, it would be barbarous,' was his answer to his remonstrating conscience, as he marked the glow of her complexion at his approach, the tremor of her hand at his pressure. 'I cannot, indeed, make her my wife. The woman whom I marry, must assist in supporting the rank which she is to fill. But Laura is not made for high life. Short commerce with the world would destroy half her witchery. Love will compensate to us for every privation. I will hide her and myself from a censorious world; she loves solitude; and, with her, solitude will be delightful.' – He forgot that solitude is delightful to the innocent alone.

Meantime, the artless Laura saw, in his highly-coloured pictures of happy love, only scenes of domestic peace and literary leisure; and, judging of his feelings by her own, dreamed not of ought that would have disgraced the loves of angels. Tedious weeks of absence had intervened since their last meeting; and Hargrave's resolution was taken. To live without her was impossible; and he was determined to try whether he had overrated the strength of her affection, when he ventured to hope that to it she would sacrifice her all. To meet her thus unexpectedly filled him with joy, and the heart of Laura throbbed quick as he expressed his rapture. Never had his professions been so ardent; and, softened by sorrow and by absence, never had Laura felt such seducing tenderness as now stole upon her. Unable to speak, and unconscious of her path, she listened with silent rapture to the glowing language of her lover, till his entreaties wrung from her a reluctant confession of her preference. Unmindful of the feeling of humiliation that makes the moment of such a confession, of all others, the least favourable to a lover's boldness, Hargrave poured forth the most vehement expressions of passion; while, shrinking into herself, Laura now first observed, that the shades of evening were closing fast, while their lonely path led through a wood that climbed the rocky hill. – She stopped. – 'I must return,' said she, 'my father will be anxious for me at this hour.' – 'Talk not now of returning,' cried Hargrave impetuously, 'trust yourself to a heart that adores you. Reward all my lingering pains, and let this happy hour begin a life of love and rapture.' – Laura, wholly unconscious of his meaning, looked up in his face with an innocent smile. 'I have often taxed you with raving,' said she, 'now, I am sure, you must admit the charge.' – 'Do not sport with me loveliest,' cried Hargrave, 'nor waste these precious moments in cold delay. Leave forms to the frozen hearts that wait them, and be from this hour mine, wholly and for ever.' Laura threw a tearful glance on her mourning habit. 'Is this like bridal attire?' said she: 'Would you bring your nuptial festivities into the house of death, and mingle the sound of your marriage vow with my mother's dying groans?' Can this simplicity be affected, thought Hargrave. Is it that she will not understand me? He examined her countenance. All there was candour and unsuspecting love. Her arm rested on his with confiding pressure, and for a moment Hargrave faltered in his purpose. The next, he imagined that he had gone too far to recede; and pressing her to his breast with all the vehemence of passion, he, in hurried half-articulate whispers, informed her of his real design. No words can express her feelings, when, the veil thus rudely torn from her eyes, she saw her pure, her magnanimous Hargrave – the god of her idolatry, degraded to a sensualist – a seducer. Casting on him a look of mingled horror, dismay, and anguish, she exclaimed, 'Are you so base?' and freeing herself, with convulsive struggle, from his grasp, sunk without sense or motion to the ground.

As he gazed on the death-pale face of Laura, and raised her lifeless form from the earth, compassion, which so often survives principle, overpowered all Hargrave's impetuous feelings; and they were succeeded by the chill of horror, as the dreadful idea occurred to him, that she was gone for ever. In vain he chafed her cold hands, tried to warm her to life in his bosom, bared her's to the evening-breeze, and distractedly called for help; while, with agony, which every moment increased, he remembered, what so lately he had thought of with delight, that no human help was near. No sign of returning life appeared. At last he recollected that, in their walk, they had at some distance crossed a little stream, and starting up with renovated hope, he ran to it with the speed of lightning; but the way, which was so short as he passed it before, now seemed lengthened without end. At last he reached it; and filling his hat with water, returned with his utmost speed. He darted forward till he found himself at the verge of the wood, and then perceived that he had mistaken the path. As he retraced his steps, a thousand times he cursed his precipitancy, and wished that he had more cautiously ascertained the sentiments of his mistress, ere he permitted his licentious purpose to be seen. After a search, prolonged by his own frantic impatience, he arrived at the spot where he left her; – but no Laura was there. He called wildly on her name – he was answered by the mountain-echo alone. After seeking her long, a hope arose that she had been able to reach the village; and thither he determined to return, that, should his hope prove groundless, he might at least procure assistance in his search.

As he approached the little garden that surrounded Captain Montreville's cottage, he with joy perceived a light in the window of Laura's apartment; and never, in the cheerfulest scenes, had he beheld her with such delight as he did now, when every gesture seemed the expression of unutterable anguish. He drew nearer, and saw despair painted on her every feature; and he felt how tender was the love that could thus mourn his degeneracy, and its own blighted hopes. If she could thus feel for his guilt, the thought irresistibly pressed on his mind, with what bitterness would she feel her own. Seduction, he perceived, would with her be a work of time and difficulty; while, could he determine to make her his wife, he was secure of her utmost gratitude and tenderness. The known honour, too, of Captain Montreville made the seduction of his daughter rather a dangerous exploit; and Colonel Hargrave knew, that, in spite of the licence of the times, should he destroy the daughter's honour, and the father's life, he would no longer be received, even in the most fashionable circles, with the cordiality he could at present command. The dignified beauty of Laura would grace a coronet, and more than excuse the weakness which raised her to that distinction: – his wife would be admired and followed, while all her affections would be his alone. In fancy he presented her glittering with splendour, or majestic in unborrowed loveliness, to his companions; saw the gaze of admiration follow wherever she turned; – and that thought determined him. He would go next morning, and in form commence honourable lover, by laying his pretensions before Captain Montreville. Should Laura have acquainted her father with the adventures of the evening, he might feel some little awkwardness in his first visit; but she might perhaps have kept his secret; and, at all events, his generous intentions would repair his offence. Satisfied with himself, he retired to rest, and enjoyed a repose that visited not the pillow of the innocent Laura.

CHAPTER II

———————————●———————————

SCARCELY had Hargrave quitted Laura, when her senses began to return, and with them an indefinite feeling of danger and alarm. The blood gushing from her mouth and nostrils, she quickly revived to a full sense of her situation, and instinctively endeavoured to quit a spot now so dark and lonely. Terror gave her strength to proceed. Every path in her native woods was familiar to her: she darted through them with what speed she could command; and, reckless of all danger but that from which she fled, she leapt from the projecting rocks, or gradually descended from the more fearful declivities, by clinging to the trees which burst from the fissures; till, exhausted with fatigue, she reached the valley, and entered the garden that surrounded her home. Here, supported no longer by the sense of danger, her spirits utterly failed her; and she threw herself on the ground, without a wish but to die.

From this state she was aroused by the voice of her father, who, on the outside of the fence, was inquiring of one of the villagers, whether she had been seen. Wishing, she scarcely knew why, to escape all human eyes, she rose, and, without meeting Captain Montreville, gained her own apartment. As she closed her door, and felt for a moment the sense of security, which everyone experiences in the chamber which he calls his own, – 'Oh!' cried she, 'that I could thus shut out the base world for ever.'

There was in Laura's chamber one spot, which had, in her eyes, something of holy, for it was hallowed by the regular devotions of her life. On *it* she had breathed her first infant prayer. *There* shone on her the eastern sun, as she offered her morning tribute of praise. *There* first fell the shades of evening that invited her to implore the protection of her God. On that spot she had so often sought consolation, so often found her chief delight, that it was associated in her mind with images of hope and comfort; and springing towards it, she now almost unconsciously dropped upon her knees. While she poured forth her soul in prayer, her anguish softened into resignation; and with the bitter tears of disappointment, those of gratitude mingled, while she thanked Him who, though He had visited her with affliction, had preserved her from guilt.

She rose, composed though wretched, resigned though hopeless; and, when summoned to supper, had sufficient recollection to command her voice, while she excused herself on the plea of a violent head-ache. Left to herself, she passed the sleepless night, now in framing excuses for her lover, now in tormenting reflections on her mistaken estimate of his character; and in bitter regrets that what seemed so excellent should be marred with so foul a stain. But Laura's thoughts were so habitually the prelude to action, that, even in the severest conflict of her powers, she was not likely to remain long in a state of ineffective meditation. 'What ought I *now* to do,' was a question which, fron childhood, Laura had every hour habitually asked herself; and the irresistible force of the habit of many years, brought the same question to her mind when she rose with the dawn.

With a heavy heart, she was obliged to confess, that delicacy, no less than prudence, must forbid all future intercourse with Hargrave. But he had for some time been a constant visitor at the cottage, till excluded by the increasing illness of Lady Harriet. He might now renew his visits, and how was it possible to prevent this? Should she now refuse to see him, her father must be made acquainted with the cause of such a refusal, and she could not doubt that the consequences would be such as she shuddered to think of. She groaned aloud as the horrid possibility occurred to her, that her father might avenge her wrongs at the expense of his virtue and his life – become for her sake a murderer, or fall by a murderer's hand. She instantly resolved to conceal for ever the insult she had received; and to this resolution she determined that all other circumstances should bend. Yet should she receive Colonel Hargrave as formerly, what might he not have the audacity to infer? How could she make him fully sensible of her indignant feelings, yet act such a part as might deceive the penetration of her father? Act a part! – deceive her father! Laura's thoughts were usually clear and distinct; and there was something in this distinct idea of evasions and deceit, that sickened her very soul. This was the first system of concealment that had ever darkened her fair and candid mind; and she wept bitterly when she convinced herself, that from such conduct there was no escape.

She sat lost in these distressing reflections, till the clock struck the hour of breakfast; then recollecting that she must not suffer her appearance to betray her, she ran to her glass, and, with more interest than she had perhaps ever before felt in the employment, proceeded to dress her countenance to advantage. She bathed her swollen eyes, shaded them with the natural ringlets of her dark hair, rubbed her wan cheeks till their colour returned, and then entered the parlour with an overacted gaiety that surprised Captain Montreville. 'I scarcely expected,' said he, 'to see you so very animated, after being so ill as to go to rest last night, for the first time in your life, without your father's blessing.'

Laura, instantly sensible of her mistake, colouring, stammered something of the cheering influence of the morning air; and then meditating on a proper medium in her demeanour, sunk into so long a silence, as Captain Montreville could not have failed to remark, had not his attention been diverted by the arrival of the newspaper, which he continued to study till breakfast was ended, when Laura gladly retired to her room.

Though the understanding of Laura was above her years, she had not escaped a mistake common to the youth of both sexes, when smarting under a recent disappointment in love, – the mistake of supposing, that all the interest of life is, with respect to them, at an end, and that their days must thenceforth bring only a dull routine of duties without incitement, and of toils without hope. But the leading principle of Laura's life was capable of giving usefulness, and almost respectability, even to her errors; and the gloom of the wilderness, through which her path seemed to lie, only brightened, by contrast, the splendour that lay beyond. 'The world,' thought she, 'has now nothing to offer that I covet, and little to threaten that I fear. What then remains but to do my duty, unawed by its threatenings, unbribed by its joys. Ere this cloud darkened all my earthly prospects, I was not untaught, though I had too much forgotten the lesson, that it was not for pastime I was sent hither. I am here as a soldier, who strives in an enemy's land; as one who must run – must wrestle – must strain every nerve – exert every power, nor once shrink from the struggle till the prize is my own. Nor do I live for myself alone. I have a friend to gratify – the poor to relieve – the sorrowful to console – a father's age to comfort – a God to serve. And shall selfish feeling disincline me to such duties as these? No, with more than seeming cheerfulness, I will perform them all. I will thank Heaven for exempting me from the far heavier task of honouring and obeying a profligate.'

A profligate! Must she apply such a name to Hargrave. The enthusiasm of the moment expired at the word, and the glow of virtuous resolution faded to the paleness of despondency and pain.

From a long and melancholy reverie, Laura was awakened by the sound of the garden gate, and she perceived that it was entered by Colonel Hargrave. Instinctively she was retreating from the window, when she saw him joined by her father; and, trembling lest candour was about to confess, or inadvertence to betray, what she so much wished to conceal, she continued with breathless anxiety to watch their conference.

Though Colonel Hargrave was certainly one of the best bred men in the kingdom, and, of consequence, entirely divested of the awkwardness of *mauvaise honte*, it must be confessed, that he entered the presence of the father of Laura with rather less than his accustomed ease; but the cordial salutaton of Captain Montreville banishing all fear that the lady had been too communicative, our lover proceeded, without any remaining embarrassment, to unfold the purpose of his visit. Nor could any one have conjectured, from the courtly condescension of the great man, that he conceived he was bestowing a benefit; nor from the manly frankness of the other, that he considered himself as receiving a favour. Not but that the Colonel was in full possession of the pleasures of conscious generosity and condescension. So complete, indeed, was his self-approbation, that he doubted not but his present magnanimous resolve would efface from the mind of Laura all resentment for his offence. Her displeasure he thought would be very short lived, if he were able to convince her that his fault was not premeditated. This he conceived to be an ample excuse, because he chose to consider the insult he had offered, apart from the base propensities, the unbridled selfishness which it indicated. As Laura had so well concealed his indiscretion, he was too good a politician himself to expose it; and he proceeded to make such offers in regard to settlements, as suited the liberality of his character.

Captain Montreville listened with undisguised satisfaction to proposals apparently so advantageous to his beloved child; but, while he expressed his entire approbation of the Colonel's suit, regard to feminine decorum made him add, 'that he was determined to put no constraint on the inclinations of his daughter.' The Colonel felt a strong conviction, that no constraint would be necessary: nevertheless, turning a neat period, importing his willingness to resign his love, rather than interfere with the happiness of Miss Montreville, he closed the conference, by entreating that the Captain would give him an immediate opportunity of learning his fate from the lips of the fair Laura herself.

Laura had continued to follow them with her eyes, till they entered the house together; and the next minute Captain Montreville knocked at her door.

'If your head-ache is not quite gone,' said he, with a significant smile, 'I will venture to recommend a physician. Colonel Hargrave is waiting to prescribe for you; and you may repay him in kind, for he tells me he has a case for your consideration.'

Laura was on the point of protesting against any communication with Colonel Hargrave; but instantly recollecting the explanation that would be necessary, 'I will go to him this instant,' she exclaimed with an eagerness that astonished her father.

'Surely, you will first smooth these reddish locks of yours,' said he, fondly stroaking his hand over her dark auburn hair. 'I fear so much haste may make the Colonel vain.'

Laura coloured violently; for, amidst all her fears of a discovery, she found place for a strong feeling of resentment, at the easy security of forgiveness that seemed intimated by a visit so immediately succeeding the offence. Having employed the few moments she passed at her toilette in collecting her thoughts, she descended to the parlour, fully resolved to give no countenance to the hopes her lover might have built on her supposed weakness.

The Colonel was alone; and as she opened the door, eagerly advanced towards her. 'My adored Laura,' cried he, 'this condescension – .' Had he staid to read the pale, but resolute countenance of his 'adored' Laura, he would have spared his thanks for her condescension.

She interrupted him. 'Colonel Hargrave,' said she, with imposing seriousness, 'I have a request to make to you. Perhaps the peace of my life depends upon your compliance.'

'Ah, Laura! what request can I refuse, where I have so much to ask?'

'Promise me, that you will never make known to my father – that you will take every means to conceal from him the – ,' she hesitated, 'the – our meeting last night,' she added, rejoiced to have found a palliative expression for her meaning.

'Oh! dearest Laura! forget it; – think of it no more.'

'Promise – promise solemnly. If indeed,' added she shuddering, while an expression of anguish crossed her features, 'if indeed promises can weigh with such a one as you.'

'For pity's sake, speak not such cutting words as those.'

'Colonel Hargrave, will you give me your promise?'

'I do promise – solemnly promise. Say, but that you forgive me.'

'I thank you, Sir, for so far ensuring the safety of my father, since he might have risked his life to avenge the wrongs of his child. You cannot be surprised, if I now wish to close our acquaintance, as speedily as may be consistent with the concealment so unfortunately necessary.'

Impatient to conclude an interview which tasked her fortitude to the utmost, Laura was about to retire. Hargrave seized her hand. 'Surely, Laura, you will not leave me thus. You cannot refuse forgiveness to a fault caused by intemperate passion alone. The only atonement in my power, I now come to offer: my hand – my fortune – my future rank.'

The native spirit, and wounded delicacy of Laura, flashed from her eyes, while she replied: 'I fear, Sir, I shall not be suitably grateful for your generosity, while I recollect the alternative you would have preferred.'

This was the first time that Laura had ever appeared to her lover, other than the tender, the timid girl. From this character she seemed to have started at once into the high-spirited, the dignified woman; and, with a truly masculine passion for variety, Hargrave thought he had never seen her half so fascinating. 'My angelic Laura,' cried he, as he knelt before her, 'lovelier in your cruelty, suffer me to prove to you my repentance – my reverence – my adoration; – suffer me to prove them to the world, by uniting our fates for ever.'

It is fit the guilty should kneel,' said Laura, turning away, 'but not to their fellow mortals. Rise, Sir, this homage to me is but mockery.'

'Say, then, that you forgive me; say, that you will accept the tenderness, the duty of my future life.'

'What! rather than control your passions, will you now stoop to receive as your wife, her whom so lately you thought vile enough for the lowest degredation? Impossible! yours I can never be. Our views, our principles, are opposite as light and darkness. How shall I call heaven to witness the prostitution of its own ordinances? How shall I ask the blessing of my Maker, on my union with a being at enmity with him?'

'Good heavens, Laura, will you sacrifice to a punctilio – to a fit of Calvinistic enthusiasm, the peace of my life, the peace of your own? You have owned that you love me – I have seen it – delighted seen it a thousand times – and will you now desert me for ever?'

'I do not act upon punctilio,' returned Laura calmly; – 'I believe I am no enthusiast. What *have* been my sentiments, is now of no importance; to unit myself with vice would be deliberate wickedness – to hope for happiness from such an union would be desperate folly.'

'Dearest Laura, bound by your charms, allured by your example, my reformation would be certain, my virtue secure.'

'Oh, hope it not! – Familiar with my form, my only hold on your regard, you would neglect, forsake, despise me; and who should say that my punishment was not just.'

'And will you then,' cried Hargrave, in an agony; 'Will you then cut me off forever? Will you drive me for ever from your heart?'

'I have now no choice – leave me – forget me – seek some woman less fastidious; or rather endeavour, by your virtues, to deserve one superior far. Then honoured, beloved, as a husband, as a father' – The fortitude of Laura failed before the picture of her fancy, and she was unable to proceed. Determined to conceal her weakness from Hargrave, she broke from him, and hurried towards the door; – but, melting into tenderness at the thought that this interview was perhaps the last, she turned. 'Oh, Hargrave,' she cried, clasping her hands as in supplication, 'have pity on yourself – have pity on me – forsake the fatal path on which you have entered, that, though for ever torn from you here, I may yet meet you in a better world.'

She then darted from the room, leaving her lover in dumb amazement, at the conclusion of an interview so different from his expectations. For the resentment of Laura he had been prepared; but upon her determined refusal, he had never calculated, and scarcely could he now admit the reality. Could he give her credit for the professed motive of her rejection? Colonel Hargrave had nothing in himself that made it natural for him to suppose passion sacrificed to reason and principle. Had he then deceived himself, – had she never really loved him? – the suggestion was too mortifying to be admitted. Had resentment given rise to her determination? She had spoken from the first with calmness, – at last with tenderness. Was all this but a scene of coquetry, designed to enhance her favours? The simple, the noble, the candid Laura guilty of coquetry? – impossible! While these thoughts darted with confused rapidity through his mind, one idea alone was distinct and permanent – Laura had rejected him. This thought was torture. Strong resentment mingled with his anguish; and to inflict, on the innocent cause of it, pangs answering to those he felt, would have afforded to Hargrave the highest gratification. Though his passion for Laura was the most ardent of which he was capable, its effects, for the present, more resembled those of the bitterest hatred. That she loved him, he would not allow himself to doubt; and, therefore, he concluded that neglect would inflict the surest, as well as the most painful wound. Swearing that he would make her feel it at her heart's core, he left the cottage, strode to the village inn, surlily ordered his horses, and, in a humour compounded of revenge, impatient passion, and wounded pride, returned to his quarters at – –. His scheme of revenge had all the success that such schemes usually have or deserve; and while, for one whole week, he deigned not, by visit or letter, to notice his mistress, the real suffering which he inflicted, did not exactly fall on her for whom he intended the pain.

CHAPTER III

TO an interview which he presumed would be as delightful as interesting, Captain Montreville chose to give no interruption; and therefore he had walked out to superintend his hay-making: But, after staying abroad for two hours, which he judged a reasonable length for a tête-à-tête, he returned, and was a little surprised to find that the Colonel was gone. Though he entertained not a doubt of the issue of the conference, he had some curiosity to know the particulars, and summoned Laura to communicate them.

'Well, my love,' said he, as the conscious Laura shut the parlour door, 'is Colonel Hargrave gone?'

'Long ago, Sir.'

'I thought he would have waited my return.'

Laura made no answer.

'When are we to see him again?'

Laura did not know.

'Well, well,' said Captain Montreville, a little impatiently, 'since the Colonel is gone without talking to me, I must just hear from you what it is you have both determined on.'

Laura trembled in every limb. 'I knew,' said she, without venturing to lift her eye, 'that you would never sacrifice your child to rank or fortune; and therefore I had no hesitation in refusing Colonel Hargrave.'

Captain Montreville started back with astonishment, – 'Refuse Colonel Hargrave?' cried he, – 'Impossible – you cannot be in earnest.'

Laura, with much truth, assured him that she never in her life had been more serious.

Captain Montreville was thunderstruck. Surprise for a few

moments kept him silent. At last recovering himself, – 'Why, Laura,' said he, 'what objection could you possibly make to Hargrave? – he is young, handsome, accomplished, and has shewn such generosity in his choice of you' –

'Generosity! Sir,' repeated Laura.

'Yes; it was generous in Colonel Hargrave, who might pretend to the first woman in the kingdom, to think of offering to share his fortune and his rank with you, who have neither.'

Laura's sentiments on this subject did not exactly coincide with her father's, but she remained silent while he continued: 'I think I have a right to hear your objections, for I am entirely at a loss to guess them. I don't indeed know a fault Hargrave has, except perhaps a few gallantries; which most girls of your age think a very pardonable error.'

A sickness, as of death, seized Laura; but she answered steadily, 'Indeed, Sir, the Colonel's views are so different from mine – his dispositions so very unlike – so opposite, that nothing but unhappiness could possibly result from such an union. But,' added she, forcing a languid smile, 'we shall, if you please, discuss all this to-morrow; for, indeed, today, I am unable to defend my own case with you. I have been indisposed all day.'

Captain Montreville looked at Laura, and, in the alarm which her unusual paleness excited, lost all sense of the disappointment she had just caused him. He threw his arm tenderly round her – supported her to her own apartment – begged she would try to rest, – ran to seek a cordial for his darling; and then, fearing that the dread of his displeasure should add to her disorder, hastened back to assure her that, though her happiness was his dearest concern, he never meant to interfere with her judgment of the means by which it was to be promoted.

Tears of affectionate gratitude burst from the eyes of Laura. 'My dear kind feather,' she cried, 'let me love – let me please you – and I ask no other earthly happiness.'

Captain Montreville then left her to rest; and, quite exhausted with illness, fatigue, and sorrow, she slept soundly for many hours.

The Captain spent most of the evening ruminating on the occurrence of the day; nor did his meditations at all diminish his surprize at his daughter's unaccountable rejection of his favourite. He recollected many instances in which he thought he had perceived her partiality to the Colonel; – he perplexed himself in vain to reconcile them with her present behaviour. He was compelled at last to defer his conclusions till Laura herself should solve the difficulty. The subject was, indeed, so vexatious to him, that he longed to have his curiosity satisfied, in order finally to dismiss the affair from his mind.

Laura had long been accustomed, when assailed by any adverse circumstance, whether more trivial or more important, to seize the first opportunity of calmly considering how far she had herself contributed to the disaster; and, as nothing is more hostile to good humour than an ill-defined feeling of self-reproach, the habit was no less useful to the regulation of our heroine's temper, than to her improvement in the rarer virtues of prudence and candour. Her first waking hour, except that which was uniformly dedicated to a more sacred purpose, she now employed in strict and impartial self-examination. She endeavoured to call to mind every part of her behaviour to Colonel Hargrave, lest her own conduct might have seemed to countenance his presumption. But in vain. She could not recall a word, a look, even a thought, that could have encouraged his profligacy. 'Yet why should I wonder,' she exclaimed, 'if he expected that temptation might seduce, or weakness betray me, since he knew me fallible, and of the Power by which I am upheld he thought not.'

Satisfied of the purity of her conduct, she next proceeded to examine its prudence: but here she found little reason for self-congratulation. Her conscience, indeed, completely acquitted her of levity or forwardness, but its charges of imprudence she could not so easily parry. Why had she admitted a preference for a man whose moral character was so little known to her? Where slept her discretion, while she suffered that preference to strengthen into passion? Why had she indulged in dreams of ideal perfection? Why had she looked for consistent virtue in a breast where she had not ascertained that piety resided? Had she allowed herself time for consideration, would she have forgotten that religion was the only foundation strong enough to support the self-denying, the purifying virtues? These prudent reflections came, in part, too late; for to love, Laura was persuaded she must henceforth be a stranger. But to her friendships, she conceived, that they might be applicable; and she determined to make them useful in her future intercourse with her own sex; to whom, perhaps, they may be applied even with more justice than to the other.

The mind of Laura had been early stored with just and rational sentiments. These were the bullion – but it was necessary that experience should give the stamp that was to make them current in the ordinary business of life. Had she called prudence to her aid, in the first stage of her acquaintance with the insinuating Hargrave, what anguish would she not have spared herself. But if the higher wisdom is to foresee and prevent misfortune, the next degree is to make the best of it when unavoidable; and Laura resolved that this praise at least should be her's. Fortified by this resolution, she quitted her apartment, busied herself in her domestic affairs, met her father almost with cheerfulness; and, when he renewed the subject of their last conversation, repeated, with such composure, her conviction of the dissimilarity of Hargrave's dispositions to her own, that Captain Montreville began to believe that he had been mistaken in his opinion of her preference. Still, however, he could not account for her rejection of an offer so unobjectionable; and he hinted a suspicion, that some of Hargrave's gallantries had been repeated to her, and perhaps with exaggeration. With trembling lips, Laura assured him she had never heard the slightest insinuation against Colonel Hargrave. Though Laura had little of romance in her composition, her father now began to imagine, that she allowed herself to cherish the romantic dream, that sympathy of souls, and exactly concordant tastes and propensities, were necessary to the happiness of wedded life. But Laura calmly declared, that her tastes were not inflexible; and that, had she intended to marry, she should have found it an easy duty to conform them to those of her husband: but that the thought of marriage was shocking to her, and she trusted no man would ever again think of her as a wife. Montreville, who for once suspected his daughter of a little affectation, made no effort to combat this unnatural antipathy, but trusted to time and nature for its cure.

As soon as her father left her, Laura, determined not to be brave by halves, began the painful task of destroying every relic of Hargrave's presence. She banished from her port-folio the designs he had made for her drawings, destroyed the music from which he had accompanied her, and effaced from her books the marks of his pencil. She had amused her solitary hours by drawing, in chalks, a portrait of features indelibly engraven on her recollection, and her fortitude failed her when about to consign it to the flames. – 'No;' she exlaimed, 'I can never part with this. This, at least, I may love unreproved,' and she pressed it in agony to her heart – inwardly vowing that no human being should fill its place. But such thoughts as these could not linger in the reasonable mind of Laura. The next moment she blushed for her weakness; and, casting away its last treasure, averted her eyes till the flames had consumed it to ashes. 'Now all is over,' she cried, as she threw herself into a chair and burst into tears. But, quickly wiping them away, she resolved that she would not wilfully bind herself to the rack of recollection, and hastened to exert herself in some of her ordinary employments.

Laura was aware that the cottage, where every walk, every shrub, every flower spoke of Hargrave, was a scene unlikely to aid her purpose of forgetting him; and, therefore, she that evening proposed to her father that they should pay their long promised visit to Mrs Douglas. He readily consented. Their journey was fixed for the following day, and Laura occupied herself in preparing for their departure, though with feelings far different from the delight with which, a few days before, she would have anticipated a meeting with her early friend.

CHAPTER IV

─────────●─────────

MRS DOUGLAS observed, with satisfaction, the improved stature and increasing gracefulness of her young favourite; but she remarked, wtih painful interest, that the hectic of pleasure which tinged the cheek of Laura, at their meeting, faded fast to the hue of almost sickly delicacy. She soon noticed that an expression, as of sudden torture, would sometimes contract, for a moment, the polished forehead of Laura; that it was now succeeded by the smothered sigh, the compressed lip, the hasty motion that spoke of strong mental effort, now subsided into the languor of deep unconquered melancholy. Such depression Mrs Douglas could not attribute to the loss of a mother, whose treatment furnished more occasions of patience than of gratitude; and she anxiously longed to discover its real cause. But it was soon evident that this was a secret which Laura had no intention to disclose. A glance from the inquiring eye of Mrs Douglas, at once recalled her to constrained cheerfulness; and the presence of Captain Montreville seemed always to put her entirely upon her guard. While he was in the room, she talked, read aloud, or played with the children, as if determined to be amused; but as soon as he retired, she relapsed, like one wearied with effort, into languor and melancholy, till recalled to herself by the scrutinizing looks of Mrs Douglas. Even in their most private conversations, the name of Hargrave never passed her lips. Months, indeed, had elapsed since Laura could have pronounced that name without painful emotion – to utter it now was become almost impossible. She felt that she had no right to publish, while she rejected, his addresses; and she felt an invincible repugnance to expose even his failings, but much more his vices, to the censure of the respectable Mrs Douglas. Soon after she first saw Hargraves, she had written to her friend a warm eulogium of his fine person, captivating manners, and elegant accomplishments. Mrs Douglas, in reply, had desired to hear more of this phoenix; but before Laura again found leisure to write, she was no longer inclined to make Hargrave her subject, and her friend had desisted from fruitless inquiries. Mrs Douglas had lately had an opportunity of judging for herself of the Colonel's attractions; and, so great did they appear to her, that it was with extreme astonishment she heard his late disappointment from Captain Montreville, who did not feel his daughter's delicacy on the subject. This communication only served to increase her perplexity as to the cause of Laura's depression; yet she felt herself relieved from the apprehension, that hopeless love for Hargrave was wasting the health and peace of her dear Laura. Still, however, she continued to watch that expressive countenance, to weigh every word that might tend to unfold the enigma. In vain; – Laura studiously avoided all approach to an explanation. Mrs Douglas's anxiety now increased to a painful extreme. She felt how necessary to female inexperience is the advice of a female, – how indispensable to feminine sorrows are the consolations of feminine sympathy; and she resolved that no false delicacy should withhold her from offering such relief as she might have power to bestow.

One morning, after the gentlemen had left them alone together, Mrs Doublas, meditating on the best means of introducing the subject she had so much at heart, had fallen into a long silence; when, looking up, she perceived that Laura had let fall her work, and was sitting with her eyes fixed, and her arms dropped, in the attitude of one whose thoughts had no connection with present objects. At the heavy sigh with which Mrs Douglas surveyed her, she started, and was rousing her attention to some indifferent subject, when Mrs Douglas, kindly taking her hand, said, 'My dear child, whatever may be necessary with others, I beseech you to be under no constraint with me. I am far from wishing to intrude into your confidence, but do not add the pain of constraint to anguish that already seems so oppressive.'

Large tears stole from under Laura's downcast eyelids; but she spoke not. Mrs Douglas continued – 'If my best advice, my most affectionate sympathy, can be of use to you, I need not say you may command them.'

Laura threw herself into the arms of her friend, and for some moments sobbed with uncontrolled emotion; but soon composing herself, she replied: 'If advice could have profited, if consolation could have reached me, where should I have sought them unless from you, respected friend of my youth; – but the warning voice of wisdom comes now too late, and even your sympathy would be bestowed in vain.'

'Heaven forbid that my dearest Laura should be beyond the reach of comfort. That is the lot of guilt alone.'

'I am grateful to Heaven,' said Laura, 'that I have been less guilty than imprudent. But, my best friend, let us quit this subject. This wretchedness cannot, shall not last. Only let me implore you not to notice it to my father. You know not what horrors might be the consequence.'

Mrs Douglas shook her head. 'Ah! Laura,' said she, 'that path is not the path of safety in which you would elude a father's eye.' Laura's glance met that of her friend; and she read suspicion there. The thought was so painful to her, that she was on the point of disclosing all; but she remembered that the reasons which had at first determined her to silence, were not altered by any one's suspicions, and she restrained herself. Colonel Hargrave had cruelly wronged and insulted her – she ought therefore to be doubly cautious how she injured him. Sympathy, in her case, she felt, would be a dangerous indulgence; and, above all, she shrunk with horror from exposing her lover, or his actions, to detestation or contempt. 'Perhaps the time may come,' said she, pursuing her reflections aloud, 'when you will be convinced that I am incapable of any clandestine purpose. At present your compassion might be a treacherous balm to me, when my best wisdom must be to forget that I have need of pity.'

Mrs Douglas looked on the open candid countenance of Laura, and her suspicions vanished in a moment; but they returned when her young friend reiterated her intreaties that she would not hint the subject to her father. Laura was, however, fortified in her resolutions of concealment, by an opinion she had often heard Mrs Douglas express, that the feelings of disappointed love should by women be kept inviolably a secret. She was decisively giving a new turn to the conversation, when it was interrupted by the entrance of the gentlemen; and Mrs Douglas, a little hurt at the steadiness of her young friend, more than half determined to renew the subject no more.

A letter lay on the table, which the post had brought for Captain Montreville; he read it with visible uneasiness, and immediately left the room. Laura perceived his emotion; and, ever alive to the painful subject nearest her heart, instantly concluded that the letter brought a confession from Hargrave. She heard her father's disordered steps pacing the apartment above, and earnestly longed, yet feared to join him. Anxiety at length prevailed; and she timidly approached the door of Captain Montreville's chamber. She laid her hand upon the lock; paused again, with failing courage, and was about to retire, when her father opened the door. 'Come in, my love,' said he, 'I wish to speak with you.' Laura, trembling, followed him into the room. 'I find,' said he, 'we must shorten our visit to our kind friends here, and travel homewords, I must prepare,' continued he, and he sighed heavily, 'I must prepare for a much longer journey.'

Laura's imagination took the alarm; and, forgetting how unlikely it was that Captain Montreville should disclose such a resolution to her, she thought only of his intending to prepare for a journey whence there is no return, before he should stake his life against that of Hargrave. She had not power to speak; but, laying her hand on her father's arm, she cast on him a look of imploring agony. 'Do not be alarmed, my love,' said he: 'I shall, in a few days, convey your commands to London; but I do not mean to be long absent.'

Laura's heart leapt light. 'To London, Sir?' said she, in a tone of cheerful inquiry.

'Yes, my dear child; I must go, and leave you alone at home – while yet I have a home to shelter you. Had you resembled any other girl of your age, I should have said no more of this – but I will have no concealments from you. Read this letter.'

It was from Captain Montreville's agent, and briefly stated, that the merchant in whose hands he had lately vested his all, in an annuity on his daughter's life, was dead; and that, owing to some informality in the deed, the heirs refused to make any payment. Having read the letter, Laura continued for some moments to muse on its contents, with her eyes vacantly fixed on the civil expression of concern with which it concluded. 'How merciful it is,' she exclaimed, 'that this blow fell not till my mother was insensible of the stroke.'

'For myself,' said Captain Montreville, 'I think I could have borne it well; but this was the little independence I thought I had secured for you, dear darling of my heart; and now' – The father's lip quivered, and his eyes filled; but he turned aside, for he could *be* tender – but would not *seem* so.

'Dearest father,' said Laura, 'think not of me. Could you have given me millions, I should still have been dependent on the care of

Providence, even for my daily bread. My dependence will now only be a little more perceptible. But perhaps,' added she cheerfully, 'something may be done to repair this disaster. Warren's heirs will undoubtedly rectify this mistake, when they find it has been merely accidental. At all events, a journey to London will amuse you; and I shall manage your harvest so actively in your absence.'

Captain Montreville had, from Laura's infancy, been accustomed to witness instances of her fortitude, to see her firm under unmerited and merciless chastisement, and patient under intense bodily suffering – but her composure on this occasion, so far surpassed his expectations, that he was inclined to attribute it less to fortitude than to inconsideration. 'How light-hearted is youth,' thought he, as he quitted her. 'This poor child has never seen the harsh features of poverty, but when distance softened their deformity, and she now beholds his approach without alarm.' He was mistaken. Laura had often taken a near survey of poverty. She had entered the cabins of the very poor – seen infancy squalid, and youth spiritless – manhood exhausted by toil, and age pining without comfort. In fancy she had substituted herself in the place of these victims of want; felt by sympathy their varieties of wretchedness; and she justly considered poverty among the heaviest of human calamities. But she was sensible that her firmness might support her father's spirits, or her weakness serve to aggravate his distress; and she wisely pushed aside the more formidable mischief, which she could not surmount, to attend to the more immediate evil, which she felt it in her power to alleviate.

The moment she was alone, Laura fell on her knees: 'Oh! Heavenly Providence,' she cried, 'save, if it be thy will, my dear father's age from poverty, though, like my great Master, I should not have where to lay my head.' She continued to pray long and fervently, for spirits to cheer her father under his misfortune; and for fortitude to endure her own peculiar sorrow, in her estimation so much more bitter. Having implored the blessing of Heaven on her exertions, she next began to practice them. She wandered out to court the exhilarating influence of the mountain air; and, studiously turning her attention to all that was gay, sought to rouse her spirits for the task she had assigned them. She was so successful, that she was that evening the life of the little friendly circle. She talked, sang, and recited – she exerted all the wit and vivacity of which she was mistress – she employed powers of humour which she herself had scarcely been conscious of possessing. Her gaiety soon became contagious. Scarcely a trace appeared of the anxious fears of Mrs Douglas, or the parental uneasiness of Captain Montreville, and fewer still of the death-stroke which disappointed confidence had carried to the peace of poor Laura. But, retired to the solitude of her chamber, her exhausted spirits found relief in tears. She felt, that long to continue her exertion would be impossible; and, in spite of reason, which told of the danger of solitude, anticipated, with pleasure, the moment when total seclusion should leave her free to undisguised wretchedness.

Laura was not yet, however, destined to the hopeless task of combating misplaced affection in entire seclusion. On the following morning she found a stranger at the breakfast-table. He seemed a man of information and accomplishments. An enthusiast in landscape, he was come to prosecute his favourite study amidst the picturesque magnificence of Highland scenery; and the appearance and manners of a gentleman, furnished him with a sufficient introduction to Highland hospitality. Relieved, by his presence, from the task of entertaining, Laura scarcely listened to the conversation, till the stranger, having risen from table, began to examine a picture which occupied a distinguished place in Mrs Douglas's parlour. It was the work of Laura, who was no mean proficient. She had early discovered what is called a genius for painting; that is to say, she had exercised much of her native invention, and habitual industry on the art. Captain Montreville added to his personal instructions, every facility which it was in his power to bestow. Even when her performances had little in them of wonderful but their number, her acquaintance pronounced them wonderful; and they obtained the more useful approbation of a neighbouring nobleman, who invited her to use, as copies, any part of his excellent collection. Her progress was now, indeed, marvellous to those who were new to the effects of unremitting industry, guided by models of exquisite skill. Having long and sedulously copied, from pieces of acknowledged merit, she next attempted an original; and having, with great care composed, and with incredible labour finished her design, she dedicated to Mrs Douglas the first fruits of her improved talents, in the picture which the stranger was now contemplating. Willing that her young friend should reap advantage from the criticisms of a judicious artist, Mrs Douglas encouraged him to speak freely of the beauties and defects of the piece. After remarking that there was some skill in the composition, much interest in the principal figure, and considerable freedom in the touch, he added: 'If this be, as I suppose, the work of a young artist, I shall not be surprised that he one day rise both to fame and fortune.'

Mrs Douglas was about to direct his praise to its rightful owner, but Laura silenced her by a look. The stranger's last expression had excited an interest which no other earthly subject could have awakened. Her labours might, it appeared, relieve the wants or increase the comforts of her father's age; and, with a face that glowed with enthusiasm, and eyes that sparkled with renovated hope, she eagerly advanced to question the critic as to the value of her work. In reply, he named a price so far exceeding her expectations, that her resolution was formed in a moment. She would accompany her father to London, and there try what pecuniary advantage was to be derived from her talent. On a scheme which was to repair all her father's losses, prudence had not time to pause; and, feeling company rather a restraint on her pleasure, Laura ran to her apartment, rather to enjoy than to reconsider her plan. Having spent some time in delighted anticipation of the pleasure which her father would take in the new team and thrashing-mill with which she would adorn his farm, and the comfort he would enjoy in the new books and easy sofa with which her labours would furnish his library, she recollected a hundred questions that she wished to ask the stranger, concerning the best means of disposing of her future productions, and she ran down stairs to renew the conversation – but the parlour was empty, the stranger was gone. No matter. No trifle could at this moment have discomposed Laura; and, with steps as light as a heart from which, for a time, all selfish griefs were banished, she crossed the little lawn in search of her father.

The moment she overtook him, locking her arm in his, and looking smilingly up in his face, she began so urgent an entreaty to be admitted as the companion of his journey, that Captain Montreville, with some curiosity, inquired what had excited in her this sudden inclination to travel? Laura blushed and hesitated; for though her plan had, in her own opinion, all the charms which we usually attribute to the new born children of our fancy, she felt that an air of more prudence and forethought mght be requisite to render it equally attractive in the eyes of Captain Montreville. She exerted, however, all the rhetoric she could at that moment command, to give her scheme a plausible appearance. With respect to herself, she was entirely successful; and she ventured to cast a look of triumphant appeal on her father. Captain Montreville, unwilling to refuse the request of his darling, remained silent; but at the detail of her plan, he shook his head. Now, to a projector of eighteen, a shake of the head is, of all gestures, the most offensive; and the smile which usually accompanies it, miserably perverts the office of a smile. Tears, half of sorrow, half of vexation, forced their way to the eyes of Laura; and she walked silently on, without courage to renew the attack, till they were joined by Mrs Douglas. Disconcerted by her ill success with her father, Laura felt little inclination to subject her scheme to the animadversions of her friend; but Captain Montreville, expecting an auxiliary, by whose aid he might conquer the weakness of yielding without conviction, called upon Mrs Douglas, in a manner which shewed him secure of her reply, to give her opinion of Laura's proposal. Mrs Douglas, who had heard, with a degree of horror, of the intention to consign Laura to solitude in her present state of suppressed dejection, and who considered new scenes and new interests as indispensable to her restoration, interpreting the asking looks of the fair petitioner, surprised Captain Montreville by a decided verdict in her favour. Rapturously thanking her advocate, Laura now renewed her intreaties with such warmth, that her father, not possessed of that facility in refusing which results from practice, gave a half-reluctant acquiescence. The delight which his consent conveyed to Laura, which sparkled in her expressive features, and animated her artless gestures, converted his half-extorted assent into cordial concurrence; for to the defects of any scheme that gave her pleasure, he was habitually blind.

In the course of the evening, Captain Montreville announced that, in order to give his daughter time to prepare for her journey, it would be necessary for them to return to Glenalbert on the following morning.

While Mrs Douglas was assisting Laura to pack up her little wardrobe, she attempted to break her guarded silence on the subject of Hargrave, by saying, 'I doubt this same journey of your's will prevent Colonel Hargrave from trying the effects of perseverance, which I used to think the most infallible resort in love, as well as in more serious undertakings.' Laura began a most diligent search for something upon the carpet. 'Poor Hargrave,' Mrs Douglas resumed, 'he is a great favourite of mine. I wish he had been more successful.' Laura continued industriously cramming a bandbox. 'All these gowns and petticoats will crush your new bonnet to pieces, my dear.' Laura suddenly desisted from her employment, rose, and turning full towards Mrs Douglas, said – 'It is unkind, it is cruel, thus to urge me, when you know that duty more than inclination keeps me silent.' 'Pardon me, my dear Laura,' said Mrs Douglas, 'I have no wish to persecute you; but you know I was ignorant that Colonel Hargrave was our interdicted subject.'

She then entered on another topic; and Laura, vexed at the partial disclosure she had inadvertently made, uneasy at being the object of constant scrutiny, and hurt at being obliged to thwart the habitual openness of her temper, felt less sorry than relieved as she sprung into the carriage that was to convey her to Glenalbert. So true is it, that concealment is the bane of friendship.

Other interests, too, quickened her desire to return home. She longed, with a feeling which could not be called hope, though it far exceeded curiosity, to know whether Hargrave had called or written during her absence; and the moment the chaise stopped, she flew to the table where the letters were deposited to wait their return. There were none for her. She interrupted Nanny's expression of joy at the sight of her mistress, by asking who had called while they were from home. 'Nobody but Miss Willis.' Laura's eyes filled with tears of bitterness. 'I am easily relinquished,' thought she – 'but it is better that it should be so;' and she dashed away the drops as they rose.

She would fain have vented her feelings in the solitude of her chamber; but this was her father's first return to a widowed home, and she would not leave him to its loneliness. She entered the parlour. Captain Montreville was already there; and, cheerfully welcoming him home, she shook up the cushion of an elbow-chair by the fire-side, and invited him to sit. 'No, love,' said he, gently compelling her, 'do you take that seat; it was your mother's.' Laura saw his lip quiver, and, suppressing the sob that swelled her bosom, she tenderly withdrew him from the room, led him to the garden, invited his attention to her new-blown carnations, and gradually diverted his regard to such cheerful objects, that, had Captain Montreville examined what was passing in his own mind, he must have confessed that he felt the loss of Lady Harriet less as a companion than an antagonist. She was more a customary something which it was unpleasant to miss from its place, than a real want which no substitute could supply. Laura's conversation, on the contrary, amusing without effort, ingenious without constraint, and rational without stiffness, furnished to her father a real and constant source of enjoyment; because, wholly exempt from all desire to shine, she had leisure to direct to the more practicable art of pleasing, those efforts by which so many others vainly attempt to dazzle.

CHAPTER V

———————●———————

THE three following days Laura employed in making arrangements for her journey. Desirous to enliven the solitude in which she was about to leave her only attendant, she consigned the care of the cottage, during her absence, to the girl's mother, who was likewise her own nurse; and cautious of leaving to the temptations of idleness, one for whose conduct she felt herself in some sort accountable, she allotted to Nanny the task of making winter clothing for some of the poorest inhabitants of Glenalbert; a task which her journey prevented her from executing herself. Nor were the materials of this little charity subtracted from her father's scanty income, but deducted from comforts exclusively her own.

Though, in the bustle of preparation, scarcely a moment remained unoccupied, Laura could not always forbear from starting at the sound of the knocker, or following with her eyes the form of a horseman winding through the trees. In vain she looked – in vain she listened. The expected stranger came not – the expected voice was unheard. She tried to rejoice at the desertion: 'I am glad of it,' she would say to herself, while bitter tears were bursting from her eyes. She often reproached herself with the severity of her language at her last interview with Hargrave. She asked herself what right she had to embitter disappointment by unkindness, or to avenge insult by disdain. Her behaviour appeared to her, in the retrospect, ungentle, unfeminine, unchristian. Yet she did not for a moment repent her rejection, nor waver for a moment in her resolution to adhere to it. Her soul sickened at the thought, that she had been the object of licentious passion merely; and she loathed to look upon her own lovely form, while she thought that it had seduced the senses, but failed to touch the soul of Hargrave.

Amidst these employments and feelings the week had closed; and the Sabbath evening was the last which Laura was to spend at Glenalbert. That evening had long been her chosen season of meditation, the village church-yard the scene where she loved to 'go forth to meditate.' The way which led to it, and to it alone, was a shady green lane, gay with veronica and hare-bell, undefaced by wheels, but marked in the middle with one distinct track, and impressed towards the sides with several straggling half-formed foot-paths. The church itself stood detached from the village, on a little knoll, on the west side of which the burial-ground sloped towards the woody bank that bounded a brawling mountain stream. Thither Laura stole, when the sun, which had been hid by the rugged hill, again rolling forth from behind the precipitous ascent, poured through the long dale his rays upon this rustic cemetery; the only spot in the valley sufficiently elevated to catch his parting beam.

'How long, how deep is the shadow – how glorious in brightness the reverse,' said she, as she seated herself under the shade of the newly raised grave-stone that marked the place of her mother's rest; and turning her mind's eye from what seemed a world of darkness, she raised it to scenes of everlasting light. Her fancy, as it soared to regions of bliss without alloy, looked back wtih something like disgust on the labours that were to prepare her for their enjoyment, and a feeling almost of disappointment and impatience accompanied the recollection, that her pilgrimage was to all appearance only beginning. But she checked the feeling as it rose, and, in penitence and resignation, raised her eyes to heaven. They rested as they fell upon a stone marked with the name and years of one who died in early youth. Laura remembered her well – she was the beauty of Glenalbert; but her lover left her for a richer bride, and her proud spirit sunk beneath the stroke. The village artist had depicted her want of resignation in a rude sculpture of the prophet's lamentation over his withered gourd. 'My gourd, too, is withered,' said Laura. 'Do I well to be angry even unto death? Will the giver of all good leave me even here without comfort? Shall I refuse to find pleasure in any duties but such as are of my own selection: Because the gratification of one passion – one misplaced passion, is refused, has this world no more to offer? this fair world, which its great Creator has stamped with his power, and stored by his bounty, and ennobled by making it the temple of his worshippers, the avenue to heaven! Shall I find no balm in the consolations of friendship, the endearments of parental love – no joy in the sweets of benevolence, the stores of knowledge, the miracles of grace! Oh! may I ever fearlessly confide in the fatherly care, that snatched me from the precipice from which my rash confidence was about to plunge me to my ruin – that opened my eyes on my danger ere retreat was impossible.'

The reflections of Laura were disturbed by the noise of some one springing over the fence; and, the next moment, Hargrave was at her side. Laura uttered neither shriek nor exclamation – but she turned; and, with steps as precipitate as would bear the name of walking, proceeded towards the gate. Hargrave followed her. 'Am I indeed so happy as to find you alone?' said he. Laura replied not, by word or look. 'Suffer me to detain you for a few moments.' Laura rather quickened her pace. 'Will you not speak to me Miss Montreville?' said Hargrave, in a tone of tender reproach. Laura continued to advance. 'Stay but one moment,' said he, in a voice of supplication. Laura laid her hand upon the gate. Hargrave's patience was exhausted. 'By heaven you *shall* hear me!' he cried, and, throwing his arm round her, compelled her to be seated on the stone-bench at the gate. Laura coldly withdrew herself. 'By what right, Sir,' said she, 'do you presume to detain me?' 'By the right of wretchedness – of misery not to be endured. Since I last saw you, I have never known rest or peace. Surely, Laura, you are now sufficiently avenged – surely your stubborn pride may now condescend to hear me.' – 'Well, Sir,' said Laura, without attempting to depart; 'what are your commands?' 'Oh, Laura, I cannot bear your displeasure – it makes me supremely miserable. If you have any pity, grant me your forgiveness.' 'If my forgiveness is of any value to you, I give it you, I trust, like a Christian – from the heart. Now, then, suffer me to go.'

'What – think you it is the frozen forgiveness of duty that will content me? Torn, as I am, by every passion that can drive man to frenzy, think you that I will accept – that I will endure this heartless, scornful pardon? Laura, you loved me once. I have doated on you – pined for you – and passion – passion only – will I accept, or bear from you.'

Laura shrunk trembling from his violence. 'Colonel Hargrave,' said she, 'if you do not restrain this vehemence, I must, I will be gone. I would fain spare you unnecessary pain; but while you thus agitate yourself, my stay is useless to you, and to me most distressing.' 'Say, then, that you accept my vows – that, hopeless of happiness but with me, you bind yourself to me alone, and for ever. Speak, heavenly creature, and bless me beyond the fairest dreams of hope!'

'Colonel Hargrave,' said Laura, 'you have my forgiveness. My – what shall I say – my esteem you have cast from you – my best wishes for your happiness shall ever be yours – more I cannot give. In pity to yourself, then – in pity to me – renounce one who can never be yours.'

Hargrave's eyes flashed fire, while his countenance faded to ghastly paleness. 'Yes;' he exclaimed, 'cold, pitiless, insensible woman – yes I renounce you. In the haunts of riot, in the roar of intemperance, will I forget that form, that voice – and, when I am lost to fame, to health, to usefulness – my ruin be on your soul.' 'Oh! Hargrave,' cried the trembling Laura, 'talk not so wildly; Heaven will hear my prayers for you. – Amidst the pursuits of wisdom – amidst the attractions of others, you will forget me.'

'Forget you! Never. While I have life, I will follow you – supplicate – persecute you. – Mine you shall be, though infamy and death ensue. Dare not,' said he, grasping her arm, – 'dare not to seek the protection of another. – Dare but to give him one smile, and his life shall be the forfeit.'

'Alas! Alas!' cried Laura, wringing her hands in anguish, 'this is real frenzy. Compose yourself, I implore you – there is no other – there never can be.' –

Her tears recalled Hargrave to something like composure. 'Dearest Laura,' said he, 'I wish to soften – I only terrify you. Fear not, beloved of my soul – speak to me without alarm. I will hear you, if it be possible, with calmness – but say not, oh! say not, that you reject me!' Laura averted her face. 'Why prolong this distressing interview,' said she, – 'You have heard my determination. I know that it is right, and I cannot relinquish it.'

The triumph of self-conquest gave firmness to her voice; and Hargrave, driven again from composure by her self-command, sprang from her side. 'It is well, Madam,' he cried; 'triumph in the destruction of my peace; but think not I will so tamely resign you. No; by Heaven. I will go this moment to your father – I will tell him my offence; and ask if he thinks it deserves such punishment. Let him take my life – I abhor it.'

'Is your promise, then, of such small avail?' said Laura, sternly.

'Shall a promise bind me to a life of wretchedness? Shall I regard

the feelings of one who takes an inhuman pleasure in my sufferings?'
At this moment Laura's eyes fell on her father, who was entering the
little avenue. Hargrave's glance followed hers, and he prepared to
join Captain Montreville. In an agony of terror, Laura grasped his
arm. 'Spare me, spare me,' she said, 'and do with me what you will!'
Captain Montreville saw that the walk was occupied; he turned from
it, and Laura had again time to breathe. 'Say, then,' said Hargrave,
softened by her emotion, – 'say that, when years of penitence have
atoned my offence, you will yet be mine.' Laura covered her face with
her hands. 'Let me not hear you – let me not look upon you,' said
Laura; – 'leave me to think, if it be possible,' – and she poured a
silent prayer to Heaven for help in this her sorest trial. The effort
composed her, and the majesty of virtue gave dignity to her form, and
firmness to her voice, while she said, – 'My father's life is in the
hands of Providence – it will still be so, when I have repeated to you,
that I dare not trust to principles such as yours the guardianship of
this the infancy of my being. I dare not incur certain guilt to escape
contingent evil. I cannot make you the companion of this uncertain
life, while your conduct is such, as to make our eternal separation the
object of my dreadful hope.'

Hargrave had trusted that the tenderness of Laura would seduce,
or his ardour overpower her firmness; but he read the expression of
her pale determined countenance, and felt assured that she was lost
to him forever. Convinced that all appeal to her feelings would be
hopeless, he would deign to make none; but in a voice made almost
inarticulate by the struggle of pride and anguish, he said, – 'Miss
Montreville, your father's life is safe from me – I will not lift my hand
against it. That he should take mine is of small importance, either to
you or myself. A violent death,' continued he, his pale lip quivering
with a smile of bitterness, – 'may perhaps procure me your tardy
pity.'

From the storm of passion, Laura had shrunk with terror and
dismay; but the voice of suppressed anguish struck her to the soul.
'Oh! Hargrave,' she cried, with tears no longer to be restrained, 'you
have my tenderest pity – would to Heaven that the purity of your
future life would restore me to the happiness of esteeming you!'

Laura's tenderness revived, in a moment, the hopes of Hargrave.
'Angel of sweetness,' he exclaimed, 'mould me to your will – say that,
when purified by years of repentance, you will again bless me with
your love; and no exertion will be too severe – no virtue too arduous.'

'No; this I dare not promise; let a higher motive influence you; for it is not merely the conduct – it is the heart that must have changed, ere I durst expose my feeble virtue to the trial of your example – your authority; ere I durst make it my duty to shut my eyes against your faults, or to see them with the indulgence of love.'

'Dearest Laura, one word from you will lure me back to the path of virtue – will you wilfully destroy even the wish to return. If for a year – for two years – my conduct should bear the strictest scrutiny – will you not accept this as a proof that my heart is changed – changed in every thing but its love for you – will you not then receive me?'

Laura had resisted entreaty – had withstood alarm – had conquered strong affection; but the hope of rousing Hargrave to the views, the pursuits, the habits of a Christian, betrayed her caution, and gladdened her heart to rapture. 'If for two years,' said she, her youthful countenance brightening with delight, 'your conduct is such as you describe – if it will bear the inspection of the wise, of the sober-minded, of the pious, – as my father's friend, as my own friend, will I welcome you.'

Thus suddenly raised from despair, Hargrave seemed at the summit of felicity. Once admitted as her 'father's friend, as her own,' he was secure of the accomplishment of his wishes. The time that must first elapse, appeared to him but a moment; and the labours of duty required of him seemed a smiling dream. Love and joy animated every feature of his fine countenance; he threw himself at the feet of Laura, and rapturously blessed her for her condescension. His extasies first made her sensible of the extent of her concession; and she feared that she had gone too far. But with her, a promise, however inadvertent, was a sacred thing, which she would neither qualify nor retract. She contented herself, therefore, with merely repeating the terms of it, emphatically guarding the conditions. Desirous now to have leisure for reflection, she reminded him that the lateness of the hour made it fit that he should depart; and, inwardly persuaded that she would not long obdurately refuse him another interview, he obeyed without much opposition.

CHAPTER VI

———————•———————

THE lovers were no sooner parted, than Hargrave began to repent that he had not more distinctly ascertained the kind and manner of the intercourse which he was to hold with his mistress during the term of his probation; and though he had little fear that she would be very rigid, he considered this as a point of such importance, that he resolved not to quit Glenalbert without having the matter settled to his satisfaction. For this reason he condescended to accept the accommodations of the little straw-roofed cottage, by courtesy called the Inn, where he had already left his horse; and thither he retired accordingly, not without some national misgivings of mind on the subject of Scotish nastiness and its consequences. His apartment, however, though small, was decent, his bed was clean, his sleep refreshing, and his dreams pleasant; nor was it till a late hour the following morning, that he rose to the homely comfort, and clumsy abundance of a Highland breakfast. As soon as he had finished his repast, he walked towards Montreville's cottage, ostensibly to pay his respects to the Captain, but, in reality, with the hope of obtaining a private interview with Laura. He entered the garden, where he expected to find Captain Montreville. It was empty. He approached the house. The shutters were barred. He knocked at the door, which was opened by the old woman; and, on inquiring for Captain Montreville, he was answered, 'Wow, Sir, him an' Miss Laura's awa' at six o'clock this morning.' 'Away,' repeated the Colonel, – 'Where are they gone?' 'To London, Sir; and I'm sure a lanely time we'll hae till they come hame again.' 'What stay do they intend making?' 'Hech, Sir, I dare say that's what they dinna ken themsels.' 'What is their address?' inquired the Colonel. 'What's your will, Sir:' 'Where are they to be found?' 'Am'n I tellan you they're in London, Sir. I'm sure ye ken whar that is?' 'But how are you to send their letters?' 'Wow! they never got mony letters but frae England; and now 'at they're in London, ye ken the folk may gie them into their ain hand.' 'But suppose you should have occasion to write to them yourself?' said Hargrave, whose small stock of patience wore fast to a close. 'Hech, Sir, sorrow a scrape can I write. They learn a' thae newfangled things now; but, trouth, i' my young days, we were na' sae upsettan.' Hargrave was in no humour to canvas the merits of the different modes of education; and, muttering an ejaculation, in which the word *devil* was distinctly audible, he turned away.

Vexed and disappointed, he wandered down the churchyard-lane, and reached the spot where he had last seen Laura. He threw himself on the seat that had supported her graceful form – called to mind her consummate loveliness – her ill-repressed tenderness – and most cordially consigned himself to Satan for neglecting to wring from her some further concessions. She was now removed from the solitude where he had reigned without a rival. Her's would be the gaze of every eye – her's the command of every heart. 'She may soon choose among numbers,' cried he, – 'she will meet with people of her own humour, and some canting hypocritical scoundrel will drive me completely from her mind.' By the time he had uttered this prediction, and bit his lip half through – he was some steps on his way to order his horses, that he might pursue his fair fugitive, in the hope of extorting from her some less equivocal kind of promise. Fortunately for his reputation for sanity, however, he recollected, before he began his pursuit, that, ere he could overtake her, Laura must have reached Edinburgh, where, without a direction, it might be difficult to discover her abode. In this dilemma, he was again obliged to have recourse to the old woman at the cottage; but she could give him no information. She neither knew how long Captain Montreville purposed remaining in Edinburgh, nor in what part of the town he intended to reside.

Thus baffled in his inquiries, Hargrave was convinced that his pursuit must be ineffectual; and, in no very placid frame of mind, he changed his destination from Edinburgh to his quarters. He arrived there in time for a late dinner, but his wine was insipid, his companions tiresome; and he retired early, that, early next morning, he might set out on a visit to Mrs Douglas, from whom he purposed to learn Captain Montreville's address.

On comparing the suppressed melancholy of Laura, her embarrassment at the mention of Hargrave, and her inadvertent disclosure, with her father's detail of her rejection of the insinuating young soldier, a suspicion not very remote from truth, had entered the mind of Mrs Douglas. She imagined that Captain Montreville had in some way been deceived as to the kind of proposals made to his daughter; and that Laura had rejected no offers but such as it would have been infamy to accept. Under this conviction, it is not surprising that her reception of the Colonel was far from being cordial; nor that, guessing his correspondence to be rather intended for the young lady than for the old gentleman, she chose to afford no facility to an intercourse which she considered as both dangerous and degrading. To Hargrave's questions, therefore, she answered, that until she should hear from London, she was ignorant of Captain Montreville's address; and that the time of his return was utterly unknown to her. When the Colonel, with the same intention, soon after repeated his visit, she quietly, but steadily, evaded all his inquiries, equally unmoved by his entreaties, and the paroxysms of impatience with which he endured his disappointment.

Hargraves was the only child of a widow – an easy, indolent, good sort of woman, who would gladly have seen him become every thing that man ought to be, provided she could have accomplished this laudable desire without recourse to such harsh instruments as contradiction and restraint. But of these she disliked the use, as much as her son did the endurance: and thus the young gentleman was educated, or rather grew up, without the slightest acquaintance of either. Of consequence, his naturally warm temper became violent, and his constitutionally strong passions ungovernable.

Hargrave was the undoubted heir of a title, and of a fine estate. Of money he had never felt the want, and did not know the value; he was, therefore, so far as money was concerned, generous even to profusion. His abilities were naturally of the highest order. To force him to the improvement of them, was an effort above the power of Mrs Hargrave; but, fortunately for him, ere his habits of mental inaction were irremediable, a tedious illness confined him to recreations in which mind had some share, however small. During the interdiction of bats and balls, he, by accident, stumbled on a volume of Peregrine Pickle, which he devoured with great eagerness; and his mother, delighted with what she was pleased to call a *turn for reading*, took care that this new appetite should not, any more than the old ones, pine for want of gratification. To direct it to food wholesome and invigorating, would have required unremitting though gentle labour: and to labour of all kinds Mrs Hargrave had a practical antipathy. But it was very easy to supply the young man with romances, poetry, and plays; and it was pleasing to mistake their intoxicating effect for the bursts of mental vigour. A taste for works of fiction, once firmly established, never after yielded to the attractions of sober truth; and, though his knowledge of history was neither accurate nor extensive, Hargrave could boast of an intimate acquaintance with all the plays, with almost all the poetry, and as far as it is attainable by human diligence, with all the myriads of romances in his mother tongue. He had chosen, of his own free-will, to study the art of playing on the flute; the violin requiring more patience than he had to bestow; and emulation, which failed to incite him to more useful pursuits, induced him to try whether he could not draw as well as his play-fellow, De Courcy. At the age of seventeen he had entered the army. As he was of good family, of an elegant figure, and furnished by nature with one of the finest countenances she ever formed, his company was courted in the highest circles, and to the ladies he was particularly acceptable. Among such associates, his manners acquired a high polish; and he improved in what is called knowledge of the world; that is, a facility of discovering, and a dexterity in managing the weaknesses of others. One year – one tedious year, his regiment had been quartered in the neighbourhood of the retirement where the afore-said De Courcy was improving his 'few paternal acres;' and, partly by his persuasion and example, partly from having little else to do, partly because it was the fashionable science of the day, Hargrave had prosecuted the study of chemistry. Thus have we detailed, and in some measure accounted for, the whole of Colonel Hargrave's accomplishments, excepting only, perhaps, the one in which he most excelled – he danced inimitably. For the rest, he had what is called a good heart; that is, he disliked to witness or inflict pain, except from some incitement stronger than advantage to the sufferer. His fine eyes had been seen to fill with tears at a tale of *elegant* distress; he could even compassionate the more vulgar sorrows of cold and hunger to the extent of relieving them, provided always that the relief cost nothing but money. Some casual instances of his feeling, and of his charity, had fallen under the observation of Laura; and upon these, upon the fascination of his manners, and the expression of his countenance, her fervid imagination had grafted every virtue that can exalt or adorn humanity. Gentle reader, excuse the delusion. Laura was only seventeen – Hargrave was the first handsome man of fashion she had ever known, the first who had ever poured into her ear the soothing voice of love.

Unprepared to find, in an obscure village in Scotland, the most perfect model of dignified loveliness, Hargrave became the sudden captive of her charms; and her manner, so void of all design, – the energy – the sometimes wild poetic grace of her language – the shrewdness with which she detected, and the simplicity with which she unveiled, the latent motives of action, whether in herself or in others, struck him with all the force of contrast, as he compared them with the moulded artificial standard of the day. His interest in her was the strongest he had ever felt, even before it was heightened by a reserve that came too late to repress or conceal the tenderness with which she repaid his passion. Yet Hargrave was not less insensible to the real charms of Laura's mind, than she was unconscious of the defects in his. Her benevolence pleased him; for bright eyes look brighter through tears of sympathy, and no smile is so lovely as that which shines on the joys of others. Her modesty charmed him; for every voluptuary can tell what allurements blushes add to beauty. But of her self-denial and humility he made no account. Her piety, never obtruded on his notice, had at first escaped his observation altogether; and, now that it thwarted his favourite pursuit, he considered it merely as a troublesome prejudice. Of all her valuable qualities, her unfailing sweetness of temper was perhaps the only one that he valued for its own sake. But her person he idolized. To obtain her no exertion would have appeared too formidable; and, remembering the conditions of their future reconciliation, he began, for the first time in his life, to consider his conduct with a view to its moral fitness.

This he found a subject of inextricable difficulty. He was ignorant of the standard by which Laura would judge him. He was willing to believe that, if she were left to herself, it would not be severe; but the words of her promise seemed to imply, that his conduct was to be subjected to the scrutiny of less partial censors, and he felt some anxiety to know who were to be his 'wise,' 'sober-minded,' 'pious' inspectors. He did not game, his expences did not much exceed his income, therefore he could imagine no change in his deportment necessary to conciliate the 'wise.' Though, under the name of sociality, he indulged freely in wine, he seldom exceeded to intoxication. Here again reform seemed needless. But, that he might give no offence to the 'sober-minded,' he intended to conduct his indispensable gallantries with great discretion, he determined to refrain from all approach to seduction, and magnanimously resolved to abstain from the molestation of innocent country-girls and decent maid-servants. Finally, to secure the favour of the 'pious,' he forthwith made a purchase of Blair's sermons, and resolved to be seen in Church once at least every Sunday.

It might be supposed, that when the scale of duty which we trace is low, we should be more likely to reach the little eminence at which we aspire; but experience shews us, that they who poorly circumscribe the Christian race, stop as much short of their humble design, as does he of his nobler purpose, whose glorious goal is perfection. The sequel will show the attainments of Colonel Hargrave in the ways of virtue. In the meantime his magnet of attraction to Perthshire was gone; he soon began to grow weary of the feeling of restraint, occasioned by supposing himself the subject of a system of *espionage*; and to kill the time, and relieve himself from his imaginary shackles, he sought the assistance of the Edinburgh races; determined, that if Laura prolonged her stay in London, he would obtain leave of absence, and seek her there.

CHAPTER VII

———•———

THE grey lights of morning shone mild on Glenalbert, as the carriage, which was conveying Laura to scenes unknown, wound slowly up the hill. With watery eyes she looked back on the quiet beauties of her native valley. She listened to the dashing of its stream, till the murmur died on her ear. Her lowly home soon glided behind the woods; but its early smoke rose peaceful from amidst its sheltering oaks, till it blended with the mists of morning; and Laura gazed on it as on the parting steps of a friend. 'Oh, vales!' she exclaimed, 'where my childhood sported – mountains that have echoed to my songs of praise, amidst your shades may my age find shelter – may your wild-flowers bloom on my grave!' – Captain Montreville pressed the fair enthusiast to his breast and smiled. It was a smile of pity – for Montreville's days of enthusiam were past. It was a smile of pleasure – for we love to look upon the transcript of our early feelings. But, whatever it expressed, it was discord with the tone of Laura's mind. It struck cold on her glowing heart; and she carefully avoided uttering a word that might call forth such another, till, bright gleaming in the setting sun, she first beheld romantic Edinburgh. 'Is it not glorious!' she cried, tears of wonder and delight glittering in her eyes, and she longed for its re-appearance, when the descent of the little eminence which had favoured their view, excluded the city from their sight.

As the travellers approached the town, Laura, whose attention was rivetted by the castle and its rocks, now frowning majestic in the shades of twilight, and by the antique piles that seemed the work of giants, scarcely bestowed a glance on the neat row of modern buildings along which she was passing, and she was sorry when the carriage turned from the objects of her admiration towards the hotel where Captain Montreville intended to lodge.

Next morning, Laura, eager to renew the pleasure of the evening, proposed a walk; not without some dread of encountering the crowd which she expected to find in such a city. Of this crowd, she had, indeed, seen nothing the night before; but she concluded, ere that she reached town, most of the inhabitants had soberly retired to rest. At the season of the year, however, when Laura reached Edinburgh, she had little cause for apprehension. The noble streets through which she passed had the appearance of being depopulated by pestilence. The houses were uninhabited, the window-shutters were closed, and the grass grew from the crevices of the pavement. The few well-dressed people whom she saw, stared upon her with such oppressive curiosity, as gave the uninitiated Laura a serious uneasiness. At first she thought that some peculiarity in her dress occasioned this embarrassing scrutiny. But her dress was simple mourning, and its form the least conspicuous possible. She next imagined, that to her rather unusual stature she owed this unenviable notice; and, with a little displeasure, she remarked to her father, that it argued a strange want of delicacy to appear to notice the peculiarities of any one's figure; and that, in this respect, the upper ranks seemed more destitute of politeness than their inferiors. Captain Montreville answered, wtih a smile, that he did not think it was her height which drew such attention. 'Well,' said she, with great simplicity, 'I must endeavour to find food for my vanity in this notice, though it is rather against my doing so, that the women stare more tremendously than the gentlemen.'

As they passed the magnificent shops, the windows, gay with every variety of colour, constantly attracted Laura's inexperienced eye; and she asked Montreville to accompany her into one where she wished to purchase some necessary trifle. The shopman observing her attention fixed on a box of artificial flowers, spread them before her; and tried to invite her to purchase, by extolling the cheapness and beauty of his goods. 'Here is a charming sprig of myrtle, ma'am; and here is a geranium-wreath, the most becoming thing for the hair – only seven shillings each, ma'am.' Laura owned the flowers were beautiful. 'But I fear,' said she, looking compassionately at the man, 'you will never be able to sell them all. There are so few people who would give seven shillings for what is of no use whatever.' 'I am really sorry for that poor young man,' said she to her father, when they left the shop. 'Tall, robust, in the very flower of his age, how he must feel humbled by being obliged to attend to such trumpery?' Why is your pity confined to him?' said Montreville. 'There were several others in the same situation.' 'Oh! but they were children, and may do something better by and by. But the tall one, I suppose, is the son of some weak mother, who fears to trust him to fight his country's battles. It is hard that she should have power to compel him to such degradation; I really felt for him when he twirled those flowers between his finger and thumb, and looked so much in earnest about nothing.' The next thing which drew Laura's attention was a stay-maker's sign. 'Do the gentlemen here wear corsets?' said she to Montreville. 'Not many of them, I believe,' said Montreville. 'What makes you inquire?' 'Because there is a *man* opposite who makes corsets. It cannot surely be for women.'

Captain Montreville had only one female acquaintance in Edinburgh, a lady of some fashion, and hearing that she was come to town to remain till after the races, he that forenoon carried Laura to wait upon her. The lady received them most graciously, inquired how long they intended to stay in Edinburgh; and on being answered that they were to leave it in two days, overwhelmed them with regrets, that the shortness of their stay precluded her from the pleasure of their company for a longer visit. Laura regretted it too; but utterly ignorant of the time which must elapse between a fashionable invitation and the consequent visit, she could not help wondering whether the lady was really engaged for each of the four daily meals of two succeeding days.

These days, Captain Montreville and his daughter passed in examining this picturesque city – its public libraries, its antique castle, its forsaken palace, and its splendid scenery. But nothing in its singular environs more charmed the eye of Laura than one deserted walk, where, though the noise of multitudes stole softened on the ear, scarcely a trace of human existence was visible, except the ruin of a little chapel which peeped fancifully from the ledge of a rock, and reminded her of the antick gambols of the red deer on her native hills, when, from the brink of the precipice, they look fearless into the dell below. Captain Montreville next conducted his daughter to the top of the fantastic mountain that adorns the immediate neighbour-hood of Edinburgh, and triumphantly demanded whether she had ever seen such a prospect. But Laura was by no means disposed to let Perthshire yield the palm to Lowland scenery. Here indeed, the prospect was varied and extensive, but the objects were too various, too distant, too gay – they glared on the eye – the interest was lost. The serpentine corn-ridges, offensive to agricultural skill; the school, with its well frequented Gean-tree; the bright green clover fields, seen at intervals through the oak coppice; the church, half hid by its venerable ash trees; the feathery birch, trembling in the breath of evening; the smoking hamlet, its soft colours blending with those of the rocks that sheltered it; the rill, dashing with fairy anger in the channel which its winter fury had furrowed – these were the simple objects which had charms for Laura, not to be rivalled by neat enclosures and whitened villas. Yet the scenes before her were delightful, and had not Captain Montreville's appeal recalled the comparison, she would, in the pleasure which they excited, have forgotten the less splendid beauties of Glenalbert.

Montreville pointed out the road that led to England. Laura sent a longing look towards it, as it wound amid woods and villages and gentle swells, and was lost to the eye in a country which smiled rich and inviting from afar. She turned her eyes where the Forth is lost in the boundless ocean, and sighed as she thought of the perils and hardships of them who go down to the sea in ships. Montreville, unwilling to subject her to the inconveniencies of a voyage, had proposed to continue his journey by land, and Laura herself could not think without reluctance of tempting the faithless deep. The scenery, too, which a journey promised to present, glowed in her fervid imagination with more than nature's beauty. Yet feeling the necessity of rigid economy, and determined not to permit her too indulgent parent to consult her accommmodation at the expence of his prudence, she it was, who persuaded Montreville to prefer a passage by sea, as the mode of conveyance best suited to his finances.

The next day our travellers embarked for London. The weather was fine, and Laura remained all day upon deck, amused with the novelty of her situation. Till she left her native solitude, she had never even seen the sea, except, when from a mountain top, it seemed far off to mingle with the sky; and to her, the majestic Forth, as it widened into an estuary, seemed itself a 'world of waters.' But when on one side the land receded from the view, when the great deep lay before her, Laura looked upon it for a moment, and shuddering, turned away. 'It is too mournful,' said she to her father – 'were there but one spot, however small, however dimly descried, which fancy might people with beings like ourselves, I could look with pleasure on the gulf between – but here there is no resting place.

Thus dismal, thus overpowering, methinks eternity would have appeared, had not a haven of rest been made known to us.' Compared with the boundless expanse of waters, the little bark in which she was floating seemed 'diminished to a point;' and Laura raising her eyes to the stars that were beginning to glimmer through the twilight, thought that such a speck was the wide world itself, amid the immeasurable space in which it rolled. This was Laura's hour of prayer, and far less inviting circumstances can recal us to the acts of a settled habit.

Five days they glided smoothly along the coast. On the morning of the sixth, they entered the river, and the same evening reached London. Laura listened with something like dismay, to the mingled discord that now burst upon her ear. The thundering of loaded carriages, the wild cries of the sailors, the strange dialect, the ferocious oaths of the populace, seemed but parts of the deafening tumult. When they were seated in the coach which was to convey them from the quay, Laura begged her father to prevail on the driver to wait till the unusual concourse of carts and sledges should pass, and heard with astonishment that the delay would be in vain. At last they arrived at the inn where Captain Montreville intended to remain till he could find lodgings; and, to Laura's great surprise, they completed their journey without being jostled by any carriages, or overturned by any waggoner – for ought she knew, without running over any children.

Being shown into a front parlour, Laura seated herself at a window, to contemplate the busy multitudes that thronged the streets; and she could not help contrasting their number and appearance with those of the inhabitants of Edinburgh. There the loitering step, the gay attire, the vacant look, or the inquisitive glance, told that mere amusement was the object of their walk, if indeed it had an object. Here, every face was full of business – none stared, none sauntered, or had indeed the power to saunter, the double tide carrying them resistlessly along in one direction or the other. Among all the varieties of feature that passed before her, Laura saw not one familiar countenance; and she involuntarily pressed closer to her father, while she thought, that among these myriads she should, but for him, be alone.

Captain Montreville easily found an abode suited to his humble circumstances; and, the day after his arrival, he removed with his daughter to the second floor above a shop in Holborn. The landlady was a widow, a decent orderly-looking person; the apartments, though far from elegant, were clean and commodious. They consisted of a parlour, two bedchambers, and a small room, or rather closet, which Laura immediately appropriated as her painting-room. Here she found amusement in arranging the materials of her art, while Captain Montreville walked to the west end of the town, to confer with his agent on the unfortunate cause of his visit to London. He was absent for some hours; and Laura, utterly ignorant of the length of his walk, and of its difficulties for one who had not seen the metropolis for twenty years, began to be uneasy at his stay. He returned at last, fatigued and dispirited, without having seen Mr Baynard, who was indisposed, and could not admit him. After a silent dinner, he threw himself upon a sofa, and dismissed his daughter, saying that he felt inclined to sleep. Laura took this opportunity to write to Mrs Douglas a particular account of her travels. She mentioned with affectionate interest some of her few acquaintances at Glenalbert, and inquired for all the individuals of Mrs Douglas's family; but the name of Hargrave did not once occur in her letter, though nothing could exceed her curiosity to know how the Colonel had borne her departure, of which, afraid of his vehemence, she had, at their last interview, purposely avoided to inform him.

Having finished her letter, Laura, that she might not appear to repress civility, availed herself of her landlady's invitation to 'come now and then,' as she expressed it, 'to have a chat;' and descended to the parlour below. On perceiving that Mrs Dawkins was busily arranging the tea equipage, with an air that showed she expected company, Laura would have retreated, but her hostess would not suffer her to go. 'No, no, Miss,' said she, 'I expects nobody but my daughter Kate, as is married to Mr Jones the haberdasher; and you mustn't go, for she can tell you all about Scotland; and it is but natural to think that you'd like to hear about your own country, now when you're in a foreign land, as a body may say.'

The good woman had judged well in the bribe she offered to her guest, who immediately consented to join her party; and who, perceiving that Mrs Dawkins was industriously spreading innumerable slices of bread and butter, courteously offered to share her toils. Mrs Dawkins thanked her, and accepted her services, adding, 'indeed it's very hard as I should have all them here things to do myself, when I have a grown up daughter in the house. But, poor thing, it a'n't her fault after all, for she never was larnt to do nothing of use.' 'That was very unfortunate,' said Laura. 'Yes, but it might'nt have been so misfortunate neither, only, you see, I'll tell you how it was. My sister, Mrs Smith, had a matter of £10,000 left her by her husband, and so she took a fancy when July was born as she'd have her called a grand name; and I'm sure an unlucky name it was for her; for many a fine freak it has put into her head. Well, and so as I was saying, she took July home to herself, and had her larnt to paint, and to make fillagree, and play on the piano, and what not; and to be sure we thought she would never do less than provide for her. But what do you think, why, two year's ago, she ran away with a young ensign, as had nothing in the varsal world but his pay; and so July came home just as she went; and what was worst of all, she could'nt do no more in the shop nor the day she was born.'

'That was hard, indeed,' said Laura.

'Wasn't it now, – but one comfort was, I had Kate brought up in another guess-way; for I larnt her plain work and writing, and how to cast accounts; and never let her touch a book, except the prayer-book a-Sundays; and see what's the upshot on't. Why, though July's all to nothing the prettiest, nobody has never made an offer for she, and Kate's got married to a warm man as any in his line hereabouts, and a man as has a house not ten doors off; and besides, as snug a box in the country as ever you seed, – so convenient you've no idear. Why, I dare say, there's a matter of ten stage-coaches pass by the door every day.'

To all this family history, Laura listened with great patience, wondering, however, what could induce the narrator to take so much trouble for the information of a stranger.

The conversation, if it deserves the name, was now interrupted by the entrance of a young woman, whom Mrs Dawkins introduced as her daughter July. Her figure was short, inclining to embonpoint – her face, though rather pretty, round and rosy, – and her whole appearance seemed the antipodes of sentiment. She had, however, a book in her hand, on which, after exchanging compliments with Laura, she cast a languishing look, and said, 'I have been paying a watery tribute to the sorrows of my fair name-sake.' Then pointing out the title-page to Laura, she added, 'You, I suppose, have often done so.'

It was the tragedy of THE MINISTER, and Laura, reading the name aloud, said, she was not acquainted with it.

'Oh,' cried Mrs Dawkins, 'that's the young woman as swears so

horridly. No, I dares to say, Miss Montreville never read no such
thing. If it an't a shame to be seen in a Christian woman hands, it is.
And if she would read it by herself, it would be nothing; but there
she goes, ranting about the house like an actress, cursing all aloud,
worser nor the drunken apple-woman at the corner of the street.'

'Pray Mamma, forbear,' said Miss Julia Dawkins, in a plaintive
tone; 'it wounds my feelings to hear you. I am sure, if Miss
Montreville would read this play, she would own that the expressions
which you austerely denominate curses, give irresistible energy to the
language.'

'This kind of energy,' said Laura, with a smile, 'has at least the
merit of being very generally attainable.' This remark was not in Miss
Julia's line. She had, therefore, recourse to her book, and with great
variety of grimace, read aloud one of Casimir's impassioned, or, as
Laura thought, frantic speeches. The curious contrast of the reader's
manner, with her appearance, of the affected sentimentality of her
air, with the robust vulgarity of her figure, struck Laura as so
irresistibly ludicrous, that, though of all young ladies, she was the
least addicted to tittering, her politeness would have been fairly
defeated in the struggle, had it not been reinforced by the entrance of
Mr and Mrs Jones. The former was a little man, in a snuff-coloured
coat, and a brown wig, who seemed to be about fifty, – the latter was
a good-humoured commonplace looking woman, of about half that
age. Laura was pleased with the cordiality with which Mr Jones shook
his mother-in-law by the hand, saying, 'Well, Mother, I's brought
you Kate pure and hearty again, and the little fellow is fine and well,
tho'f he be too young to come a wisiting.'

As soon as the commotion occasioned by their entrance was over,
and Laura formally made acquainted with the lady, Mrs Dawkins
began, 'I hopes,Kate, you ha'nt forgot how to tell about your jaunt to
Scotland; for this here young lady staid tea just o'purpose to hear it.'
'Oh, that I ha'nt,' said Mrs Jones, 'I'm sure I shall remember it the
longest day I have to live.' 'Pray Miss,' added she, turning to Laura,
'was you ever in Glasgow?' 'Never,' said Laura; 'but I have heard that
it is a fine city.' 'Ay, but I've been there first and last eleven days; and
I can say for it, it is really a handsome town, and a mort of good
white-stone houses in it. For you see, when Mr Jones married me, he
had not been altogether satisfied with his rider, and he thoft as he'd
go down to Glasgow himself and do business; and that he'd make it
do for his wedding jaunt, and that would be killing two dogs with one

stone.' 'That was certainly an excellent plan,' said Laura. 'Well,' continued Mrs Jones, 'when we'd been about a week in Glasgow, we were had to dine one day with Mr Mactavish, as supplies Mr Jones with ginghams; and he talked about some grand house of one of your Scotch dukes, and said as how we must'nt go home without seeing it. So we thought since we had come so far, we might as well see what was to be seen.' 'Certainly,' said Laura, at the pause which was made to take breath, and receive approbation. 'Well, we went down along the river, which, to say truth, is very pretty, tho'f it be not turfed, nor kept neat round the edges, to a place they call Dumbarton; where there is a rock, for all the world, like an ill-made sugar loaf, with a slice out o' the middle on't; and they told us there was a castle on it, but such a castle!' 'Pray, sister,' said Miss Julia, 'have you an accurate idea of what constitutes a castle? of the keeps, the turrets, the winding staircases, and the portcullis?' 'Bless you, my dear,' returned the traveller, 'ha'nt I seen Windsor Castle, and t'other's no more like it – no more than nothing at all. Howsoever, we slept that night at a very decent sort of an inn; and Mr Jones thought as we were so comfortable, we had best come back to sleep. So as the duke's house was but thirty miles off, we thought if we set off soon in the morning, we might get back at night. So off we set, and went two stages to breakfast, at a place with one of their outlandish names; and to be sartain, when we got there, we were as hungry as hounds. Well, we called for hot rolls; and, do but think, there was'nt no such thing to be had for love or money.'

Mrs Jones paused to give Laura time for the expression of pity; but she remained silent, and Mrs Jones resumed: 'Well, they brought us a loaf as old as St Paul's, and some good enough butter; so thinks I, I'll make us some good warm toast; for I loves to make the best of a bad bargain. So I bid the waiter bring us the toast-stool; but if you had seen how he stared, – why, the pore fellor had never heard of no such thing in his life. Then they shewed us a huge mountain, as black as a sootbag, just opposite the window, and said as we must go up there; but, thinks I, catch us at that; for if we be so bad off here for breakfast, what shall we be there for dinner. So my husband and I were of a mind upon it, to get back to Glasgow as fast as we could; for, though to be sure it cost us a power of money coming down, yet thinks we, the first loss is the best.'

'What would I have given,' cried Miss Julia, turning up the whites of her eyes, 'to have been permitted to mingle my sighs with the

mountain breezes!' Mrs Jones was accustomed to her sister's
nonsense, and she only shrugged her shoulders. But Mrs Dawkins,
provoked that her daughter should be so much more than usually
ridiculous before a stranger, said, 'Why, child, how can you be so
silly, – what in the world should you do sighing o' top of a Scotch
hill? I dare to say, if you were there you might sigh long enough
before you'd find such a comfortable cup of tea, as what you have in
your hand.' Miss Julia disdained reply; but turning to our heroine,
she addressed her in a tone so amusingly sentimental, that Laura
feared to listen to the purport of her speech, lest the manner and the
matter united should prove too much for her gravity; and rising, she
apologized for retiring, by saying, that she heard her father stir, and
that she must attend him.

When two people of very different ages meet tête à tête in a room,
where they are not thoroughly domesticated, – where there are no
books, no musical instruments, nor even that grand bond of sociality,
a fire, – it requires no common invention and vivacity to pass an
evening with tolerable cheerfulness. The little appearances of
discomfort, however, which imperceptibly lower the spirits of others,
had generally an opposite effect upon those of Laura. Attentive to the
comfort of every human being who approached her, she was always
the first to discover the existence and cause of the 'petty miseries of
life;' – but, accustomed to consider them merely as calls to exertion,
they made not the slightest impression on her spirits or temper. The
moment she cast her eyes on her father, leaning on a table, where
stood a pair of candles, that but half-lighted the room; and on the
chimney, where faded fennel occupied the place of a fire, she
perceived that all her efforts would be necessary to produce any thing
like comfort. She began her operations, by enticing her father out of
the large vacant room, into the small one, where she intended to
work. Here she prepared his coffee, gave him account of the party
below stairs, read to him her letter to Mrs Douglas, and did and said
every thing she could imagine to amuse him.

When the efforts to entertain are entirely on one side, it is scarcely
in human nature to continue them; and Laura was beginning to feel
very blank, when it luckily occurred to her, that she had brought her
little chess-board from Glenalbert. Away she flew, and in triumph
produced this infallible resort. The match was pretty equal. Captain
Montreville had more skill, Laura more resource; and she defended
herself long and keenly. At last she was within a move of being

checkmated. But the move was hers; and the Captain, in the heat of victory, overlooked a step by which the fortune of the game would have been reversed. Laura saw it, and eagerly extended her hand to the piece; but recollecting that there is something in the pride of man's nature that abhors to be beaten at chess by a lady, she suddenly desisted; and, sweeping her lily arm across the board, 'Nay, now,' she cried, wtih a look of ineffable good nature, 'if you were to complete my defeat after all my hair-breadth 'scapes, you could not be so unreasonable as to expect that I should keep my temper.' 'And how dare you,' said Captain Montreville, in great good humour with his supposed victory, 'deprive me at once of the pleasures of novelty and of triumph?' By the help of this auxiliary, the evening passed pleasantly away; and, before another came, Laura had provided for it the cheap luxury of some books from a circulating library.

CHAPTER VIII

———•———

FOR the first fortnight after Captain Montreville's arrival in London, almost every forenoon was spent in unavailing attempts to see Mr Baynard, whose illness, at the end of that time, had increased to such a degree, as left no hope that he could soon be in a condition for attending to business. Harassed by suspense, and weary of waiting for an interview which seemed every day more distant, Captain Montreville resolved to stay no longer for his agent's introduction to Mr Warren, but to visit the young heir, and himself explain his errand. Having procured Mr Warren's address from Mr Baynard's servants, he proceeded to Portland Street; and knocking at the door of a handsome house, was there informed that Mr Warren was gone to Brighton, and was not expected to return for three weeks.

Captain Montreville had now no resource but to unfold his demands to Mr Warren in writing. He did so, stating his claims with all the simple energy of truth; but no answer was returned. He fatigued himself and Laura in vain, with conjecturing the cause of this silence. He feared that, though dictated by scrupulous politeness, his letter might have given offence. He imagined that it might have miscarried, or that Mr Warren might have left Brighton before it reached him. All his conjectures were, however, wide of the truth. The letter had given no offence, for it had never been read. It safely reached the person to whom it was addressed, just as he was adding a finishing touch to the graces of a huge silk handkerchief in which he had enveloped his chin, preparatory to the exhibition of his person, and of an elegant new curricle upon the Steine. A single glance had convinced him that the letter was unworthy to encroach on this momentous concern – he had thrown it aside, intending to read it when he had nothing else to do, and had seen it no more, till on his return to London, he unrolled from it his bottle of esprit de rose, which his valet had wrapped in its folds.

The three wearisome weeks came to an end at last, as well as a fourth, which the attractions of Brighton prevailed on Mr Warren to add to his stay; and Captain Montreville, making another, almost hopeless, inquiry in Portland Street, was, to his great joy, admitted to the long desired conference. He found the young man in his nightgown, reclining on a sofa, intently studious of the *Sportsman's Magazine*, while he ever and anon refreshed himself for this his literary toil, by sipping a cup of chocolate. Being courteously invited to partake, the Captain began by apologizing for his intrusion, but pleaded that his business was of such a nature as to require a personal interview. At the mention of business, the smile forsook its prescriptive station on the smooth face of Mr Warren. 'Oh pray pardon me, Sir,' said he, 'my agent manages all my matters – I never meddle with business – I have really no head for it. Here, Du Moulin, give this gentleman Mr William's address.' 'Excuse me, Sir,' said Captain Montreville. 'On this occasion I must entreat that you will so far depart from your rule as to permit me to state my business to you in person.' 'I assure you, Sir,' said the beau rising from his luxurious posture, 'I know nothing about business – the very name of it is to me the greatest bore in life; – it always reminds me of my old dead uncle. The poor man could never talk of any thing but of bank-stock, the price of the best archangel tar, and the scarcity of hemp. Often did I wish the hemp had been cheap enough to make him apply a little of it to his own use – but the old cock took wing at last without a halter, he, he, he.'

'I shall endeavour to avoid these offensive subjects,' said Captain Montreville, smiling. 'The affair in which I wish to interest you, is less a case of law than of equity, and therefore I must beg permission to state it to your personal attention, as your agent might not think himself at liberty to do me the justice which I may expect from you.'

Mr Warren at this moment recollected an indispensable engagement, and begged that Captain Montreville would do him the favour to call another time – secretly resolving not to admit him. 'I shall not detain you two minutes,' said the Captain; 'I shall in a few words state my request, and leave you to decide upon it when you are more at leisure.' 'Well, Sir,' replied Mr Warren, with something between a sigh and an ill-suppressed yawn, 'if it must be so.' –

'About eighteen months ago,' resumed the Captain, 'my agent, Mr

Baynard, paid £1500 to your late uncle, as the price of an annuity on my daughter's life. The deed is now found to be informal, and Mr Williams has refused to make any payment. Mr Baynard's disposition has prevented me from seeing him since my arrival in London; but I have no doubt that he can produce a discharge for the price of the annuity; in which case, I presume you will allow the mistake in the deed to be rectified.'

'Certainly, certainly,' said Mr Warren, who had transferred his thoughts from the subject of the conversation to the comparative merits of nankeen pantaloons and leather-breeches. 'But even if Mr Baynard should have no document to produce,' continued Captain Montreville, 'may I not hope that you will instruct Mr Williams to examine, whether there are not in Mr Warren's books, traces of the agreement for an annuity of £80, in the name of Laura Montreville?' 'Sir?' said Warren, whose ear caught the tone of interrogation, though the meaning of the speaker had entirely escaped him. The Captain repeated his request. 'Oh, certainly I will,' said the young man, who would have promised any thing to get rid of the subject. 'I hope the matter will be found to stand as you wish. At all events, such a trifling sum can be of no sort of consequence.' 'Pardon me, Sir,' said Captain Montreville, warmly, 'to me it is of the greatest – should this trifle, as you are pleased to call it, be lost to me, my child must at my death be left to all the horrors, all the temptations of want – temptations aggravated a thousand fold, by beauty and inexperi-ence.' His last words awakened something like interest in the drowsy soul of his hearer, who said, with the returning smile of self-complacency, 'Beauty, Sir, did you say? beauty is what I may call my passion – a pretty girl is always sure of my sympathy and good offices. I shall call for Mr Williams this very day.' Captain Montreville bit his lip. 'Laura Montreville, thought he, an object of sympathy to such a thing as thou!' He bowed, however, and, said, 'I hope, Sir, you will find, upon examination, that Miss Montreville's claims rest upon your justice.' Then laying his address upon the table, he took his leave, with an air perhaps a little too stately for one who had come to ask a favour.

He returned home, however, much pleased with having at last met with Warren, and with having, as he imagined, put in train the business on account of which he had performed so long a journey, and suffered so much uneasiness. He found Laura, too, in high spirits. She had just given the finishing touches to a picture on which she had been most busily employed ever since her arrival in London. She had studied the composition, till her head ached with intensity of thought. She had laboured the finishing with care unspeakable; and she now only waited till her work could with safety be moved, to try the success of her project for the attainment of wealth. Of this success she scarcely entertained a doubt. She was sensible, indeed, that the picture had many faults, but not so many as that on which Mrs Douglas's visitor had fixed so high a price. Since painting the latter, she had improved in skill; and never had she bestowed such pains as on her present work. The stranger had said that the Scipio in Mrs Douglas's picture was interesting. The Leonidas in this was much more so – she could not doubt it, for he resembled Hargrave. She had hoped the resemblance would be apparent to no eye but her own. Her father, however, had noticed it, and Laura had tried to alter the head, but the Captain declared she had spoiled it. Laura thought so herself; and, after sketching a hundred regularly handsome countenances, could be satisfied with none that bore not some affinity to her only standard of manly beauty.

To add to the pleasure with which Laura surveyed the completion of her labours, she had that day received a letter from Mrs Douglas, in which mention was made of Hargrave.

In her first letters to Laura, Mrs Douglas had entirely avoided this subject. Almost a month Laura had waited, with sickening impatience, for some hint from which she might gather intelligence of Hargrave's motions – in vain. Her friend had been provokingly determined to believe that the subject was disagreeable to her correspondent. Laura at last ventured to add, to one of her letters, a postscript, in which, without naming the Colonel, she inquired whether the – – regiment was still at Perth. She blushed as she glanced over this postscript. She thought it had an air of contrivance and design. She was half tempted to destroy the letter; but she could not prevail on herself to make a more direct inquiry; and to forbear making any was almost impossible. An answer had this day arrived; and Laura read no part of it with such interest, as that which, with seeming carelessness, informed her that the Colonel had been several times at the parsonage: and that Mrs Douglas understood from report, that he was soon to visit London.

Again and again did Laura read this passage, and ponder every word of it with care. I am playing the fool, said she to herself, and laid the letter aside; took it up again to ascertain some particular expression, and again read the paragraph which spoke of Hargrave, and again paused upon his name. She was so employed when her father entered, and she made an instinctive motion to conceal the paper; but the next moment she held it out to him, saying, 'This is from Mrs Douglas.' 'Well, my love,' said the Captain, 'if there are no secrets in it, read it to me. I delight in Mrs Douglas's simple affectionate style.' Laura did as she was desired; but when she reached the sentence which began with the name of Hargrave, she blushed, hesitated for a moment, and then, passing over it, began the next paragraph.

Without both caution and self-command, the most upright woman will be guilty of subterfuges, where love is in question. Men can talk of the object of their affections – they find pleasure in confiding, in describing, in dwelling upon their passion – but the love of woman seeks concealment. If she can talk of it, or even of any thing that leads to it, the fever is imaginary, or it is past. 'It is very strange,' said the Captain, when Laura had concluded, 'that Mrs Douglas never mentions Hargrave, when she knows what an interest I take in him.' Laura coloured crimson, but remained silent. 'What do you think can be her reason?' asked the Captain. This was a question for which Laura could find no evasion short of actual deceit; and, with an effort far more painful than that from which her little artifice had saved her, her lovely face and neck glowing with confusion, she said: 'She does mention – only I – I. Please to read it yourself;' and she pointed it out to her father, who, prepared by her hesitation to expect something very particular, was surprised to find the passage so unimportant. 'Why, Laura,' said he, 'what was there to prevent you from reading this?' To this question Laura could make no reply; and the Captain, after gazing on her for some moments in vain hope of an explanation, dismissed the subject, saying, with a shrug of his shoulders, 'Well, well – women are creatures I don't pretend to understand.'

Laura had often and deeply reflected upon the propriety of confiding to her father her engagement with Hargrave. Vague as it was, she thought a parent had an indisputable right to be informed of it. Her promise too had been conditional, and what judge so proper as her father to watch over the fulfilment of its conditions? What judge so proper as her father to examine the character, and to inspect the conduct, of the man who might one day become her husband? But, amidst all the train of delightful visions which this thought conjured up, Laura felt that Hargrave's conduct had been such as she could not endure that her father should remember against his future son. Captain Montreville was now at a distance from Hargrave. Before they could possibly meet, her arguments, or her entreaties, might have so far prevailed over the subsiding passions of her father, as to dissuade him from a fashionable vindication of her honour. But what was to restore her lover to his present rank in the Captain's regard? What would blot from his recollection the insult offered to his child? Without mention of that insult, her tale must be almost unintelligible; and she was conscious that, if she entered on the subject at all, her father's tenderness, or his authority, might unlock every secret of her breast. The time when her engagement could produce any consequence was distant. Ere it arrived, something unforeseen might possibly remove her difficulties; or, at the worst, she hoped that, before she permitted her father to weigh the fault of Hargrave, she should be able to balance against it the exemplary propriety of his after conduct. She was not just satisfied with this reasoning; but weaker considerations can dissuade us from what we are strongly disinclined to do; and to unveiling her own partiality, or the unworthiness of its object, Laura's disinclination was extreme. She determined therefore to put off the evil hour; and withdrew her father's attention from the subject of the letter, by inquiring whether he had seen Warren, and whether he had settled his business satisfactorily? The Captain replied, that though it was not absolutely settled, he hoped it was now in a fair way of being so; and informed her of Warren's promise. 'Yet,' added he, 'any one of a thousand trifles may make such an animal forget or neglect the most important concern.' 'What sort of man did he seem?' inquired Laura. 'Man!' repeated the Captain, contemptuously. 'Why, child, he is a creature entirely new to you. He talks like a parrot, looks like a woman, dresses like a monkey, and smells like a civet-cat. You might have lived at Glenalbert for half a century, without seeing such a creature.' 'I hope he will visit us,' said Laura, 'that we may not return home without seeing at least one of the curiosities of London.'

CHAPTER IX

————————●————————

THE next day, as Captain Montreville sat reading aloud to his daughter, who was busy with her needle, Mr Warren was announced.

Laura, who concluded that he had business with her father, rose to retire; but her visitor, intercepting her, took both her hands, saying, 'Pray, Ma'am, don't let me frighten you away.' With a constitutional dislike to familiarity, Laura coolly disengaged herself, and left the room, without uttering a syllable; but not before Warren had seen enough of her to determine, that, if possible, he should see her again. He was struck with her extraordinary beauty, which was heightened by the little hectic his forwardness had called to her cheek; and he prolonged his visit to an unfashionable length, in the hope of her return. He went over all the topics which he judged proper for the ear of a stranger of his own sex; – talked of the weather, the news, the emptiness of the town, of horses, ladies, cock-fights, and boxing-matches. He informed the Captain, that he had given directions to his agent to examine into the state of the annuity; inquired how long Miss Montreville was to grace London with her presence; and was told that she was to leave it the moment her father could settle the business, on account of which alone he had left Scotland. When it was absolutely necessary to conclude his visit, Mr Warren begged permission to repeat it, that he might acquaint Captain Montreville with the success of his agent; secretly hoping, that Laura would another time be less inaccessible.

Laura meanwhile thought his visit would never have an end. Having wandered into every room to which she had access, and found rest in none of them, she concluded, rather rashly, that she should find more comfort in the one from which his presence excluded her. That disease of the mind in which by eager anticipations of the future many are unfitted for present enjoyment, was new to the active spirit of Laura. The happiness of her life, (and in spite of the caprices of her mother, it had, upon the whole, been a happy one), had chiefly arisen from a constant succession of regular, but varied pursuits. The methodical sequence of domestic usefulness, and improving study, and healthful exercise, afforded calm yet immediate enjoyment; and the future pleasure which they promised was of that indefinite and progressive kind which provokes no eager desires, no impatient expectation. Laura, therefore, had scarcely known what it was to long for the morrow; but on this day, the morrow was anticipated with wishful solicitude, – a solicitude which banished from her mind even the thoughts of Hargrave. Never did youthful bridegroom look forward to his nuptial hour with more ardour, than did Laura to that which was to begin the realization of her prospects of wealth and independence. The next day was to be devoted to the sale of her picture. Her father was on that day to visit Mr Baynard at Richmond, whither he had been removed for the benefit of a purer air; and she hoped on his return, to surprize her beloved parent with an unlooked-for treasure. She imagined the satisfaction with which she should spread before him her newly acquired riches, – the pleasure with which she would listen to his praises of her diligence; – above all, her fancy dwelt on the delight which she should feel in relieving her father from the pecuniary embarrassment, in which she knew him to be involved by a residence in London so much longer than he had been prepared to expect.

That she might add to her intended gift the pleasure of surprize, she was resolved not to mention her plan for to-morrow; and with such subjects in contemplation, how could she rest, – of what other subject could she speak? She tried to banish it from her mind, that she might not be wholly unentertaining to her father, who, on her account, usually spent his evenings at home. But the task of amusing was so laborious, that she was glad to receive in it even the humble assistance of Miss Julia Dawkins.

This young lady had thought it incumbent on her to assault our heroine with a most violent friendship; a sentiment which often made her sufficiently impertinent, though it was a little kept in check by the calm good sense and natural reserve of Laura. The preposterous affectation of Julia sometimes provoked the smiles, but more frequently the pity of Laura; for her real good nature could find no pleasure in seeing human beings make themselves ridiculous, and she applied to the cure of Miss Dawkins's foibles, the ingenuity which many would have employed to extract amusement from them. She soon found, however, that she was combating a sort of Hydra, from which, if she succeeded in lopping off one excrescence, another was instantly ready to sprout. Having no character of her own, Julia was always, as nearly as she was able, the heroine whom the last read novel inclined her to personate. But as those who forsake the guidance of nature are in imminent danger of absurdity, her copies were always caricatures. After reading Evelina, she sat with her mouth extended in a perpetual smile, and was so very timid, that she would not for the world have looked at a stranger. When Camilla was the model for the day, she became insufferably rattling, infantine, and thoughtless. After perusing the Gossip's story, she, in imitation of the rational Louisa, suddenly waxed very wise – spoke in sentences – despised romances – sewed shifts – and read sermons. But, in the midst of this fit, she, in an evil hour, opened a volume of the Nouvelle Eloise, which had before disturbed many wiser heads. The shifts were left unfinished, the sermons thrown aside, and Miss Julia returned with renewed *impetus* to the sentimental. This afternoon her studies had changed their direction, as Laura instantly guessed by the lively air with which she entered the room, saying that she had brought her netting, and would sit with her for an hour. 'But do, my dear,' added she, 'first shew me the picture you have been so busy with; Mamma says it is beautiful, for she peeped in at it the other day.'

It must be confessed, that Laura had no high opinion of Miss Dawkins's skill in painting; but she remembered Moliere's old woman, and went with great good will to bring her performance. 'Oh charming,' exclaimed Miss Julia, when it was placed before her; 'the figure of the man is quite delightful; it is the very image of that bewitching creature Tom Jones.' 'Tom Jones?' cried Laura, starting back aghast. 'Yes, my dear,' continued Julia; 'just such must have been the graceful turn of his limbs – just such his hair, his eyes, those lips, that when they touched her hand, put poor Sophia into such a flutter.' The astonishment of Laura now gave way to laughter, while she said, 'Really Miss Dawkins you must have a strange idea of Tom Jones, or I a very extraordinary one of Leonidas.' 'Leonce, you mean, in Delphine,' said Julia; 'Oh, he is a delightful creature too.' 'Delphine!' repeated Laura, to whom the name was as new as that of the Spartan was to her companion. 'No, I mean this for the Greek general taking his last leave of his wife.' 'And I think,' said Captain Montreville, approaching the picture, 'the suppressed anguish of the matron is admirably expressed, and contrasts well with the scarcely relenting ardour of the hero.' Miss Julia again declared, that the picture was charming, and that Leontine, as she was pleased to call him, was divinely handsome; but having newly replenished her otherwise empty head with Fielding's novel, she could talk of nothing else; and turning to Laura said, 'But why were you so offended, that I compared your Leontine to Tom Jones? — Is he not a favourite of yours?' 'Not particularly so,' said Laura. 'Oh why not? — I am sure he is a delightful fellow — so generous — so ardent. Come, confess — should you not like of all things to have such a lover?' 'No, indeed,' said Laura, with most unusual energy; for her thoughts almost unconsciously turned to one whose character she found no pleasure in associating with that of Fielding's hero. 'And why not?' asked Miss Julia. 'Because,' answered Laura, 'I could not admire in a lover qualities which would be odious in a husband.' 'Oh goodness!' cried Miss Julia, 'do you think Tom Jones would make an odious husband?' 'The term is a little strong,' replied Laura; 'but he certainly would not make a pleasant yoke-fellow. What is your opinion, Sir?' turning to her father. 'I confess,' said the Captain, 'I should rather have wished him to marry Squire Western's daughter than mine. But still the character is fitted to be popular.' 'I think,' said Laura, 'he is indebted for much of the toleration which he receives, to a comparison with the despicable Blifil.' 'Certainly,' said the Captain; 'and it is unfortunate for the morality of the book, that the reader is inclined to excuse the want of religion in the hero, by seeing its language made ridiculous in Thwackum, and villanous in Blifil. Even the excellent Mr Alworthy excites but feeble interest; and it is not by the character which we respect, but by that in which we are interested, that the moral effect on our minds is produced.' 'Oh,' said Miss Julia, who very imperfectly comprehended the Captain's observation, 'he might make a charming husband without being religious; and then he is so warm-hearted — so generous.' 'I shall not dispute that point with you just now,' replied Laura, 'though my opinion differs materially from yours; but Tom Jones's warmth of heart and generosity do not appear to me of that kind which qualify a man for adorning domestic life. His seems a constitutional warmth, which in his case, and I believe, in most others, is the concomitant of a warm temper, — a temper as little favourable to gentleness in those

who command, as to submission in those who obey. If by generosity
you mean the cheerful relinquishing of something which we really
value, it is an abuse of the term to apply it to the profusion with
which your favourite squanders his money.'

'If it is not generous to part with one's money,' said Miss Julia, 'I
am sure I don't know what is.'

'The quiet domestic generosity which is of daily use,' replied
Laura, 'is happily not confined to those who have money to bestow; –
but may appear in any of a thousand little acts of self-denial.' Julia,
whose ideas of generosity, culled from her favourite romances, were
on that gigantic kind of scale that makes it unfit for common
occasions, and therefore in danger of total extinction, was silent for
some moments, and then said, 'I am sure you must allow that it was
very noble in Jones to bury in his own miserable bosom his passion
for Sophia, after he knew that she felt a mutual flame.' 'If I recollect
right,' said Laura, smiling at the oddity of Julia's phrases, 'he broke
that resolution; and I fancy the merely *resolving* to do right, is a
degree of virtue, to which even the most profligate attain many times
in their lives.'

Miss Dawkins, by this time more than half-suspected her
companion of being a Methodist. 'You have such strict notions,' said
she, 'that I see Tom Jones would never have done for you.' 'No,' said
Captain Montreville, 'Sir Charles Grandison would have suited
Laura infinitely better.' 'Oh no, papa,' said Laura, laughing; 'if two
such formal personages as Sir Charles and I had met, I am afraid we
should never have had the honour of each other's acquaintance.'

'Then, of all the gentlemen who are mentioned in novels,' said
Miss Julia, 'tell me who is your favourite? – Is it Lord Orville, or
Delville, or Valancourt, or Edward, or Mortimer, or Peregrine Pickle,
or' – and she run on till she was quite out of breath, repeating what
sounded like a page of the catalogue of a circulating library.

'Really,' said Laura, when a pause permitted her to speak, 'my
acquaintance with these accomplished persons is so limited that I can
scarcely venture to decide; but, I believe, I prefer the hero of Miss
Porter's new publication – Thaddeus of Warsaw. Truly generous,
and inflexibly upright, his very tenderness has in it something manly
and respectable; and the whole combination has an air of nature that
interests one as for a real friend.' Miss Dawkins had never read the
book, and Laura applied to her father for a confirmation of her
opinion. 'Yes, my dear,' said the Captain, 'your favourite has the

same resemblance to a human character which the Belvidere Appollo has to a human form. It is so like man that one cannot absolutely call it divine, yet so perfect, that it is difficult to believe it human.'

At this moment Miss Julia was seized with an uncontrollable desire to read the book, which, she declared, she should not sleep till she had done; and she went to dispatch a servant in quest of it.

Laura followed her down stairs, to ask from Mrs Dawkins a direction to a picture-dealer, to whom she might dispose of her performance. Mrs Dawkins said she knew of no such person; but directed Laura to a printshop, the master of which was her acquaintance, where she might get the intelligence she wanted.

On the following morning, as soon as Captain Montreville had set out for Richmond, his daughter, sending for a hackney coach, departed on the most interesting business she had ever undertaken. Her heart fluttered with expectation – her step was buoyant with hope, and she sprung into the carriage with the lightness of a sylph. Stopping at the shop which her landlady recommended, she was there directed to several of the professional people for whom she was enquiring, and she proceeded to the habitation of the nearest. As she entered the house, Laura changed colour, and her breath came quick. She stopped a moment to recover herself, and then followed her conductor into the presence of the connoisseur. Struck with the sight of so elegant a woman, he rose, bowed very low, and supposing that she came to make some addition to her cabinet, threw open the door of his picture-room, and obsequiously hoped that she might find something there worthy of her attention. Laura modestly undeceived him, saying, that she had brought in the carriage which waited for her, a picture which she wished to dispose of. This statement instantly put to flight the servility of her hearer; who, with completely recovered consequence, inquired the name of the artist; and being answered, that the picture was not the work of a professional man, wrinkled his nose into an expression of ineffable contempt, and said – 'I make it a rule never to buy any of these things – they are generally such vile daubs. However to oblige so pretty a lady,' added he, (softening his contumelious aspect into a leer), 'I may look at the thing, and if it is at all tolerable' – 'There is no occasion to give you that trouble,' said Laura, turning away with an air which again half convinced the man that she must be a person of consequence. He muttered something of 'thinking it no trouble;' to which she gave no attention, but hastened to her carriage, and ordered the coachman to drive to the show-room of an Italian.

Laura did not give him time to fall into the mistake of the other, but instantly opened her business; and Mr Sonini was obligingly running himself to lift the picture from the carriage, when it was brought in by Mrs Dawkins' maid, whom Laura had requested to attend her. Having placed the picture, the Italian retreated a few paces to examine the effect, and then said – 'Ah! I do see – dis is leetle after de manner of Correggio – very pretty – very pretty, indeed.' The hopes of Laura rose high at these encouraging words; but suffered instantaneous depression, when he continued, with a shake of his head, 'but 'tis too new – quite moderne – painted in dis contri. – Painter no name – de picture may be all so good as it vil – it never vil sell. Me sorry,' added he, reading Laura's look of disappointment, 'me sorry displease such bell angela; but cannot buy.' 'I am sorry for it,' said Laura, and sighing heavily, she courtesied and withdrew.

Her next attempt was upon a little pert-looking man, in a foreign dress, and spectacles. 'Hum,' said he, 'a picture to sell – well, let us see't. – There, that's the light. Hum – a poor thing enough – no keeping – no costûme. Well, Ma'am, what do you please to ask for this?' 'I should be glad, Sir, that you would fix a price on it.' 'Hum – well – let me think – I suppose five guineas will be very fair.' At this proposal, the blood mounted to the cheeks of Laura; and she raised her eyes to examine whether the proposer really had the confidence to look her in the face. But finding his eye steadily fixed on her, she transferred her suspicions from the honesty of the bidder to the merits of her piece, and mildly answering, 'I shall not, I think, be disposed to part with it at that price,' she motioned to the servant to carry it back to the coach.

One trial still remained; and Laura ordered her carriage to an obscure street in the city. She was very politely received by Mr Collins, – a young man who had himself been an artist; but whom bad health had obliged to relinquish a profession which he loved. 'This piece has certainly great merit,' said he, after examining it, 'and most gladly would I have made the purchase; but my little room is at present overstocked, and, to own the truth to you, the picture is worth more than my wife and four little ones can afford to venture upon speculation, and such is the purchase of the work, however meritorious, of an unknown artist. But if you were to place it in the exhibition, I have no doubt that it would speedily find a purchaser.'

The prospect which the Exhibition held forth, was far too distant to meet the present exigency; for Laura well knew that her father would find almost immediate occasion for the price of her labours; and with a heavy sigh she returned to her carriage.

What now remained but to return home with the subject of so much fruitless toil. Still, however, she determined to make one effort more, and returned to inquire of the printseller, whether he knew any other person to whom she could apply? He had before given his whole list, and could make no addition to it. But observing the expression of blank disappointment which overcast her face, he offered, if she would trust him with the picture, to place it where it would be seen by his customers, and expressed a belief that some of them might purchase it. Laura thankfully accepted the offer, and after depositing with him her treasure, which had lost much of its value in her eyes, and naming the price she expected, she returned home; making on her way as many sombrous reflections on the vanity and uncertainty of all sublunary pursuits, as ever were made by any young lady in her eighteenth year.

She sat down in her now solitary parlour – suffered dinner to be placed before her and removed, without knowing of what it consisted; and when the servant who brought it disappeared, began, like a true heroine, to vent her disappointment in tears. But soon recollecting that, though she had no joyful surprize awaiting her father, she might yet gladden it with a smiling welcome, she started up from her melancholy posture – bathed her eyes – placed the tea equipage – ordered the first fire of the season to displace the faded fennel in the chimney – arranged the apartment in the nicest order – and had just given to everything the greatest popssible appearance of comfort, when her father arrived. She had need, however, of all her firmness, and of all the elation of conscious self-control, to resist the contagious depression of countenance and manner with which Captain Montreville accosted her. He had good reason for his melancholy. Mr Baynard, his early acquaintance, almost the only person known to him in this vast city, had that morning breathed his last. All access to his papers was of course at present impossible; and until a person could be chosen to arrange his affairs, it would be impracticable for Captain Montreville to ascertain whether there existed any voucher for the payment of the price of the annuity. Harassed by his repeated disappointments, and unendowed by nature with the unbending spirit that rises in disaster, he now declared to

Laura his resolution to remain in London only till a person was fixed upon for the management of Mr Baynard's affairs – to lay before him the circumstances of his case – and then to return to Scotland, and trust to a correspondence for concluding the business.

At this moment nothing could have been further from Laura's wish than to quit London. She was unwilling to forfeit her remaining hope that her picture might find a purchaser, and a still stronger interest bound her to the place which was so soon to be the residence of Hargrave. But she saw the prudence of her father's determination – she felt the necessity of relinquishing a mode of life so unsuitable to his scanty income, and she cheerfully acquiesced in his proposal of returning home. Still some time must elapse, before their departure; and she indulged a hope, that ere that time expired, the produce of her labours might lighten their pecuniary difficulties.

Captain Montreville retired early; and Laura, wearied out with the toils and the disappointments of the day, gladly resigned herself to the sleep of innocence.

Laura was indebted partly to nature, but more to her own exertion, for that happy elasticity of spirit which easily casts off lighter evil, while it readily seizes, and fully enjoys, pleasure of moderate intensity, and of frequent attainment. Few of the lesser sorrows of youth can resist the cheering influence of early morn; and the petty miseries which, in the shades of evening, assume portentous size and colour, diminish wonderfully in the light of the new-risen sun. With recovered spirits, and reviving hopes, Laura awoke to joys which the worldly know not, – the joys of pious gratitude – of devout contemplation – of useful employment; and so far was her persevering spirit from failing under the disappointments of the preceding day, that she determined to begin a new picture from the moment she was settled at Glenalbert, to compose it with more care, and finish it with greater accuracy, than the former; and to try its fate at the exhibition. She did not think the season of her father's depression a fit one for relating her moritfying adventures, and she found means to amuse him with other topics till he left her, with an intention to call in Portland Street.

He had not been gone long, when Mr Warren's curricle stopped at the door, and the young gentleman, on being informed that the Captain was abroad, inquired for Miss Montreville. After paying his compliments like one secure of a good reception, he began – 'How could you be so cruel as to refuse me the pleasure of seeing you the other day – do you know I waited here a devilish long time just on purpose, though I had promised to take the Countess of Bellamer out an airing, and she was off with Jack Villars before I came.' 'I am sorry,' said Laura, 'that I deprived her Ladyship of your company.' 'I should not have minded it much, if you had but come at last – though the Countess is the prettiest creature in London – curse me if she isn't – the present company always excepted.' 'Do you mean the exception for me, or for yourself?' said Laura. 'Oh now, how can you ask such a question? – I am sure you know that you are confoundedly handsome.' Laura gravely surveyed her own face in an opposite looking-glass, and then, with the nonchalance of one who talks of the most indifferent thing in nature, replied, – 'Yes, I think my features are uncommonly regular.' Warren was a little embarrassed by so unusual an answer to what he intended for a compliment. 'The girl,' thought he, 'must be quite a fool to own that she thinks herself so handsome.' However, after some consideration, he said, – 'It is not so much the features, as a certain *je ne sçai quoi* – a certain charm – one does not know well what to call it, that makes you look so divine.' 'I should suppose,' said Laura, 'from the subject you have chosen to amuse me, that the charm, whatever it is, has no great connection with intellect.' Warren hesitated; for he began to have some suspicions that she was laughing at him, in spite of the immoveable gravity of her countenance. 'It – it isn't – Demme, it isn't so much to amuse you; but when I see a pretty woman, I never can help telling her of it – curse me if I can.' 'And do you often find that your intelligence has the advantage of novelty?' said Laura; an arch smile beginning to dimple her cheek. 'No, 'pon honour,' replied the beau, 'the women are getting so insufferably conceited, they leave one nothing new to tell them.' 'But some gentlemen,' said Laura, 'have the happy talent of saying old things so well, that the want of novelty is not felt.' The moment the words had passed her lips, she perceived, by the gracious smile whcih they produced, that Mr Warren had applied them to himself; and the thought of being guilty of such egregious flattery, brought the colour to her face. Any explanation, however, would have been actual rudeness; and while the consciousness of her involuntary duplicity kept her silent, her companion enjoyed her confusion; which, together with the compliment, he interpreted in a way most satisfactory to his vanity, and thankfully repaid with a torrent of praises in his very best style.

So little value did Laura affix to his commendations, that she was beginning to find extreme difficulty in suppressing a yawn, when it occurred to her that it might save her father a journey to Portland Street, if she could detain Mr Warren till he arrived. Having made an observation, which has been more frequently made than profited by, that most people prefer talking to listening, she engaged her companion in a description of some of the fashionable places of public resort, none of which she had seen; in which he acquitted himself so much to his own satisfaction, that, before they separated, he was convinced that Laura was one of the most penetrating judicious women of his acquaintance; and having before remarked, that, with the help of a little rouge, and a fashionable riding-habit, she would look better in a curricle than any woman in London, he resolved, that if it depended on him, her residence in town should not be a short one. In this laudable resolution, he was confirmed by a consideration of the insolence and extravagence of a certain female, to whose place in his establishment he had some vague idea of advancing Miss Laura, though there was a stateliness about both her and her father, which he suspected might somewhat interfere with his designs in her favour. Soon after the Captain arrived, he took his leave, having no new intelligence to communicate, nor indeed any other purpose in his visit, except that which had been served by his interview with Laura.

As soon as he was gone, Laura went down stairs to beg that Miss Dawkins would accompany her after dinner to the print-shop, to inquire what had been the fate of her picture. More than one person, she was told, had admired it, and expressed a desire to become the owner; but the price had been a formidable obstacle, and it remained unsold.

Almost every evening did Laura, with Mrs Dawkins or her daughter for an escort, direct her steps to the print-shop, and return from her fruitless walk with fainter and fainter hope.

CHAPTER X

———•———

MONTAGUE DE COURCY had dined tête-à-tête with an old uncle from whom he had no expectations, and was returning home to sup quietly with his mother and sister, when his progress was arrested by a group occupying the whole breadth of the pavement, and he heard a female voice which, though unusually musical, had in it less of entreaty than of command, say, 'Pray, Sir, allow us to pass.' 'Not till I have seen the face that belongs to such a figure,' answered one of a party of young men who were rudely obstructing the passage of the lady who had spoken. With this condition, however, she seemed not to intend compliance, for she had doubled her veil, and pertinaciously resisted the attempts of her persecutors to raise it.

De Courcy had a rooted antipathy to all manner of violence and oppression, especially when exercised against the more defenceless part of the creation; and he no sooner ascertained these circumstances, than, with one thrust of his muscular arm, (which, to say the truth, was more than a match for half a dozen of the puny fry of sloth and intemperance), he opened a passage for the lady and her companion; steadily detained her tormentors till she made good her retreat; and then, leaving the gentlemen to answer, as they best could, to their own interrogatories of 'What do you mean?' and 'Who the d—l are you?' he followed the rescued damsel, with whose appearance, considering the place and the hour, he was extremely surprised.

Her height, which certainly rose about the beautiful, perhaps even exceeded the majestic; her figure, though slender, was admirably proportioned, and had all the appropriate roundness of the feminine form; her dress, though simple, and of matronly decency, was not unfashionable; while the dignity of her gait, and the composure of her motion, suited well with the majesty of her stature and mien.

While De Courcy was making these observations, he had offered the lady his arm, which she accepted, and his escort home, which she declined, saying, that she would take refuge in a shop, till a coach could be procured. Nor was he less attentive to her companion, although the latter was a little, elderly, vulgar-looking woman, imperfections which would have utterly disqualified her for the civility of many a polite gentleman.

This person had no sooner recovered the breath of which her supposed danger, and the speed of her rescue from it had deprived her, than she began, with extreme volubility, to comment on her adventure. 'Well,' she cried, 'if that was not the forwardest thing ever I seed. I am sure I have comed home afore now of an evening a matter of five hunder times, and never met with no such thing in my life. But its all along of my being so saving of your money; for I might have took a coach as you'd have had me: but its no longer ago nor last week, as I comed from my tea , at that very Mr Wilkins's, later nor this, and nobody so much as spoke to me; but catch me penny wise again. Howsoever, it's partlins your own doings; for if you hadn't staid so long a-looking at the pictures in the shop we shouldn't have met with them there men. Howsoever, Miss Montreville, you did right enough not to let that there jackanapes see your face, otherwise we mightn't have got off from them fellors tonight.'

The curiosity of De Courcy thus directed, overcame his habitual dislike to staring, and rivetted his eyes on a face, which, once seen, was destined never to be forgotten. Her luxuriant hair, (which De Courcy at first thought black, though he afterwards corrected this opinion), was carelessly divided on a forehead, whose spotless whiteness was varied only by the blue of a vein that shone through the transparent skin. As she raised her mild religious dark grey eyes, their silken lashes rested on the well-defined but delicate eye-brow; or, when her glance fell before the gaze of admiration, threw a long shade on a cheek of unequalled beauty, both for form and colour. The contour of her features, inclining to the Roman, might perhaps have been called masculine, had it not been softened to the sweetest model of maiden loveliness, by the delicacy of its size and colouring. The glowing scarlet of the lips, formed a contrast with a complexion constitutionally pale, but varying every moment; while round her easily but firmly closing mouth, lurked not a trace of the sensual or the vain, but all was calm benevolence, and saintly purity. In the contemplation of a countenance, the perfect symmetry of which was its meanest charm, De Courcy, who was a physiognomist, suffered the stream of time, as well as that of Mrs Dawkins's eloquence, to flow on without notice, and first became sensible that he had profited by neither, when the shop-boy announced that the carriage was at the door. While handing the ladies into the carriage, De Courcy again offered his attendance, which Laura, gracefully thanking him for his attentions, again declined; and they drove off just as he was about to inquire where they chose to be set down.

Now, whether it was that Laura was offended at De Courcy's inspection of her face, or whether she saw any thing disagreeable in his; whether it was that her pride disdained lodgings in Holborn, or that she desired not to be recognized by one who had met with her in such a situation, certain it is, that she chose the moment when that gentleman was placing her voluble companion in the coach, to give the coachman her directions, in sounds that escaped the ears of De Courcy. As he had no means of remedying this misfortune, he walked home, and philosophically endeavoured to forget it in a game at chess with his mother. The fidelity of a historian, however, obliges us to confess, that he this evening played in a manner that would have disgraced a school-boy. After mistaking his antagonist's men for his own, playing into check, throwing away his pieces, and making false moves, he answered his mother's question of 'Montague, what are you doing?', by pushing back his chair, and exclaiming, 'Mother, you never beheld such a woman.'

'Woman!' repeated Mrs De Courcy, settling her spectacles, and looking him full in the face. 'Woman!' said his sister, laying down Bruyere, 'Who is she?'

'I know not,' answered De Courcy, 'but had Lavater seen her, he could scarcely have believed her human.'

'What is her name?'

'The woman who attended her called her Montreville.'

'Where did you meet her?'

'In the street.'

'In the street!' cried Harriet, laughing. 'Oh, Montague, that is not half sentimental enough for you. You should have found her all in a shady bower, playing on a harp that came there nobody knows how; or, all elegant in India muslin, dandling a beggar's brat in a dirty cottage. But let us hear the whole adventure.'

'I have already told you all I know,' answered De Courcy. 'Now,

Madam, will you give me my revenge.' 'No, no,' said Mrs De Courcy, 'I will play no more; I should have no glory in conquering such a defenceless enemy.' 'Well, then,' said Montague, good-humouredly, 'give me leave to read to you, for I would rather amuse you and Harriet in any other way than by sitting quietly to be laughed at.'

After the ladies had retired for the night, De Courcy meditated for full five minutes on the descent from Laura Montreville's forehead to her nose, and bestowed a proportionable degree of consideration upon other lines in her physiognomy; but it must be confessed, that by the time he arrived at the dimple in her left cheek, he had forgotten both Lavater and his opinions, and that his recollection of her mouth was somewhat confused by that of her parting smile, which he more than once delcared aloud to himself was 'heavenly.' We are credibly informed, that he repeated the same expression three times in his sleep; and whether it was that his dreams reminded him of Mrs Dawkins's eloquence, or whether his memory was refreshed by his slumbers, he had not been long awake before he recollected that he had heard that lady mention a Mr Wilkins, and hint that he kept a print-shop. By a proper application to the London directory, he easily discovered the print-seller's abode, and thither he that very day repaired.

Mr Wilkins was not in the shop when De Courcy entered it, but the shop-boy said his master would be there in a minute. This minute appearing to De Courcy of unusual length, he, to while it away, began to examine the prints which hung around. His eye was presently attracted by the only oil picture in the shop; and his attention was fixed by observing, that it presented a striking resemblance of his old school-fellow Hargrave. He turned to make some inquiry of the shop-boy, when Mr Wilkins came in, and his interest reverted to a different object. The question, however, which he had come to ask, and which to ask would have three minutes before appeared the simplest thing in the world, now faltered on his tongue; and it was not without something like hesitation, that he inquired whether Mr Wilkins knew a Miss Montreville. Desirous to oblige a person of De Courcy's appearance, Wilkins immediately related all that he knew of Laura, either from his own observation, or from the report of her loquacious landlady; and perceiving that he was listened to with attention, he proceeded further to detail his conjectures. 'This picture is painted by her,' said he, 'and I rather think the old Captain can't be very rich, she seemed so anxious to have it sold.' De Courcy again turned to the picture, which he had before examined, and on this second inspection, was so fortunate as to discover that it bore the stamp of great genius, – an opinion in which, we believe, he would have been joined by any man of four-and-twenty who had seen the artist. 'So,' thought he, 'this lovely creature's genius is equal to her beauty, and her worth perhaps surpasses both; for she has the courage to rise superior to the silly customs of the world, and can dare to be useful to herself and to others. I knew by the noble arching of her forehead, that she was above all vulgar prejudice:' and he admired Laura the more for being a favourable instance of his own penetration, – a feeling so natural, that it lessens even our enmity to the wicked, when we ourselves have predicted their vices. It must be owned, that De Courcy was a little hasty in his judgment of Laura's worth; but the sight of such a face as hers, gives great speed to a young man's decision upon female character. He instantly purchased the picture, and recollecting that it is highly proper to patronize genius and industry, he desired Mr Wilkins to beg that a companion might be painted. He then returned home, leaving orders that his purchase should follow him immediately.

Though nature, a private education, and studious habits, made De Courcy rather reserved to strangers, he was, in his domestic circle, one of the most communicative persons in the world; and the moment he saw his mother, he began to inform her of the discoveries he had made that morning. 'Montreville!' said Mrs De Courcy, when he had ended, 'can that be William Montreville who was in the – – regiment when your father was the major of it?' 'Most likely he is,' said Montague, eagerly. 'Many a time did he hold you upon his horse, and many a paper kite did he make for you.' 'It must be the same,' said Montague; 'the name is not a common one; it certainly must be the same.' 'I can hardly believe it,' said Mrs De Courcy; 'William Montreville married that strange imprudent woman, Lady Harriet Bircham. Poor Montreville! – he deserved a better wife.' 'It cannot be he,' said De Courcy, sorrowfully; 'no such woman could be the mother of Miss Montreville.' 'He settled in Scotland immediately after his marriage,' continued Mrs De Courcy, 'and since that time I have never heard of him.' 'It is the same then,' said Montague, his countenance lightening with pleasure, 'for Miss Montreville is a Scotch woman. I remember his kindness. I think I almost recollect his face. He used to set me on his knee and sing to me; and when he sung the Babes in the Woods, I pretended to go to sleep on his bosom, for I thought it not manly to cry; but when I looked up, I saw the tears standing in his own eyes. I will go and see my old friend this very hour. 'You have forgotten,' said Mrs De Courcy, 'that you promised to escort Harriet to the park, and she will be disappointed if you engage yourself elsewhere.' De Courcy, who would have postponed any personal gratification rather than disappoint the meanest servant in his household, instantly agreed to defer his visit; and as it had never occurred to him that the claims of relationship were incompatible with those of politeness, he did not once during their walk insinuate to his sister that he would have preferred another engagement.

Never had he, either as a physiognomist or as a man, admired any woman so much as he did Laura; yet her charms were no longer his only, or even his chief, magnet of attraction towards the Montrevilles. Never before had any assemblage of features possessed such power of him, but De Courcy's was not a heart on which mere beauty could make any very permanent impression; and, to the eternal disgrace of his gallantry, it must be confessed, that he scarcely longed more for a second interview with Laura, than he did for an opportunity of paying some grateful civilities to the man who, twenty years before, had good-naturedly forgone the society of his equals in age, to sing ballads and make paper-kites for little Montague. Whatever member of his family occupied most of his thoughts, certain it is, that he spoke much more that evening of Captain Montreville than of his daughter, until the arrival of the painting afforded him occasion to enlarge on her genius, industry, and freedom from vulgar prejudice. On these he continued to descant, till Mrs De Courcy smiled, and Harriet laughed openly; a liberty at which Montague testified his displeasure, by carefully avoiding the subject for the rest of the evening.

Meanwhile the ungrateful Laura had never, from the hour in which they met, bestowed one thought upon her champion. The blackness of his eyes, and the whiteness of his teeth, had entirely escaped her observation; and, even if she had been asked, whether he was tall or short, she could scarcely have given a satisfactory reply. For this extraordinary stupidity, the only excuse is, that her heart was already occupied, the reader knows how, and that her thoughts were engrossed by an intention which her father had mentioned, of borrowing money upon his half-pay.

Though Laura had never known affluence, she was equally a

stranger to all the shames, the distresses, and embarrassments of a debtor; and the thoughts of borrowing what she could not hope by any economy to repay, gave to her upright mind the most cutting uneasiness. But no resource remained; for, even if Captain Montreville could have quitted London within the hour, he had not the means of defraying the expence of the journey. Warren's promises had hitherto produced nothing but hope, and there was no immediate prospect that the payment of the annuity would relieve the difficulty.

Laura turned a despairing wish towards her picture, lamenting that she had ever formed her presumptuous scheme, and hating herself for having, by her presence, increased the perplexities of her father. She prevailed upon him, however, to defer borrowing the money till the following day; and once more, accompanied by Julia, bent her almost hopeless steps towards the print-shop.

Silent and melancholy she passed on, equally regardless of the admiration which she occasionally extorted, and of the animadversions, called forth by the appearance of so elegant a woman on foot, in the streets of the city. As she entered the shop, she cast a half-despairing look towards the place where her picture had hung, and her heart leapt when she perceived that it was gone. 'Well, Ma'am,' said Wilkins, approaching her, 'it is sold at last, and here is the money;' and he put into her hands by far the largest sum they had ever contained. 'You may have as much more whenever you please,' continued he, 'for the gentleman who bought it wants a companion painted.'

Laura spoke not, – she had not indeed the power to speak; – but she raised her eyes with a look that intelligibly said, 'Blessed Father! thy tender mercies are over all thy works.' Recollecting herself, she thanked Wilkins, liberally rewarded him for his trouble, and taking her companion by the arm, she hastened homewards.

The sight of Laura's wealth powerfully affected the mind of Miss Dawkins, and she formed an immediate resolution, to grow rich by similar means. One little objection to this scheme occurred to her, namely, that she had learnt to draw only flowers, and that even this humble branch of the art she had discontinued since she left school. But she thought that a little practice would repair what she had lost, and that though perhaps flowers might not be so productive as historical pieces, she might better her fortune by her works; at the least, they would furnish her with clothes and pocket-money. Upon this judicious plan, she harangued with great volubility to Laura, who, buried in her own reflections, walked silently on, unconscious even of the presence of her loquacious companion. As she approached her home, she began to frame a little speech, with which she meant to present her treasure to her father; and, on entering the house, she flew with a beating heart to find him. She laid her wealth upon his knee. 'My dearest father,' she began, 'the picture' – and she fell upon his neck and burst into tears. Sympathetic tears stood in the eyes of Montreville. He had been surprized at the stoicism with which his daughter appeared to him to support her disappointment, and he was not prepared to expect from her so much sensibility to success. But though Laura had learnt from frequent experience, how to check the feelings of disappointment, to pleasure such as she now felt she was new, and she could not controul its emotions. So far was she, however, from thinking that sensibility was bestowed merely for an ornament, (an opinion which many fair ladies appear to entertain), that the expression of it was always with her an occasion of shame. Unable at this moment to contain herself, she burst from her father's embrace, and hiding herself in her chamber, poured forth a fervent thanksgiving to Him who 'feedeth the ravens when they cry to him.'

'This money is your's my love,' said Captain Montreville to her when she returned to the parlour. 'I cannot bear to rob you of it. Take it, and you can supply me when I am in want of it.' The face and neck of Laura flushed crimson. Her whole soul revolted at the thought of her father's feeling himself a pensioner on her bounty. 'No indeed, Sir,' she replied with energy, 'it is your's – it always was intended for you. But for you, I could never have acquired it.' 'I will not disappoint your generosity, my dearest,' said Montreville, 'part I will receive from you, but the rest you must keep. I know you must have many little wants.' 'No, Papa,' said Laura, 'so liberal has your kindness been to me, that I cannot at this moment name a single want.' 'Wishes, then, you surely have,' said the Captain, still pressing the money upon her; 'and let the first-fruits of your industry supply them.' 'I have no wishes,' said Laura; 'none at least which money can gratify: – and when I have,' added she, with an affectionate smile, 'let their gratification come from you, that its pleasure may be doubled to me.'

No creature could less value money for its own sake than did Laura. All her wealth, the fruit of so much labour and anxiety, would not have purchased the attire of a fashionable lady for one evening.

She, who had been accustomed to wander in happy freedom among her native hills, was imprisoned amidst the smoke and dust of a city. Without a companion, almost without an acquaintance to invigorate her spirits for the task, it was her province to revive the fainting hopes, and beguile the tedium of her father, who was depressed by disappointments in his pursuits, and disconcerted by the absence of his accustomed employments. She was at a distance from the object, not only of a tender affection, but of a romantic passion, – a passion, ardent in proportion as its object was indebted to her imagination for his power. Scarce three months had elapsed since the depravity of this idolized being had burst on her in thunder, the thought of it was still daggers to her heart, and it was very doubtful whether he could ever give such proofs of reformation as would make it safe for her to restore him to his place in her regard. Yet be it known to all who, from similar circumstances, feel entitled to fancy themselves miserable, and thus (if they live with beings of common humanity) make others really so, that no woman ever passed an evening in more heartfelt content, than Laura did that which our history is now recording. She did, indeed, possess that which, next to the overflowings of a pious heart, confers the purest happiness on this side Heaven. She felt that she was USEFUL. Nay, in one respect the consciousness of a successful discharge of duty has the advantage over the fervours of devotion; for Providence, wise in its bounty, has decreed, that while these foretastes of heavenly rapture are transient lest their delights should detach us from the business of life, we are invited to a religious practice by the permanence of its joys.

CHAPTER XI

———————•———————

CAPTAIN MONTREVILLE and his daughter were engaged in a friendly contest on the subject of a companion for the picture, when De Courcy made his visit. Though, as he entered the room, something unfashionably like a blush visited his face, his manner was free from rustic embarrassment. 'I believe,' said he, advancing towards Captain Montreville, 'I must apologize for the intrusion of a stranger. My person must have outgrown your recollection. My name, I hope, has been more fortunate. It is De Courcy.' 'The son I presume of Major De Courcy,' said Montreville, cordially extending his hand to him. 'Yes,' replied Montague, heartily taking the offered hand; 'the same whose childhood was indebted to you for so many of its pleasures.' 'My old friend Montague!' cried the Captain, 'though your present form is new to me, I remember my lovely little noble-spirited play-fellow with an interest which I have never felt in any other child except this girl.' 'And who knows,' said De Courcy, turning to Laura with a smile, 'who knows what cause I may find to rue that Miss Montreville is past the age when I might have repaid her father's kindness by assiduities to her doll?' 'That return,' said Laura, colouring, as she recollected her late champion, 'would not have been quite so arduous as the one you have already made. I hope you have had no further trouble with those rude people?' 'No, Madam,' answered De Courcy, 'nor did I expect it; the spirits that are so insolent where they dare, are submissive enough where they must.' Laura now explained to her father her obligation to De Courcy; and the Captain having thanked him for his interference, the conversation took a general turn.

Elated as he was with the successful industry and genius of his child, and pleased with the attentions of the son of his friend, the spirits of Montreville rose higher than they had ever done since his arrival in London. Won by the happy mixture of familiarity and respect, of spirit and gentleness, which distinguished the manners of De Courcy, the Captain became cheerful, and Laura almost talkative: the conversation rose from easy to animated, from animated to gay; and two hours had passed before any of the party was aware that one-fourth of that time was gone. Laura's general reserve with strangers seemed to have forsaken her while she conversed with De Courcy. But De Courcy was not a stranger. By character she knew him well. Hargrave had mentioned to her his intimacy with De Courcy. Nay, De Courcy had, at the hazard of his life, saved the life of Hargrave. Laura had heard her lover dwell with the eloquence of gratitude upon the courage, the presence of mind, with which (while others, confounded by his danger, or fearing for their own safety, left him to perish without aid), De Courcy had seized a fisher's net, and, binding one end of it to a tree, the other to his body, had plunged into the water, and intercepted Hargrave, just as the stream was hurrying him to the brink of a tremendous fall. 'All struggle was in vain,' had Hargrave said to the breathless Laura; 'but for that noble fellow, that minute would have been my last, and I should have died without awakening this interest so dear to my heart.' 'I wish I could see this De Courcy,' had Laura fervently exclaimed. 'Heaven forbid!' had been the hasty reply, 'for your habits – your pursuits – your sentiments are so similar, that he would gain without labour, perhaps without a wish, the heart that has cost me such anxious toil.' A recollection of this dialogue stole into the mind of Laura, as De Courcy was expressing an opinion which, though not a common one, coincided exactly with her own. For a moment she was absent and thoughtful; but De Courcy continued the conversation, and she resumed her gaiety.

When unwillingly at last he rose to take his leave, Captain Montreville detained him while he made some friendly inquiries into the history of the family for the last twenty years. As the questions of the Captain, however, were not impertinently minute, nor the answers of De Courcy very copious, it may not be improper to supply what was wanting in the narrative.

Major De Courcy was the representative of a family which could trace its descent from the times of the Conqueror, – an advantage which they valued above the hereditary possessions of their fathers; and if an advantage ought to be estimated by its durability, they were in the right; for the former, of necessity, was improved by time, the latter seemed tending towards decline. Frederick De Courcy was suffered to follow his inclinations in entering the army; because that was the profession the most suitable to the dignity of an ancient house. That it was of all professions the least likely to improve his fortune, was a consideration equally despised by his father and himself. When he attained his seventeenth year, a commission was purchased for him. Stored with counsels sufficient, if he followed them, to conduct him to wisdom and happiness, and with money sufficient to make these counsels of no avail, he set out from his paternal home to join his regiment. Thus was De Courcy, in his dangerous passage from youth to manhood, committed to the guidance of example, and the discretion belonging to his years; fortified, indeed, by the injunctions of his parents, and his own resolutions, never to disgrace his descent. This bulwark, he soon found, was too weak to resist the number and variety of the weapons which attacked him. The shafts of ridicule assailed him; his own passions took up arms; his pride itself turned against him. Unable to resist with vigour, he ceased to resist at all; and was hurried into every folly in which his companions wished for the assistance of his purse, or the countenance of his example.

His father's liberal allowance was soon insufficient to supply his extravagance. He contracted debts. After severe but well-merited reproof, his father paid them; and De Courcy promised amendment. A whole week of strict sobriety ensued; and the young soldier was convinced that his resolution was immutable. And so he would probably have found it, if now, for the first time since man was made, temptation had become weaker by victory, or virtue stronger by defeat. But though he had tasted the glittering bait of folly, and though he at times confessed its insipidity, the same lure again prevailed, and De Courcy was again entangled in pecuniary embarrassments. What was to be done? His father had declared his irrevocable determination no further to injure the interests of his younger children by supplying the prodigality of the eldest. By the advice of a veteran in profusion, De Courcy had recourse to Jews. As it was in his father's power to disinherit him, it was necessary to conceal these transactions; and the high spirit of Frederick was compelled to submit to all the evasions, embarrassments, and wretchedness that attend a clandestine course of action.

Often did he illustrate the trite observation that no life is more remote from happiness than a life of pleasure. The reward of all his labour was satiety; the wages of all his self-reproaches were the applause of the thoughtless for his spirit; the lamentations of the wise, that an honourable mind should be so perverted. In his twenty-second year, his father's death left him at liberty to pay his old debts, and to contract new. That which has preserved the virtue of many young men, prevented the total ruin of De Courcy. He became attached to a virtuous woman; and, influenced much by inclination, more by the wishes of her friends, she married him.

Mrs De Courcy brought no dower except the beauty which had captivated her husband, the sweetness which prolonged her power, and the good sense which made that power useful. She therefore did not think herself entitled to remonstrate very warmly on the negligence that appeared in the conduct of her husband's affairs; and it was not until after she became a mother that she judged it proper to interfere. Her gentle remonstrances, however, produced little effect beyond promises and vague resolutions, that at some '*convenient season*' the Major would examine into the real state of his fortune.

Accident at last befriended her endeavours. Soon after the birth of her second child (a daughter), a demand was made on De Courcy for a debt which he had not the means of discharging. He could not apply to the Jew; for he had solemnly pledged to Mrs De Courcy, that he would never more have recourse to that ruinous expedient. He was discussing with his wife the possibility of procuring the money by a new mortgage, while Montague, then a child of four year's old, was playing in the room. Struck by the melancholy tone of his mother's voice, the child forsook his play, and taking hold of her gown, looked anxiously from one mournful face to the other. 'I am as averse to it as you can be, my dear,' said the Major, 'but there is no other way of raising the money.' 'Wait till I am a man, Papa,' said the child; and then Betty says, I shall have a good two thousand pounds a-year, and I will give it all to you. And here,' added he, searching his little pocket, 'here is my pretty shilling that Captain Montreville gave me; take it, and don't look sorry any more.' Mrs De Courcy passionately loved this child. Overcome by the feeling of the moment, she clasped him in her arms. 'My poor wronged child!' she exclaimed, and burst into tears.

These were the first words of bitterness which Major De Courcy had ever heard from her lips; and overcome by them, and by her tears, he gave her a hasty promise, that he would, that very hour, begin the examination of his affairs. Sensible of her advantage, she permitted not his purpose to slumber, but persuaded him to a full inquiry into the extent of his debts; and in order to remove him from future temptation, she prevailed on him to sell his commission, and reside at his paternal Norwood.

After selling so much of his estate as to clear the remainder from all incumbrance, he found his income diminished to little more than a third of its original extent. His family pride reviving at the sight of the halls of his fathers, and a better affection awakening in his intercourse with the descendants of those whom his ancestors had protected, he determined to guard against the possibility of Norwood and its tenants being transferred to strangers, and entailed the remains of his property on Montague De Courcy, in the strictest form of English law. For Mrs De Courcy he made but a slender provision. For his daughter he made none: but he determined to save from his income a sum sufficient to supply this deficiency. He was still a young man, and never thought of doubting whether he might live long enough to accomplish his design, or whether the man who had found an income of £2000 a-year too small for his necessities, might be able to make savings from one of £800. In spite of the soberness of the establishment, which during the novelty of his reform he allowed Mrs De Courcy to arrange, he continued to find uses for all the money he could command. His fields wanted inclosures; his houses needed repairs; his son's education was an increasing expence; and he died while Montague was yet a boy, without having realized any part of his plans in favour of his daughter.

He left the highest testimomy to the understanding and worth of Mrs De Courcy, by making her the sole guardian of his children; and the steady rectitude and propriety of her conduct justified his confidence. Aware of the radical defect of every mode of education that neglects or severs the domestic tie, yet convinced that the house where he was master, and the dependents he could command, were dangerous scenes and companions for a youth of Montague's spirit, she committed him to the care of a clergyman, whose residence was a few miles distant from Norwood, and who also took charge of four other boys of about the same age.

This gentleman was admirably fitted for his trust; for he had a cultivated understanding, an affectionate heart, sound piety, and a calm but inflexible temper. Add to which, he had travelled, and, in his youth, associated much with men of rank, and more with men of talents; though, since he had become a pastor, the range of his moral observation had been narrowed to the hearts of a few simple villagers, which were open to him as to their father and their friend. The boys studied and played together, but they each had a separate apartment; for Mr Wentworth had himself been educated at a public school, and never recollected wthout shuddering, the hour when his youthful modesty had shrunk from sharing his bed with a stranger, and when the prayer for his parents, which he was mingling with his tears, had been disturbed by the jokes of a little rabble.

Every Saturday did Montague bend his joyful course homewards, regardless of summer's heat or winter storms. Every Sunday did his mother spend in mixing the lessons of piety with the endearments of love; in striving to connect the idea of a superintending God with all that is beautiful – all that is majestic – in nature. As her children grew up, she unfolded to them the peculiar doctrines of Christianity, so sublime, so consolatory, so suitable to the wants of man. Aware how much occasion favours the strength of impressions, she chose the hour of strong remorse on account of a youthful fault, while the culprit yet trembled before the offended Majesty of Heaven, to explain to her son the impossibility that repentance should, of itself, cancel errors past, or that the great Lawgiver should accept a few ineffectual tears, or a tardy and imperfect obedience, as a compensation for the breach of a law that is perfect. When she saw that the intended impression was made, she spoke of the great atonement that once was offered, not to make repentance unneces-sary, but to make it effectual; and, from that time, using this as one of the great landmarks of faith, she contributed to make it in the mind of De Courcy a practical and abiding principle. The peculiar precepts of Christianity she taught him to apply to his actions, by applying them herself; and the praise that is so often lavished upon boldness, dexterity, and spirit, she conscientiously reserved for acts of candour, humility, and self-denial.

Her cares were amply rewarded, and Montague became all that she wished him to be. He was a Christian from the heart, without being either forward to claim, or ashamed to own, the distinction. He was industrious in his pursuits, and simple in his pleasures. But the distinctive feature of his character, was the total absence of selfishness. His own pleasure or his own amusement he never hesitated to sacrifice to the wishes of others; or, to speak more correctly, he found his pleasure and amusement in theirs. Upon the whole, we do not say that Montague De Courcy had no faults; but we are sure he had none that he did not strive to conquer. Like other human beings, he sometimes acted wrong; but we believe he would not deliberately have neglected a known duty to escape any worldly misfortune; we are sure he would not deliberately have committed a crime to attain any earthly advantage.

Desirous that her darling should enjoy the benefits of the most liberal education, yet afraid to trust him to the temptations of an English university, Mrs De Courcy went for some years to reside in Edinburgh during the winter – in summer she returned with her family to Norwood. To his private studies, and his paternal home, Montague returned with ever new delight; for his tastes and his habits were all domestic. He had no ambitious wishes to lure him from his retreat, for his wants were even more moderate than his fortune. Except in so far as he could make it useful to others, he had no value for money, nor for anything that money could buy, exclusive of the necessaries of life, books, and implements of chemistry. The profession which he had chosen was that of improving and embellishing his estate; and, in the tranquil pleasures of a country gentleman, a man of taste, a classical sholar, and a chemist, he found means to occupy himself without injury to his health, his morals, or his fortune. His favourite amusements were drawing and physiognomy; and, like other favourites, these were sometimes in danger of making encroachments, and advancing into the rank of higher concerns. But this he prevented by an exact distribution of his time, to which he resolutely adhered.

With his mother and his sister he lived in the most perfect harmony, though the young lady had the reputation of a wit, and was certainly a little addicted to sarcasm. But she was in other respects amiable, and incapable of doing anything to offend her brother, whose indignation indeed never rose but against cruelty, meanness, or deceit.

De Courcy had just entered his twenty-fifth year, when a rheumatic fever deprived his mother of the use of her limbs; and, forsaking all his employments, he had quitted his beloved Norwood to attend her in London, whither she had come for the benefit of medical advice. He had been but a few days in town when he met with Miss Montreville, and the impression which her beauty made, the second interview tended to confirm.

Montague had never, even in imagination, been in love. The regulation of his passions, the improvement of his mind, and the care of his property, had hitherto left him no leisure for the tender folly. He had scarcely ever thought of a young woman's face, except with a reference to Lavater's opinion, nor of her manners, except to wonder how she could be so obtrusive. But in contemplating Laura's face, he forgot the rules of the physiognomist; and, in the interesting reserve of her manners, he found continually something to desire. If, at the close of his visit, he was not in love, he was at least in a fair way for being so. He was assailed at once by beauty, grace, good sense, and sweetness; and to these Laura added the singular charm of being wholly insensible to their effects upon the beholder. No side glance was sent in search of admiration; no care was taken to compose her drapery; no look of triumph accompanied her judicious remarks; no parade of sensibility disgraced her tenderness. Every charm was heightened by a matchless absence of all design; and against this formidable battery had poor De Courcy to make his stand, just at the inauspicious hour when, for the first time in his life, he had nothing else to do.

CHAPTER XII

AS soon as De Courcy was gone, Captain Montreville launched out warmly in his praise. Laura joined in the eulogium; and, the next morning, forgot that there was such a person in existence, when she read a letter from Mrs Douglas, of which the following was a part.

'Before this reaches you, Colonel Hargrave will be far on his way to London. It is possible that you may have no interest in this journey; but, lest you should, I wish to prevent your being taken by surprize. Since your departure he has repeatedly visited us; and endeavoured, both directly and indirectly, to discover your address. Perhaps you will think my caution ill-timed; but I acted according to my best judgment, in avoiding to comply with his desire. I think, however, that he has elsewhere procured the information he wanted; for his features wore an air of triumph, as he asked my commands for you. Dear child of my affections, richly endowed as you are with the dangerous gift of beauty, you have hitherto escaped, as if by miracle, from the snares of folly and frivolity. My hearts prayer for you is, that you may be as safe from the dangers that await you, in the passions of others, and in the tenderness of your own heart. But alas! my beloved Laura, distant as I am from you, ignorant as I am of the peculiarities of your situation, I can *only* pray for you. I fear to express my conjectures, lest I should seem to extort your confidence. I fear to caution, lest I should shock or offend you. Yet let me remind you, that it is easier, by one bold effort, to reject temptation, than to resist its continued allurements. Effectually to bar the access of the tempter may cost a painful effort – to parley with him is destruction. But I must stop. Tears of anxious affection blot what I have written.

'E. DOUGLAS.'

The joyful expectation of seeing Hargrave filled for a time the heart of Laura, and left no room for other thoughts. The first that found entrance was of a less pleasing cast. She perceived that Mrs Douglas suspected Hargrave of the baseness of deliberate seduction; and, with a feeling of indignation, she collected her writing materials, and sat down to exculpate him. But, as she again read her friend's expressions of affection, and considered how little her suspicions were remote from the truth, she accused herself of ingratitude and injustice in giving way to any thing like resentment. She thanked Mrs Douglas for her cautions; but assured her, that the proposals of Hargrave were honourable, unequivocal, and sanctioned by her father; that they had been rejected by herself; and, therefore, that no motive, except that of vindicating him from an unfounded suspicion, should have tempted her to betray, even to her most confidential friend, a secret which she thought a woman bound, both in delicacy and in honour, to keep inviolable. She did not once hint at the cause of her rejecting an offer so splendid, nor show a trace of the inclination which she had so nobly sacrificed to virtue, except what appeared in the warmth of her defence of her lover. For, though she felt that her story would have raised her in her friend's esteem, she scorned to purchase that advantage at the expence of another, and retained all her aversion to exposing the faults of Hargrave.

Having finished her letter, she returned to the more agreeable contemplation, and began to calculate upon the time when she might expect to see the Colonel. Her conclusion was, that he would probably visit her on the following day, and her heart throbbed with delight at the prospect.

But from the dream of joy, Laura soon returned to the more habitual consideration of the line of conduct which it was fit that she should pursue. She saw the folly of committing her happiness to the guardianship of one whose passions were his masters; and, while it was her daily prayer that she might not be led into temptation, her conscience revolted from trusting her conduct to the guidance, her virtue to the example, of a man whose principles were doubtful. For Laura's virtue was not of that saint-errant kind that sallies forth in quest of opportunities to signalize itself, and inflames its pride by meditation on the wonders it would achieve, if placed in perilous situations. Distrustful of herself – watchful to avoid occasions of falling – she had no ambition for the dangerous glory of reforming a rake into a good husband. She therefore adhered to her determination, that she would not consent to a union with her lover, till, by a course of virtuous conduct he had given proof that his offence had been the sudden fault of a moment, not the deliberate purpose of a corrupted heart.

Yet even in this mitigated view, the recollection was poison to the soul of Laura. The painful thought was far from new to her, that the passion of Hargrave was a tribute to her personal charms alone. With such a passion, even were its continuance possible, Laura felt that she could not be satisfied. To be the object of it degraded her in her own eyes. 'No, no,' she exclaimed, covering her face with her hands, 'let me not even legally occupy only the place which the vilest might fill. If I cannot be the friend, the companion, as well as the mistress, better, far better, were it that we should part for ever.'

No labour is sufficient to acquaint us fully with our own hearts. It never occurred to Laura, that she was, as much as Hargrave, the captive of mere externals; and that his character would never have deceived her penetration, had it been exhibited in the person of a little red-haired man, with bandy legs, who spoke broad Scotch, and smoked tobacco. Till the hour when he had himself dispelled the illusion, the character of Hargrave, such as she chose to imagine it, had been to her a theme of the most delightful contemplation; and to its fascinations she had willingly and entirely resigned herself. The disguise, which was rather the excuse, than the cause of her passion, had been dropped in part; yet the passion was as strong as ever. It was, indeed, no longer pleasing, no longer blind, no longer paramount; for her reason, which had before been silent, was now permitted to speak, and though it was unable to conquer, it could control. She imagined the vehemence with which Hargrave would urge her to shorten the term of his probation, and she feared that she should find it difficult, perhaps impossible, to resist his entreaties. She would not, therefore, expose her prudence to too severe a trial. 'Yes,' said she, 'I will bar the access of the tempter. I will see Hargrave only once, and that shall be to bid him farewell, till the stipulated two years are finished. If he really loves me, his affection will survive absence. If it fail in the trial, I may, though lost to happiness, find in my solitude a peace that never can visit a neglected wife.'

This philosophic conclusion was the fruit of her meditations during a restless night; and having worked herself, as she thought, into a temper decorously relentless, she proceeded, with all the consistency of her sex, to adorn her person with a care she had never before bestowed upon it. She arranged every curl for effect; chose a dress which shewed to advantage the graceful slope of her shoulders; and heightened the whiteness of her neck and arms, by contrasting it with fillets of jet. Though she was but indifferently pleased with her success, it proved sufficient for her occasions. The day passed away, and Hargrave did not appear. Laura was disappointed, but not surprized; for it was barely possible that he could have reached London on that day. On the succeeding one she thought it likely that he might come; but the succeeding one was equally barren of event.

On the third she was certain that he would arrive; and, when breakfast was over, she seated herself in expectation at the window of the front parlour, started if a carriage stopped, and listened to every voice that sounded from below stairs. Half-desirous to escape her father's observation, half-wishing that her interview with Hargrave should be without witnesses, she persuaded Captain Montreville to go and pay his respects to Mrs De Courcy. Anxiously she waited, conjectured, doubted, reconsulted Mrs Douglas's letter. The Captain returned; the hours of visiting passed away; and still no Hargrave came.

Unwilling to own, even to herself, the extent of her anxiety and disappointment, Laura talked to her father of his visit, with which he had been highly pleased. He had been amused with Harriet; charmed with Mrs De Courcy; and doubly charmed with Montague, whom he praised as a scholar and a man of sense, as an affectionate brother and a respectful son; and, to crown all these commendations, he declared, that De Courcy was more than a match for himself at chess.

When they retired for the night, Laura returned to her conjectures on the cause of Hargrave's delay. She considered that he might have been detained on the road, or that he might have found it necessary to make a visit on his way. She had little doubt, that to see her was the object of his journey to London at this unfashionable season. She had none, that he would hurry to her the first moment that it was possible. By degrees, she persuaded herself into an absolute certainty that she should see him on the following day; and on that day, she again took her anxious station in the parlour.

She was ashamed to lean over the window, and could not otherwise see who entered the house; but she left the room door a-jar, that she might have warning of his approach, held her breath to distinguish the voices from below, and listened eagerly to every footstep. At last, she imagined that she heard the wished-for inquiry. She was sure some one pronounced her name. A man's step ascended the stair; Laura trembled and her breath came short. She feared to look up, and leant her face on her hand to conceal her emotion.

The voice of her visitor made her start, and turn her head. It was Warren!

Expectation had been wound up to its highest pitch, and Laura could not instantly recover herself. She paid her compliments with a confusion and trepidation, which Warren interpreted in a way most flattering to his vanity. He approached her with a look, in which ill-suppressed triumph contended with laboured condescension; and spoke to her in a voice that seemed to say, 'Pray, endeavour to reassure yourself.' But Laura was in no humour to endure his impertinence, and she seized the first opportunity to leave the room.

Captain Montreville soon entered on the business in which he took such painful interest, by inquiring whether any traces had yet been discovered of the sale of his daughter's annuity. Warren, with abundance of regret and condolence, informed him, that Williams had as yet been able to discover no mention of the transaction in the books.

This assertion was so far true, that Williams had as yet seen no record of the business in question; for which Mr Warren could, if he had chosen, have given a very satisfactory reason. From the moment this *gentleman* had first seen Laura, he had been determined not wilfully to expedite her departure from London; and therefore he had casually dropped a hint to his man of business, that, as he was already overwhelmed with a multiplicity of affairs, it was unnecessary to hasten a concern of such trivial importance; and that he might defer inquiring into the sale of the annuity till he was at perfect leisure. Had he insinuated to Williams, that this delay was detaining from his home a man who could ill afford the consequent expence, or that it was alarming a father for the future subsistence of his only child, the man of business would have found leisure to investigate the matter, even if he had subtracted the necessary time from his hours of rest. But the upright Mr Warren had given no such intimation; and in this honourable transaction, he was, for the present, secure from detection, for he knew that business had called his agent to a distance from London.

Captain Montreville knew not what to think. He could not doubt the integrity of Mr Baynard, nor could he imagine to what purpose Warren should deny the transaction; since, if it had really taken place, the vouchers of it must be found among his deceased friend's papers. He was persuaded that to examine the books according to the date of the sale, would be the work of only a few hours; and again he inquired whether the necessary examination had taken place. Mr Warren answered, that he could not take it upon him to say that every possible search had yet been made; but his agent, he said, had examined all the most probable records of the concern, and would, on his return to town, make a still more particular scrutiny.

With this unsatisfactory answer, Captain Montreville was obliged to content himself. He had only one alternative – either to wait in London the appointment of the person who was to arrange Mr Baynard's papers, or to return to Scotland, and resign all hopes of the annuity. He feared, too, to offend Warren by urging him too strongly, since, even should a voucher of the payment of his £1500 be found, the informality in the deed would still leave room for litigation. No merely personal interest would have induced the high spirit of Montreville to conciliate a man whom he despised as a fool and a coxcomb. – For nothing that concerned himself alone, would he have submitted to the trouble and anxiety which he had lately undergone. Ill calculated by nature to struggle with difficulties, he had long been accustomed to let the lesser disasters glide by without notice, and to sink, without effort, under the greater. Disappointed in the woman of his choice, and deprived, by her folly or perverseness, of the domestic pleasures which he loved, his mind had taken a cast of melancholy. Early secluded from society, and tormented by the temper of his wife, he had concentrated all the affections which solitude confined, and caprice rejected, upon one object: and Laura became the passion of his soul. The thought of leaving her destitute, of leaving her sensibility to the scorns, her beauty to the temptations of poverty, was more than he could bear, and it sometimes almost overpowered him. He was naturally inclined to indolence, and as, like all indolent people, he was the creature of habit, his spirits had suffered much from the loss of the woman who, though too heartless for a friend, and too bitter for a companion, had, for twenty years, served him as a sort of stimulus. The same force of habit, joined to her improving graces and confirming worth, made Laura daily more dear to him, and he would willingly have given his life to secure her independence and happiness.

Brooding on the obscurity in which she must remain, whom he judged worthy to adorn the highest station – on the poverty which awaited her during his life – on the want to which his death must consign her, – removed from his habitual occupations, and deprived of the wholesome air, and exhilarating exercises to which he had long been accustomed, he allowed his spirits to grow daily more depressed. Along with the idea of the misfortunes which his death would bring upon his darling, the fear of death settled on his mind. The little ailments to which the sedentary are liable, he magnified into the symptoms of mortal disease; and momentary pain seemed to his fancy to foretell sudden dissolution. Montreville was fast sinking into a melancholy hypochondriac.

His daughter's spirits, too, failed under continued expectation, and continued disappointment; for day after day passed on, and still Hargrave came not. Her father's dejection increased her own, and her ill-disguised depression had a similar effect on him. While, however, Captain Montreville gave way without effort to his feelings, the more vigorous mind of Laura struggled to suppress the sorrow which she saw was contagious. She sometimes prevailed upon her father to seek amusement abroad, sometimes endeavoured to amuse him at home. She read to him, sung to him, exerted all her conversation talent to entertain him; and often, when all was in vain, when he would answer her by forced smiles, languid gestures, or heavy sighs, she would turn aside to wipe the tears from her eyes, then smile, and attempt her task again.

In these labours she had now, it is true, the assistance of an intelligent companion. De Courcy came often; and the Captain seemed to receive a pleasure from his visits, which even Laura's efforts could not bestow. The tenderness of his child, indeed, appeared sometimes to overpower him; for, when she was exerting herself to divert his melancholy, he would gaze upon her for a while in an agony of fondness, then suddenly desire to be left alone, and dismiss her from his presence. But De Courcy's attentions seemed always welcome. He soothed the irritated mind with respectful assiduities – he felt for its sickly sensibility – and, though ignorant of the cause of Montreville's dejection, found in alleviating it a pleasure, which was more than doubled by the undisguised approbation and gratitude of Laura.

His sister, too, came to visit Miss Montreville, and, apologizing for her mother, who was unable to accompany her, brought an invitation for the Captain and his daughter to dine in Audley Street. Laura, in hopes of amusing her father, prevailed on him to accept the invitation; and an early day was fixed for the visit. She was pleased with the frankness and gaiety of Harriet's manner, and her curiosity was roused by Captain Montreville's praises of Mrs De Courcy.

The day arrived, and Laura prepared to accompany her father, not without trepidation at the thought of entering, for the first time in her life, a room which she expected to find full of strangers. When she had finished dressing, he examined her with triumph; and thought that nothing in nature was so perfect. The thought was legible in his countenance, and Laura, with great simplicity, answered to it as if it had been spoken. 'Except to please you,' said she, 'I wish I had been neither tall nor pretty, for then I should have been allowed to move about without notice.' 'Then, too,' thought she with a heavy sigh, 'I should have been loved for my self, and not have been perhaps forgotten.'

Laura was not ignorant of her own beauty, but no human being could less value the distinction. She was aware of the regularity of her features; but as she never used a looking-glass, unless for the obvious purpose of arranging her dress, she was insensible of the celestial charm which expression added to her face. The seriousness and dignity of her manners made it difficult to address her with common-place compliment; and she had accordingly never experienced any effect of her beauty, but one which was altogether disagreeable to her, that of attracting notice. To being the subject of observation, Laura retained that Caledonian dislike which once distinguished her country-women, before they were polished into that glitter which attracts the vulgar, and paid for the acquisition by the loss of the timidity which, like the ærugo of ancient coin, adds value in the eye of taste to intrinsic worth, while it shields even baser merit from contempt.

Laura's courage failed her when, throwing open the door of a large room, Mrs de Courcy's servant announced Captain and Miss Montreville. But she revived when she perceived that the company consisted only of the mistress of the house, her son and daughter. Mrs de Courcy's appearance seemed to Laura very prepossessing. She still wore the dress of a widow; and her countenance bore the traces of what is called a green old age; for though the hair that shaded her commanding forehead was silver white, her dark eyes retained their brightness; and though her complexion was pale, it glowed at times with the roses of youth. The expression of her face, which was serious even to solemnity, brightened with a smile of inexpressible benevolence, as she received her guests; and, even in the difficulty with which she appeared to move, Laura found somewhat interesting. Her air and manners, without a tincture of fashion, spoke the gentlewoman. Her dress, her person, her demeanour, every thing about her seemed consistently respectable. The dinner was plain, but excellent. The few indispensable pieces of plate were antique and massive; and the only attendant who appeared, seemed to have grown gray in the service of the family. Laura had pleasure in observing, that the reverence with which this old man addressed his lady, softened into affectionate solicitude to please when he attended De Courcy, who, in his turn, seemed to treat him wtih the most considerate gentleness.

Mrs De Courcy behaved to Laura with distinguished politeness; addressed her often; endeavoured to draw forth her latent powers; and soon made her sensible that the impression she had given, was no less favourable than that which she had received. Montague's conversation had its accustomed effect on Montreville, and the lively Harriet gave spirit to the whole. The evening passed most agreeably; and Laura was sorry when the hour of separation arrived. Mrs De Courcy courteously thanked her for her visit, and begged her to repeat it; but Harriet sportively objected: 'No, no,' said she, 'if you come back, you will not leave a heart among all the household – even old John's seems in danger.'

'Well, Mamma,' continued she, when Laura was gone, 'what do you think of my brother's beauty?' 'I think,' said Mrs De Courcy, 'that Montague's praises did her no more than justice. She is the most lovely, the most elegant woman I ever saw.' 'She is no doubt beautiful and interesting,' returned Harriet; 'but I must still think she has too much of the buckram of the old school to be elegant.' Montague bit his lip, and tried, before he spoke, to ascertain that he was not angry. 'You are too severe, Harriet,' said Mrs De Courcy. 'Miss Montreville's reserve is not stiffness – it is not "buckram;" it is rather the graceful drapery, embellishing what it veils.' 'Mother,' cried Montague, grasping her hand, 'you have more candour, sense, and taste, than all the misses in England.' 'Oh! pray, except Miss Montreville and the present company,' said Harriet, laughing. 'She, you know, is all perfection; and *I* have really candour, sense, and taste enough to admire her more than ever I did any woman, except my little self.' De Courcy threw his arm around her – 'I see by that good-natured smile,' said he, 'that my dear Harriet has at least candour enough to pardon the folly of a wayward brother.' And, for the rest of the evening, he treated her with even more than his usual attentive kindness.

From this day Miss De Courcy frequently accompanied her brother on his visits to the Montrevilles, and Laura was a welcome guest in Audley Street. By degrees Mrs De Courcy and she discovered the real worth of each other's character, and their mutual reserve entirely disappeared. Between Laura and De Courcy, almost from the first hour of their acquaintance, there seemed (to use the language of romance) a sympathy of souls; – an expression which, if it has any meaning, must mean the facility with which simple, upright, undesigning minds become intelligible to each other. Even the sarcastic Harriet found, in the chaste propriety of Laura's character, something to command respect; and in her gentleness and warmth of heart, something to engage affection; while, in her ideas, which solitude had slightly tinged with romance, though strong sense had preserved them from absurdity, and in her language, which sometimes rose to the very verge of poetry, she found constantly somewhat to interest and amuse.

Meanwhile Montreville's dejection seemed to increase; and Laura's health and spirits, in spite of her efforts to support them, daily declined. Hargrave did not appear, and vainly did she endeavour to account for his absence. She at first conjectured that he had found it impossible to leave Scotland at the time he proposed; but a second letter from Mrs Douglas had mentioned his departure, and repeated the assurance that, however obtained, he had information of Laura's address, since he had undertaken to be the bearer of a letter from a neighbouring gentleman to Captain Montreville.

She next supposed that he had stopped on the road, or quitted it on some errand of business or pleasure – but a newspaper account of a fête champêtre at Lady Bellamer's elegant villa at Richmond, was graced, among other fashionable names, with that of the handsome Colonel Hargrave, nephew and heir of Lord Lincourt. No supposition remained to be made, except the mortifying one, that three months of absence had erased her image from the fickle heart of Hargrave. She, who had herself consigned her lover to a banishment of two years, could not bear that he should voluntarily undergo one of a few weeks. Nay, she had once herself resigned him; but to be herself resigned without effort, was more than she could endure. Her appetite, her sleep forsook her; her ordinary employments became irksome; and even the picture, the price of which was so soon to be necessary, she had not the spirits to finish.

But one who was accustomed every night to examine the thoughts and actions of the day, was not likely to remain long a prey to inactive melancholy. Not satisfied with languid efforts in the discharge of duty, she reproached herself for every failure. She upbraided herself as a wicked and slothful servant, who, when the means of usefulness were put in her power, suffered them to remain unimproved; as a rebel who had deserted the service of her rightful master, to bow to the worse than Egyptian bondage of her passions. She accused herself of having given up her love, her wishes, her hopes and fears, almost her worship, to an idol; and no sooner did this thought occur to the pious mind of Laura, than she became resigned to her loss. She even felt grateful – with such gratitude as the wretch feels under the knife which amputates the morbid limb.

Unused to let her self-reproaches pass without improvement, she resolved, by vigorous efforts, to become herself again. She even called in the aid of a decent pride. 'Shall I,' she cried, 'who have vowed to overcome the world – I who have called myself by that glorious name, a Christian, sink from these honours into a love-sick girl? Shall all my happiness, all my duties, the comfort of my father, the very means of his support, be sacrificed to a selfish passion? Or is a love, whose transient duration has proved its degenerate nature, of such value to me, that I must repay it with my whole heart and soul?'

These reflections were not made at once, nor were they at once effectual; but, when made, they were called in as oft as the image of Hargrave intruded unbidden; and constant and regular occupation was again employed to second their operation. The picture was again resorted to; but, as it afforded rather an unsocial employment, and as Laura's company was more than ever necessary to her father, it proceeded but slowly.

De Courcy was now a daily visitor. Sometimes he brought books, and would spend hours in reading aloud, an accomplishment in which he excelled. Sometimes he would amuse the Captain and his daughter by experiments in his favourite science. With a gentleness peculiar to himself, he tried to prevent the little annoyances to which hypochondriacs are subject. He invented a hundred little indulgences for the invalid; and no day passed in which Montreville was not indebted for some comfort, or some amusement, to the considerate kindness of De Courcy. At times he would gently rally the Captain on his imaginary ailments, and sometimes prevailed on him to take the air in Mrs De Courcy's carriage: though to such a height had fancy worked upon him, that Montague found it impossible to persuade him that he was able to endure the fatigue of walking.

To Laura, De Courcy's behaviour, uniformly respectful and attentive, was sometimes even tender. But, accustomed to see love only in the impassioned looks of Hargrave, to hear its accents only in his words of fire, she did not recognize it in a new form; and to consider De Courcy as a lover, never once entered her imagination. Captain Montreville was more clear-sighted, and hence arose much of the pleasure which he took in De Courcy's visits. Not that he was more knowing in the mysteries of love than his daughter; but he took it for granted, that no mortal could withstand her attractions; and he was persuaded that Laura would not withhold her heart, where she so freely expressed approbation. This opinion was a proof of the justice of the Captain's former confession, 'that women were creatures he did not understand.' Laura had never praised Hargrave. She never shrunk from De Courcy's eye, – she never felt embarrassed by his presence, – she treated him with the frankness of a sister; and though she reserved her commendations for his absence, she waited only for that to bestow them with all the warmth which his own merit and his attentions to her father could demand.

Meanwhile the Captain did not, by a premature disclosure of his hopes, endanger their completion; and De Courcy continued unconsciously to foster in his bosom, a passion that was destined to destroy his peace.

CHAPTER XIII

———————•———————

THE picture at last was finished, and Laura herself accompanied it to the print-shop. Wilkins immediately delivered to her the price, which, he said, had been for some time in his hands. It now occurred to Laura to ask who had been the purchaser of her work. 'Why, Ma'am,' said Wilkins, 'the gentleman desired me not to mention his name.' 'Indeed!' said Laura surprised. 'These were his orders, Ma'am, but I shouldn't think there could be any great harm in telling it just to you Ma'am.' 'I have no wish to hear it,' said Laura, with a look which compelled the confident to unwilling discretion; and again thanking him for the trouble he had taken, she returned home. The truth was, that De Courcy had foreseen the probability of Laura's question; and averse to be known to her under a character that savoured of patronage and protection, had forbidden the shopkeeper to mention who had purchased the pictures.

Again did Laura, delighted, present to her father the produce of her labours, her warm heart glowing with the joys of usefulness. But not as formerly did he with pleasure receive the gift. With the fretfulness of disease, he refused to share in her satisfaction. Through the gloom of melancholy, every object appeared distorted; and Captain Montreville saw in his daughter's well-earned treasure only the wages of degrading toil. 'It is hard, very hard,' said he with a deep sigh, 'that you, my lovely child, should be dependent on your daily labour for your support.' 'Oh call it not hard, my dear father,' cried Laura. 'Thanks, a thousand thanks to your kind foresight, which, in teaching me this blessed art, secured to me the only real independence, by making me independent of all but my own exertions.' 'Child,' said Montreville, fretfully, 'there is an enthusiasm about you that will draw you into ten thousand errors – you are quite mistaken in fancying yourself independent. Your boasted art depends upon the taste, the very caprice of the public for its reward; and you, of course, upon the very same caprice for your very existence.' 'It is true,' answered Laura mildly, 'that my success depends upon taste, and that the public taste is capricious; but some, I should hope, would never be wanting, who could value and reward the labours of industry – you observe,' added she with a smile, 'that I rest nothing upon genius.' 'Be that as it may,' returned Captain Montreville, with increasing querulousness, 'I cannot endure to see you degraded into an artist, and, therefore, I desire there may be no more of this traffic.'

This was the first time that Montreville had ever resorted to the method well known and approved by those persons of both sexes, who, being more accustomed to the exercise of authority than of argument, choose to wield the weapon in the use of which practice has made them the most expert. Laura looked at him with affectionate concern – 'Alas!' thought she, 'if bodily disease is pitiable, how far more deplorable are its ravages on the mind.' But even if her father had been in perfect health, she would not have chosen the moment of irritation for reply. Deeply mortified at this unexpected prohibition, she yet endeavoured to consider it as only one of the transient caprices of illness, and to find pleasure in the thought, that the hour was come, when De Courcy's daily visit would restore her father to some degree of cheerfulness.

But De Courcy's visit made no one cheerful. He was himself melancholy and absent. He said he had only a few minutes to spare, yet lingered above an hour; often rose to go, yet irresolutely resumed his seat. At last, starting up, he said, 'the longer I remain here, the more unwilling I am to go; and yet I *must* go, without even knowing when I may return.' 'Are *you* going to leave us?' said Montreville, in a tone of despondency, 'then we shall be solitary indeed.' 'I fear,' said Laura, looking with kind solicitude in De Courcy's face, 'that something distressing calls you away.' 'Distressing indeed,' said De Courcy. 'My excellent old friend Mr Wentworth has lost his only son, and I must bear the news to the parents.' 'Is there no one but you to do this painful office?' asked Montreville. 'None,' answered De Courcy, 'on whom it could with such propriety fall. Wentworth was one of my earliest friends, he was my father's early friend. I owe him a thousand obligations; and I would fain, if it be possible, soften this heavy blow. Besides,' added he, endeavouring to speak more cheerfully, 'I have a selfish purpose to serve, – I want to see how a Christian bears misfortune.' 'And can you fix no time for your return?' asked the Captain, mournfully. De Courcy shook his head. 'You will not return while your presence is necessary to Mr Wentworth,' said Laura, less anxious to regain De Courcy's society, than that he support the character of benevolence with which her imagination had justly vested him. Grieved by the prospect of losing his companion, fretted by an indefinite idea that he was wrong in his ungracious rejection of his daughter's efforts to serve him, ashamed of his distempered selfishness, yet unable to conquer it, Captain Montreville naturally became more peevish; for the consciousness of having acted wrong, without the resolution to repair the fault, is what no temper can stand. 'Your charity is mighty excursive Laura,' said he. 'If Mr De Courcy delays his return long, I shall probably not live to profit by it.' Laura, whose sweetness no captious expressions could ruffle, would have spoken to turn her father's view to brighter prospects; but the rising sob choked her voice, and courtesying hastily to De Courcy, she left the room. De Courcy now no longer found it difficult to depart. He soon bade the Captain farewell, promising to return as soon as it was possible, though he had no great faith in Montreville's dismal prediction, uttered in the true spirit of hypochondriasis, that he would come but to lay his head in his grave.

As he was descending the stairs, Laura, who never forgot in selfish feeling to provide for the comfort of others, followed him, to beg that when he had leisure, he would write to her father. Laura blushed and hesitated as she made this request, not because she had in making it any selfish motive whatever, but purely because she was unused to ask favours. Flattered by the request, but much more by her confusion, De Courcy glowed with pleasure. 'Certainly I shall write,' said he with great animation, 'if you – I mean if Captain Montreville wish it.' These words, and the tone in which they were uttered, made Laura direct a look of inquiry to the speaker's face, where his thoughts were distinctly legible; and she no sooner read then, than, stately and displeased, she drew back. 'I believe it will give my father pleasure to hear from you, sir,' said she, and coldly turned away. 'Is there no man,' thought she, 'exempt from this despicable vanity – from the insignificant Warren to the respectable De Courcy?' Poor Montague would fain have besought her forgiveness for his presumption in supposing it possible that she could have any pleasure in hearing of him; but the look with which she turned from him, left him no courage to speak to her again, and he mournfully pursued his way to Audley Street.

He was scarcely gone when Warren called, and Laura, very little displeased for his company, took shelter in her own room. Her father, however, suffered no inconvenience from being left alone to the task of entertaining his visitor, for Warren found means to make the conversation sufficiently interesting.

He began by lamenting the Captain's long detention from his home, and condoled with him upon the effects which London air had produced upon his health. He regretted that Mr Williams's absence from town had retarded the final settlement of Montreville's business; informed him that Mr Baynard's executors had appointed an agent to inspect his papers; and finally, surprised him by an unconditional offer to sign a new bond for the annuity. He could not bear, he said, to think of the Captain's being detained in London to the prejudice of his health, especially as it was evident that Miss Montreville's suffered from the same cause. He begged that a regular bond might be drawn up, which he would sign at a moment's notice, and which he would trust to the Captain's honour to destroy, if it should be found that the £1500, mentioned as the price of the annuity, had never been paid.

At this generous proposal, surprise and joy almost deprived Montreville of the power of utterance; gratefully clasping Warren's hand, 'Oh, sir,' he exclaimed, 'you have, I hope, secured an independence for my child. I thank you – with what fervour, you can never know till you are yourself a father.' Seemingly anxious to escape from his thanks, Warren again promised that he would be ready to sign the bond on the following day, or as soon as it was ready for signature. Captain Montreville again began to make acknowledgements, but Warren, who appeared rather distressed than gratified by them, took his leave, and left the Captain to the joyful task of communicating the news to Laura.

She listened with grateful pleasure. 'How much have I been to blame,' said she, 'for allowing myself to believe that a little vanity necessarily excluded every kind and generous feeling. What a pity it is that this man should condescend to such an effeminate attention to trifles!' Lost to the expectation, almost to the desire of seeing Hargrave, she had now no tie to London, but one which was soon to be broken, for Mrs and Miss De Courcy were about to return to Norwood. With almost unmixed satisfaction, therefore, she heard her father declare, that in less than a week he should be on his way to Scotland. With pleasure she looked forward to revisiting her dear Glenalbert, and anticipated the effects of its quiet shades and healthful air upon her father. Already she beheld her home, peaceful and inviting, as when, from the hill that sheltered it, she last looked back upon its simple beauties. She heard the ripple of its waters; she trod the well-known path; met the kind familiar face, and listened to the cordial welcome, with such joy as they feel who return from the land of strangers.

Nor was Montreville less pleased with the prospect of returning to his accustomed comforts and employments – of feeling himself once more among objects which he could call his own. His own! There was magic in the word, that transformed the cottage at Glenalbert into a fairy palace – the garden and the farm into a little world. To leave London interfered indeed with his hopes of De Courcy as a lover for his daughter; but he doubted not that the impression was already made, and that Montague would follow Laura to Scotland.

His mind suddenly relieved from anxiety, his spirits rose, all his constitutional good nature returned, and he caressed his daughter with a fondness that seemed intended to atone for the captious behaviour of the morning. At dinner he called for wine, a luxury in which he rarely indulged, drank to their safe arrival at Glenalbert, and obliged Laura to pledge him to the health of Warren. To witness her father's cheerfulness was a pleasure which Laura had of late tasted so sparingly, that it had the most exhilarating effect upon her spirits; and neither De Courcy nor Hargrave would have been much gratified, could they have seen the gaiety with which she supported the absence of the one, and the neglect of the other.

She was beginning to enjoy one of those cheerful domestic evenings which had always been her delight, when Miss Dawkins came to propose that she should accompany her and her mother on a visit to Mrs Jones. Laura would have excused herself, by saying, that she could not leave her father alone; but the Captain insisted upon her going, and declared that he would himself be of the party. She had therefore no apology, and, deprived of the amusement which she would have preferred, contentedly betook herself to that which was within her reach. She did not sit in silent contemplation of her own superiority, or of the vulgarity of her companions; nor did she introduce topics of conversation calculated to illustrate either; but having observed that even the most ignorant have some subject on which they can talk with ease and pleasure, and even be heard with advantage, she suffered others to lead the discourse, rightly conjecturing that they would guide it to the channel which they judged most favourable to their own powers. She was soon engaged with Mrs Dawkins in a dissertation on various branches of household economy, and to the eternal degradation of her character as a heroine, actually listened with interest to the means of improving the cleanliness, beauty, and comfort of her dwelling.

Mrs Jones was highly flattered by the Captain's visit, and exerted herself to entertain him, her husband being inclined to taciturnity by a reason which Bishop Butler has pronounced to be a good one. Perceiving that Montreville was an Englishman, she concluded that nothing but dire necessity could have exiled him to Scotland. She inquired what town he lived in; and being answered that his residence was many miles distant from any town, she held up her hands in pity and amazement. But when she heard that Montreville had been obliged to learn the language of the Highlands, and that it was Laura's vernacular tongue, she burst into an exclamation of wonder. 'Mercy upon me,' cried she, 'can you make that outlandish spluttering so as them savages can know what you says? Well, if I had been among them a thousand years, I should never have made out a word of their gibberish.'

'The sound of it is very uncouth to a stranger,' said Captain Montreville, 'but now I have learnt to like it.' 'And do them there wild men make you wear them little red and green petticoats?' asked Mrs Jones, in a tone of compassionate inquiry. 'Oh no,' said Captain Montreville, 'they never interfered with my dress. But you seem quite acquainted with the Highlands. May I ask if you have been there?' 'Aye, that I have, to my sorrow,' said Mrs Jones; and forthwith proceeded to recount her adventures, pretty nearly in the same terms as she had formerly done to Laura. 'And what was the name of this unfortunate place,' inquired the captain, when, having narrated the deficiency of hot rolls, Mrs Jones made the pause in which her auditors were accustomed to express their astonishment and horror. 'That was what I asked the waiter often and often,' replied she, 'but I could never make head or tail of what he said. Sometimes it sounded like *A rookery*; sometimes like one thing, sometimes like another. So I takes the roadbook, and looks it out, and it looked something like *A rasher*, only not right spelt. So, thinks I, they'll call it *A rasher*, because there is good bacon here; and I asked the man if they were famous for pigs; and he said, no, they got all their pigs from the manufactory in Glasgow, and that they weren't famous for any thing but fresh herrings, as are catched in that black Loch-Lomond, where they wanted me to go.'

'Kate,' said Mr Jones, setting down his tea-cup, and settling his hands upon his knees, 'you know I think you're wrong about them herrings.' 'Mr Jones,' returned the lady, with a look that shewed that the herrings had been the subject of former altercation, 'for certain the waiter told me that they came out of the loch, and to what purpose should he tell lies about it.' 'I tells you, Kate, that herrings come out of the sea,' said Mr Jones. 'Well, that loch is a great fresh water sea,' said Mrs Jones. 'Out of the salt sea,' insisted Mr Jones. 'Aye,' said Mrs Jones, 'them salt herrings as we gets here, but it stands to reason, Mr Jones, that the fresh herrings should come out of fresh water.' 'I say, cod is fresh, and does'n't it come out of the sea? answer me that, Mrs Jones.' 'It is no wonder the cod is fresh,' returned the lady, 'when the fishmongers keep fresh water running on it day and night.' 'Kate, it's of no use argufying, I say herrings come out of the sea. What say you, Sir?' turning to Captain Montreville. The Captain softened his verdict in the gentleman's favour, by saying, that Mrs Jones was right in her account of the waiter's report, though the man, in speaking of 'the loch,' meant not Loch-Lomond, but an arm of the sea. 'I know'd it,' said Mr Jones triumphantly, for haven't I read it in the newspaper as Government offers a reward to any body that'll put most salt upon them Scotch herrings, and is'n't that what makes the salt so dear?' So having settled this knotty point to his own satisfaction, Mr Jones again applied himself to his tea.

'Did you return to Glasgow by the way of Loch-Lomond?' inquired Captain Montreville. 'Ay,' cried Mrs Jones, 'that was what the people of the inn wanted us to do; but then I looked out, and seed a matter of forty of them there savages, with the little petticoats and red and white stockings, loitering and lolling about the inn-door, doing nothing in the varsal world, except wait till it was dark to rob and murder us all, bless us! So, thinks I, let me once get out from among you in a whole skin, and catch me in the Highlands again; so as soon as the chaise could be got, we just went the way we came.' 'Did you find good accommodation in Glasgow,' said the Captain. 'Yes,' replied Mrs Jones; 'but after all, Captain, there's no country like our own; – do you know, I never got so much as a buttered muffin all the while I was in Scotland?'

The conversation was here interrupted by an exclamation from Mrs Dawkins, who, knowing that she had nothing new to expect in her daughter's memoirs of her Scotish excursion, had continued to talk with Laura apart. 'Goodness me!' she cried, 'why Kate, as sure as eggs, here's Miss never seed a play in all her life!' 'Never saw a play! Never saw a play!' exclaimed the landlord and landlady at once. 'Well, that's so odd; but to be sure, poor soul, how should she, among them there hills.' 'Suppose,' said Mrs Jones, 'we should make a party, and go tonight. – We shall be just in time.' Laura was desirous to go: her father made no objection; and Mr Jones, with that feeling of good-natured self-complacency which most people have experienced, arising from the discovery that another is new to a pleasure with which he himself is familiar, offered, as he expressed it, 'to do the genteel thing, and treat her himself.'

The party was speedily arranged, and Laura soon found herself seated in the pit of the theatre. The scene was quite new to her; for her ignorance of public places was even greater than her companions had discovered it to be. She was dazzled with the glare of the lights, and the brilliancy of the company, and confused with the murmur of innumerable voices; but the curtain rose, and her attention was soon confined to the stage. The play was the Gamester, the most domestic of our tragedies; and, in the inimitable representation of Mrs Beverly, Laura fond an illusion strong enough to absorb for the time every faculty of her soul. Of the actress she thought not; but she loved and pitied Mrs Beverly with a fervour that made her insensible to the amusement which she afforded to her companions. Meanwhile her countenance, as beautiful, almost as expresssive, followed every change in that of Mrs Siddons. She wept with her; listened, started, rejoiced with her; and when Mrs Beverly repulsed the villain Stukely, Laura's eyes too flashed with 'heaven's own lightnings.' By the time the representation was ended, she was so much exhausted by the strength and rapidity of her emotions, that she was scarcely able to answer to the questions of 'How have you been amused?' and 'How did you like it?' with which her companions all at once assailed her. 'Well,' said Miss Julia, when they were arrived at home, 'I think nothing is so delightful as a play. I should like to go every night – shouldn't you?' 'No,' answered Laura. 'Once or twice in a year would be quite sufficient for me. It occupies my thoughts too much for a mere amusement.'

In the course of the two following days, Laura had sketched more than twenty heads of Mrs Siddons, besides completing the preparations for her journey to Scotland. On the third, the Captain, who could now smile at his own imaginary debility, prepared to carry the bond to receive Mr Warren's signature. The fourth was to be spent with Mrs De Courcy; and on the morning of the fifth, the travellers intended to depart.

On the appointed morning, Captain Montreville set out on an early visit to Portland Street, gaily telling his daughter at parting that he would return in an hour or two, with her dowery in his pocket. When he knocked at Mr Warren's door, the servant informed him that his master had gone out, but that expecting the Captain to call, he had left a message to beg that Montreville would wait till he returned, which would be very soon.

The Captain was then shewn into a back parlour, where he endeavoured to amuse himself with some books that were scattered round the room. They consisted of amatory poems and loose novels, and one by one he threw them aside in disgust, lamenting that one who was capable of a kind and generous action should seek pleasure in such debasing studies. The room was hung with prints and pictures, but they partook of the same licentious character; and Montreville shuddered, as the momentary thought darted across his mind, that it was strange that the charms of Laura had made no impression on one whose libertinism in regard to her sex was so apparent. It was but momentary. 'No!' thought he, 'her purity would awe the most licentious; and I am uncandid, ungrateful, to harbour even for a moment such an idea of the man who has acted towards her and me with the most disinterested benevolence.'

He waited long, but Warren did not appear; and he began to blame himself for having neglected to fix the exact time of his visit. To remedy this omission, he rang for writing materials, and telling the servant that he could stay no longer, left a note to inform Mr Warren that he would wait upon him at twelve o'clock next day. The servant, who was Mr Warren's own valet, seemed unwilling to allow the Captain to depart, and assured him that he expected his master every minute; but Montreville, who knew that there was no depending upon the motions of a mere man of pleasure, would be detained no longer.

He returned home, and finding the parlour empty, was leaving it to seek Laura in her painting-room, when he observed a letter lying on the table addressed to himself. The hand-writing was new to him. He opened it – the signature was equally so. The contents were as follows:–

'Sir,

The writer of this letter is even by name a stranger to you. If this circumstance should induce you to discredit my information, I offer no proof of my veracity but this simple one, that obviously no selfish end can be served by my present interference. Of the force of my motive you cannot judge, unless you have yourself lured to destruction the heart that trusted you, – seen it refuse all comfort, – reject all reparation, – and sink at last in untimely decay. From a fate like this, though not softened like this by anxious tenderness, nor mourned like this by remorseless pity, but aggravated by being endured for one incapable of any tender or generous feeling, it is my purpose, Sir, to save your daughter. I was last night one of a party where her name was mentioned; – where she was described as lovely, innocent, and respectable; yet the person who so described her, scrupled not to boast of a plan for her destruction. In the hope (why should I pretend a better motive) of softening the pangs of late but bitter self-reproach, by saving one fellow-creature from perhaps reluctant ruin, one family from domestic shame, I drew from him your address, and learnt that to ingratiate himself with you, and with his intended victim, he has pretended to offer as a gift, what he knew that he could not long withhold. He means to take the earliest opportunity of inveigling her from your care, secure, as he boasts, of her pardon in her attachment. Ill, indeed, does her character, even as described by him, accord with such a boast; yet even indifference might prove no guard against fraud, which, thus warned, you may defy. A fear that my intention should be frustrated by the merited contempt attached to anonymous information, inclines me to add my name, though aware that it can claim no authority with a stranger.

'I am, SIR,
    'Your obedient Servant,
        'PHILIP WILMOT.'

Captain Montreville read this letter more than once. It bore marks of such sincerity that he knew not how to doubt of the intelligence it gave; and he perceived with dismay, that the business which he had considered as closed, was as far as ever from a conclusion; for how could he accept a favour which he had been warned to consider as the wages of dishonour. For Laura he had indeed no fear. She was no less safe in her own virtue and discretion, than in the contemptuous pity with which she regarded Warren. This letter would put her upon her guard against leaving the house with him, which Captain Montreville now recollected that he had often solicited her to do, upon pretence of taking the air in his curricle.

But must he still linger in London; still be cheated with vain hopes; still fear for the future subsistence of his child; still approach the very verge of poverty; perhaps be obliged to defend his rights by a tedious law-suit? His heart sank at the prospect, and he threw himself on a seat, disconsolate and cheerless.

He had long been in the habit of seeking relief from every painful feeling in the tenderness of Laura, – of finding in her enduring spirit a support to the weakness of his own; and he now sought her in the conviction that she would either discover some advantage to be drawn from this disappointment, or lighten it to him by her affectionate sympathy. He knocked at the door. – She did not answer. He called her. – All was silent. He rang the bell, and inquired whether she was below, and was answered that she had gone out with Mr Warren in his curricle two hours before. The unfortunate father heard no more. Wildly striking his hand upon his breast, 'She is lost!' he cried, and sunk to the ground. The blood burst violently from his mouth and nostrils, and he became insensible.

The family were soon assembled round him; and a surgeon being procured, he declared that Montreville had burst a blood vessel, and that nothing but the utmost care and quiet could save his life. Mrs Dawkins, with great humanity, attended him herself, venting in whispers to the surgeon her compassion for Montreville, and her indignation against the unnatural desertion of Laura, whom she abused as a methodistical hypocrite, against whom her wrath was the stronger because she could never have suspected her.

Montreville no sooner returned to recollection, than he declared his resolution instantly to set off in search of his child. In vain did the surgeon expostulate, and assure him that his life would be the forfeit: his only answer was, 'Why should I live? She is lost.' In pursuance of his design, he tried to rise from the bed on which he had been laid; but exhausted nature refused to second him, and again he sunk back insensible.

When Montreville called in Portland Street, the servant had deceived him in saying that Warren was not at home. He was not only in the house, but expected the Captain's visit, and prepared to take advantage of it, for the accomplishment of the honourable scheme of which he had boasted to his associates. As soon, therefore, as the servant had disposed of Montreville, Warren mounted his curricle, which was in waiting at a little distance, and driving to Mrs Dawkins's, informed Laura that he had been sent to her by her father, who proposed carrying her to see the British Museum, and for that purpose was waiting her arrival in Portland Street. Entirely unsuspicious of any design, Laura accompanied him without hesitation; and though Portland Street appeared to her greatly more distant than she had imagined it, it was not till having taken innumerable turns, she found herself in an open road, that she began to suspect her conductor of having deceived her.

'Whither have you taken me, Mr Warren?' she inquired: 'This road does not lead to Portland Street.' 'Oh yes, it does,' answered Warren, 'only the road is a little circuitous.' 'Let us immediately return to the straight one then,' said Laura. 'My father will be alarmed, and conclude that some accident has happened to us.' 'Surely, my charming Miss Montreville,' said Warren, still continuing to drive on, 'you do not fear to trust yourself with me.' 'Fear *you*!' repeated Laura, with involuntary disdain. 'No, but I am at a loss to guess what has encouraged you to make me the companion of so silly a frolic. I suppose you mean this for an ingenious joke upon my father.' 'No, 'pon my soul,' said the beau, a little alarmed by the sternness of her manner, 'I meant nothing but to have an opportunity of telling you that I am quite in love with you, – dying for you, – faith I am.' 'You should first have ascertained,' answered Laura, 'whether I was likely to think the secret worth a hearing. I desire you will instantly return.'

The perfect composure of Laura's look and manner (for feeling no alarm she shewed none) made Warren conclude that she was not averse to being detained; and he thought it only necessary that he should continue to make love, to induce her quietly to submit to go on for another half mile, which would bring them to a place where he thought she would be secure. He began, therefore, to act the lover with all the energy he could muster; but Laura interrupted him. 'It is a pity,' said she, with a smile of calm contempt, 'to put a stop to such well-timed gallantry, which is indeed just such as I should have expected from Mr Warren's sense and delicacy. But I would not for the sake of Mr Warren's raptures, nor all else that he has to offer, give my father the most momentary pain, and therefore if you do not suffer me to alight this instant, I shall be obliged to claim the assistance of passengers on an occasion very little worthy of their notice.' Her contumelious manner entirely undeceived her companion in regard to her sentiments; but it had no other effect upon him, except that of adding revenge to the number of his incitements; and perceiving that they were now at a short distance from the house whither he intended to convey her, he continued to pursue his way.

Laura now rose from her seat, and seizing the reins with a force that made the horses rear, she coolly chose that moment to spring from the curricle; and walked back towards the town, leaving her inammorato in the utmost astonishment at her self-possession, as well as rage at her disdainful treatment.

She proceeded till she came to a decent-looking shop, where she entered; and, begging permission to sit down, dispatched one of the shop-boys in search of a hackney-coach. A carriage was soon procured, and Laura, concluding that her father, tired of waiting for her, must have left Portland Street, desired to be driven directly home.

As she entered the house, she was met by Mrs Dawkins. 'So Miss,' cried she, 'you have made a fine spot of work on't. You have murdered your father.' 'Good heavens!' cried Laura, turning as pale as death, 'what is it you mean? where is my father?' 'Your father is on his deathbed Miss, and you may thank your morning rides for it. Thinking you were off, he burst a blood-vessel in the fright, and the doctor says, the least stir in the world will finish him.'

Laura turned sick to death. Cold drops stood upon her forehead; and she shook in every limb. She made an instinctive attempt to ascend the stair; but her strength failed her, and she sunk upon the steps. The sight of her agony changed in a moment Mrs Dawkins's indignation to pity. 'Don't take on so, Miss,' said she, 'to be sure you didn't mean it. If he is kept quiet, he may mend still, and now that you're come back too. – By the bye, I may as well run up and tell him.' 'Oh stop!' cried Laura, reviving at once in the sudden dread that such incautious news would destroy her father, 'Stay,' said she, pressing with one hand her bursting forehead, while with the other she detained Mrs Dawkins. – 'Let me think, that we may not agitate him. Oh no! I cannot think;' and leaning her head on Mrs Dawkins' shoulder, she burst into an agony of tears.

These salutary tears restored her recollection, and she inquired whether the surgeon, of whom Mrs Dawkins had spoken, was still in the house. Being answered, that he was in Montreville's apartment, she sent to beg that he would speak with her. He came, and she entreated him to inform her father, with the caution which his situation required, that she was returned and safe. She followed him to the door of Montreville's apartment, and stood listening in trembling expectation to every thing that stirred within. At last she received the wished-for summons. She entered; she sprang towards the bed. 'My child!' cried Montreville, and he clasped her to his bosom, and sobbed aloud. When he was able to speak, 'Oh Laura,' said he, 'tell me again that you are safe, and say by what miracle, by what unheard-of mercy, you have escaped.' 'Compose yourself, my dearest father, for Heaven's sake,' cried Laura. 'I am indeed safe, and never have been in danger. When Warren found that I refused to join in his frolic, he did not attempt to prevent me from returning home.' She then briefly related the affair as it had appeared to her, suppressing Warren's rhapsodies, from the fear of irritating her father; and he, perceiving that she considered the whole as a frolic, frivolous in its intention, though dreadful in its effects, suffered her to remain in that persuasion. She passed the night by his bed-side, devoting every moment of his disturbed repose to fervent prayers for his recovery.

CHAPTER XIV

───────●───────

FROM feverish and interrupted sleep, Montreville awoke unrefreshed; and the surgeon, when he repeated his visit, again alarmed Laura with representations of her father's danger, and assurances that nothing but the most vigilant attention to his quiet could preserve his life. The anguish with which Laura listened to this sentence she suppressed, lest it should injure her father. She never approached him but to bring comfort; she spoke to him cheerfully, while the tears forced themselves to her eyes; and smiled upon him while her heart was breaking. She felt what he must suffer, should the thought occur to him that he was about to leave her to the world, unfriended and alone; and she never mentioned his illness to him unless with the voice of hope. But of the danger which she strove to disguise, Montreville was fully sensible; and though he forbore to shock her by avowing it explicitly, he could not, like her, suppress his fears. He would sometimes fervently wish that he could see his child safe in the protection of Mrs Douglas; and sometimes, when Laura was bending over him in the tenderest sympathy, he would clasp her neck, and cry, with an agony that shook his whole frame, 'What – Oh what will become of thee!'

He seemed anxious to know how long Mrs De Courcy was to remain in town, and inquired every hour whether Montague was not returned. Full well did Laura guess the mournful meaning of these questions. Full well did they remind her, that when the De Courcy family left London, she with her dying father would amidst this populous wilderness be alone. She anticipated the last scene of this sad tragedy; when, amidst busy thousands, a senseless corpse would be her sole companion. She looked forward to its close, when even this sad society would be withdrawn. Human fortitude could not support the prospect; and she would rush from her father's presence, to give vent to agonies of sorrow.

But the piety of Laura could half-invest misfortune with the character of blessing; as the mists that rise to darken the evening sun are themselves tinged with his glory. She called to mind the gracious assurance which marks the afflicted who suffer not by their own guilt or folly as the favoured of Heaven; and the more her earthly connections seemed dissolving, the more did she strive to acquaint herself with Him, from whose care no accident can sever. To this care she fervently committed her father; praying that no selfish indulgence of her grief might embitter his departure; and resolving by her fortitude to convince him that she was able to struggle with the storm from which he was no longer to shelter her.

The day succeeding that on which Montreville was taken ill had been set apart for a farewell visit to Mrs De Courcy; and Laura's note of mournful apology, was answered by a kind visit from Harriet. Unconscious of the chief cause of her father's impatience for Montague's return, Laura wishing to be the bearer of intelligence which she knew would cheer him, inquired anxiously when Miss De Courcy expected her brother. But De Courcy's motions depended upon the spirits of his venerable friend, and Harriet knew not when he might be able to leave Mr Wentworth. It was even uncertain whether for the present he would return to town at all, as in another week Mrs De Courcy meant to set out for Norwood. Laura softened this unpleasing news to her father; she did not name the particular time of Mrs De Courcy's departure, and she suffered him still confidently to expect the return of his favourite.

The next day brought a letter from De Courcy himself, full of affectionate solicitude for the Captain's health and spirits; but evidently written in ignorance of the fatal change that had taken place since his departure. In this letter the name of Laura was not mentioned, not even in a common compliment, and Montreville remarked to her this omission. 'He has forgotten it,' answered Laura, – 'his warm heart is full of his friend's distress and yours, and has not room for more ceremony.' 'I hope,' said Montreville, emphatically, 'that is not the reason.' 'What is then the reason?' inquired Laura; but Montreville did not speak, and she thought no more of De Courcy's little omission.

Her father, indeed, for the present, occupied almost all her earthly thoughts, and even her prayers rose more frequently for him than for herself. Except during the visits of Montreville's surgeon, she was Montreville's sole attendant; and, regardless of fatigue, she passed every night by his bed-side, every day in ministering to his comfort. If, worn out with watching, she dropt asleep, she started again at his slightest motion, and obstinately refused to seek in her own chamber a less interrupted repose. 'No,' thought she, 'let my strength serve me while I have duties to perform, while my father lives to need my efforts; then may I be permitted to sink to early rest, and the weary labourer, while yet it is but morning, be called to receive his hire.'

The desertion of Hargrave, whom she had loved with all the ardour of a warm heart and a fervid imagination, the death of her father so fast approaching, her separation from every living being with whom she could claim friendship or kindred, seemed signals for her to withdraw her affections from a world where she would soon have nothing left to love or to cherish. 'And be it so,' thought she, – 'let me no longer grovel here in search of objects which earth has not to offer – objects fitted for unbounded and unchangeable regard. Nor let me peevishly reject what this world really has to give, the opportunity to prepare for a better. This it bestows even on me; and a few childish baubles are all else that it reserves for those who worship it with all their soul, and strength, and mind.'

No mortal can exist without forming some wish or hope. Laura *hoped* that she should live while she could be useful to her father; and she *wished* that she might not survive him. One only other wish she had, and that was for De Courcy's return; for Montreville, whose spirits more than shared his bodily languor, now seldom spoke, but to express his longing for the presence of his favourite. Laura continued to cheer him with a hope which she herself no longer felt; for now three days only remained ere Mrs De Courcy was to quit London. The departure of their friends Laura resolved to conceal from her father, that, believing them to be near, he might feel himself the less forlorn; and this she thought might be practicable, as he had never since his illness expressed any wish to quit his bed, or to see Miss De Courcy when she came.

In Montreville's darkened apartment, without occupation but in her cares for him, almost without rest, had Laura passed a week, when she was one morning summoned from her melancholy charge, to attend a visitor. She entered the parlour. 'Mr De Courcy!' she exclaimed, springing joyfully to meet him, 'thank Heaven you are come!' But not with equal warmth did De Courcy accost her. The repulsive look she had given him at parting was still fresh in his recollection; and, with a respectful distant bow, he expressed his sorrow for Captain Montreville's illness. 'Oh he is ill, indeed!' said Laura, the faint hectic of pleasure fading suddenly from her cheek. 'Earnestly has he longed for your return; and we feared,' said she, with a violent effort suppressing her tears, 'we feared that you might not have come till – till all was over.' 'Surely Miss Montreville,' said De Courcy, extremely shocked, 'surely you are causelessly alarmed.' 'Oh no,' cried Laura, 'he cannot live!' and no longer able to contain her emotion, she burst into a passion of tears. Forced entirely from his guard by her grief, Montague threw himself on the seat beside her. 'Dearest of human beings,' he exclaimed, 'Oh that I could shield thee from every sorrow!' But absorbed in her distress, Laura heeded him not; and the next moment, sensible of his imprudence, he started from her side, and retreated to a distant part of the room.

As soon as she was again able to command herself, she went to inform her father of De Courcy's arrival. Though told with the gentlest caution, Montreville heard the news with extreme emotion. He grasped Laura's hand; and, with tears of joy streaming down his pale cheeks, said, – 'Heaven be praised! I shall not leave thee quite desolate.' Laura herself felt less desolate and she rejoiced even for herself, when she once more saw De Courcy seated beside her father.

It was only the morning before, that a letter from Harriet had informed her brother of Montreville's illness and of Laura's distress. To hear of that distress, and to remain at a distance was impossible; and Montague had left Mr Wentworth's within the hour. He had travelled all night; and, without even seeing his mother and sister, had come directly to Captain Montreville's lodgings. He was shocked at the death-like looks of Montreville, and still more at those of Laura. Her eyes were sunk, her lips colourless, and her whole appearance indicated that she was worn out with fatigue and wretchedness. Yet De Courcy felt, that never in the bloom of health and beauty, had she been so dear to him, and scarcely could he forbear from addressing her in the accents of compassion and love. Montreville wishing to speak with him alone, begged of Laura to leave him for a while to De Courcy's care, and endeavour to take some rest. She objected that Montague had himself need of rest, having travelled all night; but when he assured her, that even if she drove him away he would not attempt to sleep, she consented to retire, and seek the repose of which she was so much in want.

When they were alone, Montreville shewed De Courcy the warning letter; and related to him the baseness of Warren and Laura's escape. Montague listened to him with intense interest. He often changed colour, and his lips quivered with emotion; and, when her father described the manner in which she had accomplished her escape, he exclaimed with enthusiasm, 'Yes, she is superior to every weakness, as she is alive to every gentle feeling.' Montreville then dwelt upon her unremitting care of him – on the fortitude with which she suppressed her sorrow, even while its violence was perceptibly injuring her health. 'And is it to be wondered at,' said he, 'that I look forward with horror to leaving this lovely excellent creature in such a world, alone and friendless?' 'She shall never be friendless,' cried De Courcy. 'My mother, my sister, shall be her friends, and I will' – He stopped abruptly, and a heavy sigh burst from him.

Recovering himself, he resumed, 'You must not talk so despondingly. You will live long, I trust, to enjoy the blessing of such a child.' Montreville shook his head, and remained silent. He was persuaded that De Courcy loved his daughter, and would fain have heard an explicit avowal that he did. To have secured to her the protection of Montague would have destroyed the bitterness of death. Had Laura been the heiress of millions, he would have rejoiced to bestow her and them upon De Courcy. But he scorned to force him to a declaration, and respected her too much to make an approach towards offering her to any man's acceptance.

He was at a loss to imagine what reason withheld De Courcy from avowing an attachment which he was convinced that he felt. When he considered his favourite's grave reflecting character, he was rather inclined to believe that he was cautiously ascertaining the temper and habits of the woman with whom he meant to spend his life. But the warmth of approbation with which he mentioned Laura, seemed to indicate that his opinion of her was already fixed. It was possible, too, that De Courcy wished to secure an interest in her regard before he ventured formally to petition for it. Whatever was the cause of Montague's silence, the Captain anticipated the happiest consequences from his renewed intercourse with Laura; and he resolved that he would not, by any indelicate interference, compel him to precipitate his declaration. He therefore changed the conversation, by inquiring when Mrs De Courcy was to leave town. Montague answered, that as he had not seen his mother since his return, he did not exactly know what time was fixed for her departure: 'but,' said he, 'whenever she goes, I shall only attend her to Norwood, and return on the instant; nor will I quit you again, till you are much, much better, or till you will no longer suffer me to stay.' Montreville received this promise with gratitude and joy; and De Courcy persuaded himself, that in making it, he was actuated chiefly by motives of friendship and humanity. He remained with Montreville till the day was far advanced, and then went to take a late dinner in Audley Street.

Next morning, and for several succeeding days, he returned, and spent the greatest part of his time in attending, comforting, and amusing the invalid. He prevailed on his mother to delay her departure, that he might not be obliged immediately to leave his charge. He soothed the little impatiences of disease; contrived means to mitigate the oppressiveness of debility; knew how to exhilarate the hour of ease; and watched the moment, well known to the sickly, when amusement becomes fatigue.

Laura repaid these attentions to her father with gratitude unutterable. Often did she wish to thank De Courcy as he deserved; but she felt that her acknowledgements must fall far short of her feelings and of his deserts, if they were not made with a warmth, which to a man, and to a young man, she revolted from expressing. She imagined, too, that to one who sought for friendship, mere gratitude might be mortifying; and that it might wound the generous nature of Montague to be thanked as a benefactor, where he wished to be loved as an equal. She therefore did not speak of, or but slightly mentioned, her own and her father's obligations to him; but she strove to repay them in the way that would have been most acceptable to herself, by every mark of confidence and good will. Here no timidity restrained her; for no feeling that could excite timidity at all mingled with her regard for De Courcy. But, confined to her own breast, her gratitude became the stronger; and if she had now had a heart to give, to Montague it would have been freely given.

Meanwhile the spirits of Montreville lightened of a heavy load, by the assurance that, even in case of his death, his daughter would have a friend to comfort and protect her, his health began to improve. He was able to rise; and one day, with the assistance of Montague's arm, surprised Laura with a visit in the parlour. The heart of Laura swelled with transport when she saw him once more occupy his accustomed seat in the family-room, and received him as one returned from the grave. She sat by him, holding his hand between her own, but did not try to speak. 'If it would not make you jealous, Laura,' said Montreville, 'I should tell you that Mr De Courcy is a better nurse than you are. I have recruited wonderfully since he undertook the care of me. More indeed than I thought I should ever have done.' Laura answered only by glancing upon De Courcy a look of heartfelt benevolence and pleasure. 'And yet,' said Montague, 'it is alleged that no attentions from our own sex are so effectual as those which we receive from the other. How cheaply would bodily suffering purchase the sympathy, the endearments of' – the name of Laura rose to his lips, but he suppressed it, and changed the expression to 'an amiable woman.' 'Is it indeed so?' cried Laura, raising her eyes full of grateful tears to his face. 'Oh then, if sickness or sorrow must be your portion, may your kindness here be repaid by some spirit of peace in woman's form – some gentleness yet more feminine than De Courcy's!'

The enthusiasm and gratitude had hurried Laura into a warmth which the next moment covered her with confusion; and she withdrew her eyes from De Courcy's face before she had time to remark the effect of these, the first words of emotion that ever she had addressed to him. The transport excited by the ardour of her expressions, and the cordial approbation which they implied, instantly gave way to extreme mortification. 'She wishes,' thought he, 'that some *woman* may repay me. She would then, not only with indifference, but with pleasure, see me united to another; resign me without a pang to some mere common-place insipid piece of sweetness; and give her noble self to one who could better feel her value.'

De Courcy had never declared his preference for Laura; he was even determined not to declare it. Yet to find that she had not even a wish to secure it for herself, gave him such acute vexation, that he was unable to remain in her presence. He abruptly rose and took his leave. He soon however reproached himself with the unreasonableness of his feelings; and returned to his oft-repeated resolution to cultivate the friendship without aspiring to the love of Laura. He even persuaded himself that he rejoiced in her freedom from a passion which could not be gratified without a sacrifice of the most important duties. He had a sister for whom no provision had been made; a mother, worthy of his warmest affection, whose increasing infirmities required increased indulgence. Mrs De Courcy's jointure was a very small one; and though she consented for the present to share the comforts of his establishment, Montague knew her too well to imagine that she would accept of any addition to her income, deducted from the necessary expences of his wife and family. His generous nature revolted from suffering his sister to feel herself a mere pensioner on his bounty, or to seek dear-bought independence in a marriage of convenience, a sort of bargain upon which he looked with double aversion, since he had himself felt the power of an exclusive attachment.

Here even his sense of justice was concerned; for he knew that, if his father had lived, it was his intention to have saved from his income a provision for Harriet. From the time that the estate devolved to Montague, he had begun to execute his father's intention; and he had resolved, that no selfish purpose should interfere with its fulfilment. The destined sum, however, was as yet little more than half collected, and it was now likely to accumulate still more slowly; for, as Mrs De Courcy had almost entirely lost the use of her limbs, a carriage was to her an absolute necessary of life.

Most joyfully would Montague have sacrificed every luxury, undergone every privation, to secure the possession of Laura; but he would not sacrifice his mother's health nor his sister's independence to any selfish gratification; nor would he subject the woman of his choice to the endless embarrassments of a revenue too small for its purposes.

These reasons had determined him against addressing Laura. At their first interview he had been struck with her as the most lovely woman he had ever beheld; but he was in no fear that his affections should be entangled. They had escaped from a hundred lovely women, who had done their utmost to ensnare them, while she was evidently void of any such design. Besides, Montreville was his old friend, and it was quite necessary that he should visit him. Laura's manners had charmed De Courcy as much as her person. Still might not a man be pleased and entertained, without being in love? Further acquaintance gradually laid open to him the great and amiable qualities of her mind, and was it not natural and proper to love virtue? but this was not being in love.

Symptoms at last grew so strong upon poor De Courcy, that he could no longer disguise them from himself; but it was pleasing to love excellence. He would never reveal his passion. It should be the secret joy of his heart; and why cast away a treasure which he might enjoy without injury to any? Laura's love indeed he could not seek; but her friendship he might cherish; and who would exchange the friendship of such a woman for the silly fondness of a thousand vulgar minds?

In this pursuit he had all the success that he could desire; for Laura treated him with undisguised regard; and with that regard he assured himself that he should be satisfied. At last this 'secret joy,' this 'treasure of his heart' began to mingle pain with its pleasures; and, when called away on his mournful errand to Mr Wentworth, De Courcy confessed, that it was wise to wean himself a little from one whose presence was becoming necessary to his happiness, and to put some restraint upon a passion, which from his toy was become his master. Short absence, however, had only increased his malady; and Laura in sorrow, Laura grateful, confiding, at times almost tender, seized at once upon every avenue to the heart of De Courcy: he revered her as the best, he admired her as the loveliest, he loved her as the most amiable of human beings. Still he resolved that, whatever it might cost him, he would refrain from all attempt to gain her love; and he began to draw nice distinctions between the *very* tender friedship with which he hoped to inspire her, and the tormenting passion which he must silently endure. Happily for the success of De Courcy's self-deceit, there was no rival at hand, with whose progress in Laura's regard he could measure his own, and he never thought of asking himself what would be his sensations if her *very tender* friendship for him should not exclude love for another.

A doubt would sometimes occur to him, as to the prudence of exposing himself to the unremitting influence of her charms, but it was quickly banished as an unwelcome intruder, or silenced with the plea, that, to withdraw himself from Montreville on a sick-bed, would outrage friendship and humanity. He had, too, somewhat inadvertently, given his friend a promise that he would not leave him till his health was a little re-established; and this promise now served as the excuse for an indulgence which he had not resolution to forego. After escorting Mrs De Courcy to Norwood, he pleaded this promise to himself when he returned to London without an hour's delay; and it excused him in his own eyes for going every morning to the abode of Montreville, from whence, till the return of night drove him away, he had seldom the resolution to depart.

Meanwhile, with the health of her father, the spirits of Laura revived; and considering it as an act of the highest self-denial in a domestic man to quit his home – a literary man to suspend his studies – a young man to become stationary in the apartment of an invalid, she exerted herself to the utmost to cheer De Courcy's voluntary task. She sometimes relieved him in reading aloud, an accomplishment in which she excelled. Her pronunciation was correct, her voice varied, powerful, and melodious, her conception rapid and accurate, while the expression of her countenance was an animated comment upon the author.

De Courcy delighted to hear her sing the wild airs of her native mountains, which she did with inimitable pathos, though without skill. Her conversation, sometimes literary, sometimes gay, was always simply intended to please. Yet, though void of all design to dazzle, it happened, she knew not how, that in De Courcy's company she was always more lively, more acute, than at other times. His remarks seemed to unlock new stores in her mind; and the train of thought which he introduced, she could always follow with peculiar ease and pleasure. Safe in her preference for another, she treated him with the most cordial frankness. Utterly unconscious of the sentiment she inspired, she yet had an animating confidence in De Courcy's good will; and sometimes pleased herself with thinking, that, next to his mother and sister, she stood highest of women in his regard. No arts of the most refined coquetry could have rivetted more closely the chains of the ill-fated De Courcy; and the gratitude of the unconscious Laura, pointed the shaft that gave the death wound to his peace.

How was it possible for her to imagine, that the same sentiment could produce a demeanour so opposite as De Courcy's was from that of Hargrave. Hargrave had been accustomed to speak of her personal charms with rapture. De Courcy had never made them the subject of direct compliment; he had even of late wholly discontinued those little gallantries which every pretty woman is accustomed to receive. Hargrave omitted no opportunity to plead his passion; and though the presence of a third person of necessity precluded this topic, it restrained him not from gazing upon Laura with an eagerness from which she shrunk abashed. De Courcy had never mentioned love; and Laura observed that, when his glance met her's, he would sometimes withdraw his eye with (as she thought) almost womanly modesty. In her private interviews with Hargrave, he had ever approached her with as much vehemence and freedom of speech and manner, as her calm dignity would permit. Privacy made no change in De Courcy's manner, except to render him a little more silent – a little more distant; and to personal familiarity, he seemed to be if possible more averse than herself; for if she accidentally touched him, he coloured and drew back.

Some of these circumstances Montreville had remarked, and had drawn from them inferences very different from those of his daughter. He was convinced that the preference of De Courcy for Laura had risen into a passion, which, for some unknown reason, he wished to conceal; and he perceived, by the ease of her behaviour, that Montague's secret was unsuspected by her. Most anxiously did he wish to know the cause of his favourite's silence, and to discover whether it was likely to operate long. In Laura's absence, he sometimes led the conversation towards the subject; but De Courcy never improved the offered opportunity. Partly in the hope of inviting equal frankness, Montreville talked of his own situation, and mentioned the motive of his journey to London. Montague inquired into every particular of the business, and rested not till he had found Mr Baynard's executor, and received from him an acknowledgement, that he had in his possession a voucher for the payment of Montreville's fifteen hundred pounds to Warren.

He next, without mentioned the matter to the Captain, called upon Warren, with an intention finally to conclude the business; thinking it impossible that, since the payment of the money was ascertained, he could refuse either to pay the annuity, or refund the price of it. But the disdain of Laura yet rankled in the mind of Warren, and he positively refused to bring the affair to any conclusion, declaring, that he would litigate it to the last sixpence he was worth; to which declaration he added an excellent joke concerning the union of Scotch pride with Scotch poverty. At this effrontery the honest blood of De Courcy boiled with indignation, and he was on the point of vowing, that he too would beggar himself, rather than permit such infamous oppression; but his mother, his sister, and Laura herself, rose to his mind, and he contented himself with threatening to expose Warren to the disgrace that he merited.

Warren now began to suspect that De Courcy was the cause of Laura's contemptuous reception of his addresses, and, enraged at his interference, yet overawed by his manly appearance and decided manner, became sullen, and refused to answer Montague's expostulations. Nothing remained to be done, and De Courcy was obliged to communicate to Montreville the ill success of his negotiations.

Bereft of all hope of obtaining justice, which he had not the means to enforce, Montreville became more anxiously desirous to regain such a degree of health as might enable him to return home. In his present state, such a journey was impracticable, and he was convinced, that while he remained pent up in the polluted air of the city, his recovery could advance but slowly. Some weeks must at all events elapse before he could be in a condition to travel; and to accommodate his funds to this prolonged demand upon them, he saw that he must have recourse to some scheme of economy yet more humble than that which he had adopted.

He hoped, if he could recover strength sufficient for the search, to find in the suburbs some abode of purer air, and still more moderate expense than his present habitation. The former only of these motives he mentioned to De Courcy; for though Montreville did not affect to be rich, he never spoke of his poverty. Varius circumstances, however, had led De Courcy to guess at his friend's pecuniary embarrassment; and he too had a motive which he did not avow, in the offer which he made to secure a more healthful residence for Montreville.

Unwilling to describe the humble accommodation with which he meant to content himself, or the limited price which he could afford to offer for it, Montreville at first refused De Courcy's services; but they were pressed upon him with such warmth, that he was obliged to submit, and Montague lost no time in fulfilling his commission.

He soon discovered a situation that promised comfort. It was in the outskirts of the town, a small flower-garden belonged to the house, the apartments were airy and commodious, the furniture was handsome, and the whole most finically neat. The rent, however, exceeded that of Montreville's present lodgings; and De Courcy knew that this objection would be insurmountable. That Laura should submit to the inelegancies of a mean habitation, was what he could not bear to think of; and he determined, by a friendly little artifice, to reconcile Montreville's comfort with his economy. The surgeon had named two or three weeks as the time likely to elapse before Montreville could commence his journey. De Courcy paid in advance above half the rent of the apartments for a month, charging the landlady to keep the real rent a secret from her lodgers.

As far as the author of these memoirs has been able to learn, this was the only artifice that ever Montague De Courcy practised in his life; and it led, as artifices are wont to do, to consequences which the contriver neither wished nor foresaw.

Much to his satisfaction, Montreville was soon settled in his new abode, where De Courcy continued to be his daily visitor. A certain delicacy prevented Laura from endeavouring to procure a reversal of her father's decree, issued in a moment of peevishness, that she should paint no more with a view to pecuniary reward. She felt that he had been wrong, and she shrunk from reminding him of it, till her labours should again become necessary. But, desirous to convey to Mrs De Courcy some token of her remembrance and gratitude, she employed some of the hours which Montague spent with her father, in labouring a picture which she intended to send to Norwood. The subject was the choice of Hercules; and to make her gift the more acceptable, she presented in the hero a picture of De Courcy, while the form and countenance of Virtue, were copied from the simple majesty of her own. The figure of Pleasure was a fancied one, and it cost the fair artist unspeakable labour. She could not pourtray what she would have shrunk from beholding – a female voluptuary. Her draperies were always designed with the most chastened decency; and, after all her toil, even the form of Pleasure came sober and matronly from the hand of Laura.

Designing a little surprise for her friends, she had never mentioned this picture to De Courcy; and as she daily stole some of the hours of his visits to bestow upon it, it advanced rapidly. Montague bore these absences with impatience; but Montreville, who knew how Laura was employed, took no notice of them, and De Courcy durst not complain.

Three weeks had glided away since Montreville's removal to his new lodgings, and he remained as much as ever anxious, and as much as ever unable to guess the reason which induced De Courcy to conceal a passion which evidently increased every day. He recollected that Montague had of late never met Laura but in his presence, and he thought it natural that the lover should wish to make his first application to his mistress herself. He had an idea, that the picture might be made to assist the denouement which he so ardently desired; and with this view he privately gave orders that when next Mr De Courcy came he should be ushered into the painting-room, which he knew would be empty, as Laura never quitted him till De Courcy arrived to take her place.

Next morning accordingly Montague was shewn into the room which he had himself destined for Laura, and, for that reason, supplied with many little luxuries which belonged not to its original furniture. He looked round with delight on the marks of her recent presence. There lay her book open as she had quitted it, and the pencil with which she had marked the margin. It was one which he himself had recommended, and he thought it should ever be dear to him. On a table lay her port-folio and drawing materials: in a corner stood her easel with the picture, over which was thrown a shawl which he had seen her wear.

Not conceiving that she could have any desire to conceal her work, he approached it, and, raising the cover, stood for a moment motionless with surprise. The next, a thousand sensations, vague but delightful, darted through his mind; but before he could give a shape or distinctness to any one of them, the step approached that ever aroused De Courcy to eager expectation, and letting drop the shawl, he flew towards the door to receive Laura.

With rapture in his eyes, but confusion on his tongue, De Courcy paid his compliments, and again turned towards the picture. Laura sprung forward to prevent him from raising the covering. 'Is this forbidden, then?' said he. 'Oh yes, indeed,' said Laura, blushing, 'you must not look at it.' 'Can you be so mischievous,' cried De Courcy, a delighted smile playing on his countenance, 'as to refuse me such a pleasure?' 'I am sure,' said Laura, blushing again, and still more deeply, 'it could give you no pleasure in its present state.' 'And I am sure,' said De Courcy, ardently, 'it would give me more than I have language to express.'

De Courcy's eagerness, and the consciousness of her own confusion, made Laura now more unwilling that Montague should discover the cause of both to be his own portrait, and actually trembling with emotion, she said, putting her hand on the shawl to prevent him from raising it, 'Indeed I cannot shew you this. There is my port-folio – look at any thing but this.' 'And what inference may I draw as to the subject of a picture that Miss Montreville will not shew to the most partial – the most devoted of her friends?' 'Any inference,' replied Laura, still holding the shawl, 'that friendship or charity will permit.' 'And must I not remove this perverse little hand?' said De Courcy, laying his upon it; for all prudence was forgotten in his present emotion. Laura, a little offended at his perseverance, gravely withdrew her hand, and turned away, saying, 'Since my wishes have no power, I shall make no other trial of strength.' 'No power!' cried De Courcy, following her, 'they have more force than a thousand arms.' 'Well,' said Laura, a little surprised by his manner, but turning upon him a smile of gracious reconciliation, 'your forbearance may hereafter be rewarded by a sight of this important picture; but lest you should forfeit your recompense, had we not better remove from temptation?'

She then led the way to the parlour, and De Courcy followed her in a state of agitation that could not be concealed. He was absent and restless. He often changed colour, seemed scarce sensible of what was addressed to him, or began to reply, and the unfinished sentence died upon his lips. At last, starting up, he pleaded sudden indisposition, and was hurrying away. 'Do not go away ill and alone,' said Laura, kindly detaining him. 'Walk round the garden – the fresh air will relieve you.' 'No air will relieve me!' said De Courcy, in a voice of wretchedness. 'What then can we do for you?' said Laura, with affectionate earnestness. 'What can *you* do for me!' cried De Courcy, 'Oh nothing, nothing but suffer me to go, while yet I have the power.' He then wrung Montreville's hand, and uttering something which his emotion made inarticulate, without venturing a glance towards Laura, he quitted the house, and returned home in a state bordering on distraction.

He shut himself up in his chamber to consider of his situation, if that can be called consideration, which was but a conflict of tumultuous feeling. That Laura should have painted his portrait in a group where it held such a relation to her own; that she should keep it concealed in an apartment exclusively appropriated to herself; her alarm lest he should examine it; her confusion, which had at last risen to the most distressing height, from the idea of what De Courcy might infer, should he discover that his own portrait was the cause of so many blushes; the confiding affectionate matter in which she treated him, – all conspired to mislead De Courcy. He felt a conviction that he was beloved, and, in spite of himself, the thought was rapture.

But what availed this discovery? Could he forget the justice of his sister's claims, sacrifice to his selfish wishes the comfort of his mother, or wed his half-worshipped Laura to the distresses of an embarrassed fortune? 'Oh no,' he cried, 'let not my passions involve in disaster all that I love.'

Or could he lay open to Laura his feelings and his situation, and sue for her love, even while their union must be delayed. Her attachment, he thought, was yet in its infancy, born of gratitude, fostered by separation from other society, and, for the present, pleasing in its sensations, and transient in its nature. But he thought her capable of a love as fervent – as deep-rooted as that which she inspired; and should he wilfully awaken in her peaceful breast the cravings of such a passion as tortured his own; see her spirits, her vigour of mind, her usefulness, perhaps her health, give way to the sickness of 'hope deferred!' No, – rather let her return to the indifference in which he found her. Or, should he shackle her with a promise, of which honour might extort a reluctant fulfilment, after the affection that prompted it was perhaps withdrawn from him? Or, should he linger on from day to day in vain endeavours to conceal his affection, dishonourably sporting with the tenderness of the woman he loved, his ill-suppressed feelings every hour offering a hope which must every hour be disappointed? No! the generous heart of De Courcy would sooner have suffered a thousand deaths.

But could he return – could he see again this creature, now more than ever dear to him, and stifle the fondness – the anguish that would rend his bosom at parting? Impossible! He would see her no more. He would tear at once from his heart every hope – every joy – and dare at once all the wretchedness that awaited him. In an agony of desperation, he rang for his servant, ordered his horses, and in an hour was on his way to Norwood, with feelings which the criminal on the rack need not have envied.

CHAPTER XV

———————●———————

THE next morning, while Montreville and his daughter were expecting, with some anxiety the arrival of their daily visitor, a note was brought which De Courcy had left in Audley Street, to be delivered after his departure. Though nearly illegible, from the agitation in which it was written, it contained nothing but the simple information, that he had been suddenly obliged to leave London. It assigned no reason for his journey – it fixed no period for his absence; and Montreville endeavoured to hope that his return would not be distant. But day after day passed heavily on, and De Courcy came not. Montreville again began to feel himself a solitary deserted being; again became dejected; again became the victim of real debility and fancied disease.

All Laura's endeavours failed to animate him to cheerfulness, or rouse him to employment. If he permitted her to remain by him, he seemed rather to endure than to enjoy her presence, repressed with a languid monosyllable her attempts at conversation, or passed whole hours in listless silence. Laura, who foreboded the worst consequences from the indulgence of this depression, endeavoured to persuade him that he might now safely attempt a voyage to Scotland, and predicted beneficial effects from the sea air. But Montreville answered her with displeasure, that such an exertion would certainly destroy him, and that those who were themselves in high health and spirits, could not judge of the feelings, nor sympathize with the weakness of disease. The reproach had no more justice than is usual with the upbraidings of the sickly; for Laura's spirits shared every turn of her father's, though her stronger mind could support with grace the burden that weighed him to the earth. She desisted, however, from a subject which she saw that, for the present, he would not bear, and confined her endeavours to persuading him to undertake some light occupation, or to walk in the little garden that belonged to the house. But, even in these attempts she was commonly defeated; for Montreville would make no exertion, and the winter wind, now keen and biting, pierced through his wasted form.

None but they who have made the melancholy experiment, can tell how cheerless is the labour of supporting the spirit that will make no effort to sustain itself, of soliciting the languid smile, offering the rejected amusement, or striving, with vain ingenuity, to enliven the oft-repulsed conversation. They only know who have tried it, what it is to resist contagious depression – to struggle against the effects of the complaining voice, the languid motion, the hopeless aspect; what it is to suppress the sympathetic sigh, and restrain the little sally of impatience, so natural to those whose labours are incessant, yet unavailing. Such were the tasks that Laura voluntarily prescribed to herself. Incited by affection, and by strong sense of duty, she soothed the fretful humour, prompted the reluctant exertion, fanned the expiring hope, and seized the most favourable moment to soften by feminine tenderness, or exhilarate by youthful gaiety.

Many motives may lead to one great effort of virtue. The hope of reward, the desire of approbation, a sense of right, the natural benevolence which still affords a faint trait of the image in which man was made, all, or any of these, may produce single, or even oft-repeated acts deserving of praise; but one principle alone can lead to virtuous exertions persevering and unremitting though without success. That principle was Laura's; and even while her endeavours seemed unavailing, she was content to employ all her powers in the task selected for her by the bestower of them.

Montreville often reproached himself for the untimely burden which he was laying on the young heart of his daughter; but he could make no effort to lighten it, and self-reproach served only to embitter the spirit which it failed of stimulating to exertion. Fretful and impatient, yet conscious of his injustice, and unwilling that Laura should observe it, he would often dismiss her from her attendance, and spend whole hours in solitary gloom. These hours Laura devoted to her picture, stealing between whiles, on tiptoe, to the door of her father's apartment, to listen whether he was stirring; and sometimes venturing to knock gently for admittance.

The picture, which was far advanced when De Courcy left town, soon received the finishing touches; and Laura lost no time in transmitting it to Norwood. She wrote an affectionate letter to Harriet; in which, after thanking her for all her kindness, she offered her gift, and added, that to give her work a value which it would not otherwise have possessed, she had introduced the portrait of De Courcy; and that, glad of an opportunity of associating the remembrance of herself with an object of interest, she had admitted her own resemblance into the group. She apologized for the appearance of conceit which might attend her exhibiting her own form under the character of Virtue, by relating, with characteristic simplicity, that she had determined on her subject, chosen and half-finished her Hercules, before she designed the figures of his companions; that she had afterwards thought that her memorial would be more effectual if it contained the portrait of the giver. 'And you know,' added she, 'it would have been impossible to mould my solemn countenance into the lineaments of Pleasure.'

In the singleness of her heart, it never occurred to Laura, that any thing in the mutual relation of the figures of her piece stood in need of explanation. Had Hargrave furnished the model for her hero, she would probably have been a little more quick-sighted. As it was, she felt impatient to shew the De Courcy family, not excepting Montague himself, that she was not forgetful of their kindness; and she chose a day, when the influence of bright sunshine a little revived the spirits of Montreville, to leave him for an hour, and accompany the picture to the shop of the obliging print-seller, that it might be packed more skilfully than by herself.

After seeing it safely put up, she gave the address to Wilkins, who immediately exclaimed, 'So, Ma'am, you have found out the secret that you would not let me tell you?' 'What secret?' inquired Laura. 'The name of the gentleman, Ma'am, that bought your pictures.' 'Was it De Courcy, then?' 'Yes, Ma'am; – though to be sure it might'n't be the same. But I suppose you'll know him, Ma'am. A tall pleasant-looking gentleman, Ma'am. The pictures were sent home to Audley Street.' Laura's countenance brightened with satisfaction, and she suffered her informer to proceed. 'I am sure,' continued he, 'I managed that business to the very best of my power, and, as one might say, very dexterously.' 'Was there any occasion for management?' inquired Laura. 'Oh yes, Ma'am; for when he seemed very much taken with the first one, then I told him all about you just as I had it all from Mrs Dawkins, and how you were so anxious to have it sold; and then he said he'd have it, and paid the money into my hands; and then I told him how you looked the first day you brought it here, and that you were just ready to cry about it; and he said he must have a companion to it.

The flush, both of pride and vexation, for once stained the transparent skin of Laura. Yet it was but for a moment; and her next feeling was pleasure at the confirmation of the benevolent character with which her imagination had invested De Courcy. He had purchased her work when she was quite unknown to him, only, as she thought, from a wish to reward industry; and because he had been led to believe that the price was an object to the artist. Had another been the purchaser, she might have allowed something for the merit of the piece, but Laura was not yet cured of first imagining characters, and then bending facts to suit her theory. Sooner than bate one iota from De Courcy's benevolence, she would have assigned to her picture the rank of a sign-post.

She now remembered, that in her visits to Audley Street she had never seen her works; and in her approbation of the delicacy which prompted De Courcy to conceal that she was known to him as an artist, she forgot the little prejudice which this concealment implied. De Courcy, indeed, was himself unconscious that he entertained any such prejudice. He applauded Laura's exertions; he approved of the spirit that led a young woman of family to dare, in spite of custom, to be useful. Yet he could not help acting as if she had shared the opinion of the world, and been herself ashamed of her labours. But this was a shame that Laura knew not. She wished not indeed to intrude on the world's notice. Her choice was peaceful obscurity. But if she must be known, she would have far preferred the distinction earned by ingenious industry, to the notoriety which wealth and luxury can purchase.

On her return home, she found her father reading a letter which he had just received from De Courcy. It seemed written in an hour of melancholy. The writer made no mention of returning to town; on the contrary, he expressed a hope that Montreville might now be able to undertake a journey to Scotland. He besought the Captain to remember him, to speak of him often, and to write to him sometimes; and ended with these words – 'Farewell, my friend; the dearest of my earthly hopes is, that we may one day meet again, though years, long years, must first intervene.'

'So ends my last hope,' said Montreville, letting his head sink mournfully on his breast; 'De Courcy comes not, and thou must be left alone and unprotected.' 'The protection of so young a man,' said Laura, avoiding to answer to a foreboding which she considered merely as a symptom of her father's disease, 'might not perhaps have appeared advantageous to me in the eyes of those who are unacquainted with Mr De Courcy.' 'It would have given comfort to my dying hour,' said Montreville, 'to consign thee to such a guardian – such a husband.' 'A husband!' cried Laura, starting, and turning pale. 'Heaven be praised, that Mr De Courcy never harboured such a thought!' Montreville looked up in extreme surprise; and inquired the reason of her thankfulness. 'Oh Sir,' she replied, 'we owe so much to Mr De Courcy's friendship, that I should have hated myself for being unable to return his affection; – and pity would it have been that the love of so amiable a being should have been bestowed in vain.'

Montreville fixed his eyes upon her, as if to seek for further explanation, and continued to gaze on her face, when his thoughts had wandered from the examination of it. After some minutes of silence, he said – 'Laura, you once rejected an alliance, splendid beyond my hopes, almost beyond my wishes, and that with a man formed to be the darling of your sex; and now you speak as if even Montague De Courcy would have failed to gain you. Tell me, then, have you any secret attachment? Speak candidly, Laura; – you will not always have a father to confide in.'

Deep crimson dyed the cheeks of Laura; but, with the hesitation of a moment, she replied – 'No, Sir, I have no wish to marry. I pretend not to lay open my whole heart to you; but I may with truth assure you, that there is not at this moment a man in being with whom I would unite myself. I know you would not be gratified by extorted confidence.'

'No, Laura,' said Montreville, 'I ask no more than you willingly avow. I confide, as I have always done, in your prudence and integrity. Soon, alas! you will have no other guides. But it was my heart's wish to see you united to a man who could value and protect your worth – of late, more especially, when I feel that I so soon must leave you.'

'My dearest father,' said Laura, throwing her arm affectionately round his neck, 'do not give way to such gloomy forebodings. Your spirits are oppressed by confinement – let us but see Glenalbert again, and all will be well.'

'I shall never see Glenalbert,' said Montreville; – 'and left alone in such a place as this, without money, without friends, without a home; – where shall my child find safety or shelter?'

'Indeed, Sir,' said Laura, though a cold shuddering seized her, 'your fears have no foundation. Only yesterday Dr Flint told me that your complaints were without danger, and that a little exercise would make you quite strong again.'

Montreville shook his head. 'Dr Flint deceives you, Laura,' said he; – 'you deceive yourself.' 'No, indeed,' said Laura, though she trembled; 'you look much better, – you are much better. It is only these melancholy thoughts that retard your recovery. Trust yourself – trust me to the Providence that has hitherto watched over us.'

'I could die without alarm,' said Montreville; 'but to leave thee alone and in want – Oh! I cannot bear it.' 'Should the worst befal,' said Laura, turning pale as alabaster, 'think that I shall not be alone, I shall not want, for' – her voice failed, but she raised her eyes with an expression that filled up the ennobling sentiment. 'I believe it, my love,' said Montreville, 'but you feel these consolations more strongly than I do. Leave me for the present, I am fatigued, and wish to be alone.'

Laura retired to her own room, and endeavoured herself to practise the trust which she recommended to her father. Her meditations were interrupted by the entrance of her landlady, Mrs Stubbs, who, with many courtesies and apologies, said that she was come to present her account.

Laura, who always had pleasure in cancelling a debt the moment it was incurred, and who conceived no apology to be necessary from those who came to demand only their own, received her landlady very graciously, and begged her to be seated, while she went to bring her father's purse. Mrs Stubbs spread her bills upon the table; and Laura, after examining them, was obliged to ask an explanation.

'Why, ma'am,' returned the landlady, 'there are fourteen guineas for lodgings for six weeks, and £10, 15s. for victuals and other articles that I have furnished. I am sure I have kept an exact account.'

'I understood,' said Laura, 'that we were to have the lodgings for a guinea and a half a-week, and' – 'A guinea and a half!' cried the landlady, colouring with wrath at this disparagement of her property. 'Sure, Miss, you did not think to have lodgings such as these for a guinea and a half a-week. No, no – these lodgings have never been let for less than four guineas, and never shall, as long as my name is Bridget.'

Laura mildly pleaded her ignorance of those matters, and urged De Courcy's information as an excuse for her mistake. 'To be sure, Ma'am,' said the now pacified Mrs Stubbs, 'nobody that know'd any thing of the matter, would expect to have such rooms for less than four guineas; and that was what the gentleman said when he took them; so he paid me two guineas and a half advance for four weeks; and charged me not to let you know of it; but I can't abide them secret doings; and, besides, if I take only a guinea and a half from you, where was I to look for the rest of my rent for the last fortnight – for the young gentleman seems to have taken himself off.'

Laura suffered her loquacious hostess to proceed without interruption, for her thoughts were fully occupied. She had incurred a debt greater, by five guineas, than she had been prepared to expect; and this sum was, in her present circumstances, of great importance. Yet her predominant feeling was grateful approbation of De Courcy's benevolence; nor did her heart at all upbraid him with the consequences of his well-meant deception. 'Kind, considerate De Courcy,' thought she; 'he had hoped that, ere now, we should have ceased to need his generosity, and even have been removed from the possibility of discovering it.'

Recollecting herself, she paid the landlady her full demand; and, dismissing her, sat down to examine what remained of her finances. All that she possessed, she found amounted to no more than one guinea and a few shillings; and, dropping the money into her lap, she sat gazing on it in blank dismay.

The poverty, whose approach she had so long contemplated with a fearful eye, had now suddenly overtaken her. Husbanded with whatever care, the sum before her could minister only to the wants of a few hours. In her present habitation, it would scarcely purchase shelter for another night from the storm which a keen winter-wind was beginning to drive against her window. An immediate supply then was necessary; but where could that supply be found? It was too late to resort to the earnings of her own genius. Painting was a work of time and labour. No hasty production was likely to find favour amidst the competition of studied excellence. Even the highest effort of her art might long wait a purchaser; and tears fell from the eyes of Laura while she reflected that, even if she could again produce a Leonidas, she might never again find a De Courcy.

To borrow money on the Captain's half-pay, was an expedient which Laura had always rejected, as calculated to load their scanty income with a burden which it could neither shake off nor bear. But even to this expedient she could now no longer have recourse; for Montreville had assured her that, in his present state of health, it would be impossible to mortgage his annuity for a single guinea.

She might raise a small supply by stripping her beloved Glenalbert of some of its little luxuries and comforts; but, long before this revolting business could be transacted, she must be absolutely pennyless. Nor did she dare, without consulting her father, to give orders for dismantling his home. And how should she inform him of the necessity for such a sacrifice? Weakened both in body and in mind, how would he endure the privations that attend on real penury? His naturally feeble spirits already crushed to the earth, his kindly temper already, by anxiety and disappointment, turned to gall, his anxieties for his child alarmed even to anguish, how could he bear to learn that real want had reached him – had reached that dear child, whom the dread of leaving to poverty was poisoning the springs of life within him! 'He thinks he is about to leave me,' cried she, 'and shall I tell him that I must owe to charity even the sod that covers him from me? No; I will perish first,' and, starting from her seat, she paced the room in distressful meditation on the means of concealing from her father the extent of their calamity.

She determined to take upon herself the care of their little fund, under pretence that the trouble was too great for Montreville. He had of late shewn such listless indifference to all domestic concerns, that she hoped he might never inquire into the extent of his landlady's demand, or that his inquiries might be eluded. It seemed a light thing in Laura's eyes to suffer alone; or rather she thought not of her own sufferings, could she but spare her father the anguish of knowing himself and his child utterly destitute. She judged of his feelings by her own; felt, by sympathy, all the pangs with which he would witness wants which he could not supply; and she inwardly vowed to conceal from him every privation that she might endure, – every labour that she might undergo.

But, void of every resource, far from every friend, destitute amid boundless wealth, alone amid countless multitudes, whither should she turn for aid, or even for counsel? 'Whither,' cried she, dropping on her knees, 'except to Him who hath supplied me in yet more urgent want, who hath counselled me in yet more fearful difficulty, who hath fed my soul with angel's food, and guided it with light from heaven?' Laura rose from her devotions, more confiding in the care of Providence, more able to consider calmly of improving the means which still remained within her own power.

Before she could finish and dispose of a picture, weeks must elapse for which she could make no provision. To painting, therefore, she could not have immediate recourse. But sketches in chalk could be finished with expedition; the printseller might undertake the sale of them; and the lowness of the price might invite purchasers. Could she but hope to obtain a subsistence for her father, she would labour night and day, deprive herself of recreation, of rest, even of daily food, rather than wound his heart, by an acquaintance with poverty. 'And since his pride is hurt by the labours of his child,' said she, 'even his pride shall be sacred. He shall never know my labours.' And, so frail are even the best, that an emotion of pride swelled the bosom of Laura at the thought that the merit of her toils was enhanced by their secrecy.

The resolutions of Laura were ever the immediate prelude to action; and here was no time for delay. She again looked mournfully upon her little treasure, hpelessly re-examined the purse that contained it; again, with dismay, remembered that it was her all; then, hastily putting it into her pocket, she drew her portfolio towards her, and began to prepare for the work with the hurry of one to whom every moment seems precious. Invention was at present impossible; but she tried to recollect one of her former designs, and busied herself in sketching it till the hour of dinner arrived. She then went to summon her father from his chamber to the eating-room. 'This day,' thought she, 'I must share his precarious sustenance – another I shall be more provident. And is this then, perhaps, our last social meal?' and she turned for a moment from the door, to suppress the emotion that would have choked her utterance. 'Come in, my dear,' cried Montreville, who had heard her footstep; and Laura entered with a smile. She offered her arm to assist him in descending to the parlour. 'Why will you always urge me to go down stairs, Laura,' said he; 'you see I am unequal to the fatigue.' 'I shall not urge you to-morrow,' answered Laura: and Montreville thought the tears which stood in her eyes, were the consequence of the impatient tone in which he had spoken.

During the evening, Laura avoided all mention of restoring the purse to her father, and he appeared to have forgotten its existence. But, by no effort could she beguile those cheerless hours. Her utmost exertions were necessary to maintain the appearance of composure; and De Courcy's letter seemed to have consummated Montreville's feelings of solitude and desolation. Wilfully, and without effort, he suffered his spirits to expire. His whole train of thinking had become habitually gloomy. He was wretched, even without reference to his situation, and the original cause of his melancholy was rather the excuse than the reason of his depression. But this only rendered more hopeless all attempts to cheer him; for the woes of the imagination have this dire pre-eminence over those which spring from real evils, that, while these can warm at times in benevolent joy, or even brighten for a moment to the flash of innocent gaiety, the selfishness of the former, chequered by no kindly feeling, reflects not the sunny smile; as the dark and noisome fog drinks in vain the beam of Heaven.

Montreville, when in health, had been always and justly considered a kind-hearted, good-natured man. He had been a most indulgent husband, an easy master, and a fond father. He was honourable, generous, and friendly. Those who had witnessed his patient endurance of Lady Harriet's caprice had given his philosophy a credit which was better due to his indolence: for the grand defect of Montreville's character was a total want of fortitude and self-command; and of these failings he was now paying the penalty. His health was injured by his voluntary inaction, his fancy aggravated his real disorder, and multiplied to infinity his imaginary ailments. He had habituated his mind to images of disaster, till it had become incapable of receiving any but comfortless and doleful impressions.

After spending a few silent hours without effort towards employment or recreation, he retired for the night; and Laura experienced a sensation of relief, as, shutting herself away into her apartment, she prepared to resume her labours. After every other member of the family had retired to rest, she continued to work till her candle expired in the socket; and then threw herself on her bed to rise again wtih the first blush of dawn.

Montreville had been accustomed to breakfast in his own room; Laura therefore found no difficulty in beginning her system of abstemiousness. Hastily swallowing a few mouthfuls of dry bread, she continued her drawing, till her father rang for his chocolate. She was fully resolved to adhere to this plan, to labour with unceasing industry, and to deny herself whatever was not essential to her existence.

But neither hard fare, nor labour, nor confinement, could occasion to Laura such pain as she suffered from another of the necessities of her situation. Amidst her mournful reflections, it had occurred to her, that unless she would incur a debt which she could not hope to discharge, it would be necessary to dismiss the surgeon who attended her father. All her ideas of honour and integrity revolted from suffering a man to expend his time and trouble, in expectation of a return which she was unable to make. She was besides convinced that in Montreville's case medicine could be of no avail. But she feared to hint the subject to her father, lest she should lead to a discovery of their present circumstances; and such was her conviction of the feebleness of his spirits, and such her dread of the consequences of their increased depression, that all earthly evils seemed light compared with that of adding to his distress. Laura perhaps judged wrong; for one real evil sometimes ameliorates the condition, by putting to flight a host of imaginary calamities, and by compelling that exertion which makes any situation tolerable. But she trembled for the effects of the slightest additional suffering upon the life or the reason of her father; and she would have thought it little less than parricide to add a new bruise to the wounded spirit. On the other hand, she dreaded that Montreville, if kept in ignorance of its real cause, might consider the desertion of his medical attendant as an intimation that his case was hopeless, and perhaps become the victim of his imaginary danger.

She knew not on what to resolve. Her distress and perplexity were extreme; and if any thing could have vanquished the stubborn integrity of Laura, the present temptation would have prevailed. But no wilful fraud could be the issue of her deliberations, who was steadily convinced that inflexible justice looks on to blast with a curse even the successful schemes of villany, and to shed a blessing on the sorrows of the upright. She would not even for her father incur a debt which she could never hope to pay; and nothing remained but to consider of the best means of executing her painful determination.

Here a new difficulty occurred, for she could not decline the surgeon's further attendance without offering to discharge what she already owed. In the present state of her funds, this was utterly impossible; for though, at her instigation, his bill had been lately paid, she was sure that the new one must already amount to more than all she possessed. How to procure the necessary supply she knew not; for even if she could have secured the immediate sale of her drawings, the price of her daily and nightly toil would scarcely suffice to pay for the expensive habitation which she durst not propose to leave, and to bribe the fastidious appetite of Montreville with dainties of which he could neither bear the want nor feel the enjoyment.

Once only, and it was but for a moment, she thought of appealing to the humanity of Dr Flint, of unfolding to him her situation, and begging his attendance upon the chance of future remuneration. But Laura was destined once more to pay the penalty of her hasty judgments of character. On Montreville's first illness, Dr Flint had informed Laura, with (as she thought) great want of feeling, of her father's danger. He was a gaunt, atrabilious, stern-looking man, with a rough voice, and cold repulsive manners. He had, moreover, an uninviting name; and though Laura was ashamed to confess to herself that such trifles could influence her judgment, these disadvantages were the real cause why she always met Dr Flint with a sensation resembling that with which one encounters a cold, damp, north-east wind. To make any claim upon the benevolence of a stranger – and such a stranger! It was not to be thought of. Yet Laura's opinion, or rather her feelings, wronged Dr Flint. His exterior, it is true, was far from prepossessing. It is also true, that, considering Montreville's first illness as the effect of a very unpardonable levity on the part of Laura, he had spoken to her on that occasion with even more than his usual frigidity. Nor did he either possess or lay claim to any great share of sensibility; but he was not destitute of humanity; and had Laura explained to him her situation, he would willingly have attended her father without prospect of recompense. But Laura did not put his benevolence to the test. She suffered him to make his morning visit and depart; while she was considering of a plan which appeared little less revolting.

Laura knew that one of the most elegant houses in Grosvenor Street was inhabited by a Lady Pelham, the daughter of Lady Harriet Montreville's mother by a former marriage. She knew that, for many years, little intercourse had subsisted between the sisters; and that her father was even wholly unknown to Lady Pelham. But she was ignorant, that the imprudence of her mother's marriage served as the excuse for a coldness, which had really existed before it had any such pretext.

With all her Scotish prejudice in favour of the claims of kindred (and Laura in this and many other respects was entirely a Scotch woman), she could not, without the utmost repugnance, think of applying to her relation. To introduce herself to a stranger whom she had never seen – to appear not only as an inferior, but as a supplicant – a beggar! Laura had long and successfully combated the innate pride of human nature; but her humility almost failed under this trial. Her illustrious ancestry – the dignity of a gentlewoman – the independence of one who can bear to labour and endure to want, all rose successively to her mind; for pride can wear many specious forms. But she had nearer claims than the honour of her ancestry – dearer concerns than her personal importance; and when she thought of her father, she felt that she was no longer independent.

Severe was her struggle, and bitter were the tears which she shed over the conviction that it was right that she should become a petitioner for the bounty of a stranger. In vain did she repeat to herself, that she was a debtor to the care of Providence for her daily bread, and was not entitled to choose the means by which it was supplied. She could not conquer her reluctance. But she could act right in defiance of it. She could sacrifice her own feelings to the comfort of her father – to a sense of duty. Nay, upon reflection, she could rejoice that circumstances compelled her to quell that proud spirit with which, as a Christian, she maintained a constant and vigorous combat.

While these thoughts were passing in her mind, she had finished her drawing; and, impatient to know how far this sort of labour was likely to be profitable, she furnished her father with a book to amuse him in her absence; and, for the first time since they had occupied their present lodgings, expressed a wish to take a walk for amusement. Had Montreville observed the blushes that accompanied this little subterfuge, he would certainly have suspected that the amusement which this walk promised was of no common kind; but he was in one of his reveries, hanging over the mantle-piece, with his forehead resting on his arm, and did not even look up while he desired her not to be long absent.

She resolved to go first to Lady Pelham, that coming early she might find her disengaged, and afterwards to proceed to the print-shop.

The wind blew keen across the snow as Laura began her reluctant pilgrimage. Her summer attire, to which her finances could afford no addition, ill defended her from the blast. Through the streets of London she was to explore her way unattended. Accustomed to find both beauty and pleasure in the solitude of her walks, she was to mix in the throngs of a rude rabble, without protection from insult. But no outward circumstances could add to the feelings of comfortless dismay with which she looked forward to the moment, when, ushered through stately apartments into the presence of self-important greatness, she should announce herself a beggar. Her courage failed – she paused, and made one step back towards her home. But she recalled her former thoughts. 'I have need to be humbled,' said she; and again proceeded on her way.

As she left the little garden that surrounded her lodgings, she perceived an old man who had taken shelter by one of the pillars of the gate. He shivered in the cold, which found easy entrance through the rags that covered him, and famine glared from his hollow eye. His gray hair streamed on the wind, as he held out the tattered remains of a hat, and said, 'Please to help me, Lady. – I am very poor.' He spoke in the dialect of her native land, and the accents went to Laura's heart; – for Laura was in the land of strangers. She had never been deaf to the petitions of the poor; for all the poor of Glenalbert were known to her; and she knew that what she spared from her own comforts, was not made the minister of vice. Her purse was already in her hand, ere she remembered that to give was become a crime.

As the thought crossed her, she started like one who had escaped from sudden danger. 'No, I must not give you money,' said she, and returned the purse into her pocket, with a pang that taught her the true bitterness of poverty. 'I am cold and hungry,' said the man still pleading, and taking encouragement from Laura's relenting eye. 'Hungry!' repeated Laura, 'then come with me, and I will give you bread;' and she returned to the house to bestow on the old man the humble fare which she had before destined to supply her own wants for the day, glad to purchase by a longer fast the right to feed the hungry.

'In what respect am I better than this poor creature,' said she to herself, as she returned with the beggar to the gate, 'that I should offer to him with ease, and even with pleasure, what I myself cannot ask without pain. Surely I do not rightly believe that we are of the same dust! The same frail, sinful, perishable, dust!'

But it was in vain that Laura continued to argue with herself. In this instance she could only do her duty; she could not love it. Her heart filled, and the tears rose to her eyes. She dashed them away – but they rose again.

When she found herself in Grosvenor Street, she paused for a moment. 'What if Lady Pelham should deny my request? dismiss me as a bold intruder? Why, then,' said Laura, raising her head, and again advancing with a firmer step, 'I shall owe no obligation to a stranger.'

She approached the house – she ascended the steps. Almost

breathless she laid her hand upon the knocker. At that moment she imagined her entrance through files of insolent domestics into a room filled with gay company. She anticipated the inquisitive glances – shrunk in fancy from the supercilious examination; and she again drew back her hand. 'I shall never have courage to face all this,' thought she. While we hesitate, a trifle turns the scale. Laura perceived that she had drawn the attention of a young man on the pavement, who stood gazing on her with familiar curiosity; and she knocked, almost before she was sensible that she intended it.

The time appeared immeasurable till the door was opened by a maid-servant. 'Is Lady Pelham at home?' inquired Laura, taking encouragement from the sight of one of her own sex. 'No, Ma'am,' answered the maid, 'my lady is gone to keep Christmas in – –shire, and will not return for a fortnight.' Laura drew a long breath, as if a weight had been lifted from her breast; and, suppressing an ejaculation of 'thank Heaven,' sprung in the lightness of her heart at one skip from the door to the pavement.

CHAPTER XVI

———————————●———————————

LAURA'S exultation was of short continuance. She had gone but a few steps ere she reflected that the wants which she had undertaken so painful a visit to supply were as clamant as ever, and now further than ever from a chance of relief. Mournfully she pursued her way towards the print-shop, hopelessly comparing her urgent and probably prolonged necessities with her confined resources.

The utmost price which she could hope to receive for the drawing she carried, would be far from sufficient to discharge her debt to the surgeon; and there seemed now no alternative but to confess her inability to pay, and to throw herself upon his mercy. To this measure, however, she was too averse to adopt it without reconsidering every other possible expedient. She thought of appealing to the friendship of Mrs Douglas, and of suffering Dr Flint to continue his visits till an answer from her friend should enable her to close the connection. But Mrs Douglas's scanty income was taxed to the uttermost by the maintenance and education of a numerous family, by the liberal charities of its owners, and by the hospitable spirit, which, banished by ostentation from more splendid abodes, still lingers by the fireside of a Scotch clergyman. Laura was sure that Mrs Douglas would supply her wants at whatever inconvenience to herself; and this very consideration withheld her from making application to her friend.

Laura had heard and read that ladies in distress had found subsistence by the sale of their ornaments. But by their example she could not profit; for her ornaments were few in number and of no value. She wore indeed a locket, which she had once received from her mother, with a strong injunction neither to lose nor give it away; but Laura, in her profound ignorance of the value of trinkets, attached no estimation to this one, except as the only unnecessary gift which she had ever received from her mother. 'It contains almost as much gold as a guinea,' said she, putting her hand to it, 'and a guinea will soon be a great treasure to me.' Still she determined that nothing short of extremity should induce her to part with it; but desirous to ascertain the extent of this last resort, she entered the shop of a jeweller, and presenting the locket, begged to know its value.

After examining it, the jeweller replied that he believed it might be worth about five guineas, 'for though,' said he, 'the setting is antiquated, these emeralds are worth something.'

At the mention of this sum, all Laura's difficulties seemed to vanish. Besides enabling her to pay the surgeon, it would make an addition to her little fund. With rigorous abstinence on her part, this little fund, together with the price of her incessant labour, would pay for her lodgings, and support her father in happy ignorance of his poverty, till he was able to remove to Glenalbert. Then, when he was quite well and quite able to bear it, she would tell him how she had toiled for him, and he would see that he had not lavished his fondness on a thankless child.

These thoughts occupied far less time than the recital; and yet, ere they were passed, Laura had untied the locket from her neck, and put it into the hands of the jeweller. It was not till she saw it in the hands of another, that she felt all the pain of parting with it. She asked to see it once more; as she gazed on it for the last time, tears trickled from her eyes; but speedily wiping them away, and averting her head, she restored the locket to its new owner, and taking up the money, departed.

She soon arrived at the print-shop, and finding Wilkins disengaged, produced her drawing, and asked him to purchase it. Wilkins looked at it, and inquired what price she had put upon it. 'I am quite unacquainted with its real value,' answered she, 'but the rapid sale of my work is at present such an object to me, that I shall willingly make it as cheap as possible, or allow you to fix your own price.' 'Have you any more to dispose of, Ma'am?' asked Wilkins. 'I have none finished, but I could promise you six more in a week if you are inclined to take them.' 'I think,' said Wilkins, 'after some consideration, I might venture to take them if you could afford them for half a guinea each.' 'You shall have them,' said Laura, with a sigh; 'but I think half-a-guinea rather a low – a high, I believe, I mean. – '

Laura did not at this moment exactly know what she meant; for her eyes had just rested on a gentleman, who, with his back towards her, was busied in examining a book of caricatures. She thought she could not be mistaken in the person. Only one form upon earth was endowed with such symmetry and grace; and that form was Hargrave's. He slightly turned his head, and Laura was certain.

Though Laura neither screamed nor fainted, this recognition was not made without extreme emotion. She trembled violently, and a mist spread before her eyes; but she remembered the apparently wilful desertion of her lover; and, determined neither to claim his compassion nor gratify his vanity by any of the airs of a forsaken damsel, she quietly turned away from him, and leant against the counter to recover strength and composure.

She was resolved to quit the shop the instant that she was able; and yet, perhaps she would have become sooner sensible of her recovered powers of motion, had it not been for a latent hope that the caricatures would not long continue so very interesting. No one however, accosted her; and next came the idea that Hargrave had already observed her, without wishing to claim her acquaintance. Before the mortifying thought could take a distinct form, Laura was already on her way towards the door.

'You have left your half-guinea, Ma'am,' said Wilkins, calling after her; and Laura, half angry at being detained, turned back to fetch it. At this moment Hargrave's eye fell upon her half averted face. Surprise and joy illuminating his fine countenance, 'Laura!' he exclaimed, 'is it possible! have I at last found you?' and springing forward, he clasped her to his breast, regardless of the inquisitive looks and significant smiles of the spectators of his transports. But to the scrutiny of strangers, to the caresses of Hargrave, even to the indecorum of her situation, poor Laura was insensible. Weakened by the fatigue and emotion of the two preceding days, overcome by the sudden conviction that she had not been wilfully neglected, her head sunk upon the shoulder of Hargrave, and she lost all consciousness.

When Laura recovered, she found herself in a little parlour adjoining to the shop, with no attendant but Hargrave, who still supported her in his arms. Her first thought was vexation at her own ill-timed sensibility; her next, a resolution to make no further forfeiture of her respectability, but rather, by the most stoical composure, to regain what she had lost. For this purpose, she soon disengaged herself from her perilous support, and unwilling to speak till secure of maintaining her firmness, she averted her head, and returned all Hargrave's raptures of love and joy with provoking silence.

As soon as she had completely recovered her self-possession, she rose, and apologizing for the trouble she had occasioned him, said she would return home. Hargrave eagerly begged permission to accompany her, saying that his carriage was in waiting, and would convey them. Laura, with cold politeness, declined his offer. Though a little piqued by her manner, Hargrave triumphed in the idea that he retained all his former influence. 'My bewitching Laura,' said he, taking her hand, 'I beseech you to lay aside this ill-timed coquetry. After so sweet, so interesting a proof, that you still allow me some power over your feelings, must I accuse you of an affectation of coldness?' 'No, sir,' said Laura indignantly, 'rather of a momentary weakness, for which I despise myself.'

The lover could not indeed have chosen a more unfavourable moment to express his exultation; for Laura's feelings of humiliation and self-reproach were just then raised to their height, by her perceiving the faces of two of the shop-boys peeping through the glass door with an aspect of roguish curiosity. Conscious of her inability to walk home, and feeling her situation quite intolerable, she called to one of the little spies, and begged that he would instantly procure her a hackney coach.

Hargrave vehemently remonstrated against this disorder. 'Why this unkind haste?' said he. 'Surely after so tedious, so tormenting an absence, you need not grudge me a few short moments.' Laura thought he was probably himself to blame for the absence of which he complained, and coldly answering, 'I have already been detained too long,' was about to quit the room, when Hargrave, impatiently seizing her hand, exclaimed, 'Unfeeling Laura! does that relentless pride never slumber? Have I followed you from Scotland, and sought you for three anxious months, to be met without one kind word, one pitying look!'

'Followed me!' repeated Laura with surprise.

'Yes, upon my life, my journey hither had no other object. After you so cruelly left me, without warning or farewell, how could I endure to exist in the place which you once made delightful to me. Indeed I could not bear it. I resolved to pursue you wherever you went, to breathe at least the same air with you, sometimes to feast my fond eyes with that form, beyond imagination lovely – perhaps to win that beguiling smile which no heart can withstand. The barbarous caution of Mrs Douglas in refusing me your address, has caused the disappointment of all my hopes.'

Hargrave had egregiously mistaken the road to Laura's favour when he threw a reflection upon her friend. 'Mrs Douglas certainly acted right,' said she. 'I have equal confidence in her prudence and in her friendship.' 'Probably then,' said Hargrave, reddening with vexation, 'this system of torture originated with you. It was at your desire that your friend withstood all my entreaties.' 'No,' answered Laura, 'I cannot claim the merit of so much forethought. I certainly did not expect the honour that you are pleased to say you have done me, especially when you were doubtful both of my abode and of your own reception.'

'Insulting girl,' cried Hargrave, 'you know too well, that, however received, still I must follow you. And, but for a series of the most tormenting accidents, I should have defeated the caution of your cold-hearted favourite. At the Perth post-office I discovered that your letters were addressed to the care of Mr Baynard; and the very hour that I reached London, I flew to make inquiries after you. I found that Mr Baynard's house was shut up, and that he was gone in bad health to Richmond. I followed him, and was told that he was too ill to be spoken with, that none of the servants knew your abode, as the footman who used to carry messages to you had been dismissed, and that your letters were now left at Mr Baynard's chambers in town. Thither I went, and learnt that, ever since your removal to Richmond, you had yourself sent for your letters, and that, of course, the clerks were entirely ignorant of your residence. Imagine my disappointment. The people, however, promised to make inquiries of your messenger, and to let me know where you might be found; and day after day did I haunt them, the sport of vain hope and bitter disappointment. No other letter ever came for you, nor did you ever inquire for any.'

'After Mr Baynard's removal to Richmond,' said Laura, 'I directed Mrs Douglas to address her letters to our lodgings.'

'Ah Laura, think what anxieties, what wretchedness I have suffered in my fruitless search! Yet you meet me only to drive me coldly from your presence. Once you said that you pardoned the folly – the madness that offended you; but too well I see that you deceived yourself or me – that no attachment, no devotion can purchase your forgiveness.' 'Indeed,' said Laura, melted by the proof which she had received of her lover's affection, yet fearful of forfeiting her caution,

'I am incapable of harbouring enmity against the worst of human beings, and – '

'Enmity!' interrupted Hargrave, 'Heavens, what a word!' 'I mean,' said Laura, faltering, 'that I am not insensible to the regard – '

'Madam, the coach is at the door,' said the shop-boy, again peeping slily into the room; and Laura, hastily bidding Hargrave good morning, walked towards the carriage. Having herself given the coachman his directions, she suffered Hargrave to hand her in, giving him a slight bow in token of dismissal. He continued, however, to stand for some moments with his foot upon the step, waiting for a look of permission to accompany her; but, receiving none, he sprung into the seat by her side, and called to the man to drive on. Laura offended at his boldness, gave him a very ungracious look, and drew back in silence. 'I see you think me presumptuous,' said he, 'but, just found, how can I consent to leave you? Oh Laura, if you knew what I have suffered from an absence that seemed endless! Not for worlds would I endure such another.'

'The stipulated two years are still far from a close,' said Laura coldly; 'and, till they are ended, our intercourse cannot be too slight.'

'Surely,' cried Hargrave, 'when you fixed this lingering probation, you did not mean to banish me from your presence for two years!' Laura could not with truth aver that such a banishment had been her intention. 'I believe,' said she, suppressing a sigh, 'that would have been my wisest meaning.' 'I would sooner die,' cried Hargrave, vehemently. 'Oh, had I sooner found you,' added he, a dark expression which Laura could not define clouding his countenance, 'what wretchedness would have been spared! But now that we have at last met,' continued he, his eyes again sparkling with love and hope, 'I will haunt you, cling to you, supplicate you, till I melt you to a passion as fervent as my own.' While he spoke he dropped upon his knee by her side, and drew his arm passionately round her. Time had been, that Laura, trembling with irrepressible emotion, would have withdrawn from the embrace, reproaching herself for sensations from which she imagined that the more spotless heart of her lover was free, and hating herself for being unable to receive as a sister, the caresses of a fondness pure as a brother's love. But Hargrave had himself torn the veil from her eyes; and shrinking from him as if a serpent had crossed her path, she cast on him a look that struck like an ice-bolt on the glowing heart of Hargrave. 'Just Heaven!' he cried, starting up with a convulsive shudder, 'this is abhorrence! Why, why have you deceived me with a false show of sensibility? Speak it at once,' said he, wildly grasping her arm; 'say that you detest me, and tell me too who has dared to supplant me in a heart once wholly mine.'

'Be calm, I implore you,' said Laura, terrified at his violence, 'no one has supplanted you. I am, I ever shall be, whatever you deserve to find me.'

Laura's soothing voice, her insinuating look, retained all their wonted power to calm the fierce passions of her lover. 'Oh I shall never deserve you,' said he in a tone of wretchedness, while his face was again crossed by an expression of anguish, which the unsuspecting Laura attributed to remorse for his former treatment of herself.

The carriage at this moment stopped, and anxious to calm his spirits at parting, Laura smiled kindly upon him, and said, 'Be ever thus humble in your opinion of your own merits, ever thus partial in your estimate of mine, and then,' added she, the tears trembling in her lovely eyes, 'we shall meet again in happier circumstances.' 'You must not, shall not leave me thus,' cried Hargrave impatiently, 'I will not quit this spot, till you have consented to see me again.' 'Do not ask it,' replied Laura. 'A long, long time must elapse, much virtuous exertion must be undergone, ere I dare receive you with other than this coldness, which appears to be so painful to you. Why then sport with your own feelings and with mine?' 'Ah Laura,' said Hargrave in a voice of supplication, 'use me as you will, only suffer me to see you.' Moved with the imploring tone of her lover, Laura turned towards him that she might soften by her manner the meditated refusal; but, in an evil hour for her resolution, she met the fine eyes of Hargrave suffused with tears, and, wholly unable to utter what she intended, she remained silent. Hargrave was instantly sensible of his advantage, and willing to assist her acquiescence by putting his request into a less exceptionable form, he said, 'I ask not even for your notice, suffer me but to visit your father.' 'My father has been very ill,' returned Laura, who, unknown to herself, rejoiced to find an excuse for her concession, 'and it may give *him* pleasure to see you; but *I* can claim no share in the honour of your visits.' Hargrave, delighted with his success, rapturously thanked her for her condescension; and springing from the carriage, led her, but half satisfied with her own conduct, into the house.

She ushered him into the parlour, and before he had time to detain her, glided away to acquaint her father with his visit. She found the Captain wrapt in the same listless melancholy in which she had left him; the book which she had meant to entertain him, used only as a rest for his arm. Laura was now beset with her old difficulty. She had not yet learnt to speak of Hargrave without sensible confusion; and to utter his name while any eye was fixed upon her face, required an effort which no common circumstances could have tempted her to make. She therefore took refuge behind her father's chair, before she began her partial relation of her morning's adventure.

'And is he now in the house,' cried Montreville, with an animation which he had long laid aside. 'I rejoice to hear it. Return to him immediately, my love. I will see him in a few minutes.' 'As soon as you choose to receive him,' said Laura; 'I shall carry your commands. I shall remain in the dressing-room.' 'For shame, Laura!' returned Montreville. 'I thought you had been above these silly airs of conquest. Colonel Hargrave's rejected passion gives you no right to refuse him the politeness due to all your father's guests.' 'Certainly not, Sir, but' – she stopped, hesitating – 'however,' added she, 'since *you* wish it, I will go.'

It was not without embarrassment that Laura returned to her lover; to offer him another tête à tête seemed so like soliciting a renewal of his ardours. In this idea she was stopping at the parlour door, collecting her courage, and meditating a speech decorously repulsive, when Hargrave, who had been listening for her approach, impatiently stepped out to look for her, and in a moment spoiled all her concerted oratory, by taking her hand and leading her into the room.

Though Hargrave could at any time take Laura's feelings by surprise, an instant was sufficient to restore her self-possession; and withdrawing her hand, she said, 'In a few minutes, Sir, my father will be glad to see you, and at his desire I attend you till he can have that honour.' 'Bless him for the delay!' cried Hargrave, 'I have a thousand things to say to you.' 'And I, Sir,' said Laura, solemnly, 'have one thing to say to you, of more importance to me, probably, than all the thousand.'

Hargrave bit his lip; and Laura proceeded, her colour, as painful recollection rose, fading from the crimson that had newly flushed it, to the paleness of anguish. 'Six months ago,' said she, speaking with an effort that rendered her words scarcely articulate – 'Six months ago you made me a promise. Judge of my anxiety that you should keep it, when to secure its fulfilment I can call up a subject so revolting – so dreadful.' She paused – a cold shudder running through her limbs: but Hargrave, abashed and disconcerted, gave her no interruption, and ventured not even to raise his eyes from the ground. 'My father,' she continued, 'is no longer able to avenge his child; – the bare mention of her wrongs would destroy him. If then you value my peace – if you dread my detestation – let no circumstance seduce, no accident surprise from you this hateful secret.'

While she spoke, the blushes which had deserted her cheek were transferred to that of Hargrave; for though, to his own conscience, he had palliated his former outrage till it appeared a very venial trespass, he was not proof against the unaffected horror with which it had inspired the virtuous Laura. Throwing himself at her feet, and hiding his face in her gown, he bitterly, and for the moment sincerely, bewailed his offence, and vowed to devote his life to its expiation. Then, starting up, he struck his hand wildly upon his forehead, and exclaimed, 'Madman that I have been! Oh, Laura, thy heavenly purity makes me the veriest wretch. No – thou canst never pardon me!'

The innocent Laura, who little suspected all his causes of self-reproach, wept tears of joy over his repentance, and, in a voice full of tenderness, said, 'Indeed I have myself too many faults to be unrelenting. Contrition and amendment are all that Heaven requires – why should I ask more?' Hargrave saw that she attributed all his agitation to remorse for his conduct towards herself; but the effects of her mistake were too delightful to suffer him to undeceive her; and perceiving at once that he had found the master-spring of all her tenderness, he overpowered her with such vows, protestations, and entreaties, that, before their conference was interrupted, he had, amidst tremors, blushes, and hesitation, which spoke a thousand times more than her words, wrung from her a confession that she felt a more than friendly interest in the issue of his probation.

Indeed Montreville was in no haste to break in upon their dialogue. That any woman should have refused the hand of the handsome – the insinuating – the gallant Colonel Hargrave, had always appeared to him little less than miraculous. He had been told, that ladies sometimes rejected what they did not mean to relinquish; and though he could scarcely believe his daughter capable of such childish coquetry, he was not without faith in a maxim, which, it must be confessed, receives sanction from experience, namely, that in all cases of feminine obduracy, perseverance is an infallible recipé. This recipé, he had no doubt, was now to be tried upon Laura; and he fervently wished that it might be with success. Though he was too affectionate a father to form on this subject a wish at variance with his daughter's happiness, he had never been insensible to the desire of seeing her brow graced by a coronet. But now more important considerations made him truly anxious to consign her to the guardianship of a man of honour.

The unfortunate transaction of the annuity would, in the event of his death, leave her utterly destitute. That event, he imagined, was fast approaching; and with many a bitter pang he remembered that he had neither friend nor relative with whom he could entrust his orphan child. His parents had long been dead; his only surviving brother, a fox-hunting squire of small fortune, shared his table and bed with a person who had stooped to these degrading honours from the more reputable situation of an innocent dairy-maid. With Lady Harriet's relations (for friends she had none), Montreville had never maintained any intercourse. They had affected to resent his intrusion into the family, and he had not been industrious to conciliate their favour. Except himself, therefore, Laura had no natural protector; and this circumstance made him tenfold more anxious that she should recal her decision in regard to Hargrave.

He had no doubt that the present visit was intended for Laura; and he suffered as long a time to elapse before he claimed any share in it, as common politeness would allow. He had meant to receive the Colonel in his own apartment, but an inclination to observe the conduct of the lovers, induced him to make an effort to join them in the parlour, where he with pleasure discovered by the countenances of both, that their conversation had been mutually interesting. Hargrave instantly recovered himself, and paid his compliments with his accustomed grace; but Laura, by no means prepared to stand inspection, disappeared the moment her father entered the room.

This was the first time that the gentlemen had met, since the day when Montreville had granted his fruitless sanction to the Colonel's suit. Delicacy prevented the father from touching upon the subject, and it was equally avoided by Hargrave, who had not yet determined in what light to represent his repulse. However, as it completely occupied the minds of both, the conversation, which turned on topics merely indifferent, was carried on with little spirit on either side, and was soon closed by Hargrave's taking leave, after begging permission to repeat his visit.

Colonel Hargrave had promised to spend that evening with the most beautiful woman in London; but the unexpected rencounter of the morning, left him in no humour to fulfil his engagement. He had found his Laura, – his lovely, his innocent Laura, – the object of his only serious passion, – the only woman whose empire reached beyond his senses. He had found her cautious, reserved, severe; yet feeling, constant, and tender. He remembered the overwhelming joy which made her sink fainting on his bosom; called to mind her ill-suppressed tears – her smothered sighs – her unbidden blushes; and a thousand times assured himself that he was passionately beloved. He triumphed the more in the proofs of her affection, because they were not only involuntary but reluctant; and, seen through the flattering medium of gratified pride, her charms appeared more than ever enchanting. On these charms he had formerly suffered his imagination to dwell, till to appropriate them seemed to him almost the chief end of existence; and, though in absence his frenzy had a little intermitted, his interview with Laura roused it again to double violence.

No passion of Hargrave's soul (and all his passions were of intense force), had ever known restraint, or control, or even delay of gratification, excepting only this, the strongest that had ever governed him. And must he now pine for eighteen lingering months, ere he attained the object of such ardent wishes? Must he submit, for a time that seemed endless, to the tyranny of this intolerable passion, – see the woman on whom he doated receive his protestations with distrust, and spite of her affection, shrink from his caresses with horror? No! – he vowed that if there were persuasion in man, or frailty in woman, he would shorten the period of his trial, – that he would employ for this purpose all the power which he possessed over Laura's heart, and, if that failed, that he would even have recourse to the authority of the father.

But he had yet a stronger motive than the impetuosity of his passions for striving to obtain immediate possession of his treasure. He was conscious that there was a tale to tell, which, once known, (and it could not long be concealed), would shake his hopes to the foundation. But on this subject he could not now dwell without disgust, and he turned from it to the more inviting contemplation of Laura's beauty and Laura's love; and with his head and his heart, every nerve, every pulse full of Laura, he retired to pursue in his dreams, the fair visions that had occupied his waking thoughts.

While he was thus wilfully surrendering himself to the dominion of his frenzy, Laura, the self-denied Laura, was endeavouring, though it must be owned without distinguished success, to silence the pleadings of a heart as warm, though better regulated, by attending to the humble duties of the hour.

When she quitted Hargrave, she had retired to offer up her fervent thanks to Heaven, that he was become sensible of the enormity of his former conduct. Earnestly did she pray, that, though earth should never witness their union, they might be permitted together to join a nobler society – animated by yet purer love – bound by yet holier ties. She next reconsidered her own behaviour towards Hargrave; and, though vexed at the momentary desertion of her self-command, saw, upon the whole, little cause to reproach herself, since her weakness had been merely that of body, to which the will gave no consent. She resolved to be guardedly cautious in her future demeanour towards him; and since the issue of his probation was doubtful, since its close was at all events distant, to forfeit the enjoyment of her lover's company, rather than, by remaining in the room during his visits, appear to consider them as meant for herself.

As soon as Hargrave was gone, Montreville returned to his chamber; and there Laura ordered his small but delicate repast to be served, excusing herself from partaking of it, by saying that she could dine more conveniently in the parlour. Having in the morning bestowed on the beggar the meagre fare that should have supplied her own wants, she employed the time of her father's meal, in the labour which was to purchase him another; pondering meanwhile on the probability that he would again enter on the discussion of Hargrave's pretensions. To this subject she felt unconquerable repugnance; and though she knew that it must at last be canvassed, and that she must at last assign a reason for her conduct, she would fain have put off the evil hour.

She delayed her evening visit to her father, till he grew impatient for it, and sent for her to his apartment. The moment she entered the room, he began, as she had anticipated, to inquire into the particulars of her interview with Hargrave. The language of Laura's reply was not very perspicuous; the manner of it was more intelligible: and Montreville instantly comprehended the nature of her conference with the Colonel. 'He has then given you an opportunity of repairing your former rashness,' said Montreville, with eagerness, – 'and your answer?' 'Colonel Hargrave had his answer long ago, Sir', replied Laura, trembling at this exordium. Montreville sighed heavily, and, fixing his eyes mournfully upon her, remained silent. At last, affectionately taking her hand, he said, 'My dear child, the time has been, when even your caprices on this subject were sacred with your father. While I had a shelter, however humble – an independence, however small, to offer you, your bare inclination determined mine. But now your situation is changed – fatally changed; and no trivial reasons would excuse me for permitting your rejection of an alliance so unexceptionable, so splendid. Tell me, then, explicitly, what are your objections to Colonel Hargrave?'

Laura remained silent, for she knew not how to frame her reply. 'Is it possible that he can be personally disagreeable to you?' continued Montreville. 'Disagreeable!' exclaimed Laura, thrown off her guard by astonishment. 'Colonel Hargrave is one whom any woman might – whom no woman could know without – ' 'Without what?' said Montreville, with a delighted smile. But Laura, shocked at the extent of her own admission, covered her face with her hands, and almost in tears, made no reply.

'Well, my love,' said Montreville, more cheerfully than he had spoken for many a day. 'I can interpret all this, and will not persecute you. But you must still suffer me to ask what strange reasons could induce you to reject wealth and title, offered by a man not absolutely *disagreeable*?' Laura strove to recollect herself, and deep crimson dying her beautiful face and neck, she said without venturing to lift her eyes, 'You yourself have told me, Sir, that Colonel Hargrave is a man of gallantry, and, believe me, with such a man I should be most miserable.'

'Come, come, Laura,' said Montreville, putting his arm around her, 'confess, that some little fit of jealousy made you answer Hargrave unkindly at first, and that now a little female pride, or the obstinacy of which we used to accuse you fifteen years ago, makes you unwilling to retract.'

'No, indeed,' returned Laura, with emotion, 'Colonel Hargrave has never given me cause to be jealous of his affection. But jealousy would feebly express the anguish with which his wife would behold his vices, degrading him in the eyes of men, and making him vile in the sight of Heaven.'

'My love,' said Montreville, 'your simplicity and ignorance of the world make you attach far too great importance to Hargrave's little irregularities. I am persuaded that a wife whom he loved would have no cause to complain of them.'

'She would at least have no *right* to complain,' returned Laura, 'if, knowing them, she chose to make the hazardous experiment.'

'But I am certain,' said Montreville, 'that a passion such as he evidently feels for you, would ensure his perfect reformation; and that a heart so warm as Hargrave's, would readily acknowledge all the claims upon a husband's and a father's love.'

Laura held down her head, and, for a moment, surrendered her fancy to prospects, rainbow-like, bright but unreal. Spite of the dictates of sober sense, the vision was cheering; and a smile dimpled her cheek while she said, 'But since this reformation is so easy and so certain, would it be a grievous delay to wait for its appearance.'

'Ah Laura!' Montreville began, 'this is no time for – ' 'Nay, now,' interrupted Laura, sportively laying her hand upon his mouth, 'positively I will be no more lectured tonight. Besides I have got a new book for you from the library, and the people insisted upon having it returned to-morrow.' 'You are a spoiled girl,' said Montreville, fondly caressing her, and he dropped the subject with the less reluctance, because he believed that his wishes, aided as he perceived they were, by an advocate in Laura's own breast, were in a fair train for accomplishment. He little knew how feeble was the influence of inclination over the decisions of her self-controlling spirit.

To prevent him from returning to the topic he had quitted, she read aloud to him till his hour of rest; and then retired to her chamber to labour as formerly, till the morning was far advanced.

CHAPTER XVII

———————●———————

LAURA had it now in her power to discharge her debt to the surgeon, and she was resolved that it should immediately be paid. When, therefore, he called in the morning to make his daily visit, she met him before he entered Montreville's chamber, and requested to speak with him in the parlour.

She began by saying, she feared that medicine could be of little use to her father, to which Dr Flint readily assented, declaring, in his dry way, that generous food and open air would benefit him more than all the drugs in London. Laura begged him to say explicitly so to the Captain, and to give that as a reason for declining to make him any more professional visits. She then presented him a paper containing four guineas, which she thought might be the amount of his claim. He took the paper, and deliberately unfolding it, returned one-half of its contents; saying, that his account had been settled so lately, that the new one could not amount to more than the sum he retained. Laura, who having now no favour to beg, no debt that she was unable to pay, was no longer ashamed of her poverty, easily opened to Dr Flint so much of her situation as was necessary to instruct him in the part he had to act with Montreville. He made no offer to continue his visits, even as an acquaintance, but readily undertook all that Laura required of him, adding, 'Indeed, Miss Montreville, I should have told your father long ago that physic was useless to him, but whimsical people must have something to amuse them, and if he had not paid for my pills, he would for some other man's.' He then went to Montreville, and finding him in better spirits than he had lately enjoyed, actually succeeded in persuading him, for that day at least, that no new prescription was necessary, and that he could continue to use the old without the inspection of a surgeon.

Laura's mind was much relieved by her having settled this affair to her wish; and when the Doctor was gone, she sat down cheerfully to her drawing. Her meeting with Hargrave had lightened her heart of a load which had long weighed upon it more heavily than she was willing to allow; and, spite of poverty, she was cheerful. 'I have now only hunger and toil to endure,' thought she, smiling as gaily as if hunger and toil had been trifles; 'but light will be my labours, for by them I can in part pay back my debt of life to my dear kind father. I am no more forlorn and deserted, for he is come who is sunshine to Laura's soul. The cloud that darkened him has passed away, and he will brighten all my after life. Oh fondly beloved! with thee I would have been content to tread the humblest path; but, if we must climb the steeps, together we will court the breeze, together meet the storm. No time shall change the love I bear thee. Thy step, when feeble with age, shall still be music to Laura's ear. When the lustre of the melting eyes is quenched, when the auburn ringlet fades to silver, dearer shalt thou be to me than in all the pride of manly beauty. And when at last the dust shall cover us, one tree shall shelter our narrow beds, and the wind that fans the flowers upon thy grave, shall scatter their fallen leaves upon mine.'

Casting these thoughts into the wild extempore measures which are familiar to the labourers of her native mountains,* Laura was singing them to one of the affecting melodies of her country, her sweet voice made more sweet by the magic of real tenderness, when the door opened, and Hargrave himself entered.

He came, resolved to exert all his influence, to urge every plea which the affection of Laura would allow him, in order to extort her consent to their immediate union; and he was too well convinced of his power to be very diffident of success. Laura ceased her song in as much confusion as if her visitor had understood the language in which it was composed, or could have known himself to be the subject of it. He had been listening to its close, and now urged her to continue it, but was unable to prevail. He knew that she was particularly sensible to the charms of music. He had often witnessed the effect of her own pathetic voice upon her feelings; and he judged that no introduction could be more proper to a conference in which he intended to work on her sensibility. He therefore begged her to sing a little plaintive air with which she had often drawn tears from

---

* See Jamieson's Popular Ballads, Vol. ii, p. 558.

his eyes. But Laura knew that, as her father was still in bed, she could not without rudeness avoid a long tête à tête with Hargrave, and therefore she did not choose to put her composure to any unnecessary test. She excused herself from complying with his request, but glad to find any indifferent way to pass the time, she offered to sing, if he would allow her to choose her own song, and then began a lively air, which she executed with all the vivacity that she could command. The style of it was quite at variance with Hargrave's present humour and design. He heard it with impatience; and scarcely thanking her said, 'Your spirits are high this morning, Miss Montreville.'

'They are indeed,' replied Laura, gaily, 'I hope you have no intention to make them otherwise.'

'Certainly not; though they are little in unison with my own. The meditations of a restless, miserable night, have brought me to you.'

'Is it the usual effect of a restless night to bring you abroad so early the next morning?' said Laura, anxious to avoid a trial of strength in a sentimental conference.

'I will be heard seriously,' said Hargrave, colouring with anger, 'and seriously too I must be answered.'

'Nay,' said Laura, 'if you look so tremendous I shall retreat without hearing you at all.'

Hargrave, who instantly saw that he had not chosen the right road to victory, checked his rising choler – 'Laura,' said he, 'you have yourself made me the victim of a passion ungovernable – irresistible; and it is cruel – it is ungenerous in you to sport with my uneasiness.'

'Do not give the poor passion such hard names,' said Laura, smiling. 'Perhaps you have never tried to resist or govern it.'

'As soon might I govern the wind,' cried Hargrave, vehemently, – 'as soon resist the fires of Heaven. And why attempt to govern it?'

'Because,' answered Laura, 'it is weak, it is sinful, to submit unresisting to the bondage of an imperious passion.'

'Would that you too would submit unresisting to its bondage!' said Hargrave, delighted to have made her once more serious. 'But if this passion is sinful,' continued he, 'my reformation rests with you alone. Put a period to my lingering trial. Consent to be mine, and hush all these tumults to rest.'

'Take care how you furnish me with arguments against yourself,' returned Laura, laughing. 'Would it be my interest, think you, to lull all these transports to such profound repose?'

'Be serious Laura, I implore you. Well do you know that my love can end only with my existence, but I should no longer be distracted with these tumultuous hopes and fears if – ' 'Oh,' cried Laura, interrupting him, 'hope is too pleasing a companion for you to wish to part with that; and,' added she, a smile and a blush contending upon her cheek, 'I begin to believe that your fears are not very troublesome.' 'Ah Laura,' said Hargrave sorrowfully, 'you know not what you say. There are moments when I feel as if you were already lost to me – and the bare thought is distraction. Oh if you have pity for real suffering,' continued he, dropping on his knees, 'save me from the dread of losing you; forget the hour of madness in which I offended you. Restore to me the time when you owned that I was dear to you. Be yet more generous, and give me immediate, unalienable right to your love.'

'You forget, Colonel Hargrave,' said Laura, again taking sanctuary in an appearance of coldness; 'you forget that six months ago I fixed two years of rectitude as the test of your repentance, and that you were then satisfied with my decision.'

'I would then have blessed you for any sentence that left me a hope, however distant; but now the time when I may claim your promise seems at such a hopeless distance – Oh Laura, let me but prevail with you; and I will bind myself by the most solemn oaths to a life of unsullied purity.'

'No oaths,' replied Laura with solemnity, 'can strengthen the ties that already bind you to a life of purity. That you are of noble rank, calls you to be an example to others; and the yet higher distinction of an immortal spirit bids you strive after virtues that may never meet the eye of man. Only convince me that such are the objects of your ambition, and I shall no longer fear to trust with you my improvement and my happiness.'

As she spoke unusual animation sparkled in her eyes, and tinged her delicate cheek with brighter colouring. 'Lovely, lovely creature!' cried Hargrave, in transport, 'give but thyself to these fond arms, and may Heaven forsake me if I strive not to make thee blest beyond the sweetest dreams of youthful fancy.'

'Alas!' said Laura, 'even your affection would fail to bless a heart conscious of acting wrong.'

'Where is the wrong,' said Hargrave, gathering hope from the relenting tenderness of her voice, 'Where is the wrong of yielding to the strongest impulse of nature – or, to speak in language more like your own, where is the guilt of submitting to an ordinance of Heaven's own appointment?'

'Why,' replied Laura, 'will you force me to say what seems unkind? Why compel me to remind you that marriage was never meant to sanction the unholy connection of those whose principles are discordant?'

'Beloved of my heart,' said Hargrave, passionately kissing her hand, 'take me to thyself, and mould me as thou wilt. I swear to thee that not even thine own life shall be more pure, more innocent than mine. Blest in thy love, what meaner pleasure could allure me. Oh yield then, and bind me for ever to virtue and to thee.'

Laura shook her head. 'Ah Hargrave,' said she, with a heavy sigh, 'before you can love and practice the purity which reaches the heart, far other loves must warm, far other motives inspire you.'

'No other love can ever have such power over me,' said Hargrave with energy. 'Be but thou and thy matchless beauty the prize, and every difficulty is light, every sacrifice trivial.'

'In little more than a year,' said Laura, 'I shall perhaps ask some proofs of the influence you ascribe to me; but till then' –

'Long, long before that time,' cried Hargrave, striking his forehead in agony, 'you will be lost to me for ever,' and he paced the room in seeming despair. Laura looked at him with a pity not unmixed with surprise. 'Hear me for a moment,' said she, with the soothing voice and gentle aspect, which had always the mastery of Hargrave's feelings, and he was instantly at her side, listening with eagerness to every tone that she uttered, intent on every variation of her countenance.

'There are circumstances,' she continued, her transparent cheek glowing with bright beauty, tears in her downcast eyes trembling through the silken lashes – 'There are circumstances that may change me, but time and absence are not of the number. Be but true to yourself, and you have nothing to fear. After this assurance, I trust it will give you little pain to hear that, till the stipulated two years are ended, if we are to meet, it must not be without witnesses.'

'Good Heavens! Laura, why this new, this intolerable restriction – What can induce you thus wilfully to torment me?'

'Because,' answered the blushing Laura, with all her natural simplicity, 'because I might not always be able to listen to reason and duty rather than to you.'

'Oh that I could fill thee with a love that should for ever silence the cold voice of reason!' cried Hargrave, transported by her confession; and, no longer master of himself, he would have clasped her in his arms. But Laura, to whose mind his caresses ever recalled a dark page in her story, recoiled as from pollution, the glow of ingenuous modesty giving place to the paleness of terror.

No words envenomed with the bitterest malice, could have stung Hargrave to such frenzy as the look and the shudder with which Laura drew back from his embrace. His eyes flashing fire, his pale lips quivering with passion, he reproached her with perfidy and deceit; accused her of veiling her real aversion under the mask of prudence and principle; and execrated his own folly in submitting so long to be the sport of a cold-hearted, tyrannical, obdurate woman. Laura stood for some minutes gazing on him with calm compassion. But displeased at his groundless accusations, she disdained to soothe his rage. At last, wearied of language which, for the present, expressed much more of hatred than of love, she quietly moved towards the door. 'I see you can be very calm, Madam,' said Hargrave, stopping her, 'and I can be as calm as yourself,' added he, with a smile like a moon-beam on a thunder cloud, making the gloom more fearful.

'I hope you soon will be so,' replied Laura coldly. 'I am so now,' said Hargrave, his voice half-choked with the effort to suppress his passion. 'I will but stay to take leave of your father, and then free you for ever from one so odious to you.'

'That must be as you please, Sir,' said Laura, with spirit; 'but, for the present, I must be excused from attending you.' She then retired to her own chamber, which immediately adjoined the painting-room; and with tears reflected on the faint prospects of happiness that remained for the wife of a man whose passions were so ungovernable. Even the ardour of his love, for which vanity would have found ready excuse in many a female breast, was to Laura subject of unfeigned regret, as excluding him from the dominion of better motives, and the pursuit of nobler ends.

Hargrave was no sooner left to himself than his fury began to evaporate. In a few minutes he was perfectly collected, and the first act of his returning reason was to upbraid him with his treatment of Laura. 'Is it to be wondered that she shrinks from me,' said he, the tears of self-reproach rising to his eyes, 'when I make her the sport of all my frantic passions? But she shall never again have cause to complain of me – let but her love this once excuse me, and henceforth I will treat her with gentleness like her own.'

There is no time in the life of a man so tedious, as that which passes between the resolution to repair a wrong, and the opportunity to make the reparation. Hargrave wondered whether Laura would return to conduct him to her father; feared that she would not – hoped that she would – thought he heard her footstep – listened – sighed – and tried to beguile the time by turning over her drawings.

Almost the first that met his eye, was a sketch of features well known to him. He started and turned pale. He sought for a name upon the reverse; there was none, and he again breathed more freely. 'This must be accident,' said he; 'De Courcy is far from London – yet it is very like;' and he longed more than ever for Laura's appearance. He sought refuge from his impatience in a book which lay upon the table. It was the Pleasures of Hope, and marked in many parts of the margins with a pencil. One of the passages so marked was that which begins,

> 'Thy pencil traces on the lover's thought
> 'Some cottage home, from towns and toil remote,
> 'Where love and lore may claim alternate hours,' &c.

And Hargrave surrendered himself to the pleasing dream that Laura had thought of him, while she approved the lines. 'Her name, written by her own snowy fingers, may be here,' said he, and he turned to the title-page, that he might press it, with a lover's folly, to his lips – The title-page was inscribed with the name of Montague De Courcy.

The glance of the basilisk was not more powerful. Motionless he gazed on the words, till all the fiends of jealousy taking possession of his soul, he furiously dashed the book upon the ground 'False, false siren,' he cried, 'is this the cause of all your coldness – your loathing?' And without any wish but to exclude her for ever from his sight, he rushed like a madman out of the house.

He darted forward, regardless of the snow that was falling on his uncovered head, till it suddenly occurred to him that he would not suffer her to triumph in the belief of having deceived him. 'No,' cried he, 'I will once more see that deceitful face; reproach her with her treachery; enjoy her confusion, and then spurn her from me for ever.'

He returned precipitately to the house; and, flying up stairs, saw Laura, the traces of melancholy reflection on her countenance, waiting for admission at her father's door. 'Madam', said he, in a

voice scarcely articulate, 'I must speak with you for a few minutes.'
'Not for a moment, Sir,' said Laura, laying her hand upon the lock.
'Yes, by Heaven, you shall hear me,' cried Hargrave; and rudely
seizing her, he forced her into the painting-room, and bolted the
door.

'Answer me,' said he fiercely, 'how came that book into your
possession?' pointing to it as it still lay upon the floor. 'When have
you this infernal likeness? Speak!'

Laura looked at the drawing, then at the book, and at once
understood the cause of her lover's frenzy. Sincere compassion filled
her heart; yet she felt how unjust was the treatment which she
received; and, with calm dignity, said, 'I will answer all your
questions, and then you will judge whether you have deserved that I
should do so.'

'Whom would not that face deceive?' said Hargrave, gnashing his
teeth in agony. 'Speak sorceress – tell me, if you dare, that this is not
the portrait of De Courcy – that he is not the lover for whom I am
loathed and spurned.'

'That *is* the portrait of De Courcy,' replied Laura, with the simple
majesty of truth. 'It is the sketch from which I finished a picture for
his sister. That book too is his,' and she stooped to lift it from the
ground. 'Touch not the vile thing,' cried Hargrave in a voice of
thunder. With quiet self-possession, Laura continued, 'Mr De
Courcy's father was, as you know, the friend of mine. Mr De Courcy
himself was, when an infant, known to my father; and they met,
providentially met, when we had great need of a considerate friend.
That friend Mr De Courcy was to us, and no selfish motive sullied
his benevolence; for he is not, nor ever was, nor, I trust, ever will be,
known to me as a lover!'

The voice of sober truth had its effect upon Hargrave, and he said,
more composedly, 'Will you then give me your word, that De Courcy
is not, nor ever will be, dear to you?'

'No!' answered Laura, 'I will not say so, for he must be loved
wherever his virtues are known; but I have no regard for him that
should disquiet you. It is not such,' continued she, struggling with the
rising tears – 'it is not such as would pardon outrage, and withstand
neglect, and humble itself before unjust aspersion.'

'Oh Laura,' said Hargrave, at once convinced and softened, 'I
must believe you, or my heart will burst.'

'I have a right to be believed,' returned Laura, endeavouring to rally her spirits. 'Now, then, release me, after convincing me that the passion of which you boast so much, is consistent with the most insolent disrespect, the most unfounded suspicion.' But Hargrave was again at her feet, exhausting every term of endearment, and breathing forth the most fervent petitions for forgiveness.

Tears, which she could no longer suppress, now streamed down Laura's cheeks, while she said, 'How could you suspect me of the baseness of pretending a regard which I did not feel, of confirming engagements from which my affections revolted!' Hargrave, half wild with the sight of her tears, bitterly reproached himself with his injustice; vowed that he believed her all perfection; that, with all a woman's tenderness, she possessed the truth and purity of angels, and that, could she this once pardon his extravagance, he would never more offend. But Laura, vexed and ashamed of her weakness, insisted on her release in a tone that would be obeyed, and Hargrave, too much humbled to be daring, unwillingly suffered her to retire.

In the faint hope of seeing her again, he waited till Montreville was ready to admit him; but Laura was not with her father, nor did she appear during the remainder of his visit. Desirous to know in what light she had represented their affair, in order that his statement might tally with hers, he again avoided the subject, resolving that next day he should be better prepared to enter upon it. With this view, he returned to Montreville's lodgings early in the next forenoon, hoping for an opportunity to consult with Laura before seeing her father. He was shewn into the parlour, which was vacant. He waited long, but Laura came not. He sent a message to beg that she would admit him, and was answered that she was sorry it was not in her power. He desired the messenger to say that his business was important, but was told that Miss Montreville was particularly engaged. However impatient, he was obliged to submit. He again saw Montreville without entering upon the subject so near his heart; and left the house without obtaining even a glimpse of Laura.

The following day he was equally unsuccessful. He indeed saw Laura; but it was only in the presence of her father, and she gave him no opportunity of addressing her particularly. Finding that she adhered to the resolution she had expressed, of seeing him no more without witnesses, he wrote to her, warmly remonstrating against the barbarity of her determination, and beseeching her to depart from it, if only in a single instance. The billet received no answer, and Laura continued to act as before.

Fretted almost to fever, Hargrave filled whole pages with the description of his uneasiness, and complaints of the cruelty which caused it. In conclusion, he assured Laura that he could no longer refrain from confiding his situation to her father; and entreated to see her, were it only to learn in what terms she would permit him to mention their engagement. This letter was rather more successful than the former; for, though Laura made no reply to the first part, she answered the close by a few cautious lines, leaving Hargrave, excepting in one point, at full liberty as to his communications with her father.

Thus authorized, he seized the first opportunity of conversing with Montreville. He informed him that he had reason to believe himself not indifferent to Laura; but that, some of his little irregularities coming to her knowledge, she had sentenced him to a probation which was yet to continue for above a year. Though Hargrave guarded his words so as to avoid direct falsehood, the conscious crimson rose to his face as he uttered this subterfuge. But he took instant refuge in the idea that he had no choice left; and that, if there was any blame, it in fact belonged to Laura, for forcing him to use concealment. He did yet more. He erected his head, and planted his foot more firmly, as he thought, that what he dared to do he dared to justify, were he not proud to yield to the commands of love, and humanely inclined to spare the feelings of a sick man. He proceeded to assure Montreville, that though he must plead guilty to a few youthful indiscretions, Laura might rely upon his constancy and fidelity. Finally, addressing himself to what he conceived to be the predominant failing of age, he offered to leave the grand affair of settlements to Montreville's own decision; demanding only in return, that the father would use his interest, or even his authority, if necessary, to obtain his daughter's consent to an immediate union.

Montreville answered, that he had long desisted from the use of authority with Laura, but that his influence was at the Colonel's service; and he added, with a smile, that he believed that neither would be very necessary.

In consequence of this promise, Montreville sought an opportunity of conversing on this subject with his daughter; but she shewed such extreme reluctance to enter upon it, and avoided it with such sedulous care, that he could not immediately execute his design. He observed, too, that she looked ill, that she was pale and languid. Though she would not confess any ailment, he could not help fearing that all was not right; and he waited the appearance of recovered strength, ere he should enter on a topic which was never heard by her without strong emotion. But Laura looked daily more wretched. Her complexion became wan, her eyes sunk, and her lips colourless.

Hargrave observed the change, and, half persuaded that it was the effect of his own capricious behaviour at their last interview, he became more anxious for a private conference, in which his tenderness might sooth her to forgetfulness of his errors. When she was quitting the room, he often followed her to the door, and entreated to be heard for a single moment. But the utmost he could obtain was a determined 'I cannot,' or a hasty 'I dare not,' and in an instant she had vanished.

Indeed watching and abstinence, though the chief, were not the only causes of Laura's sickly aspect. Hargrave's violence had furnished her with new and painful subjects of meditation. While yet she thought him all perfeciton, he had often confessed to her the warmth of his temper, with a candour which convinced her (anxious as she was to be so convinced) that he was conscious of his natural tendency, and vigilantly guarded it from excess; consequently, that to the energy of the passionate he united the justice of the cool. She had never witnessed any instance of his violence; for since their first acquaintance, she had herself, at least while she was present, been his only passion. All things unconnected with it were trivial in his estimation; and till the hour which had roused her caution, she had unconsciously soothed this tyrant of his soul with perpetual incense, by proofs of her tenderness, which, though unobserved by others, were not lost upon the vanity of Hargrave. Successful love shedding a placid gentleness upon his really polished manners, he had, without intention to deceive, completely misled Laura's judgment of his character. Now he had turned her eyes from the vision, and compelled her to look upon the reality; and with many a bitter tear she lamented that ever she suffered her peace to depend upon an union which, even if accomplished, promised to compensate transient rapture with abiding disquiet.

But still fondly attached, Laura took pleasure in persuading herself that a mere defect of temper was not such a fault as entitled her to withdraw her promise; and having made this concession, she soon proceeded to convince herself, that Hargrave's love would make ample amends for occasional suffering, however severe. Still she assured herself that if, at the stipulated time, he produced not proofs of real improvement, much more if that period were stained with actual vice, she would, whatever it might cost her, see him no more. She determined to let nothing move her to shorten his probation, nor to be satisfied without the strictest scrutiny into the manner in which it had been spent.

Aware of the difficulty of withstanding the imploring voice, the pleading eyes of Hargrave, she would not venture into temptation for the mere chance of escape; and adhered to her resolution of affording him no opportunity to practise on her sensibility. Nor was this a slight exercise of self-denial, for no earthly pleasure could bring such joy to Laura's heart, as the assurance, however oft repeated, that she was beloved. Yet, day after day, she withstood his wishes, and her own; and generally spent the time of his visits in drawing.

Meanwhile, her delicate face and slender form gave daily greater indications of malady. Montreville, utterly alarmed, insisted upon sending for medical advice; but Laura, with a vehemence most unusual to her, opposed this design, telling him, that if he persisted in it, vexation would cause the reality of the illness which at present was merely imaginary.

The Captain was however the only member of the family who did not conjecture the true cause of Laura's decay. The servant who attended her, reported to her mistress, that the slender repast was always presented, untouched by Laura, to her father; that her drink was only water, her fare coarse and scanty; and that often, a few morsels of dry bread were the only sustenance of the day. Mrs Stubbs, who entertained a suitable contempt for poverty, was no sooner informed of these circumstances, than she recollected with indignation the awe with which Laura had involuntarily inspired her; and determined to withdraw part of her misplaced respect. But Laura had an air of command, a quiet majesty of demeanour, that seemed destined to distance vulgar impertinence; and Mrs Stubbs was compelled to continue her unwilling reverence. Determined, however, that though her pride might suffer, her interest should not, she dropped such hints as induced Laura to offer the payment of the lodgings a week in advance, an offer which was immediately accepted.

In spite of Laura's utmost diligence, this arrangement left her almost pennyless. She was obliged, in that inclement season, to give up even the comfort of a fire; and more than once passed the whole night in labouring to supply the wants of the following day.

In the meantime, Hargrave continued to pay his daily visits, and Laura to frustrate all his attempts to speak with her apart. His patience was entirely exhausted. He urged Montreville to the performance of his promise, and Montreville often approached the subject with his daughter, but she either evaded it, or begged with such pathetic earnestness to be spared a contest which she was unable to bear, that, when he looked on the sickly delicacy of her frame, he had not courage to persecute her further. Convinced, however, that Laura's affections were completely engaged, he became daily more anxious that she should not sacrifice them to what he considered as mistaken prudence; especially since Hargrave had dropped a hint, which, though not so intended, had appeared to Montreville to import, that his addresses, if rejected in the present instance, would not be renewed at the distant date to which Laura chose to postpone them.

The father's constant anxiety for the health and happiness of his child powerfully affected both his strength and spirits; and he was soon more languid and feeble than ever. His imagination, too, betrayed increased symptoms of its former disease, and he became more persuaded that he was dying. The selfishness of a feeble mind attended his ailments, and he grew less tender of his daughter's feelings, less fearful to wound her sensibility. To hints of his apprehensions for his own life, succeeded direct intimations of his conviction that his end was approaching; and Laura listened, with every gradation of terror, to prophetic forebodings of the solitude, want, and temptation, to which she must soon be abandoned.

Pressed by Hargrave's importunities, and weary of waiting for a voluntary change in Laura's conduct towards her lover, Montreville at last resolved that he would force the subject which she was so anxious to shun. For this purpose, detaining her one morning in his apartment, he entered on a melancholy description of the perils which await unprotected youth and beauty; and explicitly declared his conviction, that to these perils he must soon leave his child. Laura endeavoured, as she was wont, to brighten his dark imagination, and to revive his fainting hope. But Montreville would now neither suffer her to enliven her prospects, nor to divert him from the contemplation of them. He persisted in giving way to his dismal anticipations, till, spite of her efforts, Laura's spirits failed her, and she could scarcely refrain from shedding tears.

Montreville saw that she was affected; and fondly putting his arm round her, continued, 'Yet still, my sweet Laura, you, who have been the pride of my life, you can soften to me the bitterness of death. Let me but commit you to the affection of the man whom I know that you prefer, and my fears and wishes shall linger no more in this nether world.'

'Oh Sir,' said Laura, 'I beseech, I implore you to spare me on this subject.' 'No!' answered Montreville, 'I have been silent too long. I have too long endangered your happiness, in the dread of giving you transient pain. I must recur to' –

'My dear father,' interrupted Laura, 'I have already spoken to you on this subject – spoken to you with a freedom which I know not where I found courage to assume. I can only repeat the same sentiments; and indeed, indeed, unless you were yourself in my situation, you cannot imagine with what pain I repeat them.'

'I would willingly respect your delicacy,' said Montreville, 'but this is no time for frivolous scruples. I must soon leave thee, child of my affections! My eyes must watch over thee no more; my ear must be closed to the voice of thy complaining. Oh then, give me the comfort to know that other love will console, other arms protect thee.'

'Long, long,' cried Laura, clasping his neck, 'be your affection my joy – long be your arms my shelter. But alas! what love could console me under the sense of acting wrong – what could protect me from an avenging conscience?'

'Laura, you carry your scruples too far. When I look on these wan cheeks and lustreless eyes, you cannot conceal from me that you are sacrificing to these scruples your own peace, as well as that of others.'

'Ah Sir,' said Laura, who from mere despair of escape, gathered courage to pursue the subject, 'What peace can I hope to find in a connexion which reason and religion alike condemn?'

'That these have from childhood been your guides, has ever been my joy and my pride,' returned Montreville. 'But in this instance you forge shackles for yourself, and then call them the restraints of reason and religion. It were absurd to argue on the reasonableness of preferring wealth and title, with the man of your choice, to a solitary struggle with poverty, or a humbling dependence upon strangers. And how, my dear girl, can any precept of religion be tortured into a restriction on the freedom of your choice?'

'Pardon me, Sir, the law which I endeavour to make my guide is here full and explicit. In express terms it leaves me free to marry whom I will, but with this grand reservation, that I marry "only in the Lord." It cannot be thought that this limitation refers only to a careless assent to the truth of the Gospel, shedding no purifying influence on the heart and life. And can I hope for happiness in a wilful defiance of this restriction?'

'If I could doubt,' said Montreville, avoiding a reply to what was unanswerable – 'if I could doubt that a union with Colonel Hargrave would conduce to your happiness, never should I thus urge you. But I have no reason to believe that his religious principles are unsound, though the follies incident to his sex, and the frailty of human nature, may have prevailed against him.'

'My dear Sir,' cried Laura impatiently, 'how can you employ such qualifying language to express – what my soul sickens at. How can my father urge his child to join to pollution this temple, (and she laid her hand emphatically on her breast) which my great master has offered to hallow as his own abode? No! the express command of Heaven forbids the sacrilege, for I cannot suppose that when *man* was forbidden to degrade himself by a union with vileness, the precept was meant to exclude the sex whose feebler passions afford less plea for yielding to their power.'

'Whither does this enthusiasm hurry you?' said Montreville, in displeasure. 'Surely you will not call your marriage with Colonel Hargrave a union with vileness.' 'Yes,' returned Laura, all the glow of virtuous animation fading to the paleness of anguish, 'if his vices make him vile, I must call it so.'

'Your language is much too free, Laura, as your notions are too rigid. Is it dutiful, think you, to use such expressions in regard to a connexion which your father approves? Will you call it virtue to sport with your own happiness, with the peace of a heart that doats upon you – with the comfort of your dying parent?'

'Oh my father,' cried Laura, sinking on her knees, 'my spirit is already bowed to the earth – do not crush it with your displeasure. Rather support my feeble resolution, lest, knowing the right, I should not have power to choose it.'

'My heart's treasure,' said Montreville, kissing the tears from her eyes, 'short ever is my displeasure with thee: for I know that though inexperience may mislead thy judgment, no pleasure can bribe, no fear betray thy inflexible rectitude. Go on then – convince me if thou canst, that thou art in the right to choose thy portion amidst self-denial, and obscurity, and dependence.'

'Would that I were able to convince you,' returned Laura, 'and then you would no longer add to the difficulties of this fearful struggle. Tell me then, were Colonel Hargrave your son, and were I what I cannot name, could any passion excuse, any circumstances induce you to sanction the connexion for which you now plead?'

'My dear love,' said Montreville, 'the cases are widely different. The world's opinion affixes just disgrace to the vices in your sex, which in ours it views with more indulgent eyes.' 'But I,' returned Laura, 'when I took upon me the honoured name of Christian, by that very act became bound that the opinion of the world should not regulate my principles, nor its customs guide my practice. Perhaps even the worst of my sex might plead that the voice of a tempter lured them to perdition; but what tongue can speak the vileness of that tempter! – Could I promise to *obey* him who wilfully leads others to their ruin! Could I *honour* him who deceives the heart that trusteth in him! Could I *love* him who could look upon a fellow creature – once the image of the highest, now humbled below the brutes that perish – upon the heir of immortality, immortal only to misery, and who could, unmoved, unpitying, seek in the fallen wretch a minister of pleasure! – Love!' continued Laura, forgetting in the deformity of the hideous image that it was capable of individual application, 'words cannot express the energy of my abhorrence!'

'Were Hargrave such – or to continue such' – said Montreville – 'Hargrave!' cried Laura, almost with a shriek, 'Oh God forbid – And yet' – She covered her face with her hands, and cold drops stood on her forehead, as she remembered how just cause she had to dread that the portrait might be his.

'Hargrave,' continued Montreville, 'is not an abandoned profligate, though he may not have escaped the follies usual to men of his rank; and he has promised, if you will be favourable to him, to live henceforward in irreproachable purity. Heaven forgives the sins that are forsaken, and will you be less lenient?'

'Joyfully will I forgive,' replied Laura, 'when I am assured that they are indeed abhorred and forsaken' – 'They are already forsaken,' said Montreville; 'it rests with you to confirm Hargrave in the right, by consenting to his wishes.'

'I ask but the conviction which time alone can bring,' said Laura, 'and then' –

'And how will you bear it, Laura, if, weary of your perverse delays, Hargrave should relinquish his suit? How would you bear to see the affections you have trifled with transferred to another?'

'Better, far better,' answered Laura, 'than to watch the deepening of those shades of iniquity, that close at last into outer darkness: better than to see each guilty day advance and seal our eternal separation. To lose his affection,' continued she with a sickly smile, 'I would bear as I strive to bear my other burdens; and should they at last prove too heavy for me, they can but weigh me to the earth, where they and I must soon rest together.'

'Talk not so, beloved child,' said Montreville, 'a long life is before you. All the joys that ambition, all the joys that love can offer, are within your power. A father invites, implores, I will not say commands, you to accept them. The man of your choice, to whom the proudest might aspire, whom the coldest of your sex might love, entreats you to confirm him in the ways of virtue. Consent then to this union, on which my heart is set, while yet it can be hallowed by the blessing of your dying father.'

'Oh take pity on me,' Laura would have said, and 'league not with my weak heart to betray me,' but convulsive sobs were all that she could utter. 'You consent then,' said Montreville, choosing so to interpret her silence – 'you have yielded to my entreaties, and made me the happiest of fathers.' 'No! no!' cried Laura, tossing her arms distractedly, 'I will do right though my heart should break. No, my father, my dear honoured father, for whom I would lay down my life, not even your entreaties shall prevail.'

'Ungrateful child,' said Montreville; 'what could you have pleaded for, that your father would have refused – your father whom anxiety for your welfare has brought to the gates of the grave, whose last feeling shall be love to you, whose last words shall bless you.'

'Oh most merciful, most gracious,' cried Laura, clasping her hands, and raising her eyes in resigned anguish, 'wilt thou suffer me to be tempted above what I am able to bear! Oh my dear father, if you have pity for misery unutterable, misery that cannot know relief, spare me now, and suffer me to think – if to think be yet possible.'

'Hear me but for one moment more,' said Montreville, who from the violence of her emotion gathered hopes of success. 'Oh no! no!' cried Laura, 'I must leave you while yet I have the power to do right.' And, darting from his presence, she shut herself into her chamber. There, falling on her knees, she mingled bitter expressions of anguish, with fervent prayers for support, and piteous appeals for mercy.

Becoming by degrees more composed, she endeavoured to fortify her resolution by every argument of reason and religion which had formerly guided her determination. She turned to the passages of Scripture which forbid the unequal yoke with the unbeliever; convinced that the prohibition applies no less to those whose lives are unchristian, than to those whose faith is unsound. She asked herself whether she was able to support those trials (the severest of all earthly ones,) which the wife of a libertine must undergo; and whether, in temptations which she voluntarily sought, and sorrows which she of choice encountered, she should be entitled to expect the divine support. 'Holy Father,' she cried, 'what peace can enter where thy blessing is withheld! and shall I dare to mock thee with a petition for that blessing on a union which thou has forbidden! May I not rather fear that this deliberate premeditated guilt may be the first step in a race of iniquity! May I not dread to share in the awful sentence of those who are joined to their idols, and be "let alone" to wander in the way that leadeth to destruction?'

Yet, as oft as her father's entreaties rose to her recollection, joined with the image of Hargrave – of Hargrave beseeching, of Hargrave impassioned – Laura's resolution faltered; and half-desirous to deceive herself, she almost doubted of the virtue of that firmness that could withstand a parent's wish. But Laura was habitually suspicious of every opinion that favoured her inclinations, habitually aware of the deceitfulness of her own heart; and she did not, unquestioned, harbour for a moment the insidious thought that flattered her strongest wishes. 'And had my father commended me to marry where I was averse,' said she, 'would I then have hesitated? Would my father's command have prevailed on me then to undertake duties which I was unlikely to perform? No: there I would have resisted. There, authority greater than a father's would have empowered me to resist; and I know that I should have resisted even unto death. And shall mere inclination give more firmness than a sense of duty! Yet, Oh dear father, think me not unmindful of all your love – or forgetful of a debt that began with my being. For your sake cold and hunger shall be light to me – for you poverty and toil shall be pleasing. But what solitary sorrow could equal the pang with which I should blush before my children for the vices of their father! What is the wasting of famine to the mortal anguish of watching the declining love, the transferred desires, the growing depravity of my husband!'

In thoughts and struggles like these, Laura passed the day alone.

Montreville, though disappointed at his ill success with his daughter, was not without hope that a lover's prayers might prevail where a father's were ineffectual; and believing that the season of Laura's emotion was a favourable one for the attempt, he was anxious for the daily visit of Hargrave.

But, for the first time since his meeting with Laura, Hargrave did not appear. In her present frame, Laura felt his absence almost a relief; but Montreville was uneasy and half alarmed. It was late in the evening when a violent knocking at the house door startled Montreville, who was alone in his apartment; and the next minute, without being announced, Hargrave burst into the room. His hair was dishevelled, his dress neglected, and his eyes had a wildness which Montreville had never before seen in them. Abruptly grasping Montreville's hand, he said, in a voice of one struggling for composure, 'Have you performed your promise – have you spoken with Laura?'

'I have,' answered Montreville; 'and have urged her, till, had you seen her, you would yourself have owned that I went too far. But you look' –

'Has she consented,' interrupted Hargrave – 'will she give herself to me?'

Montreville shook his head. 'Her affections are wholly yours,' said he, 'you may yourself be more successful – I fervently wish that you may. But why this strange emotion? What has happened?'

'Nothing, nothing,' said Hargrave, 'ask me no questions; but let me speak instantly with Laura.'

'You shall see her,' returned Montreville, opening the door, and calling Laura, 'Only I beseech you to command yourself, for my poor child is already half distracted.' 'She is the fitter to converse with me,' said Hargrave, with a ghastly smile, 'for I am upon the very verge of madness.'

Laura came at her father's summons; but when she saw Hargrave, the colour faded from her face, an universal tremour seized her, she stopped, and leaned on the door for support. 'Colonel Hargrave wishes to speak with you alone,' said Montreville, 'go with him to the parlour.'

'I cannot,' answered Laura, in words scarcely audible – 'this night I cannot.'

'I command you to go,' said the father in a tone which he had seldom employed, and Laura instantly prepared to go. 'Surely,

surely,' said she, 'Heaven will not leave me to my own weakness, whilst I act in obedience to you.'

Perceiving that she trembled violently, Hargrave offered her the support of his circling arm; but Laura instantly disengaged herself. 'Will you not lean on me, dearest Laura,' said he; 'perhaps it is for the last time.'

'I hope,' answered Laura, endeavouring to exert her spirit, 'it will be the last time that you will avail yourself of my father's authority to constrain me.'

'Spare me your reproaches, Laura,' said Hargrave, 'for I am desperate. All that I desire on earth – my life itself depends upon this hour.'

They entered the parlour, and Laura, sinking into a seat, covered her eyes with her hand, and strove to prepare for answering this new call upon her firmness.

Hargrave stood silent for some moments. Fain would he have framed a resistless petition; for the events of that day had hastened the unravelling of a tale which, once known to Laura, would, he knew, make all his petitions vain. But his impatient spirit could not wait to conciliate; and, seizing her hand, he said, with breathless eagerness, 'Laura, you once said that you loved me, and I believed you. Now to the proof – and if that fail – But I will not distract myself with the thought. You have allowed me a distant hope. Recall your sentence of delay. Circumstances which you cannot – must not know, leave you but one alternative. Be mine now, or you are for ever lost to me.'

Astonished at his words, alarmed by the ill-suppressed vehemence of his manner, Laura tried to read his altered countenance, and feared she knew not what. 'Tell me what you mean?' said she. 'What mean these strange words – these wild looks. Why have you come at this late hour?'

'Ask me nothing,' cried Hargrave, 'but decide. Speak. Will you be mine – now – to-morrow – within a few hours. Soon, very soon, it will be no longer possible for you to choose.'

A hectic of resentment kindled in Laura's cheek at the threat of desertion which she imagined to lurk beneath the words of Hargrave. 'You have,' said she, 'I know not how, extended my conditional promise to receive you as a friend far beyond what the terms of it could warrant. In making even such an engagement, perhaps I condescended too far. But, admitting it in your own sense, what right have you to suppose that I am to be weakly terrified into renouncing a resolution formed on the best grounds?'

'I have no right to expect it,' said Hargrave, in a voice of misery. 'I came to you in desperation. I cannot – will not survive the loss of you; and if I prevail not now, you must be lost to me.'

'What means this strange, this presuming haste?' said Laura. 'Why do you seem thus wretched?'

'I am, indeed, most wretched. Oh Laura, thus on my knees I conjure you to have pity on me; – or, if it will cost you a pang to lose me, have pity on yourself. And if thy love be too feeble to bend thy stubborn will, let a father's wishes, a father's prayers, come to its aid.'

'Oh Hargrave,' cried Laura, bursting into tears, 'how have I deserved that you should lay on me this heavy load – that you should force me to resist the entreaties of my father.'

'Do not – Oh do not resist them. Let a father's prayers – let the pleadings of a wretch whose reason, whose life depends upon you, prevail to move you.'

'Nothing shall move me,' said Laura, with the firmness of despair, 'for I am used to misery, and will bear it.'

'And will you bear it too if driven from virtuous love – from domestic joy, I turn to the bought smile of harlots, forget you in the haunts of riot, or in the grave of a suicide?'

'Oh for mercy,' cried the terrified Laura, 'talk not so dreadfully. Be patient – I implore you. Fear not to lose me. Be but virtuous, and no power of man shall wrest me from you. In poverty – in sickness – in disgrace itself I will cleave to you.'

'Oh, I believe it,' said Hargrave, moved even to woman's weakness, 'for thou art an angel. But wilt though cleave to me in –'

'In what', said Laura.

'Ask me nothing – but yield to my earnest entreaty. Save me from the horrors of losing you; and may Heaven forsake me if ever again I give you cause to repent of your pity.'

Softened by his imploring looks and gestures, overpowered by his vehemence, harassed beyond her strength, Laura seemed almost expiring. But the upright spirit shared not the weakness of its frail abode. 'Cease to importune me,' said she; – 'everlasting were my cause of repentance, should I wilfully do wrong. You may break my heart – it is already broken, but my resolution is immoveable.'

Fire flashed from the eyes of Hargrave; as, starting from her feet, he cried, in a voice of frenzy, 'Ungrateful woman, you have never loved me! You love nothing but the fancied virtue to which I am sacrificed. But tremble, obdurate, lest I dash from me this hated life, and my perdition be on your soul!'

'Oh no,' cried Laura, in an agony of terror, 'I will pray for you – pity you, – what shall I say – love you as never man was loved. Would that it were possible to do more!'

'Speak then your final rejection,' said Hargrave, grasping her hand with convulsive energy; 'and abide by the consequence.' 'I must not fear consequences,' said Laura, trembling in every limb. 'They are in the hands of Heaven.' 'Then be this first fond parting kiss our last!' cried Hargrave, and frantickly straining her to his breast, he rushed out of the room.

Surprise, confusion, a thousand various feelings kept Laura for a while motionless; till, Hargrave's parting words ringing in her ears, a dreadful apprehension took possession of her mind. Starting from her seat, and following him with her arms as if she could still have detained him, 'Oh Hargrave, what mean you?' she cried. But Hargrave was already beyond the reach of her voice; and, sinking to the ground, the wretched Laura found refuge from her misery in long and deep insensibility.

In the attitude in which she had fallen, her lily arms extended on the ground, her death-like cheek resting upon one of them, she was found by a servant who accidentally entered the room, and whose cries soon assembled the family. Montreville alarmed hastened down stairs, and came in just as the maid with the assistance of the landlady was raising Laura, to all appearance dead.

'Merciful Heaven!' he exclaimed, 'what is this?' The unfeeling landlady immediately expressed her opinion that Miss Montreville had died of famine, declaring that she had long feared as much. The horror-struck father had scarcely power to ask her meaning. 'Oh Sir,' said the maid, sobbing aloud, 'I fear it is but too true – for she cared not for herself, so you were but well – for she was the sweetest lady that ever was born – and many a long night has she sat up toiling when the poorest creature was asleep – for she never cared for herself.'

The whole truth flashed at once upon Montreville, and all the storm, from which his dutiful child so well had sheltered him, burst upon him in a moment. 'Oh Laura,' he cried, clasping her lifeless form, 'my only comfort – my good – my gentle – my blameless child, has thou nourished thy father with thy life! Oh why didst thou not let me die!' Then laying his cheek to hers, 'Oh she is cold – cold as clay,' he cried, and the old man wrung his hands, and sobbed like an infant.

Suddenly he ceased his lamentation; and pressing his hands upon his breast, uttered a deep groan, and sunk down by the side of his senseless child. His alarm and agitation burst again the blood-vessel, which before had been slightly healed, and he was conveyed to bed without hope of life. A surgeon was immediately found, but he administered his prescription without expecting its success; and, departing, left the dying Montreville to the care of the landlady.

The tender-hearted Fanny remained with Laura, and at last succeeded in restoring her to animation. She then persuaded her to swallow a little wine, and endeavoured to prevail upon her to retire to bed. But Laura refused. 'No, my kind, good girl,' said she, laying her arm gratefully on Fanny's shoulder. 'I must see my father before I sleep. I have thwarted his will today, and will not sleep without his blessing.' Fanny then besought her so earnestly not to go to the Captain's chamber, that Laura, filled as every thought was with Hargrave, took alarm, and would not be detained. The girl, dreading the consequences of the shock that awaited her, threw her arms round her to prevent her departure. 'Let me go,' cried Laura, struggling with her. 'he is ill; I am sure he is ill, or he would have come to watch and comfort his wretched child.'

Fanny then, with all the gentleness in her power, informed Laura that Montreville, alarmed by the sight of her fainting, had been suddenly taken ill. Laura, in terror which effaced the remembrance of all her former anguish, scarcely suffered her attendant to finish her relation; but broke from her, and hurried as fast as her tottering limbs would bear her to her father's chamber.

Softly, on tiptoe, she stole to his bed-side, and drew the curtain. His eyes were closed, and death seemed already stamped on every feature. Laura shuddered convulsively, and shrunk back in horror. But the dread of scaring the spirit from its frail tenement suppressed the cry that was rising to her lips. Trembling she laid her hand upon his. He looked up, and a gleam of joy brightened in his dying eyes as they rested on his daughter. 'Laura, my beloved,' said he, drawing her gently towards him, 'thou has been the joy of my life. I thank God that thou art spared to comfort me in death.'

Laura tried to speak the words of hope; but the sounds died upon her lips.

After a pause of dread silence, Montreville said, 'This is the hour when thy father was wont to bless thee. Come, and I will bless thee still.'

The weeping Laura sank upon her knees, and Montreville laid one hand upon her hand, while she still held the other, as if wishing to detain him. 'My best – my last blessing be upon thee, child of my heart,' said he. 'The everlasting arms be around thee, when mine can embrace thee no more. The Father of the fatherless be a parent to thee; support thee in sorrow; crown thy youth with joy – thy gray hairs with honour; and, when thou art summoned to thy kindred angels, may thy heart throb its last on some breast kind and noble as thine own.'

Exhausted by the effort which he had made, Montreville sunk back on his pillow; and Laura, in agony of supplication, besought Heaven to spare him to her. 'Father of mercies!' she inwardly ejaculated, 'if it be possible, save me, oh save me from this fearful stroke, – or take me in pity from this desolate wilderness to the rest of thy chosen.'

The dead of night came on, and all but the wretched Laura was still. Montreville breathed softly. Laura thought he slept, and stifled even her sighs, lest they should wake him. In the stillness of the dead, but in agony of suspence that baffles description, she continued to kneel by his bed-side, and to return his relaxing grasp, till she felt a gentle pressure of her hand, and looked up to interpret the gesture. It was the last expression of a father's love. Montreville was gone!

CHAPTER XVIII

COLONEL HARGRAVE had been the spoiled child of a weak mother, and he continued to retain one characteristic of spoiled children; some powerful stimulant was with him a necessary of life. He despised all pleasures of regular recurrence and moderate degree; and even looked down upon those who could be satisfied with such enjoyments, as on beings confined to a meaner mode of existence. For more than a year Laura had furnished the animating principle which kept life from stagnation. When she was present, her beauty, her reserve, her ill-concealed affection, kept his passions in constant play. In her absence, the interpretations of looks and gestures, of which she had been unconscious, and the anticipation of concessions which she thought not of making, furnished occupation for the many hours which, for want of literary habit, Colonel Hargrave was obliged to pass in solitude and leisure, when deprived of fashionable company, public amusements, and tolerable romances. In a little country town, these latter resources were soon exhausted, and Hargrave had no associates to supply the blank among his brother officers; some of whom were low both in birth and education, and others, from various reasons, rather repelling, than courting his intimacy. One had a pretty wife, another an unmarried daughter; and the phlegmatic temperament and reserved manners of a third tallied not with Hargrave's constitutional warmth. The departure of Laura, therefore, deprived him at once of the only society that amused, and the only object that interested him. He was prevented by the caution of Mrs Douglas from attempting a correspondence with his mistress; and his muse was exhausted with composing amatory sonnets, and straining half-imaginary torments into reluctant rhimes.

He soon tired of making sentimental visits to the now deserted

Glenalbert, and grew weary of inspecting his treasures of pilfered gloves and stray shoe-bows. His new system of reform, too, sat rather heavily upon him. He was not exactly satisfied with its extent, though he did not see in what respect he was susceptible of improvement. He had some suspicion that it was not entitled to the full approbation of the 'wise, the pious, the sober-minded' observers, whom he imagined that Laura had charged with the inspection of his conduct; and he reflected, with a mixture of fear and impatience, that by them every action would be reported to Laura, with all the aggravation of illiberal comment. For though he did not distinctly define the idea to himself, he cherished a latent opinion, that the 'wise' would be narrow-minded, the 'pious' bigotted, and the 'sober-minded' cynical. The feeling of being watched is completely destructive of comfort, even to those who have least to conceal; and Colonel Hargrave sought relief at once from restraint and ennui, in exhibiting, at the Edinburgh races, four horses which were the envy of all the gentleman, and a person which was the admiration of all the ladies. His thoughts dissipated, and his vanity gratified, his passion had never, since its first existence, been so little troublesome as during his stay in Edinburgh; and once or twice, as he caught a languishing glance from a gay young heiress, he thought he had been a little precipitate in changing his first designs in regard to Laura. But alas! the races endure only for one short week; Edinburgh was deserted by its glittering birds of passage; and Hargrave returned to his quarters, to solitude, and to the conviction that, however obtained, the possession of Laura was necessary to his peace.

Finding that her return was as uncertain as ever, he resolved to follow her to London; and the caution of Mrs Douglas baffling his attempts to procure her address from any other quarter, he contrived to obtain it by bribing one of the under attendants of the Post Office to transcribe for him the superscription of a letter to Miss Montreville. Delighted with his success, he could not refuse himself the triumph of making it known to Mrs Douglas; and, by calling to ask her commands for her young friend, occasioned the letter of caution from her to Laura, which has been formerly mentioned.

The moment he reached London, he hastened to make inquiries after the abode of Captain Montreville; but his search was disappointed by the accidents which he afterwards related to Laura. Day after day, he hoped that Laura, by sending to Mr Baynard's chambers, would afford him the means of discovering her residence.

But every day ended in disappointment; and Hargrave, who, intending to devote all his time to her, had given no intimation to his friends of his arrival in town, found himself as solitary, listless, and uncomfortable as before he quitted Scotland.

One evening, when, to kill the time, he had sauntered into the Theatre, he renewed his acquaintance with the beautiful Lady Bellamer. Two years before, Hargrave had been the chief favourite of Lady Bellamer, then Miss Walpole. Of all the danglers whom beauty, coquetry, and fifty thousands pounds attracted to her train, none was admitted to such easy freedom as Hargrave. She laughed more heartily at his wit, whispered more familiarly in his ear, and slapped him more frequently on the cheek than any of his rivals. With no other man was she so unreasonable, troublesome, and ridiculous. In short, she ran through the whole routine of flirtation, till her heart was entangled, so far at least as the heart of a coquette is susceptible of that misfortune. But whatever flames were kindled in the lady's breast, the gentleman, as is usual on such occasions, escaped with a very slight tinge. While Miss Walpole was present, his vanity was soothed by her blandishments, and his senses touched by her charms; but, in her absence, he consoled himself with half a dozen other affairs of the same kind.

Meanwhile Lord Bellamer entered the lists, and soon distinguished himself from his competitors, by a question, which, with all her admirers, Miss Walpole had not often answered. The lady hesitated; for she could not help contrasting the insignificant starvling figure of her suitor with the manly beauty of Hargrave's person. But Lord Bellamer had a title in possession; Hargrave's was only reversionary. His Lordship's estate, too, was larger than the Colonel's expectations. Besides, she began to have doubts whether her favourite ever intended to propose the important question; for though, to awaken his jealousy, she had herself informed him of Lord Bellamer's pretensions, and though she had played off the whole artillery of coquetry to quicken his operations, the young man maintained a resolute and successful resistance. So, after some fifty sighs given to the well turned leg and sparkling eyes of Hargrave, Miss Walpole became Lady Bellamer; and this was the only change which marriage effected in her; for no familiarity could increase her indifference to Lord Bellamer, and no sacredness of connection can warm the heart of a coquette. She continued equally assiduous in courting admiration, equally daring in defying censure; and was content to purchase the adulation of fools, at the expence of being obliged to the charity of those who were good-natured enough to say, 'to be sure Lady Bellamer is a little giddy, but I dare say she means no harm.'

Her husband's departure with his regiment for the continent, made no change in her way of life, except to save her the trouble of defending conduct which she would not reform. She continued in London, or at her villa at Richmond Hill, to enter into every folly which others proposed, or herself to project new ones.

Meanwhile Hargrave's duty called him to Scotland, where Lady Bellamer and all her rivals in his attention were entirely forgotten amidst the superior attractions of Laura; attractions which acted with all the force of novelty upon a heart accustomed to parry only premeditated attacks, and to resist charms that were merely corporeal. From an early date in his acquaintance with Miss Montreville, he had scarcely recollected the existence of Lady Bellamer, till he found himself in the next box to her at the theatre. The pleasure that sparkled in the brightest blue eyes in the world, the flush that tinged her face, wherever the rouge permitted its natural tints to appear, convinced Hargrave in a moment that her Ladyship's memory had been more tenacious; and he readily answered to her familiar nod of invitation, by taking his place at her side.

They entered into conversation with all the frankness of their former intimacy. Lady Bellamer inquired how the Colonel had contrived to exist during eighteen months of rustication; and gave him in return memoirs of some of their mutual acquaintances. She had some wit, and an exuberance of animal spirits; and she seasoned her nonsense with such lively sallies, sly scandal, and adroit flattery, that Hargrave had scarcely ever passed an evening so gaily. Once or twice, the composed grace, the artless majesty of Laura, rose to his recollections, and he looked absent and thoughtful. But his companion rallied him with so much spirit, that he quickly recovered himself, and fully repaid the amusement which he received. He accepted Lady Bellamer's invitation to sup with her after the play, and left her at a late hour, with a promise to visit her again the next day. From that time, the freedom of their former intercourse was renewed; with this difference only, that Hargrave was released from some restraint, by his escape from the danger of entanglement which necessarily attends particular assiduities towards an unmarried woman.

Let the fair enchantress tremble who approaches even in thought the utmost verge of discretion. If she advance but one jot beyond that magic circle, the evil spirit is ready to seize her, which before, feared even to rise in her presence. Lady Bellamer became the victim of unpardonable imprudence on her own part, and mere constitutional tendency on that of her paramour. To a most blameable levity she sacrificed whatever remained to be sacrificed, of her reputation, her virtue, and her marriage vow; while the crime of Hargrave was not palliated by one sentiment of genuine affection; for she by whom he fell was no more like the object of his real tenderness, than those wandering lights that arise from corruption and glimmer only to betray, are to the steady sunbeam which enlightens, and guides, and purifies where it shines.

Their intercourse continued, with growing passion on the side of the lady, and expiring inclination on that of the gentleman, till Lady Bellamer informed him that the consequences of their guilt could not long be concealed. Her Lord was about to return to his disgraced home; and she called upon Hargrave to concert with her the means of exchanging shackles which she would no longer endure for bonds which she could bear with pleasure, and himself to stand forth the legal protector of his unborn child. Hargrave heard her with a disgust which he scarcely strove to conceal; for at that moment Laura stood before him, bewitching in chastened love – respectable in saintly purity. He remembered that the bare proposal of a degradation which Lady Bellamer had almost courted, had once nearly banished the spotless soul from a tenement only less pure than itself. In fancy he again saw through her casement the wringing of those snowy hands, those eyes raised in agony, and the convulsive heavings of that bosom which mourned his unlooked-for baseness; and he turned from Lady Bellamer, inwardly cursing the hour when his vows to Laura were sacrificed to a wanton.

The very day after this interview was that in which he accidentally encountered Laura; and from that moment his whole desire was to make her his own, before public report should acquaint her with his guilt. He durst not trust to the strength of her affection for the pardon of so foul an offence. He could not hope that she would again place confidence in vows of reformation which had been so grossly violated. When the proper self-distrust of Laura refused him the opportunity of making a personal appeal to her sensibilties, he hoped that her father might successfully plead his cause; and that before his guilt was known to her, he might have made it at once her interest and her duty to forget it. But the storm was about to burst even more speedily than he apprehended. Lady Bellamer little suspected that her conduct was watched with all the malice of jealousy, and all the eagerness of interest. She little suspected that her confidential servant was the spy of her injured husband, bound to fidelity in this task by ties as disgraceful as they were strong, and that this woman waited only for legal proof of her mistress's guilt, to lay the particulars before her lord. That proof was now obtained; and Lord Bellamer hastened to avail himself of it. He arrived in London on the morning of the last day of Montreville's life; and, charging his guilty wife with her perfidy, expelled her from his house.

She flew to Hargrave's lodgings, and found him preparing for his daily visit to Laura. Though provoked at being delayed, he was obliged to stay and listen to her, while she hastily related the events of the morning. She was about to speak of her conviction, that, by making her his wife, he would shield her from the world's scorn, and that he would not, by any legal defence, retard her emancipation. But Hargrave suffered her not to proceed. He perceived that his adventure must now be public. It must immediately find its way into the public prints; and in a few hours it might be in the hands of Laura. He bitterly upbraided Lady Bellamer with her want of caution in the concealment of their amour; cursed her folly as the ruin of all his dearest hopes; and, in the frenzy of his rage, scrupled not to reveal the cutting secret, that while another was the true object of his affections, Lady Bellamer had sacrificed her all to an inclination as transient as it was vile. The wretched creature, terrified at his rage, weakened by her situation, overcome by the events of the morning, and stung by a reception so opposite to her expectations, sunk at his feet in violent hysterics. But Hargrave could at that moment feel for no miseries but his own; and consigning her to the care of the woman of the house, he was again about to hasten to Montreville's, when he was told that a gentleman wished to speak wtih him upon particular business.

This person was the bearer of a note from Lord Bellamer, importing that he desired to meet Colonel Hargrave on that or the following day, at any hour and place which the Colonel might appoint. After the injuries given and received, their meeting, he said, could have but one object. Hargrave, in no humour to delay, instantly replied that in three hours he should be found in a solitary field, which he named, at a few miles distant from town, and that he should bring with him a friend and a brace of pistols. He then went in search of this friend, and finding him at home, the business was speedily settled.

Nothing, in the slight consideration of death which Hargrave suffered to enter his mind, gave him so much disturbance as the thought that he might, if he fell, leave Laura to the possession of another. He willingly persuaded himself that she had an attachment to him too romantic to be transferable. But she was poor; she might in time make a marriage of esteem and convenience; and Laura, the virtuous Laura, would certainly love her husband, and the father of her children. The bare idea stung like a scorpion, and Hargrave hastened to his man of business, where he spent the time which yet remained before the hour of his appointment, in dictating a bequest of five thousand pounds to Laura Montreville; but true to his purpose, he added a clause, by which, in case of her marriage, she forfeited the whole.

He then repaired to meet Lord Bellamer; and, the ground being taken, Hargrave's first ball penetrated Lord Bellamer's left shoulder, who then fired without effect, and instantly fell. Hargrave, whose humanity had returned with his temper, accompanied his wounded antagonist to a neighbouring cottage to which he was conveyed, anxiously procured for him every possible comfort, and heard with real joy, that if he could be kept from fever, his wound was not likely to be mortal. The gentleman who had been Hargrave's second, offered to remain near Lord Bellamer, in order to give warning to his friend should any danger occur; and it was late in the evening before Hargrave, alone and comfortless, returned to town.

Never had his own thoughts been such vexatious companions. To his own scared conscience his crimes might have seemed trivial; but when he placed them before him in the light in which he knew that they would be viewed by Laura, their nature seemed changed. He knew that she would find no plea in the custom of the times, for endangering the life of a fellow-creature, and that her moral vocabulary contained no qualifying epithet to palliate the foulness of adultery. The next day would give publicity to his duel and its cause; and should the report reach Laura's ear, what could he hope from her favour? The bribes of love and ambition he had found too poor to purchase her sanction to the bare intention of a crime. Even the intention seemed forgiven only in the hope of luring him to the paths of virtue: and when she should know the failure of that hope, would not her forgiveness be withdrawn?

But Laura, thus on the point of being lost, was more dear to him than ever; and often did he wish that he had fallen by Lord Bellamer's hand, rather than that he should live to see himself the object of her indifference, perhaps aversion. Time still remained, however, by one desperate effort to hurry or terrify her into immediate compliance with his wishes; and, half-distracted with the emotions of remorse, and love, and hope, and fear, he ordered his carriage to Montreville's house. Here passed the scene which has been already described. Hargrave was too much agitated to attend to the best methods of persuasion, and he quitted Laura in the full conviction that she would never be his wife. He threw himself into his carriage, and was driven home, now frantickly bewailing his loss, now vowing, that rather than endure it, he would incur the penalties of every law, divine and human. All night he paced his apartment, uttering imprecations on his own folly, and forming plans for regaining by fraud, force, or persuasion, his lost rights over Laura. At last his vehemence having somewhat spent itself, he threw himself on a couch, and sunk into feverish and interrupted sleep.

It was not till next morning, that he thought of inquiring after the unfortunate partner of his iniquity; and was told that, too ill to be removed, she had been carried to bed in the house, where she still remained.

Intending to renew the attempt of the preceding night, he again repaired to Laura's house; but his intention was frustrated by the death of Montreville. On receiving the information, he was at first a good deal shocked at the sudden departure of a man, whom, a few hours before, he had left in no apparent danger. But that feeling was effaced when once he began to consider the event as favourable to his designs upon Laura. Left to solitude, to poverty, perhaps to actual want, what resource had she so eligible as the acceptance of offers splendid and disinterested like his. And he would urge her acceptance of them with all the ardour of passion. He would alarm her with the prospects of desolateness and dependence, he would appeal to the wishes of her dead father. Such pleadings must, he thought, have weight with her; and again the hopes of victory revived in his mind. Should the principle, to which she so firmly adhered, outweigh all these considerations, he thought she would forfeit by her obstinacy all claim to his forbearance, and his heart fluttered at the idea that she had now no protector from his power. He resolved to haunt, to watch her, to lose no opportunity of pressing his suit. Wherever she went he was determined to follow; 'and surely,' thought he, 'she must have some moments of weakness, she cannot be always on her guard.'

For some days he continued to make regular visits at her lodgings, though he had no hope of seeing her till after Montreville was consigned to the dust; and he rejoiced that the customary seclusion was likely to retard her knowledge of his misconduct. To make inquiries after the health and spirits of Laura, was the ostensible, but not the only motive of his visits. He wished to discover all that was knwon to the people of the house of her present situation and future plans. On the latter subject they could not afford him even the slightest information, for Laura had never dropped a hint of her intentions. But he received such accounts of her pecuniary distresses, and of the manner in which she supported them, as at once increased his reverence for her character, and his hopes that she would take refuge from her wants in the affluence which he offered her.

From Fanny, who officiated as porter, and who almost adored Laura, he received most of his intelligence; and while he listened to instances of the fortitude, the piety, the tenderness, the resignation of his beloved, a love of virtue, sincere though transient, would cross his soul; he would look back with abhorrence on a crime which had hazarded the loss of such a treasure; and vow, that, were he once possessed of Laura, his life should be a copy of her worth. But Hargrave's vows deceived him; for he loved the virtues only that were associated with an object of pleasure, he abhorred the vices only which threatened him with pain.

On the day succeeding the funeral, he ventured on an attempt to see Laura, and sent her a message, begging permission to wait upon her; but was answered that she received no visitors. He then wrote to her a letter full of the sentiments which she inspired. He expressed his sympathy with her misfortunes, and fervently besought her to accept of a protector who would outdo in tenderness the one she had lost. He implored her to add the strongest incentive to the course of virtue, in which, if she would listen to his request, he solemnly promised to persevere. He again insinuated that she must speedily decide; that, if her decision were unfavourable, he might be driven to seek forgetfulness amidst ruinous dissipation; and he adjured her, by the wishes of her dead father, a claim which he thought would with her be irresistible, to consent to dispense with his further probation.

He said he would visit her late in the following forenoon, in the hope of receiving his answer from her own lips; and concluded by telling her that, lest the late unfortunate event had occasioned her any temporary difficulties, he begged to be considered as her banker, and enclosed a bill for a hundred pounds.

He gave this letter to Fanny, with injunctions to deliver it immediately, and then went to inquire for Lord Bellamer, whom it gave him real pleasure to find pronounced out of danger. Lady Bellamer, too, had ceased to reproach and molest him. She had recovered from her indisposition, and removed to the house of a relation, who humanely offered to receive her. His hopes were strong of the effect of his letter; and he passed the evening in greater comfort than had lately fallen to his share. Often did he repeat to himself that Laura must accede to his proposals. What other course could she pursue – Would her spirit allow her to become a burden on the scanty income of her friend Mrs Douglas – Would she venture to pursue, as a profession, the art in which she so greatly excelled – Would she return to live alone at Glenalbert? This last appeared the most probable to Hargrave, because the most desirable. Alone, without any companion whose frozen counsel could counteract the softness of her heart, in a romantic solitude, watched, as he would watch, importuned as he would importune her, strange if no advantage could be wrested from her affection or her prudence, her interest or her fears! To possess Laura was the first wish of his soul; and he was not very fastidious as to the means of its gratification; for even the love of a libertine is selfish. He was perfectly sincere in his honourable proposals to Laura. He might have been less so had any others possessed a chance of success.

He rose early the next morning, and impatiently looked for the hour which he had appointed for his visit. He wished that he had fixed on an earlier one, took up a book to beguile the minutes, threw it down again, looked a hundred times at his watch, ordered his carriage to the door two hours before it was wanted, feared to go too soon, lest Laura should refuse to see him, and yet was at her lodgings, long before his appointment. He inquired for her, and was answered that she had discharged her lodgings, and was gone. 'Gone! Whither?' – Fanny did not know; Miss Montreville had been busy all the evening before in preparing for her removal, and had left the house early that morning. 'And did she leave no address where she might be found?' 'I heard her tell the coachman,' said Fanny, 'to stop at the end of Grosvenor-street, and she would direct him where she chose to be set down. But I believe she has left a letter for you, Sir.' 'Fool!' cried Hargrave, 'why did you not tell me so sooner – give it me instantly.'

He impatiently followed the girl to the parlour which had been Montreville's. The letter lay on the table. He snatched it, and hastily tore it open. It contained only his bill, returned with Miss Montreville's compliments and thanks. He twisted the card into atoms, and cursed with all his soul the ingratitude and cold prudence of the writer. He swore that if she were on earth, he would find her; and vowed that he would make her repent of the vexation which he said she had always taken a savage delight in heaping upon him.

Restless, and yet unwilling to be gone, he next wandered into Laura's painting-room, as if hoping in her once-favourite haunt to find traces of her flight. He had never entered it since the day when the discovery of De Courcy's portrait had roused his sudden frenzy. Association brought back the same train of thought. He imagined that Laura, while she concealed herself from him, had taken refuge with the De Courcys; and all his jealousy returned. After, according to custom, acting the madman for a while, he began as usual to recover his senses. He knew he could easily discover whether Miss Montreville was at Norwood, by writing to a friend who lived in the neighbourhood; and he was going home to execute this design, when, passing through the lobby, he was met by the landlady. He stopped to renew his inquiries whether any thing was known, or guessed, of Laura's retreat. But Mrs Stubbs could give him no more information on that subject than her maid, and she was infinitely more suprised at his question than Fanny had been; for having made certain observations which convinced her that Hargrave's visits were in the character of a lover, she had charitably concluded, and actually asserted, that Laura had accepted of his protection.

Hargrave next inquired whether Laura had any visitors but himself? 'No living creature,' was the reply. 'Could Mrs Stubbs conjecture whither she was gone?' 'None in the world,' answered Mrs Stubbs; 'only this I know, it can't be very far off – for to my certain knowledge, she had only seven shillings in her pocket, and that could not carry her far, as I told the gentleman who was here this morning.' 'What gentleman?' cried Hargrave. 'One Mr De Courcy, Sir, that used to call for her; but he has not been here these six weeks before; and he seemed quite astounded as well as yourself, Sir.' Hargrave then questioned her so closely concerning De Courcy's words and looks, as to convince himself that his rival was entirely ignorant of the motions of the fugitive. In this belief he returned home, uncertain what measures he should pursue, but determined not to rest till he had found Laura.

When De Courcy quitted Laura, he had no intention of seeing her again till circumstances should enable him to offer her his hand. No sacrifice could have cost him more pain; but justice and filial duty did not permit him to hesitate. Neither did he think himself entitled to sadden with a face of care his domestic circle, nor to make his mother and sister pay dear for their comforts, by shewing that they were purchased at the expence of his peace. Nor did he languidly resign to idle love-dreams the hours which an immortal spirit claimed for its improvement, and which the social tie bound him to enliven and cheer. But to appear what he was not, to introduce constraint and dissimulation into the sacred privacies of home, never occurred to De Courcy. He therefore strove not to *seem* cheerful but to *be* so. He returned to his former studies, and even prosecuted them with alacrity, for he knew that Laura respected a cultivated mind. His faults, he was if possible more than ever studious to correct, for Laura loved virtue. And when occasion for a kind considerate or self-denying action presented itself, he eagerly seized it, saying in his heart, 'this is like Laura.'

Sometimes the fear that he might be forgotten, forced from him the bitterest sigh that he had ever breathed; but he endeavoured to comfort himself with the belief that she would soon be screened from the gaze of admiration, and that her regard for him, though yet in its infancy, would be sufficient to secure her from other impressions. Of the reality of this regard he did not allow himself to doubt, or if he hesitated for a moment, he called to mind the picture, Laura's concealment of it, her confusion at his attempt to examine it, and he no longer doubted.

The arrival of the picture itself might have explained all that related to it, had De Courcy chosen to have it so explained. But he turned his eye from the unpleasing sight, and sheltered his hopes by a hundred treasured instances of love which had scarcely any existence but in his fancy.

His efforts to be cheerful were however less successful, after Laura, in a few melancholy lines, informed Miss De Courcy that Montreville's increased illness made their return to Scotland more uncertain than ever. He imagined his dear Laura the solitary attendant of a sickbed; no kind voice to comfort, no friendly face to cheer her; perhaps in poverty, that poverty increased too by the artifice which he had used to lessen it. He grew anxious, comfortless, and at length really miserable. Every day the arrival of the letters was looked for with extreme solicitude in hope of more cheering news; but every day brought disappointment, for Laura wrote no more. His mother shared in his anxiety, and increased it by expressing her own. She feared that Miss Montreville was ill, and unable to write; and the image of Laura among strangers, sick and in poverty, obliterated Montague's prudent resolutions of trusting himself no more in the presence of his beloved. He set out for London, and arrived at the door of Laura's lodgings about an hour after she had quitted them.

Mrs Stubbs, of whom he made personal inquiries, was abundantly communicative. She gave him, as far as it was known to her, a full history of Laura's adventures since he had seen her; and, where she was deficient in facts, supplied the blank by conjecture. With emotion indescribable, he listened to a coarse account of Miss Montreville's wants and labours. 'How could you suffer all this?' cried he, indignantly, when he was able to speak. 'Times are hard, Sir,' returned Mrs Stubbs, the jolly purple deepening in her cheeks. 'Besides, Miss Montreville had always such an air with her, that I could not for my very heart have asked her to take pot-luck with us.'

The colour faded from De Courcy's face as Mrs Stubbs proceeded to relate the constant visits of Hargrave. 'I'll warrant,' said she, growing familiar as she perceived that she excited interest, 'I'll warrant he did not come here so often for nothing. People must have ears, and use them too; and I heard him myself swearing to her one day, that he loved her better than his life, or something to that purpose; and that, if she would live with him, he would make her dreams pleasant, or some such stuff as that; and now, as sure as can be, she has taken him at his word, and gone to him.'

'Peace, woman!' cried De Courcy, in a tone which he had never used to any of the sex, 'how dare you –?'

Mrs Stubbs, who had all that want of nerve which characterizes vulgar arrogance, instantly shrunk into her shell. 'No offence, Sir,' said she. 'Its all mere guess-work with me; only she does not know a creature in London, and she had nothing to carry her out of it; for she had just seven shillings in her pocket. I gave her seventeen and sixpence of change this morning, and she gave half-a-guinea of that to the kitchen-maid. Now it stands to reason, she would not have been so ready parting with her money if she had not known where more was to be had.'

De Courcy, shocked and disgusted, turned from her in displeasure; and finding that nothing was to be learnt from her of the place of Laura's retreat, betook himself to the print-shop, where he remembered that he had first procured Miss Montreville's address. Mr Wilkins declared his ignorance on the subject of Montague's inquiries; but, seeing the look of disappointment with which De Courcy was leaving the shop, goodnaturedly said, 'I dare say, Sir, if you wish to find out where Miss Montreville lives, I could let you know by asking Colonel Hargrave. He comes here sometimes to look at the caricatures. And,' added Mr Wilkins, winking significantly, 'I am mistaken if they are not very well acquainted.'

De Courcy's heart rose to his mouth. 'Perhaps so,' said he, scarcely conscious of what he said. 'There was a famous scene between them here about three weeks ago,' proceeded the print-seller, anxious to justify his own sagacity. 'I suppose they had not met for a while, and there such a kissing and embracing' – ' 'Tis false!' cried De Courcy, lightning flashing from his eyes, 'Miss Montreville would have brooked such indignities from no man on earth.' 'Nay,' said Wilkins, shrugging up his shoulders, 'the shop-lads saw it as well as I – she fainted away in his arms, and he carried her into the back-room there, and would not suffer one of us to come near her; and Mr Finch there saw him down on his knees to her.' 'Cease your vile slanders,' cried De Courcy, half-distracted with grief and indignation, 'I abhor – I despise them. But at your peril dare to breathe them into any other ear.' So saying, he darted from the shop, and returned to his hotel, infinitely more wretched than ever he had been.

The happy dream was dispelled that painted him the master of Laura's affections. Another possessed her love; and how visible, how indelicately glaring, must be the preference that was apparent to every vulgar eye! But, bitter as was his disappointment, and cruel the pangs of jealousy, they were ease compared to the torture with which he admitted a thought derogatory to Laura's worth. A thousand times he reproached himself for suffering the hints and conjectures of a lowbred woman to affect his mind; – a thousand times assured himself, that no poverty, no difficulties, would overpower the integrity of Laura. 'Yet Hargrave is a libertine,' said he, 'and if she can love a libertine, how have I been deceived in her! No! it cannot be! – She is all truth – all purity. It is she that is deceived. He has imposed upon her by a false show of virtue, and misery awaits her detection of his deceit. She gone to him! I will never believe it. Libertine as he is, he dared not but to think of it. Extremity of want – lingering famine would not degrade her to this,' – and tears filled De Courcy's manly eyes at the thought that Laura was indeed in want.

He had no direct means of supplying her necessities; but he hoped that she might inquire at her former abode for any letters that might chance to be left for her, and that she might thus receive any packet which he addressed to her. 'She shall never be humbled,' said he with a heavy sigh, 'by knowing that she owes this trifle to an indifferent, forgotten stranger;' and inclosing fifty pounds in a blank cover, he put both into an envelope to Mrs Stubbs, in which he informed her, that if she could find no means of conveying the packet to Miss Montreville, the anonymous writer would claim it again at some future time, on describing its contents.

Before dispatching the letter, however, he resolved on making an attempt to discover whether Hargrave was acquainted with Laura's retreat. He shrunk from meeting his rival. His blood ran cold as he pictured to his fancy the exulting voice, the triumphant glance which would announce the master of Laura's fate. But any thing was preferable to his present suspense; and the hope that he might yet be useful to Laura, formed an incitement still more powerful. 'Let me but find her,' said he, 'and I will yet wrest her from destruction. If she is deceived I will warn; if she is oppressed, I will protect her.'

He imagined that he should probably find Hargrave at the house of his uncle Lord Lincourt, and hastened thither to seek him; but found the house occupied only by servants, who were ignorant of the Colonel's address. De Courcy knew none of Hargrave's places of resort. The habits and acquaintance of each lay in a different line. No means therefore of discovering him occurred to Montague, except that of inquiring at the house of Mrs Stubbs, where he thought it probable that the place of Hargrave's residence might be known. Thither, then, he next bent his course.

The door was opened to him by Fanny; who replied to his questions, that none of the family knew where Colonel Hargrave lived, and lamented that De Courcy had not come a little earlier, saying that the Colonel had been gone not above a quarter of an hour. De Courcy was turning disappointed away; when Fanny, stopping him, said with a courtesy and a half-whisper, 'Sir, an't please you, my mistress was all wrong about Miss Montreville, for the Colonel knows no more about her than I do.' 'Indeed!' said De Courcy, all attention. 'Yes indeed Sir – when I told him she was away, he was quite amazed, and in such a passion! So then I thought I would give him the letter. –' 'What letter?' cried De Courcy, the glow of animation fading in his face. 'A letter that Miss Montreville left for him, Sir, but when he got it he was ten times angrier than before, and swore at her for not letting him know where she was going. So I thought, Sir, I would make bold to tell you, Sir, as Mistress had been speaking her mind, Sir; for it's a sad thing to have one's character taken away; and Miss Montreville, I am sure, wouldn't do hurt to nobody.'

'You are a good girl, a very good girl,' said De Courcy, giving her, with a guinea, a very hearty squeeze of the hand. He made her repeat the particulars of Hargrave's violent behaviour; and satisfied from them that his rival had no share in Laura's disappearance, he returned to his hotel, his heart lightened of half the heaviest load that ever it had borne.

Still, however, enough remained to exclude for a time all quiet from his breast. He could not doubt that Laura's affections were Hargrave's. She had given proof of it palpable to the most common observer; and resentment mingled with his grief while he thought, that to his fervent respectful love, she preferred the undistinguishing passion of a libertine. 'All women are alike,' said he, 'the slaves of mere outward show:' – An observation for which the world was probably first indebted to circumstances somewhat like De Courcy's.

Restless and uncomfortable, without any hope of finding Laura, he would now have left London without an hour's delay. But, though he forgot his own fatigues, he was not unmindful of those of the grey-haired domestic who attended him. He therefore deferred his journey to the following morning; and then set out on his return to Norwood, more depressed and wretched than he had quitted it.

CHAPTER XIX

———————•———————

ALL was yet dark and still, when Laura, like some unearthly being, stood by the bed where Fanny slept. The light which she bore in her wasted hand, shewed faintly the majestic form, darkened by its mourning garments; and shed a dreary gleam upon tearless eyes, and a face whence all the hues of life were fled. She made a sign for Fanny to rise; and, awe-struck by the calm of unutterable grief, Fanny arose, and in silence followed her. They entered the chamber of death. With noiseless steps Laura approached the body, and softly drew back the covering. She beckoned Fanny towards her. The girl comprehended that her aid was wanted in performing the last duties to Montreville; and, shrinking with superstitious fear, said, in a low tremulous whisper, 'I dare not touch the dead.' Laura answered not; but raising her eyes to Heaven, as if there to seek assistance in her mournful task, she gently pressed her hand upon the half-closed eyes that had so often beamed fondness on her. Unaided, and in silence, she did the last offices of love. She shed no tears. She uttered no lamentation. The dread stillness was broken only by the groans that burst at times from her heavy heart, and the more continued sobs of her attendant, who vented in tears her fear, her pity, and her admiration.

When the sad task was finished, Laura, still speechless, motioned to the servant to retire. In horror at the thoughts of leaving Laura alone with the dead, yet fearing to raise her voice, the girl respectfully grasped her mistress's gown, and, in a low but earnest whisper, besought her to leave this dismal place, and to go to her own chamber. Scarcely sensible of her meaning, Laura suffered her to draw her away; but when the door closed upon all that remained of her father, she shuddered convulsively, and struggled to return.

Fanny, however, gathered courage to lead her to her own apartment. There she threw herself prostrate on the ground; a flood of tears came to relieve her oppressed heart, and her recovered utterance broke forth in an act of resignation. She continued for some hours to give vent to her sorrow – a sorrow unallayed by any less painful feeling, save those of devotion. She had lost the affectionate guide of her youth, the fond parent, whose love for her had brought him untimely to the grave; and, in the anguish of the thought that she should watch his smile and hear his voice no more, she scarcely remembered that he had left her to want and loneliness.

The morning was far advanced, when her sorrows were broken in upon by her landlady, who came to ask her directions in regard to the funeral. Laura had been unable to bend her thoughts to the consideration of this subject; and she answered only by her tears. In vain did Mrs Stubbs repeat that 'it was folly to take on so,' – 'that we must all die;' 'and that as every thing has two handles, Laura might comfort herself that she should now have but one mouth to feed.' Laura seemed obstinate in her grief, and at last Mrs Stubbs declared that whether she would hear reason or not, something must without delay be settled about the funeral; as for her part she could not order things without knowing how they were to be paid for. Laura, putting her hand to her forehead, complained that her head felt confused, and, mildly begging her persecutor to have a little patience with her, promised, if she might be left alone for the present, to return to the conversation in half an hour.

Accordingly, soon after the time appointed, the landlady was surprised to see Laura enter the parlour, her cheek indeed colourless and her eyes swelled with weeping, but her manner perfectly calm and collected. 'Here are my father's watch and seals,' said she, presenting them. 'They may be disposed of. That cannot wound him now,' – and she turned away her head, and drew her hand across her eyes. 'Have the goodness to order what is necessary, for I am a stranger, without any friend.' Mrs Stubbs, examining the watch, declared her opinion that the sale of it would produce very little. 'Let every thing be plain, but decent,' said Laura, 'and when I am able I will work day and night till all is paid.' 'I doubt, Miss,' answered Mrs Stubbs, 'it will be long before your work will pay for much; besides you will be in my debt for a week's lodgings – we always charge a week extra when there is a death in the house.' 'Tell me what you would have me to do, and I will do it,' said the unfortunate Laura, wholly unable to contend with her hard-hearted companion. 'Why, Miss,' said Mrs Stubbs, 'there is your beautiful rose-wood work-table and the foot-stools, and your fine ivory work-box that Mr De Courcy sent here before you came; if you choose to dispose of them, I will take them off your hands.' 'Take them,' said Laura, 'I knew not that they were mine.' Mrs Stubbs then conscientiously offered to give a fourth part of the sum which these toys had cost De Courcy three months before, an offer which Laura instantly accepted; and the landlady having settled this business much to her own satisfaction, cheerfully undertook to arrange the obsequies of poor Montreville.

Though the tragical scenes of the night had left Laura no leisure to dwell upon her fears for Hargrave, it was not without thankfulness that she heard of his safety and restored composure. Her mind was at first too much occupied by her recent loss, to attempt accounting for his extravagant behaviour; and, after the first paroxysms of her sorrow were past, she retained but an imperfect recollection of his late conversation with her. She merely remembered his seeming distraction and threatened suicide; and only bewildered herself by her endeavours to unravel his mysterious conduct. Sometimes a suspicion not very remote from truth would dart into her mind; but she quickly banished it, as an instance of the causeless fears that are apt to infest the hearts of the unfortunate.

An innate delicacy which, in some degree, supplied to Laura the want of experience, made her feel an impropriety in the daily visits which she was informed that Hargrave made at her lodgings. She was aware that they might be liable to misrepresentation, even though she should persist in her refusal to see him; and this consideration appeared to add to the necessity already so urgent, for resolving on some immediate plan for her future course of life. But the future offered to Laura no attractive prospect. Wherever she turned, all seemed dark and unpromising. She feared not to labour for her subsistence; no narrow pride forbade her use of any honourable means of independence. But her personal charms were such as no degree of humility could screen from the knowledge of their possessor, and she was sensible how much this dangerous distinction increased the disqualifications of her sex and age for the character of an artist. As an artist, she must be exposed to the intrusion of strangers, to public observation if successful; to unpitied neglect if she failed in her attempt. Besides, it was impossible to think of living alone and unprotected, in the human chaos that surrounded her. All her father's dismal forebodings rose to her remembrance; and she almost regarded herself as one who would be noticed only as a mark for destruction, beguiled by frauds which no vigilance could detect, overwhelmed by power which she could neither resist nor escape.

Should she seek in solitude a refuge from the destroyer, and return to mourn at her deserted Glenalbert, the stroke that had left it like her lonely and forlorn, want lurked amidst its shades; for with her father had died not only the duties and the joys of life, but even the means of its support. Her temporary right to the few acres which Montreville farmed, was in less than a year to expire; and she knew that, after discharging the claim of the landlord, together with some debts which the long illness of Lady Harriet and the ill-fated journey had obliged Montreville to contract, little would remain from the sale of her effects at Glenalbert.

Laura was sure, that the benevolent friend of her youth, the excellent Mrs Douglas, would receive her with open arms – guide her inexperience with a mother's counsel – comfort her sorrows with a mother's love. But her spirit revolted from a life of indolent dependence, and her sense of justice from casting a useless burden upon an income too confined to answer claims stronger and more natural than hers. Mrs Douglas was herself the preceptress of her children, and both by nature and education amply qualified for the momentous task. In domestic management, her skill and activity were unrivalled. Laura, therefore, saw no possibility of repaying, by her usefulness in any department of the family, the protection which she might receive; and she determined that nothing but the last necessity should induce her to tax the generosity of her friend, or to forego the honourable independence of those who, though 'silver or gold they have none,' can barter for the comforts they enjoy their mental treasures or their bodily toil.

To undertake the tuition of youth occurred to her as the most eligible means of procuring necessary subsistence, and protection, more necessary still. It appeared to her that, as a member of any reputable family, she should be sheltered from the dangers which her father had most taught her to dread. She reviewed her accomplishments, and impartially examined her ability to communicate them with temper and perseverance. Though for the most part attained with great accuracy, they were few in number, and unobtrusive in kind. She read aloud with uncommon harmony and grace. She spoke and wrote with fluency and precision. She was grammatically acquainted with the French and Latin languages, and an adept in the common rules of arithmetic. Her proficiency in painting has been already noticed; and she sang with inimitable sweetness and expression.

But though expert in every description of plain needle-work, she was an utter novice in the manufacture of all those elegant nothings, which are so serviceable to fine ladies in their warfare against time. Though she moved with unstudied dignity and peerless grace, we are obliged to confess, that the seclusion of her native village had doomed her to ignorance of the art of dancing, that she had never entered a ball-room less capacious than the horizon, nor performed with a partner more illustrious than the schoolmaster's daughter. Her knowledge of music, too, was extremely limited. Lady Harriet had indeed tried to teach her to play on the piano-forte; but the attempt, after costing Laura many a full heart, and many a watery eye, was relinquished as vain. Though the child learnt with unusual facility whatever was taught her by her father or Mrs Douglas, and though she was already remarkable for the sweetness with which she warbled her woodnotes wild, she no sooner approached the piano-forte, than an invincible stupidity seemed to seize on all her faculties. This was the more mortifying, as it was the only one of her ladyship's accomplishments which she ever personally attempted to communicate to her daughter. Lady Harriet was astonished at her failure. It could proceed, she thought, from nothing but obstinacy. But the appropriate remedy for obstinacy, only aggravated the symptoms, and, after all, Laura was indebted to Colonel Hargrave's tuition for so much skill as enabled her to accompany her own singing.

Laura had more than once felt her deficiency in these fashionable arts, on seeing them exhibited by young ladies, who, to use their own expression, had returned from *finishing themselves* at a boarding-school, and she feared that this blank in her education might prove a fatal bar to her being employed as a governess. But another and a greater obstacle lay before her – she was utterly unknown. The only patrons whose recommendation she could command, were distant and obscure; and what mother would trust the minds and the manners of her children to the formation of a stranger? She knew not the ostrich-like daring of fashionable mothers. This latter objection seemed equally hostile to her being received in quality of companion by those who might be inclined to exchange subsistence and protection for relief from solitude; and Laura, almost despairing, knew not whither to turn her eye.

One path indeed invited her steps, a path bright with visions of rapture, warm with the sunshine of love and pleasure; but the flaming sword of Heaven guarded the entrance; and as often as her thoughts reverted that way, the struggle was renewed which forces the choice from the pleasing to the right. No frequency of return rendered this struggle less painful. Laura's prudence had slept, when a little vigilance might have saved her many an after pang; and she had long paid, was still long to pay, the forfeit of neglecting that wisdom which would guard 'with all diligence' the first beginnings of even the most innocent passions. Had she curbed the infant-strength of an attachment which, though it failed to warp her integrity, had so deeply wounded her peace, how had she lessened the force of that temptation, which lured her from the rugged ascent, where want and difficulty were to be her companions; which enticed her to the flowery bowers of pleasure with the voice and with the smile of Hargrave!

Yet Laura had resisted a bribe more powerful than any consideration merely selfish could supply; and she blushed to harbour a thought of yielding to her own inclinations what she had refused to a parent's wants, to a parent's prayer. Her heart filled as she called to mind how warmly Montreville had seconded the wishes of her lover, how resolutely she had withstood his will; and it swelled even to bursting at the thought that the vow was now fatally made void, which promised, by every endearment of filial love, to atone for this first act of disobedience. 'Dearest, kindest of friends,' she cried, 'I was inflexible to thy request – thy last request! and shall I now recede? now, when, perhaps, thou art permitted to behold and to approve my motive; perhaps permitted to watch me still – permitted with higher power to guard, with less erring wisdom to direct me! And, Thou, who, in matchless condescension, refusest not to be called Father of the fatherless – Thou, who, in every difficulty canst guide, from every danger canst protect thy children, let, if Thou see it good, the Heavens, which are thy throne, be all my covering, the earth, which is thy footstool, be all my bed; but suffer me not to wander from Thee, the only source of peace and joy, to seek them in fountains unhallowed and forbidden.'

Religious habits and sentiments were permanent inmates of Laura's breast. They had been invited and cherished, till, like familiar friends, they came unsolicited; and, like friends, too, their visits were most frequent in adversity. But the more ardent emotions of piety, are, alas! transient guests with us all; and, sinking from the flight which raised her for a time above the sorrows and the wants of earth, Laura was again forced to shrink from the gaunt aspect of poverty, again to turn a wistful eye towards a haven of rest on this side the grave.

Young as she was, however, she had long been a vigilant observer of her own actions, and of their consequences; and the result was an immutable conviction, that no heartfelt comfort could, in any circumstances, harbour with wilful transgression. As wilful transgression, she considered her marriage with a man whose principles she had fatal reason to distrust. As a rash defiance of unknown danger; as a desperate daring of temptations whose force was yet untried, as a desertion of those arms by which alone she could hope for victory in her Christian combat, Laura considered the hazardous enterprize which, trusting to the reformation of a libertine, would expose her to his example and his authority, his provocations and his associates. Again she solemnly renewed her resolution never, by wilfully braving temptation, to forego the protection of Him who can dash the fulness of worldly prosperity with secret bitterness, or gladden with joys unspeakable the dwelling visited by no friend but Him, cheered by no comfort save the light of his countenance.

Hargrave's letter served rather to fortify the resolution which it was intended to shake; for Laura was not insensible to the indelicacy which did not scorn to owe to her necessities a consent which he had in vain tried to extort from her affection. Though pleased with his liberality, she was hurt by his supposing that she could have so far forgotten the mortal offence which he had offered her, as to become his debtor for any pecuniary favour; and, as nothing could be further from her intention than to owe any obligation to Colonel Hargrave, she did not hesitate a moment to return the money. When she had sealed the card in which she inclosed it, she again returned to the contemplation of her dreary prospects; and half hopelessly examined the possibilities of subsistence. To offer instruction to the young, or amusement to the old, in exchange for an asylum from want and danger, still appeared to her the most eligible plan of life; and again she weighed the difficulty of procuring the necessary recommendations.

Lady Pelham occurred to her. Some claim she thought she might have had to the patronage of so near a relation. But who should identify her? who should satisfy Lady Pelham that the claim of relationship did indeed belong to Laura? Had she been previously known to her aunt, her difficulties would have been at an end; now she would probably be rejected as an impostor; and she gave a sigh to the want of foresight which had suffered her to rejoice in escaping an interview with Lady Pelham.

After much consideration, she determined to solicit the recommendations of Mrs Douglas and the De Courcy family; and, until she could avail herself of these, to subsist, in some obscure lodging, by the labour of her hands. In the meantime, it was necessary to remove immediately from her present abode. The day following was the last when she could claim any right to remain there; and she proceeded to make preparations for her departure.

With a bleeding heart she began to arrange whatever had belonged to Montreville; and paused, with floods of tears, upon every relic now become so sacred. She entered his closet. His was the last foot that had pressed the threshold. His chair stood as he had risen from it. On the ground lay the cushion yet impressed with his knees – his Bible was open as he had left it. One passage was blistered with his tears; and there Laura read with emotions unutterable – 'Leave to me thy fatherless children, and I will preserve them alive.' Her recent wounds thus torn open, with agony which could not be restrained, she threw herself upon the ground; and, with cries of anguish, besought her father to return but for one short hour to comfort his desolate child. 'Oh I shall never, never see him more,' said she, – 'all my cries are vain,' – and she wept the more because they were in vain. Soon, however, she reproached herself with her immoderate sorrow, soon mingled its accents with those of humble resignation; and the vigorous mind recovering in devotion all its virtuous energy, she returned, wtih restored composure, to her melancholy labours.

In her father's writing desk she found an unfinished letter. It began 'My dear De Courcy,' – and Laura was going to read it with the awe of one who listens to the last words of a father, when she remembered having surprised her father while writing it, and his having hastily concealed it from her sight. She instantly folded it without further acquaintance with its contents, except that her own name caught her eye. Continuing to arrange the papers, she observed a letter addressed to herself in a hand which she did not remember to have seen. It was Lady Pelham's answer to that in which Laura had announced her mother's death. She perceived that it might furnish an introduction to her aunt; and with a sensation of gratitude she remembered that she had been accidentally prevented from destroying it.

Lady Pelham was elder by several years than her sister Lady Harriet. Her father, a saving painstaking attorney, died a few months after she was born. His widow, who, from an idea of their necessity, had concurred in all his economical plans, discovered with equal surprise and delight, that his death had left her the entire management of five-and-forty thousand pounds. This fortune, which she was to enjoy during her life, was secured, in the event of her demise, to little Miss Bridget; and this arrangement was one of the earliest pieces of information which little Miss Bridget received. For seven years the little heiress was, in her mother's undisguised opinion, and consequently in her own, the most important personage upon the face of this terrestrial globe. But worldly glories are fleeting. Lord Winterfield's taste in stewed carp had been improved by half a century's assiduous cultivation. Now the widow Price understood the stewing of carp better than any woman in England, so his Lordship secured to himself the benefit of her talent by making her Lady Winterfield. In ten months after her marriage, another young lady appeared, as much more important than Miss Bridget, as an earl is than an attorney. Fortune, however, dispensed her gifts with tolerable equality. Beauty and rank, indeed, were all on the side of Lady Harriet, but the wealth lay in the scale of Miss Price; for Lord Winterfield, leaving the bulk of his property to the children of his first marriage, bequeathed to his youngest daughter only five thousand pounds. These circumstances procured to Miss Price another advantage, for she married a baronet with a considerable estate, while Lady Harriet's fate stooped to a lieutenant in a marching regiment. After ten years, which Lady Pelham declared were spent in uninterrupted harmony, Sir Edward Pelham died. The exclusive property of his wife's patrimony had been strictly secured to her; and, either thinking such a provision sufficient for a female, or moved by a reason which we shall not at present disclose, Sir Edward bestowed on the nephew who inherited his title, his whole estate, burthened only with a jointure of five hundred pounds a-year, settled upon Lady Pelham by her marriage-contract. Of his daughter, and only child, no mention was made in his testament; but Sir Edward, during the last years of his life, had acquired the character of an oddity, and nobody wondered at his eccentricities. At the commencement of her widowhood, Lady Pelham purchased a villa in — —shire, where she spent the summer, returning in the winter to Grosvenor Street; and this last was almost the only part of her history which was known to Laura. Even before Lady Harriet's marriage, little cordiality had existed between the sisters. From the date of that event, their intercourse had been almost entirely broken off; and the only attention which Laura had ever received from her aunt, was contained in the letter which she was now thankfully contemplating. Her possession of this letter, together with her acquaintance with the facts to which it related, she imagined would form sufficient proof of her identity; and her national ideas of the claims of relationship, awakened a hope of obtaining her aunt's assistance in procuring some respectable situation.

Determined to avail herself of her fortunate discovery, she quitted her father's apartments; and, carrying with her her credential, lost no time in repairing to Grosvenor Street. Nor did she experience the reluctance which she had formerly felt towards an interview with Lady Pelham; for she was fully sensible of the difference between a petitioner for charity and a candidate for honourable employment. Besides, there is no teacher of humility like misfortune; and Laura's spirits were too completely subdued to anticipate or to notice diminutive attacks upon her self-consequence. She still, however, with constitutional reserve, shrunk from intruding upon a stranger; and she passed and repassed the door, examining the exterior of the house, as if she could thence have inferred the character of its owner, before she took courage to give one gentle knock.

A footman opened the door, and Laura, faltering, inquired if Lady Pelham was within. From Laura's single knock, her humble voice, and her yet more humble habit, which, in ten month's use, had somewhat faded from the sober magnificence of black, the man had formed no very lofty idea of the visitor's rank. He answered, that he believed his lady was not at home; but half-afraid of dismissing some person with whom she might have business, he spoke in a tone which made Laura a little doubt the truth of his information. She inquired at what time she might be likely to gain access to Lady Pelham; and, as she spoke, threw back her cape veil, unconscious how successfully she was pleading her own cause. Struck with a countenance whose candour, sweetness, and beauty, won a way to every heart, the man gazed at her for a moment with vulgar admiration, and then throwing open the door of a little parlour, begged her to walk in, while he inquired whether his lady were visible. He soon returned, telling

Laura that Lady Pelham would receive her in a few minutes.

During these few minutes, Laura had formed a hundred conjectures concerning her aunt's person, voice, and manner. She wondered whether she resembled Lady Harriet; whether her own form would recal to Lady Pelham the remembrance of her sister. At every noise her heart fluttered – at every step she expected the entrance of this relation, on whom perhaps so much of her future fate might depend; and she held her breath that she might distinguish her approach. A servant at last came to conduct her to his mistress; and she followed him, not without a feeling of awe, into the presence of her mother's sister.

That sentiment, however, by no means gathered strength when she took courage to raise her eyes to the plain little elderly person to whom she was introduced, and heard herself addressed in the accents of cheerful familiarity. Laura, with modest dignity, made known her name and situation. She spoke of her mother's death, and the tears trickled from her eyes – of her father's, and in venting the natural eloquence of grief, she forgot that she came to interest a stranger. Lady Pelham seemed affected; she held her handkerchief to her eyes, and remained in that attitude for some time after Laura had recovered self-possession. Then, throwing her arms round her lovely niece, she affectionately acknowledged the relationship, adding, 'Your resemblance to my poor sister cannot be overlooked, and yet in saying so, I am far from paying you a compliment.'

After shewing Lady Pelham her own letter, and mentioning such circumstances as tended to confirm her identity, Laura proceeded to detail her plans, to which her Ladyship listened with apparent interest. She inquired into Laura's accomplishments, and seemed pondering the probability of employing them with advantage to the possessor. After a few moments silence, she said, 'That short as their acquaintance had been, she thought she could perceive that Laura had too much sensibility for a dependent situation. But we shall talk of that hereafter,' continued she. 'At present, your spirits are too weak for the society of strangers; – and mine,' added her Ladyship, with a sigh, 'are not much more buoyant than your own.' Laura looked up with the kindly interest which, whether she herself were joyful or in sadness, sorrow could always command with her; and her aunt answered her glance of inquiry, by relating, that her only daughter and heiress, had eloped from her a few days before, with an artful young fellow without family or fortune. 'She deceived me by a train of the basest artifices,' said Lady Pelham, 'though she might have known that her happiness was my chief concern; and that, to secure it, I might have been brought to consent to any thing. Yet with the closest secrecy she misled – with the most unfeeling coldness left me. Her disobedience I might have forgiven – her deceit I never can; or, if as a Christian I forgive, I never, never can forget it.'

Lady Pelham had talked herself out of breath; and Laura, not quite understanding this kind of Christian forgiveness, was silent, because she did not well know what to say. She felt, however, compassion for a parent, deserted by her only child, and the feeling was legible in a countenance peculiarly fitted for every tender expression.

There are some degrees of sorrow which increase in acuteness, at least which augment in vehemence of expression, by the perception of having excited sympathy. Weak fires gather strength from radiation. After a glance at Laura, Lady Pelham melted into tears, and continued, 'I know not how I had deserved such treatment from her; for never had she reason to complain of me. I have always treated her with what I must call unmerited kindness.'

Laura now ventured a few conciliating words. 'She will feel her error, Madam, – she will strive by her after-life to atone –' Lady Pelham immediately dried her eyes, 'No, no, my dear,' interrupted she, 'you don't know her – you have no idea of the hardness of her unfeeling heart. Rejoice, sweet girl, that you have no idea of it. For my part, though sensibility is at best but a painful blessing, I would not exchange it for the most peaceful apathy that can feel for nothing but itself. I must have something to love and cherish. You shall be that something. You shall live with me, and we shall console each other.'

On another occasion, Laura might have been disposed to canvass the nature of that sensibility which could thus enlarge to a stranger on the defects of an only child. Indeed she was little conversant even with the name of this quality. Her own sensibility she had been taught to consider as a weakness to be subdued, not as an ornament to be gloried in; and the expansion of soul which opens to all the sorrows and to all the joys of others, she had learnt to call by a holier name – to regulate by a nobler principle. But she was little disposed to examine the merits of a feeling to which she owed the offer of an unsolicited asylum. Her heart swelling with gratitude, she clasped Lady Pelham's hand between her own, and while tears streamed down her face, 'Kind considerate friend,' she cried, 'why,

why were you not known to us while my father could have been sensible to your kindness!'

After Lady Pelham had repeated her proposal in more detail, and Laura had thankfully acceded to it, they remained in conversation for some time longer. Lady Pelham shewed that she had much wit, much vivacity, and some information; and, after settling that Laura should next day become an inmate in Grosvenor Street, they separated, mutually delighted with each other. Lady Pelham applauded herself for a generous action, and, to the interest which Laura awakened in every breast, was added in Lady Pelham's all the benevolence of self-complacency. Laura, on the other hand, did not dream that any fault could harbour in the unsuspicious liberal heart which had believed the tale, and removed the difficulties of a stranger. She did not once dream that she owed her new asylum to any motives less noble than disinterested goodness.

No wonder that her Ladyship's motive escaped the penetration of Laura, when it even evaded her own. And yet no principle could be more simple in its nature, or more constant in its operation, than that which influenced Lady Pelham; but the Proteus put on so many various forms, that he ever evaded detection from the subject of his sway. In the meantime, the desire of performing a generous action – of securing the gratitude of a feeling heart – of patronizing a poor relation, were the only motives which her Ladyship acknowledged to herself, when she offered protection to Laura. An idea had, indeed, darted across her right honourable mind, that she might now secure a humble companion at a rate lower than the usual price of such conveniences: a momentary notion, too, she formed of exciting the jealousy of her daughter, by replacing her with so formidable a competitor for favour; but these, she thought, were mere collateral advantages, and by no means the circumstances which fixed her determination. The resolution upon which she acted, was taken, as her resolutions generally were, without caution; and she expressed it, as her custom was, the moment it was formed. Laura was scarcely gone, however, when her aunt began to repent of her precipitancy, and to wish, as she had often occasion to do, that she had taken a little more time for consideration. But she comforted herself, that she could at any time get rid of her charge, by recommending Laura to one of the situations which she had mentioned as her choice; and the lady knew it would not be difficult to find one more lucrative than that upon which her niece was entering; for how could she possibly offer wages to so near a relation, or insult with the gift of a trifling sum a person of Laura's dignity of deportment? These reasons, Lady Pelham alleged to herself, as sufficient grounds for a resolution never to affront her niece by a tender of pecuniary favours.

While these thoughts were revolving in Lady Pelham's mind, Laura had reached her home; and, on her knees, was thanking Providence for having raised up for her a protector and a friend, and praying that she might be enabled to repay, in affectionate and respectful duty, a part of the debt of gratitude which she owed to her benefactress. The rest of the evening she spent in preparing for her removal – in ruminating on her interview with her aunt, and in endeavouring to compose, from the scanty materials which she possessed, a character of this new arbitress of her destiny. From Lady Pelham's prompt decision in favour of a stranger, from her unreserved expression of her feelings, from her lively manner and animated countenance, Laura concluded that she was probably of a warm temper, susceptible, and easily wounded by unkindness or neglect, but frank, candid, and forgiving. Laura wished that she had better studied her aunt's physiognomy. What she recollected of it was quite unintelligible to her. She laboured in vain to reconcile the feminine curvatures of the nose and forehead with the inflexible closing of the mouth, and the hard outline of the chin, where lurked no soft relenting line.

But however the countenance might puzzle conjecture, of the mind she harboured not a doubt; Lady Pelham's, she was persuaded, was one of those open generous souls, which the young and unwary are always prepared to expect and to love – souls having no disguise, and needing none. Now this was precisely the character which Lady Pelham often and sincerely drew of herself: and who ought to have been so intimately acquainted with her Ladyship's dispositions?

CHAPTER XX

—————————•—————————

IT was not without hesitation that Laura formed her resolution to conceal from Hargrave her place of abode. She felt for the uneasiness which this concealment would cause him. She feared that her desertion might remove one incitement to a virtuous course. But she considered, that while their future connection was doubtful, it was imprudent to strengthen by habitual intercourse their need of each other's society; and she reflected, that she could best estimate his character from actions performed beyond the sphere of her influence. Her watchful self-distrust made her fear to expose her resolution to his importunities; and she felt the impropriety of introducing into her aunt's family, a person who stood on terms with her which she did not choose to explain. These reasons induced her to withhold from Hargrave the knowledge of her new situation; and, certain that if it were known to Mrs Stubbs or her servants he would soon be master of the secret, she left no clue by which to trace her retreat. Perhaps, though she did not confess it to herself, she was assisted in this act of self-command by a latent hope, that as she was now to be introduced to a society on his own level, Hargrave might not find the mystery quite inscrutable.

She was kindly welcomed by Lady Pelham, and took possession of a small but commodious apartment, where she arranged her drawing-materials, together with the few books she possessed, intending to make that her retreat as often as her aunt found amusement or occupation independent of her. She resolved to devote her chief attention to making herself useful and entertaining to her patroness. In the first, she derived hopes of success, from Lady Pelham's declared incapacity for all employments that are strictly feminine. The second, she thought, would be at once easy and pleasant, for

Lady Pelham was acute, lively, and communicative. This latter quality she possessed in an unusual degree, and yet Laura found it difficult to unravel her character. In general, she saw that her aunt's understanding was bright; she was persuaded that in general her heart was warm and generous; but the descent to particulars baffled Laura's penetration. Lady Pelham could amuse – could delight; she said many wise, and many brilliant things; but her wisdom was not always well-timed, and her brilliant things were soap-bubbles in the sun, sparkling and highly coloured, but vanishing at the touch of him who would examine their structure. Lady Pelham could dispute with singular acuteness. By the use of ambiguous terms, by ingenious sophistry, by dexterously shifting from the ground of controversy, she could baffle, and perplex, and confound her opponents: but she could not argue; she never convinced. Her opinions seemed fluctuating, and Laura was sometimes ready to imagine that she defended them, not because they were just, nor even because they were her own, but merely because she had called them so; for with a new antagonist she could change sides, and maintain the opposite ground with equal address.

In spite of all the warmth of heart for which she gave her heart credit, Laura soon began to imagine that Lady Pelham had no friends. Among all the acquaintances whom she attracted and amused, no one seemed to exchange regard with her. The gaiety of pleasure never softened in her presence into the tenderness of affection. Laura could not discover that there existed one being from whose failings Lady Pelham respectfully averted her own sight, while reverently veiling them from the eyes of others. A few, a very few, seemed to be the objects of Lady Pelham's esteem; those of her love Laura could not discover. Towards her, however, her aunt expressed a strong affection; and Laura continued to persuade herself, that if Lady Pelham had no friends, it was because she was surrounded by those who were not worthy of her friendship.

As she appeared to invite and to desire unreserved confidence, Laura had soon made her acquainted with the narrative of her short life, excepting in so far as it related to Hargrave. At the detail of the unworthy advantage which Warren had taken of Montreville's inability to enforce his claim for the annuity, Lady Pelham broke out into sincere and vehement expressions of indignation and contempt; for no one more cordially abhorred oppression, or despised meanness in others. She immediately gave directions to her man of business to attempt bringing the affair to a conclusion, and even to threaten Warren with a prosecution in case of his refusal. Virtuous resistance of injustice was motive sufficient for this action. Pity that Lady Pelham should have sought another in the economy and ease with which it promised to provide for an indigent relative! Mr Warren was no sooner informed that the poor obscure unfriended Laura was the niece of Lady Pelham, and the inmate of her house, than he contrived to arrive at a marvellous certainty that the price of the annuity had been paid, and that the mistake in the papers relating to it originated in mere accident. In less than a fortnight the informality was rectified, and the arrears of the annuity paid into Laura's hands; the lawyer having first, at Lady Pelham's desire, deducted the price of his services.

With tears in her eyes, Laura surveyed her wealth, now of diminished value in her estimation. 'Only a few weeks ago,' said she, 'how precious had this been to me. – But now! – Yet it is precious still,' said she, as she wiped the tears away, 'for it can minister occasions of obedience and usefulness.' That very day she dispatched little presents for each of Mrs Douglas's children, in which use was more considered than show; and in the letter which announced her gifts, she inclosed half the remaining sum to be distributed among her own poor at Glenalbert. That her appearance might not discredit her hostess, she next proceeded to renew her wardrobe; and though she carefully avoided unnecessary expence, she consulted not only decency but elegance in her attire. In this, and all other matters of mere indifference, Laura was chiefly guided by her aunt; for she had early observed that this lady, upon all occasions, small as well as great, loved to exercise the office of dictatrix. No person could have been better fitted than Laura to conciliate such a temper; for on all the lesser occasions of submissions she was as gentle and complying as she was inflexible upon points of real importance. In their conversations, too, though Laura defended her own opinions with great firmness, she so carefully avoided direct contradiction or sarcastic retort, impatience in defeat, or triumph in victory, that even Lady Pelham could scarcely find subject of irritation in so mild an antagonist. In some respects, their tempers seemed to tally admirably. Lady Pelham had great aptitude in detecting errors, Laura a genius for remedying them. Difficulty always roused her Ladyship's impatience, but she found an infallible resource in the perseverance of Laura. In short, Laura contrived so many opportunities, or seized with such happy art those which presented themselves, of ministering to the comfort or convenience of her aunt, that she became both respectable and necessary to her; and this was, generally speaking, the utmost extent of Lady Pelham's attachments.

Lady Pelham sometimes spoke of her daughter, and Laura never missed the opportunity of urging a reconciliation. She insisted that the rights of natural affection were unalienable; that as they did not rest upon the merits, so neither could they be destroyed by the unworthiness either of parents or of children. The mother answered, with great impatience, that Laura's argument was entirely founded on prejudice; that it was true that for the helplessness of infancy, a peculiar feeling was provided; but that in all animals this peculiar feeling ceased as soon as it was no longer essential to the existence of the individual. 'From thenceforth,' added she, 'the regard must be founded on the qualities of the head and heart; and if my child is destitute of these, I can see no reason why I should prefer her to the child of any other woman.' 'Ah!' said Laura, tears of grateful recollection rushing down her cheek, 'some parents have loved their child with a fervour which no worth of hers could merit.' The gush of natural sensibility for this time averted the rising storm; but the next time that Laura renewed her conciliatory efforts, Lady Pelham, growing more vehement as she became herself convinced that she was in the wrong, burst into a paroxysm of rage; and, execrating all rebellious children, and their defenders, commanded Laura in future to confine her attention to what might concern herself.

The humbling spectacle of a female face distorted with passion was not quite new to Laura. Undismayed, she viewed it with calm commiseration; and mildly expressing her sorrow for having given offence, took up her work and left the ferment to subside at leisure. Her Ladyship's passion soon cooled; and, making advances with a sort of surly condescension, she entered on a new topic. Laura answered exactly as if nothing disagreeable had happened; and Lady Pelham could not divine whether her niece commanded her countenance, or her temper. Upon one principle of judging the lady had grounds for her doubt; she herself had sometimes commanded her countenance – her temper never.

Laura not only habitually avoided giving or taking offence, but made it a rule to extinguish its last traces by some act of cordiality and good-will. This evening, therefore, she proposed, with a grace which seemed rather to petition a favour than to offer a service, to attempt a portrait of her aunt. The offer was accepted wth pleasure, and the portrait begun on the following day. It proved a likeness, and a favourable one. Lady Pelham was kinder than ever. Laura avoided the prohibited subject, and all was quiet and serene. Lady Pelham at last herself reverted to it; for indeed she could not long forbear to speak upon any topic that roused her passions. No dread of personal inconvenience could deter Laura from an act of justice or mercy, and she again steadily pronounced her opinion. But aware that one who would persuade must be careful not to irritate, she expressed her sentiments with still more cautious gentleness than formerly; and perceiving that her aunt was far more governed by passion than by reason, she quitted argument for entreaty. By these means she avoided provoking hostility, though she failed to win compliance. Lady Pelham seemed to be utterly impenetrable to entreaty, or to take pride in resisting it, and Laura had only to hope that time would favour her suit.

Lady Pelham mentioned an intention of moving early to the country, and Laura rejoiced in the prospect of once more beholding the open face of Heaven – of listening to nature's own music – of breathing the light air of spring. She longed to turn her ear from the discords of the city to the sweet sounds of peace – her eye from countenances wan with care, flushed with intemperance, or ghastly with famine, to cheeks brown with wholesome exercise, or ruddy with health and contentment – to exchange the sight of dusky brick walls, and walks overlooked by thousands, for the sunny slope or the sheltered solitary lane. Lady Pelham took pleasure in describing the beauties of Walbourne, and Laura listened to her with interest, anticipating eagerly the time when she should inhabit so lovely, so peaceful scene. But that interest and eagerness rose to the highest, when she accidentally discovered that the De Courcy family were Lady Pelham's nearest neighbours in the country.

The want of something to love and cherish, which was with her Ladyship a mere form of speech, was with Laura a real necessity of nature; and though it was one which almost every situation could supply, since every creature that approached her was the object of her benevolence, yet much of the happiness of so domestic a being depended on the exercise of the dearer charities, and no one was more capable of a distinguishing preference than Laura. She had a hearty regard for the De Courcy family. She revered Mrs De Courcy; she liked Harriet; and bestowed on Montague her cordial esteem and gratitude. This gratitude had now acquired a sacred tenderness; for it was associated in her mind with the remembrance of a parent. De Courcy's self-denial had cheered her father's sick-bed, his benevolence gladdened her father's heart, and his self-denial appeared more venerable, his benevolence more endearing.

Having written to inform Harriet of the change in her situation, she discovered from her answer a new proof of De Courcy's friendship, in the fruitless journey which he had made to relieve her, and she regretted that her caution had deprived her of an opportunity of seeing and thanking him for all his kindness. 'Yet, if we had met,' said she, 'I should probably have acted as I have done a thousand times before; left him to believe me an insensible, ungrateful creature, for want of courage to tell him that I was not so.' She longed, however, to see De Courcy; for with him she thought she could talk of her father – to him lament her irreparable loss, dwell with him on the circumstances that aggravated her sorrow – on the prospects which mingled that sorrow with hope. This was a subject on which she never entered with Lady Pelham any farther than necessity required – real sorrow has its holy ground, on which no vulgar foot must tread. The self-command of Laura would have forbidden her, in any situation, to darken with a settled gloom the sunshine of domestic cheerfulness; but Lady Pelham had in her somewhat which repels the confidence of grief. Against all the arrows of misfortune, blunted at least as they rebound from the breasts of others, she seemed to 'wear a charmed life.' She often indeed talked of sensibility, and reprobated the want of it as the worst of faults; but the only kind of it in which she indulged rather inclined to the acrimonious than the benevolent, and Laura began to perceive, that however her aunt might distinguish them in others, irascible passions and keen feelings were in herself synonymous.

After the effort of giving and receiving the entertainment which Lady Pelham constantly offered, and as constantly exacted in return, Laura experienced a sensation of recovered freedom when the arrival of a visitor permitted her to escape to her own apartment. She saw nobody but her aunt, and never went abroad except to church. Thus, during a fortnight which she had passed in Grosvenor Street she had heard nothing of Hargrave. She was anxious to know whether he visited Lady Pelham; for, with rustic ignorance, she imagined that all people of condition who resided in the same town must be known to each other; but she had not courage to ask, and searched in vain for his name among the cards that crowded the table in the lobby. Though she was conscious of some curiosity to know how he employed the hours which her absence left vacant, she did not own to herself that she was at all concerned in a resolution which she took, to inquire in person whether any letters had been left for her with Mrs Stubbs. She did not choose to commit the inquiry to a servant, because she would not condescend to enjoin her messenger to secrecy as to the place of her abode; and she continued resolved to give her lover no clue to discover it.

Accordingly, she early one morning set out in a hackney-coach, which she took the precaution to leave at some distance from her old lodgings, ordering it to wait her return. Fanny was delighted to see her, and charmed with the improvement of her dress, and the returning healthfulness of her appearance; but the landlady eyed her askance, and surlily answered to her inquiry for her letters, that she would bring the only one she had got; muttering, as she went to fetch it, something of which the words 'secret doings' were all that reached Laura's ear. 'There, Miss,' said the ungracious Mrs Stubbs, 'there's your letter, and there's the queer scrawl it came wrapped up in.' 'Mr De Courcy's hand,' cried Laura surprised, but thinking, from its size, that some time would be required to read it, she deferred breaking the seal till she should return to her carriage. 'I suppose you're mistaken, Miss,' said Mrs Stubbs; 'Mr De Courcy was here twice the day it came, and he never said a word of it.'

Laura now tremulously inquired whether she might be permitted to visit her father's room; but being roughly answered that it was occupied, she quietly prepared to go. As Fanny followed her through the garden, to open the gate for her, Laura, a conscious blush rising to her face, inquired whether any body else had inquired for her since her departure. Fanny, who was ready to burst with the news of Hargrave's visit, and who was just meditating how she might venture to introduce it, improved this occasion of entering on a full detail of his behaviour. With the true waiting-maid-like fondness for romance, she enlarged upon all his extravagancies, peeping side-long now and then under Laura's bonnet, to catch encouragement from the complacent simper with which such tales are often heard. But no smile repaid her eloquence. With immoveable seriousness did Laura listen to her, gravely revolving the strange nature of that love which could so readily amalgamate with rage and jealousy, and every discordant passion. She was hurt at the indecorum which exposed these weaknesses to the observation of a servant; and with a sigh reflected, that, to constitute the happiness of a woman of sense and spirit, a husband must be possessed of qualities respectable as well as amiable.

Fanny next tried, whether what concerned De Courcy might not awaken more apparent interest; and here she had at least a better opportunity to judge of the effect of her narrative, for Laura stopped and turned full towards her. But Fanny had now no transports to relate, except De Courcy's indignation of Mrs Stubbs' calumny; and it was not without hesitating, and qualifying, and apologizing, that the girl ventured to hint at the insinuation which her mistress had thrown out. She had at last succeeded in raising emotion, for indignant crimson dyed Laura's cheeks, and fire flashed from her eyes. But Laura seldom spoke while she was angry; and again she silently pursued her way. 'Pray, Madam,' said the girl as she was opening the gate, 'do be so good as to tell me where you live now, that nobody may speak ill of you before me?' 'I thank you, my good girl,' returned Laura, a placid smile again playing on her countenance; 'but my character is in no danger. – You were kind to us, Fanny, when you knew that we could not reward you; accept of this from me;' and she put five guineas into her hand. 'No, indeed, Ma'am,' cried Fanny, drawing back her hand and colouring; 'I was civil for pure good will, and –.' Laura, whose sympathy with her inferiors was not confined to her bodily wants, fully understood the feeling that revolts from bartering for gold alone the service of the heart. 'I know it my dear,' answered she, in an affectionate tone; 'and believe me, I only mean to acknowledge, not to repay, your kindness.' Fanny, however, persisted in her refusal, and Laura obliged her to leave her at the gate, where, with tears in her eyes, the girl stood gazing after her till she was out of sight. 'I'm sure,' said she, turning towards the house as Laura disappeared, 'I'm sure she was made to be a queen, for the more one likes her, the more she frightens one.'

As soon as Laura was seated in her carriage, she opened her packet, and with momentary disappointment examined its contents. 'Not one line!' she cried in a tone of mortification; and then turned to the envelope addressed to Mrs Stubbs. Upon comparing this with the circumstances which she had lately heard, she at once comprehended De Courcy's intention of serving her by stealth, foregoing the credit due to his generosity. She wondered, indeed, that he had neglected to disguise his hand-writing in the superscription. 'Did he think,' said she, 'that I could have forgotten the writing that has so often brought comfort to my father?' She little guessed how distant from his mind was the repose which can attend to minute contrivance.

Delighted to discover a trait of character which tallied so well with her preconceived opinion, she no sooner saw Lady Pelham than she related it to her aunt, and began a warm eulogium on De Courcy's temper and dispositions. Lady Pelham coldly cut her short, by saying, 'I believe Mr De Courcy is a very good young man, but I am not very fond of prodigies. One can't both wonder and like at a time; your men with two heads are always either supposititious or disgusting.' This speech was one of the dampers which the warm heart abhors; real injury could not more successfully chill affection or repress confidence. It had just malice and just truth enough to be provoking; and for the second time that day Laura had to strive with the risings of anger. She was upon the point of saying, 'So, aware of the impossibility of being at once wonderful and pleasing, your Ladyship, I suppose, aims at only one of these objects;' but ere the sarcasm found utterance, she checked herself, and hastened out of the room, with the sensation of having escaped from danger. She retired to write to De Courcy a letter of grateful acknowledgement; in which, after having received Lady Pelham's approbation, she inclosed his gift, explaining the circumstances which now rendered it unnecessary.

Lady Pelham was not more favourable to the rest of the De Courcy family than she had been to Montague. She owned, indeed, that Mrs De Courcy was the best woman in the world, but a virtue, she said, so cased in armour, necessarily precluded all grace or attraction. Harriet she characterized as a little sarcastic coquette. Laura, weary of being exposed to the double peril of weakly defending, or angrily supporting her attacked friends, ceased to mention the De Courcys at all; though, with a pardonable spirit of contradiction, she loved them the better for the unprovoked hostility of Lady Pelham. The less she talked of them, the more she longed for the time when she might, unrestrained, exchange with them testimonies of regard. The trees in the Park, as they burst into leaf, stimulated Laura's desire for the country; and while she felt the genial air of spring, or listened to the early song of some luckless bird caged in a neighbouring window, or saw the yellow glories of the crocus peeping from its unnatural sanctuary, she counted the days till her eyes should be gladdened with the joyous face of nature. Only a fortnight had now to pass before her wish was to be gratified, for Lady Pelham intended at the end of that time to remove to Walbourne.

Laura was just giving the finishing touches to her aunt's portrait when a visitor was announced; and, very unwilling to break off at this interesting crisis, Lady Pelham having first scolded the servant for letting in her friend, desired him to shew the lady into the room where Laura was at work. The usual speeches being made, the lady began – 'Who does your ladyship think bowed to me *en passant* just as I was getting out of the carriage? – Why, Lady Bellamer! – Can you conceive such effrontery?' 'Indeed, I think, in common modesty, she should have waited for your notice!' 'Do you know, I am told on good authority that Hargrave is determined not to marry her.' Laura's breath came short. – 'He is very right,' returned Lady Pelham. 'A man must be a great fool to marry where he has had such damning proofs of frailty.' Laura's heart seemed to pause for a moment, and then to redouble its beating. – 'What Hargrave can this be?' thought she; but she durst not inquire. 'I hear,' resumed the lady, 'that his uncle is enraged at him, and more for the duel than the *crim. con.*' The pencils dropped from Laura's hand. – Fain would she have inquired, what she yet so much dreaded to know; but her tongue refused its office. 'I see no cause for that,' returned Lady Pelham; 'Hargrave could not possibility refuse to fight after such an affair.' 'Oh certainly not!' replied the lady; 'but Lord Lincourt thinks, that in such a case, Hargrave ought to have insisted upon giving Lord Bellamer the first fire, and then have fired his own pistol in the air. – But, bless me, what ails Miss Montreville,' cried the visitor, looking at Laura, who, dreadfully convinced, was stealing out of the room. 'Nothing,' answered Laura; and fainted.

Lady Pelham called loudly for help; and, while the servants were administering it, stood by conjecturing what could be the cause of Laura's illness; wondering whether it could have any possible connection with Colonel Hargrave; or whether it were the effect of mere constitutional habit.

The moment Laura shewed signs of recollection, Lady Pelham began her interrogation. 'What has been the matter my dear? What made you ill? Did any thing affect you? Are you subject to faintings?' Laura remained silent, and, closing her eyes, seemed deaf to all her aunt's questions. After a pause, Lady Pelham renewed the attack. – 'Have you any concern with Colonel Hargrave, Laura?' 'None,' answered Laura, with a smile of ineffable bitterness; and again closing her eyes, maintained an obstinate silence. Weary of ineffectual inquiries, Lady Pelham quitted her, giving orders, that she should be assisted into bed, and recommending to her to take some rest.

Vain advice! Laura could not rest! From the stupor which had overpowered her faculties, she awoke to the full conviction, that all her earthly prospects were for ever darkened. Just entering on life, she seemed already forsaken of all its hopes, and all its joys. The affections which had delighted her youth were torn from the bleeding soul; no sacred connection remained to bless her maturity; no endearment awaited her decline. In all her long and dreary journey to the grave, she saw no kindly resting-place. Still Laura's hopes and wishes had never been bounded to this narrow sphere; and when she found here no rest for the sole of her foot, she had, in the promises of religion, an ark whither she could turn for shelter. But how should she forget that these promises extended not to Hargrave. How shut her ear to the dread voice which, in threatening the adulterer and the murderer, denounced vengeance against Hargrave! With horror unspeakable she considered his incorrigible depravity; with agony, revolved its fearful consequences.

Yet, while the guilt was hateful in her eyes, her heart was full of love and compassion for the offender. The feeling with which she remembered his unfaithfulness to her had no resemblance to jealousy. 'He has been misled,' she cried; 'vilely betrayed by a wretch, who has taken advantage of his weakness. Oh how could she look on that form, that countenance, and see in them only the objects of a passion, vile as the heart that cherished it.' – Then she would repent of her want of candour. – 'I am unjust, I am cruel,' she said, 'thus to load with all the burden of this foul offence, her who had perhaps the least share in it. – No! He must have been the tempter; it is not in woman to be so lost.'

But in the midst of sorrow, whose violence seemed at times almost to confuse her reason, she never hesitated for a moment on the final dissolution of her connection with Hargrave. She formed no resolution on a subject where no alternative seemed to remain, but assumed, as the foundation of all her plans of joyless duty, her eternal separation from Hargrave; a separation final as death. By degrees she became more able to collect her thoughts; and the close of a sleepness night found her exercising the valuable habit of seeking in herself the cause of her misfortunes. The issue of her self-examination was the conviction, that she had bestowed on a frail fallible creature, a love disproportioned to the merits of any created thing; that she had obstinately clung to her idol after she had seen its baseness; and that now the broken reed whereon she had leaned was taken away, that she might restore her trust and her love where alone they were due. That time infallibly brings comfort even to the sorest sorrows – that if we make not shipwreck of faith and a good conscience, we save from the storms of life the materials of peace at least – that lesser joys become valuable when we are deprived of those of keener relish – are lessons which even experience teaches but slowly: and Laura had them yet in a great measure to learn. She was persuaded that she should go on mourning to the grave. What yet remained of her path of life seemed to lie through a desert waste, never more to be warmed with the sunshine of affection; never more to be brightened with any ray of hope, save that which beamed from beyond the tomb. She imagined, that lonely and desolate she should pass through life, and joyfully hail the messenger that called her away; like some wretch, who, cast alone on a desert rock, watches for the sail that is to waft him to his native land.

The despair of strong minds is not listless or inactive. The more Laura was convinced that life was lost as to all its pleasing purposes, the more was she determined that it should be subservient to useful ends. Earthly felicity, she was convinced, had fled for ever from her grasp; and the only resolution she could form, was never more to pursue it; but, in the persevering discharge of the duties which yet remained to her, to seek a preparation for joys which earth has not to bestow. That she might not devote to fruitless lamentation the time which was claimed by duty, she, as soon as it was day, attempted to rise, intending to spend the morning in acts of resignation for herself, and prayers that pardon and repentance might be granted to him whose guilt had destroyed her peace. But her head was so giddy, that, unable to stand, she was obliged to return to her bed. It was long ere she was again able to quit it. A slow fever seized her, and brought her to the brink of the grave. Her senses, however, remained uninjured, and she had full power and leisure to make those reflections which force themselves upon all who are sensible of approaching dissolution. Happy were it, if all who smart under disappointment, would anticipate the hour which will assuredly arrive, when the burden which they impatiently bear shall appear to be lighter than vanity! The hand which is soon to be cold, resigns without a struggle the baubles of the world. Its cheats delude not the eye that is for ever closing. A deathbed is that holy ground where the charms of the enchanter are dissolved; where the forms which he had clothed with unreal beauty, or aggravated to gigantic horror, are seen in their true form and colouring. In its true form and colouring did Laura behold her disappointment; when, with characteristic firmness, she had wrung from her attendants, a confession of her danger. With amazement she looked back on the infatuation which could waste on any concern less than eternal, the hopes, the fears, and the wishes which she had squandered on a passion which now seemed trivial as the vapour scattered by the wind.

At last, aided by the rigid temperance of her former life, and her exemplary patience in suffering, the strength of her constitution began to triumph over her disorder. As she measured her steps back to earth again, the concerns which had seemed to her reverting eye diminished into nothing, again swelled into importance; but Laura could not soon forget the time when she had seen them as they were; and this remembrance powerfully aided her mind in its struggle to cast off its now disgraceful shackles. Yet bitter was the struggle; for what is so painful as to tear at once from the breast what has twined itself with every fibre, linked itself with every hope, stimulated every desire, and long furnished objects of intense, of unceasing interest. The heart which death leaves desolate, slowly and gently resigns the affection to which it has fondly clung. It is permitted to seek indulgence in virtuous sorrow, to rejoice in religious hope; and even memory brings pleasure dear to the widowed mind. But she who mourned the depravity of her lover, felt that she was degraded by her sorrow; hope was, as far as he was concerned, utterly extinguished; and memory presented only a mortifying train of weaknesses and self-deceptions.

But love is not that irremediable calamity which romance has delighted to paint, and the vulgar to believe it. Time, vanity, absence, or any of a hundred other easy remedies, serves to cure the disease in the mild form in which it affects feeble minds, while more Herculean spirits tear off the poisoned garment, though it be with mortal anguish. In a few weeks, the passion which had so long disturbed the peace of Laura was hushed to lasting repose; but it was the repose of the land where the whirlwind has passed; dreary and desolate. Her spirits had received a shock from which it was long, very long, ere she could rouse them. And he who had ceased to be an object of passion, still excited an interest which no other human being could awaken.

Many a wish did she breathe for his happiness; many a fervent prayer for his reformation. In spite of herself, she lamented the extinguished love, as well as the lost lover; and never remembered, without a heavy sigh, that the season of enthusiastic attachment was, with her, passed never to return.

But she cordially wished that she might never again behold the cause of so much anguish and humiliation. She longed to be distant from all chance of such a meeting, and was anxious to rcover strength sufficient for her journey to Walbourne. Lady Pelham only waited for her niece's recovery; and, as soon as she could bear the motion of a carriage, they left London.

CHAPTER XXI

———————•———————

THEY travelled slowly, and Laura's health seemed improved by the journey. The reviving breeze of early spring, the grass field exchanging its winter olive for a bright green, the ploughman's cheerful labour, the sower whistling to his measured step, the larch trees putting forth the first and freshest verdure of the woods, the birds springing busy from the thorn, were objects whose cheering influence would have been lost on many a querulous child of disappointment. But they were industriously improved to their proper use by Laura, who acknowledged in them the kindness of a father, mingling with some cordial drop even the bitterest cup of sorrow. The grief which had fastened on her heart she never obtruded on her companion. She behaved always with composure, sometimes with cheerfulness. She never obliquely reflected upon Providence, by insinuations of the hardness of her fate, nor indulged in splenetic dissertations on the inconstancy and treachery of man. Indeed she never, by the most distant hint, approached the ground of her own peculiar sorrow. She could not, without the deepest humiliation, reflect that she had bestowed her love on an object so unworthy. She burnt with shame at the thought of having been so blinded, so infatuated, by qualities merely external. While she remembered, with extreme vexation, that she had suffered Hargrave to triumph in the confession of her regard, she rejoiced that no other witness existed of her folly – that she had never breathed the mortifying secret into any other ear.

In this frame of mind, she repelled with calm dignity every attempt which Lady Pelham made to penetrate her sentiments; and behaved in such a manner that her aunt could not discover whether her spirits were affected by languor of body or by distress of mind. Laura,

indeed, had singular skill in the useful art of repulsing without
offence; and Lady Pelham, spite of her curiosity, found it impossible
to question her niece with freedom. Notwithstanding her youth, and
her almost dependent situation, Laura inspired Lady Pelham with
involuntary awe. Her dignified manners, her vigorous understanding,
the inflexible integrity which descended even to the regulation of her
forms of speech, extorted some degree of respectful caution from one
not usually over careful of giving offence. Lady Pelham was herself at
times conscious of this restraint; and her pride was wounded by it. In
Laura's absence, she sometimes thought of it with impatience, and
resolved to cast it off at their next interview; but whenever they met,
the unoffending majesty of Laura effaced her resolution, or awed her
from putting it in practice. She could not always, however, refrain
from using that sort of innuendo which is vulgarly called *talking at*
one's companions; a sort of rhetoric in great request with those who
have more spleen than courage, and which differs from common
scolding only in being a little more cowardly and a little more
provoking. All her Ladyship's dexterity and perseverance in this
warfare were entirely thrown away. Whatever might be meant, Laura
answered to nothing but what met the ear; and, with perverse
simplicity, avoided the particular application of general propositions.
Lady Pelham next tried to coax herself into Laura's confidence. She
redoubled her caresses and professions of affection. She hinted, not
obscurely, that if Laura would explain her wishes, they would meet
with indulgence, and even assistance, from zealous friendship. Her
professions were received with gratitude – her caresses returned with
sensibility; but Laura remained impenetrable. Lady Pelham's temper
could never brook resistance; and she would turn from Laura in a
pet: – the pitiful garb of anger which cannot disguise, and dares not
show itself. But Laura never appeared to bestow the slightest notice
on her caprice, and received her returning smiles with unmoved
complacency. Laura would fain have loved her aunt; but in spite of
herself, her affection took feeble root amidst these alternations of
frost and sunshine. She was weary of hints and insinuations; and felt
not a little pleased that Lady Pelham's fondness for improving and
gardening seemed likely to release her, during most of the hours of
daylight, from this sort of sharpshooting warfare.

   It was several days after their arrival at Walbourne before they
were visited by any of the De Courcy family. Undeceived in his hopes
of Laura's regard, Montague was almost reluctant to see her again.

Yet from the hour when he observed Lady Pelham's carriage drive up the avenue, he had constantly chosen to study at a window which looked towards Walbourne. Laura, too, often looked towards Norwood, excusing to herself the apparent neglect of her friends, by supposing that they had not been informed of her arrival. Lady Pelham was abroad superintending her gardeners, and Laura employed in her own apartment, when she was called to receive De Courcy. For the first time since the wreck of all her hopes, joy flushed the wan cheek of Laura, and fired her eye with transient lustre. 'I shall hear the voice of friendship once more,' said she, and she hastened down stairs with more speed than suited her but half-recovered strength. 'Dear Mr De Courcy,' she cried, joyfully advancing towards him! De Courcy scarcely ventured to raise his eyes. Laura held out her hand to him. 'She loves a libertine!' thought he, and, scarcely touching it, he drew back. With grief and surprise, Laura read the cold and melancholy expression of his face. Her feeble spirits failed under so chilling a reception; and while, in a low tremulous voice, she inquired for Mrs and Miss De Courcy, unbidden tears wandered down her cheeks. In replying, Montague again turned his eyes towards her; and, shocked at the paleness and dejection of her altered countenance, remembered only Laura ill and in sorrow. 'Good Heavens!' he exclaimed, with a voice of the tenderest interest, 'Laura – Miss Montreville, you are ill – you are unhappy!' Laura, vexed that her weakness should thus extort compassion, hastily dried her tears. 'I have been ill,' said she, 'and am still so weak that any trifle can discompose me.' Montague's colour rose. 'It is then a mere trifle in her eyes,' thought he, 'that I should meet her with coldness.' 'And yet,' continued Laura, reading mortification in his face, 'it is no trifle to fear that I have given offence where I owe so much gratitude.' 'Talk not of gratitude, I beseech you,' said De Courcy, 'I have no claim, no wish, to excite it.' 'Mr De Courcy,' cried Laura, bursting into tears of sad remembrance, 'has all your considerate friendship, all your soothing kindness to him who is gone, no claim to the gratitude of his child!' Montague felt that he stood at this moment upon dangerous ground, and he gladly availed himself of this opportunity to quit it. He led Laura to talk of her father, and of the circumstances of his death; and was not ashamed to mingle sympathetic tears with those which her narrative wrung from her. In her detail, she barely hinted at the labour by which she had supported her father; and avoided all allusion to the wants which she had endured. If any thing could have exalted her in the opinion of De Courcy, it would have been the humility which sought no praise to recompense exertion – no admiration to reward self-denial. 'The praise of man is with her as nothing,' thought he, gazing on her wasted form and faded features with fonder adoration than ever he had looked on her full blaze of beauty. 'She has higher hopes and nobler aims. And can such a creature love a sensualist! – Now, too, when his infamy cannot be unknown to her! Yet it must be so – she has never named him, even while describing scenes where he was daily present; and why this silence if he were indifferent to her? If I durst mention him! – but I cannot give her pain.'

From this reverie De Courcy was roused by the entrance of Lady Pelham, whose presence brought to his recollection the compliments and ceremonial which Laura had driven from his mind. He apologized for having delayed his visit; and excused himself for having made it alone, by saying that his sister was absent on a visit to a friend, and that his mother could not yet venture abroad; but he warmly entreated that the ladies would wave etiquette, and see Mrs De Courcy at Norwood. Lady Pelham, excusing herself for the present on the plea of her niece's indisposition, urged De Courcy to direct his walks often towards Walbourne; in charity, she said, to Laura, who being unable to take exercise, spent her forenoons alone, sighing, she supposed, for some Scotch Strephon. Laura blushed; and Montague took his leave, pondering whether the blush was deepened by any feeling of consciousness.

'She has a witchcraft in her that no language can express – no heart withstand –,' said De Courcy, suddenly breaking a long silence, as he and his mother were sitting tête à tête after dinner. 'Marriage is an excellent talisman against witchcraft,' said De Courcy, gravely; 'but Miss Montreville has charms that will delight the more the better they are known. There is such noble simplicity, such considerate benevolence, such total absence of vanity and selfishness in her character, that no woman was ever better fitted to embellish and endear domestic life.' 'Perhaps in time,' pursued De Courcy, 'I might have become not unworthy of such a companion – But now it matters not,' – and, suppressing a very bitter sigh, he took up a book which he had of late been reading to his mother. 'You know, Montague,' said Mrs De Courcy, 'I think differently from you upon this subject. I am widely mistaken in Miss Montreville, if she could bestow her preference on a libertine, knowing him to be such.' Montague took involuntary pleasure in hearing this opinion repeated; yet he had less faith in it than he usually had in the opinions of his mother. 'After the emotion which his presence excited,' returned he, – 'an emotion which even these low people – I cannot think of it with patience,' cried he, tossing away the book, and walking hastily up and down the room. 'To betray her weakness, her *only* weakness, to such observers – to the wretch himself.' 'My dear De Courcy, do you make no allowance for the exaggeration, the rage for the romantic, so common to uneducated minds?' 'Wilkins could have no motive for inventing such a tale,' replied De Courcy; 'and if it had *any* foundation, there is no room for doubt.' 'Admitting the truth of all you have heard,' resumed Mrs De Courcy, 'I see no reason for despairing of success. If I know any thing of character, Miss Montreville's attachments will ever follow excellence, real or imaginary. Your worth is real, Montague; and, as such, it will in time approve itself to her.' 'Ah, Madam, had her affection been founded even on imaginary excellence, must it not now have been completely withdrawn – now, when she cannot be unacquainted with his depravity. Yet she loves him still. – I am sure she loves him. Why else this guarded silence in regard to him? – Why not mention that she permitted his daily visits – saw him even on the night when her father died?' 'Supposing,' returned Mrs De Courcy, 'that her affection had been founded on imaginary excellence, might not traces of the ruins remain percep- tible, even after the foundation had been taken away? Come, come, Montague, you are only four-and-twenty, you can afford a few years patience. If you act prudently, I am convinced that your perseverance will succeed; but if it should not, I know how you can bear disappointment. I am certain that your happiness depends not on the smile of any face, however fair.' 'I am ashamed,' said De Courcy, 'to confess how much my peace depends upon Laura. You know I have no ambition – all my joys must be domestic. It is as a husband and a father that all my wishes must be fulfilled – and all that I have ever fancied of venerable and endearing, so meet in her, that no other woman can ever fill her place.' 'That you have no ambition,' replied De Courcy, 'is one of the reasons why I join in your wishes. If your happiness had any connection with splendour, I should have regretted your choice of a woman without fortune. But all that is necessary for your comfort you will find in the warmth of heart with which Laura will return your affection – the soundness of principle with which she will assist you in your duties. Still, perhaps, you might find these qualities in others, though not united in an equal degree; but I confess to you, Montague, I despair of your again meeting with a woman whose dispositions and pursuits are so congenial to your own; – a woman, whose cultivated mind and vigorous understanding, may make her the companion of your studies as well as of your lighter hours.' 'My dear mother,' cried De Courcy, affectionately grasping her hand, 'it is no wonder that I persecute you with this subject so near to my heart for you always, and you alone, support my hopes. Yet should I even at last obtain this treasure, I must ever regret that I cannot awaken the enthusiasm which belongs only to a first attachment.' 'Montague,' said Mrs De Courcy, smiling, 'from what romance have you learnt that sentiment? However I shall not attempt the labour of combating it, for I prophesy that, before the change can be necessary, you will learn to be satisfied wth being loved with reason.' 'Many a weary day must pass before I can even hope for this cold preference. Indeed, if her choice is to be decided by mere rational approbation, why should I hope that it will fall upon me? Yet, if it be possible, her friendship I will gain – and I would not exchange it for the love of all her sex.' 'She already esteems you – highly esteems you,' said Mrs De Courcy; 'and I repeat that I think you need not despair of animating esteem into a warmer sentiment. But will you profit by my knowledge of my sex, Montague? You know, the less use we make of our own wisdom, the fonder we grow of bestowing it on others in the form of advice! Keep your secret carefully, Montague. Much of your hope depends on your caution. Pretensions to a pre-engaged heart are very generally repaid with dislike.' Montague promised attention to his mother's advice; but added, that he feared he should not long be able to follow it. 'I am a bad dissembler,' said he, 'and on this subject, it is alleged, that ladies are eagle-eyed.' 'Miss Montreville, of all women living, has the least vanity,' returned Mrs De Courcy; 'and you may always reinforce your caution, by recollecting that the prepossessions which will certainly be against you as a lover, may be secured in your favour as a friend.'

The next day found De Courcy again at Walbourne; and again he enjoyed a long and private interview with Laura. Though their conversation turned only on indifferent subjects, De Courcy observed the settled melancholy which had taken possession of her mind. It was no querulous complaining sorrow, but a calm sadness, banishing all the cheerful illusions of a life which it still valued as the preparation for a better. To that better world all her hopes and wishes seemed already fled; and the saint herself seemed waiting, with resigned desire, for permission to depart. De Courcy's fears assigned to her melancholy its true cause. He would have given worlds to know the real state of her sentiments, and to ascertain how far her attachment had survived the criminality of Hargrave. But he had not courage to probe the painful wound. He could not bear to inflict upon Laura even momentary anguish; perhaps he even feared to know the full extent of those regrets which she lavished on his rival. With scrupulous delicacy he avoided approaching any subject which could at all lead her thoughts towards the cause of her sorrow, and never even seemed to notice the dejection which wounded him to the soul.

'The spring of her mind is for ever destroyed,' said he to Mrs De Courcy, 'and yet she retains all her angelic benevolence. She strives to make pleasing to others, the objects that will never more give pleasure to her.' Mrs De Courcy expressed affectionate concern, but added, 'I never knew of a sorrow incurable at nineteen. We must bring Laura to Norwood, and find employments for her suited to her kindly nature. Meanwhile do you exert yourself to rouse her; and, till she is well enough to leave home, I shall freely resign to her all my claims upon your time.' De Courcy faithfully profited by his mother's permission, and found almost every day an excuse for visiting Walbourne. Sometimes he brought a book which he read aloud to the ladies; sometimes he borrowed one, which he chose to return in person; now he wished to shew Laura a medal, and now he had some particularly fine flower-seeds for Lady Pelham. Chemical experiments were an excellent pretext; for they were seldom completed at a visit, and the examination of one created a desire for another. Laura was not insensible to his attentions. She believed that he attributed whatever was visible of her depression to regrets for her father; and she was by turns ashamed of permitting her weakness to wear the mask of filial piety, and thankful that she escaped the degradation of being pitied as a love-sick girl. But love had now no share in Laura's melancholy. Compassion, strong indeed to a painful excess, was the only gentle feeling that mingled with the pain of remembering Hargrave. Who that, in early youth, gives way to the chilling conviction, that nothing on earth will ever again kindle a wish or a hope, can look without sadness on the long pilgrimage that spreads before them? Laura looked upon hers with resigned sadness, and a thousand times repeated to herself that it was but a point, compared with what lay beyond. Hopeless of happiness, she yet forced herself to seek short pleasure in the charms of nature, and the comforts of affluence; calling them the flowers which a bountiful hand had scattered in the desert which it was needful that she should tread alone. It was with some surprise that she found De Courcy's visits produced pleasure without requiring an effort to be pleased; and with thankfulness she acknowledged that the enjoyments of the understanding were still open to her, though those of the heart were for ever withdrawn.

In the meantime her health improved rapidly, and she was able to join in Lady Pelham's rambles in the shrubbery. To avoid particularity, De Courcy had often quitted Laura to attend on these excursions; and he rejoiced when her recovered strength allowed him to gratify, without imprudence, the inclination which brought him to Walbourne. It often, however, required all his influence to persuade her to accompany him in his walks with Lady Pelham. Her Ladyship's curiosity had by no means subsided. On the contrary, it was rather exasperated by her conviction that her niece's dejection had not been the consequence of ill health, since it continued after that plea was removed; and Laura was constantly tormented with oblique attempts to discover what she was determined should never be known.

Lady Pelham's attacks were now become the more provoking, because she could address her hints to a third person, who, not aware of their tendency, might strengthen them by assent, or unconsciously point them as they were intended. She contrived to make even her very looks tormenting, by directing, upon suitable occasions, sly glances of discovery to Laura's face; where, if they found out nothing, they at least insinuated that there was something to find out. She was inimitably dexterous and indefatigable in improving every occasion of innuendo. Any subject, however irrelevant, furnished her with the weapons of her warfare. 'Does this flower never open any further?' asked Laura, shewing one to De Courcy – 'No,' said Lady Pelham, pushing in between them; 'that close thing, wrapped up in itself, never expands in the genial warmth; it never shews its heart.' 'This should be a precious book with so many envelopes,' said Laura, untying a parcel. – 'More likely,' said Lady Pelham, with a sneer, 'that what is folded in so many doublings won't be worth looking into.' 'This day is cold for the season,' said De Courcy, one day warming himself after his ride. 'Spring colds are the most chilling of any,' said Lady Pelham. 'They are like a repulsive character in youth; one is not prepared for them. The frosts of winter are more natural.'

Lady Pelham was not satisfied with using the occasions that presented themselves; she invented others. When the weather confined her at home, and she had nothing else to occupy her, she redoubled her industry. 'Bless me, what a sentiment!' she exclaimed, affecting surprise and consternation, though she had read the book which contained it above twenty times before. – "Always live with a friend as if he might one day become an enemy!" I can conceive nothing more detestable. A cold-hearted suspicious wretch! Now to a friend I could not help being all open and ingenuous but a creature capable of having such a thought, could never have a friend.' Lady Pelham ran on for a while, contrasting her open ingenuous self, with the odious character which her significant looks appropriated to her niece, till even the mild Laura was provoked to reply. Fixing her eyes upon her aunt with calm severity, 'If Rochefoucault meant,' said she, 'that a friend should be treated with suspicious confidence, as if he might one day betray, I agree with your Ladyship in thinking such a sentiment incompatible with friendship; but we are indebted to him for a useful lesson, if he merely intended to remind us that it is easy to alienate affection without proceeding to real injury, and very possible to forfeit esteem without incurring serious guilt.' – The blood mounted in Lady Pelham's face, but the calm austerity of Laura's eye imposed silence, and she continued to turn over the pages of her book, while her niece rose and left the room. She then tossed it away, and walked angrily up and down, fretting between baulked curiosity and irritated pride. Finding every other mode of attack unsuccessful, she once more resolved to have recourse to direct interrogation. This intention had been frequently formed, and as often defeated by the dignified reserve of Laura; but now that Lady Pelham felt her pride concerned, she grew angry enough to be daring. It was so provoking to be kept in awe by a mere girl, a dependent. Lady Pelham could at any time meditate herself into a passion; she did so on the present occasion; and accordingly resolved and executed in the same breath. She followed Laura to her apartment, determined to insist upon knowing what affected her spirits. Laura received her with a smile so gracious, that, spite of herself, her wrath began to evaporate. Conceiving it proper, however, to maintain an air of importance, she began with an aspect that announced hostility, and a voice in which anger increased intended gravity into surliness. 'Miss Montreville, if you are at leisure I wish to speak with you.' 'Quite at leisure, Madam,' said Laura in a tone of the most conciliating good humour, and motioning her aunt to a seat by the fire. 'It is extremely unpleasant,' said Lady Pelham, tossing her head to escape the steady look of inquiry which Laura directed towards her; 'It is extremely unpleasant (at least if one has any degree of sensibility) to live with persons who always seem unhappy, and are always striving to conceal it, especially when one can see no cause for their unhappiness.' 'It must indeed be very distressing,' returned Laura mentally preparing for her defence. 'Then I wonder,' said Lady Pelham, with increased acrimony of countenance, 'why you choose to subject me to so disagreeable a situation. It is very evident that there is something in your mind which you are either afraid or ashamed to tell.' 'I am sorry,' said Laura, with unmoved self-possession, 'to be the cause of any uneasiness to your Ladyship. I do not pretend that my spirits are high, but I should not have thought their depression unaccountable. The loss of my only parent, and such a parent! is reason for lasting sorrow; and my own so recent escape from the jaws of the grave, might impose seriousness upon levity itself.' – 'I have a strong notion, however, that none of these is the true cause of your penseroso humours. Modern misses don't break their hearts for the loss of their parents. – I remember you fainted away just when Mrs Harrington was talking to me of Colonel Hargrave's affair; and I know he was quartered for a whole year in your neighbourhood.'

Lady Pelham stopped to reconnoitre her niece's face, but without success; for Laura had let fall her scissors, and was busily seeking them on the carpet. 'Did you know him?' inquired Lady Pelham. 'I have seen him,' answered Laura, painfully recollecting how little she had really known him. 'Did he visit at Glenalbert?' resumed her Ladyship, recovering her temper, as she thought she had discovered a clue to Laura's sentiments. 'Yes, Madam, often;' replied Laura, who having, with a strong effort, resumed her self-possession, again submitted her countenance to inspection. 'And he was received there as a lover I presume?' said Lady Pelham, in a tone of interrogation. Laura fixed on her aunt one of her cool commanding glances. 'Your Ladyship,' returned she, 'seems so much in earnest, that if the question were a little less extraordinary, I should almost have thought you expected a serious answer.' Lady Pelham's eyes were not comfortably placed, and she removed them by turns to every piece of furniture in the apartment. Speedily recovering herself, she returned to the charge. 'I think, after the friendship I have shewn, I have some right to be treated with confidence.' 'My dear Madam,' said Laura, gratefully pressing Lady Pelham's hand between her own, 'believe me, I am not forgetful of the kindness which has afforded me shelter and protection; but there are some subjects of which no degree of intimacy will permit the discussion. It is evident, that whatever proposals have hitherto been made to me, have received such an answer as imposes discretion upon me. No addresses which I accept shall ever be a secret from your Ladyship – those which I reject I am not equally entitled to reveal.' 'By which I understand you to say, that you have rejected Colonel Hargrave?' said Lady Pelham. 'By no means,' answered Laura, with spirit, 'I was far from saying so. I merely intended to express my persuasion, that you are too generous to urge me on a sort of subject where I ought not to be communicative.' 'Very well, Miss Montreville,' cried Lady Pelham, rising in a pet, 'I comprehend the terms on which you choose that we should live. I may have the honour of being your companion, but I must not aspire to the rank of a friend.' 'Indeed, my dear aunt,' said Laura, in a voice irresistibly soothing, 'I have no earthly wish so strong as to find a real friend in you: but,' added she, with an insinuating smile, 'I shall never earn the treasure with tales of luckless love.' 'Well, Madam,' said Lady Pelham, turning to quit the room, 'I shall take care for the future not to press myself into your confidence; 'and as it is not the most delightful thing in the world to live in the midst of ambuscades, I shall intrude as little as possible on your more agreeable engagements.' 'Pray, don't go,' said Laura with perfect good humour, and holding upon her delicate fingers a cap which she had been making, 'I have finished your cap. Pray have the goodness to let me try it on.' Female vanity is at least a *sexagénaire*. Lady Pelham sent a side glance towards the cap. 'Pray do,' said Laura, taking her hand, and coaxingly pulling her back. 'Make haste then,' said Lady Pelham, sullenly, 'for I have no time to spare.' 'How becoming,' cried Laura, as she fixed on the cap, 'I never saw you look so well in any thing. Look at it;' and she held a looking-glass to her aunt. The ill humour which had resisted the graces of the loveliest face in the world, could not stand a favourable view of her own; and Lady Pelham quitted Laura with a gracious compliment to her genius for millinery, and a declaration, that the cap should be worn the next day, in honour of a visit from Mr De Courcy and Harriet.

The next day the expected guests dined at Walbourne. As Harriet had just returned from her excursion, this was the first time that she had seen Laura, and the meeting gave them mutual pleasure. Harriet seemed in even more than usual spirits; and Laura, roused by the presence of persons whom she loved and respected, shewed a cheerfulness more unconstrained than she had felt since her father's death. Montague, who watched her assiduously, was enchanted to perceive that she could once more smile without effort; and, in the joy of his heart, resumed a gaiety which had of late been foreign to him. But the life of the party was Lady Pelham; for who could be so delightful, so extravagantly entertaining as Lady Pelham could be when she pleased? And she did please this afternoon; for a train of fortunate circumstances had put her into high good humour. She not only wore the becoming cap; but had hit, without difficulty, the most becoming mode of putting it on. The cook had done her office in a manner altogether faultless; and the gardener had brought in such a sallad! its like had never been seen in the county.

Miss De Courcy was extremely anxious that Laura should pass a few days at Norwood. But Laura, remembering the coolness which had of late subsisted between herself and Lady Pelham, and unwilling to postpone her endeavours to efface every trace of it, objected that she could not quit her aunt for such a length of time. Harriet immediately proposed to invite Lady Pelham. – 'I'll set about it this instant, while she's in the vein,' said she. 'This sunshine is too bright to last.' Laura looked very grave, and Harriet hastened to execute her purpose. There is no weakness of their neighbours which mankind so instinctively convert to their own use as vanity. Except to secure Laura's company, Harriet had not the slightest desire for Lady Pelham's. Yet she did not even name her friend while she pressed Lady Pelham so earnestly to visit Norwood, that she succeeded to her wish, and obtained a promise that the ladies should accompany her and her brother home on the following day.

When at the close of an agreeable evening, Laura attended her friend to her chamber, Harriet, with more sincerity than politeness, regretted that Lady Pelham was to join their party to Norwood. 'I wish the old lady would have allowed you to go without her,' said she. 'She'll interrupt a thousand things I had to say to you. However, my mother can keep her in conversation. She'll be so delighted to see you, that she'll pay the penalty without a grudge.' 'I shall feel the more indebted to your mother's welcome,' said Laura, with extreme gravity, 'because she will extend it to a person to whom I owe obligations that cannot be repaid.' Harriet, blushing, apologized for her freedom; and Laura accepting the apology with smiles of courtesy and affection, the friends separated for the night.

CHAPTER XXII

———————•———————

NORWOOD had appeared to Laura to be little more than a mile distant from Walbourne. The swellings of the ground had deceived her. It was more than twice that distance. As the carriage approached Norwood, Laura perceived traces of a noble park, changed from its former purpose to one more useful, though less magnificent. The corn fields were intermixed by venerable avenues, and studded with gigantic elm and oak. Through one of these avenues, straight as a dart, and darkened by the woods that closed over it, the party drove up to a massive gate. In the door of a turreted lodge, overgrown with hornbeam, stood the grey-haired porter, waiting their arrival. He threw open the gate with one hand, and respectfully stood with his hat in the other, while De Courcy checked his horse to inquire for the old man's family.

The avenue now quitted its formality, to wind along the bank of a rapid stream, till the woods suddenly opening to the right, discovered the lawn, green as an emerald, and kept with a neatness truly English. A variety of flowering shrubs were scattered over it, and here and there a lofty forest-tree threw its quivering shadow; while tall spruce-firs, their branches descending to the ground, formed a contrast to its verdure. At the extremity of this lawn stood Norwood, a large castellated building; and, while Laura looked on it, she imagined the interior dull with baronial magnificence.

The carriage drove up to the door, and Laura could not helping smiling at the cordial welcome that seemed to await De Courcy. The great Newfoundland dog that lay upon the steps leapt upon him, and expressed his joy by a hundred clumsy gambols; while John, the old servant whom she had seen in Audley Street, busied himself about his master, with an officiousness that evidently came from the heart, leaving Lady Pelham's attendants to wait upon their mistress and her companions. De Courcy, giving his hand to Lady Pelham, conducted her, followed by Harriet and Laura, into the room where Mrs De Courcy was sitting; and the next moment his heart throbbed with pleasure, while he saw the beloved of his soul locked in his mother's arms.

When the first joy of the meeting was over, Laura had leisure to observe the interior of the mansion, which differed not less from her expectations than from any thing she had before seen. Though it was equally remote from the humble simplicity of her cottage of Glenalbert, and the gaudiness of Lady Pelham's more modern abode, she saw nothing of the gloomy splendour which she had fancied; every thing breathed comfort and repose. The furniture, though not without magnificence, was unadorned and substantial, grandeur holding the second place to usefulness. The marble hall through which she had entered, was almost covered with matting. In the spacious room in which she was sitting, the little Turkey carpet of our forefathers had given place to one of homelier grain but far larger dimensions. The apartment was liberally stored with couches, footstools, and elbow chairs. A harp occupied one window, a piano-forte stood near it; many books were scattered about, in bindings which shewed they were not meant for ornament: and in the chimney blazed a fire which would have done credit to the days of Elizabeth.

The dinner hour was four; and punctual to a moment the dinner appeared, plain, neat, and substantial. It was served without tumult, partaken of with appetite, and enlivened by general hilarity, and good will. When the ladies rose from table, Harriet offered to conduct Laura through the other apartments, which exactly corresponded with those she had seen. The library was spacious; and besides an excellent collection of books, contained globes, astronomical instruments, and cabinets of minerals and coins. A smaller room which opened from it, used as De Courcy's laboratory, was filled with chemical and mechanical apparatus. Comfort, neatness, and peace reigned everywhere, and Norwood seemed a fit retreat for literary leisure and easy hospitality.

Between music, work, and conversation, the evening passed away cheerfully; nor did Laura mark its flight till the great house clock struck nine. The conversation suddenly paused; Harriet laid aside her work; Mrs De Courcy's countenance assumed a pleasing seriousness; and Montague, quitting his place by Laura's side, seated himself in a patriarchal-looking chair at the upper end of the room. Presently John entered, followed by all the domestics of the family. He placed before his master a reading desk and a large bible, and then sat down at a distance with his fellow servants.

With a manner serious and earnest, as one impressed with a just sense of their importance, Montague read a portion of the Holy Scriptures. He closed the volume; and all present sunk upon their knees. In plain but solemn language, he offered a petition in the name of all, that all might be endowed with the graces of the Christian spirit. In the name of all he confessed that they were unworthy of the blessings they implored. In the name of all, he gave thanks for the means of improvement, and for the hopes of glory. He next, more particularly, besought a blessing on the circumstances of their several conditions. Among the joyous faces of this happy household, Laura had observed one alone clouded with sorrow. It was that of a young modest-looking girl in deep mourning, whose audible sobs attested that she was the subject of a prayer which commended an orphan to the Father of the fatherless. The worship was closed; the servants withdrew. A silence of a few moments ensued; and Laura could not help gazing with delight, not unmingled with awe, on the traces of serene benevolence and manly piety, which lingered on the countenance of De Courcy.

'Happy Harriet,' said she, when she was alone with her friend, 'Would that I had been your sister!' Harriet laughed. 'You need not laugh, my dear,' continued Laura, with most unembarrassed simplicity, 'I did not mean your brother's wife, but his sister, and Mrs De Courcy's daughter.'

Though Miss De Courcy was much less in Montague's confidence than her mother, she was not ignorant of his preference for Laura; but Mrs De Courcy had so strongly cautioned her against even hinting this preference to the object of it, that, though she but half guessed the reasons of her mother's injunction, she was afraid to disobey. That Laura was even acquainted with Hargrave was unknown to Harriet; for De Courcy was almost as tenacious of Laura's secret as she herself was, and would as soon have thought of giving up his own heart to the frolics of a kitten, as of exposing that of Laura to the *badinage* of his sister. This kind precaution left Laura perfectly at her ease with Harriet, an ease which would quickly have vanished, had she known her to be acquainted with her humiliating story.

The young ladies had rambled over half the grounds of Norwood before the family had assembled at a cheerful breakfast; and as soon as it was ended, Harriet proposed that Laura should assist her with her advice in composing a water-colour drawing from one of her own pictures. 'We'll leave Lady Pelham and my mother in possession of the drawing-room,' said she, 'for the pictures all hang in the library. I wanted them put up in the sitting-room, but Montague would have them where they are – and so he carried his point, for mamma humours him in everything.' 'Perhaps,' returned Laura, 'Mrs De Courcy thinks that he has some right to dictate in his own house.' 'Well, that's true,' cried Harriet. 'I protest I had forgotten that this house was not my mother's.'

The picture which Miss De Courcy had fixed upon, was that of Leonidas, and Laura would far rather have been excused from interference; yet, as she could not with propriety escape, nothing remained but to summon her composure, and to study anew this resemblance of her unworthy lover. She took her work, and began quietly to superintend Harriet's progress. Their employments did not interrupt conversation; and though Laura's was at first a little embarrassed, she soon recovered her ease. 'Do touch the outline of the mouth for me,' said Harriet; 'I can't hit the resemblance at all.' Laura excused herself, saying, that since her fever, her hand had been unsteady. 'Oh, here's Montague; he'll do it. Come hither Montague, and sketch a much prettier mouth than your own.' De Courcy, who had approached his sister before he understood her request, shrunk back. She could scarcely have proposed an employment less agreeable to him; and he was hastily going to refuse it, when, happening to meet the eye of Laura, in the dread that she should detect his consciousness, he snatched the pencil and began.

Harriet having thus transferred her work, quickly found out other occupation. 'Oh, by the by, my dear,' said she to Laura, 'your Leonidas is the greatest likeness in the world of my old beau, Colonel Hargrave. Bless me, how she blushes! Ah! I see Hargrave has not been so long in Scotland for nothing!' 'Take away that thing, Harriet,' cried De Courcy, quite thrown off his guard, and pushing the drawing from him. 'I see no reason why *everybody* should do for you what you ought to be doing for yourself.' 'Hey-day, what ails the man,' cried Harriet, looking after her brother to the window, whither he had retreated. 'You need not be so angry at me for making Laura blush. I dare say she likes it; it becomes her so well.' 'If you are accustomed to say such strange things to your friends, my dear Harriet,' said Laura, 'the blushes you raise will not always have that advantage. The colourings of anger are not generally becoming.' 'So, with that meek face of yours, you would have me believe that it is downright rage that has made you all scarlet. No, no, my dear – there is rage, and there is the colour of it, too, (pointing to Montague's face); and if you'll put your two heads together before the glass, you will see whether the colours are a bit alike!' Montague, recovering his temper, tried to laugh, and succeeded very ill. 'I don't wonder you laugh,' said Laura, not venturing to look round to him, 'at hearing Harriet, on such slender grounds, exalt such a matter-of-fact person as myself, into the heroine of a romance. But, to spare your imagination, Harriet, I will tell you, that your old beau, as you call him, being the handsomest man I had seen, I saw no harm in making use of his beauty in my picture.' 'Well, I protest,' cried Harriet, 'it was quite by accident I thought of mentioning it, for I had not the least idea that ever you had seen Hargrave.' 'And, now that you have made that mighty discovery,' said De Courcy, endeavouring to appear unconcerned, 'I suppose you'll poison Miss Montreville; for you know you were so in love with Hargrave, that I was obliged to put a rail round the fish-pond to prevent *felo de se*.' 'In love,' said Harriet, yawning, 'ay, so I was indeed, for three whole days when I had nothing else to do. But only think of the sly girl never even to name him to me! Well! well! I shall worm it all out of her when we are by ourselves, though she won't blab before you.' 'I will give you an opportunity this moment,' said De Courcy, who, quite unable to bear the subject any longer, determined to make his mother interrupt it, and immediately went in search of her. In a few minutes Mrs De Courcy appeared, and dismissed her unwilling daughter to escort Lady Pelham to the flower-garden, while Laura preferred remaining at home.

At the next opportunity, Harriet executed her threat, in so far as depended upon her. She did what she could to rally Laura out of her secret, but she totally failed of success. Laura, now upon her guard, not only evaded making any discovery, but, by the easy indifference of her answers, convinced Harriet that there was nothing to discover. Indeed, her suspicion was merely a transient thought, arising from Laura's confusion at her sudden attack, and scarcely outlived the moment that gave it birth; though the emotion which Montague had shewn, confirmed his sister in the belief of his attachment to Laura.

The subject thus entirely dropped which Laura could never approach without pain, the time of her visit to Norwood glided away in peace and comfort, every day lessening the dejection which she had believed, nay almost wished, would follow her to the grave. Still, however, the traces of it were sufficiently visible to the observant eye of love; and Montague found in it an interest not to be awakened by the brightest flashes of gaiety. 'There is a charm inexpressible in her sadness,' said he to Mrs De Courcy. 'I think,' said De Courcy, 'I can observe that that charm is decaying. I think, if it should entirely disappear before your fates are more closely united, you need not lament its departure. These cypresses look graceful bending over the urn there in the vista, but I should not like them to darken the sitting-room.'

The only habit, common to love-lorn damsels, in which Laura indulged, was that of preferring solitary rambles; a habit, however, which had been imbibed long before she had any title to that character. Delighted with the environs of Norwood, she sometimes wandered beyond the dressed ground into the park, where art still embellished without restraining nature. The park might, indeed, have better deserved the name of an ornamented farm; for the lawns were here and there diversified by cornfields, and enlivened by the habitations of the labourers necessary to the agriculturist. These cottages, banished by fashion far from every lordly residence, were contrived so as to unite beauty with usefulness; they gave added interest to the landscape even to the eye of a stranger, but far more to that of De Courcy, for he knew that every one of them contained useful hands or graceful hearts; youth for whom he provided employment, or age whose past services he repaid. Here the blue smoke curled from amidst the thicket; there the white wall enlivened the meadow; here the casement flashed bright with the setting sun; there the woodbine and the creeping rose softened the colouring that would have glared on the eye.

Laura had followed the windings of a little green lane, till the woods which darkened it suddenly opened into a small field, sheltered by them on every side, which seemed to form the territory of a cottage of singular neatness and beauty. In a porch covered with honeysuckle, which led through a flower-garden to the house, a lovely little boy about three years old was playing with De Courcy's great Newfoundland dog. The child was stretching on tiptoe to hug with one arm the neck of his rough companion; while, with the other hand, he was playfully offering the animal a bit of bread, and then snatching it in sport away. Neptune, not used to be so tantalized, made a catch at his prey; but the child succeeded in preserving his prize, and, laughing, hid it behind him. The next moment Laura saw the dog throw him down, and heard a piercing cry. Fearless of personal danger, she ran to his assistance. The child was lying motionless on his face; while, with one huge paw laid on his back, Neptune was standing over him, wagging his tail in triumph. Convinced that the child was unhurt, and that the scream had been caused merely by fear, Laura spoke to the dog, who immediately quitted his posture to fawn upon her. She lifted the child from the ground and carried him towards the cottage. The poor little fellow, pale with terror, clung round her neck; but he no sooner saw himself in safety, than, recovering his suspended faculties, he began to roar with all his might. His cries reached the people in the house, who hastened to inquire into their cause; and Laura was met in the door of the cottage by De Courcy's grey-haired servant, John, who seemed its owner, and a decent old woman, who was his wife.

Laura prefaced her account of the accident by an assurance that the child was not hurt, and the old woman, taking him in her arms, tried to sooth him, while John invited Miss Montreville to enter. She followed him into a room, which, unacquainted as she was with the cleanliness of the English cottages, appeared to her quite Arcadian. While Margaret was busy with her little charge, Laura praised the neatness and comfort of John's abode. 'It is as snug a place as heart can desire, please you, Ma'am,' answered John, visibly gratified; 'and we have every thing here as convenient as in the king's palace, or as my master himself has, for the matter of that.' 'I thought, John, you had lived in Mr De Courcy's house,' said Laura. 'Yes, please you, Ma'am, and so I did, since I was a little fellow no higher than my knee, taken in to run messages, till my young master came of age, and then he built this house for me, that I might just have it to go to when I pleased, without being turned away like; for he knew old folks liked to have a home of their own. So now, of a fine evening, I come home after prayers, and stay all night; and when it's bad weather, I have the same bed as I have had these forty years; not a penny worse than my master's own.' 'And if you are employed all day at Norwood,' said Laura, 'how do you contrive to keep your garden in such nice order?' 'Oh! for the matter of that, Ma'am, my master would not grudge me a day's work of the under gardener any time; no, nor to pay a man to work the little patch for me; but only, as he says, the sweetest flowers are of one's own planting, so, of a fine day he often sends me home for an hour or two in the cool, just to put the little place in order.' 'Mr De Courcy seems attentive to the comfort of every body that comes near him,' said Laura. 'That he is, Madam; one would think he had an affection, like, for every mortal creature, and particularly when they grow old and useless, like me and Margaret. I know who offered him twenty pounds a-year for this house and the bit of field; but he said old folks did not like moving, and he would not put us out of this, even though he could give us one twice as good.' 'And your rent is lower than twenty pounds, I suppose?' said Laura. 'Why sure, Ma'am, we never pay a penny for it. My master,' said John, drawing up his head, and advancing his chest, 'my master has the proper true spirit of a gentleman, and he had it since ever he was born; for it's bred in the bone with him, as the saying is. Why, Ma'am, he had it from a child. – I have seen him, when he was less than that boy there, give away his dinner when he was as hungry as a hound, just because a beggar asked it. – Ay, I remember, one day, just two-and-twenty years ago come July, that he was sitting at the door on my knee, eating his breakfast, and he had asked it half a dozen times from Mrs Martin, for he was very hungry; and she did not always attend to him very well. So, up came a woman leading a little ragged creature; and it looked at Master Montague's bread and milk, and said, 'I wish I had some too.' So, says my master, "here take you some, and I'll take what you leave." – Well, Ma'am, the brat snapped it up all in a trice, and I waited to see what little master would do. – Well, he just laughed as good naturedly! Then I was gong to have got him another breakfast, but my Lady would not let me. "No, No, John!" said my Lady, "we must teach Montague the connection between generosity and self-denial." – These were my Lady's very words.'

By this time Margaret had succeeded in quieting the child; and a double allowance of bread and butter restored all his gaiety. 'Come, Nep,' said he, squatting himself on the ground where Neptune was lying at Laura's feet; 'come, Nep, I'll make friends; and there's half for you, Henry's own dear Nep.' 'Will you sit upon my knee?' said Laura, who was extremely fond of children. The boy looked steadily in her face for a few moments, and then holding out his arms to her, said, 'Yes, I will.' 'Whose charming child is this?' inquired Laura, twisting his golden ringlets round her fingers. The colour rose to old Margaret's furrowed cheek as she answered, 'He is an orphan, Ma'am.' – 'He is our grandson,' said John, and drew his hand across his eyes. Laura saw that the subject was painful, and she inquired no further. She remained for a while playing with little Henry, and listening to John's praises of his master; and then returned homewards.

She was met by De Courcy and Harriet, who were coming in search of her. She related her little adventure, and praised the extraordinary beauty of the child. 'Oh, that's Montague's protegé!' cried Harriet. 'By the by he has not been to visit us since you came; I believe he was never so long absent before since he could see. I have a great notion my brother did not want to produce him to you.' – 'To me!' exclaimed Laura in surprise; 'Why not?' But receiving no answer from Harriet, who had been effectually silenced by a look from De Courcy, she turned for explanation to Montague; who made an awkward attempt to laugh off his sister's attack, and then as awkwardly changed the subject.

For some minutes Laura gravely and silently endeavoured to account for his behaviour. 'His generosity supports this child,' thought she, 'and he is superior to blazoning his charity.' So having, as great philosophers have done, explained the facts to agree with her theory, she was perfectly satisfied, and examined them no more. Association carrying her thoughts to the contemplation of the happiness which De Courcy seemed to diffuse through every circle where he moved, she regretted that she was so soon to exchange the enjoyment of equable unobtrusive kindness, for starts of officious fondness mingling with intervals of cold neglect or peevish importunity.

'Norwood is the Eden of the earth,' said she to Harriet, as they drew their chairs towards the fire, to enjoy a *tête a tête* after the family were retired for the night; 'and it is peopled with spirits fit for paradise. – Happy you, who need never think of leaving it!' 'Bless you, my dear,' cried Harriet, 'there is nothing I think of half so much. – You would not have me be an old maid to comb lapdogs and fatten cats, when I might be scolding my own maids and whipping my own children.' 'Really,' said Laura, 'I think you would purchase even *these* delightful recreations too dearly by the loss of your present society. Sure it were a mad venture to change such a blessing for any uncertainty!' 'And yet, Mrs Graveairs, I have a notion that a certain gallant soldier could inspire you with the needful daring. – Now, look me in the face, and deny it if you can.' Laura did as she was desired; and, with cheeks flushed to crimson, but a voice of sweet austere composure, replied, 'Indeed, Miss De Courcy, I am hurt that you should so often have taxed me, even in sport, with so discreditable a partiality. You cannot be serious in supposing that I would marry an' – adulterer, Laura would have said; but to apply such an epithet to Hargrave was too much for human firmness, and she stopped. 'I declare she is angry,' cried Harriet. 'Well, my dear, since it displeases you, I shan't tease you any more; at least not till I find a new subject. But, pray now, do you intend to practise as you preach. Have your made a vow never to marry?' 'I do not say so,' answered Laura; 'it is silly to assert resolutions which nobody credits. Besides my situation sadly differs from yours. Like the moon, that is rising yonder, I must pursue my course alone. Thousands around me might perhaps warm and enlighten me; but far distant, their influence is lost ere it reaches me. You are in the midst of a happy family, endeared to you by all that is lovely in virtue; all that is sacred in kindred. – I know not what would tempt me to resign your situation.' – 'What would tempt you?' cried Harriet. 'Why a pretty fellow would. But I verily believe you have been taking your cue from Montague; these are precisely his ideas. I think he has set his heart upon making me lead apes.' 'What makes you think so?' inquired Laura. 'Because he finds out a hundred faults to every man that talks nonsense to me. One is poor; and he thinks it folly to marry a beggar. Another is old, though he's rich; and that would be downrightly selling myself. One's a fool, and t'other's cross; and in short there's no end to his freaks. Only the other day he made me dismiss a creature that I believe I should have liked well enough in time. I have not half forgiven him for it yet. Poor Wilmot – and I should have had a nice barouche too!' 'What could possibly weigh with your brother against the barouche?' said Laura, smiling. 'Why, my dear, the saucy wretch told me, as plainly as he civilly could, that Wilmot and I had not a grain of prudence between us; ergo, that we should be ridiculous and miserable. Besides, poor Wilmot once persuaded a pretty girl to play the fool; and though he afterwards did every thing he could to prevail on her to be made an honest woman, the silly thing chose rather to break her heart and die; and, ever since, poor Wilmot has been subject to fits of low spirits.' 'Is it possible, Harriet, that you can talk so lightly of a crime so black in its nature, so dreadful in its consequences: Can it seem a trifle to you to destroy the peace, the innocence of a fellow-creature? Can you smile at remorse that pursued its victim even to the grave?' Tears filled the eyes of Harriet. 'Oh no, my dearest,' she cried, throwing her arms round Laura's neck; 'do not think so hardly of me. – I am a rattle, it is true, but I am not unprincipled.' – 'Pardon my injustice, dearest Harriet,' said Laura, 'in believing, even for a moment, that you were capable of such perversion; and join with me in rejoicing that your brother's influence has saved you from witnessing, from sharing, the pangs of unavailing repentance.' 'Indeed,' said Harriet, 'Montague's influence can do any thing with me; and no wonder. I should be the most ungrateful wretch on earth if I could oppose his wishes. I cannot tell you the thousandth part of the affection he has shewn me. Did you ever hear, my dear, that my father had it not in his power to make any provision for me?' Laura answered that she had never heard the circumstances of the family at all mentioned. 'Do you know,' continued Harriet, 'I am certain that Montague is averse to my marrying, because he is afraid that my poverty, and not my will, consents. But he has himself set that matter to rest; for the very morning after I gave Wilmot his *congé*, Montague presented me with bills for two thousand pounds. The generous fellow told me that he did not offer his gift while Wilmot's suit was pending, lest I should think he bought a right to influence my decision.' 'This is just what I should have expected from Mr De Courcy,' said Laura, the purest satisfaction beaming in her countenance. 'He is ever considerate, ever generous.' 'To tell you that he gives me money,' cried Harriet, rapturously, 'is nothing; he gives me his time, his labour, his affection. Do love him, dear Laura! He is the best of all creatures!' 'Indeed I believe it,' said Laura, 'and I have the most cordial regard for him.' – 'Ah but you must' – Harriet's gratitude to her brother had very nearly been too strong for his secret, and she was on the point of petitioning Laura to return a sentiment warmer than cordial regard, when, recollecting her mother's commands, she desisted; and to fly from the temptation, wished Laura good night, and retired.

It was with sincere regret that Laura, the next day, took leave of her kind hosts. As De Courcy handed her into the carriage, the tears were rising to her eyes: but they were checked by a glance from Lady Pelham, in which Laura thought she could read mingled scorn and anger. Lady Pelham had remarked the improved spirits of her niece; but, instead of rejoicing that any medicine should have 'ministered to a mind diseased,' she was offended at the success of a remedy applied by any other than herself. She was nettled at perceiving that the unobtrusive seriousness of Mrs De Courcy, and the rattling gaiety of Harriet, had effected what all her brilliant powers had not achieved. Her powers, indeed, had been sometimes directed to entertain, but never to console; they had been exerted to purchase admiration, not to win confidence; yet, with a common perverseness, she was angry at their ill success, not sorry for their wrong direction. She did not consider, that real benevolence, or an excellent counterfeit, is the only road to an unadulterated heart. It appeared to her a proof of an ungrateful temper in her niece, that she should yield in so short a time to strangers to whom she owed nothing, what she refused to a relation to whom she owed so much. She had been unable to forbear from venting her spleen in little spiteful remarks, and sly stings, sometimes so adroitly given, that they were unobserved, except by the person who was by degrees becoming accustomed to expect them. The presence of the De Courcy family, however, restrained the expression of Lady Pelham's ill humour; and, as she detested restraint, (a detestation which she always ascribed to a noble ingenuousness of mind), she nestled, with peculiar complacency, into the corner of the carriage which was to convey her to what she called freedom, namely, the liberty to infrine, with impunity, the rights of others. Laura felt that her reluctance to quit Norwood was a bad compliment to her aunt, and she called a smile to her face as she kissed her hand to her kind friends; yet the contrast between their affectionate looks, and the 'lurking devil' in Lady Pelham's eye, did not lessen her regret at the exchange she was making.

Lady Pelham saw the tone of Laura's mind, and she immediately struck up a discord. 'Heaven be praised,' she cried, 'we have at last escaped out of that stupid place! I think it must be something extraordinary that tempts me to spend four days there again.' Laura remained silent; for she disliked direct contradiction, and never spoke what she did not think. Lady Pelham continued her harangue, declaring, 'that your good sort of people were always intolerably tiresome; that clock-work regularity was the dullest thing in nature; that Norwood was another cave of Trophonius; Mrs De Courcy inspired with the soul of a starched old maid; Harriet animated by the joint spirit of a magpie and a monkey; and Montague by that of a methodist parson.' Finally, she again congratulated herself on her escape from such society, and wondered how any body could submit to it without hanging himself. Laura was accustomed to support Lady

Pelham's attacks upon herself with perfect equanimity; but her temper was not proof against this unjust, this unexpected philippic against her friends; and she reddened with anger and disdain, though she had still so much self-command as to reply only, 'Your Ladyship is fortunate in being able to lose, without regret, what *others* find it so difficult to replace.'

Lady Pelham fully understood the emphasis which was laid on the word *others*, but the mortification to her vanity was compensated by the triumph of discovering the vulnerable side of her niece's temper. This was the first time that she had been conscious of power over it, and severely did Laura pay for the momentary negligence which had betrayed the secret. Some persons never feel pleasure without endeavouring to communicate it. Lady Pelham acted upon the converse of this amiable principle; and, as an ill-regulated mind furnished constant sources of pain, a new channel of participation was a precious discovery. As often, therefore, as spleen, jealousy, or malice prompted her to annoyance, she had recourse henceforth to this new-found weapon; and she varied her warfare through all the changes of hints, insinuations, and that mode of attack the most provoking of all, which, aiming at no particular point, becomes the more difficult to parry. During several months, she made it the occasional instrument of her vengeance for the jealousy which she entertained of Laura's increasing intimacy with the De Courcys; an intimacy which she chose to embitter, though she could not break it off, without depriving herself of acquaintances who were visited by the first people in the county.

Her industry in teazing was not confined to Laura. She inflicted a double stroke, by the petulance or coldness with which she sometimes treated the De Courcys. But though Laura was keenly sensible to these petty wrongs done her friends, the injury passed them over without much notice. Harriet repaid them with laughter or sarcasm; while Montague seemed to consider them as wholly unworthy of attention. He continued his visits to Walbourne, and accident at last furnished an excuse for their frequency.

In the course of Lady Pelham's improvements, a difficulty chanced to occur, which a slight knowledge of the elements of mathematics would have enabled her to solve. To supply the want of this knowledge, she had recourse to Mr De Courcy, who removed her perplexity with the ease of one conversant with his subject, and the accuracy of one who speaks to a reasoning creature. Lady Pelham was charmed! She was convinced that 'of all studies that of mathematics must be the most delightful. She imagined it might not be quite impracticable even for a lady, supposing she were so fortunate as to meet with a friend who could assist her.' De Courcy, laughing, offered his services, not, it must be owned, with any idea that they would be accepted. Her Ladyship, however, eagerly embraced the offer; for she was little accustomed to forecast the difficulties of any scheme that entered her brain. In this triumphant expectation that all difficulty would yield to her acuteness, and her brighter abilities gain in a comparison with the plain good-sense of her niece, she obliged Laura to join her in this new pursuit. Upon the study of this science, so little in favour with a sex who reserve cultivation for faculties where it is least wanting, Laura entered with a pleasure that surprised herself, and she persevered in it with an industry that astonished her teacher. Lady Pelham was, for a little while, the companion of her labours; but, at the first difficulty, she took offence at the unaccommodating thing, which shewed no more indulgence to female than to royal indolence. – Forthwith she was fired with a strong aversion to philosophers in bibs, and a horror at *she*-pedants, a term of reproach which a dexterous side-glance could appropriate to her niece, though the author of those memoirs challenges any mortal to say that ever Laura Montreville was heard to mention ellipse or parabola, or to insinuate her acquaintance with the properties of circle or polygon. Nothing moved by Lady Pelham's sneers, Laura continued her studies, impelled partly by the duty of improving the most valuable faculty of an immortal mind, partly by the pleasure which she derived from the study itself. It is true, that her Ladyship's indiscreet use of the secret, made Laura's labours the cause of much merriment to titterers of both sexes; but we have never discovered that De Courcy esteemed her the less for her persevering industry, or loved her the less for this new subject of mutual interest. He watched with delight the restoration of her mind to its full vigour; and as he had never known her in the blaze of youthful gaiety, he was scarcely sensible of the shade which blended the radiance of her mid-day of life with the sober tints of evening.

The impression of her early disappointment was indeed indelible, but it was no longer overwhelming. She had given the reins to her imagination – it had fatally misled her; but its power had sustained an irrecoverable shock, and the sway was transferred to reason. She had dreamed of an earthly heaven, and seen that it was but a dream. All her earthly joys had vanished – yet misery had been almost as transient as delight, and she learned the practical use of a truth which all acknowledge in theory. In the course of four months residence at Walbourne, she recovered a placid cheerfulness, which afterwards continued to be the habitual tenor of her mind. If she looked forward to the future events of her life, it was to resolve that they should be subservient to the great end of her being. If she glanced backward, it was less to lament her disappointment, than to blame the error which had led to it; and she never allowed her thoughts to dwell upon her unworthy lover, except when praying that he might be awakened to a sense of his guilt.

She was chiefly concerned to improve and to enjoy the present; and in this she was successful in spite of the peevish humours of Lady Pelham, mixed occasionally with ebullitions of rage. Those who are furious where they dare, or when the provocation is sufficient to rouse their courage, sometimes chide with impotent perseverance where they are awed from the full expression of their fury: as the sea, which the lightest breeze dashes in billows over the sandbank, frets in puny ripples against the rock that frowns over it. If Lady Pelham's temper had any resemblance to this stormy element, it was not wholly void of likeness to another – for it 'changed as it listed,' without any discoverable reason. It would have lost half its power to provoke, and Laura half the merit of her patient endurance, if it had been permanently diabolical. The current, not only serene but sparkling, would reflect wth added beauty every surrounding object, then would suddenly burst into foam, or settle into a stagnant marsh. Laura threw oil upon the torrent, and suffered the marsh to clear itself. She enjoyed Lady Pelham's wit and vivacity in her hours of good humour, and patiently submitted to her seasons of low spirits, as she complaisantly called them.

Laura at last, undesignedly, opened a new direction to her aunt's spleen. From her first introduction to Lady Pelham, she had laboured assiduously to promote a reconciliation between her aunt and her daughter, Mrs Herbert. Her zeal appeared surprising to Lady Pelham, who could not estimate the force of her motive for thus labouring, to the manifest detriment of her own interest, she being (after Mrs Herbert) the natural heiress of her aunt's fortune. She had seized the moment of complacency; watched the relentings of nature; by turns tried to sooth and to convince; and, in the proper spirit of a peace-maker, adhered to her purpose with meek perseverance.

According to the humour of the hour, Lady Pelham was alternately flattered by solicitations that confessed her power, or rendered peevish by entreaties which she was determined to reject, or fired to rage by the recollection of her wrongs. If the more placid frame prevailed, she could ring eternal changes on the same oft-refuted arguments, or adroitly shift the subject by some lively sally of wit, or some neat compliment to her niece. In her more stormy tempers, she would profess a total inability to pardon; nay, a determination never to attempt it; and took credit for scorning to pretend a forgiveness which she could not practise.

Still Laura was not discouraged: for she had often observed that what Lady Pelham declared on one day to be wholly impossible, on the next became, without any assignable reason, the easiest thing in nature; and that what to-day no human force could wrest from her, was yielded to-morrow to no force at all. She therefore persisted in her work of conciliation; and her efforts at last prevailed so far, that, though Lady Pelham still protested implacability, she acknowledged, that, as there was no necessity for her family feuds being known to the world, she was willing to appear upon decent terms with the Herberts; and, for that purpose, would receive them for a few weeks at Walbourne.

Of this opening, unpromising as it was, Laura instantly availed herself; and wrote to convey the frozen invitation to her cousin, in the kindest language which she was permitted to use. It was instantly accepted; and Mrs Herbert and her husband became the inmates of Walbourne.

Mrs Herbert had no resemblance to her mother. Her countenance was grave and thoughtful; her manners uniformly cold and repulsive. Laura traced in her unbending reserve, the apathy of one whose genial feelings had been blunted by early unkindness. Frank, high-spirited, and imprudent, Herbert was his wife's opposite; and Laura had not been half an hour in his company, before she began to tremble for the effects of these qualities on the irascible temper of her aunt. But her alarm seemed causeless; for the easy resoluteness with which he maintained his opinions, appeared to extort from Lady Pelham a sort of respect; and, though she privately complained to Laura of what she called his assurance, she exempted him, while present, from her attacks, seeming afraid to exert upon him her skill in provoking. Laura began to perceive, that a termagant is not so untameable an animal as she had once imagined, since one glimpse

of the master-spirit is of sovereign power to lay the lesser imps of
spleen. But though Lady Pelham seemed afraid to measure her
strength with spirits of kindred irascibility, she was under no restraint
with Mrs Herbert, upon whom she vented a degree of querulousness
that appeared less like the ebullitions of ill-temper, than the
overflowings of settled malice. Every motion, every look, furnished
matter of censure or of sarcasm. The placing of a book, the
pronunciation of a word, the snuffing of a candle, called forth
reprehension; and Laura knew not whether to be most astonished at
the ingenious malice which contrived to convert 'trifles light as air,'
into certain proofs of degeneracy, or at the apathy on which the
venomed shaft fell harmless. Mrs Herbert received all her mother's
reprimands in silence, without moving a muscle, without announcing,
by the slightest change of colour, that the sarcasm had reached
further than her ear. If, as not unfrequently happened, the reproof
extended into a harangue, Mrs Herbert unmoved withdrew no part of
her attention from her netting, but politely suppressed a yawn.

These discourteous scenes were exhibited only in Mr Herbert's
absence; his presence instantly suspended Lady Pelham's warfare;
and Laura inferred that his wife never made him acquainted with her
mother's behaviour. That behaviour formed an exception to the
general unsteadiness of Lady Pelham; for to Mrs Herbert she was
consistently cruel and insulting. Nothing could be more tormenting
to the benevolent mind of Laura, than to witness this system of
aggression; and she repented having been instrumental in renewing
an intercourse that could lead to no pleasing issue.

But the issue was nearer than she expected. One day, in Herbert's
absence, Lady Pelham began to discuss with his wife, or rather *to* her,
the never-failing subject of her duplicity and disobedience. She was
not interrupted by any expression of regret or repentance from the
culprit, who maintained a stoical silence, labouring the while to
convey mathematical precision to the crimping of a baby's cap, an
employment upon which Lady Pelham seemed to look with peculiar
abhorrence. From the turpitude of her daughter's conduct, she
proceeded to its consequences. She knew no right, she said, that
people had to encumber their friends with hosts of beggarly brats.
She vowed that none such should ever receive her countenance or
protection. Her rage kindled as she spoke. She inveighed against Mrs
Herbert's insensibility; and at last talked herself into such a pitch of
fury, as even to abuse her for submitting to the company of one who

could not conceal detestation of her; – a want of spirit which she directly attributed to the most interested views; – views which, however, she absolutely swore that she would defeat. In the energy of her declamation, she did not perceive that Herbert had entered the room, and stood listening to her concluding sentences, with a face of angry astonishment. Advancing towards his wife, he indignantly inquired the meaning of the tumult. 'Nothing,' answered she, calmly surveying her handywork; 'only my mother is a little angry, but I have not spoken a word.' He then turned for explanation to Lady Pelham, whom the flashing of his eye reduced to instantaneous quiet; and, not finding, in her stammering abstract of the conversation, any apology for the insult which he had heard, he took his wife by the arm, and instantly left the house, giving orders that his baggage should follow him to a little inn in the neighbouring village. Thus did the insolence of one person, and the hasty spirit of another, undo what Laura had for months been labouring to effect. The Herberts never made any attempt at reconciliation, and Lady Pelham would never afterwards hear them mentioned, wiothout breaking out into torrents of abuse, and even imprecation, which made Laura's blood run cold. Yet, with her usual inconsistency, Lady Pelham was vexed at the suspension of her intercourse with the Herberts; because she thus lost even the shadow of power over her daughter. Not that she acknowledged this cause of regret. No! she eloquently bewailed her hard fate, in being exposed to the censure of the world as at variance with her nearest relatives. She complained that, with a heart 'warm as melting charity,' she had no one to love or to cherish. Yet Laura could not always forbear smiling at the perverse direction of her aunt's regrets. Lady Pelham was angry, not that her own unkindness had driven her children from her, but that Laura's officious benevolence had brought them to her house; a measure from which, she was pleased to say that no person of common sense could have expected a different issue.

CHAPTER XXIII

———————— • ————————

IF Lady Pelham repined at the desertion of the Herberts, it was not because their departure consigned her to solitude. Never had Walbourne attracted so many visitors. Lady Pelham's beautiful niece drew thither all the gentlemen of the neighbourhood. The ladies followed them of course. The beauty and modesty of Laura charmed the men, while the women were half-inclined to think it an unfounded slander that such a good-natured, obliging, neat-handed creature studied mathematics, and read Tacitus in the original.

Among the society to which she was introduced by Lady Pelham, and still more among that in which she mingled at Norwood, Laura met with persons of distinguished ability, rank, and politeness. In such company she rapidly acquired that ease of address which alone was wanting to make her manners as fascinating as they were correct. She grew accustomed to find herself the object of attention, and though no habit could reconcile her to the gaze of numbers, she gradually learnt to carry into these lesser occasions, the self-command which distinguished her in more important concerns. In real modesty and humility she improved every day; for it was the study of her life to improve in them. She retained all the timidity which is the fruit of genuine sensibility and quick perception of impropriety, while she lost that bashfulness which owes its growth to solitude and inexperience. Her personal charms, too, increased as they approached maturity. The symmetry of her form and features was indeed scarcely susceptible of improvement; but added gracefulness gave new attractions to her figure; while the soul lent its improving strength and brightness to animate her face with charms which mere symmetry knows not.

With such qualifications Laura could not fail to excite admiration;

yet never perhaps did beauty so seldom listen to its own praises. It was labour lost to compliment one who never rewarded the flatterer with one smile of gratified vanity, or repaid him with one complaisant departure from the simple truth. To the everyday nothings of the common herd she listened with a weariness which politeness could sometimes scarcely suppress. 'Oh would,' thought she, 'that civil nothings, as they are called, required no answer, – or that one obliging gentleman would undertake the labour of replying to the rest!' If addressed in the language of common-place compliment by one whom she respected, her look of mortification intelligibly said, 'Has then your penetration searched me deeper than I know myself, and detected in me the more than childish weakness of valuing myself on such distinctions as those you are praising?'

Laura had no personal vanity; and therefore it required no effort to withstand such praise. She had more merit in the more strenuous but less successful exertions which she made to resist the silent flattery of the respectful glance that awaited her decision, besought her approbation, or reflected her sentiments. Sometimes she thought Montague De Courcy an adept in this sort of flattery. But more frequently, when administered by him, she forgot to call it by that name; and she was the less upon her guard against his homage, because it was never offered in any more palpable form.

Fortified by the advice of his mother, who had convinced him that a premature disclosure of his sentiments would be fatal to his hopes, and aware, that were he even successful with Laura, some further provision must be made for his sister, ere he could with justice increase the expence of his household, he acted with such caution as baffled the penetration of common observers. The neighbouring tea-tables were rather inclined to consign his affections to a lively young heiress, whose estate had formerly been dismembered from that of Norwood; for he had flirted with her at a review, and danced with her at the county ball. Moreover, the charitable declared, 'that if he was backward it was not for want of encouragement, that Miss allowed herself strange liberties; though, to be sure, heiresses might do any thing.'

In spite of the lynx eye in detecting embryo passion, which is ascribed to the sex, Montague's secret was safe even from Laura herself; or if a momentary suspicion had glanced across her mind, she chid it away with self accusations of vanity, and recollections of the ten thousand opportunities for a declaration which he had

suffered to pass unimproved. Besides, Mrs De Courcy had once
hinted that Montague's little fits of melancholy and absence were
occasioned by his partiality for a lady whose affections were pre-
engaged, and Laura was sure that the hint could not refer to herself.
Her humiliating secret, she was thankful, was safely lodged in her
own breast, and could never be divulged to cover her with
mortification.

That which any effort of imagination can ascribe to the influence
of Cupid, no woman ever attributed to any other power; and if, at any
time, a shade crossed the open countenance of Montague, Laura
called to mind his mother's hint, and added to her truly sisterly
affection a pity which lent indescribable softness to her manners
towards him. Indeed she always treated him with undisguised regard,
and Montague tried to be satisfied. Yet he could not help longing to
read, in some inadvertent glance, a proof that all the heart was not
freely shewn. In vain! – the heart was open as the day; and all was
there that could delight the friend, but nothing that could satisfy the
lover.

He had, however, none of the temptations of jealousy to betray his
secret, for his rivals were neither numerous nor formidable. Laura
was known to have no fortune; she had little talent for chit chat, and
still less for flattery; thus amid universal admiration and general
good-will, she had only two professed adorers – one, who haunted
her while present, toasted her when absent, and raved of her charms,
both in prose and rhime, without ever suffering his pretensions to
become so serious as to afford her a pretext for seriously repulsing
them – the other, a prudent elderly widower, who, being possessed of
a good fortune, and a full-grown daughter, thought himself entitled
to consult his taste without regard to pecuniary views, and conceived
that Laura might be useful to the young lady in the double capacities
of companion and example. Laura's answer to his proposals was a
firm but gentle refusal, while she assured him, that she would not
abuse his confidence nor betray the trust he had reposed in her.
Elderly gentlemen are seldom inclined to publish a repulse. The
widower never mentioned his even to Lady Pelham; and Laura, on
this occasion, owed to her principle an escape from many a tedious
remonstrance, and many a covert attack.

The summer had almost glided away, and Montague continued to
fluctuate between hope and fear, his mother to cherish his hopes and
allay his apprehensions, Laura to be tranquil, Harriet to be gay, and

Lady Pelham to exhibit, by turns, every various degree of every various humour, when one morning Miss De Courcy, who had lately returned from a visit to a companion, accompanied her brother on horseback to Walbourne. Lady Pelham was, as usual, engaged in her garden, but the visitors had no sooner entered the room where Laura sat, then she observed that they seemed to have exchanged characters. Harriet looked almost thoughtful, while the countenance of De Courcy sparkled with unusual animation. He was gay even to restlessness. He offered to give Laura her lesson in mathematics; and before it was half over, having completely bewildered both himself and his pupil, he tossed away the book, declaring that he never in his life was so little fit for thinking. Pleasure spoke in every tone of his voice, or sported in his eye when he was silent.

After a short visit, enlivened by a hilarity which Laura found more infectious than the gravity of Harriet, he proposed leaving his sister with her friend, while he rode on to call for a gentleman in the neighbourhood. 'Begone, then,' cried Laura, gaily, 'for I long to question Harriet what has given you such enviable spirits this morning.' 'Ah, she must not betray me,' said De Courcy, half smiling, half sighing, 'or I forfeit my only chance of being remembered when I am out of sight. If she can be silent, curiosity may perhaps befriend me.' 'How very humble!' cried Laura, – 'as if curiosity were the only name you could find for the interest I take in what makes you gay, or Harriet grave!' 'Dear Laura,' said De Courcy, ardently, 'give the cause what name you will, if you will but think of me.' Then snatching her lily hands, he pressed them to his lips, and the next moment was gone.

Confused, surprised, a little displeased, Laura stood silently revolving his behaviour. He had never before made the slightest approach to personal familiarity. Had her frankness invited the freedom? 'Dear Laura!' It was the first time he had ever called her by any name less respectful than Miss Montreville. 'Well, and what then – it were mere prudery to be displeased at such a trifle. What,' thought she, 'can have delighted him so much? Perhaps the lady is kind at last. He need not, however, have vented his transports upon me.' And Laura was a little more angry than before.

During her cogitation, Laura forgot that she might apply to her companion for a solution of the mystery; perhaps she did not even recollect that Harriet was in the room, till happening to turn her head, she met a glance of sly inquisition, which, however, was instantly withdrawn. Harriet made no comment on the subject of her observation. 'The man is as much elated,' cried she, 'as if I were five-and-forty, and had never had a lover before.'

'You, my dear Harriet,' exclaimed Laura, instantly recovering her good humour, 'is it a conquest of yours that has pleased Mr De Courcy so much?' 'Even so,' returned Harriet – 'Heigho!'

'I congratulate you: and yet it does not seem to delight you quite so much as it does your brother.'

'Really Laura I am not sure whether it does or not; so I am come to ask you.'

'Me! Indeed you have too much confidence in my penetration; but you have, fortunately, abler, and more natural advisers. Your mother' –

'Oh, my mother is so cautious, so afraid of influencing me! when to be influenced is the very thing I want. I do hate caution. Then I can't talk it over with her as I could with you. And then, there's Montague looks so provokingly pleased; and yet he pretends to prim up his mouth, and say, "really it is a subject on which he neither can, nor ought to give an opinion." Pray, advise me, my dear.'

'What! before I know who the gentleman is; when perhaps you have even no right to inform me!'

'Pshaw! nonsense. – It is Bolingbroke. But I believe you have never met with him.' 'So you would have me advise you to marry a man whom I have never seen; for of course that is the advice you want. Had the balance lain on the other side, no advice would have been thought necessary.' 'Poh,' cried Harriet pouting. 'I don't want to be advised to marry him.' 'Are you sure,' returned Laura, smiling, 'that you know what you want.' – 'Saucy girl! I would have you tell me whether I am ever likely to marry him!' 'Do you think I am by birth entitled to the second-sight, that I should foresee this before I know any thing of the gentleman's merits, or, what is of more consequence, of their rank in your estimation?' 'The man has good legs,' said Harriet, plaiting the fingers of her glove with great industry. 'Legs! really, Harriet, I was in hopes I had for once found you serious.' – 'So I am, my dear; I never was so serious before, and hope I never shall again. Yet I don't know what to think; so I shall just tell you honestly how the matter stands, and you shall think for me.'

'I will not promise that; but I own I have some curiosity to hear your *honest* confession.' – 'Oh you need not peep so archly askance under those long eyelashes; I can stand a direct look, I assure you; for at this moment I have not the slightest preference in the world for Bolingbroke over half a score of others.' 'Then what room is there for hesitation?' 'Why, my dear, in the first place, he has a noble fortune: though that goes for nothing with you; secondly, he is really a good creature, and far from a fool; then, to talk in your style, I have had advantages in observing his temper and dispositions such as I shall never have with any other man; for his sister and I have been companions from childhood, and I have lived under his roof for months; then, which will weigh with you more than all, he is Montague's particular favourite.' 'Great recommendations these, Harriet; sufficient at least to bias any woman who intends to marry. I should like to know Mr Bolingbroke.' 'Here is his letter, my dear,' said Harriet; 'it came inclosed in one to my brother. There is a good deal of the man's turn in it.'

Laura took the letter, and read as follows:

'I will not wrong your penetration so much as to suppose that this letter will surprise you, or that you will fail to anticipate the subject on the first glance at the signature. Nor do I write to tell you, in the hackneyed phrase, that the happiness of my whole life depends upon you, because, next to your affection, nothing is so desirable to me as your esteem, and the hope that, though you should reject my suit, you will continue to respect my understanding. But I may with truth declare, that I prefer you to all women; that I love you, not only in spite of your faults, but, perhaps, even the more for them; and that, to forfeit the hope of your affection, would dispel many a long-cherished vision of domestic peace, and even some lighter dreams of rapture. Dearest Harriet, do not, in return for this confession, write me a cold profession of esteem. I know already that you esteem me, for you have long known me possessed of qualities that inevitably engage esteem; but I am conscious of a deficiency in the gifts that excite passion, and I dread that I may never awaken sentiments like those I feel. Yet it is no small compliment which I offer, when I suppose you superior to the attractions which captivate the vulgar of your sex; and you may value it the more, because it is perhaps the only one I shall ever pay you.

'To say all this, or something like it, has long been in my thoughts; and, during your late visit to my sister, occupied them more than I shall own; but a dread of I know not what, forced me to let you depart without offering to your acceptance all that I have to offer. I felt a certainty that I was not yet beloved, and, I believe I feared that you, in your lively way, (so I must call it, since no epithet that implies reproof must flow from a lover's pen), would give utterance to the feeling of the moment, and bid me think of you no more. Is it presumption to say, that I hope more from a more considerate decision? Ask your own heart, then, dear Miss De Courcy, whether time and the assiduities of respectful love can beguile you of such tenderness as is due to a confiding affectionate husband. Ask yourself, whether you can ever return my warm attachment, to such a degree as will make the duties of a wife easy and pleasant to you. I need not assure you that I am not the selfish wretch who could find joy in receiving those which were painfully and reluctantly per-formed. Be candid with yourself then I adjure you. Fear not that I shall persecute you with importunity or complaint. If it must be so, I will see you no more for some months; and, at the end of that time, shall expect, in reward of my self-conquest, to be received with cordiality as your brother's friend. If your sentence be against me, save yourself the pain of telling me so; for I know that it must be painful to you. Yet judge of the strength of that regard which is thus anxious to shield you from uneasiness, at the moment when it anticipates such pain from your hands. If you can give me hope (and, observe, when I say hope, I do not mean certainty), do not tax your delicacy for studied phrases of acceptance, but write me even a common card of invitation to Norwood, and the tenderest billet that ever was penned by woman, never gave more pleasure than it will bring to your very affectionate and obedient servant,

'EDWARD BOLINGBROKE.'

Laura could not help smiling at the composed style of this epistle, so different from the only ones of its kind with which she was conversant. A lover confess that his mistress had faults, and that he was sensible of them! – insinuate that he expected not only duty, but willing and grateful duty from his wife! – have the boldness to expect, that, if his passion were unsuccessful, he should quickly be able to conquer it! Laura felt no inclination to envy her friend a lover so fully in the exercise of his judgment and foresight; but she was pleased with the plain honest rationality of the letter; and, with the materials before her, immediately busied her imagination in its favourite work of sketching and adorning character.

She was called from her meditation by another petition for advice.

'You see,' said Harriet, 'he pretends not to expect certainty; but it is much the same whether one run one's neck into the noose, or gets entangled so that one can't decently get off. If I could *creditably* contrive to keep him dangling till I had made up my mind,' continued she, illustrating the metaphor with her watch-chain. 'Do assist me, my dear; I am sure you have managed a dozen of them in your time.'

'My experience is not so extensive,' replied Laura, 'and I can really assist you to no *creditable* method of trifling.'

'You would not have me resolve to marry a man whom I don't care a farthing for.' 'No, indeed! but I think Mr Bolingbroke would have a right to complain, if you gave hopes which you did not fulfil.' 'You would have me dismiss him at once then?' 'By no means; but I would have you think for yourself on a subject of which no other person can judge; and remember, my dear, that, as your decision has neither been wrested from you by surprise, nor seduced from you by persuasion, you have no excuse for forming a weak or wavering resolution.'

Determined that on such a subject she would deliver no opinion, Laura was relieved from some embarrassment by the return of De Courcy. His reflections during his ride had effectually quelled the exuberance of his spirits, and he endeavoured to repair his unguardedness by distant politeness. His manner increased the feeling of restraint of which Laura could not at that time divest herself; and after a short and constrained sequel to a visit which had begun so differently, Montague hurried his sister away.

'I shall never conquer her indifference,' said he to his mother, after relating the folly of the morning. 'Had you seen her frozen look of displeasure, you would have been convinced.' 'And how, my dear Montague, could you expect Miss Montreville to receive such freedom? like a little village coquette gasping at the prospect of a first lover? If you are convinced that your secret would still be heard without pleasure, you must redouble your caution to preserve it. But suffer me to warn you against the extreme of reserve in which I have sometimes observed that you are apt to fall. It can only confirm suspicions if they are excited; if not, it will disgust by an appearance of caprice.'

Montague promised to be guarded; and withdrew to seek in his laboratory a refuge from despondence. Those who pursue worldly gains and vulgar pleasures, must cheerlessly toil on, waiting for their reward till their end is attained; but the pursuits of science and of virtue have this advantage peculiar to themselves, that there is reward in the labour, even though the success be only partial; and, in half an hour, all Montague's cares were absorbed in the muriatic acid. In a few days he again saw Laura, and her sunny smile of welcome revived hopes which she little thought of fulfilling.

When a woman of ordinary delicacy is brought to hesitate upon the proposal of a lover, it is easy, provided prudence be on his side, to conjecture how the balance will turn. Mr Bolingbroke received his card of invitation to Norwood; and his suit advanced prosperously, though slowly. He was a plain unpretending man, seven years at least beyond excuse for any youthful indiscretion, habitually silent, though sure of commanding attention when he spoke. The perfect fairness and integrity of his mind had secured him the respect of all his acquaintance in a degree which he appeared to have precisely estimated. and he never seemed to expect less or to exact more. His calm unobtrusive manners never captivated a stranger, nor gave offence to an intimate. He was kind and generous to a sister, who, twenty years before, had succeeded as his play-thing to tops and marbles; and uniformly respectful to a maiden aunt who had, about the same date, replaced his mother as directress of the family.

His father had been long dead, and in consequence of his steady resistance of all the batteries of charms opened against him, or rather against his £7000 a-year, the ladies had begun to shake their heads, and pronounce him a determined bachelor. But, notwithstanding their decision, Mr Bolingbroke was resolved to marry, for he considered marriage as one of the duties of his station.

Harriet amused, became customary, pleasing, necessary, to him. 'Our dissimilarity will assist us to correct each other's failings,' thought he, and his choice was fixed. He was aware that a grave elderly man might find some difficulty in attaching a volatile girl; and though he could not condescend to flatter even his mistress, he was assiduous to please. He bestowed an infinity of little attentions, which were the more gratifying, because, from a man of his temper, they were wholly unexpected. His books, his horses, his carriage, waited but a half-expressed wish. He planned little excursions and parties of pleasure, or contrived to add some agreeable surprise to those which were proposed by others. Far from shewing any paltry jealousy, he treated Miss De Courcy's favourites of both sexes with distinguished politeness; and perhaps he owed his success with a heart which had withstood more attractive admirers, partly to the agreeable associations which he found means to raise, partly to vanity, pleased with power over the philosophic Mr Bolingbroke.

Montague watched the progress of his friend with keen interest, but he conscientiously avoided influencing Harriet's decision. On the contrary, lest the dread of future dependence should weigh with her, he informed her, that, should she prefer a single life, or should other circumstances render such a sum important to her, he was determined to double the little fortune he had already given.

While he was anxious to see his sister's happiness secured by her union with an estimable man, he felt that her marriage with Mr Bolingbroke would immediately remove one grand obstacle to his own wishes; for the little dower which he was determined ere he settled in life to save for Harriet, would form an addition altogether insignificant to the splendid settlement which was now in her power. There was nothing Quixotic in the justice and generosity of De Courcy; and he had no intention of incurring real difficulty and privation for the sake of adding a trifle to the stores of affluence. He therefore considered his sister's marriage as leaving him at full liberty to pursue his inclinations with regard to Laura, if the time should ever arrive when he could declare them without hazarding the forfeiture of even his present stinted measure of favour.

CHAPTER XXIV

———•———

ONE day Miss De Courcy expressed a wish to shew Laura the collection of paintings at a celebrated seat in the neighbourhood. Mr Bolingbroke immediately undertook to procure the permission of the noble owner, who was his relation; and the party was speedily arranged. Mrs Penelope's sociable, as Mr Bolingbroke always called it, was to convey his aunt, his sister, Harriet, and Mrs De Courcy, to whom the genial warmth of the season had partially restored the use of her limbs. Mrs Penelope piqued herself upon rising with the lark, and enforcing the same wholesome habit upon the whole household; the Bolingbrokes were, therefore, to take an early breakfast at Norwood, and then to proceed on their excursion. De Courcy and Mr Bolingbroke were to ride. Lady Pelham and Laura were to join the party in the grounds.

The weather proved delightful; and, after spending some hours in examining the paintings, in which Laura derived additional pleasure from the skilful comments of De Courcy, the party proceeded to view the grounds, when she, with almost equal delight, contemplated a finished specimen of modern landscape-gardening. Pursuing, as usual, his cautious plan, Montague divided his attentions pretty equally between the elder ladies and Miss Bolingbroke, bestowing the least part upon her for whom he would willingly have reserved all; while Harriet, in good humour with herself, and with all around her, frankly gave her arm to her lover; and sometimes laughing, sometimes blushing, suffered herself to loiter, to incline her head in listening to somewhat said in a half-whisper, and to answer it in an under tone; without recollecting that she had resolved, till she had *quite* made up her mind, to restrain her habitual propensity to flirting.

De Courcy was certainly above the meannness of envy, yet he

could not suppress a sigh as, with Mrs Penelope and his mother leaning on his arms, while Laura walked behind with Miss Bolingbroke, he followed Harriet and his friend into the darkened path that led to a hermitage. The walk was shaded by yew, cypress, and other trees of dusky foliage, which, closing into an arch, excluded the gaudy sunshine. As they proceeded, the shade deepened into twilight, and the heats of noon gave place to refreshing coolness. The path terminated in a porch of wicker-work, forming the entrance to the hermitage, the walls of which were composed of the roots of trees, on the outside rugged as from the hand of nature, but within polished and fancifully adorned with shells and fossils. Opposite to the entrance, a rude curtain of leopard skin seemed to cover a recess; and Harriet, hastily drawing it aside, gave to view a prospect gay with every variety of cheerful beauty. The meadows, lately cleared from their burden, displayed a vivid green, and light shadows quickly passed over them and were gone. The corn-fields were busy with the first labours of the harvest. The village spires were thickly sown in the distance. More near, a rapid river flashed bright to the sun; yet the blaze came chastened to the eye, for it entered an awning close hung with the graceful tendrils of the passion-flower.

The party were not soon weary of so lovely a landscape, and returning to the more shady apartment, found an elegant collation of fruits and ices, supplied by the gallantry of Mr Bolingbroke. Never was there a more cheerful repast. Lady Pelham was luckily in good humour, and therefore condescended to permit others to be so too. Laura, happily for herself, possessed a faculty not common to beauties – she could be contented where another was the chief object of attention; and she was actually enjoying the court that was paid to her friend, when, accidentally raising the vine leaf which held the fruit she was eating, she observed some verses pencilled on the rustic table in a hand-writing familiar to her recollection.

Sudden instinct made her hastily replace the leaf, and steal a glance to see whether any other eye had followed her's. No one seemed to have noticed her; but Laura's gaiety had vanished. The lines were distinct, as if recently traced; and Laura's blood ran chill at the thought, that, had she even a few hours sooner visited this spot, she might have met Colonel Hargrave. 'He may still be near,' thought she; and she wished, though she could not propose, to be instantly gone. None of her companions, however, seemed inclined to move. They continued their merriment, while Laura, her mind wholly occupied with one subject, again stole a glimpse of the writing. It was undoubtedly Hargrave's; and, deaf to all that was passing around her, she fell into a reverie, which was first interrupted by the company rising to depart.

Though she had been in such haste to be gone, she was now the last to go. In her momentary glance at the sonnet, she had observed that it was inscribed to her. 'Of what possible consequence,' thought she, 'can it be to me?' yet she lingered behind to read it. In language half passionate, half melancholy, it complained of the pains of absence and the cruelty of too rigid virtue; but it broke off abruptly, as if the writer had been suddenly interrupted.

So rapidly did Laura glance over the lines, that her companions had advanced but a few paces, ere she was hastening to follow them. On reaching the porch, she saw that the walk was just entered by two gentlemen. An instant convinced her that one of them was Hargrave. Neither shriek nor exclamation announced this discovery, but Laura, turning pale, shrunk back out of view. Her first feeling was eager desire of escape; her first thought, that, returning to the inner apartment, she might thence spring from the lofty terrace, on the verge of which the hermitage was reared. She was deterred, by recollecting the absurd appearance of such an escape, and the surprise it would occasion. But what was to be done? There was no third way of leaving the place where she stood, and if she remained, in a few moments Hargrave would be there.

These ideas darted so confusedly through her mind, that it seemed rather by instinct than design, that she drew her hat over her face, and doubled her veil in order to pass him unnoticed. She again advanced to the porch; but perceived, not without consternation, that Hargrave had joined her party, and stood talking to Lady Pelham in an attitude of easy cordiality. Laura did not comment upon the free morality which accorded such a reception to such a character; for she was sick at heart, and trembled in every limb. Now there was no escape. He would certainly accost her, and she must answer him – answer him without emotion! or how would Mr De Courcy – how would his mother construe her weakness! What would Hargrave himself infer from it! What, but that her coldness sprung from mere passing anger! or, more degrading still, from jealousy! The truant crimson now rushed back unbidden; and Laura proceeded with slow but steady steps.

During her short walk she continued to struggle with herself. 'Let me but this once command myself,' said she. 'And wherefore should I not? It is he who ought to shrink. – It is he who ought to tremble!' Yet it was Laura who trembled, when, advancing towards her, Lady Pelham introduced her to Colonel Hargrave as her niece. Laura's inclination of the head, cold as indifference could make it, did not seem to acknowledge former intimacy; and when Hargrave, with a manner respectful even to timidity, claimed her acquaintance, she gave a short answer of frozen civility, and turned away. Shrinking from even the slightest converse with him, she hastily passed on; then, determined to afford him no opportunity of speaking to her, she glided in between Mrs De Courcy, who stood anxiously watching her, and Harriet, who was studying the contour of Hargrave's face; and offering an arm to each, she gently drew them forward.

Mr Bolingbroke immediately joined them, and entered into conversation with Harriet; while Mrs De Courcy continued to read the legible countenance of Laura, who silently walked on, revolving in her mind the difference between this and her last unexpected meeting with Hargrave. The freedom of his address to the unfriended girl who was endeavouring to exchange the labour of her hands for a pittance to support existence, (a freedom which had once found sympathetic excuse in the breast of Laura), she now, not without indignation, contrasted with the respect offered to Lady Pelham's niece, surrounded by the rich and the respectable. Yet while she remembered what had then been her half-affected coldness, her ill-restrained sensibility; and compared them with the total alienation of heart which she now experienced, she could not stifle a sigh which rose at the recollection, that in her the raptures of love and joy were chilled never more to warm. 'Would that my preference had been more justly directed,' thought she, her eye unconsciously wandering to De Courcy; 'but that is all over now!'

From idle regrets, Laura soon turned to more characteristic meditation upon the conduct most suitable for her to pursue. Hargrave had joined her party; had been acknowledged, by some of them at least, as an acquaintance; and had particularly attached himself to Lady Pelham, with whom he followed in close conversation. Laura thought he would probably take the first opportunity of addressing himself to her; and if her manner towards him corresponded with the bent of her feelings, consciousness made her fear, that in her distance and constraint Lady Pelham's already suspicious eye would read more than merely dislike to a vicious character. Hargrave himself, too, might mistake who so nearly resembled her former manner for the veil of her former sentiments. She might possibly escape speaking to him for the present, but if he was fixed in the neighbourhood, (and something of the woman whispered that he would not leave it immediately), they would proabably meet where to avoid him was not in her power. After some minutes of close consideration, she concluded, that to treat Colonel Hargrave with easy civil indifference, best accorded with what she owed to her own dignity; and was best calculated, if he retained one spark of sensibility or discernment, to convince him that her sentiments had undergone an irrevocable change. This method, therefore, she determined to pursue; making, with a sigh, this grand proviso, that she should find it practicable.

Mrs De Courcy, who guessed the current of her thoughts, suffered it to proceed without interruption; and it was not till Laura relaxed her brow, and raised her head, like one who has taken his resolution, that her companion, stopping, complained of fatigue; proposing, as her own carriage was not in waiting, to borrow Lady Pelham's, and return home, leaving the other ladies to be conveyed in Mrs Penelope's sociable to Norwood, where the party was to dine. Not willing to direct the proposal to Laura, upon whose account chiefly it was made, she then turned to Mrs Penelope, and inquired whether she did not feel tired with her walk; but that lady, who piqued herself upon being a hale active woman of her age, declared herself able for much greater exertion, and would walk, she said, till she had secured an appetite for dinner. Laura, who had modestly held back till Mrs Penelope's decision was announced, now eagerly offered her attendance, which Mrs De Courcy, with a little dissembled hesitation, accepted, smiling to perceive how well she had divined her young favourite's inclinations.

The whole party attended them to the spot where the carriages were waiting. On reaching them, Mr Bolingbroke, handing in Mrs De Courcy, left Laura's side for the first time free to Hargrave, who instantly occupied it; while Montague, the drops standing on his forehead, found himself shackled between Mrs Penelope and Miss Bolingbroke. 'Ever dear, ever revered Miss Montreville' – Hargrave began in an insinuating whisper. 'Sir!' cried Laura, starting with indignant surprise. 'Nay, start not,' continued he in an under voice; 'I have much, much to say. Lady Pelham allows me to visit Walbourne; will you permit me to' – Laura had not yet studied her lesson of easy civility, and therefore the courtesy of a slight inclination of the head was contradicted by the tone in which she interrupted him, saying, 'I never presume, Sir, to select Lady Pelham's visitors.'

She had reached the door of the carriage, and Hargrave took her hand to assist her in entering. Had Laura been prepared, she would have suffered him, though reluctantly, to do her this little service; but he took her unawares, and snatching back her hand as from the touch of a loathsome reptile, she sprang, unassisted, into her seat.

As the carriage drove off, Mrs De Courcy again apologized for separating Laura from her companions; 'though I know not,' added she, 'whether I should not rather take credit for withdrawing you from such dangerous society. All ladies who have stray hearts must guard them either in person or by proxy, since this formidable Colonel Hargrave has come among us.' 'He has fortunately placed the more respectable part of us in perfect security,' returned Laura, with a smile and voice of such unembarrassed simplicity as fully satisfied her examiner.

Had Laura spent a lifetime in studying to give pain, which, indeed, was not in all her thoughts, she could not have inflicted a sharper sting on the proud heart of Hargrave, than by the involuntary look and gesture with which she quitted him. The idea of inspiring with disgust, unmixed irresistible disgust, the woman upon whose affections, or rather upon whose passions, he had laboured so zealously and so long, had ever been more than he could bear, even when the expression of her dislike had no witness; but now she had published it to chattering misses and prying old maids, and more favoured rivals. Hargrave bit his lip till the blood came; and, if the lightning of the eye could scathe, his wrath had been far more deadly to others.

After walking for some minutes surly and apart, he began to comfort himself with the hopes of future revenge. 'She had loved him, passionately loved him, and he was certain she could not be so utterly changed. Her behaviour was either all affectation, or a conceit of the strength of her own mind, which all these clever women were so vain of. But the spark still lurked somewhere, whatever she might imagine, and if he could turn her own weapons against herself.' – Then, recollecting that he had resolved to cultivate Lady Pelham, he resumed his station by her side, and was again the courtly, insinuating Colonel Hargrave.

Hargrave had lately acquired a friend, or rather an adviser (the dissolute have no friends), who was admirably calculated to supply the deficiencies of his character as a man of pleasure. Indeed, except in so far as pleasure was his constant aim, no term could, with less justice, have been applied to Hargrave; for his life was chiefly divided between the goadings of temptations to which he himself lent arms, and the pangs of self-reproach which he could not exclude, and would not render useful. The strait and narrow way he never had a thought of treading, but his wanderings were more frequent than he intended, his returns more lingering. The very strength of his passions made him incapable of deep or persevering deceit; he was humane to the suffering that pressed itself on his notice, if it came at a convenient season; and he was disinterested, if neglect of gold deserve the name. Lambert, his new adviser, had no passions, no humanity, no neglect of gold. He was a gamester.

The practice of this profession, for, though a man of family and fortune he made it a profession, had rendered him skilful to discern, and remorseless to use the weaknesses of his fellow creatures. His estate lay contiguous to −, the little town where Hargrave had been quartered when he visited at Norwood; but the year which Hargrave passed at − was spent by Lambert almost entirely alone in London. He had returned however to the country, had been introduced to Hargrave, and had just fixed upon him as an easy prey, when the soldier was saved for a time, by receiving intimation of his promotion, and orders to join his regiment in a distant county.

They met again in an evil hour, just as Hargrave had half-determined to abandon as fruitless his search after Laura. The necessity of a stimulant was as strong as ever. Another necessity too was strong, for £10,000 of damages had been awarded to Lord Bellamer; Hargrave could not easily raise the money, and Lord Lincourt refused to advance a shilling. 'A pretty expensive pleasure has this Lady Bellamer been to me,' said Hargrave, bestowing on her Ladyship a coarse enough epithet; for even fine gentlemen will sometimes call women what they have found them to be. He was prevailed on to try the gaming-table for the supply of both his wants, and found that pleasure fully twice as expensive. His friend introduced him to some of those accommodating gentlemen who lend money at illegal interest, and was generous enough to supply him when they would venture no more upon an estate in reversion. Lambert had accidentally heard of the phœnix which had appeared at Walbourne; and, on comparing the description he received of her with that to which with politic patience he had often listened, he had no doubt of having found the object of Hargrave's search. But, as it did not suit his present views that the lover should renew the pursuit, he dropt not a hint of his discovery, listening, with a gamester's insensibility, to the regrets which burst forth amidst the struggles of expiring virtue, for her whose soft influence would have led to peace and honour.

At last a dispute arising between the worthy Mr Lambert and his respectable coadjutors, as to the partition of the spoil, it occurred to him that he could more effectually monopolize his prey in the country; and thither accordingly he was called by pressing business. There he was presently so fortunate as to discover a Miss Montreville, on whose charms he descanted in a letter to Hargrave in such terms, that, though he averred she could not be Hargrave's Miss Montreville, Hargrave was sure she could be no other; and, as his informer expected, arrived in − −shire as soon as a chaise and four could convey him thither.

Lambert had now a difficult game to play, for he had roused the leading passion, and the collateral one could act but feebly; but they who often tread the crooked path, find pleasure in its intricacy, vainly conceiting that it gives proof of their sagacity, and Lambert looked with pleasure on the obstacles in his way. He trusted, that while the master-spirit detained Hargrave within the circle of Walbourne, he might dexterously practise with the lesser imp of evil.

Had his letter afforded a clue to Laura's residence, Hargrave would have flown directly to Walbourne, but he was first obliged to stop at −; and Lambert, with some difficulty, persuaded him, that, as he was but slightly known to Lady Pelham, and probably in disgrace with her protegée, it would be more politic to delay his visit, and first meet them at Lord −'s, where he had information that they were to go on the following day. 'You will take your girl at unawares,' said he, 'if she be your girl; and that is no bad way of feeling your ground.' The vanity of extorting from Laura's surprise some unequivocal token of his power prevailed on the lover to delay the interview till the morning; and, after spending half the evening in dwelling upon the circumstances of his last unexpected meeting with her, which distance softened in his imagination to more than its actual tenderness, he, early in the morning set out with Lambert for −, where he took post in the hermitage, as a place which no stranger omitted to visit.

Growing weary of waiting, he dispatched Lambert as a scout; and, lest he should miss Laura, remained himself in the hermitage, till his emissary brought him information that the party were in the picture gallery. Thither he hastened; but the party had already left the house, and thus had Laura accidental warning of his approach. No reception could have been so mortifying to him, who was prepared to support her sinking under the struggle of love and duty, of jealousy and pride. No struggle was visible; or, if there was, it was but a faint strife between native courtesy and strong dislike. He had boasted to Lambert of her tenderness; the specimen certainly was not flattering. Most of her companions were little more gracious. De Courcy paid him no more attention than bare civility required. – With the Bolingbrokes he was unacquainted, but the character of his companion was sufficient reason for their reserve. Lady Pelham was the only person present who soothed his wounded vanity. Pleased with the prospect of unravelling the mystery into which she had pried so long in vain, charmed with the easy gallantry and adroit flattery of which Hargrave, in his cooler moments, was consummate master, she accepted his attentions with great cordiality; while he had the address tacitly to persuade her that they were a tribute to her powers of entertaining.

Before they parted, she had converted her permission to visit Walbourne into a pressing invitation, nay, had even hinted to De Courcy the propriety of asking the Colonel to join the dinner party that day at Norwood. The hint, however, was not taken; and therefore, in her way home, Lady Pelham indulged her fellow-travellers with sundry moral and ingenious reflections concerning the folly of being 'righteous over much;' and on the alluring accessible form of the true virtue, contrasted with the repulsive, bristly, hedge-hog-like make of the false. Indeed, it must be owned, that for the rest of the evening her Ladyship's conversation was rather sententious than agreeable; but the rest of the party, in high good humour, overlooked her attacks, or parried them in play.

Montague had watched the cold composure of Laura on Hargrave's first accosting her, and seen the gesture which repulsed him at parting; and though in the accompanying look he lost volumes, his conclusions, on the whole, were favourable. Still a doubt arose, whether her manner sprung not from the fleeting resentment of affection; and he was standing mournfully calculating the effects of Hargrave's perseverance, when his mother, in passing him as she followed her guests to the eating-room, said, in an emphatical whisper, 'I am satisfied. There is no worm in the bud.'

Mrs De Courcy's encouraging assertion was confirmed by the behaviour of Laura herself; for she maintained her usual serene cheerfulness; nor could even the eye of love detect more than one short fit of distraction; and then the subject of thought seemed any thing rather than pleasing retrospect, or glad anticipation. The company of his friends, Harriet's pointedly favourable reception of Mr Bolingbroke's assiduities, and the rise of his own hopes, all enlivened Montague to unusual vivacity, and led him to a deed of daring which he had often projected, without finding courage to perform it. He thought, if he could speak of Hargrave to Laura, and watch her voice, her eye, her complexion, all his doubts would be solved. With this view, contriving to draw her a little apart, he ventured, for the first time, to name his rival; mentioned Lady Pelham's hint; and, faltering, asked Laura whether he had not done wrong in resisting it.

'Really,' answered Laura with a very *naïve* smile, and a very faint blush, 'I don't wonder you hesitate in offering me such a piece of flattery as to ask my opinion.'

'Do not tax me with flattering you,' said De Courcy earnestly; 'I would as soon flatter an apostle; but tell me candidly what you think.'

'Then, candidly,' said Laura, raising her mild unembarrassed eye to his, 'I think you did right, perfectly right, in refusing your countenance to a person of Colonel Hargrave's character. While vice is making her encroachments on every hand, it is not for the friends of virtue to remove the ancient landmarks.'

Though this was one of the stalest pieces of morality that ever Montague had heard Laura utter, he could scarcely refrain from repaying it by clasping her to his heart. Convinced that her affections were free, he could not contain his rapture, but exclaimed, 'Laura, you are an angel! and, if I did not already love beyond all power of expression, I should be' – He raised his eyes to seek those of Laura, and met his mother's, fixed on him with an expression that compelled him to silence. – 'You should be in love with me;' said Laura, laughing, and filling up the sentence as she imagined it was meant to conclude. 'Well, I shall be content with the second place.'

Mrs De Courcy, who had approached them, now spoke on some indifferent subject, and saved her son from a very awkward attempt at explanation. She drew her chair close to Laura, and soon engaged her in a conversation so animated, that Montague forgot his embarrassment, and joined them with all his natural ease and cheerfulness. The infection of his ease and cheerfulness Laura had ever found irresistible. Flashes of wit and genius followed the collision of their minds; and the unstudied eloquence, the poetic imagery of her style, sprung forth at his touch, like blossoms in the steps of the fabled Flora.

Happy with her friends, Laura almost forgot the disagreeable adventure of the morning; and, every look and word mutually bestowing pleasure, the little party were as happy as affection and esteem could make them, when Lady Pelham, with an aspect like a sea fog, and a voice suitably forbidding, inquired whether her niece would be pleased to go home, or whether she preferred sitting chattering there all night. Laura, without any sign of noticing the rudeness of this address, rose, and said she was quite ready to attend her Ladyship. In vain did the De Courcys entreat her to prolong her visit till the morning. To dare to be happy without her concurrence, was treason against Lady Pelham's dignity; and unfortunately she was not in a humour to concur in the joy of any living thing. De Courcy's reserve towards her new favourite she considered as a tacit reproof of her own cordiality; and she had just such a conviction that the reproof was deserved, as to make her thoroughly out of humour with the reprover, with herself, and consequently with everybody else. Determined to interrupt pleasure which she would not share, the more her hosts pressed her stay, the more she hastened her departure; and she mingled her indifferent good nights to them with more energetic reprimands to the tardiness of her coachman.

'Thank heaven,' said she, thrusting herself into the corner of her carriage with that jerk in her motion which indicates a certain degree of irritation, 'to-morrow we shall probably see a civilized being.' A short pause followed. Laura's plain integrity and prudence had gained such ascendancy over Lady Pelham, that her niece's opinion was to her Ladyship a kind of second conscience, having, indeed, much the same powers as the first. Its sanction was necessary to her quiet, though it had not force to controul her actions. On the present occasion she wished, above all things, to know Laura's sentiments; but she would not condescend to ask them directly. 'Colonel Hargrave's manners are quite those of a gentleman,' she resumed. The remark was entirely ineffectual; for Laura coolly assented, without inquiring whether he were the civilized being whom Lady

Pelham expected to see. Another pause. 'Colonel Hargrave will be at Walbourne to-morrow,' said Lady Pelham, the tone of her voice sharpening with impatience. 'Will he, Ma'am?' returned Laura, without moving a muscle. 'If Miss Montreville has no objections,' said Lady Pelham, converting by a toss of her head and a twist of her upper lip, the words of compliment into an insult. 'Probably,' said Laura, with a smile, 'my objections would make no great difference.' – 'Oh, to be sure!' returned Lady Pelham, 'it would be lost labour to state them to such an obstinate, unreasonable person as I am! Well, I believe you are the first who ever accused me of obstinacy.' If Lady Pelham expected a compliment to her pliability, she was disappointed; for Laura only answered, 'I shall never presume to interfere in the choice of your Ladyship's visitors.'

That she should be thus compelled to be explicit was more than Lady Pelham's temper could endure. Her eyes flashing with rage, 'Superlative humility indeed!' she exclaimed with a sneer; but, awed, in spite of herself, from the free expression of her fury, she muttered it within her shut teeth in a sentence of which the words 'close' and 'jesuitical' alone reached Laura's ear. A long and surly silence followed; Lady Pelham's pride and anger struggling with her desire to learn the foundation and extent of the disapprobation which she suspected that her conduct excited. The latter, at last, partly prevailed; though Lady Pelham still disclaimed condescending to direct consultation.

'Pray, Miss Montreville,' said she, 'if Colonel Hargrave's visits were to *you*, what mighty objections might your sanctity find to them?' – Laura had long ago observed that a slight exertion of her spirit was the best *quietus* to her aunt's ill humour; and, therefore, addressing her with calm austerity, she said, 'Any young woman, Madam, who values her reputation, might object to Colonel Hargrave's visits, merely on the score of prudence. But even my "superlative humility" does not reconcile me to company which I despise; and my "sanctity," as your Ladyship is pleased to call it, rather shrinks from the violator of laws divine and human.'

Lady Pelham withdrew her eyes to escape a glance which they never could stand; but, bridling, she said, 'Well, Miss Montreville, I am neither young nor sanctimonious, therefore your objections cannot apply to Colonel Hargrave's visits to me; and I am determined,' continued she, speaking as if strength of voice denoted strength of resolution, 'I am determined, that I will not throw away the society of an agreeable man, to gratify the whims of a parcel of narrow-minded bigots.'

To this attack Laura answered only with a smile. She smiled to see herself classed with the De Courcys; for she had no doubt that they were the 'bigots' to whom Lady Pelham referred. She smiled, too, to observe that the boasted freedom of meaner minds is but a poor attempt to hide from themselves the restraint imposed by the opinions of the wise and good.

The carriage stopped, and Laura took sanctuary in her own apartment; but at supper she met her aunt with smiles of unaffected complacency, and, according to the plan which she invariably pursued, appeared to have forgotten Lady Pelham's fit of spleen; by that means enabling her aunt to recover from it with as little expence to her pride as possible.

CHAPTER XXV

———————●———————

LADY PELHAM was not disappointed in her expectation of seeing Colonel Hargrave on the following day. He called at Walbourne while her Ladyship was still at her toilette; and was shown into the drawing-room, where Laura had already taken her station. She rose to receive him, with an air which shewed that his visit gave her neither surprise nor pleasure; and, motioning him to a distant seat, quietly resumed her occupation. Hargrave was a little disconcerted. He expected that Laura would shun him, with marks of strong resentment, or perhaps with the agitation of offended love; and he was prepared for nothing but to entreat the audience which she now seemed inclined to offer him.

Lovers are so accustomed to accuse ladies of cruelty, and to find ladies take pleasure in being so accused, that unlooked-for kindness discomposes them; and a favour unhoped is generally a favour undesired. The consciousness of ill desert, the frozen serenity of Laura's manner, deprived Hargrave of courage to use the opportunity which she seemed voluntarily to throw in his way. He hesitated, he faltered; while, all unlike her former self, Laura appeared determined that he should make love, for she would not aid his dilemma even by a comment on the weather. All the timidity which formerly marked her demeanour, was now transferred to his; and, arranging her work with stoical composure, she raised her head to listen, as Hargrave approaching her stammered out an incoherent sentence expressive of his unalterable love, and his fears that he had offended almost beyond forgiveness.

Laura suffered him to conclude without interruption; then answered, in a voice mild but determined, 'I had some hopes, Sir, from your knowledge of my character and sentiments, that, after what has passed, you could have entertained no doubts on this subject. – Yet, lest even a shadow of suspense should rest on your mind, I have remained here this morning on purpose to end it. I sincerely grieve to hear that you still retain the partiality you have been pleased to express, since it is now beyond my power to make even the least return.'

The utmost bitterness of reproach would not have struck so chilly on the heart of Hargrave as these words, and the manner in which they were uttered. From the principles of Laura he had indeed dreaded much; but he had feared nothing from her indifference. He had feared that duty might obtain a partial victory; but he had never doubted that inclination would survive the struggle. With a mixture of doubt, surprise, and anguish, he continued to gaze upon her after she was silent; then starting, he exclaimed – 'I will not believe it; it is impossible. Oh, Laura, choose some other way to stab, for I cannot bear this!' – 'It pains me,' said Laura, in a voice of undissembled concern, 'to add disappointment to the pangs which you cannot but feel; yet it were most blameable now to cherish in you the faintest expectation.' – 'Stop,' cried Hargrave, vehemently, 'if you would not have me utterly undone. I have never known peace or innocence but in the hope of your love; leave me a dawning of that hope, however distant. Nay, do not look as if it were impossible. When you thought me a libertine, a seducer – all that you can now think me, you suffered me to hope. Let me but begin my trial now, and all woman-kind shall not lure me from you.'

'Ah,' said Laura, 'when I dreamt of the success of that trial, a strange infatuation hung over me. Now it has passed away for ever. Sincerely do I wish and pray for your repentance, but I can no longer offer to reward it. My desire for your reformation will henceforth be as disinterested as sincere.'

Half distracted with the cutting calmness of her manner, so changed since the time when every feature spoke the struggles of the heart, when the mind's whole strength seemed collected to resist its tenderness, Hargrave again vehemently refused to believe in her indifference. ' 'Tis but a few short months,' he cried, grasping her hand with a violence that made her turn pale; ' 'tis but a few short months since you loved me with your whole soul, since you said that your peace depended upon my return to virtue. And dare you answer it to yourself to cast away the influence, the only influence that can secure me?'

'If I have any influence with you,' returned Laura, with a look and an attitude of earnest entreaty, 'let it but this once prevail, and then be laid aside for ever. Let me persuade you to the review of your conduct; to the consideration of your prospects as an accountable being, of the vengeance that awaits the impenitent, of the escape offered in the gospel. As you value your happiness, let me thus far prevail. Or if it will move you more,' continued she, the tears gushing from her eyes,' 'I will beseech you to grant this, my only request; in memory of a love that mourned your unworthiness almost unto death.'

The sight of her emotions revived Hargrave's hopes; and, casting himself at her feet, he passionately declared, while she shuddered at the impious sentiment, that he asked no heaven but her love, and cared not what were his fate if she were lost. 'Ah, Sir,' said she, with pious solemnity, 'believe me, the time is not distant when the disappointment of this passion will seem to you a sorrow light as the baffled sports of childhood. Believe the testimony of one who but lately drew near to the gates of the grave. On a death-bed, guilt appears the only real misery; and lesser evils are lost amidst its horror like shadows in a midnight-gloom.'

The ideas which Laura was labouring to introduce into the mind of Hargrave were such as he had of late too successfully endeavoured to exclude. THey had intruded like importunate creditors; till, oft refused admittance, they had ceased to return. The same arts which he had used to disguise from himself the extent of his criminality, he now naturally employed to extenuate it in the sight of Laura. He assured her that he was less guilty than she supposed; that she could form no idea of the force of the temptation which had overcome him; that Lady Bellamer was less the victim of his passions than of her own; he vehemently protested that he despised and abhorred the wanton who had undone him; and that, even in the midst of a folly for which he now execrated himself, his affections had never wandered from their first object. While he spoke, Laura in confusion cast down her eyes, and offended modesty suffused her face and neck with crimson. She could indeed form no idea of a heart which, attached to one woman, could find any temptation in the allurements of another. But when he ended, virtuous indignation flashing in her countenance, 'For shame, Sir!' said she. 'If any thing could degrade you in my eyes it were this mean attempt to screen yourself behind the partner of your wickedness. Does it lessen your guilt that it had

not even the poor excuse of passion; or think you that, even in the
hours of a weakness for which you have given me such just reason to
despise myself, I could have prized the affections of a heart so
depraved? You say you detest your crime; I fear you only detest its
punishment; for, were you really repentant, my opinion, the opinion
of the whole world, would seem to you a trifle unworthy of regard,
and the utmost bitterness of censure be but an echo to your own self-
upbraidings.'

Hargrave had no inclination to discuss the nature of repentance.
His sole desire was to wrest from Laura some token, however slight,
of returning tenderness. For this purpose he employed all the
eloquence which he had often found successful in similar attempts.
But no two things can be more different in their effects, than the
language of passion poured into the sympathizing bosom of mutual
love, or addressed to the dull ear of indifference. The expressions
which Laura once thought capable of warming the coldest heart
seemed now the mere ravings of insanity; the lamentations which she
once thought might have softened rocks, now appeared the weak
complainings of a child for his lost toy. With a mixture of pity and
disgust she listened and replied; till the entrance of Lady Pelham put
a period to the dialogue, and Laura immediately quitted the room.

Lady Pelham easily perceived that the conversation had been
particular; and Hargrave did not long leave her in doubt as to the
subject. He acquainted her with his pretensions to Laura, and begged
her sanction to his addresses; assuring her that his intercourse with
Lady Bellamer was entirely broken off, and that his marriage would
secure his permanent reformation. He complimented Lady Pelham
upon her liberality of sentiment and knowledge of the world; from
both of which he had hopes, he said, that she would not consider one
error as sufficient to blast his character. Lady Pelham made a little
decent hesitation on the score of Lady Bellamer's prior claims; but
was assured that no engagement had ever subsisted there. 'She
hoped Lord Lincourt would not be averse.' She was told that Lord
Lincourt anxiously desired to see his nephew settled. 'She hoped
Colonel Hargrave was resolved that his married life should be
irreproachable. Laura had a great deal of sensibility, it would break
her heart to be neglected; and Lady Pelham was sure, that in that
case the thought of having consented to the dear child's misery would
be more than she could support!' Her Ladyship was vanquished by
an assurance, that for Laura to be neglected by her happy husband

was utterly impossible.

'Laura's inclinations then must be consulted; every thing depended upon her concurrence, for the sweet girl had really so wound herself round Lady Pelham's heart, that positively her Ladyship could not bear to give her a moment's uneasiness, or to press her upon a subject to which she was at all averse.' And, strange as it may seem, Lady Pelham at that moment believed herself incapable of distressing the person whom, in fact, she tormented with ceaseless ingenuity! Hargrave answered by confessing his fears that he was for the present less in favour than he had once been; but he disclosed Laura's former confessions of partiality, and insinuated his conviction that it was smothered rather than extinguished.

Lady Pelham could now account for Laura's long illness and low spirits; and she listened with eager curiosity to the solution of the enigma, which had so long perplexed her. She considered whether she should relate to the lover the sorrows he had caused. She judged (for Lady Pelham often *judged* properly) that it would be indelicate thus to proclaim to him the extent of his power; but, with the usual inconsistency between her judgment and her practice, in half an hour she had informed him of all that she had observed, and hinted all that she suspected. Hargrave listened, was convinced, and avowed his conviction that Lady Pelham's influence was alone necessary to secure his success. Her Ladyship said, 'that she should feel some delicacy in using any strong influence with her niece, as the amiable orphan had no friend but herself, had owed somewhat to her kindness, and might be biassed by gratitude against her own inclination. The fortune which she meant to bequeath to Laura might by some be thought to confer a right to advise; but, for her part, she thought her little all was no more than due to the person whose tender assiduities filled the blank which had been left in her Ladyship's maternal heart by the ingratitude and disobedience of her child.' This sentiment was pronounced in a tone so pathetic, and in language so harmonious, that, though it did not for a moment impose upon her hearer, it deceived Lady Pelham herself; and she shed tears, which she actually imagined to be forced from her by the mingled emotions of gratitude and of disappointed tenderness.

Lady Pelham had now entered on a subject inexhaustible; her own feelings, her own misfortunes, her own dear self. Hargrave, who in his hours of tolerable composure was the most polite of men, listened, or appeared to listen, with unconquerable patience, till he fortunately recollected an appointment which his interest in her Ladyship's conversation had before banished from his mind; when he took his leave, bearing with him a very gracious invitation to repeat his visit.

With him departed Lady Pelham's fit of sentimentality; and, in five minutes, she had dried her eyes, composed the paragraph which was to announce the marriage of Lord Lincourt (for she killed off the old peer without ceremony) to the lovely heiress of the amiable Lady Pelham; taken possession of her niece's barouche and four, and heard herself announced as the benefactress of this new wonder of the world of fashion. She would cut off her rebellious daughter with a shilling; give her up to the beggary and obscurity which she had chosen, and leave her whole fortune to Lady Lincourt; for so, in the fulness of her content, she called Laura. After some time enjoying her niece's prospects, or to speak more justly her own, she began to think of discovering how near they might be to their accomplishment; and, for this purpose, she summoned Laura to a conference.

Lady Pelham loved nothing on earth but herself; yet vanity, gratified curiosity, and, above all, the detection of a mere human weakness reducing Laura somewhat more to her own level awakened in her breast an emotion resembling affection; as, throwing her arms round her niece, she, in language half sportive, half tender, declared her knowledge of Laura's secret, and reproached her with having concealed it so well. Insulted, wronged, and forsaken by Hargrave, Laura had kept his secret inviolable, for she had no right to disclose it; but she scorned, by any evasion, to preserve her own. Glowing with shame and mortification, she stood silently shrinking from Lady Pelham's looks; till, a little recovering herself, she said, 'I deserve to be thus humbled for my folly in founding my regards, not on the worth of their object, but on my own imagination; and more, if it be possible, do I deserve, for exposing my weakness to one who has been so ungenerous as to boast of it. But it is some compensation to my pride,' continued she, raising her eyes, 'that my disorder is cured beyond the possibility of relapse.' Lady Pelham smiled at Laura's security, which she did not consider as an infallible sign of safety. It was in vain that Laura proceeded solemnly to protest her indifference. Lady Pelham could allow for self-deceit in another's case, though she never suspected it in her own. Vain were Laura's comments upon Hargrave's character; they were but the fond revilings of offended love. Laura did not deny her former preference;

she even owed that it was the sudden intelligence of Hargrave's crimes which had reduced her to the brink of the grave; therefore Lady Pelham was convinced that a little perseverance would fan the smothered flame; and perseverance, she hoped, would not be wanting. Nevertheless, as her Ladyship balanced her fondness for contradicting by her aversion to being contradicted, and as Laura was too much in earnest to study the qualifying tone, the conference concluded rather less amicably than it began; though it ended by Lady Pelham's saying, not very consistently with her sentiments an hour before, that she would never cease to urge so advantageous a match, conceiving that she had a right to influence the choice of one whom she would make the heiress of forty thousand pounds. Laura was going to insist that all influence would be ineffectual, but her aunt quitted her without suffering her to reply. She would have followed to represent the injustice of depriving Mrs Herbert of her natural rights; but she desisted on recollecting that Lady Pelham's purposes were like wedges, never fixed but by resistance.

The time had been when Lady Pelham's fortune would have seemed to Hargrave as dust in the balance, joined with the possession of Laura. He had gamed, had felt the want of money; and money was no longer indifferent to him. But Laura's dower was still light in his estimation, compared with its weight in that of Lambert, to whom he accidentally mentioned Lady Pelham's intention. That prudent person calculated that £40,000 would form a very handsome addition to a fund upon which he intended to draw pretty freely. He had little doubt of Hargrave's success; he had never known any woman with whom such a lover could fail. He thought he could lead his friend to bargain for immediate possession of part of his bride's portion, and, for certainty of the rest in reversion, before parting with his liberty. He allowed two, or perhaps even three months for the duration of Laura's influence; during which time he feared he should have little of her husband's company at the gaming-table; but from thenceforth, he judged that the day would be his own, and that he should soon possess himself of Hargrave's property, so far as it was alienable. He considered that, in the meantime, Laura would furnish attraction sufficient to secure Hargrave's stay at −, and he trusted to his own dexterity for improving that circumstance to the best advantage. He failed not, therefore, to encourage the lover's hopes, and bestowed no small ridicule on the idea that a girl of nineteen should desert a favourite on account of his gallantry.

Cool cunning would engage with fearful odds against imprudence, if it could set bounds to the passions, as well as direct their course. But it is often deceived in estimating the force of feelings which it knows only by their effects. Lambert soon found that he had opened the passage to a torrent which bore all before it. The favourite stimulus found, its temporary substitute was almost disregarded; and Hargrave, intoxicated with his passion, tasted sparingly of the poisoned cup which his friend designed for him. His time and thoughts were again devoted to Laura, and gaming was only sought as a relief from the disappointment and vexation which generally attended his pursuit. The irritation of his mind, however, made amends for the lessened number of opportunities for plundering him, by rendering it easier to take advantage of those which remained.

The insinuating manners and elegant person of Hargrave gained daily on the favour of Lady Pelham; for the great as well as the little vulgar are the slaves of mere externals. She permitted his visits at home and his attendance abroad, expatiating frequently on the liberality of sentiment which she thus displayed. At first these encomiums on her own conduct were used only to disguise from herself and others her consciousness of its impropriety; but she repeated them till she actually believed them just, and considered herself as extending a charitable hand to rescue an erring brother from the implacable malignity of the world.

She was indefatigable in her attempts to promote his success with Laura. She lost no opportunity of pressing the subject. She obstinately refused to be convinced of the possibility of overcoming a strong prepossession. Laura, in an evil hour for herself, thoughtlessly replied, that affection was founded on the belief of excellence, and must of course give way when the foundation was removed. This observation had just fallacy sufficient for Lady Pelham's purpose. She took it for her text, and harangued upon it with all the zeal and perseverance of disputation. She called it Laura's theory; and insisted that, like other theorists, she would shut her eyes against the plainest facts, nay, stifle the feelings of her own mind, rather than admit what might controvert her opinion. She cited all the instances which her memory could furnish of agricultural, and chemical, and metaphysical theorism; and, with astonishing ingenuity, contrived to draw a parallel between each of them and Laura's case. It was in vain that Laura qualified, almost retracted her unlucky observation. Her adversary would not suffer her to desert the untenable ground. Delighted with her victory, she returned again and again to the attack, after the vanquished had appealed to her mercy; and much more than 'thrice she slew the slain.'

Sick of arguing about the possibility of her indifference, Laura at length confined herself to simple assertions of the fact. Lady Pelham at first merely refused her belief; and, with provoking pity, rallied her niece upon her self-deceit; but, finding that she corroborated her words by a corresponding behaviour to Hargrave, her Ladyship's temper betrayed its accustomed infirmity. She peevishly reproached Laura with taking a coquettish delight in giving pain; insisted that her conduct was a tissue of cruelty and affectation; and upbraided her with disingenuousness in pretending an indifference which she could not feel. 'And does your Ladyship communicate this opinion to Colonel Hargrave?' said Laura, one day, fretted almost beyond her patience by a remonstrance of two hours continuance. 'To be sure I do,' returned Lady Pelham. 'In common humanity I will not allow him to suffer more from your perverseness than I can avoid.' 'Well, Madam,' said Laura, with a sigh and a shrug of impatient resignation, 'nothing remains but that I shew a consistency, which, at least is not common to affectation.'

Lady Pelham's representations had their effect upon Hargrave. They brought balm to his wounded pride, and he easily suffered them to counteract the effect of Laura's calm and uniform assurances of her indifference. While he listened to these, her apparent candour and simplicity, the regret she expressed at the necessity of giving pain, brought temporary conviction to his mnd; and, with transports of alternate rage and grief, he now execrated her inconstancy, then his own unworthiness; now abjured her, then the vices which had deprived him of her affection. But the joint efforts of Lady Pelham and Lambert always revived hopes sufficient to make him continue a pursuit which he had not indeed the fortitude to relinquish.

His love (if we must give that name to a selfish desire, mingled at times with every ungentle feeling), had never been so ardent. The well-known principle of our nature which adds charms to what is unattainable, lent new attractions to Laura's really improved loveliness. The smile which was reserved for others seemed but the more enchanting; the hand which he was forbidden to touch seemed but the more soft and snowy; the form which was kept sacred from his approach, bewitched him with more resistless graces. Hargrave had been little accustomed to suppress any of his feelings, and he gave vent to this with an entire neglect of the visible uneasiness which it occasioned to its subject. He employed the private interviews, which Lady Pelham contrived to extort for him, in the utmost vehemence of complaint, protestation, and entreaty. He laboured to awaken the pity of Laura; he even condescended to appeal to her ambition; and persevered, in spite of unequivocal denials, till Laura, disgusted, positively refused ever again to admit him without witnesses.

His public attentions were, if possible, still more distressing to her. Encouraged by Lady Pelham, he, notwithstanding the almost repulsive coldness of Laura's manner, became her constant attendant. He pursued her wherever she went; placed himself, in defiance of propriety, so as to monopolize her conversation; and seemed to have laid aside all his distinguishing politeness, while he neglected every other woman to devote his assiduities to her alone. He claimed the station by her side till Laura had the mortification to observe that others resigned it at his approach; he snatched every opportunity of whispering his adulations in her ear; and, far from affecting any concealment in his preference, seemed to claim the character of her acknowledged adorer. It is impossible to express the vexation with which Laura endured this indelicate pre-eminence. Had Hargrave been the most irreproachable of mankind, she would have shrunk from such obtrusive marks of his partiality; but her sense of propriety was no less wounded by the attendance of such a companion, than her modesty was shocked by her being thus dragged into the notice, and committed to the mercy of the public. The exclusive attentions of the handsome Colonel Hargrave, the mirror of gallantry, the future Lord Lincourt, were not, however undesired, to be possessed unenvied. Those who unsuccessfully angled for his notice, avenged themselves on her to whom they imputed their failure, by looks of scorn, and by sarcastic remarks, which they sometimes contrived should reach the ear of the innocent object of their malice. Laura, unspeakably averse to being the subject of even laudatory observation, could sometimes scarcely restrain the tears of shame and mortification that were wrung from her by attacks which she could neither resent nor escape. In spite of the natural sweetness of her temper, she was sometimes tempted to retort upon Colonel Hargrave the vexation which he caused to her: and his officiousness almost compelled her to forsake the civility within the bounds of which she had determined to confine her coldness.

He complained bitterly of this treatment, and reproached her with taking ungenerous advantage of his passion. 'Why then,' said she, 'will you force me into the insolence of power. If you will suffer me to consider you as a common acquaintance, I shall never claim a right to avenge on you the wrongs of society; but approach no nearer. – I am unwilling to express a sentiment less respectful than dislike.' The proud spirit of Hargrave, however, could ill brook the repulses which he constantly provoked; and often in transports of rage he would break from Laura, swearing that he would no more submit to be thus made the sport of an insensible tyrannical woman.

At first she submitted with patience to his injurious language, in the hope that he would keep his oaths; but she soon found that he only repaid her endurance of his anger by making her submit to what was yet more painful, a renewal of his abject supplications. All her caution could not prevent the private interviews which she granted so unwillingly. He haunted her walks, stole upon her unannounced, detained her almost by force at these accidental meetings, or at those which he obtained by the favour of Lady Pelham. His whole conduct conspired to make him an object of real dread to Laura, though her watchful self-command and habitual benevolence preserved him from her aversion.

Sometimes she could not help wondering at the obstinacy of her persecutor. 'Surely,' said she to him, 'after all I have said, after the manner in which I have said it, you cannot expect any fruit from all these rhapsodies; you must surely think your honour bound to keep them up, at whatever hazard to the credit of your understanding.' Laura had never herself submitted to be driven into a course of actions contrary to reason, and it never occurred to her that her lover had no reason for his conduct, except that he was not sufficiently master of himself to desist from his pursuit.

From the importunities of Hargrave, however, Laura could sometimes escape. Though they were frequent, they were of necessity intermitting. He could not always be at Walbourne; he could not intrude into her apartment. She visited sometimes where he was not admitted, or she could decline the invitation which she knew extended to him. But her persecutions by Lady Pelham had no intermission; from them she had no retreat. Her chamber was no sanctuary from so familiar a friend; and the presence of strangers only served to exercise her Ladyship in that ingenious species of conversation which addresses to the *sense* of one of the company what it conveys to the *ear* of the rest.

For some time she employed all her forces in combating Laura's supposed affectation; and when, not without extreme difficulty, she was convinced that she strove against a phantom of her own creation, she next employed her efforts to alter her niece's determination. She tried to rouse her ambition; and again and again expatiated on all the real and on all the imaginary advantages of wealth and title. The theme in her Ladyship's hands seemed inexhaustible, though Laura repeatedly declared that no earthly thing could be less in her esteem than distinctions which she must share with such a person as Hargrave. Every day and all day, the subject was canvassed, and the oft-confuted argument vamped up anew, till Laura was thoroughly weary of the very names of rank, and influence, and coronets, and coaches.

Next, her Ladyship was eloquent upon Laura's implacability. 'Those who were so very unforgiving,' she supposed, 'were conscious that they had no need to be forgiven. Such people might pretend to be Christians, but in her opinion such pretensions were mere hypocrisy.' Laura stood amazed at the strength of self-deception which could produce this sentiment from lips which had pronounced inextinguishable resentment against an only child. Recovering herself, she calmly made the obvious reply, 'that she entertained no enmity against Hargrave; that on the contrary she sincerely wished him every blessing, and the best of all blessings, a renewed mind; but that the Christian precept was never meant to make the vicious and the impure the denizens of our bosoms.' It might be thought that such a reply was quite sufficient, but Lady Pelham possessed one grand qualification for a disputant; she defied conviction. She could shift, and turn, and bewilder, till she found herself precisely at the point from whence she set out.

She had a practice, too, of all others the most galling to an ingenuous and independent spirit – she would invent a set of opinions and sentiments, and then argue upon them as if they were real. It was in vain for Laura to disclaim them. Lady Pelham could prove incontrovertibly that they were Laura's sentiments; or, which was the same thing, proceeded as if she had proved it. She insisted that Laura acted on a principle of revenge against Hargrave, for the slight his inconstancy had put upon her; and argued most convincingly on the folly and wickedness of a revengeful spirit. Laura in vain protested her innocence. Lady Pelham was certain of the fact;

and she dilated on the guilt of such a sentiment, and extenuated the temporary recession of Hargrave, till a bystander must have concluded that Laura was the delinquent, and he her harmless victim. Her Ladyship declared, that, 'she did not wonder at her niece's obduracy. She had never, in her life, known a person of cool temper who was capable of forgiving. She had reason, for her own part, to be thankful that, if she had the failings of a warm temper, she had its advantages too. She had never, except in one instance, known what it was to feel permanent displeasure.'

On this topic Lady Pelham had the more room for her eloquence, because it admitted of no reply; and, perhaps, for this reason it ws the sooner exhausted; for it had not been discussed above half a dozen times, before she forsook it in order to assert her claims to influence her niece's decision. And here her Ladyship was suddenly convinced of the indefensible rights of relationship. 'She stood in the place of Laura's parents, and in their title might claim authority.' But finding Laura firmly of opinion that parental authority extended no further than a negative voice, Lady Pelham laid aside the imperative tone to take up that of entreaty. 'She would not advance the claim which her tried friendship might give her to advise; she would only beseech, conjure. She hoped her importunities would be forgiven, as they could proceed only from the tenderest regard to her dear girl's wishes. Laura was her only hope; the sole being on earth to whom her widowed heart clung with partial affection – and to see her thus throw away her happiness was more than her Ladyship could bear.' Closely as Laura had studied her aunt's character, and well as it was now known to her, she was sometimes overpowered by these expressions of love and sorrow; and wept as she was compelled to repeat that her happiness and her duty must alike be sacrificed ere she could yield to the wishes of her friend. But as she never, even in these moments of softness, betrayed the smallest symptom of compliance, Lady Pelham had not patience to adhere to the only method of attack that possessed a chance of success.

Of all her arts of teazing, this was indeed the most distressing to a person of Laura's sensibility, and she felt not a little relieved when, exasperated by the failure of all her efforts, Lady Pelham burst into vehement upbraidings of her niece's hardness of heart. 'She could not have conceived,' she said, 'such obduracy in one so young; in woman too; a creature who should be all made up of softness. Laura might pique herself upon her stoicism, but a Zeno in petticoats was, in her opinion, a monster. For her part she could never resist entreaty in her life.'

'Then I beseech you Madam,' said Laura, after having patiently submitted to be baited thus for three full hours, 'do not make mine an exception; but for pity's sake be prevailed upon to drop this subject. I assure you it can have no effect but to distress me.'

'You may be determined, Miss Montreville, that all my endeavours shall be in vain, but I shall certainly never be so far wanting to my duty as to neglect pressing upon you a match so much for your honour and advantage.'

'Is it possible,' cried Laura, losing patience at this prospect of the continuation of her persecutions, 'that your Ladyship can think it for my "advantage" to marry a man I despise; for my "honour" to share the infamy of an adulterer!'

'Upon my word, Miss Montreville,' returned Lady Pelham, reddening with anger, 'I am constrained to admire the delicacy of your language; so very suitable to the lips of so very delicate a lady.'

A smile, not wholly free from sarcasm, played on Laura's lips. 'If delicacy,' said she, 'be henceforth to find so strenuous a supporter in your Ladyship, I shall hope to be exempted in future from all remonstrance on the subject of this evening's altercation.'

If Laura really entertained the hope she mentioned, she was miserably disappointed; for Lady Pelham remitted not a jot of her tormentings. Her remonstrances were administered in every possible form, upon every possible occasion. They seasoned every tête à tête, were insinuated into every conversation. Laura's attempts to avoid the subject were altogether vain. The discourse might begin with the conquests of Gengis Khan, but it always ended with the advantages of marrying Colonel Hargrave.

Teazed and persecuted, disturbed in every useful occupation and every domestic enjoyment, Laura often considered of the possibility of delivering herself from her indefatigable tormentors, by quitting the protection of her aunt and taking refuge with Mrs Douglas. But this plan she had unfortunately deprived herself of the means of executing.

Laura knew that her cousins, the Herberts, were poor. She knew that Mrs Herbert was in a situation which needs comforts that poverty cannot command, and it was vain to expect these comforts from the maternal compassion of Lady Pelham. She therefore determined to supply them, as far as possible, from her own little fund; and fearing that a gift from her might revolt the high spirit of Herbert, she inclosed almost all her half-year's annuity in a blank cover, and conveyed it to her cousin. All that she retained was a sum far too small to defray the expence of a journey to Scotland; and several months were to elapse before she could recruit her fund. Till then, she had no resource but patience; and she endeavoured to console herself with a hope that in time the perseverance of her adversaries would fail.

Often did she with a sigh turn her eyes towards Norwood – Norwood, the seat of all the peaceful domestic virtues; where the voice of contention was unheard, where courtly politeness, though duly honoured, held the second place to the courtesy of the heart. But Mrs De Courcy had never hinted a wish that Laura should be a permanent inmate of her family, and, even if she had, there would have been a glaring impropriety in forsaking Lady Pelham's house for one in its immediate neighbourhood. De Courcy, too, she thought, was not the kind friend he was wont to be. She had of late seen him seldom, which was probably caused by the marked coolness of Lady Pelham's reception; but it had happened unfortunately that he had twice surprised her in the midst of Hargrave's extravagancies, when she almost feared to speak to him, lest she should awaken the furious jealousy to which her tormentor was subject, and she dreaded that her father's friend (for so she loved to call him) suspected her of encouraging the addresses of such a lover. During these visits he had looked, she thought, displeased, and had early taken leave. Was it kind to judge her unheard? Perhaps, if an opportunity had been given her, she might have assumed courage to exculpate herself; but, without even calling to ask her commands, De Courcy was gone with Mr Bolingbroke to London, to make arrangements for Harriet's marriage.

CHAPTER XXVI

———•———

THOUGH Laura could not escape the attacks of Lady Pelham, she sometimes found means to elude those of Hargrave. She watched his approach; and whenever he appeared, intrenched herself in her own apartment. She confined herself almost entirely to the house, and excused herself from every visit where she thought he might be of the party. He besieged her with letters; she sent them back unopened. Lady Pelham commanded her to be present during his visits; she respectfully, but peremptorily, refused to comply.

She had thus remained a sort of prisoner for some weeks, when her aunt one morning entered her room with an aspect which Laura could not well decipher. 'Well, Miss Montreville,' said she, 'you have at last accomplished your purpose; your capricious tyranny has prevailed at last; Colonel Hargrave leaves – this morning.' 'Dear Madam,' cried Laura, starting up overjoyed, 'what a deliverance!' 'Oh to be sure, mighty cause you have to congratulate yourself upon a deliverance from a man who might aspire to the first woman in England! But you will never have it in your power to throw away such another offer. You need hardly expect to awaken such another passion.'

'I hope, with all my heart, I shall not; but are you certain he will go?' 'Oh, very certain. He has written to tell me so!' 'I trust he will keep his word,' said Laura; 'and when I am sure he is gone, I will beg of your Ladyship to excuse me for a few hours, while I walk to Norwood. I have been so shackled of late! but the first use I make of my liberty shall be to visit my friends.' 'I am afraid, my dear,' returned Lady Pelham, with more gentleness than she was accustomed to use in contradiction, 'you will scarcely find time to visit Mrs De Courcy. I have long promised to pass some time with my friend Mrs Bathurst; and I propose setting off to-morrow. I should die of *ennui* here, now I have lost the society that has of late given me so much pleasure.' – 'Mrs Bathurst, Madam? she who was formerly' – 'Poh, poh, child,' interrupted Lady Pelham, 'don't stir up the embers of decayed slander – Will you never learn to forget the little mistakes of your fellow-creatures? Mrs Bathurst makes one of the best wives in the world; and to a man with whom everybody would not live so well.'

Practice had made Laura pretty expert in interpreting her aunt's language, and she understood more in the present instance than it was meant she should comprehend. She had heard of Mrs Bathurst's fame, and, knowing that it was not quite spotless, was rather averse to being the companion of Lady Pelham's visit; but she never, without mature deliberation, refused compliance with her aunt's wishes; and she resolved to consider the matter before announcing opposition. Besides she was determined to carry her point of seeing Mrs De Courcy, and therefore did not wish to introduce any other subject of altercation. 'Though I should accompany you to-morrow, Madam,' said she, 'I shall have time sufficient for my walk to Norwood. The preparations for my journey cannot occupy an hour; and, if I go to Norwood now,' added she, tying on her bonnet, 'I can return early. Good morning, Madam; to-day I may walk in peace.'

Laura felt as if a mountain had been lifted from her breast as she bounded across the lawn, and thought that Colonel Hargrave was, by this time, miles distant from Walbourne; but as she pursued her way, she began to wonder that Lady Pelham seemed so little moved by his departure. It was strange that she, who had remonstrated so warmly, so unceasingly, against Laura's behaviour to him, did not more vehemently upbraid her with its consequences. Lady Pelham's forbearance was not in character – Laura did not know how to explain it. 'I have taken her by surprise,' thought she, 'with my excursion to Norwood, but she will discuss it at large in the evening; and probably in many an evening – I shall never hear the last of it.'

It was needless, however, to anticipate evil, and Laura turned her thoughts to the explanation which she was bent on making to her friends. The more she reflected, the more she was persuaded that De Courcy suspected her of encouraging the addresses of Hargrave; addresses now provokingly notorious to all the neighbourhood. He had most probably communicated the same opinion to his mother; and Laura wished much to exculpate herself, if she could do so without appearing officiously communicative. If she could meet Mr De Courcy alone, if he should lead to the subject, or if it should accidentally occur, she thought she might be able to speak freely to him; more freely than even to Mrs De Courcy. 'It is strange, too,' thought she, 'that I should feel so little restraint with a person of the other sex; less than ever I did with one of my own. – But my father's friend ought not to be classed with other men.'

Her eyes yet swam in tears of grateful recollection, when she raised them to a horseman who was meeting her. It was Montague De Courcy; and, as he leisurely advanced, Laura's heart beat with a hope that he would, as he had often done before, dismount to accompany her walk. But Montague, though evidently in no haste to reach the place of his destination, stopped only to make a slight inquiry after her health, and then passed on. Laura's bosom swelled with grief, unmixed with resentment. 'He thinks,' said she, 'that I invite the attentions of a libertine; and is it surprising that he should withdraw his friendship from me! But he will soon know his error.' And again she more cheerfully pursued her way.

Her courage failed her a little as she entered Norwood. 'What if Mrs De Courcy too should receive me coldly,' thought she; 'Can I notice it to her? Can I beg of her to listen to my justification?' These thoughts gave Laura an air of timidity and embarrassment as she entered the room where Mrs De Courcy was sitting alone. Her fears were groundless. Mrs De Courcy received her with kindness, gently reproaching her for her long absence. Laura assured her that it was wholly involuntary, but 'of late,' said she, hesitating, 'I have been very little from home.' Mrs De Courcy gave a faint melancholy smile; but did not inquire what had confined her young friend. 'Harriet has just left me,' said she, 'to pay some visits, and to secure the presence of a companion for a very important occasion. She meant also to solicit yours, if three weeks hence you are still to be capable of acting as a bridemaid.' Laura smiling was about to reply, that being in no danger of forfeiting that privilege, she would most joyfully attend Miss De Courcy; but she met a glance of such marked, such mournful scrutiny, that she stopped; and the next moment was covered with blushes. 'Ah!' thought she, 'Mrs De Courcy indeed believes all that I feared, and more than I feared – What can I say to her?'

Her embarrassment confirmed Mrs De Courcy's belief; but, unwilling further to distress Laura, she said, 'Harriet herself will talk over all these matters with you, and then your own peculiar manner will soften the refusal into somewhat almost as pleasing as consent; if indeed you are obliged to refuse.' 'Indeed, Madam,' said Laura, 'nothing can be further from my thoughts than refusal; I shall most willingly, most gladly, attend Miss De Courcy; but may I – will you allow me to – to ask you why you should expect me to refuse?' 'And if I answer you,' returned Mrs De Courcy, 'will you promise to be candid with me on a subject where ladies think that candour may be dispensed with?' 'I will promise to be candid with you on every subject,' said Laura, rejoiced at this opportunity of entering on her justification. 'Then I will own to you,' said Mrs De Courcy, 'that circumstances have conspired with public report to convince me that you are yourself about to need the good office which Harriet solicits from you. Colonel Hargrave and you share between you the envy of our little world of fashion.' 'And have you, Madam – has Harriet – has Mr De Courcy given credit to this vexatious report!' cried Laura, the tears of mortification filling her eyes. 'Ah how differently should I have judged of you!' – 'My dearest girl,' said Mrs De Courcy, surprised but delighted, 'I assure you that none of us would, upon slight grounds, believe any thing concerning you, that you would not wish us to credit. But, in this instance, I thought my authority indisputable; Lady Pelham' – 'Is it possible,' cried Laura, 'that my aunt could propagate such a report, when she knew the teasing, the persecution that I have endured.' 'Lady Pelham did not directly assure me of its truth;' answered Mrs De Courcy; 'but when I made inquiries, somewhat, I own, in the hope of being empowered to contradict the rumour, her answer was certainly calculated to make me believe that you were soon to be lost to us.' – 'Lost indeed!' exclaimed Laura. 'But what could be my aunt's intention. Surely she cannot still expect to prevail with me. My dear friend, if you knew what I have suffered from her importunities. – But she has only my advantage in view, though, surely, she widely mistakes the means.'

Laura now frankly informed Mrs De Courcy of the inquietude she had suffered from the persevering remonstrances of Lady Pelham, and the obtrusive assiduities of Hargrave. Mrs De Courcy, though she sincerely pitied the comfortless situation of Laura, listened with pleasure to the tale. 'And is all this confidential?' said she, 'so confidential that I must not mention it even to Montague or Harriet?' 'Oh no, inded, Madam,' cried Laura; 'I wish, above all things, that Mr De Courcy should know it; tell him all, Madam; and tell him too, that I would rather be in my grave than marry Colonel Hargrave.'

Laura had scarcely spoken ere she blushed for the warmth with which she spoke, and Mrs De Courcy's smile made her blush again, and more deeply. But the plea which excused her to herself she the next moment urged to her friend. 'Ah, Madam,' said she, 'if you had witnessed Mr De Courcy's kindness to my father; if you had known how my father loved him, you would not wonder that I am anxious for his good opinion.' 'I do not wonder, my love,' said Mrs De Courcy, in a tone of heartfelt affection. 'I should be much more surprised if such a mind as yours could undervalue the esteem of a man like Montague. But why did not my sweet Laura take refuge from her tormentors at Norwood, where no officious friends, no obtrusive lovers would have disturbed her quiet?'

Laura excused herself, by saying that she was sure her aunt would never have consented to her absence for more than a few hours; but she promised, now that Lady Pelham's particular reason for detaining her was removed, that she would endeavour to obtain permission to spend some time at Norwood. 'I fear I must first pay a much less agreeable visit,' continued Laura, 'for my aunt talks of carrying me to-morrow to the house of a Mrs Bathurst, of whom you probably have heard.' Mrs De Courcy knew that Lady Pelham was on terms of intimacy with Mrs Bathurst, yet she could not help feeling some surprise that she should choose to introduce her niece to such a *chaperon*. She did not, however, think it proper, by expressing her opinion, to heighten Laura's reluctance towards what she probably could not prevent; and therefore merely expressed a strong wish that Lady Pelham would permit Laura to spend the time of her absence at Norwood. Laura, though she heartily wished the same, knew her aunt too well to expect that a purpose which she had once announced she would relinquish merely because it would interfere with the inclinations of others. Still it was not impossible that it might be relinquished. A thousand things might happen to alter Lady Pelham's resolution, though they were invincible by entreaty. Laura lingered with Mrs De Courcy for several hours, and when at last she was obliged to go, received, at parting, many a kind injunction to remember her promised visit. As she bent her steps homeward, she revolved in her mind every chance of escape from being the companion of her aunt's journey. She was the more averse to attend Lady Pelham because she conjectured that they would not return before Miss De Courcy's marriage, on which occasion Laura was unwilling to be absent. But she was sensible that neither this nor any other reason she could urge, would in the least affect Lady Pelham's motions. Derham Green, the seat of Mrs Bathurst, was above ninety miles from Walbourne; and it was not likely that Lady Pelham would travel so far with the intention of making a short visit.

Laura had quitted the avenue of Norwood and entered the lane which led to that of Walbourne, when the noise of singing, for it could not be called music, made her look round; and she perceived that she was overtaken by a figure in a dingy regimental coat, and a rusty hat, which, however, regained some of its original shade by a contrast with the grey side-locks which blew up a-thwart it. This person was applying the whole force of his lungs to the utterance of 'Hearts of Oak,' in a voice, the masculine bass of which was at times oddly interrupted by the weak treble tones of age, while, with a large crabstick, he beat time against the sides of a starveling ass upon which he was mounted. The other hand was charged with the double employment of guiding the animal, and of balancing a large portmanteau, which was placed across its shoulders. Laura, retaining the habits of her country, addressed the man with a few words of courtesy, to which he replied with the frankness and garrulity of an old Englishman; and as they proceeded at much the same pace, they continued the conversation. It was, however, soon interrupted. At the gate of a grass field, with which the ass seemed acquainted, the creature made a full stop. – 'Get on,' cried the man, striking it with his heel. It would not stir. The rider applied the crabstick more vigorously than before. It had no effect; even an ass can despise the chastisement with which it is too familiar. The contention was obstinate; neither party seemed inclined to yield. At last fortune decided in favour of the ass. The portmanteau slipped from its balance, and fell to the ground. The man looked dolefully at it. 'How the plague shall I get it up again?' said he. 'Don't dismount,' said Laura, who now first observed that her companion had but one leg – 'I can lift it up for you.'

As she raised it, Laura observed that it was directed to Mr Jones, at Squire Bathurst's, Derham Green, – –shire. Though the name was too common to excite any suspicion, the address struck her as being the same place which had so lately occupied her thoughts. 'Have you far to go,' said she to the man. 'No, Ma'am,' answered he, 'only to Job Wilson, the carrier's, with this portmanteau, for Colonel Hargrave's gentleman. The Colonel took Mr Jones with himself in the chay, but he had only room for one or two of his boxes, so he left this with the groom, and the groom gave me a pot of porter to go with it.'

The whole affair was now clear. Lady Pelham, finding Laura unmanageable at home, was contriving that she should meet Colonel Hargrave at a place where, being among strangers, she would find it less possible to avoid him. Mrs Bathurst too was probably a good convenient friend, who would countenance whatever measures were thought necessary. In the first burst of indignation at the discovery of her aunt's treachery, Laura thought of retracing her steps to Norwood, never more to enter the presence of her unworthy relation; but, resentment cooling at the recollection of the benefits she owed to Lady Pelham, she determined on returning to Walbourne, to announce in person her refusal to go with her aunt; conceiving this to be the most respectful way of intimating her intentions.

As soon as she returned home she retired to her chamber without seeing Lady Pelham; and immediately dispatched the following note to Mrs De Courcy. 'My dear Madam, an accident has happened which determines me against going to Derham Green. Will you think I presume too soon on your kind invitation, if I say that I shall see you to-morrow at breakfast? Or will not your benevolence rather acquire a new motive in the shelterless condition which awaits your very affectionate L.M.'

She then proceeded to make arrangements for her departure, reflecting, with tears, on the hard necessity which was about to set her at variance with the only living relation who had ever acknowledged her. She knew that Lady Pelham would be enraged at the frustration of a scheme, to accomplish which she had stooped to such artifice; and she feared that, however gentle might be the terms of her intended refusal, her aunt would consider it as unpardonable rebellion. She was, however, firmly resolved against compliance, and all that remained was to use the least irritating mode of denial.

They met at dinner. Lady Pelham in high good humour, Laura grave and thoughtful. Lady Pelham mentioned her journey; but, dreading to rouse her aunt's unwearied power's of objurgation, Laura kept silence; and her just displeasure rendering her averse to Lady Pelham's company, she contrived to spend the evening alone.

As the supper hour approached, Laura began to tremble for the contest which awaited her. She felt herself more than half inclined to withdraw from the storm, by departing without warning, and leaving Lady Pelham to discover the reason of her flight after she was beyond the reach of her fury. But she considered that such a proceeding must imply an irreconcilable breach with one to whom she owed great and substantial obligations; and would carry an appearance of ingratitude which she could not bear to incur. Summoning her courage, therefore, she resolved to brave the tempest. She determined, that whatever provocation she might endure, she would offer none but such as was unavoidable; though, at the same time, she would maintain that spirit which she had always found the most effectual check to her aunt's violence.

The supper passed in quiet; Laura unwilling to begin the attack; Lady Pelham glorying in her expected success. Her Ladyship had taken her candle, and was about to retire, before Laura durst venture on the subject. 'Good night, my dear,' said Lady Pelham. 'I fear,' replied Laura, 'I may rather say farewell, since it will be so long ere I see you again.' 'How do you mean!' inquired Lady Pelham. 'That I cannot accompany you to Mrs Bathurst's,' replied Laura; fetching, at the close of her speech, a breath longer than the speech itself. 'You won't go?' exclaimed Lady Pelham, in a voice of angry astonishment. 'Since it is your wish that I should,' returned Laura meekly, 'I am sorry that it is not in my power.' 'And pray what puts it out of your power?' cried Lady Pelham, wrath working in her countenance. 'I cannot go where I am to meet Colonel Hargrave.' For a moment Lady Pelham looked confounded, but presently recovering utterance, she began – 'So! this is your Norwood intelligence; and your charming Mrs De Courcy – your model of perfection – sets spies upon the conduct of all the neighbourhood!'

Laura reddened at this vulgar abuse of the woman on earth whom she most revered; but she had set a guard on her temper, and only answered, that it was not at Norwood she received her information. 'A fortunate, I should rather say a providential accident,' said she, 'disclosed to me the whole' – the word 'strategem' was rising to her lips, but she exchanged it for one less offensive.

'And what if Colonel Hargrave is to be there?' said Lady Pelham, her choler rising as her confusion subsided. 'I suppose, forsooth, my pretty prudish Miss cannot trust herself in the house with a man!' 'Not with Colonel Hargrave, Madam,' said Laura coolly.

Lady Pelham's rage was now strong enough to burst the restraints of Laura's habitual ascendancy. 'But I say you shall go, Miss,' cried she in a scream that mingled the fierceness of anger with the insolence of command. 'Yes I say you shall go; we shall see whether I am always to truckle to a baby-faced chit, a creature that might have died in a workhouse but for my charity.' 'Indeed, Madam,' said Laura, 'I do not forget – I never shall forget – what I owe you; nor that when I was shelterless and unprotected, you received and cherished me.' 'Then shew that you remember it, and do what I desire,' returned Lady Pelham, softened in spite of herself, by the resistless sweetness of Laura's look and manner. 'Do not, I beseech you, Madam,' said Laura, 'insist upon this proof of my gratitude. If you do, I can only thank you for your past kindness, and wish that it had been in my power to make a better return.' 'Do you dare to tell you that you will not go?' cried Lady Pelham, stamping till the room shook. 'I beg, Madam,' said Laura entreatingly, 'I beg of you not to command what I shall be compelled to refuse.' 'Refuse at your peril!' shrieked Lady Pelham, in a voice scarce articulate with passion, and grasping Laura's arm in the convulsion of her rage.

Laura had some times been the witness, but seldom the object of her aunt's transports; and while Lady Pelham stood eyeing her with a countenance 'fierce as ten furies,' she, conscious with what burning shame she would herself have shrunk from making such an exhibition, sympathetically averted her eyes as if the virago had been sensible of the same feeling. 'I say refuse at your peril!' cried Lady Pelham. – 'Why dont you speak? obstinate' – 'Because,' answered Laura with saintlike meekness, 'I can say nothing but what will offend you – I cannot go to Mrs Bathurst's.'

Angry opposition Lady Pelham might have retorted with some small remains of self-possession, but the serenity of Laura exasperating her beyond all bounds, she was so far transported as to strike her a violent blow. Without uttering a syllable, Laura took her candle and quitted the room; while Lady Pelham, herself confounded at the outrage she had committed, made no attempt to detain her.

Laura retired to her chamber, and sat quietly down to consider the state of her warfare, which she determined to conclude by letter, without exposing her person to another assault; but in a few minutes she was stormed in her citadel, and the enemy entered, conscious of mistake, but with spirit unbroken. Lady Pelham had gone too far to retract, and was too much in the wrong to recant her error; her passion, however, had somewhat exhausted itself in the intemperate exercise which she had allowed it; and though as unreasonable as ever, she was less outrageous. Advancing towards Laura with an air intended to express offended majesty (for studied dignity is generally the disguise chosen by conscious degradation), she began, 'Miss Montreville, do you, in defiance of my commands, adhere to your resolution of not visiting Mrs Bathurst?' 'Certainly, Madam;' replied Laura, provoked that Lady Pelham should expect to intimidate her by a blow; 'I have seen no reason to relinquish it.' – 'There is a reason, however,' returned Lady Pelham, elevating her chin, curling her upper lip, and giving Laura the side-glance of disdain, 'though probably it is too light to weigh with such a determined lady, and that is, that you must either prepare to attend me to-morrow, or return to that beggary from which I took you, and never more enter my presence.' 'Then, Madam,' said Laura, rising with her native mien of calm command, 'we must part; for I cannot go to Mrs Bathurst's.'

Laura's cool resistance of a threat which was expected to be all powerful, discomposed Lady Pelham's heroics. Her eyes flashing fire, and her voice sharpening to a scream, 'Perverse ungrateful wretch!' she cried, 'Get out of my sight – leave my house this instant.' 'Certainly, if you desire it, Madam,' answered Laura, with unmoved self-possession; 'but, perhaps, if you please, I had better remain here till morning. I am afraid it might give rise to unpleasant observations if it were known that I left your house at midnight.'

'I care not who knows it – I would have the world see what a viper I have fostered in my bosom. Begone, and never let me see your hypocritical face again.'

'Then I hope,' said Laura, 'your Ladyship will allow a servant to accompany me to Norwood. At this hour it would be improper for me to go alone.' 'Oh to be sure,' cried Lady Pelham, 'do go to your friend and favourite and make your complaint of all your harsh usage, and descant at large upon poor Lady Pelham's unlucky failings. No, no, I promise you, no servant of mine shall be sent on any such errand.' 'There is fine moonlight,' said Laura looking calmly from the window, 'I dare say I shall be safe enough alone.' 'You shall not go to Norwood!' cried Lady Pelham – 'I'll take care to keep you from that prying, censorious old hag. You two shan't be allowed to sit primming up your mouths, and spitting venom on all the neighbourhood.' Weary of such low abuse, Laura took her bonnet, and was leaving the room. Lady Pelham placed herself between her and the door. 'Where are you going?' she demanded, in a voice in which rage was a little mingled with dread. 'To the only shelter that England affords me,' returned Laura; 'to the only friends from whom death or distance does not sever me.' 'I shall spoil your dish of scandal for to-night,

however,' said Lady Pelham, flouncing out of the room; and, slapping
the door with a force that made the windows rattle, she locked it on
the outside. Laura making no attempt to obtain release, quietly sat
down expecting a renewal of the charge. Soon, however, all the
household seemed still, and Laura having mingled with the prayer
that commended herself to the care of heaven, a supplication for
pardon and amendment to her aunt, retired to sound and refreshing
rest.

On quitting Laura, Lady Pelham went to bed, pride and anger in
her breast fiercely struggling against a sense of blame. But the
darkness, the silence, the loneliness of night assuage the passions
even of a termagant; and by degrees she turned from re-acting and
excusing her conduct, to fretting at its probable consequences.

The courage of a virago is no more than the daring of intoxication.
Wait till the paroxysms be past, and the timid hare is not more the
slave of fear. Lady Pelham began to feel, though she would scarcely
acknowledge it to herself, how very absurdly her contest would figure
in the mouths of the gossips round Walbourne. If her niece left her
house in displeasure, if a breach were known to subsist between
them, was it not most likely that Laura would in her own defence
relate the treatment to which she had been subjected? At all events, if
she went to Norwood before a reconciliation took place, she would
certainly explain her situation to Mrs De Courcy; and Lady Pelham
could not brave the contempt of the woman whom she disliked and
abused. Anger has been compared to a short madness, and the
resemblance holds in this respect, that in both cases, a little terror is
of sovereign use in restoring quiet. Lady Pelham even feared the
calm displeasure of Laura, and shrunk from meeting the reproving
eye of even the dependent girl whom she had persecuted and
reproached and insulted. By degrees, Laura's habitual ascendancy
was completed restored, perhaps with added strength for its
momentary suspension; for she had rather gained in respectability by
patient endurance, while Lady Pelham was somewhat humbled by a
sense of misconduct. Besides, in the course of eight months
residence under her roof, Laura was become necessary to her aunt.
Her prudence, her good temper, her various domestic talents, were
ever at hand to supply the capital defects of Lady Pelham's character.
Lady Pelham could not justly be said to love any mortal, but she felt
the advantages of the method and regularity which Laura had
introduced into her family; Laura's beauty gratified her vanity;

Laura's sweetness bore with her caprice; Laura's talents amused her solitude; and she made as near an approach as nature would permit to loving Laura. What was of more consequence, Laura was popular in the neighbourhood; her story would be no sooner told than believed; and Lady Pelham's lively imagination strongly represented to her the aggravation, commentary, and sarcasm, with which such an anecdote would be circulated.

But though these ideas floated in Lady Pelham's mind, let it not be thought that she once supposed them to be the motives of her determination to seek a reconcilement! No. Lady Pelham had explained, and disguised, and adorned her failings, till she had converted the natural shame of confession into a notion that a candid avowal atoned for any of her errors; and no sooner did she begin to think of making concessions to her niece, than the consciousness of blame was lost in inward applause of her own candour and condescension. An observing eye, therefore, would have seen more of conceit than of humility in her air, when early in the morning, she entered Laura's apartment. Laura was already dressed, and returned her aunt's salutation more coldly than she had ever formerly done, though with perfect good humour. Lady Pelham approached and took her hand; Laura did not withdraw it. 'I fear,' said Lady Pelham, 'you think I behaved very absurdly last night.' Laura looked down and said nothing. 'I am willing to own I was to blame,' continued her Ladyship, 'but people of strong feelings, you know, my dear, cannot always command themselves.' Laura was still silent. 'We must forgive and forget the failings of our friends,' proceeded her Ladyship. Laura, who dreaded that these overtures of peace only covered a projected attack, still stood speechless. 'Will you not forgive me, Laura?' said Lady Pelham coaxingly, her desire of pardon increasing, as she began to doubt of obtaining it. 'I do, Madam,' said Laura, clasping Lady Pelham's hand between her own. 'I do from my heart forgive all, and if you will permit me, I will forget all — all but that when I was an orphan, alone in the wide world, you sheltered and protected me.' 'Thank you, my good girl,' returned Lady Pelham, sealing the reconciliation with a kiss. 'I knew you would think it a duty to excuse an error arising merely from my natural warmth, and the interest I take in you — "A bad effect from a noble cause." It is a melancholy truth that those who have the advantages of a feeling heart, must share its weaknesses too.' Laura had so often listened to similar nonsense, that it had ceased to provoke a smile. 'Let us talk of this no more,' said she; 'let me rather try to persuade you not only to excuse, but to sanction the obstinacy that offended you.' 'Ah Laura,' returned Lady Pelham, smiling, 'I must not call you obstinate, but you are very firm. If I could but prevail on you to go with me only for a day or two, I should make my visit as short as you please; for now it has been all arranged I must go, and it would look so awkward to go without you!' 'If the length of your visit depend upon me,' answered Laura, waving a subject on which she was determined not to forfeit her character for firmness, 'it shall be short indeed, for I shall long to offer some reparation for all my late perverseness and disobedience.'

At another time Lady Pelham's temper would have failed her at this steady opposition of her will; but fear kept her in check. After a few very gentle expostulations, she gave up the point, and inquired whether her niece still intended to spend the time of her absence at Norwood. Laura answered that she did; and had promised to breakfast there that morning. Upon this Lady Pelham overwhelmed her with such caresses and endearments, as she intended should obliterate the remembrance of her late injurious behaviour. She extolled Laura's prudence, her sweet and forgiving disposition, her commendable reserve with strangers, and her caution in speaking of herself or of her own affairs. Unfortunately for the effect of the flattery, Laura recollected that some of these qualities had at times been the subject of Lady Pelham's severe reprehension. She had, besides, sufficient penetration to detect the motive of her Ladyship's altered language; and she strove to suppress a feeling of contempt, while she replied to her aunt's thoughts as freely as if they had been frankly spoken; assuring her that she should be far from publishing to strangers the casual vexations of her domestic life. Lady Pelham reddened, as her latent thoughts were thus seized and exposed naked to her view; but fear again proved victorious, and she redoubled her blandishments. She even had recourse to a new expedient, and for the first time made Laura an offer of money. With infinite difficulty did Laura suppress the indignation which swelled her breast. She had forgiven abuse and insult, but it was beyond endurance that her aunt should suppose that her pardon and silence might be bought. Restraining her anger, however, she positively refused the money; and bidding Lady Pelham farewell, departed, amidst pressing injunctions to remain at Norwood no longer than till her aunt returned to Walbourne; her Ladyship protesting that her own home would not be endurable for an hour without the company of her dear

Laura.

Lady Pelham unwillingly set out on a journey of which the first intention had been totally defeated; but she had no alternative, since, besides having promised to visit Mrs Bathurst, she had made an appointment to meet Hargrave at the stage where she was to stop for the night, and it was now too late to give him warning of his disappointment. Even Hargrave's politeness was no match for his vexation, when he saw Lady Pelham, late in the evening, alight from her carriage, unaccompanied by Laura. He listened with impatience to her Ladyship's apology and confused explanations; and more than half resolved upon returning to − to carry on his operations there. But he too had promised to Mrs Bathurst, whom for particular reasons he wished not to disoblige. The travellers, therefore, next day pursued their journey to Derham Green, beguiling the way by joint contrivances to conquer the stubbornness of Laura.

CHAPTER XXVII

————•————

LAURA had proceeded but a short way towards Norwood when she was met by De Courcy, who, with a manner the most opposite to his coldness on the preceding day, sprang forward to meet her, his countenance radiant with pleasure. Laura, delighted with the change, playfully reproached him wth his caprice. Montague coloured, but defended himself with spirit; and a dialogue, more resembling flirtation than any in which Laura had ever engaged, occupied them till, as they loitered along the dark avenue of Norwood, a shade of the sentimental began to mingle with their conversation. De Courcy had that morning resolved, firmly resolved, that while Laura was his guest at Norwood, he would avoid a declaration of his sentiments. Convinced, as he now was, that he no longer had any thing to fear from the perseverance of Hargrave, he was yet far from being confident of his own success. On the contrary, he was persuaded that he had hitherto awakened in Laura no sentiment beyond friendship, and that she must become accustomed to him as a lover, before he could hope for any farther grace. He considered how embarrassing would be her situation in a house of which the master was a repulsed, perhaps a rejected, admirer; and he had determined not to hazard embittering to her a residence from which she had at present no retreat. Yet the confiding manner, the bewitching loveliness of Laura, the stillness, shade, and solitude of their path had half-beguiled him of his prudence, when, fortunately for his resolution, he saw Harriet advancing to meet her friend. Harriet's liveliness soon restored gaiety to the conversation; and the party proceeded less leisurely than before to Norwood, where Laura was received with affectionate cordiality by Mrs De Courcy.

Never had the time appeared to Laura to fly so swiftly as now.

Every hour was sacred to improvement, to elegance, or to benevolence. Laura had a mind capable of intense application; and therefore could exalt relaxation into positive enjoyment. But the pleasure which a vigorous understanding takes in the exercise of its powers, was now heightened in her hours of study, by the assistance, the approbation of De Courcy; and the hours of relaxation he enlivened by a manner which, at once frank and respectful, spirited and kind, seemed peculiarly fitted to adorn the domestic circle. A part of each day was employed by Mrs De Courcy in various works of charity; and, joining in these, Laura returned with satisfaction to a habit which she had unwillingly laid aside during her residence in London, and but imperfectly resumed at Walbourne. Amiable, rational, and pious, the family at Norwood realized all Laura's day-dreams of social happiness; and the only painful feeling that assailed her mind arose from the recollection that the time of her visit was fast stealing away. Her visit was, however, prolonged by a fortunate cold which detained Lady Pelham at Derham Green; and Laura could not regret an accident which delayed her separation from her friends. Indeed she began to dread Lady Pelham's return, both as the signal of her departure from Norwood, and as a prelude to the renewal of her persecutions on account of Hargrave. Far from having, as Lady Pelham had insinuated, renounced his pursuit, he returned in a few days from Mrs Bathurst's; again established himself with Lambert; and, though he could not uninvited intrude himself into Norwood, contrived to beset Laura as often as she passed its bounds. In the few visits which she paid, she generally encountered him; and he regularly waylaid her at church. But he had lost an able coadjutor in Lady Pelham; and now, when no one present was concerned to assist his designs, and when Laura was protected by kind and considerate friends, she generally found means to escape his officious attentions; though, remembering his former jealousy of Montague, and the irritability of his temper, she was scrupulously cautious of marking her preference of De Courcy, or of appearing to take sanctuary with him from the assiduities of Hargrave. Indeed, notwithstanding the mildness of De Courcy's disposition, she was not without fear that he might be involved in a quarrel by the unreasonable suspicions of Hargrave, who had often taxed her with receiving his addresses, ascribing his own failure to their success. She had in vain condescended to assure him that the charge was groundless. He never met De Courcy without shewing evident marks of dislike. If he accosted him, it was in a tone and manner approaching to insult. The most trivial sentence which De Courcy addressed to Laura, drew from Hargrave looks of enmity and defiance; while Montague, on his part, returned these aggressions by a cool disdain, the most opposite to the conciliating frankness of his general manners. Laura's alarm lest Hargrave's ill-concealed aversion should burst into open outrage, completed the dread with which he inspired her; and she felt like one subjected to the thraldom of an evil genius, when he one day announced to her that he had procured leave to remove his regiment to —; in order, as he said, 'that he might be at hand to assert his rights over her.'

He conveyed this information as, rudely preventing Mr Bolingbroke and De Courcy, he led her from Mrs De Courcy's carriage into church. Laura durst not challenge his presumptuous expression, for Montague was close by her side, and she dreaded that his aversion to arrogance and oppression should induce him to engage in her quarrel. Silently therefore, though glowing with resentment, she suffered Hargrave to retain the place he had usurped, while Montague followed, with a countenance which a few short moments had clouded with sudden care. 'Ah,' thought he, 'those rights must indeed be strong which he dares thus boldly, thus publickly assert.' It was some time ere the service began, and Laura could not help casting glances of kind inquiry on the saddened face, which, a few minutes before, she had seen bright with animation and delight. Hargrave's eye followed her's with a far different expression. While she observed him darting a scowl of malice and aversion on the man to whom he owed his life, Laura shuddered; and wondering at the infatuation which had so long disguised his true character, bent her head, acknowledged her short-sightedness, and resigned the future events of her life to the disposal of heaven. It was the day immediately preceding Harriet's marriage, and neither she nor Mrs De Courcy was in church; Laura therefore returned home tête à tête with Montague. Ignorant that Hargrave's provoking half-whisper had been overheard by De Courcy, she could not account for the sudden change in his countenance and manner; yet though she took an affectionate interest in his melancholy, they had almost reached home before she summoned courage to inquire into its cause. 'I fear you are indisposed,' said she to him in a voice of kind concern. De Courcy thanked her. 'No, not indisposed,' said he, with a faint smile. 'Disturbed, then,' said Laura. De Courcy was silent for a moment, and then taking her hand, said, 'May I be candid with you?' 'Surely,' returned Laura. 'I trust I shall ever meet with candour in you.' 'Then I will own,' resumed De Courcy, 'that I am disturbed. And can the friend of Montreville be otherwise when he hears a right claimed over you by one so wholly unworthy of you?' 'Ah,' cried Laura, 'you have then heard all. I hoped you had not attended to him.' 'Attended!' exclaimed De Courcy, 'Could any right be claimed over you and I be regardless?' 'It were ungrateful to doubt your friendly interest in me,' replied Laura. 'Believe me Colonel Hargrave has no right over me, nor ever shall have.' 'Yet I did not hear your resist the claim,' returned De Courcy. 'Because,' answered Laura, 'I feared to draw your attention. His violence terrifies me, and I feared that – that you might' – She hestitated, stopped, and blushed very deeply. She felt the awkwardness of appearing to expect that De Courcy should engage in a quarrel on her account, but the simple truth ever rose so naturally to her lips, that she could not even qualify it without confusion. 'Might what?' cried De Courcy eagerly; 'Speak frankly I beseech you.' 'I feared,' replied Laura, recovering herself, 'that the interest you take in the daughter of your friend might expose you to the rudeness of this overbearing man.' 'And did you upon my account, dearest Laura, submit to this insolence?' cried De Courcy, his eyes sparkling with exultation. 'Is my honour, my safety then dear to you? Could you think of me even while Hargrave spoke!' With surprise and displeasure Laura read the triumphant glance which accompanied his words. 'Is it possible,' thought she, 'that, well as he knows me, he can thus mistake the nature of my regard! or can he, attached to another, find pleasure in the idle dream. Oh man! thou art altogether vanity!' Snatching away the hand which he was pressing to his lips, she coldly replied, 'I should have been equally attentive to the safety of any common stranger had I expected his interference, and Colonel Hargrave's speeches cannot divert my attention even from the most trivial object in nature.' Poor De Courcy, his towering hopes suddenly levelled with the dust, shrunk from the frozen steadiness of her eye. 'Pardon me, Miss Montreville,' said he in a tone of mingled sorrow and reproach, 'pardon me for the hope that you would make any distinction between me and the most indifferent. I shall soon be cured of my presumption.' Grieved at the pain she saw she had occasioned, Laura would fain have said something to mitigate the repulse which she had given: but a new light began to dawn upon her, and she feared to conciliate the friend lest she should encourage the lover. Fortunately for the relief of her embarrassment the carriage stopped. De Courcy gravely and in silence handed her from it; and, hurrying to her chamber, she sat down to reconsider the dialogue she had just ended.

De Courcy's manner more than his words recalled a suspicion which she had oftener than once driven from her mind. She was impressed, she scarcely knew why, with a conviction that she was beloved. For some minutes this idea alone filled her thoughts; the next that succeeded was recollection that she ought sincerely to lament a passion which she could not return. It was her duty to be sorry, very sorry indeed, for such an accident; to be otherwise would have argued the most selfish vanity, the most hard-hearted ingratitude towards the best of friends, and the most amiable of mankind. Yet she was not *very* sorry; it was out of her power to convince herself that she was; so she imputed her philosophy under her misfortune to doubtfulness of its existence. 'But after all,' said she to herself, 'his words could not bear such a construction; and for his manner – who would build any thing upon a manner! While a woman's vanity is so apt to deceive her, what rational creature would give credit to what may owe so much to her own imagination! Besides, did not Mrs De Courcy more than hint that his affections were engaged. Did he not even himself confess to me that they were. And I taxed him with vanity! – Truly, if he could see this ridiculous freak of mine he might very justly retort the charge. And see it he will. What could possess me with my absurd prudery to take offence at his expecting that I, who owe him ten thousand kind offices, should be anxious for his safety? – How could I be so false, so thankless as to say I considered him as a common acquaintance? – The friend of my father, my departed father! the friend who supported him in want, and consoled him in sorrow! No wonder that he seemed shocked! What is so painful to a noble heart as to meet with ingratitude? But he shall never again have reason to think me vain or ungrateful;' and Laura hastened down stairs that she might lose no time in convincing De Courcy that she did not suspect him of being her lover, and highly valued him as a friend. She found him in the drawing-room, pensively resting his forehead against the window sash; and approaching him, spoke some trifle with a smile so winning, so gracious, that De Courcy soon forgot both his wishes and his fears, enjoyed the present, and was happy.

The day of Harriet's marriage arrived; and for once she was grave and silent. She even forgot her bridal finery; and when Laura went to inform her of Mr Bolingbroke's arrival, she found her in the library, sitting on the ground in tears, her head resting on the seat of an old-fashioned elbow chair. She sprang up as Laura entered; and dashing the drops from her eyes, cried, 'I have been trying to grow young again for a few minutes, before I am made an old woman for life. Just there I used to sit when I was a little little thing, and laid my head upon my father's knee; for this was his favourite chair, and there old Rover and I used to lie at his feet together. I'll beg this chair of my mother, for now I love every thing at Norwood.' Laura drew her away, and she forgot the old elbow-chair when she saw the superb diamonds which were lying on her dressing-table. The ceremonial of the wedding was altogether adjusted by Mrs Penelope; and though, in compliance with Mr Bolingbroke's whims, she suffered the ceremony to be privately performed, she invited every creature who could claim kindred with the names of Bolingbroke or De Courcy to meet and welcome the young bride to her home. Mr Bolingbroke having brought a licence, the pair were united at Norwood. Mr Wentworth officiated, and De Courcy gave his sister away. Mrs Bolingbroke's own new barouche, so often beheld in fancy, now really waited to convey her to her future dwelling; but she turned to bid farewell to the domestics who had attended her infancy, and forgot to look at the new barouche.

Mr Bolingbroke was a great man, and could not be allowed to marry quietly. Bonfires were lighted, bells were rung, and a concourse of his tenantry accompanied the carriages which conveyed the party. The admiration of the company whom Mrs Penelope had assembled in honour of the day, was divided between Mrs Bolingbroke's diamonds and her bride-maid; and as the number of each sex was pretty equal, the wonders shared pretty equally.

'Did you ever see any thing so lovely as Miss Montreville?' said Sophia Bolingbroke to the young lady who sat next her. 'I never can think any body pretty who has red hair,' was the reply. 'If her hair be red,' returned Sophia, 'it is the most pardonable red hair in the world, for it is more nearly black. Don't you admire her figure?' 'Not particularly; she is too much of the May-pole for me; besides, who can tell what her figure is when she is so muffled up. I dare say she is stuffed, or she would shew a little more of her skin.' 'She has at least an excellent taste in stuffing, then,' said Sophia, 'for I never saw any thing so elegantly formed.' 'It is easy to see,' said the critic, 'that she thinks herself a beauty by her dressing so affectedly. To-night when every body else is in full dress, do but look at her's!' 'Pure, unadorned, virgin white,' said Miss Bolingbroke, looking at Laura; 'the proper attire of angels!' The name of Miss Montreville had drawn the attention of De Courcy to this dialogue. 'I protest,' cried he to Mr Wentworth, who stood by him. 'Sophy Bolingbroke is the most agreeable plain girl I ever saw.' He then placed himself by her side; and while she continued to praise Laura, gave her credit for all that is most amiable in woman.

The moment he left her she ran to rally Laura upon her conquest. 'I give you joy, my dear,' said she, 'De Courcy is certainly in love with you.' 'Nonsense,' cried Laura, colouring crimson; 'what can make you think so?' 'Why he will talk of nothing but you, and he looked so delighted when I praised you; and paid me more compliments in half an hour than ere I received in my whole life before.' 'If he was so complimentary,' said Laura, smiling, 'it seems more likely that he is in love with you.' 'Ah,' said Sophia, sighing, 'that is not very probable.' 'Full as probable as the other,' answered Laura; and turned away to avoid a subject which she was striving to banish from her thoughts.

During the few days which Laura and the De Courcys spent with the newly-married pair, Miss Bolingbroke's observations served to confirm her opinion; and merely for the pleasure of speaking of Montague, she rallied Laura incessantly on her lover. In weighing credibilities, small weight of testimony turns the scale; and Laura began alternately to wonder what retarded De Courcy's declaration, and to tax herself with vanity in expecting that he would ever make one. She disliked her stay at Orfordhall, and counted the hours till her return to Norwood. De Courcy's attentions she had long placed to the account of a regard which, while she was permitted to give it the name of friendship, she could frankly own that she valued above any earthly possessions. These attentions were now so familiar to her, that they were become almost necessary, and she was vexed at being constantly reminded that she ought to reject them. She had therefore a latent wish to return to a place where she would have a legitimate claim to his kindness, and where at least there would be no one to remind her that she ought to shrink from it. Besides, she was weary of the state and magnificence that surrounded her. While Harriet glided into the use of her finery as if she had been accustomed to it from her cradle, Laura could by no means be reconciled to it. She endured with impatience a meal of three hours long; could not eat while six footmen were staring at her; started, if she thoughtlessly leant her head against the white damask wall; and could not move with ease, where every gesture was repeated in endless looking-glasses. With pleasure, therefore, she saw the day arrive which was to restore her to easy hospitality, and respectable simplicity at Norwood; but that very day she received a summons to attend her aunt at Walbourne.

Unwilling as Laura was to quit her friends, she did not delay to comply with Lady Pelham's requisition. Mrs De Courcy judged it improper to urge her to stay; and Montague in part consoled himself for her departure, by reflecting, that he would now be at liberty to disclose his long-concealed secret. 'No doubt you are at liberty,' said Mrs De Courcy, when he spoke to her of his intentions, 'and I am far from pretending to advise or interfere. But, my dear Montague, you must neither be surprised, nor in despair, if you be at first unsuccessful. Though Laura esteems you, perhaps more than esteems you, she is convinced that she is invulnerable to love; and it may be so, but her fancied security is all in your favour.' Weary of suspense, however, De Courcy often resolved to know his fate; and often went to Walbourne, determined to learn ere he returned, whether a circle of pleasing duties was to fill his after life, or whether it was to be spent alone, 'loveless, joyless, unendeared;' but when he met the friendly smile of Laura, and remembered that, his secret told, it might vanish like the gleaming of a wintry sun, his courage failed, and the intended disclosure was again delayed. Yet his manner grew less and less equivocal, and Laura, unwilling as she was to own the conviction to herself, could scarcely maintain her wilful blindness.

She allowed the subject to occupy the more of her thoughts, because it came disguised in a veil of self-condemnation and humility. Sometimes she repeated to herself, that she should never have known the vanity of her own heart, had it not been visited by so absurd a suspicion; and sometimes that she should never have been acquainted with its selfishness and obduracy, had she not borne with such indifference, the thoughts of what must bring pain and disappointment to so worthy a breast. But, spite of Laura's efforts to be miserable, the subject cost her much more perplexity than distress; and, in wondering whether De Courcy really were her lover, and what could be his motive for concealing it if he were, she often forgot to deplore the consequences of her charms.

Meanwhile Hargrave continued his importunities; and Lady Pelham seconded them with unwearied perseverance. In vain did Laura protest that her indifference was unconquerable; in vain assure him that though a total revolution in his character might regain her esteem, her affection was irrecoverably lost. She could at any time exasperate the proud spirit of Hargrave, till in transports of fury he would abjure her for ever; but a few hours always brought the 'for ever' to an end, and Hargrave back, to supplicate, to importune, and not unfrequently to threaten. Though her unremitting coldness, however, failed to conquer his passion, it by degrees extinguished all of generous or kindly that had ever mingled with the flame; and the wild unholy fire which her beauty kept alive, was blended with the heart-burnings of anger and revenge. From such a passion Laura shrunk with dread and horror. She heard its expressions as superstition listens to sounds of evil omen; and saw his impassioned glances with the dread of one who meets the eye of the crouching tiger. His increasing jealousy of De Courcy, which testified itself in haughtiness, and even ferocity of behaviour towards him, and Montague's determined though cool resistance of his insolence, kept her in continual alarm. Though she never on any other occasion voluntarily entered Hargrave's presence, yet if De Courcy found him at Walbourne, she would hasten to join them, fearing the consequences of a private interview between two such hostile spirits; and this apparent preference not only aggravated the jealousy of Hargrave, but aroused Lady Pelham's indefatigable spirit of remonstrance. The subject was particularly suited for an episode to her Ladyship's harangues in favour of Hargrave; and she introduced and varied it with a dexterity all her own. She taxed Laura with a passion for De Courcy; and in terms not eminently delicate, reproached her with facility in transferring her regards. While the charge was privately made, it appeared to Laura too groundless to affect her temper. But Lady Pelham, whose whole life might be said to form one grand experiment upon the powers of provocation, took occasion to rally her upon it before some of her companions; hinting not obscurely at the secret which Laura had so religiously kept, and confessed with so much pain. The attempt was partly successful, for Laura was really angry; but she commanded herself so far as to parry the attack, secretly vowing that her candour should never again commit her to the discretion of Lady Pelham.

Sometimes assuming the tone of a tender monitress, Lady Pelham would affect to be seriously convinced that her niece entertained a passion for De Courcy, and treating all Laura's denials as the effect of maiden timidity, would pretend to sympathize in her sufferings, advising her to use her strength of mind to conquer this unfortunate partiality; to transfer her affections from one to whom they appeared valueless to him who sued for them with such interesting perseverance. Above all, she entreated her to avoid the appearance of making advances to a man who probably never bestowed a thought on her in return; thus intimating that Laura's behaviour might bear so provoking a construction. Laura, sometimes irritated, oftener amused by these impertinences, could have endured them wtih tolerable patience; but they were mere interludes to Lady Pelham's indefatigable chidings on the subject of Hargrave. These were continued with a zeal and industry worthy of better success. And yet they could not be said to be wholly unsuccessful, while, though they could not persuade, they could torment. In vain did Laura recount the reasons which, even amidst the utmost strength of inclination, would have deterred her from a connection with a person of Hargrave's character. To reason with Lady Pelham was a labour at once severe and unavailing. She was so dexterous in the use of indefinite language, so practised in every art of shift and evasion, that the strongest argument failed to conquer; or if forced from her ground, she on the next occasion occupied it again, just as if she had always maintained it undisputed. Remonstrance and entreaty were not more successful. In defiance of both, Lady Pelham continued to ring endless changes on the same endless theme, till Laura's patience would have failed her, had she not been consoled by reflecting that the time now drew near when the payment of her annuity would enable her to escape from her unwearied persecutors. She heartily wished, however, that a change of system might make her residence with Lady Pelham endurable; for strong as was her attachment to Mrs Douglas, it was no longer her only friendship; and she could not without pain think of quitting, perhaps for ever, her valued friends at Norwood.

Winter advanced; Lady Pelham began to talk of her removal to town; and Laura was not without hopes, that when removed to a distance from Hargrave, her aunt would remit somewhat of her diligence in his cause. Laura expected that his duty would generally confine him to head-quarters, and she hoped to find in his absence a respite from one half of her plague. At all events, from London she thought she could easily procure an escort to Scotland, and she was determined rather finally to forfeit the protection of Lady Pelham, than submit to such annoyance as she had of late endured. Laura could not help wondering sometimes that her aunt, while she appeared so anxious to promote the success of Hargrave, should meditate a step which would place him at a distance from the object of his pursuit; but Lady Pelham's conduct was so generally inconsistent, that Laura was weary of trying to reconcile its contradictories. She endeavoured to hope that Lady Pelham, at last becoming sensible of the inefficacy of her efforts, was herself growing desirous to escape the Colonel's importunity; and she thought she could observe, that as the time of their departure approached, her Ladyship relaxed somewhat of her industry in teazing.

But the motives of Lady Pelham's removal did not at all coincide with her niece's hopes; and nothing could be further from her intention, than to resign her labours in a field so rich in controversy and provocation. She imagined that Laura's obstinacy was occasioned, or at least strengthened by the influence of the De Courcys, and she expected that a more general acquaintance with the world would remove her prejudices. At Walbourne, Laura, if offended, could always take refuge with Mrs De Courcy. In London, she would be more defenceless. At Walbourne, Lady Pelham acted under restraint, for there were few objects to divide with her the observation of her neighbours, and she felt herself accountable to them for the propriety of her conduct; but she would be more at liberty in a place where, each immersed in his own business or pleasure, no one had leisure to comment on the concerns of others. She knew that Hargrave would find means to escape the duty of remaining with his regiment, and indeed had concerted with him the whole plan of her operations.

Meanwhile Laura, altogether unsuspicious of their designs, gladly prepared for her journey, considering it as a fortunate instance of the instability of Lady Pelham's purposes. She paid a parting visit to Mrs Bolingbroke, whom she found established in quiet possession of all the goods of fortune. By the aid of Mrs De Courcy's carriage, she contrived, wtihout molestation from Hargrave, to spend much of her time at Norwood, where she was always received with a kindness the most flattering, and loaded with testimonies of regard. De Courcy still kept his secret; and Laura's suspicions rather diminished when she considered that, though he knew she was to go without any certainty of returning, he suffered numberless opportunities to pass without breathing a syllable of love.

The day preceding that which was fixed for the journey arrived; and Laura begged Lady Pelham's permission to spend it entirely with Mrs De Courcy. Lady Pelham was rather unwilling to consent, for she remembered that her last excursion had been rendered abortive by a visit to Norwood; but, flattering herself that her present scheme was secure from hazard of failure, she assumed an accommodating humour, and not only permitted Laura to go but allowed the carriage to convey her, stipulating that she should return it immediately, and walk home in the evening. She found the De Courcys alone, and passed the day less cheerfully than any she had ever spent at Norwood. Mrs De Courcy, though kind, was grave and thoughtful; Montague absent, and melancholy. Harriet's never-failing spirits no longer enlivened the party, and her place was but feebly supplied by the infantine gaiety of De Courcy's little protegé Henry. This child, who was the toy of all his patron's leisure hours, had, during her visits to Norwood, become particularly interesting to Laura. His quickness, his uncommon beauty, his engaging frankness, above all, the innocent fondness which he shewed for her, had really attached her to him, and he repaid her with all the affections of his little heart. He would quit his toys to hang upon her; and, though at other times, as restless as any of his kind, was never weary of sitting quietly on her knee, clasping her snowy neck in his little sun-burnt arms. His prattle agreeably interrupted the taciturnity into which the little party were falling, till his grandfather came to take him away. 'Kiss your hand Henry, and bid Miss Montreville farewell,' said the old man as he was about to take him from Laura's arms. 'It will be a long time before you see her again.' 'Are you going away?' said the child, looking sorrowfully in Laura's face. 'Yes, far away,' answered Laura. 'Then Henry will go with you, Henry's dear pretty lady. 'No no,' said his grandfather. 'You must go to your mammy; good boys love their mammies best.' 'Then you ought to be Henry's mammy,' cried the child, sobbing, and locking his arms round Laura's neck, 'for Henry loves you best.' 'My dear boy!' cried Laura, kissing him with a smile that half-consented to his wish; but, happening to turn her eye towards De Courcy, she saw him change colour, and, with an abruptness unlike his usual manner, he snatched the boy from her arms, and, regardless of his cries, dismissed him from the room.

This little incident did not contribute to the cheerfulness of the group. Grieved to part with her favourite, and puzzled to account for De Courcy's behaviour, Laura was now the most silent of the trio. She saw nothing in the childish expression of fondness which should have moved De Courcy; yet it had evidently stung him with sudden uneasiness. She now recollected that she had more than once inquired who were the parents of this child, and that the question had always been evaded. A motive of curiosity prompted her now to repeat her inquiry, and she addressed it to Mrs De Courcy. With a slight shade of embarrassment Mrs De Courcy answered, 'His mother was the only child of our old servant; a pretty, meek-spirited, unfortunate girl; and his father' – 'His father's crimes,' interrupted De Courcy, hastily, 'have brought their own punishment; a punishment beyond mortal fortitude to bear;' – and, catching up a book, he asked Laura whether she had seen it, endeavouring to divert her attention by pointing out some passages to her notice. Laura's curiosity was increased by this appearance of concealment, but she had no means of gratifying it, and the subject vanished from her mind when she thought of bidding farewell to her beloved friends, perhaps for ever.

When she was about to go, Mrs De Courcy affectionately embraced her. 'My dear child,' said she, 'second in my love and esteem only to my own Montague, almost the warmest wish of my heart is to retain you always with me; but, if that is impossible, short may your absence be, and may you return to us as joyfully as we shall receive you.' Weeping, and reluctant to part, Laura at last tore herself away. Hargrave had so often stolen upon her walks that the fear of meeting him was become habitual to her, and she wished to escape him by reaching home before her return could be expected. As she leant on De Courcy's arms, ashamed of being unable to suppress her sensibility, she averted her head, and looked sadly back upon a dwelling endeared to her by many an innocent, many a rational pleasure.

Absorbed in her regrets, Laura had proceeded a considerable way before she observed that she held a trembling arm; and recollected that De Courcy had scarcely spoken since their walk began. Her tears ceased suddenly, while confused and disquieted, she quickened her pace. Soon recollecting herself, she stopped; and thanking him for his escort, begged that he would go no further. 'I cannot leave you yet,' said De Courcy in a voice of restrained emotion, and again he led her onwards. A few short sentences were all that passed till they had almost reached the antique gate which terminated the winding part of the avenue. Here Laura again endeavoured to prevail upon her companion to return, but without success. With more composure than before, he refused to leave her. Dreading to encounter Hargrave while De Courcy was in such evident agitation, she besought him to go, telling him that it was her particular wish that he should proceed no farther. He instantly stopped, and, clasping her hand between his, 'Must I then leave you, Laura,' said he; 'you whose presence has so long been the charm of my existence!' The blood rushed violently into Laura's face, and as suddenly retired. 'And can I,' continued De Courcy, 'can I suffer you to go without pouring out my full heart to you?' Laura breathed painfully, and she pressed her hand upon her bosom to restrain its swelling. 'To talk to you of passion,' resumed De Courcy, 'is nothing. You have twined yourself with every wish and every employment, every motive, every hope, till to part with you is tearing my heart-strings.' Again he paused. Laura felt that she was expected to reply, and, though trembling and breathless, made an effort to speak. 'This is what I feared,' said she, 'and yet I wish you had been less explicit, for there is no human being whose friendship is so dear to me as yours; and now I fear I ought' – The sob which had been struggling in her breast now choked her utterance, and she wept aloud. 'It is the will of heaven,' said she, 'that I should be reft of every earthly friend.' She covered her face and stood labouring to compose herself; while, heart-struck with a disappointment which was not mitigated by all the gentleness with which it was conveyed, De Courcy was unable to break the silence.

'Ungrateful! selfish that I am,' exclaimed Laura suddenly dashing the tears from her eyes, 'thus to think only of my own loss, while I am giving pain to the worthiest of hearts. – My best friend, I cannot indeed return the regard with which you honour me, but I can make you cease to wish that I should. And I deserve the shame and anguish I shall suffer. She, whom you honour with your love,' continued she, the burning crimson glowing in her face and neck, 'has been the sport of a passion, strong as disgraceful – disgraceful as its object is worthless.'

Her look, her voice, her manner conveyed to De Courcy the strongest idea of the torture which this confession cost her; and no sufferings of his own could make him insensible to those of Laura. 'Cease, cease,' he cried, 'best and dearest of women, do not add to my wretchedness the thought of giving pain to you.' Then, after a few moments pause, he continued, 'it would be wronging your noble candour to doubt that you have recalled your affections.' 'In doing so,' answered Laura, 'I can claim no merit. Infatuation itself could have been blind no longer.' 'Then why, dearest Laura,' cried De Courcy, his heart again bounding with hope, 'why may not time and the fond assiduities of love' – 'Ah!' interrupted Laura, 'that is impossible. A mere preference I might give you, but I need not tell you that I have no more to give.' 'My heavenly Laura,' cried De Courcy, eager joy beaming in his eyes, 'give me but this preference, and I would not exchange it for the fondest passion of woman-kind.' 'You deceive yourself,' said Laura mournfully, 'miserably deceive yourself. Such a sentiment could never content you. You would miss a thousand little arts of happiness which love alone can teach; observe a thousand nameless coldnesses which no caution could conceal; and you would be unhappy without knowing perhaps of what to complain. You, who would deserve the warmest affection to be content with mere endurance! Oh no, I should be wretched in the bare thought of offering you so poor a return.'

'Endurance, Laura! I should indeed be a monster to find joy in any thing which you could describe by such a word. But must I despair of awakening such affection as will make duty delightful, such as will enjoy the bliss which it bestows?'

'Believe me, my dear friend,' said Laura in a voice as sweet, as soothing, as ever conveyed the tenderest confession, 'believe me I am not insensible to the value of your regard. It adds a new debt of gratitude to all that Montreville's daughter owes you. My highest esteem shall ever be yours, but after what I have confided to you, a moment's consideration must convince you that all beyond is impossible.' 'Ah!' thought De Courcy, 'what will it cost me to believe that it is indeed impossible.' But Laura's avowal was not quite so fatal to his hopes as she imagined; and while she supposed that he was summoning fortitude to endure their final destruction, he stood silently pondering Mrs De Courcy's oft repeated counsel to let love borrow the garb of friendship, nor suffer him undisguised to approach the heart where, having once been dethroned as an usurper, all was in arms against him.

'If I must indeed renounce every dearer hope,' resumed he, 'then in your friendship, my ever dear Miss Montreville, I must seek the happiness of my after-life, and surely' – 'Oh no,' interrupted Laura, 'that must not be – the part, the little part of your happiness which will depend upon earthly connections, you must find in that of some fortunate woman who has yet a heart to give.' 'How can you name it to me?' cried De Courcy half indignantly! 'Can he who has known you Laura, admired in you all that is noble, loved in you all that is enchanting, transfer his heart to some common-place being? – You are my business – you are my pleasure – I toil but to be worthy of you – your approbation is my sweetest reward – all earthly things are precious to me but as you share in them – even a better world borrows hope from you. And is this a love to be bestowed on some soulless thing? No, Laura, I cannot, I will not change. If I cannot win your love, I will admit no substitute but your friendship.'

'Indeed, Mr De Courcy,' cried Laura, unconsciously pressing, in the energy of speech, the hand which held hers. 'Indeed it is to no common-place woman that I wish to resign you. Lonely as my own life must be, its chief pleasures must arise from the happiness of my friends, and to know that you are happy.' – Laura stopped, for she felt her own voice grow tremulous. 'But we will not talk of this now,' resumed she, 'I shall be absent for some months at least, and in that time you will bring yourself to think differently. Promise me at least to make the attempt.'

'No, Laura,' answered De Courcy, 'that I cannot promise. I will never harass you with importunity or complaint, but the love of you shall be my heart's treasure, it shall last though life – beyond life – and if you cannot love me, give in return only such kind thoughts as you would bestow on one who would promote your happiness at the expence of his own. And promise me, dearest Laura, that when we meet, you will not receive me with suspicion or reserve, as if you feared that I should presume on your favour, or persecute you with solicitations. Trust to my honour, trust to my love itself for sparing you all unavailing entreaty. Promise me then, ever to consider me as a friend, a faithful tender friend; and forget, till my weakness reminds you of it, that ever you knew me as a lover.'

'Ah, Mr De Courcy,' cried Laura, tears filling her eyes, 'what thoughts but the kindest can I ever have of him who comforted my father's sorrows, who relieved – in a manner that made relief indeed a kindness – relieved my father's wants? And what suspicion, what coldness can I ever feel towards him whom my father loved and honoured! Yes I will trust you; for I know that you are as far above owing favours to compassion as to fear.'

'A thousand thanks, beloved Laura,' cried De Courcy, kissing her hands, 'and thus I seal our compact. One thing more; shall I trespass on your noble frankness, if I ask you whether, had not another stolen the blessing, I might have hoped to awaken a warmer regard? whether any labour, any cares could have won for me what he has forfeited?'

Silent and blushing, Laura stood for a few moments with her eyes fixed on the ground, then raising them, said, 'From you I fear no wrong construction of my words, and will frankly own to you that for my own sake, as well as your's, I wish you had been known to me ere the serpent wound me in his poisoned folds. I believe, indeed, that no mortal but himself could have inspired the same – what shall I call an infatuation with which reason had nothing to do. But you have the virtues which I have been taught to love, and – and – But what avails it now? I *was* indeed a social creature; domestic habits, domestic wishes strong in me. But what avails it now!'

'And was there a time when you could have loved me, Laura? Blessings on you for the concession. It shall cheer my exiled heart when you are far distant; sooth me with delightful day-dreams of what might have been; and give my solitude a charm which none but you could bring to the most social hour.'

'Your solitude, my honoured friend,' replied Laura, 'needs it not; it has better and nobler charms; the charms of usefulness, of piety; and long may these form your business and delight. But what makes me linger with you. I meant to have hastened home that I might avoid one as unlike to you as confidence is to fear; the feelings which you each inspire – Farewell. I trust I shall soon hear that you are well and happy.'

Loath to part, De Courcy endeavoured to detain her while he again gave utterance to his strong affection; and when she would be gone, bade her farewell in language so solemn, so tender, that all her self-command could not repress the tears which trickled down her cheeks. They parted; he followed her to beg that she would think of him sometimes. Again she left him; again he had some little boon to crave. She reached the gate, and looking back saw De Courcy standing motionless where she had last quitted him. She beckoned a farewell. The gate closed after her, and De Courcy felt as if one blank dreary waste had blotted the fair face of nature.

CHAPTER XXVIII

———————•———————

THE evening was closing, when Laura proceeded on her way. She had outstaid her purposed time, and from every bush by the path side she expected to see Hargrave steal upon her; in every gust of the chill November wind she thought she heard his footstep. She passed the last cottages connected with Norwood. The evening fires glanced cheerfully through the casements, and the voice of rustic merriment came softened on the ear. 'Amiable De Courcy!' thought Laura. 'The meanest of his dependents finds comfort in his protection, while the being on whom I have lavished the affection which might have rejoiced that worthy heart, makes himself an object of dread, even to her whom he pretends to love.' She reached home, however, without interruption, and was going to join Lady Pelham in the sitting-room; when happening to pass a looking-glass, she observed that her eyes still bore traces of the tears she had been shedding, and, in dread of the merciless raillery of her aunt, she retired to her own room. There, with an undefined feeling of despondence, she sat down to re-consider her conversation with De Courcy.

Never was task more easy, or more unprofitable. She remembered every word that De Courcy had uttered; remembered the very tone, look, and gesture with which they were spoken. She recollected too all that she had said in reply; but she could by no means unravel the confused effects of the scene upon her own mind. She certainly pitied her lover to a very painful degree. 'Poor De Courcy!' said she, accompanying the half-whisper with a heavy sigh. But having, in the course of half an hour's rumination, repeated this soliloquy about twenty times, she began to recollect that De Courcy had borne his disappointment with considerable philosophy, and appeared to derive no small comfort from the prospect of an intercourse of mere friendship. This fortunate recollection, however, not immediately relieving her, she endeavoured to account for her depression by laying hold of a vague idea which was floating in her mind, that she had not on this occasion acted as she ought. Friendships between young persons of different sexes were proverbial fomenters of the tender passion; and though she was herself in perfect safety, was it right to expose to such hazard the peace of De Courcy? Was it generous, was it even honourable to increase the difficulties of his self-conquest, by admitting him to the intimacy of friendship? It was true he had voluntarily sought the post of danger: but then he was under the dominion of an influence which did not allow him to weigh consequences; and was it not unpardonable in her, who was in full possession of herself, to sanction, to aid his imprudence? Yet how could she have rejected a friendship which did her so much honour? the friendship of the man whom her father had so loved and respected! of the man to whom her father had wished to see her connected by the closest ties! the man to whom she owed obligations never to be repaid? Alas! how had she acknowledged these obligations? By suffering the most amiable of mankind to sport with his affections, while she had weakly thrown away her own. But the mischief was not yet totally irremediable; and dazzled by the romantic generosity of sacrificing her highest earthly joy to the restoration of her benefactor's quiet, she snatched a pen intending to retract her promise. An obsolete notion of decorum was for once favourable to a lover, and Laura saw the impropriety of writing to De Courcy. Besides, it occurred to her that she might withdraw into Scotland, without formally announcing the reason of her retreat; and thus leave herself at liberty to receive De Courcy as a friend whenever discretion should warrant this indulgence. After her most magnanimous resolves however, feeling her mind as confused and comfortless as before, she determined to obtain the benefit of impartial counsel, and changed the destination of the paper on which she had already written 'My dear friend,' from De Courcy to Mrs Douglas.

With all her native candour and singleness of heart did Laura detail her case to the monitress of her youth. To reveal De Courcy's name was contrary to her principles; but she described his situation, his mode of life, and domestic habits. She enlarged upon his character, her obligations to him, and the regret which, for his sake, she felt, that particular circumstances rendered her incapable of such an attachment as was necessary to conjugal happiness. She mentioned her compliance with her lover's request of a continuance of their former intimacy; confessed her doubts of the propriety of her concession; and entreated Mrs Douglas's explicit opinion on the past, as well as her directions for the future.

Her mind thus unburdened, she was less perplexed and uneasy; and the next morning cheerfully commenced her journey, pleasing herself with the prospect of being released from the harassing attendance of Hargrave. On the evening of the second day the travellers reached Grosvenor Street; and the unsuspecting Laura, with renewed sentiments of gratitude to her aunt, revisited the dwelling which had received her when she could claim no other shelter.

Her annuity having now become due, Laura, soon after her arrival in town, one day borrowed Lady Pelham's chariot, that she might go to receive the money, and purchase some necessary additions to her wardrobe. Remembering, however, the inconveniencies to which she had been subjected by her imprudence in leaving herself without money, she regulated her disbursements by the strictest economy; determined to reserve a sum, which, besides a little gift to her cousin, might defray the expences of a journey to Scotland.

Her way chancing to lie through Holborn, a recollection of the civilities of her old landlady, induced her to stop and inquire for Mrs Dawkins. The good woman almost compelled her to alight; overwhelmed her with welcomes, and asked a hundred questions in a breath, giving in return a very detailed account of all her family affairs. She informed Laura, that Miss Julia, having lately read the life of a heroine who in the capacity of a governess captivated the heart of a great lord, had been seized with the desire to seek adventures under a similar character; but finding that recommendations for experience were necessary to her admission into any family of rank, she had condescended to serve her apprenticeship in the tuition of the daughters of an eminent cowfeeder. The good woman expressed great compassion for the pupils of so incompetent a teacher, from whom they could learn nothing useful. 'But that was,' she observed, 'their father's look out, and in the mean time, it was so far well that July was doing something towards her keeping.' After a visit of some length Laura wished to be gone, but her hostess would not suspend her eloquence long enough to suffer her to take leave. She was at last obliged to interrupt the harangue; and breaking from her indefatigable entertainer, hurried home, not a little alarmed lest her stay should expose her on her return home to oratory of a different kind. Lady Pelham, however, received her most graciously, examined all her purchases, and enquired very particularly into the cost of each. She calculated the amount, and the balance of the annuity remaining in Laura's possession. 'Five and thirty pounds!' she exclaimed – 'what in the world, Laura, will you do with so much money?' 'Perhaps five and thirty different things,' answered Laura, smiling; 'I have never had, nor ever shall have, half so much money as I could spend.' 'Oh you extravagant thing!' cried Lady Pelham patting her cheek. 'But take care that some one does not save you the trouble of spending it. You should be very sure of the locks of your drawers. You had better let me put your treasures into my bureau.' Laura was about to comply, when recollecting that there might be some awkwardness in asking her aunt for the money while she concealed its intended destination, she thanked Lady Pelham, but said she supposed it would be perfectly safe in her own custody; and then, as usual, avoided impending altercation by hastening out of the room. She thought Lady Pelham looked displeased; but as that was a necessary effect of the slightest contradiction, she saw it without violent concern; and the next time they met, her Ladyship was again all smiles and courtesy.

Three days, 'three wondrous days', all was sunshine and serenity. Lady Pelham was the most ingenious, the most amusing, the most fascinating of woman-kind. 'What a pity,' thought Laura, 'that my aunt's spirits are so fluctuating! How delightful she can be when she pleases!' In the midst of these brilliant hours, Lady Pelham one morning ran into the room where Laura was at work – 'Here's a poor fellow,' said she, with a look and voice all compassion, 'who has sent me his account, and says he must go to jail if it is not paid instantly. But it is quite impossible for me to get the money till to-morrow.' 'To jail!' cried Laura, shocked – 'What is the amount?' 'Forty pounds,' said Lady Pelham, 'and I have not above ten in the house.' 'Take mine,' cried Laura, hastening to bring it. Lady Pelham stopped her. 'No, my dear good girl,' said she, 'I wont take away your little store, perhaps you may want it yourself.' 'Oh no,' said Laura, 'I cannot want it, pray let me bring it.' 'The poor man has a large family,' said Lady Pelham, 'but indeed I am very unwilling to take –' Her Ladyship spared further regrets, for Laura was out of hearing. She returned in a moment with the whole of her wealth, out of which, Lady Pelham, after some further hesitation, was prevailed upon to take thirty pounds; a robbery to which she averred that she would never have consented, but for the wretched situation of an innocent family, and her own certainty of repaying the debt in a day or two at farthest. Several days, however, passed away, and Lady Pelham made no mention of discharging her debt. Laura wondered a little that her aunt should forget a promise so lately and so voluntarily given; but her attention was entirely diverted from the subject by the following letter from Mrs Douglas.

'You see, my dear Laura, I lose no time in answering your letter, though, for the first time, I answer you with some perplexity. The weight which you have always kindly allowed to my opinion, makes me at all times give it with timidity; but that is not the only reason of my present hesitation. I confess that in spite of the apparent frankness and perspicuity with which you have written, I am not able exactly to comprehend you. You describe a man of respectable abilities, of amiable dispositions, of sound principles, and engaging manners. You profess that such qualities, aided by intimacy, have secured your cordial friendship, while obligations beyond return have enlivened this friendship by the warmest gratitude. But, just as I am about to conclude that all this has produced its natural effect, and to prepare my congratulations for a happy occasion, you kill my expectations with a dismal sentence, expressing your regrets for having been obliged to reject the addresses of this excellent person. Now this might have been intelligible enough, supposing you were pre-occupied by a stronger attachment. But so far from this, you declare yourself absolutely incapable of any exclusive affection, or of such a regard as is necessary to any degree of happiness in the conjugal state. I know not, my dear Laura, what ideas you may entertain of the fervency suitable to wedded love; but, had you been less peremptory, I should have thought it not unlikely to spring from a young woman's "most cordial esteem" and "warmest gratitude" towards a young man with "expressive black eyes," and "the most benevolent smile in the world."

'From the tenor of your letter, as well as from some expressions you have formerly dropped, I am led to conjecture that you think an extravagant passion necessary to the happiness of married life. You will smile at the expression; but if it offends you, change it for any other descriptive of a feeling beyond tender friendship, and you will find the substitute nearly synonymous with the original. Now this idea appears to me rather erroneous; and I cannot help thinking that calm, dispassionate affection, at least on the side of the lady, promises more permanent comfort.

'All male writers on the subject of love, so far as my little knowledge extends, represent possession as the infallible cure of passion. A very unattractive picture, it must be confessed, of the love of that lordly sex! but they themselves being the painters, the deformity is a pledge of the resemblance, and I own my small experience furnishes no instance to contradict their testimony. Taking its truth then for granted, I need not inquire whether the passions of our own sex be equally fleeting. If they be, the enamoured pair soon find themselves at best in the same situation with those who marry from sober sentiments of regard; that is, obliged to seek happiness in the esteem, the confidence, the forbearance of each other. But if, in the female breast, the fervours of passion be less transient, I need not describe to you the sufferings of feminine sensibility under half-returned ardour, nor the stings of feminine pride under the unnatural and mortifying transference of the arts of courtship. I trust, my dear child, that should you even make a marriage of passion, your self-command will enable you to smother its last embers in your own bosom, while your prudence will improve the short advantage which is conferred by its empire in that of your husband, to lay the foundation of an affection more tender than friendship, more lasting than love.

'Again, it is surely of the utmost consequence to the felicity of wedded life, that a just and temperate estimate be formed of the character of him to whose temper we must accommodate ourselves; whose caprices we must endure; whose failings we must pardon, whether the discord burst upon us in thunder, or steal on amid harmonies which render it imperceptible, perhaps half-pleasing. Small chance is there that passion should view with the calm extenuating eye of reason the faults which it suddenly detects in the god of its idolatry. The once fervent votary of the idol, finding it unworthy of his worship, neglects the useful purposes to which he might apply the gold which it contains.

'I have other reasons for thinking that passion is at best unnecessary to conjugal happiness; but even if I should make you a proselyte to my opinion, the conviction would, in the present case, probably come too late. Such a man as you describe will probably be satisfied with the answer he has received. He will certainly never importune you, nor poorly attempt to extort from your pity what he could not win from your love. His attachment will soon subside into a friendly regard for you, or be diverted into another channel by virtues similar to those which first attracted him. I only wish, my dear Laura, that after this change takes place, the "circumstances" may remain in force which render you "for ever incapable of repaying him with a love like his own." If you are sure that these circumstances are decisive, I foresee no evil which can result from your cultivating a friendship so honourable and advantageous to you, as that of a man of letters and a Christian; whose conversation may improve your mind, and whose experience may supply that knowledge of the world which is rarely attainable by women in the more private walks of life.

'To him I should suppose that no danger could arise from such an intercourse. We are all apt to over-rate the strength and durability of the attachments we excite. I believe the truth is, that in a vigorous, well-governed, and actively employed mind, love rarely becomes that resistless tyrant which vanity and romances represent him. His empire is divided by the love of fame or the desire of usefulness, the eagerness of research or the triumph of discovery. But even solitude, idleness, and imagination cannot long support his dominion without the assistance of hope; and I take it for granted from your tried honour and generosity, that your answer has been too explicit to leave your lover in any doubt that your sentence is final.

'I own I could have wished, that the virtues of my ever dear Laura had found in the sacred characters of wife and mother a larger field than a state of celibacy can afford; but I have no fear that your happiness or respectability should ever depend upon outward circumstances. I have no doubt that moderate wishes and useful employments will diffuse cheerfulness in the loneliest dwelling, while piety will people it with guests from heaven.

'Thus, my beloved child, I have given my opinion with all the freedom you can desire. I have written a volume rather than a letter. The passion for giving advice long survives that which is the subject of our correspondence; but to shew you that I can lay some restraint on an old woman's rage for admonition, I will not add another line except that which assures you that I am, with all a mother's love, and all a friend's esteem,

'Your affectionate

'E. DOUGLAS.'

Laura read this letter often, and pondered it deeply. Though she could not deny that it contained some truths, she was not satisfied with the doctrine deduced from them. She remembered that Mrs Douglas was the most affectionate of wives; and concluded that in one solitary instance her judgment had been at variance with her practice; and that, having herself made a marriage of love, she was not an adequate judge of the disadvantages attending a more dispassionate connection. Some passages too she could well have spared; but as these were prophetic rather than monitory, they required little consideration; and after the second reading, Laura generally omitted them in the perusal of her friend's epistle. Upon the whole, however, it gave her pleasure. Her conscience was relieved by obtaining the sanction of Mrs Douglas to her promised intimacy with De Courcy, and already she looked forward to the time when it should be renewed.

Since her arrival in town, her aunt, all kindness and complacency, had scarcely named Hargrave; and, with the sanguine temper of youth, Laura hoped that she had at last exhausted the perseverance of her persecutors. This fruitful source of strife removed, she thought she could without much difficulty submit to the casual fits of caprice to which Lady Pelham was subject; and considering that her aunt, with all her faults, was still her most natural protector, and her house her most proper abode, she began to lay aside thoughts of removing immediately to Scotland, and to look towards Walbourne as her permanent home.

In the meantime she promised herself that the approaching winter would bring her both amusement and information. The capital, with all its wonders, of which she had hitherto seen little, the endless diversity of character which she expected its inhabitants to exhibit, the conversation of the literary and the elegant, of wits, senators, and statesmen, promised an inexhaustible fund of instruction and delight. Nay, the patriotic heart of Laura beat high with the hope of meeting some of those heroes who, undaunted by disaster, where all but honour is lost maintain the honour of Britain, or who, with happier fortune, guide the triumphant navies of our native land. She was yet to learn how little of character appears through the varnish of fashionable manners, and how little a hero or a statesman at a rout differs from a mere man of fashion in the same situation.

Lady Pelham seemed inclined to furnish her with all the

opportunities of observation which she could desire, introducing her to every visitor of distinction, and procuring for her the particular atention of two ladies of high rank, who constantly invited her to share in the gaieties of the season. But Laura, instructed in the value of time, and feeling herself accountable for its employment, stopped far short of the dissipation of her companions. She had long since established a criterion by which to judge of the innocence of her pleasure, accounting every amusement, from which she returned to her duties with an exhausted frame, languid spirits, or distracted attention, to be at best dangerous, and contrary to all rational ends of recreation. Of entertainments which she had never before witnessed, curiosity generally induced her for once to partake; but she found few that could stand her test; and to those which failed in the trial, she returned as seldom as possible.

One species alone, if it deserves to be classed with entertainments, she was unwillingly obliged to except from her rule. From card-parties Laura always returned fatigued both in mind and body; while present at them she had scarcely any other wish than to escape; and she quitted them unfit for any thing but rest. Lady Pelham, however, sometimes made it a point that her niece should accompany her to these parties; and, though she never asked Laura to play, was occasionally at pains to interest her in the game, by calling her to her side, appealing to her against ill-fortune, or exacting her congratulations in success. A few of these parties excepted, Laura's time passed pleasantly. Though the calm of her aunt's temper was now and then disturbed by short gusts of anger, it returned as lightly as it fled; and the subject, fertile in endless chiding, seemed almost forgotten.

A fortnight had passed in this sort of quiet, when one morning Lady Pelham proposed to carry Laura to see the Marquis of $-$'s superb collection of pictures. Laura, obliged by her aunt's attention to her prevailing taste, eagerly accepted the proposal, and hastened to equip herself for the excursion. Light of heart, she was returning to the drawing-room to wait till the carriage drew up, when, on entering, the first object she beheld was Colonel Hargrave, seated confidentially by the side of Lady Pelham.

Laura, turning sick with vexation, shrunk back; and, bewailing the departure of her short-lived quiet, returned, half angry, half sorrowful, to her own room. She had little time, however, to indulge her chagrin, for Lady Pelham almost immediately sent to her to let her know that the carriage waited. Disconcerted, and almost out of

humour, Laura had tossed aside her bonnet, and was about to retract
her consent to go, when, recollecting that the plan had been proposed
on her account, without any apparent motive unless to oblige her, she
thought her aunt would have just reason to complain of such an
ungracious rejection of her civility.

'Besides, it is like a spoiled child,' thought she, 'to quarrel with any
amusement, because one disagreeable circumstance attends it;' and,
readjusting her bonnet, she joined Lady Pelham, not without a secret
hope that Hargrave might not be of the party. The hope deceived
her. He was ready to hand her into the carriage, and to take his seat
by her side.

Her sanguine expectations thus put to flight, the habitual
complacency of Laura's countenance suffered a sudden eclipse. She
answered almost peevishly to Hargrave's inquiries for her health; and
so complete was her vexation, that it was long ere she observed how
much his manner towards her was changed. He whispered no
extravagancies in her ear; offered her no officious attentions; and
seized no opportunities of addressing her, but such as were
consistent with politeness and respect. He divided his assiduities not
unequally between her and Lady Pelham; and even without any
apparent reluctance, permitted a genteel young man, to whom the
ladies curtsied in passing, to share in his office of escort, and almost
to monopolize Laura's conversation. Having accompanied the ladies
home, he left them immediately, refusing Lady Pelham's invitation to
dinner; and Laura, no less pleased than surprised at this unexpected
turn, wished him good morning more graciously than she had of late
spoken to him.

The next day he dined in Grosvenor Street, and the same
propriety of manner continued. The following evening Laura again
met with him in a large party. He did not distinguish her particularly
from any of her fair competitors. Laura was delighted. She was
convinced that he had at last resolved to abandon his fruitless pursuit;
but what had so suddenly wrought this happy change, she could not
divine.

He did not visit Lady Pelham daily, yet it so happened that Laura
saw him every day, and still he was consistent. Laura scarcely
doubted, yet durst scarcely trust her good fortune.

The violent passions of Hargrave, however, in some degree
unfitted him for a deceiver; and sometimes the fiery glance of
impatience, of admiration, or of jealousy, belied the serenity of his

manner. Laura did not fail to remark this; but she possessed the happy faculty of explaining every ambiguity in human conduct, in a way favourable to the actor, – a faculty which, though it sometimes exposed her to mistake and vexation, was, upon the whole, at once a happiness and a virtue. She concluded that Hargrave, determined to persecute her no further, was striving to overcome his passion; that the appearances she had remarked were only the struggles which he could not wholly supress; and she felt herself grateful to him for making the attempt, – the more grateful from her idea of its difficulty.

With her natural singleness of heart, she one day mentioned to Lady Pelham the change in Hargrave's behaviour. 'I suppose,' added she smiling, 'that, finding he can make nothing more of me, he is resolved to lay me under obligation by leaving me at peace, having first contrived to make me sensible of its full value.' Lady Pelham was a better dissembler than Colonel Hargrave; and scarcely did a change of colour announce the deception, while, in a tone of assumed anger, she answered by reproaching her niece with having at last accomplished her purpose, and driven her lover to despair. Yet Lady Pelham was aware that Hargrave had not a thought of relinquishing his pursuit. His new-found self-command was merely intended to throw Laura off her guard, that Lady Pelham might have an opportunity of executing a scheme which Lambert had conceived, to entangle Laura beyond the possibility of escape.

Many an action, harmless in itself, is seen, by a discerning bystander, to have in it 'nature that in time will venom breed, though no teeth for the present.' It happened that Lambert, while at Walbourne, had once seen Laura engaged in a party at chess; and her bent brow and flushed cheek, her palpitating bosom, her trembling hand, her eagerness for victory, above all, her pleasure in success, restrained but not concealed, inspired him with an idea that play might be made subservient to the designs of his friend; designs which he was the more disposed to promote, because, for the present, they occupied Hargrave to the exclusion of that folly of which Lambert had so well availed himself.

It was Lambert's proposal that he should himself engage Laura in play; and having won from her, by means which he could always command, that he should transfer the debt to Hargrave. The scheme was seconded by Lady Pelham, and, in part, acquiesced in by Hargrave. But though he could consent to degrade the woman whom he intended for his wife, he could not endure that any other than himself should be the instrument of her degradation; and, sickening at the shackles which the love of gaming had imposed upon himself, he positively refused to accede to that part of the plan, which proposed to make Laura's entanglement with him the branch of a habit previously formed. Besides, the formation of a habit, especially one so contrary to previous bias, was a work of time; and a strategem of tedious execution did not suit the impatience of Hargrave's temper. He consented, however, to adopt a more summary modification of the same artifice. It was intended that Laura should at first be induced to play for a stake too small to alarm her, yet sufficiently great to make success desirable; that she should at first be allowed to win; that the stake should be increased until she should lose a sum which it might incommode her to part with; and then that the stale cheat of gamblers, hope of retrieving her loss, should be pressed on her as a motive for venturing nearer to destruction.

The chief obstacle to the execution of this honourable enterprise lay in the first step, the difficulty of persuading Laura to play for any sum which could be at all important to her. For obviating this, Lady Pelham trusted to the diffidence, the extreme timidity, the abhorrence of notoriety, which nature strengthened by education had made a leading feature in the character of Laura. Her Ladyship determined that the first essay should be made in a large company, in the presence of persons of rank, of fame, of talent, of every qualification which could augment the awe almost amounting to horror, with which Laura shrunk from the gaze of numbers.

Partly from a craving for a confident, partly in hope of securing assistance, Lady Pelham communicated her intention to the honourable Mrs Clermont, a dashing widow of five-and-thirty. The piercing black eyes, the loud voice, the free manner, and good-humoured assurance of this lady, had inspired Laura with a kind of dread, which had not yielded to the advances which the widow condescended to make. Lady Pelham judged it most favourable to her righteous purpose, that the first attempt should be made in the house of Mrs Clermont, rather than in her own; both because that lady's higher circle of acquaintance could command a more imposing assemblage of visitors; and because this arrangement would leave her Ladyship more at liberty to watch the success of her scheme, than she could be where she was necessarily occupied as mistress of the ceremonies.

The appointed evening came, and Lady Pelham, though with the utmost kindness of manner, insisted upon Laura's attendance. Laura would rather have been excused; yet, not to interrupt a humour so harmonious, she consented to go. Lady Pelham was all complacency. She condescended to preside at her niece's toilette, and obliged her to complete her dress by wearing for that evening a superb diamond aigrette, one of the ornaments of her own earlier years. Laura strenuously resisted this addition to her attire, accounting it wholly unsuitable to her situation; but her aunt would take no denial, and the affair was not worthy of a more serious refusal. This important concern adjusted, Lady Pelham viewed her niece with triumphant admiration. She burst forth into praises of her beauty, declaring, that she had never seen her look half so lovely. Yet, with skilful malice, she contrived to awaken Laura's natural bashfulness, by saying, as they were alighting at Mrs Clermont's door, 'Now my dear don't mortify me to-night by any of your Scotch *gaucheries*. Remember every eye will be turned upon you.' 'Heaven forbid,' thought Laura, and timidly followed her aunt to a couch where she took her seat.

For a while Lady Pelham's words seemed prophetic, and Laura could not raise her eyes without meeting the gaze of admiration or of scrutiny; but the rooms began to be crowded by the great and the gay, and Laura was relieved from her vexatious distinction. Lady Pelham did not long suffer her to enjoy her release, but rising, proposed that they should walk. Though Laura felt in her own majestic stature a very unenviable claim to notice, a claim rendered more conspicuous by the contrast offered in the figure of her companion, she could not with politeness refuse to accompany her aunt, and giving Lady Pelham her arm, they began their round.

Laura, little acquainted with the ease which prevails in town parties, could not help wondering at the nonchalance of Mrs Clermont, who, leaving her guests to entertain themselves as they chose, was lounging on a sofa playing piquet with Colonel Hargrave. 'Mrs Clermont at piquet,' said Lady Pelham. 'Come Laura, piquet is the only civilized kind of game you play. You shall take a lesson;' and she led her niece forwards through a circle of misses, who, in hopes of catching the attention of the handsome Colonel Hargrave, were tittering and talking nonsense most laboriously. This action naturally drew the eyes of all upon Laura, and Lady Pelham, who expected to find useful engines in her timidity and embarrassment, did not fail to make her remark the notice which she excited. From this notice

Laura would have escaped, by seating herself near Mrs Clermont; but Lady Pelham perceiving her intention, placed herself there without ceremony, so as to occupy the only remaining seats, leaving Laura standing alone, shrinking at the consciousness of her conspicuous situation. No one was near her to whom she could address herself, and her only resource was bending down to overlook Mrs Clermont's game.

She had kept her station long enough to be fully sensible of its awkwardness, when Mrs Clermont, suddenly starting up, exclaimed, 'Bless me! I had quite forgotten that I promised to make a loo-table for the Dutchess. Do, my dear Miss Montreville, take my hand for half an hour.' 'Excuse me, Madam,' said Laura, drawing back, 'I play so ill.' 'Nay, Laura,' interrupted Lady Pelham, 'your teacher is concerned to maintain your skill, and I insist on it that you play admirably.' 'Had not your Ladyship better play?' 'Oh no, my dear; I join the loo-table.' 'Come,' said Mrs Clermont, offering Laura the seat she had just quitted, 'I will take no excuse; so sit down, and success attend you!' The seat presented Laura with an inviting opportunity of turning her back upon her inspectors, she was averse from refusing such a trifling request, and rather willing to give Hargrave a proof that she was not insensible to the late improvement in his behaviour. She therefore quietly took the place assigned her, while the trio exchanged smiles of congratulation on the facility with which she had fallen into the snare.

Something, however, yet remained to be arranged, and Lady Pelham and her hostess still kept their stations by her side. While dividing the cards, Laura recollected having observed that, in town, every game seemed played for money; and she asked her antagonist what was to be the stake. He of course referred that point to her own decision; but Laura, in profound ignorance of the arcana of card-tables, blushed, hesitated, and looked at Lady Pelham and Mrs Clermont for instructions. 'We don't play high in this house, my dear,' said Mrs Clermont, 'Colonel Hargrave and I were only playing guineas.' 'Laura is only a beginner,' said Lady Pelham, 'and perhaps half a guinea' – Laura interrupted her aunt by rising and deliberately collecting the cards, 'Colonel Hargrave will excuse me,' said she. 'That is far too great a stake for me.' 'Don't be absurd, my dear,' said Lady Pelham, touching Laura's sleeve, and affecting to whisper; 'why should not you play as other people do?' Laura not thinking this a proper time to explain her conscientious scruples, merely answered, that she could not afford it; and, more embarrassed than before, would have glided away, but neither of her guards would permit her to pass. 'You need not mind what you stake with Hargrave,' said Lady Pelham apart; 'you play so much better than he that you will infallibly win.' 'That does not at all alter the case,' returned Laura. 'It would be as unpleasant to me to win Colonel Hargrave's money as to lose my own.' 'Whatever stake Miss Montreville chooses must be equally agreeable to me,' said Colonel Hargrave; but Laura observed that the smile which accompanied these words had in it more of sarcasm than of complacency. 'I should be sorry, Sir,' said she, 'that you lowered your play on my account. Perhaps some of these young ladies,' continued she, looking round to the talkative circle behind – 'Be quiet, Laura,' interrupted Lady Pelham, again in an under tone; 'you will make yourself the town-talk with your fooleries.' 'I hope not,' returned Laura, calmly; 'but if I do, there is no help; little inconveniencies must be submitted to for the sake of doing right.' 'Lord, Miss Montreville,' cried Mrs Clermont aloud, 'what odd notions you have! Who would mind playing for half a guinea. It is nothing; absolutely nothing. It would not buy a pocket handkerchief.' It would buy a week's food for a poor family, thought Laura; and she was confirmed in her resolution; but not willing to expose this reason to ridicule, and a little displeased that Mrs Clermont should take the liberty of urging her, she coolly, yet modestly replied, 'That such matters must greatly depend on the opinions and circumstances of the parties concerned, of which they were themselves the best judges.' 'I insist on your playing,' said Lady Pelham, in an angry half-whisper. 'If you will make yourself ridiculous, let it be when I am not by to share in the ridicule.' 'Excuse me, Madam, for to-night,' returned Laura, pleadingly. 'Before another evening I will give you reasons which I am sure will satisfy you.' 'I am sure,' said Hargrave, darting a very significant look towards Laura, 'if Miss Montreville, instead of cards, prefer allowing me to attend her in your absence, I shall gain infinitely by the exchange.' Laura, to whom his glance made this hint very intelligible, reddened; and, saying she would by no means interrupt his amusement, was again turning to seek a substitute among her tittering neighbours, when Mrs Clermont prevented her, by calling out to a lady at a considerable distance. 'My dear Dutchess, do have the goodness to come hither, and talk to this whimsical beauty of ours. She is seized with an economical fit, and has taken it into her pretty little head that I am quite a gambler because I fix her stake at half-a-guinea.' 'What may not youth and beauty do!' said her Grace, looking at Laura with a smile half-sly half-insinuating. 'When I was the Miss Montreville of my day, I too might have led the fashion of playing for pence, though now I dare not venture even to countenance it.' The mere circumstance of rank could never discompose Laura; and, rather taking encouragement from the charming though faded countenance of the speaker, she replied, 'But, in consideration of having no pretensions to lead the fashion, may I not claim exemption from following it?' 'Oh, by no means,' said her Grace. 'When once you have entered the world of fashion, you must either be the daring leader or the humble follower. If you choose the first, you must defy the opinions of all other people; and, if the last, you must have a suitable indifference for your own.' 'A gentle intimation,' returned Laura, 'that in the world of fashion I am quite out of place, since nothing but my own opinion is more awful to me than that of others.' 'Miss Montreville,' said Lady Pelham, with an aspect of vinegar, 'we all await your pleasure.' 'Pray, Madam,' answered Laura, 'do not let me detain you a moment; I shall easily dispose of myself.' 'Take up your cards this instant, and let us have no more of these airs,' said Lady Pelham, now without affectation whispering, in order to conceal from her elegant companions the wrath which was, however, distinctly written in her countenance.

It now occurred to Laura as strange, that so much trouble should be taken to prevail upon her to play for more than she inclined. Hargrave, though he had pretended to release her, still kept his seat, and his language had tended rather to embarrass than relieve her. Mrs Clermont had interfered further than Laura thought either necessary or proper; and Lady Pelham was eager to carry her point. Laura saw that there was something in all this which she did not comprehend; and, looking up to seek an explanation in the faces of her companions, she perceived that the whole trio seemed waiting her decision with looks of various interest. The piercing black eyes of Mrs Clermont were fixed upon her with an expression of sly curiosity. Hargrave hastily withdrew a sidelong glance of anxious expectation; while Lady Pelham's face was flushed with angry impatience of delay. 'Has your Ladyship any particular reason for wishing that I should play for a higher stake than I think right?' said Laura, fixing on her aunt a look of calm scrutiny. Too much out of humour to be completely on her guard, Lady Pelham's colour deepened several shades, while she answered, 'I child! what should make you think so? 'I don't know,' said Laura. 'People sometimes try to *convince* from mere love of victory; but they seldom take the trouble to *persuade* without some other motive.' 'Any friend,' said Lady Pelham, recollecting herself, 'would find motive enough for what I have done, in the absurd appearance of these littlenesses to the world, and the odium that deservedly falls on a young miser.' 'Nay, Lady Pelham,' said the Dutchess, 'this is far too severe. Come,' added she, beckoning to Laura, with a gracious smile, 'you shall sit by me, that I may endeavour to enlarge your conceptions on the subject of card-playing.'

Laura, thus encouraged, instantly begged her aunt's permission to pass. Lady Pelham could not decently refuse; and, venting her rage, by pinching Laura's arm till the blood came, and muttering through her clenched teeth, 'obstinate wretch,' she suffered her niece to escape. Laura did not condescend to bestow any notice upon this assault, but, pulling her glove over her wounded arm, took refuge beside the Dutchess. The fascinating manners of a high-bred woman of fashion, and the respectful attentions offered to her whom the Dutchess distinguished by her particular countenance, made the rest of the evening pass agreeably, in spite of the evident ill-humour of Lady Pelham. Her ladyship restrained the further expression of her rage till Laura and she were on their way home; when it burst out in reproaches of the parsimony, obstinacy, and perverseness which had appeared in her niece's refusal to play. Laura listened to her in silence; sensible, that while Lady Pelham's passion overpowered the voice of her own reason, it was vain to expect that she should hear reason from another. But, next day, when she judged that her aunt had had time to grow cool, she took occasion to resume the subject; and explained, with such firmness and precision, her principles in regard to the uses of money and the accountableness of its possessors, that Lady Pelham laid aside thoughts of entangling her by means of play; since it was vain to expect that she would commit to the power of chance that which she habitually considered as the sacred deposit of a father, and specially destined for the support and comfort of his children.

CHAPTER XXIX

HARGRAVE no sooner perceived the futility of his design to involve
Laura in a debt of honour, than he laid aside the disguise which had
been assumed to lull her vigilance, and which he had never worn
without difficulty. He condescended, however, to save appearance, by
taking advantage of the idea which Laura had herself suggested to
Lady Pelham, and averred that he had made a powerful effort to
recover his self-possession; but he declared that, having totally failed
in his endeavours to obtain his liberty, he was determined never to
renew them, and would trust to time and accident for removing
Laura's prejudice. In vain did she assure him that no time could
produce such a revolution in her sentiments as would at all avail him;
that though his eminent improvement in worth might secure her
esteem, her affections were alienated beyond recall. The old system
was resumed, and with greater vigour than before, because with less
fear of observation and more frequent opportunities of attack. Every
meal, every visit, every public place, furnished occasions for his
indefatigable assiduities, from which Laura found no refuge beyond
the precincts of her own chamber.

Regardless of the vexation which such a report might give her, he
chose to make his suit a subject of the tittle-tattle of the day. By this
manœuvre, in which he had before found his advantage, he hoped
that several purposes might be served. The publicity of his claim
would keep other pretenders at a distance; it would oblige those who
mentioned him to Laura to speak, if not favourably, at least with
decent caution; and it might possibly at last induce her to listen with
less reluctance to what every one spoke of as natural and probable.
Lady Pelham seconded his intentions, by hints of her niece's
engagement, and confidential complaints to her friends of the

mauvaise honte which made Laura treat with such reserve the man to whom she had long been affianced. The consequence of their manœuvring was, that Hargrave's right to persecute Laura seemed universally acknowledged. The men, at his approach, left her free to his attendance; the women entertained her with praises of his person, manners, and equipage; with hints of her situation, too gentle to warrant direct contradiction; or charges made with conviction too strong to yield any form of denial.

Lady Pelham, too, resumed her unwearied remonstrances, and teased, chided, argued, upbraided, entreated, and scolded, through every tedious hours in which the absence of visitors left Laura at her mercy. Laura had at one time determined against submitting to such treatment, and had resolved, that, if it were renewed, she would seek a refuge far from her persecutors, and from England. But that resolution had been formed when there appeared no immediate necessity for putting it in practice; and England contained somewhat to which Laura clung almost unconsciously. Amidst all her vexations, Mrs De Courcy's letters soothed her ruffled sprits; and more than once, when she renewed her determination to quit Lady Pelham, a few lines from Norwood made her pause in its fulfilment, reminding her that a few months, however unpleasing, would soon steal away, and that her return to the country would at least bring some mitigation of her persecutions.

Though Mrs De Courcy wrote often, and confidentially, she never mentioned Montague further than was necessary to avoid particularity. She said little of his health, nothing of his spirits or occupations, and never hinted any knowledge of his rejected love. Laura's inquiries concerning him were answered with vague politeness; and thus her interest in the state of his mind was constantly kept awake. Often did she repeat to herself, that she hoped he would soon learn to consider her merely as a friend; and that which we have often repeated as truth, we in time believe to be true.

Laura had been in town about a month, when one of her letters to Norwood was followed by a longer silence than usual. She wrote again, and still the answer was delayed. Fearing that illness prevented Mrs De Courcy from writing, Laura had endured some days of serious anxiety, when a letter was brought her, addressed in Montague's hand. She hastily tore it open, and her heart fluttered between pleasure and apprehension, when she perceived that the whole letter was written by him. It was short and cautious. He apologized for the liberty he took, by saying, that a rheumatic affection having prevented his mother from using her pen, she had employed him as her secretary, fearing to alarm Laura by longer silence. The letter throughout was that of a kind yet respectful friend. Not a word betrayed the lover. The expressions of tender interest and remembrance with which it abounded, were ascribed to Mrs De Courcy, or at least shared with her, in a manner which prevented any embarrassment in the reply. Laura hesitated for a moment, whether her answer should be addressed to Mrs De Courcy, or to Montague; but Montague was her benefactor, their intimacy was sanctioned by her best friend, and it is not difficult to imagine how the question was decided. Her answer produced a reply, which again was replied to in its turn; and thus a correspondence was established, which, though at first constrained and formal, was taught by Montague's prudent forbearance, to assume a character of friendly ease.

This correspondence, which soon formed one of Laura's chief pleasures, she never affected to conceal from Lady Pelham. On the contrary, she spoke of it with perfect openness and candour. Unfortunately, however, it did not meet with her Ladyship's approbation. She judged it highly unfavourable to her designs in regard to Hargrave. She imagined that, if not already an affair of love, it was likely soon to become so; and she believed that, at all events, Laura's intercourse with the De Courcys would foster those antiquated notions of morality to which Hargrave owed his ill success. Accordingly, she at first objected to Laura's new correspondence; then lectured on its impropriety and imprudence; and, lastly took upon her peremptorily to prohibit its continuance. Those who are already irritated by oppression, a trifle will at last rouse to resistance. This was an exercise of authority so far beyond Laura's expectations, that it awakened her resolution to submit no longer to the importunity and persecution which she had so long endured, but to depart immediately for Scotland. Willing, however, to execute her purpose with as little expence of peace as possible, she did not open her intentions at the moment of irritation. She waited a day of serenity to propose her departure.

In order to procure the means of defraying the expence of her journey, it was become necessary to remind Lady Pelham of her loan, which appeared to have escaped her Ladyship's recollection. Laura, accordingly, one day gently hinted a wish to be repaid. Lady Pelham at first looked surprised, and affected to have forgotten the whole transaction; but, upon being very distinctly reminded of the particulars, she owned that she recollected something of it, and carelessly promised to settle it soon; adding that she knew Laura had no use for the money. Laura then frankly announced the purpose to which she meant to apply it; saying, that, as her aunt was now surrounded by more agreeable society, she hoped she might, without inconvenience, be spared, and would therefore relieve Lady Pelham of her charge, by paying a visit to Mrs Douglas. Rage flamed in Lady Pelham's countenance, while she burst into a torrent of invective against her niece's ingratitude, and coldness of heart; and it mingled with triumph as she concluded by saying, – 'Do, Miss; by all means go to your precious Scotland, but find the means as you best can; for not one penny will I give your for such a purpose. I have long expected some such fine freak as this, but I thought I should disappoint it.' Not daunted by this inauspicious beginning, Laura, taking encouragement from her aunt's known instability, again and again renewed the subject; but Lady Pelham's purposes, however easily shaken by accident or caprice, were ever inflexible to entreaty. 'She possessed,' she said, 'the means of preventing her niece's folly, and she was determined to employ them.' Laura burnt with resentment at the injustice of this determination. She acknowledged no right which Lady Pelham possessed to detain her against her own consent, and she considered the detention of her lawful property as little else than fraud. But perceiving that remonstrance was useless, she judged it most prudent not to embitter, by vain recriminations, an intercourse from which she could not immediately escape. Without further complaint or upbraiding, she submitted to her fate; content with resolving to employ more discreetly the next payment of her annuity, and with making a just but unavailing appeal to her aunt's generosity, by asserting the right of defencelessness to protection. Lady Pelham had not the slightest idea of conceding any thing to this claim. On the contrary, the certainty that Laura could not withdraw from her power, encouraged her to use it with less restraint. She invited Hargrave to a degree of familiarity which he had not before assumed; admitted him at all hours; sanctioned any freedom which he dared to use with Laura; and forced or inveigled her into frequent tête-à-têtes with him.

Fretted beyond her patience, Laura's temper more than once failed under this treatment, and she bitterly reproached Hargrave as the source of all her vexation. As it was, however, her habitual study to convert every event of her life to the purposes of virtue, it soon occurred to her, that, during these compulsory interviews, she might become the instrument of awakening her unworthy lover to more noble pursuits. Like a ray of light, the hope of usefulness darted into her soul, shedding a cheering beam on objects which before were dark and comfortless; and, with all the enthusiastic warmth of her character, she entered on her voluntary task; forgetting, in her eagerness to recal a sinner from the error of his ways, the weariness, disgust, and dread with which she listened to the ravings of selfish passion. She no longer endeavoured to avoid him, no longer listened to him with frozen silence or avowed disdain. During their interviews, she scarcely noticed his protestations, but employed every interval in urging him, with all the eloquence of dread, to retreat from the gulf which was yawning to receive him; in assuring him, with all the solemnity of truth, that the waters of life would repay him a thousand-fold for the poisoned cup of pleasure. Truth, spoken by the loveliest lips in the world, confirmed by the lightnings of a witching eye, kindled at times in Hargrave a something which he mistook for the love of virtue. He declared his abhorrence of his former self, asserted the innocence of his present manner of life, and vowed that, for the future, he should be blameless. But when Laura rather incautiously urged him to give proof of his reformation, by renouncing a passion whose least gratifications were purchased at the expence of justice and humanity, he insisted that she required more than nature could endure, and vehemently protested that he would never, but with life, relinquish the hope of possessing her. Her remonstrances had however one effect, of which she was altogether unconscious. Hargrave could not estimate the force of those motives which led her to labour so earnestly for the conversion of a person wholly indifferent to her; and though she often assured him that her zeal was disinterested, he cherished a hope that she meant to reward his improvement. In this hope he relinquished, for a while, the schemes which he had devised against the unsuspecting Laura, till accident again decided him against trusting to her free consent for the accomplishment of his wishes.

Among other exercises of authority to which Lady Pelham was emboldened by her niece's temporary dependence on her will, she adhered to her former prohibition of Laura's correspondence with De Courcy. Laura, unwilling to make it appear a matter of importance, promised that she would desist; but said that she must first write to Mr De Courcy to account for her seeming caprice. Lady Pelham consented, and the letter was written. It spoke of Laura's situation, of her sentiments, of her regret for Hargrave's strange perseverance, of the dread and vexation to which he occasionally subjected her. To atone for its being the last, it was more friendly, more communicative than any she had formerly written. Laura meant to disguise under a sportive style the effects which oppression had produced upon her spirits; and the playful melancholy which ran throughout, gave her expressions an air of artless tenderness. Lady Pelham passed through the hall as this letter was lying upon the table, waiting for the servant who was to carry it to the post; she looked at it. The sheet was completely filled. She wondered what it could contain. She took it up and examined it, as far as the seal would permit her. What she saw did but increase her curiosity. It was only wafered, and therefore easily opened; but then it was so dishonourable to open a letter. Yet what could the letter be the worse? A girl should have no secrets from her near relations. Still, to break a seal! – It was felony by the law. Lady Pelham laid down the letter and walked away, already proud of having disdained to do a base action; but she heard the servant coming for his charge; she thought it best to have time to consider the matter. She could give him the letter at any time – and she slipped it into her pocket.

Sad sentence is produced against 'the woman who deliberates:' Lady Pelham read the letter; and then, in the heat of her resentment at the manner in which her favourite was mentioned, shewed it to Hargrave. As he marked the innocent confiding frankness, the unconstrained respect, the chastened yet avowed regard, with which Laura addressed his rival, and contrasted them with the timid caution which, even during the reign of passion, had characterized her intercourse with himself, – contrasted them too with the mixture of pity, dislike, and dread, which had succeeded her infatuation, all the pangs of rage and jealousy took hold on the soul of Hargrave. He would have vented his frenzy by tearing the letter to atoms, but Lady Pelham snatched it from his quivering grasp, and dreading detection, sealed and restored it to its first destination.

The first use which he made of his returning powers of self-command, was to urge Lady Pelham's concurrence in a scheme which he had before devised, but which had been laid aside in consequence of his ill-founded hopes. He entreated that her Ladyship would, by an opportune absence, assist his intention; which was, he said, to alarm Laura with the horrors of a pretended arrest for an imaginary debt, and to work upon the gratefulness of her disposition, by himself appearing as her deliverer from her supposed difficulty. Lady Pelham in vain urged the futility of this strategem, representing the obstacles to its accomplishment, and the certainty of early detection. Hargrave continued to importune, and she yielded.

Yet Hargrave himself was as far as Lady Pelham from expecting any fruits from the feeble artifice which he had detailed to her. He had little expectation that Laura could ever be induced to receive any pecuniary obligation at his hands, and still less that she would consider a loan which she might almost immediately repay, as a favour important enough to be rewarded with herself. He even determined that his aid should be offered in terms which would ensure its rejection. Though he durst not venture to unfold his whole plan to Lady Pelham, his real intention was merely to employ the disguise of the law in removing Laura from even the imperfect protection of her aunt, to a place where she would be utterly without defence from his power. To the baseness of his purpose he blinded himself by considering the reparation which he should make in bestowing wealth and title on his victim; its more than savage brutality he forgot in anticipation of the gratitude with which Laura, humbled in her own eyes, and in those of the world, would accept the assiduities which now she spurned. He little knew the being whom he thus devoted to destruction! Incited by jealousy and resentment, he now resolved on the immediate execution of his design; and he did not quit Lady Pelham till he had obtained her acquiescence in it so far as it was divulged to her. He then hastened to prepare the instruments of his villainy; and ere he gave himself time to cool, all was in readiness for the scheme which was to break the innocent heart that had loved and trusted him in seeming virtue, and pitied and prayed for him and warned him in guilt. How had the shades of evil deepened since the time when Hargrave first faltered between his infant passion and a virtuous purpose! He had turned from the path which 'shineth more and more unto the perfect day.' On that in which he trode the night was stealing, slow but sure, which closes at last in outer darkness.

One morning at breakfast, Lady Pelham, with more than usual civility, apologized for leaving Laura alone during the rest of the day, saying that business called her but a few miles out of the town, but that she would return in the evening. She did not say whither she was going; and Laura, never imagining that it could at all concern her to know, did not think of inquiring. Pleasing herself with the prospect of one day of peace and solitude, she saw her aunt depart, and then sat down to detail to the friend of her youth her situation, her wishes, and her intentions. She was interrupted by a servant who came to inform her that two men below desired to speak with her. Wondering who in that land of strangers could have business with her, Laura desired that they should be shewn up stairs. Two coarse robust-looking men, apparently of the lower rank, entered the room. Laura was unable to divine what could have procured her a visit from persons of their appearance; yet, with her native courtesy, she was motioning them to a seat, when one of them stepped forward; and, laying on her shoulder a stick which he held, said, in a rough ferocious voice, 'Laura Montreville, I arrest you at the suit of John Dykes.' Laura was surprised but not alarmed. 'This must be some mistake,' said she, 'I know no such person as John Dykes.' 'He knows you though, and that is enough,' answered the man. 'Friend,' returned Laura, mildly, 'you mistake me for some other person.' 'What, Miss,' said the other man, advancing, 'do you pretend tht you are not Laura Montreville, daughter of the late Captain William Montreville, of Glenalbert in Scotland?' Laura, now changing colour, owned that she was the person so described. 'But,' said she, recovering herself, 'I cannot be arrested. I do not owe five shillings in the world.' 'Mayhap not, Miss,' said the man, 'but your father did; and you can be proved to have intermeddled with his effects as his heiress, which makes you liable for all his debts. So you'll please pay me the two hundred pounds which he owed to Mr John Dykes.' 'Two hundred pounds!' exclaimed Laura. 'The thing is impossible. My father left a list of his debts in his own hand-writing, and they have all been faithfully discharged by the sale of his property in Scotland.' The men looked at each other for a moment, and seemed to hesitate; but the roughest of the two presently answered, 'What nonsense do you tell me of lists? who's to believe all that? I have a just warrant; so either pay the money or come along.' 'Surely, friend,' said Laura, who now suspected the people to be mere swindlers, 'you cannot expect that I should pay such a sum without inquiring into your right to demand it. If your claim be a just one, present it in a regular account, properly attested, and it shall be paid to-morrow.' 'I have nothing to do with to-morrow, Miss,' said the man. 'I must do my business. It's all one to me whether you pay or not. It does not put a penny in my pocket: only if you do not choose to pay, come along; for we can't be standing here all day.' 'I cannot procure the money just now, even though I were willing,' answered Laura, with spirit, 'and I do not believe you have any right to remove me.' 'Oh, as for the right, Miss, we'll let you see that. There is our warrant, properly signed and sealed. You may look at it in my hand, for I don't much like to trust you with it.'

The warrant was stamped, and imposingly written upon parchment. With the tautology which Laura had been taught to expect in a law-paper, it rung changes upon the permission to seize and confine the person of Laura Montreville, as heiress of William Montreville, debtor to John Dykes of Pimlico. It was signed as by a magistrate, and marked with the large seals of office. Laura now no longer doubted; and, turning pale and faint, asked the men whether they would not stay for an hour while she sent to Finsbury Square to beg the advice of Mr Derwent, Lady Pelham's man of business. 'You may send for him to the lock-up house,' said the savage. 'We have no time to spare.' 'And whither will you take me?' cried Laura, almost sinking with horror. 'Most likely,' answered the most gentle of the two ruffians, 'you would not like to be put into the common prison; and you may have as good accommodations in my house as might serve a dutchess.'

Spite of her dismay Laura's presence of mind did not entirely forsake her. She hesitated whether she should not send to beg the assistance of some of Lady Pelham's acquaintance, or at least their advice in a situation so new to her. Among them all there was none with whom she had formed any intimacy; none whom, in her present circumstances of embarrassment and humiliation, she felt herself inclined to meet. She shrunk at the thought of the form in which her story might be represented by the malignant or the misjudging, and she conceived it her best course to submit quietly to an inconvenience of a few hours continuance, from which she did not doubt that her aunt's return would that evening relieve her. Still the idea of being a prisoner; of committing herself to such attendants; of being an inmate of the abodes of misery, of degradation, perhaps of vice, filled her with dread and horror, while, sinking on a couch, she covered her pale face with her hands, and inwardly commended herself to the care of heaven.

The men, meanwhile, stood whispering apart, and seemed to have forgotten the haste which they formerly expressed. At last one of them, after looking from the window into the street, suddenly approached her, and, rudely seizing her arm, cried, 'Come, Miss, the coach can't wait all day. It's of no use crying; we're too well used to that, so walk away if you don't choose to be carried.' Laura dashed the tears from her eyes, and, faintly trying to disengage her arm, was silently following her conductor to the door, when it opened and Hargrave entered.

Prepared as he was for a scene of distress, determined as he was to let no movement of compassion divert his purpose, he could not resist the quiet anguish which was written in the lovely face of his victim; and turning with real indignation to her tormentor, he exclaimed, 'Ruffian! what have you done to her?' But quickly recollecting himself, he threw his arm familiarly round her, and said, 'My dearest Laura, what is the meaning of all this? What can these people want with you?' 'Nothing which can at all concern you Sir,' said Laura, her spirit returning at the boldness of his address. 'Nay, my dear creature,' said Hargrave, 'I am sure something terrible has happened. Speak, fellows,' said he, turning to his emissaries, 'what is your business with Miss Montreville?' 'No great matter, Sir,' answered the man; 'only we have a writ against her for two hundred pounds, and she does not choose to pay it; so we must take her to a little snug place, that's all.' 'To a prison! You, Laura, to a prison! Heavens! it is not to be thought of. Leave the room fellows, and let me talk with Miss Montreville.' 'There is no occasion, Sir,' said Laura. 'I am willing to submit to a short confinement. My aunt returns this evening, and she will undoubtedly advance the money. It ought to be much the same to me what room I inhabit for the few intervening hours.' 'Good heaven! Laura do you consider what you say? Do you consider the horrors – the disgrace? Dearest girl, suffer me to settle this affair, and let me for once do something that may give you pleasure.' Laura's spirit revolted from the freedom with which this was spoken. Suffering undeserved humiliation, never had she been more jealous of her claim to respect. 'I am obliged to you, Sir,' said she, 'but your good offices are unnecessary. Some little hardship, I find, I must submit to; and I believe the smallest within my choice is to let these people dispose of me till Lady Pelham's return.' Hargrave reddened. 'She prefers a prison,' thought he, 'to owing even the smallest obligation to me. But her pride is near a fall;' and he smiled with triumphant pity on the stately mien of his victim.

He was, in effect, almost indifferent whether she accepted or rejected his proffered assistance. If she accepted it, he was determined that it should be clogged with a condition expressly stated, that he was for the future to be received with greater favour. If she refused, and he scarcely doubted that she would, he had only to make the signal, and she would be hurried, unresisting, to destruction. Yet, recollecting the despair, the distraction, with which she would too late discover her misfortune; the bitter upbraidings with which she would meet her betrayer; the frantic anguish with which she would mourn her disgrace, if, indeed, she survived it, he was inclined to wish that she would choose the more quiet way of forwarding his designs, and he again earnestly entreated her to permit his interference. Laura's strong dislike to being indebted for any favour to Hargrave, was somewhat balanced in her mind by the horror of a prison, and by the consideration that she could immediately repay him by the sale of part of her annuity. Though she still resisted his offer, therefore, it was less firmly than before. Hargrave continued to urge her. 'If,' said he, 'you dislike to allow me the pleasure of obliging you, this trifling sum may be restored whenever you please; and if you afterwards think that any little debt remains, it is in your power to repay it a thousand fold. One kind smile, one consenting look, were cheaply purchased with a world.' The hint which concluded this speech seemed to Laura manifestly intended to prevent her acceptance of the offer which he urged so warmly. 'Are you not ashamed, Sir,' said she, with a disdainful smile, 'thus to make a parade of generosity which you do not mean to practise? I know you do not — cannot expect, that I should poorly stoop to purchase your assistance.' 'Upon my soul, Laura,' cried Hargrave, seizing her hands, 'I am most earnest, most anxious, that you should yield to me in this affair; nor will I quit this spot till you have consented — nor till you have allowed me to look upon your consent as a pledge of your future favour.' Laura indignantly snatched her hands from his grasp. 'All that I comprehend of this,' said she, 'is insult, only insult. Leave me, Sir! It is unworthy even of you to insult the misfortunes of a defenceless woman.' Hargrave would not be repulsed. He again took her hand and persevered in his entreaties, not forgetting, however, to insinuate the conditions. Laura, in silent scorn, turned from him, wondering what could be the motive of his strange conduct, till it suddenly occurred to her that the arrest might be a mere plot contrived by Hargrave himself for the purpose of terrifying her into the acceptance of the conditions necessary to her escape. This suspicion once formed gained strength by every circumstance. The improbability of the debt; the time chosen when Lady Pelham was absent; the opportune arrival of Hargrave; the submission of the pretended bailiffs to his order; his frequent repetition of the conditions of his offer, at the same time that he appeared to wish for its acceptance; all conspired to convince Laura that she was intended to be made the dupe of a despicable artifice. Glowing with indignation, she again forced herself from Hargrave. 'Away with this contemptible mockery,' she cried, 'I will hear no more of it. While these people choose to guard me in this house, it shall be in an apartment secure from your intrusion.' Then, before Hargrave could prevent her, she left him, and shut herself into her own chamber.

Here, at greater liberty to think, a new question occurred to her. In case of her refusal to accept of Hargrave's terms – in case she actually preferred intrusting herself to the pretended bailiffs, whither could they intend to convey her? Laura's blood ran cold at the thought. If they were indeed the agents of Hargrave, what was there of dreadful that she had not to fear! Yet she could scarcely believe that persons could be found to attempt so daring a villany. Would they venture upon an outrage for which they must answer to the laws! an outrage which Lady Pelham would certainly feel herself concerned to bring to immediate detection and punishment. 'Unfortunate chance!' cried Laura, 'that my aunt should be absent just when she might have saved me. And I know not even where to seek her. – Why did she not tell me whither she was going? She who was wont to be so open! – Can this be a part of this cruel snare? Could she – Oh it is impossible! My fears make me suspicious and unjust.'

Though Laura thus endeavoured to acquit Lady Pelham, her suspicion of Hargrave's treachery augmented every moment. While she remembered that her father, though he had spoken to her of his affairs with the most confidential frankness, had never hinted at such a debt, never named such a person as his pretended creditor – while she thought of the manner of Hargrave's interference, the improbability that her own and her father's name and address, as well as the casualty of Lady Pelham's absence should be known to mere strangers – the little likelihood that common swindlers would endeavour to extort money by means so hazardous and with such small chance of success – her conviction rose to certainty; and she determined that nothing short of force should place her in the power of these impostors. Yet how soon might that force be employed! How feeble was the resistance which she could offer! And who would venture to aid her in resisting the pretended servants of law! 'Miserable creature that I am!' cried she, wringing her hands in an agony of grief and terror, 'must I submit to this cruel wrong? – Is there no one to save me – no friend near? – Yes! yes, I have a friend from whom no treachery of man can tear me – who can deliver me from their violence – who can do more – can make their cruelty my passport to life eternal. Let me not despair then – Let me not be wanting to myself. – With His blessing the feeblest means are mighty.'

After a moment's consideration Laura rung her bell, and the maid who usually attended her appeared. 'Catherine,' said Laura, endeavouring to speak composedly, 'will you oblige me by going to Finsbury Square, to Mr Derwent, and begging of him to come hither instantly?' 'Bless me, Madam,' cried the girl, 'you look as if you were just going to faint! can I get you any thing?' 'No, no, I shall not faint,' said Laura. 'Go my dear – go quickly – if you would save a wretch from destruction. Stop not a moment I implore you!' – Oh Catherine, more than life depends on you!' The girl's curiosity was strongly excited by these words, as well as by the strange visit of the men who were waiting in the lobby. She would fain have staid to make inquiries, but the imploring anguish of Laura's look and manner was irresistible, and she hastened out of the room. Laura then double-locking the door determined that by force only it should be entered, and throwing herself on a seat, strove to rally the spirits she was so soon to need. In a few minutes, however, Catherine returned, and through the key hole informed Laura that she had been intercepted by the men below stairs, who would not suffer any one to leave the house. 'All is then as I feared,' cried Laura in a voice of desperation. 'And thus has he made his cruel plot so sure! Is there no escape! Oh Catherine! cannot you steal away from them? Is there no means to save me?' Moved by the voice of anguish, the girl promised to do her utmost, but confessed that she had little hope of succeeding.

For a moment Laura believed her fate sealed, and almost gave herself up to despair; but, now convinced of the treachery of Hargrave, and unwillingly obliged to suspect Lady Pelham's connivance, indignation at such unexampled baseness and cruelty again roused her fainting spirit. Again she determined to resist to the uttermost, and if dragged by force from her place of refuge, to appeal to the humanity of the passengers in the street. 'Surely,' thought she, 'even common strangers will not permit such oppression.' The windows of her chamber looked towards the gardens behind the house; and she now regretted that she had not rather shut herself up in one of the front apartments, from whence she could have explained her situation to the passers by. Seeing no other chance of escape, she resolved on attempting to change her place of refuge, and was approaching the door to listen whether any one was near, when she was startled by the rough voice of one of the pretended bailiffs. 'Come along Miss,' he cried, 'we are quite tired of waiting. Come along.' The shuddering Laura made no reply. 'Come, come Miss,' cried the man again; 'you have had time enough to make ready.' Laura continued silent, while the ruffian called to her again and again, shaking the door violently. He threatened, with shocking oaths, that he would burst it open, and that she would be punished for resisting the officers of justice. All was in vain. Laura would not answer a single word. Trembling in every limb, she listened to his blasphemies and vows of vengeance, till she had wearied out her persecutor, and her ear was gladdened with the sound of his departing. He was almost immediately succeeded by his less ferocious companion, who more civilly begged her to hasten, as their business would not permit any longer delay. Finding that she would not answer, he reminded her of the consequences of obstructing the execution of the law; and threatened, if she continued obstinate, to use force. Laura sat silent and motionless, using every momentary interval of quiet, in breathing a hasty prayer for deliverance. The least violent of the fellows proved the most persevering; yet at last she had the satisfaction to hear him also retire. Presently a lighter step approached, and Hargrave called to her. 'Miss Montreville! Laura! Miss Montreville!' Laura was still silent. He called again, without success. 'Miss Montreville is ill,' cried he aloud, as if to some one at a distance. 'She is insensible. The door must be forced.' 'No! No!' cried Laura, determined not to leave him this pretence, 'I am not insensible, nor ill, if you would leave me in peace.' 'For heaven's sake, then,' returned he, 'let me speak a few words to you.' 'No,' answered Laura, 'you can say nothing that I wish to hear.' 'I beseech you, I implore you,' said Hargrave, 'only by one word put it in my power to save you from these miscreants – say but that one little word, and you are free.' 'Man, man!' cried Laura, vehemently, 'why will you make me abhor you? I want no freedom but from your

persections! Begone!' 'Only promise me,' said Hargrave, lowering his
voice, 'only promise me that you will give up that accursed De
Courcy, and I will dismiss these men.' 'Do you curse him who saved
your life! Monster! Leave me! I detest you.' Hargrave gnawed his lip
with passion. 'You shall dearly pay for this obstinacy,'said he, and
fiercely strode away.

   In the heat of his wrath, he commanded his coadjutors to force the
door; but the law which makes the home of an Englishman a sacred
sanctuary, extends its precious influence, in some faint degree, to the
breasts even of the dregs of mankind; and these wretches, who would
have given up Laura to any other outrage, hesitated to perpetrate this.
They objected the danger. 'Does your Honour think,' said one of
them, 'that the servants will stand by and allow us to break open the
door.' 'I tell you,' said Hargrave, 'all the men-servants are from
home. What do you fear from a parcel of women?' 'Women can bear
witness as well as men, your Honour; and it might be as much as our
necks are worth to be convicted. But if your Honour could entice her
out, we'd soon catch her.' Hargrave took two or three turns along the
lobby, and then returned to Laura. 'Miss Montreville,' said he, 'my
dearest Miss Montreville, I conjure you to admit me only for a
moment. These savages will wait no longer. They are determined to
force your door. Once more I implore you, before it is too late, let me
speak with you. I expect them every moment.' Laura's breast swelled
with indignation at this vile pretence of kindness. 'Acting under your
commands, Sir,' said she, 'I doubt not that they may even dare this
outrage. And let them at their peril. If the laws of my country cannot
protect, they shall avenge me.' For a moment Hargrave stood
confounded at this detection, till anger replacing shame, – 'Very well,
Madam,' he cried; 'insult me as you please, and take the
consequences.' He then rejoined his emissaries; and by bribery and
threats endeavoured to prevail upon them to consummate their
violence. The men, unwilling to forfeit the reward of the hazard and
trouble they had already undergone, allured by Hargrave's promises,
and fearing his vengeance, at last agreed to drag their hapless victim
to her doom.

   Having taken such instruments as they could find, for the purpose
of forcing the door, they followed Hargrave up stairs, and prepared to
begin their work. At this near prospect of the success of all his
schemes, Hargrave's rage began to cool; and a gleam of tenderness
and humanity reviving in his heart, he shrunk from witnessing the

anguish which he was about to inflict. 'Stop,' said he to his people, who were approaching the door; 'stay a few moments;' and, putting his hand to his forehead, he walked about, not wavering in his purpose, but endeavouring to excuse it to himself. 'It is all the consequence of her own obstinancy,' said he, suddenly stopping. 'You may go on – No; stay, let me first get out of this house. Her cries would drive me mad. – Make haste – lose no time after I am gone. It is better over.'

Besides the motive which he owned, Hargrave was impelled to depart by the dread of meeting Laura's upbraiding eye, and by the shame of appearing even to the servants, who were so soon to know his baseness, an inactive spectator of Laura's distress. He hastened from the house, and the men proceeded in their work. With dread and horror did Laura listen to their attempts. Pale, breathless, her hands clenched in terror, she fixed her strained eyes upon the door, which every moment seemed yielding; then flying to the window, surveyed in despair the height, which made escape an act of suicide; then again turning to the door, tried with her feeble strength to aid its resistance. In vain! It yielded, and the shock threw Laura upon the ground. The ruffians raised her, more dead then alive, and were seizing her lily arms to lead her away; but, with all her native majesty, she motioned them from her. 'You need not touch me,' said she, 'you see I can resist no further.' With the composure of despair, she followed them to the hall, where, her strength failing, she sunk upon a seat. The servants now in pity and amazement approaching her, she addressed herself to one of them. 'Will you go with me, my good friend,' said she, 'that you may return and tell Lady Pelham where to find her niece's corpse!' The girl consented with tears in her eyes; but one of the fellows cried, 'No; no; she may run after the coach if she likes, but she don't go within side.' 'Why not?' said the other, with a brutal leer. 'They may both get home again together. They'll be free enough soon.' Laura shuddered. 'Where wandered my senses,' said she, 'when I thought of subjecting any creature to the chance of a fate like mine! Stay here, my dear, and tell Lady Pelham, that I charge her, by all her hopes here and hereafter, to seek me before she sleeps. Let her seek me wherever there is wickedness and wo – and there, living or dead, I shall be found.' 'Let's have done with all this nonsense,' said one of the men. 'John, make the coach draw up close to the door.' The fellow went to do as he was desired; while the other with a handkerchief prepared to stifle the cries of

Laura, in case she should attempt to move the pity of passengers in the street. Laura heard the carriage stop, she heard the step let down, and the sound was like her death knell.

The man hurried her through the hall. He opened the street door – and Catherine entered with Mr Derwent. Laura, raising her bowed-down head, uttered a cry of joy. 'I am safe!' she cried, and sunk into the arms of Catherine.

Mr Derwent immediately directed his servants to seize the fellow who had held Laura, the other having made his escape upon seeing the arrival of her deliverers. Laura, soon recovering, told her tale to Mr Derwent, who ordering the man to be searched, examined the warrant, and declared it to be false. The danger attending forgery, however, had been avoided, for there was no magistrate of the same name with that which appeared in the signature. Hargrave's villany thus fully detected, Laura wished to dismiss his agent; but Mr Derwent would not permit such atrocity to go unpunished, and gave up the wretch to the arm of law. He then quitted Laura, leaving his servant to attend her till Lady Pelham's return and, worn out with the emotion she had undergone, she threw herself on a bed to seek some rest.

Early in the evening Lady Pelham returned, and immediately inquired for her niece. The servants, always attentive and often uncharitable spectators of the actions of their superiors, had before observed the encouragement which their mistress gave to Hargrave, and less unwilling to suspect than Laura, were convinced of Lady Pelham's connivance in his purpose. None of them therefore choosing to announce the failure of a scheme in which they believed her so deeply implicated, her questions produced no information except that Miss Montreville was gone indisposed to bed. The habitual awe with which the good sense and discernment of Laura had inspired Lady Pelham, was at present augmented almost to fear by the consciousness of duplicity. She shrunk from encountering the glance of quiet scrutiny, the plain direct question which left no room for prevarication, no choice between simple truth and absolute falsehood. But curiosity to know the success of the plot, and still more a desire to discover how far she was suspected of abetting it, prevailed over her fears; and having before studied the part she was to play, she entered Laura's apartment.

She found her already risen and prepared to receive her. 'My dear child,' said her Ladyship in one of her kindest tones, 'I am told you have been ill. What is the matter?' 'My illness is nothing, Madam,' answered Laura, 'but I have been alarmed in your absence by the most daring, the most unprincipled outrage!' 'Outrage, my dear!' cried Lady Pelham in a voice of the utmost surprise; 'What outrage?' Laura then, commanding by a powerful effort the imagination which swelled her heart, related her injuries without comment; pausing at times to observe how her aunt was affected by the recital. Lady Pelham was all amazement; which, though chiefly pretended, was partly real. She was surprised at the lengths to which Hargrave had gone, and even suspected his whole design, though she was far from intending to discover her sentiments to her niece. 'This is the most extraordinary thing I ever heard of!' cried she when Laura had ended. 'What can have been the meaning of this trick? What can have incited the people?' 'Colonel Hargrave, Madam,' said Laura without hesitation. 'Impossible, my dear! Hargrave can be no further concerned in it, than so far as taking advantage of the accident to extort the promise of a little kindness from you. He would never have ventured to send the men into my house on such an errand.' 'One of them confessed to Mr Derwent, before the whole family, that Colonel Hargrave was his employer.' 'Astonishing!' cried Lady Pelham. 'And what do you suppose to have been Hargrave's intention?' 'I doubt not, Madam,' returned Laura, commanding her voice, though resentment flashed from her eyes, 'I doubt not that his intentions were yet more base and inhuman than the means he employed. But whatever they were, I am certain he would never have dared to entertain them, had it not been for the encouragement which your Ladyship has thought proper to give him.' 'I, child!' cried Lady Pelham, truth in her colour contradicting the falsehood of her tongue, 'Surely you do not think that I would encourage him in such a plot!' 'No, Madam,' answered Laura, 'I hope and believe that you are incapable of consenting to such wickedness. I allude only to the general countenance which you have always shewn to Colonel Hargrave.' Lady Pelham could implicitly rely upon Laura's word; and finding that she was herself unsuspected, she had leisure to attempt palliating the offence of her *protegé*. 'That countenance,' returned she, 'shall be completely withdrawn for the future, if Hargrave does not explain this strange frolic to my satisfaction.' 'Frolic, Madam!' cried Laura indignantly. 'If that name belongs to crimes which would disgrace barbarians, then call this a frolic!' 'Come, my dear girl,' said Lady Pelham, coaxingly throwing

her arm round Laura, 'you are too much, and I must own, according
to present appearances, justly irritated, to talk of this affair coolly to-
night. To-morrow we shall converse about it. Now let's go to tea.'
'No, Madam,' said Laura with spirit, for she saw through her aunt's
intention of glossing over Hargrave's villany – 'I will never again
expose myself to the chance of meeting a wretch whose crimes are
my abhorrence. I will not leave this room till I quit it for ever.
Madam, you have often called me firm. Now I will prove to you that I
am so. Give me the means to go hence in a manner becoming your
niece, or my own limbs shall bear me to Scotland, and on the charity
of my fellow-creatures will I rely for support.' 'I protest, my love,'
cried Lady Pelham, 'you are absolutely in a passion, I never saw you
so angry till now.' 'Your Ladyship never saw me have such reason for
anger,' replied Laura. 'I own I am angry, yet I know that my
determination is right, and I assure you it will outlive the heat with
which it is expressed.'

Had Laura's purpose been more placidly announced it would
have roused Lady Pelham to fury; but even those who have least
command over their tempers have generalship enough to perceive the
advantage of the attack; and the passion of a virago has commonly a
patriarchal submission for its elder-born brother. Lady Pelham
saw that Laura was in no humour for trifling; she knew that
her resolutions were not easily shaken; and she quitted her upon
pretence of fatigue, but in reality that she might consider how
to divert her from the purpose which she had announced so
peremptorily.

Laura was every day becoming more necessary to her aunt, and
to think of parting with her was seriously disagreeable. Besides,
Laura's departure would effectually blast the hopes of Hargrave;
and what would then become of all Lady Pelham's prospects of
borrowing consequence from the lovely young Countess of Lincourt?
Never wanting in invention, Lady Pelham thought of a hundred
projects for preventing her niece's journey to Scotland. Her choice
was fixed by a circumstance which she could not exclude from
her consideration. The story of Hargrave's seditious plot was likely
soon to be made public. It was known to Mr Derwent, and to
all her own household. Her conscience whispered that her
connivance would be suspected. Mr Derwent might be discreet;
but what was to be expected from the discretion of servants? The
story would spread from the footmen to the waiting-maids, and from

these to their ladies, till it would meet her at every turn. Nor had her imprudent consent left her the power of disclaiming all concern in it, by forbidding Hargrave her house, since he would probably revenge himself by disclosing her share in the strategem. Lady Pelham saw no better success of palliating these evils, than by dismissing her establishment and returning immediately to Walbourne; and she hoped, at the same time, that it might not be impossible to prevail on Laura to change the direction of her journey. For this purpose she began by beseeching her niece to lay aside thoughts of retiring to Scotland; and was beginning to recount all the disadvantages of such a proceeding; but Laura would listen to no remonstrance on the subject; declaring that, if after what had happened, she remained in a place where she was liable to such outrage, she should be herself accountable for whatever evil might be the consequence. Lady Pelham then proposed an immediate removal to Walbourne, artfully insinuating that, if any cause of complaint should there arise, Laura would be near the advice and assistance of her friends at Norwood, and of Mrs Bolingbroke. Laura was not without some wishes that pointed towards Walbourne; but she remembered the importunities which she had there endured, and she firmly resisted giving occasion to their renewal. Lady Pelham had then recourse to tender upbraidings. 'Was it possible that Laura, the only hope and comfort of her age, would quit her now, when she had so endeared herself to the widowed heart, reft of all other treasure – now when increasing infirmity required her aid – now when the eye which was so soon to close, was fixed on her as on its last earthly treasure! Would Laura thus cruelly punish her for a crime in which she had no share; a crime which she was willing to resent to the utmost of her niece's wishes!' Lady Pelham talked herself into tears, and few hearts of nineteen are hard enough to resist the tears of age. Laura consented to accompany her aunt to Walbourne, provided that she should never be importuned on the subject of Hargrave, nor even obliged to see him. These conditions Lady Pelham solemnly promised to fulfil, and, well pleased, prepared for her journey. Hargrave, however, waited on her before her departure, and excused himself so well on the score of his passion, his despair, and his eager desire to be allied to Lady Pelham, that, after a gentle reprimand, he was again received into favour, informed of the promises which had been made against him, and warned not be discouraged if their performance could not immediately be dispensed with. Of this visit

Laura knew nothing; for she adhered to her resolution of keeping her apartment, nor ever crossed its threshold, till, on the third day after her perilous adventure, the carriage was at the door which conveyed her to Walbourne.

CHAPTER XXX

As Lady Pelham's carriage passed the entrance of the avenue which led to Norwood, Laura sunk into a profound reverie; in the course of which she settled most minutely the behaviour proper for her first meeting with De Courcy. She decided on the gesture of unembarrassed cordiality with which she was to accost him; intending her manner to intimate that she accounted him a friend, and only a friend. The awkwardness of a private interview she meant to avoid by going to Norwood next day, at an hour which she knew that Montague employed in reading aloud to his mother. All this excellent arrangement, however, was unfortunately useless. Laura was taking a very early ramble in what had always been her favourite walk, when, at a sudden turn, she saw De Courcy not three steps distant. Her white gown shining through the still leafless trees had caught his attention, the slightest glimpse of her form was sufficient for the eye of love, and he had advanced prepared to meet her; while she, thus taken by surprise, stood before him conscious and blushing. At this confusion, so flattering to a lover, De Courcy's heart gave one bound of triumphant joy; but he was too modest to ascribe to love what timidity might so well account for, and he prudently avoided reminding Laura, even by a look, of either his hopes or his wishes. Quickly recollecting herself, Laura entered into a conversation which, though at first reserved and interrupted, returned by degrees to the confidential manner which De Courcy had formerly won from her under the character of her father's friend.

This confidence, so precious to him, De Courcy was careful never to interrupt. From the time of Laura's return, he saw her almost daily. She made long visits to Mrs De Courcy; he came often to Walbourne; they met in their walks, in their visits; they spent a week together under Mr Bolingbroke's roof; yet De Courcy religiously kept his promise, nor ever wilfilly reminded Laura that he had a wish beyond her friendship. Always gentle, respectful and attentive, he never invited observation by distinguishing her above others who had equal claims on his politeness. She only shared his assiduities with every other woman whom he approached; nor did he betray uneasiness when she, in her turn, received attentions from others. His prudent self-command, had the effect which he intended; and Laura, in conversing with him, felt none of the reserve which may be supposed to attend intercourse with a rejected admirer. His caution even at times deceived her. She recollected Mrs Douglas's prophecy, that 'his attachment would soon subside into friendly regard,' and imagined she saw its accomplishment. 'How happy are men in having such flexible affections,' thought she with a sigh. 'I wonder whether he has entirely conquered the passion which, three short months ago, was to "last through life – beyond life?" I hope he has,' whispered she with a deeper sigh; and she repeated it again – 'I hope he has,' – as if by repeating it, she would have ascertaned that it was her real sentiment. Yet, at other times, some little inadvertency, unheeded by less interested observers, would awaken a doubt of De Courcy's self-conquest; and in that doubt Laura unconsciously found pleasure. She often reconsidered the arguments which her friend had used to prove that passion is unnecessary to the happiness of wedded life. She did not allow that she was convinced by them; but she half wished that she had had an opportunity of weighing them before she had decided her fate with regard to De Courcy. Meanwhile, much of her time was spent in his company, and his presence had ever brought pleasure with it. Week after week passed agreeably away, and the close of the winter atoned for the disquiet which had marked its commencement.

During all this time, Laura saw nothing of Hargrave. His visits, indeed, to Walbourne were more frequent than she supposed, but the only one of which she had been informed, Lady Pelham affected to announce to her, advising her to avoid it by spending that day at Norwood. Since their return from town, her Ladyship had entirely desisted from her remonstrances in his favour, and Laura hoped that his last outrage had opened her aunt's eyes to the deformity of his character. And, could Lady Pelham's end have been pursued without annoyance to any living being, it would long before have shared the perishable nature of her other purposes. But whatever conferred the invaluable occasion of tormenting, was cherished by Lady Pelham as the dearest of her concerns; and she only waited fit opportunity to shew that she could be as stubborn in thwarting the wishes of others, as capricious in varying her own. De Courcy's attachment could not escape her penetration; and as she was far from intending to desert the cause of Hargrave, she saw, with displeasure, the progressive advancement of Laura's regard for the friend of her father. Though she was sufficiently acquainted with Laura to know that chiding would effect no change in her sentiments or conduct, she had not temper enough to restrain her upbraidings on this subject, but varied them with all the skill and perseverance of a veteran in provocation. 'She did not, she must confess, understand the delicacy of ladies whose affections could be transferred from one man to another. She did not see how any modest woman could find two endurable men in the world. It was a farce to tell her of friendship and gratitude, and such like stuff. Everybody knew the meaning of a friendship between a girl of nineteen and a good-looking young fellow of five-and-twenty. She wondered whether Laura was really wise enough to imagine that De Courcy could afford to marry her; or whether, if he were mad enough to think of such a thing, she could be so ungenerous as to take advantage of his folly, to plunge him into irretrievable poverty; and this too, when it was well known that a certain young heiress had prior claims upon him.' Laura at first listened to these harangues with tolerable *sang froid*; yet they became, she was unconscious why, every day more provoking. Though she had self-command enough to be silent, her changing colour announced Lady Pelham's victory, and it was followed up without mercy or respite. It had, however, no other effect than that of imposing a restraint when her Ladyship happened to be present; for De Courcy continued his attentions, and Laura received him with increasing favour.

Lady Pelham omitted none of the minor occasions of disturbing this harmonious intercourse. She interrupted their tête à têtes, beset them in their walks, watched their most insignificnt looks, pried into their most common-place messages, and dexterously hinted to the one whatever foible she could see or imagine in the other. A casual breath of scandal soon furnished her with a golden opportunity of sowing dissension, and she lost no time in taking advantage of the hint. 'It is treating me like a baby,' said she once to Laura, after opening in form her daily attack; 'it is treating me like a mere simpleton to expect that you are to deceive me with your flourishing sentiments about esteem and gratitude. Have esteem and gratitude the blindness of love? Don't I see that you overlook in your beloved Mr Montague De Courcy faults which in another you would think sufficient excuse for any ill treatment that you chose to inflict?' Laura kept silence; for of late she had found that her temper could not stand a charge of this kind. 'What becomes of all your fine high-flown notions of purity, and so forth,' continued Lady Pelham, 'when you excuse his indiscretions with his mother's *protegée*, and make a favourite and a plaything of his spoilt bantling?' Laura turned pale, then reddened violently. 'What protegée? what bantling?' cried she, quite thrown off her guard. 'I know of no indiscretions – I have no playthings.' – 'What! you pretend not to know that the brat he takes so much notice of is his own. Did you never hear of his affair with a pretty girl whom his mamma was training as a waiting-maid for her fine-lady daughter.' 'Mr De Courcy, Madam!' cried Laura, making a powerful struggle with her indignation – 'He seduce a girl who as a member of his family was doubly entitled to his protection! Is it possible that your Ladyship can give credit to such a calumny?' 'Hey-day,' cried Lady Pelham, with a provoking laugh, 'a most incredible occurrence to be sure! And pray why should your immaculate Mr De Courcy be impeccable any more than other people?' 'I do not imagine, Madam,' returned Laura, with recovered self-possession, 'that Mr De Courcy, or any of the human race, is perfectly sinless; but nothing short of proof shall convince me that he is capable of deliberate wickedness; or even that the casual transgressions of such a man can be so black in their nature, so heinous in their degree. It were next to a miracle if one who makes conscience of guarding his very thoughts, could, with a single step, make such progress in iniquity.' 'It were a miracle indeed,' said Lady Pelham, sneeringly, 'if you could be prevailed upon to believe any thing that contradicts your romantic vagaries. As long as you are determined to worship Mr De Courcy, you'll never listen to any thing that brings him down from his pedestal.' 'It is wasting time,' returned Laura calmly, 'to argue on the improbability of this malicious tale. I can easily give your Ladyship the pleasure of being able to contradict it. Mrs Bolingbroke is at Norwood. She will tell me frankly who is the real father of little Henry, and I shall feel no difficulty in asking her. Will you have the goodness to lend me the carriage for an hour?' 'A pretty expedition truly!' cried Lady Pelham, 'and mighty delicate and dignified it is for a young lady, to run about inquiring into the pedigree of all the bastards in the county! I assure you, Miss Montreville, I shall neither countenance nor assist such a scheme!' 'Then, Madam,' answered Laura coolly, 'I shall walk to Norwood. The claims of dignity, or even of delicacy, are surely inferior to those of justice and gratitude. But though it should subject me to the scorn of all mankind, I will do what in me lies to clear his good name whose kindness ministered the last comforts that sweetened the life of my father.'

The manner in which these words were pronounced, shewed Lady Pelham that resistance was useless. She was far from wishing to quarrel with the De Courcy family, and she now began to fear that she should appear the propagator of this scandal. Having little time to consult the means of safety, since Laura was already leaving the room, she hastily said, 'I suppose in your explanations with Mrs Bolingbroke, you will give me up for your authority?' 'No, Madam,' replied Laura, with a scorn which she could not wholly suppress, 'your Ladyship has no right to think so at the moment when I am shewing such concern for the reputation of my friends.' Lady Pelham would have fired at this disdain, but her *quietus* was at hand – she was afraid of provoking Laura to expose her, and therefore she found it perfectly possible to keep her temper. 'If you are resolved to go,' said she, 'you had better wait till I order the carriage; I fear we shall have rain.' Laura at first refused; but Lady Pelham pressed her, with so many kind concerns for a slight cold which she had, that though she saw through the veil, she suffered her Ladyship to wear it undisturbed. The carriage was ordered, and Laura hastened to Norwood.

Though she entertained not the slightest doubt of De Courcy's integrity, she was restless and anxious. It was easy to see that her mind was pre-occupied during the few minutes which passed before, taking leave of Mrs De Courcy, she begged Mrs Bolingbroke to speak with her apart. Harriet followed her into another room; and Laura, with much more embarrassment than she had expected to feel, prepared to begin her interrogation. Harriet, from the thoughtful aspect of her companion, anticipating something of importance, stood gravely waiting to hear what she had to say; while Laura was confused by the awkwardness of explaining her reason for the question she was about to ask. 'I have managed this matter very ill,' said she at last, pursuing her thoughts aloud. 'I have entered on it with so much formality, that you must expect some very serious affair; and, after all, I am only going to ask a trifling question. Will you tell me who is the father of my pretty little Henry?' Harriet looked surprised, and answered, – 'Really, my dear, I am not sure that I dare. You inquired the same thing once before; and just when I was going to tell you, Montague looked so terrible, that I was forced to hold my tongue. But what makes you ask? What! You won't tell? Then I know how it is. My prophecy has proved true, and the good folks have given him to Montague himself. Ah! What a tell-tale face you have, Laura! And who has told you this pretty story?' 'It is of no consequence,' replied Laura, 'that you should know my authority, provided that I have yours to contradict the slander.' 'You shall have better authority than mine,' returned Harriet. 'Those who were malicious enough to invent such a tale of Montague, might well assert that his sister employed falsehood to clear him. You shall hear the whole from nurse Margaret herself; and her evidence cannot be doubted. Come, will you walk to the cottage and hear what she has to say?'

They found Margaret alone; and Harriet, impatient till her brother should be fully justified, scarcely gave herself time to answer the old woman's civilities, before she entered on her errand. 'Come, nurse,' said she, with all her natural frankness of manner, 'I have something particular to say to you. Let's shut the door and sit down. Do you know somebody has been malicious enough to tell Miss Montreville that Montague is little Henry's father.' Margaret lifted up her hands and eyes. 'My young master, Madam!' cried she – 'He go to bring shame and sorrow into any honest man's family! If you'll believe me, Miss,' continued she, turning to Laura, 'this is, begging your pardon, the wickedest lie that ever was told.' Laura was about to assure her that she gave no credit to the calumny, but Harriet, who had a double reason for wishing that her friend should listen to Margaret's tale, interrupted her, saying, 'Nurse, I am sure nothing could convince her so fully as hearing the whole story from your own lips. I brought her hither on purpose; and you may trust her, I assure you, for she is just such a wise prudent creature as you always told me that I ought to be.' 'Ah, Madam,' answered Margaret, 'I know that; for John says she is the prettiest-behaved young lady he ever saw; and says how fond my lady is of her, and others too besides my lady, though it is not for servants to be making remarks.' 'Come, then, nurse,' said Harriet, 'sit down between us; and tell us the whole sad story of my poor foster-sister, and clear your friend Montague from this aspersion.' Margaret did as she was desired. 'Ah, yes!' said she, tears lending to her eyes a transient brightness, 'I can talk of it now! Many a long evening John and I speak of nothing else. She always used to sit between us, – but now we both sit close together. But we are growing old,' continued she, in a more cheerful tone, 'and in a little while we shall see them all again. We had three of the prettiest boys! – My dear young lady, you will soon have children of your own, but never set your heart upon them, nor be too proud of them, for that is only provoking Providence to take them away.' 'I shall probably never have so much reason,' said Harriet, 'as you had to be proud of your Jessy.' The mother's pride had survived its object; and it brightened Margaret's faded countenance, as, pressing Harriet's hand between her own, she cried, 'Ah, bless you! you were always kind to her. She was indeed the flower of my little flock; and when the boys were taken away, she was our comfort for all. But I was too proud of her. Five years since, there was not her like in all the country round. A dutiful child, too, and never made us sad or sorrowful till – and such a pretty modest creature! But I was too proud of her.'

Margaret stopped, and covered her face with the corner of her apron. Sympathizing tears stood in Laura's eyes; while Harriet sobbed aloud at the remembrance of the play-fellow of her infancy. The old woman first recovered herself. 'I shall never have done at this rate,' said she, and, drying her eyes, turned to address the rest of her tale to Laura. 'Well, Ma'am, a gentleman who used to come a-visiting to the castle, by ill fortune chanced to see her; and ever after that he noticed her and spoke to her; and flattered me up, too, saying, what a fine-looking young creature she was, and so well brought up too, and what a pity it was that she should be destined for a tradesman's wife. So, like a fool as I was, I thought no harm of his fine speeches, because Jessy always said he behaved quite modest and respectful like. But John, to be sure, was angry, and said that a tradesman was her equal, and that he hoped her rosy cheeks would never give her notions above her station; and, says he, – I am sure many and many a time I have thought of his words – says he, 'God grant I never see worse come of her than to be an honest tradesman's wife.' My young master, too, saw the gentleman one day speaking to her; and he was so good as advise her himself, and told her that the gentleman meant nothing honest by all his fine speeches. So after that, she would never stop with him at all, nor give ear to a word of his flatteries; but always ran away from him, telling him to say those fine things to his equals. So, one unlucky day I had some matters to be done in the town, and Jessy said she would like to go, and poor foolish I was so left to myself that I let her go. So she dressed herself in her clean white gown. – I remember it as were it but yesterday. I went to the door with her, charging her to be home early. She shook hands with me. Jessy, says I, you look just like a bride. So she smiled. No, mother, says she, I shan't leave home so merrily the day I leave it for all – and I never saw my poor child smile again. So she went, poor lamb, little thinking! – and I stood in the door looking after her, thinking, like a fool as I was, that my young master need not have thought it strange though a gentleman had taken her for a wife, for there were not many ladies that looked like her.'

Margaret rested her arms upon her knees, bent her head over them, made a pause, and then began again. 'All day I was merry as a lark, singing and making every thing clean in our little habitation here, where I thought we should sit down together so happy when John came home at night from the castle. So it was getting darkish before my work was done, and then I began to wonder what was become of Jessy; and many a time I went across the green to see if there was any sight of her. At last John came home, and I told him that I was beginning to be frightened; but he laughed at me, and said she had perhaps met with some of her comrades, and was gone to take her tea with them. So we sat down by the fire; but I could not rest, for my mind misgave me sadly; so says I, John, I will go and see after my girl. Well, says he, we may as well go and meet her. – Alas! Alas! a sad meeting was that! We went to the door; I opened it, and somebody fell against me. – It was Jessy. She looked as dead as she did the day I laid her in her coffin; and all her pretty cheek was blue, and her pretty mouth, that used to smile so sweetly in my face when she was a baby on my knee, it was all bloody. And her pretty shining hair that I used to comb so often – Oh woe, woe is me! How could I see such a sight and live.'

The mother wrung her withered hands, and sobbed as if her heart were breaking. Laura laid her arms kindly round old Margaret's neck, for misfortune made the poor and the stranger her equal and her friend. She offered no words of unavailing consolation, but pitying tears trickled fast down her cheeks; while Mrs Bolingbroke, her eyes flashing indignant fires, exclaimed, 'Surely the curse of heaven will pursue that wretch!' 'Alas!' said Margaret, 'I fear I cursed him too; but I was in a manner beside myself then. God forgive both him and me! My poor child never cursed him. All that I could say she would not tell who it was that had used her so. She said she should never bring him to justice; and always prayed that his own conscience might be his only punishment. So from the first we saw that her heart was quite broken; for she would never speak nor look up, nor let me do the smallest thing for her, but always said it was not fit that I shoudl wait on such a one as she. Well, one night, after we were all a-bed, a letter was flung in at the window of Jessy's closet, and she crept out of her bed to take it. I can shew it you, Miss, for it was under her pillow when she died.' Margaret, unlocking a drawer, took out a letter and gave it to Laura, who read in it these words:

'My dear Jessy, I am the most miserable wretch upon earth. I wish I had been upon the rack the hour I met you. I am sure I have been so ever since. Do not curse me, dear Jessy! Upon my soul, I had far less thought of being the ruffian I have been to you, than I have at this moment of blowing out my own brains. I wish to heaven that I had been in your own station that I might have made you amends for the injury I have done. But you know it is impossible for me to marry you. I inclose a bank-bill for £100, and I will continue to pay you the same sum annually while you live, though you should never consent to see me more. If you make me a father, no expence shall be spared to provide the means of secrecy and comfort. No accommodation which a wife could have shall be withheld from you. Tell me if there be any thing more than I can do for you. I shall never forgive myself for what I have done. I abhor myself, and from this hour, I forswear all woman-kind for your sake. Once more, dear Jessy, pardon me I impore you.'

This letter was without signature; but the hand-writing was familiar to Laura, and could not be mistaken. It was Hargrave's. Shuddering at this new proof of his depravity, Laura inwardly offered a thanksgiving that she had escaped all connection with such a monster. 'You may trust my friend with the wretch's name,' said Harriet, anxious that Laura's conviction should be complete. 'She will make no imprudent use of it.' 'I should never have known it myself had it not been for this letter,' answered Margaret. 'But my poor child wished to answer it, and she was not able to carry the answer herself, so she was obliged to ask her father to go with it. And first she made us both promise on the Bible, never to bring him either to shame or punishment; and then she told us that it was that same Major Hargrave that used to speak her so fair. Here is the scroll that John took of her answer.'

'Sir, I return your money, for it can be of no use where I am going. I will never curse you; but trust I shall to the last have pity on you, who had no pity on me. I fear your sorrow is not right repentance; for, if it was, you would never think of committing a new sin by taking your own life, but rather of making reparation for the great evil you have done. Not that I say this in respect of wishing to be your wife. My station makes that unsuitable, more especially now when I should be a disgrace to any man. And I must say, a wicked person would be as unsuitable among my friends; for my parents are honest persons, although their daughter is so unhappy as to bring shame on them. I shall not live long enough to disgrace them any farther, so pray inquire no more of me, nor take the trouble to send me money, for I will not buy my coffin with the wages of shame; and I shall need nothing else. So, wishing that my untimely end may bring you to a true repentance, I remain, Sir, the poor dying disgraced,

'JESSY WILSON.'

'Ah, Miss,' continued Margaret, wiping from the paper the drops which had fallen on it, 'my poor child's prophecy was true. She always said she would just live till her child was born, and then lay her dishonoured head and her broken heart in the grave. My Lady and Miss Harriet there were very kind, and my young master himself was so good as promise that he would act the part of a father to the little orphan. And he used to argue with her that she should submit to the chastisement that was laid upon her, and that she might find some comfort still; but she always said that her chastisement was less than she deserved, but that she could never wish to live to be 'a very scorn of men, an outcast and an alien among her mother's children.' So the day that little Henry was born, she was doing so well that we were in hopes she would still be spared to us; but she knew better; and, when I was sitting by her, she pulled me close to her and said, 'Mother,' says she, looking pleased like, 'the time of my release is at hand now,' and then she charged me never to give poor little Henry to his cruel father. I had not the power to say a word to her, but sat hushing the baby, with my heart like to break. So, by and by, she said to me again; but very weak and low like, 'my brothers lie side by side in the churchyard, lay me at their feet; it is good enough for me.' So she never spoke more, but closed her eyes, and slipped quietly away, and left her poor old mother.'

A long paused followed Margaret's melancholy tale. 'Are you convinced, my friend,' said Mrs Bolingbroke at length. 'Fully,' answered Laura, and returned to silent and thankful meditation. 'My master,' said Margaret, 'has made good his promise to poor Jessy. He has shewn a father's kindness to her boy. He paid for his nursing, and forces John to take a board for him that might serve any gentleman's son; and now it will be very hard if the end of all his goodness is to get himself ill spoken of; and nobody saying a word against him that was the beginning of all this mischief. But that is the way of the world.' 'It is so,' said Laura. 'And what can better warn us that the earth was never meant for our resting-place. The "raven" wings his way through it triumphant. The "dove" finds no rest for the sole of her foot, and turns to the ark from whence she came.'

Mrs Bolingbroke soon after took leave of her nurse, and the ladies proceeded in their walk towards Walbourne. Harriet continued to express the warmest detestation of the profligacy of Hargrave, while Laura's mind was chiefly occupied in endeavouring to account for De Courcy's desire to conceal from her the enormity which had just come to her knowledge. Unable to divine his reason, she applied to Harriet. 'Why my dear,' said she, 'should your brother have silenced you on a subject which could only be mentioned to his honour?' 'He never told me his reasons,' said Harriet smiling, 'but if you will not be angry I may try to guess them.' 'I think,' said Laura, 'that thus cautioned, I may contrive to keep my temper; so speak boldly.' 'Then, my dear,' said Harriet, 'I may venture to say that I think he suspected you of a partiality for this wretch, and would not shock you by a full disclosure of his depravity. And I know,' added she, in a voice tremulous with emotion, 'that in him this delicacy was virtue; for the peace of his life dpends on securing your affectionate, your exclusive preference.' 'Ah, Harriet, you have guessed right. – Yes! I see it all. Dear generous De Courcy!' cried Laura, and burst into tears. Harriet had not time to comment upon this agitation; for the next moment De Courcy himself was at her side. For the first time, Laura felt embarrassed and distressed by his presence. The words she had just uttered still sounded in her ear, and she trembled lest they had reached that of De Courcy. She was safe. Her exclamation was unheard by Montague, – but he instantly observed her tears, and they banished from his mind every other idea than that of Laura in sorrow. He paid his compliments like one whose attention was distracted, and scarcely answered what his sister addressed to him. Mrs Bolingbroke inwardly enjoying his abstraction and Laura's embarrassment, determined not to spoil an opportunity which she judged so favourable to her brother's suit. 'This close walk,' said she with a sly smile, 'was never meant for a trio. It is just fit for a pair of lovers. Now I have letters to write, and if you two will excuse me' – De Courcy colouring crimson, had not presence of mind to make any reply, while Laura, though burning with shame and vexation, answered with her habitual self-command, 'Oh, pray my dear, use no ceremony. Here are none but *friends*.' The emphasis which she laid upon the last word, wrung a heavy sigh from De Courcy; who, while his sister was taking leave, was renewing his resolution not to disappoint the confidence of Laura.

The very circumstances which Mrs Bolingbroke had expected should lead to a happy eclaircissement, made this interview the most reserved and comfortless which the two friends had ever had. Laura was too conscious to talk of the story which she had just heard, and she was too full of it to enter easily upon any other subject. With her gratitude for the delicacy which De Courcy had observed towards her, was mingled a keen feeling of humiliation at the idea that he had discovered her secret before it had been confided to him; for we can sometimes confess a weakness which we cannot without extreme mortification see detected. Her silence and depression infected De Courcy; and the few short constrained sentences which were spoken during their walk, formed a contrast to the general vivacity of their conversations. Laura however recovered her eloquence as soon as she found herself alone with Lady Pelham. With all the animation of sensibility, she related the story of the ill-fated Jessy; and disclosing in confidence the name of her destroyer, drew, in the fulness of her heart, a comparison between the violator of laws human and divine, owing his life to the mercy of the wretch whom he had undone, and the kind adviser of inexperienced youth, the humane protector of forsaken infancy. Lady Pelham quietly heard her to an end; and then wrinkling her eyelids, and peeping through them with her glittering blue eyes, she began, 'Do you know, my dear, I never met with prejudices so strong as yours? When will you give over looking for prodigies? Would any mortal but you expect a gay young man to be as correct as yourself? As for your immaculate Mr De Courcy, with his sage advices, I think it is ten to one that he wanted to keep the girl for himself. Besides, I'll answer for it, Hargrave would have bid farewell to all his indiscretions if you would have married him.' 'Never name it, Madam,' cried Laura warmly, 'if you would not banish me from your presence. His marriage with me would have been itself a crime; a crime aggravated by being, as if in mockery, consecrated to heaven. For *my* connection with such a person no name is vile enough.' 'Well, well,' said Lady Pelham, shrugging her shoulders, 'I prophesy that one day you will repent having refused to share a title with the handsomest man in England.' 'All distinctions between right and wrong,' returned Laura, 'must first be blotted from my mind. The beauty of his person is no more to me than the shining colours of an adder; and the rank which your Ladyship prizes so highly, would but render me a more conspicuous mark for the infamy in which his wife must share.'

Awed by the lightnings of Laura's eye, Lady Pelham did not venture to carry the subject farther for the present. She had of late been watching an opportunity of procuring the re-admission of Hargrave to the presence of his mistress; but this fresh discovery had served, if possible, to widen the breach. Hargrave's fiery temper submitted with impatience to the banishment which he had so well deserved, and he constantly urged Lady Pelham to use her authority on his behalf. Lady Pelham, though conscious that this authority had no existence, was flattered by having power ascribed to her, and promised at some convenient season to interfere. Finding herself, however, considerably embarrassed by a promise which she could not fulfil without hazarding the loss of Laura, she was not sorry that an opportunity occurred of evading the performance of her agreement. She therefore acquainted Hargrave with Laura's recent discovery, declaring that she could not ask her niece to overlook entirely so great an irregularity. From a regard to the promise of secrecy which she had given to Laura, as well as in common prudence, Lady Pelham had resolved not to mention the De Courcy family as the fountain from which she had drawn her intelligence. Principle and prudence sometimes governed her Ladyship's resolutions, but seldom swayed her practice. In the first interview with Hargrave which followed this rational determination, she was led by the mere vanity of a babbler to give such hints as not only enabled him to trace the story of his shame to Norwood, but inclined him to fix the publishing of it upon Montague.

From the moment when Hargrave first unjustly suspected Laura of a preference for De Courcy, his heart had rankled with an enmity which a sense of its ingratitude served only to aggravate. The cool disdain with which De Courcy treated him – a strong suspicion of his attachment, – above all, Laura's avowed esteem and regard – inflamed this enmity to the bitterest hatred. Hopeless as he was of succeeding in his designs by any fair or honourable means, he might have entertained thoughts of relinquishing his suit; and of seeking, in a match of interest, the means of escape from his embarrassments: but that Laura, with all her unequalled charms, should be the prize of De Courcy, that in her he should obtain all that beauty, affluence, and love could give, was a thought not to be endured. Lady Pelham, too, more skilled to practise on the passions of others than to command her own, was constantly exciting him, by hints of De Courcy's progress in the favour of Laura; while Lambert, weary of waiting for the tedious accomplishment of his own scheme, continually goaded him, with sly sarcasms on his failure in the arts of persuasion, and on his patience in submitting to be baffled in his wishes by a haughty girl. In the heat of his irritation, Hargrave often swore that no power on earth should long delay the gratification of his love and his revenge. But to marry a free-born British woman against her consent, is, in these enlightened times, an affair of some difficulty; and Hargrave, in his cooler moments, perceived that the object of three years eager pursuit was farther than ever from his attainment.

Fortune seemed in every respect to oppose the fulfilment of his designs, for his regiment at this time received orders to prepare to embark for America; and Lord Lincourt, who had discovered his nephew's ruinous connection with Lambert, had influence to procure, from high authority, a hint that Hargrave would be expected to attend his duty on the other side of the Atlantic.

The news of this arrangement Hargrave immediately conveyed to Lady Pelham, urging her to sanction any means which could be devised for making Laura the companion of his voyage. Lady Pelham hesitated to carry her complaisance so far; but she resolved to make the utmost use of the time which intervened to promote the designs of her favourite. Her Ladyship was not at any time much addicted to the communication of pleasurable intelligence, and the benevolence of her temper was not augmented by a prospect of the defeat of a plan in which her vanity was so much interested. She therefore maliciously withheld from her niece a piece of information so likely to be heard with joy. It reached Laura, however, by means of one who was ever watchful for her gratification. De Courcy no sooner ascertained the truth of the report, than he hastened to convey it to Laura.

He found her alone, and was welcomed with all her accustomed cordiality. 'I am sorry,' said he, with a smile which contradicted his words, 'I am sorry to be the bearer of bad news to you; but I could not deny myself the edification of witnessing your fortitude – Do you know that you are on the point of losing the most assiduous admirer that ever woman was blessed with? In three weeks Colonel Hargrave embarks for America. Nay, do not look incredulous. I assure you it is true.' 'Thank Heaven,' cried Laura, 'I shall once more be in peace and safety!' 'Oh, fie! Is this your regret for so ardent a lover? Have you no feeling?' 'Just such a feeling as the poor man had when he escaped from beneath the sword that hung by a hair. Indeed, Mr De Courcy, I cannot tell you to what a degree he has embittered the two last years of my life. But I believe,' continued she, blushing very deeply, 'I need not explain to you any of my feelings towards Colonel Hargrave, since I find you have I know not what strange faculty of divining them.' Assisted by a conversation which he had had with his sister, De Courcy easily understood Laura's meaning. Respectfully taking her hand, 'Pardon me,' said he, in a low voice, 'if I have ever ventured to guess what it was your wish to conceal from me.' 'Oh, believe me,' cried Laura, with a countenance and manner of mingled candour and modesty, 'there is not a thought of my heart that I wish to conceal from you; since from you, even my most humbling weaknesses are sure of meeting with delicacy and indulgence. But since you are so good an augur,' added she, with an ingenuous smile, 'I trust you perceive that I shall need no more delicacy or indulgence upon the same score.' The fascinating sweetness of her looks and voice, for the first time beguiled De Courcy of his promised caution. 'Dear, dear Laura,' he cried, fondly pressing her hand to his breast, 'it is I who have need of indulgence, and I must – I must sue for it. I must repeat to you that –' Laura's heart sprung to her lips, and unconsciously snatching away her hand, she stood in breathless expectation of what was to follow. 'Madman, that I am!' cried De Courcy, recalled to recollection by her gesture, – 'whither am I venturing!' That was precisely what of all things Laura was most desirous to know; and she remained with her eyes fixed on the ground, half dreading the confidence, half the timidity of her lover. A momentary glance at the speaking countenance of Laura, glowing with confusion, yet brightened with trembling pleasure, awakened the strongest hopes that ever had warmed De Courcy's bosom. 'Beloved Laura,' said he, again tenderly approaching her, 'remember I am but human. Cease to treat me with this beguiling confidence. Cease to bewitch me with these smiles, which are so like all that I wish, or suffer me to –' Laura started, as her attention was drawn by some one passing close to the ground window near which they were standing. 'Ah!' cried she, in a tone of vexation, 'there is my evil genius. Colonel Hargrave is come into the house. He will be here this instant. Excuse me for driving you away. I beseech you do not remain a moment alone with him.'

Laura was not mistaken. She had scarcely spoken, ere, with a dark cloud on his brow, Hargrave entered. He bowed to Laura, who was advancing towards the door. 'I am afraid, Madam, I interrupt you,' said he, darting a ferocious scowl upon De Courcy. Laura, without deigning even a single glance in reply, left the room. Hargrave, as he passed the window, had observed the significant attitude of the lovers; and his jealousy and rage were inflamed to the uttermost by the scorn which he had endured in the presence of his rival. Fiercely stalking up to De Courcy, 'Is it to you, Sir,' said he, 'that I am indebted for this insolence?' 'No Sir,' answered De Courcy, a little disdainfully. 'I have not the honour of regulating Miss Montreville's civilities.' 'This is a paltry evasion,' cried Hargrave. 'Is it not to your misrepresentations of a youthful indiscretion that I owe Miss Montreville's present displeasure?' 'I am not particularly ambitious of the character of an informer,' answered De Courcy; and taking his hat wished Hargrave a stately good morning. 'Stay, Sir!' cried Hargrave, roughly seizing him by the arm. 'I must have some further conversation with you – You don't go yet.' 'I am not disposed to ask your permission,' returned De Courcy; and coolly liberating his arm, walked out of the house. Boiling with rage, Hargrave followed him. 'It is easy to see, Sir,' said he, 'from whence you borrow a spirit that never was natural to you – Your presumption builds upon the partiality of that fickle capricious woman. But observe, Sir, that I have claims on her; claims which she herself was too happy in allowing; and no man shall dare to interfere with them.' 'I shall dare,' returned De Courcy, anger kindling in his eyes, 'to inquire by what right you employ such expressions in regard to Miss Montreville; and whether my spirit be my own or not, you shall find it sufficient to prevent your holding such language in my presence.' 'In your presence, or the presence of all the devils,' cried De Courcy, 'I will maintain my right; and, if you fancy that it interferes with any claim of yours, you know how to obtain satisfaction. There is but one way to decide the business.' 'I am of your opinion,' replied De Courcy, 'that there is one way, provided that we can mutually agree to bide by it; and that is, an appeal to Miss Montreville herself.' Hargrave turned pale, and his lip quivered with rage. 'A mode of decision, no doubt,' said he, 'which your vanity persuades you will be all in your favour! No, no, Sir, our quarrel must be settled by means in which even your conceit cannot deny my equality.' 'By a brace of pistols, you mean of course,' said De Courcy, coolly; 'but I frankly tell you, Colonel Hargrave, that my notions must have changed before I can find the satisfaction of a gentleman in being murdered; and my principles, before I shall seek it in murdering you.' 'Curse on your hypocrisy!' cried Hargrave. 'Keep this canting to cozen girls, and let me avenge my wrongs like a man, or the world shall know you, Sir.' 'Do you imagine,' said De Courcy, with a smile of calm disdain, 'that I am to be terrified into doing what I tell you I think wrong, by the danger of a little misrepresentation? You may, if you think fit, tell the world that I will not stake my life in a foolish quarrel, nor wilfully send an unrepenting sinner to his great account; and, if you go on to ascribe for my forbearance any motive which is derogatory to my character, I may, if *I* think fit, obtain justice as a peacable citizen ought; or I may leave you undisturbed the glory of propagating a slander which even you yourself believe to be groundless.'

De Courcy's coolness served only to exasperate his adversary. 'Truce with this methodistical jargon!' cried he fiercely. 'It may impose upon women, but I see through it, Sir – see that it is but a miserable trick to escape what you dare not meet.' 'Dare not!' cried De Courcy, lightnings flashing from his eye. 'My nerves have failed me, then, since' – He stopped abruptly, for he scorned at such a moment to remind his antagonist of the courageous effort to which he owed his life. 'Since when!' cried Hargrave, more and more enraged, as the recollection which De Courcy had recalled, placed before him the full turpitude of his conduct. – 'Do you think I owe you thanks for a life which you have made a curse to me, by cheating me of its dearest pleasures. But may tortures be my portion if I do not foil you!'

The latter part of this dialogue was carried on in a close shady lane which branched off from the avenue of Walbourne. The dispute was proceeding with increasing warmth on both sides when it was interrupted by the appearance of Laura. From a window she had observed the gentlemen leave the house together; had watched Hargrave's angry gestures, and seen De Courcy accompany him into the by-path. The evil which she had so long dreaded seemed now on the point of completion; and alarm leaving no room for reserve, she followed them with her utmost speed.

'Oh, Mr De Courcy,' she cried, with a look and attitude of most earnest supplication, 'for mercy leave this madman! – If you would not make me for ever miserable, carry this no further – I entreat – I implore you. Fear for me, if you fear not for yourself.' The tender solicitude for the safety of his rival, which Hargrave imagined her words and gestures to express, the triumphant delight which they called up to the eyes of De Courcy, exasperated Hargrave beyond all bounds of self-command. Frantic with jealousy and rage, he drew, and rushed fiercely on De Courcy; but Montague having neither fear nor anger to disturb his presence of mind, parried the thrust with his cane, closed with his adversary before he could recover, wrested the weapon from his hand; and having calmly ascertained that no person could be injured by its fall, threw it over the fence into the adjoining field. Then taking Hargrave aside, he whispered that he would immediately return to him; and, giving his arm to Laura, led her towards the house.

She trembled violently, and big tears rolled down her colourless cheeks, as, vainly struggling with her emotion, she said, 'Surely you will not endanger a life so precious, so' – She was unable to proceed; but, laying her hand on De Courcy's arm, she raised her eyes to his face, with such a look of piteous appeal as reached his very soul. Enchanted to find his safety the object of such tender interest, he again forgot his caution; and, fondly supporting with his arm the form which seemed almost sinking to the earth, 'What danger would I not undergo,' he cried, 'to purchase such concern as this! Be under no alarm, dear Miss Montreville. Even if my sentiments in regard to duelling were other than they are, no provocation should tempt me to implicate your revered name in a quarrel which would, from its very nature, become public.' Somewhat tranquillized by his words, Laura walked silently by his side till they reached the house, when, in a cheerful tone, he bade her farewell. 'A short farewell,' said he, 'for I must see you again this evening.' Laura could scarcely prevail on herself to part from him. 'May I trust you?' said she, with a look of anxiety that spoke volumes. 'Securely, dearest Laura,' answered he. 'He whom you trust needs no other motive for rectitude.' He then hastened from her into the field, whither he had thrown Hargrave's sword; and having found it, sprung over into the lane where he had left its owner. Gracefully presenting it to him, De Courcy begged pardon for having deprived him of it, 'though,' added he, 'I believe you are now rather disposed to thank me for preventing the effects of a momentary irritation.' Hargrave took his sword, and, in surly silence walked on; then, suddenly stopping, he repeated that there was only one way in which the quarrel could be decided; and asked De Courcy whether he was determined to refuse him satisfaction. 'The only satisfaction,' returned De Courcy, 'which is consistent with my notions of right and wrong, I will give you now, on the spot. It is not to my information that you owe Miss Montreville's displeasure. Circumstances, which I own were wholly foreign to any consideration of your interests, induced me to keep your secret almost as if it had been my own; and it is from others that she has learnt a part of your conduct, which, you must give me leave to say, warrants, even on the ground of modern honour, my refusal to treat you as an equal.' 'Insolent!' cried Hargrave, 'Leave me – avoid me, if you would not again provoke me to chastise you, unarmed as you are.' 'My horses wait for me at the gate,' said De Courcy, coolly proceeding by his side, 'and your way seems to lie in the same direction as mine.'

The remainder of the way was passed in silence. At the gate, De Courcy mounting his horse, bid his rival good morning, which the other returned with an ungracious bow. De Courcy rode home, and Hargrave, finding himself master of the field, returned to Walbourne. There he exerted his utmost influence with Lady Pelham to procure an opportunity of excusing himself to Laura. Lady Pelham confessed that she could not venture to take the tone of command, lest she should drive Laura to seek shelter elsewhere; but she promised to contrive an occasion for an interview which he might prolong at his pleasure, provided such a one could be found without her apparent interference. With this promise he was obliged for the present to content himself, for, during his stay, Laura did not appear. She passed the day in disquiet. She could not rest. She could not employ herself. She dreaded lest the interview of the morning should have been only preparatory to one of more serious consequence. She told herself a hundred times that she was sure of De Courcy's principles; and yet feared as if they had been unworthy of confidence. He had promised to see her in the evening, and she anxiously expected the performance of his promise. She knew that if he came while Lady Pelham was in the way, her Ladyship would be too vigilant a guard to let one confidential word be exchanged. She therefore, with a half-pardonable cunning, said not a word of De Courcy's promised visit; and as soon as her aunt betook herself to her afternoon's nap, stole from the drawing-room to receive him. Yet perhaps she never met him with less semblance of cordiality. She blushed and stammered while she expressed her hopes that the morning's dispute was to have no further consequences, and apologized for the interest she took in it, in language more cold than she would have used to a mere stranger. Scarcely could the expression of tenderness have delighted the lover like this little ill-concealed affectation, the first and the last which he ever witnessed in Laura Montreville. 'Ah, dearest Laura,' cried he, 'it is too late to retract – You have said that my safety was dear to you; owned that it was for *me* you feared this morning, and you shall not cancel your confession.' Laura's colour deepened to crimson, but she made no other reply. Then, with a more timid voice and air, De Courcy said, 'I would have told you *then* what dear presumptuous hopes your anxiety awakened, but that I feared to extort from your agitation what perhaps a cooler moment might refuse me. My long-loved, ever dear Laura, will you pardon me these hopes? Will you not speak to me? – Not one little word to tell me that I am not too daring.' Laura spoke not even that little word. She made a faint struggle to withdraw the hand which De Courcy pressed. Yet the lover read the expressions of her half-averted face, and was satisfied.

CHAPTER XXXI

———————●———————

'Pray,' said Lady Pelham to her niece, 'what might you and your paragon be engaged in for the hour and a half you were together this evening?'

'We were discussing a very important subject, Madam,' answered Laura, mustering all her confidence.

'May I be permitted to inquire into the nature of it?' returned Lady Pelham, covering her spleen with a thin disguise of ceremony.

'Certainly, Madam,' replied Laura. 'You may remember I once told you that if ever I received addresses which I could with honour reveal, I should bespeak your Ladyship's patience for my tale. Mr De Courcy was talking of marriage, Madam; and – and I –'

'Oh, mighty well, Miss Montreville,' cried Lady Pelham, swelling with rage, 'I comprehend you perfectly. You may spare your modesty. Keep all these airs and blushes till you tell Colonel Hargrave, that all your fine high-flown passion for him has been quite at the service of the next man you met with!'

Laura's eyes filled with tears of mortification, yet she meekly answered, 'I am conscious that the degrading attachment of which I was once the sport merits your upbraidings; and indeed they have not been its least punishment.' She paused for a moment, and then added with an insinuating smile. 'I can bear that you should reproach me with my new choice, for inconstancy is the prescriptive right of woman, and nothing else can be objected to my present views.'

'Oh, far be it from me!' cried Lady Pelham, scorn and anger throwing her whole little person into active motion, 'far be it from me to make any objection to your immaculate swain! I would have you understand, however, that no part of my property shall go to enrich a parcel of proud beggars. It was indeed my intention, if you had made a proper match, to give you the little all that I have to bestow; but if you prefer starving with your methodist parson to being the heiress of five-and-forty thousand pounds, I have no more to say. However, you had better keep your own secret. The knowledge of it might probably alter Mr De Courcy's plans a little.'

'Your Ladyship,' answered Laura, with spirit, 'has good access to know that the love of wealth has little influence on my purposes; and I assure you that Mr De Courcy would scorn upon any terms to appropriate what he considers as the unalienable right of your own child. Though we shall not be affluent, we shall be too rich for your charity, and that is the only claim in which I could compete with Mrs Herbert.'

This mention of her daughter exasperated Lady Pelham to fury. In a voice half-choked with passion, she cried, 'Neither that rebellious wretch nor any of her abbettors or imitators shall ever have countenance or assistance from me. No! Not though they should beg with their starved bantlings from door to door.' To this intemperate speech Laura made no reply, but quietly began to pour out the tea. Lady Pelham continued to hurry up and down the room, chafing, and venting her rage in common abuse; for a scold in the drawing-room is not very unlike a scold at a green-stall. The storm meeting with no opposition, at length spent itself; or subsided into short growlings, uttered at the intervals of a surly silence. To these, as no answer was absolutely necessary, none was returned. Laura did not utter a syllable, till Lady Pelham's wrath beginning to give place to her curiosity, she turned to her niece, saying, 'Pray, Miss Montreville, when and where is this same wise marriage of yours to take place?'

'The time is not quite fixed, Madam,' answered Laura. 'As soon as you can conveniently spare me, I intend going to Scotland; and when you, and Mrs De Courcy wish me to return, Mr De Courcy will escort me back.'

'I spare you!' returned Lady Pelham with a sneer – 'Oh, Ma'am, if that is all, pray don't let me retard your raptures. You may go to-morrow, or to-night, Ma'am if you please. – Spare you indeed! Truly while I can afford to pay a domestic, I need not be dependent on your assistance; and in attachment or gratitude any common servant may supply your place.'

The rudeness and ingratitude of this speech again forced the tears to Laura's eyes; but she mildly replied, 'Well, Madam, as soon as you find a substitute for me, I shall be ready to depart.' Then to escape further insult she quitted the room.

Lady Pelham's wrath at the derangement of her plan would not suffer her to rest till she had communicated the disaster to Colonel Hargrave. Early next morning, accordingly, she dispatched a note requiring his immediate presence at Walbourne. He obeyed the summons, and was as usual privately received by Lady Pelham. He listened to her intelligence with transports of rage rather than of sorrow. He loaded his rival with execrations, declaring that he would rather see Laura torn in pieces than know her to be the wife of De Courcy. He swore that he would circumvent their schemes, and that though his life should be the forfeit, he would severely revenge the sufferings he had endured.

Lady Pelham had not courage to encounter the evil spirit which she had raised. Subdued, and crouching before his violence, she continued to give a terrified assent to every extravagance he uttered, till he announced his resolution of seeing Laura on the instant, that he might know whether she dared to confirm this odious tale. Lady Pelham then ventured to represent to him that Laura might be so much offended by this breach of contract, as to take refuge with Mrs De Courcy, a measure which would oppose a new obstacle to any scheme for breaking off the intended marriage. She assured him that she would grant every reasonable assistance in preventing a connection so injurious to her niece's interest, though she knew Laura's obstinacy of temper too well to hope any thing from direct resistance. She hinted that it would be most prudent to give the desired interview the appearance of accident, and she promised to contrive the occasion as soon as Hargrave was sufficiently calm to consider of improving it to best advantage.

But calm was a stranger to the breast of Hargrave. The disquiet which is the appointed portion of the wicked, raged there beyond control. To the anguish of disappointment were added the pangs of jealousy, and the heart-burnings of hatred and revenge. Even the loss of the object of three years eager pursuit was less cutting than the success of De Courcy; and the pain of a forfeiture which was the just punishment of a former crime, was heightened to agony by the workings of such passions as consummate the misery of fiends.

The associates of the wicked must forego the consolations of honest sympathy. All Hargrave's tortures were aggravated by the sarcasms of Lambert; who, willing to hasten the fever to its crisis, goaded him with coarse comments upon the good fortune of his rival, and advices (which he well knew would act in a direction opposite to their seeming purpose) to desist from further competition. After spending four-and-twenty hours in alternate fits of rage and despair, Hargrave returned to Lady Pelham, informing her, that whatever were the consequences, he would no longer delay seeing Laura. Lady Pelham had foreseen this demand; and though not without fear of the event, had prepared for compliance. She had already arranged her scheme, and the execution was easy.

Laura's favourite walk in the shrubbery led to a little summer-house, concealed in a thicket of acacias. Thither Lady Pelham had conveyed some dried plants, and had requested Laura's assistance in classing them. Laura had readily agreed, and that very morning had been allotted for the task. Lady Pelham, having first directed Hargrave where to take his station, accompanied her unsuspecting niece to the summer-house, and there for a while joined in her employment. Soon, however, feigning a pretext for half an hour's absence, she quitted Laura, intending at first to loiter in the shrubbery, as a kind of safeguard against the ill consequences of her imprudent connivance; but meeting with a gardener who was going to transplant a bed of favourite auriculas, she followed him to watch over their safety, leaving her niece to guard her own.

Scarcely had Laura been a minute alone, ere she was startled by the entrance of Hargrave, and seriously alarmed by seeing him lock the door, and deliberately secure the key. 'What is it you mean, Sir?' said she, trembling.

'To decide your fate and mine!' answered Hargrave, with a look and voice that struck terror to her soul. 'I am told you are a bride, Laura,' said he, speaking through his clenched teeth. 'Say,' continued he, firmly grasping her arm. 'Speak! is it so?'

'I know no right,' said Laura, recovering herself, 'that you have to question me – nor meanly thus to steal –'

'No evasions!' interrupted Hargrave, in a voice of thunder. 'I have rights – rights which I will maintain while I have being. Now tell me, if you dare, that you have transferred them to that abhorred –'

He stopped, – his utterance choked by the frenzy into which he had worked himself. 'What has transported you to this fury, Colonel Hargrave?' said Laura, calmly. 'Surely you must be sensible, that whatever claims I might once have allowed you, have long since been made void by your own conduct. I will not talk to you of principle, though that were of itself sufficient to sever us forever; but ask yourself what right you can retain over the woman whom you have insulted, and forsaken, and oppressed, and outraged?'

'Spare your taunts, Laura. They will only embitter the hour of retribution. And may hell be my portion, if I be not richly repaid for all the scorn you have heaped upon me. I will be revenged, proud woman. You shall be at my mercy, where no cool canting villain can wrest you from me!'

His threats, and the frightful violence with which they were uttered, filled Laura with mingled dread and pity. 'Command yourself, I beseech you, Colonel Hargrave,' said she. 'If you resent the pain which, believe me, I have most unwillingly occasioned, you are amply revenged. You have already caused me sufferings which mock description.'

'Yes, yes. I know it,' cried Hargrave in a milder voice. 'You were not then so hard. You could feel when that vile wanton first seduced me from you. Then think what I now endure, when this cold-blooded – but may I perish if I do not snatch his prize from him. And think not of resistance, Laura; for, by all that I have suffered, resistance shall be vain.'

'Why do you talk so dreadfully to me?' said Laura, making a trembling effort to release her arm, which he still firmly grasped. 'Why, why will you not cease to persecute me? I have never injured you. I have forgiven, pitied, prayed for you. How have I deserved this worse than savage cruelty?'

'Laura,' said Hargrave, moved by the pleadings of a voice which would have touched a murderer's heart, 'you have still a choice. Promise to be mine. Permit me only, by slow degrees, to regain what I have lost. Say that months – that years hence you will consent, and you are safe.'

'Impossible!' said Laura. 'I cannot bind myself. Nor could you trust a promise extorted by fear. Yet be but half what I once thought you, and I will esteem –'

'Esteem!' interrupted Hargrave, with a ghastly smile. 'Yes! And shrink from me, as you do now, while you hang on that detested wretch till even his frozen heart warm to passion. No!' continued he, with an awful adjuration, 'though the deed bring me to the scaffold, you shall be mine. You shall be my wife, too, Laura, – but not till you have besought me – sued at my feet for the title you have so often despised. I will be master of your fate, of that reputation, that virtue which you worship – and your minion shall know it, that he may writhe under jealousy and disappointment.'

'Powers of Mercy!' cried Laura, raising her eyes in strong compunction, 'have I made this mine idol!' Then, turning on Hargrave a look of deep repentance, 'Yes,' she continued, 'I deserve to see thee as thou art, without mitigation vile; since on thee my sacrilegious heart bestowed such love as was due to the Infinite alone!'

'Oh, Laura,' cried Hargrave, softened by the remembrance of her youthful affection, 'let but one faint spark of that love revive, and I will forget all your scorns, and feel again such gentle wishes as blest our first hours of tenderness. Or only swear that you will renounce that bane of my existence – that you will shrink from him, shun him like a serpent! – Or give me your word only, and I will trust it. Your liberty, your person, shall be as sacred as those of angels. Promise them –'

'Why do you attempt to terrify me?' said Laura, her indignation rising as her alarm subsided. 'I have perhaps no longer the right – even if I had the inclination – to utter such a vow. I trust that, in this land of freedom, I am safe from your violence. My reputation, frail as it is, you cannot harm without permission from on high; and if, for wise purposes, the permission be given, I doubt not that I shall be enabled to bear unjust reproach, – nay, even to profit by the wrong.'

Hargrave suffered her to conclude; rage bereft him, for a time, of the power of utterance. Then, bursting into a torrent of reproach, he upbraided her in language the most insulting. 'Do you dare to own,' said he, 'that your base inclinations favour that abhorred – that this accursed marriage is your choice – your free choice?' He paused in vain for a reply. Laura would not irritate him further, and scorned to disguise the truth. 'Then, Laura,' said he, and he confirmed the sentence with a dreadful oath, 'you have sealed your fate. Think you that your De Courcy shall foil me? By Heaven, I will see you perish first. I will tear you from him, though I answer it with my life and soul. Let this be the pledge of my triumph' – and he made a motion to clasp her rudely in his arms. With a cry of dread and horror, Laura sprung from him, and, throwing open the casement, called loudly for assistance. Hargrave forced her back. 'Spare your alarms, my lovely proud one,' said he, with a smile, which made her blood run cold. 'You are safe till we meet where cries will be useless. What! may I not even kiss this pretty hand, as earnest that you shall soon be mine beyond the power of fate?' 'Silence, audacious!' cried Laura, bursting into tears of mingled fear and indignation, while she struggled violently to disengage her hands. 'Nay, this rosy cheek will content me better,' cried Hargrave, and was again attempting to clasp her – when the door was burst suddenly open, and De Courcy appeared.

'Ruffian!' he exclaimed, approaching Hargrave, who, in his surprise, permitted his prey to escape. Her fears now taking a new direction, Laura flew to intercept De Courcy. 'Ah!' she cried, 'my folly has done this. Fly from this madman, I entreat you. I have nothing to fear but for you. Begone, I implore you.'

'And leave you to such treatment! Not while I have life! When you choose to go, I will attend you. For you, Sir! – But I must stoop below the language of a gentleman ere I find words to describe your conduct.'

'For Heaven's sake,' cried Laura, 'dear De Courcy, provoke him no further. Let us fly this place;' and clinging to De Courcy's arm, she drew him on; while, with the other, he defended her from Hargrave, who had advanced to detain her. Her expression of regard, her confiding attitude, exasperated the frenzy of Hargrave to the uttermost. Almost unconscious of his actions, he drew a pistol from his pocket and fired. Laura uttered a cry of terror, clasping her lover's arm more closely to her breast. 'Be not alarmed love,' whispered De Courcy. 'It is nothing!' – and staggering forward a few paces, he fell to the ground.

Laura, in desperation rushed from the summer-house, calling wildly for help; then struck with the fearful thought that Hargrave might complete his bloody work, she hastened back. During the few moments of her absence, De Courcy addressed his murderer, whose rage had given place to a mild stupor. 'I fear this is an unlucky stroke, Hargrave. Save yourself. My horse is at the gate.' Hargrave answered only with a groan; and, striking his clenched hand on his forehead, turned away. His crime was unpremeditated. No train of self-deceit had reconciled his conscience to its atrocity. The remembrance of the courage which had saved his life; the generous concern of De Courcy for his safety; humility, the last virtue which utterly forsakes us, all awakened him to remorse, keen and overwhelming, like every other passion of Hargrave. Not bearing to look upon his victim, he stood fixed and motionless; while Laura, on her knees, watched, in dismay, the changing countenance of De Courcy, and strove to staunch the blood which was streaming from his wound.

De Courcy once more tried to cheer Laura with words of comfort.

'Were it not,' said he, 'for the pleasure this kind concern gives me, I might tell you that I do not suffer much pain. I am sure I could rise, if I could trust this slender arm,' laying his hand gently upon it. Laura eagerly offered her assistance as he attempted to raise himself; but the effort overpowered him, and he sunk back fainting.

In the strong language of terror, Laura besought Hargrave to procure help. Still motionless, his forehead resting against the wall, his hands clenched as in convulsion, Hargrave seemed not to heed her entreaties. 'Have you no mercy?' cried she, clasping the arm from which she had so lately shrunk in horror. 'He saved your life. Will you let him perish without aid?' 'Off, woman!' cried Hargrave, throwing her from him. 'Thy witchcraft has undone me;' and he distractedly hurried away.

Laura's terror was not the passive cowardice of a feeble mind. She was left alone to judge, to act, for herself – for more than herself. Immediate, momentous decision was necessary. And she did decide by an effort of which no mind enfeebled by sloth or selfishness would have been capable. She saw that loss of blood was the cause of De Courcy's immediate danger, a danger which might be irremediable before he could receive assistance from more skilful hands than her's. Such remedy, then, as she could command she hastened to apply.

To the plants which their beauty had recommended to Lady Pelham, Laura had added a few of which the usefulness was known to her. Agaric of the oak was of the number, and she had often applied it where many a hand less fair would have shrunk from the task. Nor did she hesitate now. The ball had entered near the neck; and the feminine, the delicate Laura herself disengaged the wound from its coverings; the feeling, the tender Laura herself performed an office from which false sensibility would have recoiled in horror.

She was thus employed when she was found by a woman whom Hargrave had met and sent to her assistance, with an indistinct message, from which Laura gathered that he was gone in search of a surgeon. The woman no sooner cast her eyes on the bloody form of De Courcy, and on the colourless face of Laura, more death-like than his, than, with noisy imbecility, she began to bewail and ejaculate. Laura, however, instantly put a stop to her exclamations by dispatching her for cordials and assistance. In a few minutes all the household was assembled round De Courcy; yet such was the general curiosity, horror, or astonishment, that he would have remained unaided but for the firmness of her who was most interested in the scene. She dismissed every one whose presence was unnecessary, and silenced the rest by peremptory command. She administered a cordial to recruit the failing strength of De Courcy; and causing him to be raised to the posture which seemed the least painful, made her own trembling arms his support.

Nothing further now remained to be done, and Laura began to feel the full horrors of her situation; to weigh the fearful probability that all her cares were vain; to upbraid herself as the cause of this dire tragedy. Her anguish was too great to find relief in tears. Pale and cold as marble, chilly drops bursting from her forehead, she sat in the stillness of him who waits the sentence of condemnation, save when a convulsive shudder expressed her suffering.

The mournful quiet was interrupted by the entrance of Lady Pelham, who, quite out of breath, began a string of questions, mixed with abundance of ejaculation. 'Bless my soul!' she cried, 'how has all this happened? For heaven's sake, Laura, tell me the meaning of all this. Why don't you speak, girl? Good Lord! could you not have prevented these madmen from quarrelling? What brought De Courcy here? How did he find you out? Why don't you speak. Mercy on me! Is the girl out of her senses?'

The expression of deep distress with which Laura now raised her eyes, reminded Lady Pelham of the sensibility requisite upon such an occasion, which her Ladyship's curiosity had hitherto driven from her recollection. Approaching, therefore, to De Courcy, she took a hasty look at this dismal spectacle; and exclaiming, 'Oh what a sight is here! Unfortunate Laura! Dear wretched girl!' she began first to sob, and then to scream violently. Laura motioned to the attendants to lead her away; and she suffered them to do so without resistance; but she had no sooner crossed the threshold, than, perceiving the spectators whom curiosity had collected in the shrubbery, she redoubled her shrieks, struggled, beat herself; and, but for the untoward strength of her nerves, would have soon converted her pretended fit into reality. Wearied with her efforts, she was beginning to relax them, when the surgeon appeared, and her Ladyship was more vociferous than ever. Mr Raby, a quiet sensible man, undertook her care before he proceeded to his more serious business; and, either guided by his previous acquaintance with his patient, or by his experience in similar cases, gave a prescription which, though simple was perfectly efficacious. He directed that the lady should be instantly secluded in her own chamber, with only one attendant; and the remedy proved so beneficial, that her Ladyship enjoyed a night of tranquil repose.

He next turned his attention to De Courcy; and judging it proper to extract the ball without delay, advised Laura to retire. Without opposition she prepared to obey; and, seeing De Courcy about to speak, put her hand on his lips to save him the exertion, and herself the pain of a farewell. Yet, as she resigned her charge, raising her eyes to heaven, once more to commend De Courcy to the divine protection, the fervour of her supplication burst into words. 'Oh if it be possible! if it be possible!' – she cried. 'Yes it is possible,' said De Courcy, comprehending the unfinished sentence. 'Your firmness, noble creature, has made it possible.' Reproaching herself with having allowed De Courcy to perceive her alarm, she hastened away; and seating herself on the steps that led to the door, awaited in silence the event of the operation.

Here, as she sorrowfully called to mind the various excellencies of De Courcy, his piety, his integrity, his domestic virtues, so lately known, so soon to be lost to her, she suddenly recollected the heavier calamity of the mother deprived of such a son, and perceived the inhumanity of permitting the stroke to fall without preparation. Having access to no messenger more tender than a common servant, she determined, though with unspeakable reluctance, herself to bear the tidings to Mrs De Courcy. 'I will know the worst,' thought she, 'and then' –

She started at a faint noise that sounded from the summer-house. Steps approached the door from within. She sprung up, and the surgeon appeared. 'I have the happiness to tell you,' said he, 'that, if no fever take place, our friend is safe. The chief danger has been from loss of blood; and your presence of mind – Ah! – Do you feel faint?' –

The awful interest which had supported the spirits of Laura thus suddenly withdrawn, the tide of various feeling overpowered them; and she sunk into one of those long and deep faintings which were now unhappily become in some degree constitutional with her. Mr Raby having given directions for her recovery, placed De Courcy in Lady Pelham's carriage, and himself attended him to Norwood; where he mitigated Mrs De Courcy's horror and distress by assuring her of her son's safety, which he again delighted Montague by ascribing to the cares of Laura.

It was late in the evening before Laura was sufficiently collected to review with composure the events of the day! As soon, however, as she was capable of considering all the circumstances, a suspicion occurred that her unfortunate interview with Hargrave had been sanctioned, if not contrived by Lady Pelham. That he should know the place and the hour in which he might surprise her alone; – that to this place, which because of its loneliness she had of late rather deserted, she should be conducted by her aunt; – that at this moment she should upon a trivial pretence be left in solitude, – seemed a coincidence too strong to be merely accidental. She recollected some symptoms of private communication between Lady Pelham and Hargrave. Suspicions of connivance in the infamous strategem of her arrest again revived in her mind. Lady Pelham, she perceived, had afforded her a protection at best imperfect, perhaps treacherous. Hargrave's late threats too, as she revolved them in her thoughts, appeared more like the intimations of setled design than the vague ravings of passion. Prudence, therefore, seemed to require that she should immediately provide for her own safety: and indignation at her aunt's breach of confidence, hastened the purpose which she formed, to leave Walbourne without delay. She determined to go the next morning to Norwood, there to remain till De Courcy shewed signs of convalescence, and then perform her long-projected journey to Scotland.

In order to avoid unpleasant altercation, she resolved to depart without warning Lady Pelham of her intention; merely announcing by letter the reasons of her conduct. The affectionate Laura would not have parted from the meanest servant without a kindly farewell; but her innate abhorrence of treachery steeled her heart, and she rejoiced that it was possible to escape all present intercourse with her deceitful kinswoman.

As soon as the dawn appeared she arose; and on her knees thankfully acknowledged the protecting care which had watched over her, since first as a destitute orphan she applied to Lady Pelham. She blessed the goodness which had softened in her favour a heart little subject to benevolent expressions, which had restored her in sickness, consoled her in sorrow, delivered her from the snares of the wicked, and opened to her the joys of virtuous friendship. And where is the wretch so miserable that he may not in the review of eighteen months find subjects of gratitude still more numerous! Laura began no important action of her life without imploring a blessing on the event; and she now proceeded to commend herself and her future prospects to the same care of which she had glad experience.

The proper business of the morning ended, she had begun to make arrangements for her immediate departure; when she heard Lady Pelham's bell ring, and the next instant heard a noise like that occasioned by the fall of something heavy. She listened for a while, but all was again still. The rest of the family were yet buried in sleep, and Laura hearing no one stirring to answer Lady Pelham's summons, began to fear that her aunt was ill, perhaps unable to make any further effort to procure assitance. At this idea, all her just indignation subsiding in a moment, she flew to Lady Pelham's chamber.

Lady Pelham was lying on the floor, having apparently fallen in an attempt to rise from her bed. She was alive though insensible; and her face, though altered, was still florid. Laura soon procuring help, raised her from the ground; and guessing that apoplexy was her disorder, placed her in an upright posture, loosened her night-clothes, and having hurried away a servant for Mr Raby, ventured, until his arrival, upon such simple remedies as she knew might be safely administered. In little more than an hour the surgeon arrived; and having examined his patient, declared her to be in extreme danger. Before he left her, however, he succeeded in restoring her to some degree of recollection; yet, far from changing his first opinion, he advised Laura to lose no time in making every necessary use of an amendment which he feared would be only transient.

From Lady Pelham, he went to Norwood; and returning to Walbourne in the evening, brought the pleasing intelligence that De Courcy continued to do well. This second visit produced no change in his sentiments, and he remained persuaded that though Lady Pelham might continue to linger for a time, the shock had been too great to allow of complete recovery. Laura now rejoiced that she had not executed her purpose of leaving Walbourne; since, had her aunt's illness succeeded to the rage which her departure would have excited, she could never have ceased to blame herself as the cause. She looked with profound compassion, too, upon the condition of an unfortunate being, whose death-bed was neither smoothed by affection, nor cheered by pious hope. 'Unhappy woman!' thought she, as she sat watching an unquiet slumber into which her aunt had fallen, 'to whom the best gifts of nature and of fortune have, by some fatality, been useless, or worse than useless; whose affluence has purchased no higher joys than half-grudged luxuries; whose abilities have dazzled others and bewildered herself, but lent no steady light to guide her way; whose generosity has called forth no gratitude, whose kindness has awakened no affection; to whom length of days has brought no reverence, and length of intimacy no friends! Even the sacred ties of nature have been to her unblessed. Her only child, driven from her in anger, dares not approach to share the last sad offices with me, who, in performing them, must forgive as well as pity. Favourite of fortune! what has been wanting to thee save that blessing which "bringeth no sorrow with it." But that blessing was light in thine esteem; and amidst the glitter of thy toys, the "pearl of great price" was disregarded.'

For some days Lady Pelham continued much in the same situation. She suffered no pain, yet gave no signs of amendment. On the sixth morning from her first attack she grew suddenly and materially worse. It was soon discovered that her limbs were paralyzed, and the surgeon declared that her end could not be very distant. Her senses, however, again returned, and she continued free from pain. She shewed little apprehension of her own danger; and Laura debated with herself whether she should permit her aunt to dream away the last precious hours of probation, or endeavour to awaken her to a sense of her condition.

Laura had no faith in death-bed repentance. She knew that resolution of amendment which there is no longer time to practise, and renunciation of sin made under the immediate prospect of punishment, are at best suspicious. She kew that, in the ordinary course of providence, the grace which has been long despised is at length justly withdrawn. Yet she saw that she had no right to judge Lady Pelham as wholly impenitent; and she considered a death-bed as highly suitable to the renewal, though not to the beginning of repentance. She knew too, that the call *might* be made effectual at the 'eleventh hour;' and the bare chance was worth the toil of ages. She felt how little she herself would have valued the mistaken pity which could suffer her to enter on the 'dark valley' without a warning to cling closer to the 'staff and rod' of comfort: – She therefore ventured to hint gently to Lady Pelham the opinion of her medical friends, and to remind her of the duty of preparing for the worst.

Lady Pelham at first appeared a good deal shocked; and lay for some time apparently meditating upon her situation. At last, recovering her spirits, she said, 'Your nerves, Laura, were always so coarse, that you seemed to me to take a pleasure in thinking of shocking things; but I am sure it is abominably barbarous in you to tease me with them now I am ill. Do keep your horrid fancies to yourself, or keep away till you are cured of the vapours – I dare say it is your dismal face that makes me dream so unpleasantly.'

Laura, however, was not to be so discouraged. She took occasion to represent that no harm could ensue from preparing to meet the foe; since his march was not to be retarded by shutting our eyes on his advances, nor hastened by the daring which watched his approach. She at length thought she had succeeded in convincing her aunt of her danger. Lady Pelham *said* that she feared she was dying, and she believed that she said the truth. But Lady Pelham had had sixty years practice in self-deceit. The fear might flutter in her imagination, but was not strong enough to touch her heart. Laura, however, made use of her acknowledgement to press upon her the duties of forgiveness and charity towards all mindkind, and especially towards her child; reminding her of the affecting parity of situation between offending man and his disobedient offspring. Lady Pelham at first answered impatiently that she would not be argued on this subject; but as her spirits began to fail under the first confinement which she had ever endured, she became more tractable. 'God knows,' said she to Laura, one day, 'we all have much need to be forgiven; and therefore we must forgive in our turn. For my part I am sure I die in charity with all mankind, and with that creature among the rest. However, I shall take my friend the Spectator's advice, and remember the difference between giving and *for*giving.'

Laura often begged permission to send for Mrs Herbert; but Lady Pelham sometimes postponed it till she should get better, sometimes till she should grow worse. Laura was in the meantime her constant attendant; bearing with her peevishness, soothing her caprice, and striving to rouse in her feelings suitable to her condition. Finding, however, that she made but little progress in her pious work, she begged that she might be allowed to take the assistance of a clergyman. 'A clergyman, child!' cried Lady Pelham. 'Do you imagine me to be a papist? Or do you think me capable of such weak superstition as to place more reliance on a parson's prayers than on yours, or my maid Betty's? No, no! I trust I have been no worse than other people; and I hope, though I may be weak, I shall never be fanatical. Besides, I have too high a sense of the Divine Justice to think that our Maker would first give us ungovernable passions, and then punish us for yielding to them. A phlegmatic being like you, may indeed be called to strict account; but people of strong feelings must be judged by a different standard.' 'Oh, Madam,' said Laura, 'be assured that our Maker gives us no unconquerable passions. If we ourselves have made them so, it becomes us to be humbled in the dust, not to glory in the presumptuous hope that He will soften the sanctions of his law to favour our remissness.'

Driven from the strong hold of justice, rather by the increase of her bodily languor, than by the force of truth, the dying sinner had recourse to mercy, – a mercy, however, of her own composing. 'It is true,' said she one day to Laura, 'that I have done some things which I have reason to regret, and which, I must confess, deserve punishment. But Divine Mercy towards believers, we are told, is infinite; and though I may at times have doubted, I have never disbelieved.' Laura, shuddering at this awful blindness, was striving to frame a useful reply, when she saw her aunt's countenance change. It was distorted by a momentary convulsion, and then fixed for ever in the stillness of death.

CHAPTER XXXII

———————•———————

LAURA was more shocked than afflicted by the death of a person whom she was unable to love, and had no reason to respect. She lost no time in conveying the news to Mrs Herbert, begging that she would herself come and give the necessary directions. Thinking it proper to remain at Walbourne till after her aunt's funeral, she refused Mrs De Courcy's invitation to spend at Norwood the time which intervened. De Courcy continued to recover fast; and Laura, thinking she might soon leave him without anxiety, again fixed an early day for her journey to Scotland.

Notwithstanding Laura's knowledge of the phlegmatic temperament of her cousin, she was surprised at the stoicism with which Mrs Herbert supported the death of her mother. She examined the dead body with a cold comment on its appearance; gave orders for the interment in an unfaltering voice; and neither seemed to feel nor to affect the slightest concern. Nor did her philosophy appear to fail her one jot, when, upon opening the will, she was found to be left without inheritance. The paper, which had been drawn up a few months before, evinced Lady Pelham's adherence to her scheme for her niece's advancement; and this, with her obstinate enmity to Mrs Herbert, furnished the only instance of her consistency or perseverance, which were ever known to the world. Her whole property she bequeathed to Laura Montreville, and to her second son upon taking the name of Pelham, provided that Laura married Colonel Hargrave, or a peer, or the eldest son of a peer; but if she married a commoner, or remained unmarried, she was to inherit only ten thousand pounds, the bulk of the property going to a distant relation.

The very hour that this will was made public, Laura informed the contingent heir that he might possess himself of his inheritance, since she would certainly never perform the conditions which alone could destroy his claim. Not acquiescing in the justice of excluding Mrs Herbert from her natural rights she would instantly have offered to share with her cousin the bequest of Lady Pelham; but considering that her engagement with De Courcy entitled him to decide on the disposal of whatever belonged to his future wife, she hastened to ask his sanction to her purpose. De Courcy, without hesitation, advised that the whole should be given up to its natural owner. 'We shall have enough for humble comfort, dear Laura,' said he, 'and have no need to grasp at a doubtful claim.' Laura, however, differed from him in opinion. She thought she might, in strict justice, retain part of the bequest of so near a relation; and she felt pleased to think that she should enter the De Courcy family not altogether portionless. She therefore reserved two thousand pounds, giving up the rest unconditionally to Mrs Herbert.

These points being settled, nothing now remained to retard Laura's journey to Scotland. Mrs De Courcy, indeed, urged her to postpone it till Montague should acquire a right to be her escort; but Laura objected that it was her wish to give a longer time to her old friend than she thought it proper to withdraw De Courcy from his business and his home. She reflected, too, with a light heart, that a protector in her journey was now less necessary, since her mad lover, as Harriet called Colonel Hargrave, had embarked for America. Laura had heard of his departure before her aunt's death; and she gladly observed that favourable winds were speeding him across the Atlantic.

The day preceding that on which she meant to leave Walbourne, she spent with Mrs De Courcy and Montague; who, though not entirely recovered, was able to resume his station in the family-room. De Courcy, with the enthusiasm of youth and love, spoke of his happy prospects; his mother, with the sober eye of experience, looked forward to joys as substantial, though less dazzling; while feminine modesty suppressed the pleasure with which Laura felt that she was necessary to these schemes of bliss. With the confidence of mutual esteem they arranged their plan of life, – a plan at once embracing usefulness and leisure, retirement and hospitality. Laura consented that one month, 'one little month,' should begin the accomplishment of these golden dreams; for she permitted De Courcy to follow her at the end of that time to Scotland. A few weeks they were to spend in wandering through the romantic scenes of her native land; and then join Mrs De Courcy at Norwood, which was to continue her permanent abode.

Laura remained with her friends till the evening was closing; then, avoiding the solemnity of a farewell by a half-promise of stopping as she passed the next day, she sprung into Mrs De Courcy's carriage, and drove off. Tears rushed to De Courcy's eyes as the carriage was lost to his sight. 'I am still weak,' thought he as he dashed them away. 'She will soon return to bring gladness to every heart, and double joy to mine. To-morrow too I shall see her,' thought he; yet he continued depressed, and soon retired to his chamber.

Mrs De Courcy and her son met early the next morning, expecting that Laura would early begin her journey. Montague stationed himself at the window to watch for her appearance; half fearing that she would not keep her promise, yet every minute repeating that it was impossible she could go without bidding farewell. The breakfast hour arrived, and still Laura came not. De Courcy, impatient, forgot his weakness, and insisted upon walking to the gate that he might inquire whether a carriage had passed from Walbourne.

He had scarcely left the house when old John, with a face that boded evil, hastily came to beg that his Lady would speak with a servant of Lady Pelham's. Mrs De Courcy, somewhat alarmed, desired that the servant might come in. 'Please, Madam,' said he, 'let me know where I may find Miss Montreville. The carriage has waited for her these three hours?' 'Good heavens!' cried Mrs De Courcy, in consternation. 'Is Miss Montreville not at Walbourne?' 'No, Madam, she has not been there since yesterday morning.' Mrs De Courcy, now in extreme alarm, summoned her coachman, and desired to know where he had left Miss Montreville the evening before. He answered, that, at Laura's desire, he had set her down at the gate of Walbourne; that he had seen her enter; and afterwards, in turning the carriage, had observed her walking along the avenue towards the house. Inexpressibly shocked, Mrs De Courcy had yet the presence of mind to forbid alarming her son with these fearful tidings. As soon as she could recollect herself, she dispatched old Wilson, on whose discretion she thought she might rely, to inform De Courcy that a message from Walbourne had made her cease to expect Laura's visit. Montague returned home, sad and disappointed. His melancholy questions and comments increased the distress of his mother. 'Did she not even write one line?' said he. 'Could you have believed that she would go without one farewell – that she could have passed our very gate?' 'She was willing to spare you the pain of a farewell,' said Mrs De Courcy, checking the anguish of her heart. 'She will write soon, I hope.'

But day after day passed, and Laura did not write. Mrs De Courcy, still concealing from her son a misfortune which she thought him yet unequal to bear, used every possible exertion to trace the fugitive. She offered high rewards to whoever could afford the smallest clue to discovery. She advertised in every newspaper except that which De Courcy was accustomed to read. Her suspicions at first falling upon Hargrave, she caused particular inquiry to be made whether any of his domestics had been left in England with orders to follow him; but she found that he with his whole suite had sailed from Europe more than a fortnight before Laura's disappearance. She employed emissaries to prosecute the search in almost every part of the kingdom. Judging the metropolis to be the most likely place of concealment, she made application to the officers of police for assistance in her inquiries there. All was in vain. No trace of Laura was to be found.

For a while De Courcy amused himself from day to day with the hope of hearing from her; a hope which his mother had not the courage to destroy. He calculated that she would reach the end of her journey on the sixth day after that on which she left him. On the seventh she would certainly write; therefore in four or five more he should undoubtedly hear from her. The expected day came and passed as others had done, without bringing news of Laura. Another and another came, and ended only in disappointment. De Courcy was miserable. He knew not how to account for a silence so adverse to the considerate kindness of Laura's character, except by supposing that illness made her unable to write. This idea gathering strength in his mind, he resolved to follow her immediately to Scotland, tracing her through the route which he knew she intended to take. Mrs De Courcy in vain attempted to dissuade him from the prosecution of his design, and to sooth him with hopes which she knew too well would prove deceitful. He was resolute, and Mrs De Courcy was at last obliged to prevent his fruitless journey by unfolding the truth. The utmost tenderness of caution was insufficient to prevent the effects of this blow on De Courcy's bodily frame. In a few hours strong fever seized him; and his wound, which had hitherto worn a favourable appearance, gave alarming symptoms of inflammation. Three weeks did Mrs De Courcy watch by his bedside in all the anguish of a mother's fears; forgetting, in her anxiety for his life, that he must for a time live only to sorrow. The balance long hung doubtful. At length the strength of his constitution and his early habits of temperance prevailed. By slow degrees his health was restored, though his spirits were still oppressed by a dejection which long withstood every effort of reason and religion.

To divert his sorrow rather than in the hope of removing its cause, he left his home and wandered through the most unfrequented parts of England, making anxious, yet almost hopeless, inquiries for his lost treasure. Sometimes, misled by false intelligence, he was hurried from place to place in all the eagerness of expectation, but bitter disappointment closed the pursuit; and the companion of his relaxation, his encouragement in study, his pattern in virtue, the friend, the mistress, almost the wife, was lost beyond recal.

While De Courcy was thus languishing on a sick-bed or wandering restless and miserable, Laura too was a wanderer, a prey to care more deep, more hopeless.

The soft shades of twilight were stealing on as she cast a last look back towards Norwood; and were deepening fast as with a sigh, half-pleasing, half-melancholy, she surveyed the sheltering chestnut tree where she had once parted from De Courcy. As she approached her home, the stars coming forth poured their silent language into the ear of piety. Never deaf to this holy call, Laura dismissed her attendants that she might meditate alone. She proceeded slowly along till she came to the entrance of a woody lane, which branched off from the avenue. She stopped, half-inclined to enter; a sensation of fear made her pause. The next moment the very consciousness of that sensation induced her to proceed. 'This is mere childish superstition,' said she, and entered the lane. She had taken only a few steps when she felt herself suddenly seized from behind; one person forcibly confining her arms while another prevented her cries. Vainly struggling against masculine strength, she was hurried rapidly forward, till, her breath failing, she could resist no farther. Her conductors, soon quitting the beaten path, dragged her on through a little wood that sheltered the lawn towards the east; till reaching a gap which appeared to have been purposely made in the park wall, Laura perceived a carriage in waiting. Again exerting the strength of desperation, she struggled wildly for freedom; but the unequal contest soon was closed; she was lifted into the carriage; one of the men took his place by her side, and they drove off with the speed of lightning.

From the moment when she recovered recollection, Laura had not a doubt that she owed this outrage to Hargrave. She was convinced that his pretence of leaving the kingdom had been merely intended to throw her off her guard, and that he was now waiting, at no distant place, the success of his daring villany. At this idea, a horrible dread seized her, she threw herself back in the carriage, and wept in despair. Her attendant perceiving that she no longer struggled, with a coarse expression of pity, released her from his grasp; and taking the handkerchief from her mouth, told her 'she might cry as long as she pleased, for he knew it did a woman's heart good to cry.' Laura now besought him to tell her whither she was going. 'You'll know that by and by,' said he. 'Let me alone. I am going to sleep; do you the same.'

The bare mention of his purpose revived Laura's hopes. 'Surely,' thought she, 'while he sleeps, I may escape. In spite of this fearful speed I may spring out; and if I could but gain a few steps, in this darkness I should be safe.' Full of this project, she remained still as the dead; fearing by the slightest sound or motion to retard the sleep of her guard. At last his breathing announced that he was asleep; and Laura began, with trembling hands, to attempt her escape. The blinds were drawn up; and if she could let down that on the side of the carriage where she sat, she might without difficulty open the door. She tried to stir the blind. It refused to yield. She used her utmost force, but it remained firm. She ventured, cautious and trembling, to attempt that on the other side. It dropt; and Laura thought she was free. It only remained to open the door of the chaise and leap out. She tried it; but the door was immoveable, and, in despair, she shrunk back. Again she started up; for it occurred to her that, though with more danger, she might escape by the window. Cautiously stepping across her guard, she leant out and placed her hands on the top of the carriage, that, trusting to her arms for supporting her weight, she might extricate herself, and drop from thence into the road. Raising herself upon the edge of the step, she fixed her hands more firmly. She paused a moment to listen whether her guard were undisturbed. He still slept soundly; and resting her limbs upon the window frame, she prepared to complete her escape.

A moment more and she had been free; when a horseman riding up, pushed her fiercely back, upbraiding, with tremendous oaths, the carelessness of his companion. The fellow, rousing himself, retorted upon the wretched Laura the abuse of his comrade, swearing that 'since he saw she was so cunning, he would keep better watch on her for the future.'

The desponding Laura endured his reproaches in silence. Finding herself thus doubly guarded, she resigned all hope of escaping by her own unaided exertions; and mingling silent prayers with her fearful anticipations, she strove to reanimate her trust that she should not be wholly forsaken. Sometimes her habitual confidence prevailed, and she felt assured, that she should not be left a prey to the wicked. Yet the dreadful threats, the fiery passions of Hargrave rose to her recollection, and she again shuddered in despair. She suddenly remembered Jessy Wilson, Starting, with an exclamation of horror and affright, she sought some weapon which might dispense to her a death less terrible; and instinctively grasping her pen-knife hid it in her bosom. The next moment she shrunk from her purpose, and doubted the lawfulness of such defence. 'Will he dare his own life, too?' thought she. 'Oh, Heaven! in mercy spare me the necessity of sending a wretch to his great account, with all his crimes unrepented on his head – or pardon him and me?'

She continued to commend herself to Heaven, till her terrors by degrees subsided. She began again to feel the steady trust which is acquired by all who are habituated to a grateful consideration of the care which they experience; a trust that even the most adverse events shall terminate in their real advantage; that the rugged and slippery ways of this dark wilderness, shall, at the dawn of everlasting day, be owned as the fittest to conduct us to the house of our Father. She began, too, to regain the confidence which strong minds naturally put in their own exertions. She resolved not to be wanting to herself; nor, by brooding over her terrors, to disable herself from taking advantage of any providential circumstance which might favour her escape.

Morning at length began to dawn, but the blinds being closely drawn up, Laura could make no observations on the country through which she was passing. She remarked that the furious speed with which she had first been driven, had slackened to a slow pace; and she judged that the wearied cattle could not proceed much further. She hoped that it would soon be necessary to stop; and that during the few minutes in which they halted to change horses, she might find means of appealing to the justice of her fellow-creatures. 'Surely,' said she, 'some heart will be open to me.'

After proceeding slowly for some time the carriage stopped. Laura listened for the sounds of human voices, but all was silent. She heard the trampling of horses as if led close by the carriage. Some one was certainly near who had no interest in this base oppression. 'Help! Oh help me,' cried Laura. 'I am cruelly and wrongfully detained. I have friends that will reward you. Heaven will reward you! – Help me! for kind mercy, help me!' 'Heyday!' cried the fellow in the carriage, with something between a grin and a stare, 'who is the girl speaking to? What! did you imagine we should be wise enough to bring you within holla of a whole yardful of stable boys and piping chambermaids? Reward indeed! Set your heart at rest, Miss; we shall be rewarded without your friends or Heaven either.'

The carriage again proceeded with the same speed as at first, and Laura strove to support with composure this new blow to her hopes. Her companion, now producing a bottle of wine and some biscuits, advised her to share with him; and that she might not wilfully lavish her strength and spirits, she consented. Once more in the course of the day the travellers stopped to change horses, and Laura once more, though with feebler hopes, renewed her appeals to justice and mercy. No answer greeted her. Again she was hurried on her melancholy way.

The day, as it advanced, seemed rough and gloomy. The wind swept in gusts through the trees, and the rain beat upon the carriage. The evening was drawing on when Laura remarked that the motion was changed. The chaise proceeded slowly over soft uneven ground, and she guessed, with dismay, that it had quitted all frequented paths. In renewed alarm, she again besought her companion to tell her whither he meant to conduct her, and for what end she was thus cruelly forced from her home. 'Why, how should I tell you what I do not know myself?' answered the man. 'I shan't conduct you much farther – and a good riddance. As for the end you'll see that when it comes.'

About an hour after quitting the road, the carriage stopped; and the man letting down the blind, Laura perceived through the dusk, that they were on a barren moor. Waste and level, it seemed to spread before her; but the darkness prevented her from distinguishing its features or its boundaries. Suddenly, as the gust died away, she fancied she heard the roar of waters. She listened; but the wind swelled again, and she heard only its howlings over the heath. The horseman, who had rode away when the carriage stopped, now gallopped back, and directed the postilion to proceed. They went on for a few hundred yards, and again they stopped. The roar of waters again burst on Laura's ear, now swelling in thunder, now sinking in a sullen murmur. She saw a light glimmer at a distance. It was tossed by the billows of the ocean.

The door of the chaise was opened, and she was lifted from it. Gliding from the arms of the ruffian who held her, and clasping his knees, 'Oh! if you have the heart of a man,' she cried, 'let me not be torn from my native land – let me not be cast on the merciless deep. Think what it is to be an exile – friendless in a strange land – the sport, the prey of a pitiless enemy. Oh! if you have need of mercy, have mercy upon me.' – 'Holla! Robert,' shouted the ruffian, 'take away this girl. She's enough to make a man play the fool and whimper.' The other fellow now approaching, lifted Laura, more dead than alive, from the ground, and, wrapping her in a large cloak, bore her towards the beach.

In a creek sheltered by rocks from the breakers, lay a small boat. One man sat near the bow, roaring a hoarse sea-song. As the party approached, he rose, and pushing the boat ashore, received the half lifeless Laura in his brawny arms, cursing her with strange oaths for having made him wait so long. Then, on his uttering a discordant yell, two of his companions appeared; and after exchanging with Laura's guards a murmuring account of the trouble they had undergone, pushed off from the land. The keel grated along the pebbles; the next moment it floated on the waves, and Laura starting up, threw back the cloak from her face, and with strained eyes gazed on her parting native land, till all behind was darkness.

A pang of anguish striking to her heart, she made once more a desperate effort to awaken pity. Stretching her clasped hands towards the man who sat near her, she cried, in the piercing voice of misery, 'Oh take pity on me! I am an orphan. I have heard that sailors have kindly hearts – Have pity then – land me on the wildest coast, and I will fall down and pray for you!' The person to whom she spoke having eyed her a moment in silence, coolly drew in his oar; and rising, wrapped her close in the cloak and laid her down in the bottom of the boat, advising her with an oath to 'keep snug or she would capsize them.' In despair she renounced all further effort. Silent and motionless she lay, the cold spray dashing over her unheeded; till wet, chilled, and miserable, she was lifted on board a small brig which lay about half a mile from the shore. She was carried down to the cabin, which was more decent than is usual in vessels of that size. A clean-looking woman attended to undress her; night-clothes were in readiness for her; and every accommodation provided which her situation rendered possible. Every thing served to convince her of the care and precaution with which this cruel scheme had been concerted, and to shew her the depth of the snare into which she had fallen.

She was laid in her narrow crib, ere it occurred to her that Hargrave might be near to watch his prey. Exhausted as she was, sleep fled at the thought. She listened for his voice, for his footstep, amid the unwonted discord that disturbed her ear. Daylight returned, and no sound reached her more terrible than that of the gale rattling in the cordage and dashing the waves against the vessel's side. Worn out with fatigue and suffering, she slept at length; and a mid-day sun glanced by fits through her grated window ere she awoke to a new sense of sorrow. She rose, and going upon deck, looked sadly back upon the way she had unconsciously passed. Behind, the blue mountains were sinking in the distance; on the left lay a coast unknown to her; before her stretched the boundless deep, unvaried save by the whitening surge.

Laura spent most of her time upon deck, the fresh air reviving her failing spirits. One male and one female attendant seemed appropriated to her, and served her with even officious assiduity. Hoping that some opportuny might occur of transmitting an account of her situation to England, she begged these obsequious attendants to supply her with writing materials; but was firmly, though respectfully, refused.

The third morning came, and Laura looked in vain for any object to vary the immeasurable waste. The sun rose from one unbending line, and sunk again in naked majesty. She observed that the course of the vessel was in general directly west; and if she had before doubted, this circumstance would have convinced her of her destination. She once ventured to inquire whither the ship was bound, but was answered that 'she should know that when she reached the port.'

It was on the fourth of May that Laura began her ill-omened voyage. On the twelfth of June, land! All ran to gaze with glad eyes on what seemed a low cloud, faintly descried on the verge of the horizon – all but Laura, who looked sadly forward, as to the land of exile, of degradation, – of death. Day after day that dreaded land approached; till, by degrees, the boundless ocean was narrowed to a mighty river, and the unfrequent sail, almost too distant for mortal sight, was multiplied to a busy fleet, plying in every direction their cheerful labours. At length a city appeared in view, rising like an amphitheatre, and flashing bright with a material unknown to European architecture. Laura inquired what town it was; and, though refused all information, surmised that Quebec lay before her.

Opposite the town, the ship hove to; a boat was launched, and Laura expected to be sent on shore. Nor did she unwillingly prepare to go. 'Surely,' thought she, 'in this populous city some one will be found to listen to my tale, and wrest me from the arm of the oppressor.' The boat however departed without her, carrying ashore the man who had hitherto attended her. After remaining on shore for several hours, the man returned, and the vessel again proceeded in her voyage. Laura now imagined that Montreal was her destined port; and again she strove to hope that, among numbers, she should find aid.

A still cloudy evening had succeeded to a sultry day, when Laura observed an unusual bustle upon deck. It was growing dark, when, as she leant over the rail, to watch the fire-flies that flashed like stars in the air, the captain approaching her, told her that she must go ashore, and immediately lifted her into a boat which lay along-side. Her attendants and baggage were already there; the sailors had taken their oars; and, roaring to their companions a rough 'good night,' made towards the land. Instead, however, of gaining the nearest point, they rowed into what in the darkness seemed a creek; but Laura soon perceived that, having left the great river on which they had hitherto sailed, they were following the course of one of its tributary streams. The darkness prevented her from distinguishing objects on the banks, though now and then a light, glimmering from a casement, shewed that the haunts of man were near. She could not even discern the countenances of the sailors; but she observed, that he who seemed to direct the others, spoke in a voice which was new to her ear. All night the rowers toiled up the stream. The day dawned; and Laura perceived that, passing an open cultivated plain, she was pursuing her course towards woods impervious to the light. Dark and tangled they lowered over the stream, till they closed round, and every cheerful object was blotted from the scene.

CHAPTER XXXIII

———————•———————

THE travellers had proceeded for some time shaded by the overhanging woods, the distance lengthened by the dreary sameness of their way, when a wild halloo smote Laura's ear; and she perceived that three Indians stood at the water-edge, making signs for the boat to land. To her unspeakable surprise, the sailors joyfully obeyed the signal. They ran their bark into a creek to which the Indians pointed, and cheerfully busied themselves in discharging their cargo. Placed with her attendants on a little eminence, which rose above the swampy margin of the river, Laura took a fearful survey of the scene around her. Save where the sluggish stream opened to the day, her view was bounded to a few yards of marshy ground, rank with unwholesome vegetation. No track appeared to lead from this desolate spot. Between the gigantic pines, brushwood and coarse grass spread in sad luxuriance. No trace was here of human footstep. All was dreary and forlorn, as the land which the first wanderers visited unwilling.

She had not long continued her melancholy survey, when the two stoutest of the Indians approached; and one of them, after talking apart with her attendants, lifted her female servant in his arms, and walked on. The other, making some uncouth gestures, prepared to raise Laura from the ground. She shrunk back alarmed; but the Indian, in broken French, assured her that he would not hurt her; and, pointing towards the woods, reminded her of the difficulty of passing them on foot. Her valet, too, represented the fatigue she must undergo, if she refused the assistance of the Indian. But Laura preferring a toilsome march to such a mode of conveyance, persevered in her refusal; and, bidding them lead the way, followed into the pathless wild.

They continued their journey for several hours, no object meeting their sight that might mark the stages of their way. No work of man appeared, not even the faintest trace that ever man had toiled through this wilderness; yet Laura perceived that the Indians proceeded without hesitation. The position of the grass, the appearance of the leaves, gave indication sufficient to guide them in their route. One of them carried a bag of provisions; and having reached a spot where the ground was firm and dry, he invited Laura to sit down and take some refreshment. Faint with fatigue, Laura thankfully acceded. Scarcely, however, had she seated herself on the grass, ere her attention was drawn by a slight though unusual noise; and she was told that it was caused by a rattlesnake. At this intelligence her maid, screaming, started up, and was going to dart forward into the wood. The Indians beheld her terror with silent contempt, while Laura calmly detained her with gentle force. 'Stay, Mary,' said she. 'If you tread on the animal you are gone! If we are quiet, we may probably see and avoid it.' The influence which Laura always acquired over those with whom she lived, prevailed over Mary's dread; and in a few moments the serpent was seen by one of the Indians, who killed it with a single blow.

Their hasty meal ended, the party proceeded on their way; but they had not gone far ere Laura, worn out with toil and sorrow, sunk upon the ground. She had now no choice; and the Indian, lifting her with the same ease as she would have done an infant, went on with more speed than before.

Towards the close of the day, the woods suddenly opened into a small field, surrounded by them on every side, which appeared to have been itself imperfectly redeemed from the same state of waste luxuriance. In the centre stood a house, or rather cabin, rudely constructed of the material which nature so lavishly supplied. Around it a small patch, inclosed by a palisade, bore marks of forsaken cultivation. Beyond this inclosure, logs of prodigious size lay scattered through the field, and the roots, which had not been cleared from the ground, were again shooting luxuriantly. With a faint sensation of gladness, Laura beheld traces of humankind. Yet no living creature appeared. Here reigned primeval stillness. The winds had died away. A sultry calm filled the air. The woods were motionless. The birds were silent. All was fixed as in death, save where a dull stream stole under the tall canes that deformed its margin.

Mary's exclamations of grief and surprise first informed Laura that she had reached her home. To Laura the dreariness of the scene was of small concern. No outward circumstances could add to the horrors with which her fears were familiar. While her attendant bewailed aloud that ever thirst of gain had lured her from happy England, Laura was inwardly striving to revive the hope that sudden death might snatch her from the grasp of the oppressor; and renewing her oft repeated prayer, – 'Oh that Thou wouldst hide me in the grave.' But no selfish sorrow could make her regardless of the woes of others. 'Courage, Mary,' said she, with a foreboding smile, 'we shall soon be released; and both, I hope, find shelter in our Father's house.'

The cabin was divided into three apartments, each entering from the other. To the innermost Laura was conducted; and she saw that it had been arranged for her. The window was secured with iron. The furniture, unlike that of the other rooms, was new and not inelegant. Laura looked round to observe whether any trace of Hargrave's presence was visible. None appeared. She examined every recess and corner of her new abode, as one who fears the lurking assassin. She ascertained that Hargrave was not its inmate; and thanked Heaven for the prospect of one night of peace. It was in vain, however, that she tried to discover how long this reprieve might last. The servants either could not or would not give her any information. She was too well acquainted with the character of her oppressor to hope that he would long delay his coming. 'To-morrow, perhaps' – thought she; and the cold shivering came over her, which now ever followed her anticipation of the future. 'Yet why do I despair?' said she. 'Is any time too short, are any means too feeble for the Power – for the wisdom in which I trust? But since the hour of trial may be so near, let me not waste the time which should prepare for it, – prepare to cast off this poor clog of earth, and rise beyond its sorrows and its stains.'

Laura's bodily frame, however, could not long keep pace with the efforts of her mind, for her health and strength were failing under the continued influence of grief and fear. The form, once rounded in fair proportion, was wasted to a shadow. The once graceful neck bent mournfully forward. The lily arms hung down in listless melancholy. The cheek, once of form inimitable, was sunk and hollow now. The colour, once quick to tell the modest thought, was fixed in the paleness of the dead. And death was ever present to her thoughts, –

sole point to which her hope turned steadily!

One only desire lingered on earth. She wished that some friend should pity her hard fate, and know that the victim had shrunk from it, though in vain. Intending to leave behind her some attestation of her innocence, she besought Mary to procure for her the means of writing. 'Why should you fear to trust me?' said she. 'To whom upon earth can my complaint reach now? You may see all I write, Mary; and perhaps when I am gone you will yourself convey it to my friend. Your master will not prevent you then; for then he will have pity on me, and wish that he had not dealt with me so hardly.' The irresistible sweetness of Laura had won the heart of her attendant, and Mary promised that she would endeavour to gratify her. She said that the writing materials were kept carefully locked up by Robert, the man-servant; that his master's orders on that subject had been peremptory; that she was sure he would not venture to disobey while there remained a possibility of conveying intelligence from the place of their confinement; that two of the Indians were to depart on the following day; that after they were gone, no means of access to the habitable world remaining, Robert might possibly relax his strictness, and permit Laura to amuse herself with writing. Mary's words awakened in Laura's mind an idea that all was not yet lost. The Indians were suspected of favouring her. They might then bear her appeal to human pity, to human justice. If she could find means to speak with them apart, she would plead so earnestly that even savages would be moved to mercy! At these thoughts a ray of hope once more kindled in her breast. It was the last. All day she watched for an opportunity to address one of the Indians. In vain! Robert guarded her with such relentless fidelity, that she found it impossible to effect her purpose. The Indians departed. Mary performed her promise, and the unfortunate Laura wrote the following letter, which was afterwards, with Hargrave's permission, conveyed to Mrs Douglas.

'From this dreary land of exile, to whom shall I address myself save to you, mine own friend, and my father's friend? Where tell my sad fate save to you, who first taught me the hope that lives beyond it? And let it comfort your kind heart to know, that while you are shedding tears over this last memorial of your Laura, I shall be rejoicing in the full consummation of that hope.

'There is indeed another friend! One to whom my last earthly thoughts are due! But I cannot tell him, that she who was almost the wife of his bosom is gone down to a dishonoured grave. I have not time to soften my sad tale to him, nor to study words of comfort; for the moments are precious with me now. A few, a very few, are all that remain for preparation. I must not rob them of their awful right. Tell him my story as he is able to bear it. Tell him my innocence, and he will believe it, for he knew my very soul. But I must hasten, lest the destroyer come, ere, in these lines, I close my connection with this world of trial.'

[She then proceeded to give a simple narrative of her wrongs. She expressed no bitterness against the author of them. She spoke of him as a misguided being, and pitied the anguish which he was preparing for himself.] 'Tell Mr De Courcy,' she proceeded, 'that I charge him, by all the love he bears me, to forgive my enemy, even from the heart forgive him. Let him do more. Let him pray for him; and if they meet, admonish him. It may be that his heart will soften when he remembers me.'

[The remainder of the letter was written at intervals. Laura spent her time chiefly in acts of devotion, of self-examination, and repentance. It was only when exhausted nature could no longer follow these exercises of the soul, that she returned to add another line to her picture of wretchedness.]

'The saints who resisted unto blood striving against sin, who gave up their lives in defence of the truth, looked forward to the hour of their departure rejoicing. But I must go to the grave laden with shame and sorrow. My soul is weary of my life, and yet I must fear to die. Yet let my enemy a little while delay his coming and my death also will be joyful. Let him stay only a few days, and I shall be deaf to the voice of the oppressor. I am wasting fast away. If he haste not to catch the shadow, it will be gone.–

'The people whom he has appointed to guard his poor prisoner, no longer watch me as they once did. It is useless now. A few short steps and my feeble limbs bend to the earth, reminding me whither I am hastening.–

'When I am gone, Mary will carry you the ringlets which you were wont to twine round your finger. Send one of them to her who should have been my sister; but give not any to my own Montague, for he will pine over them when he might be happy in some new connection. Yet tell him that I loved him to the end. I believe he sometimes doubted of my love; but tell him that I bore him a firm affection. Passion is unfit for the things of this world.–

'I have a letter from my enemy. In two days more.–

'I have a knife concealed in my bosom. All night it is hidden beneath my pillow; and when my weary eyes close for a moment, I grasp it, and the chill touch rouses me again. Mine own dear friend, did you think when first you taught me to join my little hands in prayer, that these hands should be stained with murder?–

'Is it a crime to die when I can no longer live with innocence? When there is no escape but in the grave, is it forbidden to hide me there? My mind grows feeble now. I cannot discern between good and evil.–

'Why is my soul bowed down to the dust, as if the fountain of compassion were sealed? I will yet trust Him who is the helper of those who have no help in man. It may be that he will melt the heart of my enemy, and move him to let me die in peace. Or perhaps even the sight of my persecutor may be permitted to burst the rending heart – to scare the trembling spirit from its prison.–

'This day is my last, and it is closing now! The silence of midnight is around me. Ere it again return a deeper night shall close for me, and the weary pilgrim shall sink to rest. It is time that I loosen me from the earth; I will not give my last hours to this land of shadows. Then fare you well, mine own dear friend! You first pointed my wishes to that better world where I shall not long wait your coming. And far thee well, mine own Montague! Take comfort. I was not fit to linger here; for I had desires that earth could not satisfy; and thirstings after a perfection which this weak heart could not attain. Farewell – I will look back no more.'

HARGRAVE'S LETTER TO LAURA.

'My dearest Laura – The tantalizing business which has so long thwarted my wishes will still detain me for two days. Your gentle mind cannot imagine what this delay costs me. My only recompense is, that it affords me an opportunity of shewing you somewhat of that consideration with which I could always wish to treat you. I willingly forego the advantage of surprise for the sake of allowing you to exercise that decision which you are so well qualified to use discreetly. You know Laura how I have doated on you. For near four long years you have been the desire of my soul; and now that my happy daring has placed me within reach of my utmost wishes, I would fain attain them without distress to you. This is no time for concealment; and you must pardon me if I am explicit with you. I have known the disposition of Lady Pelham's fortune from the hour when it was made. You know that with all my faults I am not sordid; but circumstances have rendered money necessary to me. Except in the event of Lord Lincourt's death, I cannot return to England otherwise than as your husband. I will own, too, dearest Laura, that after all I have done, and all that I may be compelled to do, I dare not trust for pardon to your pity alone. I must interest your duty in my cause. Consider your situation, then, my beloved, and spare me the pain of distressing you. I have watched you, implored you, pined for you – I have borne your coldness, your scorn. I have ventured my life to obtain you. Judge whether I be of a temper to be baulked of my reward. You must be mine, bewitching Laura. No cool, insulting, plausible pretender can cheat me of you now. Trackless woods divide you from all human kind. I have provided against the possibility of tracing your retreat. It rests with you then to choose whether you will bless my love with a willing and honourable reward, or force me to extort the power of bestowing obligation. My charming Laura, for now indeed I may call you mine, pardon, in consideration of its sincerity, the abrupt language I am compelled to hold. – One thing more. In three weeks I must return hither. The engagement of your British attendants expires before that time. I cannot for a moment allow myself to suppose that you will prefer a hopeless solitary exile to the reparation which I shall even then be so anxious to make; to the endearments of a fond husband, of an impassioned lover; to the envy and the homage of an admiring world. Suffer me rather, dear lovely girl, to exult in the hope that you will receive, without reluctance, the man to whom fate assigns you, and that you will recal somewhat of the tenderness you once confessed for your own ever-devoted,

'VILLIERS HARGRAVE.'

LAURA'S ANSWER

(sent with the foregoing to Mrs Douglas:)

'I thought my spirit had been broken, crushed never more to rise. Must the glow of indignation mingle with the damps of death? But I will not upbraid you. The language of forgiveness best befits me now. The measure of your injuries to me is almost full; while those which you have heaped upon yourself are yet more deep and irreparable. My blasted fame, my life cut off in its prime, even the horrible dread that has overwhelmed me, are nothing to the pangs of hopeless remorse, the unaccepted struggle for repentance. – Yet a little while, and this darkness shall burst into light ineffable. Yet a little while, and this sorrow shall be as the remembrance of a troubled dream. But you – Oh Hargrave, have pity on yourself!

'It was not to warn, it was to plead with you, that I won on my knees the consent of your messenger to bear my reply. I will strive to hope; for you were not always pitiless. I have seen you feel for the sufferings of a stranger, and have you no mercy for me? Alas! in those pitying tears I saw you shed, began this long train of evil; for then began my base idolatry, and justly have you been made the instrument of my punishment.

'My mind wanders. I am weaker than a child. Oh Hargrave, if you have human pity let the feeble spark expire in peace. Here, where no Christian footstep shall hallow the turf that covers me, nor song of Christian praise rise near my grave, here let me lay me down and die – and I will bless you that I die in peace. I dare not spend my parting breath in uttering unholy vows, nor die a voluntary partner in your crimes. Nor would I, had my life been prolonged, have joined to pollution this dust, which, perishable as it is, must rise to immortality – which, vile as it is, more vile as it soon may be, shall yet "put on incorruption." Why then should you come hither? Will it please you to see this poor piece of clay, for which you have ventured your soul, faded to an object of horror? – cast uncoffined into the earth, robbed of the decencies which Christians pay even to the worst of sinners? When you look upon my stiffened corpse will you then triumph in the security of your possession? Will you again exult in hope when you turn from my grave and say, "here lies the wretch whom I have undone!"

'Come not I charge you, if you would escape the anguish of the murderer. When did the evil of your deeds stop within your first intention? Do not amuse your conscience with the dream of reparation. I am fallen indeed, ere you dare insult me with the thought! Will you wed the dead? Or could I outlive your injuries, think you that I would sink so low as to repay them with myself? – reward with vows of love a crime more black than murder! Though my name, already degraded through you, must no more claim alliance with the good and worthy, think you that I would bind myself before heaven to a wretch who owed his very life to my undeserved mercy?

Inhuman! Your insults have roused the failing spirit. Yet I must quell these last stirrings of nature. Instant, full, and free must be my forgiveness; for such is the forgiveness which I shall soon require.

'Perhaps, as now you seem to think me fit for any baseness, you will suppose my forebodings a poor deceit to win you from your purpose. See then if you can trace in these unsteady lines the vigour of health. Ask him who bears them to you, how looks now the face which you call lovely? Ask him if the hand which gave this letter looks soft and graceful now? I love to gaze upon it. It bids me hope, for it is like no living thing. Inquire minutely. Ask if there remains one charm to lure you on to farther guilt. And if death has already seized on all, if he has spared nothing to desire, will you yet hurry him on his prey? You have made life a burden too heavy for the weary frame. Will you make death too dreadful to be endured? Will you add to its horrors till nature and religion shrink from it in agony.

'I cannot plead with you as I would. My strength fails. My eyes are dim with weeping. Oh grant that this farewell may be the last – that we may meet no more till I welcome you with the joy which angels feel over the sinner that repenteth.'

The whole of the night preceding Hargrave's arrival, was passed by Laura in acts of devotion. In her life, blameless as it had appeared to others, she saw so much ground for condemnation, that, had her hopes rested upon her own merit, they would have vanished like the sunshine of a winter storm. Their support was more mighty; and they remained unshaken. The raptures of faith beamed on her soul. By degrees they triumphed over every fear; and the first sound that awoke the morning, was her voice raised in a trembling hymn of praise.

Her countenance elevated as in hope; her eyes cast upwards; her hands clasped; her lips half open in the unfinished adoration; her face brightened with a smile, the dawn of eternal day – she was found by her attendant. Awe-struck, the woman paused, and at a reverend distance gazed upon the seraph; but her entrance had called back the unwilling spirit from its flight; and Laura, once more a feeble child of earth, faintly inquired whether her enemy were at hand. Mary answered that her master was not expected to arrive before the evening; and entreated that Laura would try to recruit her spirits, and accept of some refreshment. Laura made no opposition. She unconsciously swallowed what was placed before her; unwittingly suffered her attendant to lead her abroad; nor once heeded ought that was done to her, nor ought that passed before her eyes, till her exhausted limbs found rest upon the trunk of a tree, which lay mouldering near the spot where its root was sending forth a luxuriant thicket.

The breath of morning blew chill on the wasted form of Laura, while it somewhat revived her to strength and recollection. Her attendant seeing her shiver in the breeze, compassionately wrapped her more closely in her cloak, and ran to seek a warmer covering. 'She feels for my bodily wants,' said Laura. 'Will she have no pity for the sufferings of the soul? Yet what relief can she afford: What help is there for me in man? Oh be Thou my help who art the guard of the defenceless! Thou who canst shield in every danger – Thou who canst guide in every difficulty!'

Her eye rested as it fell, upon a track as of recent footsteps. They had brushed away the dew, and the rank grass had not yet risen from their pressure. The unwonted trace of man's presence arrested her attention; and her mind, exhausted by suffering, and sharing the weakness of its frail abode, admitted the superstitious thought that these marks afforded a providential indication for her guidance. Transient animation kindling in her frame, she followed the track as it wound round a thicket of poplar; then, suddenly recollecting herself, she became conscious of the delusion, and shed a tear over her mental decay.

She was about to return, when she perceived that she was near the bank of the river. Its dark flood was stealing noiseless by, and Laura, looking on it, breathed the oft repeated wish that she could seek rest beneath its waves. Again she moved feebly forward. She reached the brink of the stream, and stood unconsciously following its course with her eye; when a light wind stirring the canes that grew down to the water edge, she beheld close by her an Indian canoe. With suddenness that mocks the speed of light, hope flashed on the darkened soul; and, stretching her arms in wild ecstasy, 'Help, help,' cried Laura, and sprung towards the boat. A feeble echo from the further shore alone returned the cry. Again she called. No human voice replied. But delirious transport lent vigour to her frame. She sprung into the bark; she pressed the slender oar against the bank. The light vessel yielded to her touch. It floated. The stream bore it along. The woods closed around her prison. 'Thou hast delivered me!' she cried; and sunk senseless.

A meridian sun beat on her uncovered head ere Laura began to revive. Recollection stole upon her like the remembrance of a feverish dream. As one who, waking from a fearful vision, still trembles in his joy, she scarcely dared to hope that the dread hour was past, till raising her eyes she saw the dark woods bend over her, and steal slowly away as the canoe glided on with the tide. The raptures of fallen man own their alliance with pain, by seeking the same expression. Joy and gratitude too big for utterance long poured themselves forth in tears. At length returning composure permitting the language of extasy, it was breathed in the accents of devotion; and the lone wild echoed to a song of deliverance.

The saintly strain rose unmixed with other sound. No breeze moaned through the impervious woods. No ripple broke the stream. The dark shadows trembled for a moment in its bosom as the little bark stole by, and then reposed again. No trace appeared of human presence. The fox peeping from the brushwood, the wild duck sailing stately in the stream, saw the unwonted stranger without alarm, untaught as yet to flee from the destroyer.

The day declined; and Laura, with the joy of her escape, began to mingle a wish, that, ere the darkness closed around her, she might find shelter near her fellow beings. She was not ignorant of the dangers of her voyage. She knew that the navigation of the river was interrupted by rapids. A cataract which broke its course had been purposely described in her hearing. She examined her frail vessel and trembled; for life was again become precious, and feeble seemed her defence against the torrent. The canoe, which could not have contained more than two persons, was constructed of a slender frame of wood, covered with the bark of the birch. It yielded to the slightest motion, and caution was necessary to poise in it even the light form of Laura.

Slowly it floated down the lingering tide; and, when a pine of larger size or form more fantastic than his fellows enabled her to measure her progress, she thought that through wilds less impassible her own limbs would have borne her more swiftly. In vain behind each tangled point did her fancy picture the haunt of man. Vainly amid the mists of eve did she trace the smoke of sheltered cottages. In vain at every winding of the stream she sent forward a longing eye in search of human dwelling. The narrow view was bounded by the dark wilderness, repeating ever the same picture of dreary repose.

The sun went down. The shadows of evening fell; not such as in her happy native land blend softly with the last radiance of day; but black and heavy, harshly contrasting with the light of a naked sky reflected from the waters, where they spread beyond the gloom of impending woods. Dark, and more dark the night came on. Solemn even amid the peopled land, in this vast solitude it became more awful. Ignorant how near the place of danger might be, fearing to pursue darkling her perilous way, Laura tried to steer her light bark to the shore, intending to moor it, to find in it a rude resting place, and in the morning to pursue her way. Laboriously she toiled, and at length reached the bank in safety; but in vain she tried to draw her little vessel to land. Its weight resisted her strength. Dreading that it should slip from her grasp and leave her without means of escape, she re-entered it, and again glided on in her dismal voyage. She had found in the canoe a little coarse bread made of Indian corn; and this, with the water of the river, formed her whole sustenance. Her frame worn out with previous suffering, awe and fear at last yielded to fatigue; and the weary wanderer sunk to sleep.

It was late on the morning of a cloudy day, when a low murmuring sound stealing on the silence awoke Laura from the rest of innocence. She listened. The murmur seemed to swell on her ear. She looked up. The dark woods still bent over her. But they no longer touched the margin of the stream. They stretched their giant arms from the summit of a precipice. Their image was no more reflected unbroken. The gray rocks which supported them but half lent their colours to the rippling water. The wild duck, no longer tempting the stream, flew screaming over its bed. Each object hastened on with fearful rapidity, and the murmuring sound was now a deafening roar.

Fear supplying super-human strength, Laura strove to turn the course of her vessel. She strained every nerve; she used the force of desperation. Half-hoping that the struggle might save her, half-fearing to note her dreadful progress, she toiled on till the oar was torn from her powerless grasp, and hurried along with the tide.

The fear of death alone had not the power to overwhelm the soul of Laura. Somewhat might yet be done perhaps to avert her fate, at least to prepare for it. Feeble as was the chance of life, it was not to be rejected. Fixing her cloak more firmly about her, Laura bound it to the slender frame of the canoe. Then commending herself to heaven with the fervour of a last prayer, she, in dread stillness, awaited her doom.

With terrible speed the vessel hurried on. It was whirled round by the torrent – tossed fearfully – and hurried on again. It shot over a smoothness more dreadful than the eddying whirl. It rose upon its prow. Laura clung to it in the convulsion of terror. A moment she trembled on the giddy verge. The next, all was darkness!

CHAPTER XXXIV

———•———

WHEN Laura was restored to recollection, she found herself in a plain decent apartment. Several persons of her own sex were humanely busied in attending her. Her mind retaining a confused remembrance of the past, she inquired where she was, and how she had been brought thither. An elderly woman, of a prepossessing appearance, answered with almost maternal kindness, 'that she was among friends all anxious for her safety; begged that she would try to sleep; and promised to satisfy her curiosity when she should be more able to converse.' This benevolent person, whose name was Falkland, then administered a restorative to her patient; and Laura, uttering almost incoherent expressions of gratitude, composed herself to rest.

Awakening refreshed and collected, she found Mrs Falkland and one of her daughters still watching by her bed-side. Laura again repeated her questions, and Mrs Falkland fulfilled her promise, by relating that her husband, who was a farmer, having been employed with his two sons in a field which overlooked the river, had observed the canoe approach the fall; that seeing it too late to prevent the accident, they had hurried down to the bed of the stream below the cataract, in hopes of intercepting the boat at its reappearance: That being accustomed to float wood down the torrent, they knew precisely the spot where their assistance was most likely to prove effectual: That the canoe, though covered with foam for a moment, had instantly risen again, and that Mr Falkland and his sons had, not without danger, succeeded in drawing it to land. She then, in her turn, inquired by what accident Laura had been exposed to such a perilous adventure; expressing her wonder at the direction of her voyage, since Falkland farm was the last inhabited spot in that district. Laura, mingling her natural reserve with a desire to satisfy her kind hostess, answered, that she had been torn from her friends by an inhuman enemy, and that her perilous voyage was the least effect of his barbarity. 'Do you know,' said Mrs Falkland, somewhat mistaking her meaning, 'that to his cruelty you partly owe your life; for had he not bound you to the canoe, you must have sunk while the boat floated on.' Laura heard with a faint smile the effect of her self-possession; but considering it as a call to pious gratitude rather than a theme of self-applause, she forbore to offer any claim to praise; and suffered the subject to drop without further explanation.

Having remained for two days with this hospitable family, Laura expressed a wish to depart. She communicated to Mr Falkland her desire of returning immediately to Europe; and begged that he would introduce her to some asylum where she might wait the departure of a vessel for Britain. She expressed her willingness to content herself with the poorest accommodation, confessing that she had not the means of purchasing any of a higher class. All the wealth, indeed, which she could command, consisted in a few guineas which she had accidentally had about her when she was taken from her home; and a ring which Mrs De Courcy had given her at parting. Her hosts kindly urged her to remain with them till they should ascertain that a vessel was immediately to sail, in which she might secure her passage; assuring her that a week scarcely ever elapsed without some departure for her native country. Finding, however, that she was anxious to be gone, Mr Falkland himself accompanied her to Quebec. They travelled by land. The country at first bore the characters of a half redeemed wilderness. The road wound at times through dreary woods, at others through fields where noxious variety of hue bespoke imperfect cultivation. At last it approached the great river; and Laura gazed with delight on the ever-changing, rich and beautiful scenes which were presented to her view; scenes which she had passed unheeded when grief and fear veiled every prospect in gloom. One of the nuns in the Hotel Dieu was the sister of Mrs Falkland; and to her care Mr Falkland intended to commit his charge. But before he had been an hour in the town, he received information that a ship was weighing anchor for the Clyde, and Laura eagerly embraced the opportunity. The captain being informed by Mr Falkland, that she could not advance the price of her passage, at first hesitated to receive her; but when, with the irresistible candour and majesty that shone in all her looks and words, she assured him of his reward, when she spoke to him in the accents of his native land, the Scotsman's heart melted; and having satisfied himself that she was a Highlander, he closed the bargain, by swearing that he was sure he might trust her. With tears in her eyes, Laura took leave of her benevolent host; yet her heart bounded with joy as she saw the vessel cleaving the tide, and each object in the dreaded land of exile swiftly retiring from her view. In a few days that dreaded land disappeared. In a few more the mountains of Cape Breton sunk behind the wave. The brisk gales of autumn wafted the vessel cheerfully on her way; and often did Laura compute her progress.

In a clear frosty morning towards the end of September, she heard once more the cry of land! – now music to her ear. Now with a beating breast she ran to gaze upon a ridge of mountains indenting the disk of the rising sun; but the tears of rapture dimmed her eyes, when every voice at once shouted, 'Scotland!'

All day Laura remained on deck, oft measuring, with the light splinter, the vessel's course through the deep. The winds favoured not her impatience. Towards evening they died away, and scarcely did the vessel steal along the liquid mirror. Another and another morning came, and Laura's ear was blessed with the first sounds of her native land. The tolling of a bell was borne along the water; now swelling loud, and now falling softly away. The humble village church was seen on the shore; and Laura could distinguish the gay colouring of her country-women's Sunday attire, – the scarlet plaid, transmitted from generation to generation, pinned decently over the plain clean coif, – the bright blue gown, the trophy of more recent housewifery. To her every form in the well-known garb seemed the form of a friend. The blue mountains in the distance, – the scattered woods, – the fields yellow with the harvest, – the river sparkling in the sun, seemed, to the wanderer returning from the land of strangers, fairer than the gardens of Paradise.

Land of my affections! – when 'I forget thee, may my right hand forget her cunning!' Blessed be thou among nations! Long may thy wanderers return to thee rejoicing, and their hearts throb with honest pride when they own themselves thy children!

The vessel at last cast anchor, and all was cheerful bustle; every one eager to hurry ashore. Some hastened to launch the boat; some ran below to seek out the little offerings of love which they had brought for their friends. Never had Laura heard sound so animating as the cry of 'all ready!' followed by the light short stroke of the oar that sent her swiftly forward. Many a wistful glance did the rowers turn. 'There's mother on the pier-head!' cried one. 'I see Annie and the bairns!' cried another; and the oar was plied more swiftly. They landed. The shout of joy, and the whisper of affection were exchanged on every side. Laura stood back from the tumult, breathing a silent thanksgiving on behalf of herself and her companions. 'Poor lassie!' said the captain, approaching her, 'is there naebody to welcome thee? Come! I'm going up to Glasgow the night to see my wife and the owners; and if ye like to gang wi' me, ye'll be sae far on your way to your friends.' Laura thankfully accepted the proposal; and the fly-boat being just about to sail up the river, she placed in it the little packet of necessaries which she had collected at Quebec; and accompanied the good-natured sailor to his home.

She was kindly received by his wife and daughter, and furnished wtih the best accommodations they could command. The next morning she gave the captain a draft for the price of her passage; and producing her purse and Mrs De Courcy's ring, offered them as further security; saying, that as she was now in her own country, a few shillings would support her till she reached her friends, since she might travel to Perthshire on foot. The sailor, however, positively refused to accept of any thing more than the draft, swearing that if he were deceived in Laura, he would never trust woman again. He then, at her desire, procured her a seat in the stage-coach, and once more she proceeded on her journey.

At a small village, a few miles from Perth, she desired to be set down. A by-road led from the village to Mr Douglas's parish. The distance was said to be only seven miles; and Laura, forgetting the latitude allowed to Scotish measurement, thought she might easily reach the parsonage before night-fall. Leaving her little parcel at the village, she hastened forward; – now pausing a moment as some well-known peak or cliff met her eye, now bounding on with the light step of joy. She pictured the welcome of affection; already she saw the mild countenance of her early friend; already she felt the embrace of love.

Darkness surprised her when she had yet much of her journey to perform, and had shrouded every object ere she reached the well-known gate, and saw across the narrow lawn the lights streaming from the window. She stopped – fear stealing on her joy. In five months what changes might not have happened! Her friend, her mother, might be ill, might be dead! So must weak men mitigate with the prospect of evil the transports which belong not to his inheritance! She again proceeded. She entered the hall. The parlour door was open. A group of cheerful faces appeared, ruddy with youth and health; but Laura's eye rested on one of more mature, more interesting grace, – one shaded with untimely silver, and lighted up with milder fires. She remained motionless, fearing to surprise her friend by too suddenly appearing, till one of the girls, observing her, exclaimed, in a transport of joy, 'Laura! Mamma! Laura!' Mrs Douglas sprung from her seat; and the welcome of affection, the embrace of love were reality!

The first burst of gladness was succeeded by the solicitous inquiry, by the interesting narrative; and Laura beguiled her friend of many tears by the story of her sad voyage, her hopeless captivity, her perilous escape. Tears, too, of real bitterness rose to her eyes, at the thought that, although she had escaped from the cruelty of her oppressor, yet its consequences must be lasting as her life; and that she was now pouring her story perhaps into the only ear that would be open to her protestations of innocence. But she would not cloud the hour of joy by calling the attention of her friend to the shade that rested on her prospects; nor diminish her own gratitude for deliverance from more real misfortune, by anticipating the scorns of the world. She uttered not the faintest foreboding of evil, but continued with serene cheerfulness to 'charm as she was wont to do,' till at a late hour the friendly party separated for the night.

Weary as she was, Laura could not rest. She had a task to perform too painful to be thought of with indifference. It was necessary to write to De Courcy; and to damp all the pleasure which a knowledge of her safety would convey, by retracting engagements wich had been made when her alliance inferred no dishonour. She well knew that De Courcy himself, convinced of her innocence, would spurn the idea of forsaking her in misfortune, – of giving, by his desertion, a sanction to calumny. And should she take advantage of his honour and his love to fix in his heart the incurable anguish of following to the wife of his bosom the glance of suspicion or of scorn! The world's neglect was trivial in her estimation. Even its reproach might be endured by one who could appeal from its sentence to a higher tribunal. But what should ease the heart whose best affections were turned to poison by domestic shame; the heart jealous of the honour which it could not defend, bleeding at the stab from which it dared not recoil?

Laura had already taken her resolution, and the next day saw it effected. She wrote to De Courcy, detailing minutely every event that had befallen her from the hour of their separation till her landing in Britain. There her narrative closed. She told not in what spot the wanderer had found rest. She did not even intimate in what part of the island she had disembarked, lest it should furnish a clue to her present retreat. Nor did she, by expressions of tenderness and regret, aggravate the pang which she was compelled to inflict. In words like these she proceeded. 'And now, my respected friend, I imagine you are pausing to offer a thanksgiving for yourself and for me. Let it not damp your just gratitude that somewhat of evil is permitted to mingle with this signal deliverance. Let not my escape from misfortune the most dreadful be forgotten, even though the world should refuse to believe in that escape. For thus it must be. Known to have been in the power of that bad man, will the harsh-judging world believe me innocent? Will it be believed that he ventured to cast his very life upon my mercy, by dragging me unwilling from my home? So long the sport of his ungoverned passions, will it be believed that I have not even seen him?

'I know it will be difficult to convince you that an unjust sentence can be pronounced against me. Certain yourself of the truth of my story, you imagine that it will find easy credence with others. But even if we could change the nature of man, and teach strangers to judge with the candour of friendship, who shall furnish them with the materials for judging? Not he, who, in corroborating my tale, must publish his own disgrace! Not the weak Laura, who, by a constitutional defect, shrinks even from the eye where she cannot read distrust!

'Consider all this, and you will at once perceive the reasons which induce me to conceal myself from you for a time. Engagements formed under circumstances now so materially changed I cannot consider as binding. You, I fear, may think otherwise, and be hurried on by your generous nature to tempt a fate which that very turn of mind would render insupportable. My own part in this fate I think I can bear. The share which would fall upon you, I own would crush me to the dust. My spirits are not yet what they have been. I am weary of struggling with a perverse heart, ever leading me aside from duty. I will not lend it arms by exposing myself to entreaties and arguments to which I cannot yield without betraying my best friend to anguish unpitied and hopeless; anguish which would bear with double pressure on myself.

'A stain is fallen on my good name, and "the glory has departed from me." Be it so! He who doth all things well hath chosen my lot, and his choice shall be mine. I trust I shall be enabled to act as becomes one who is degraded in the public eye. I have sometimes shrunk from the approbation of the world – that little circle I mean which we are apt to call the world. Now I will hide me from its censure; and shall find in the duties which peculiarly belong to the fallen – the duties of humility, of charity and of devotion – enough to make life still no unpleasing pilgrimage. A good name has been justly likened to a jewel – precious, not necessary. But if you, my dear friend, covet fame for me, look forward to the time when an assembled universe shall behold my acquittal, when a Judge, before whom the assembled universe is as nothing, shall proclaim me for his own.'

This letter Laura accompanied with another, in which she begged Mrs De Courcy's assistance in reconciling her son to the change in his prospects. Both were inclosed by Mr Douglas to a friend in London, who was directed to forward them by post; thus avoiding any trace of the quarter from whence they came.

Her lot thus chosen, Laura began to make arrangements for entering on a mode of life befitting her situation. Fearing that the shaft of slander should glance aside from herself to the friends who still clung to her, she steadily resisted Mrs Douglas's warm invitations to make the parsonage her home. Her father's little farm at Glenalbert had been annexed to one of larger size. The cottage remained untenanted, and thither Laura determined to retire. Her fortune, however far from affluent, she thought would suffice to support the humble establishment which she meant to retain. One servant was sufficient for her who had been accustomed to make few claims on the assistance of others. To obviate the impropriety of living alone while yet extreme youth made even nominal protection valuable, she invited an elderly widow lady, poor, but respectable, to preside in her household. In necessary preparations for her removal to Glenalbert, in affectionate assiduities to the friends with whom she resided, in compensating to her own poor for her long, though involuntary neglect of their claims, Laura sought a refuge from painful reflection; and, if a sigh arose at the review of her altered prospects, she called to mind her deliverance, and regret was exchanged for thankfulness. The vain might have bewailed a seclusion thus untimely, thus permanent; the worldly-minded might have mourned the forfeiture of earthly prosperity; any spirit unsupported by religion must have sunk under unmerited disgrace, embittered by keen sense of shame and constitutional timidity. Laura was a Christian, and she could even at times rejoice that the spirit of vanity was mortified, the temptations of the world withdrawn; even where the blow was more painful, she humbly believed that it was necessary, and thankfully owned that it was kind.

The arrangements for her new establishment were soon completed, and the time came when Laura was to begin her life of seclusion. The day before her intended removal she completed her twentieth year; and Mrs Douglas would have assembled a little group of friends to celebrate the occasion, but Laura steadily opposed it. 'Let not one who is suspected,' said she, 'assume the boldness of innocence! yet since the suspicion wrongs me I will not wear the melancholy of guilt. Give the children a holiday for my sake, and I shall be as playful and as silly as the youngest of them.' The holiday was granted; and Laura, amidst the joyful noisy little company that soon assembled round her, forgot that she was an outcast.

She was busily searching every corner for the hidden handkerchief, the little rogue who had concealed it in his shoe laughing the while and clapping his hands in delight, when she started at the voice of a stranger in the lobby; who was announcing that he had a letter for Mrs Douglas, which he could deliver to no person but herself. The next moment the stranger was shewn in to the room, and Laura with amazement beheld her American attendant. The amazement on his part was still greater. He started, he trembled, he at first shrunk from Laura, then eagerly advancing towards her, 'Bless my soul, Madam!' he exclaimed, 'are you alive? Then Mary's words are true, and the angels watch over you.'

It was some time before the man's astonishment would permit him to declare his errand. At last when his curiosity had been partially satisfied, he was prevailed upon to enter his narrative. 'You may remember, Madam,' said he, addressing himself to Laura, 'it was the morning we expected my master, (though I told Mary, for a make-believe, that he would not come till evening,) that morning Mary took you out and left you; for which I was mortal angry with her, for my mind misgave me that some mischief would come of it. So she ran down to the place where she left you sitting, but you were not there. Then she looked all about, but she could see you nowhere. She was afraid to go among the canes, for fear of the rattlesnakes, so she ran home and told me. So I went with her, scolding her to be sure all the way. Well we sought and sought, till at last, half in the water, and half on the shore, we found your hat and then to be sure none of us never doubted that you had drowned yourself; and Mary cried and wrung her hands like a distracted creature, saying that my master was a wicked wretch that had broken your heart, and often and often she wished that we could find you to give you Christian burial, for she said she was sure your ghost would never let her rest in her bed. But we had no drags, nor anything to take you up with out of the water. Well, we were just in the midst of all our troubles when my master came. "Well, Robert," says he, in his hearty way, "Where is my angel?" I had not the heart to say a word; so with that Mary ran forward sobbing like a baby, and says she, just off hand, "Miss Montreville is in a watery grave, and I am sure, Sir, some heavy judgment will light on him that drove her to it." So my master stood for a moment thunderstruck, as it were, and then he flew upon us both like a tiger, and shook us till he scarce left breath in us, and swore that it was all a trick, and that he would make us produce you or he would have our lives. So I tried to pacify him the best I could; but Mary answered him, that it was all his own doing, and that he might seek you in the river where he would find your corpse. This put my master quite beside himself; and he catched her up, and flung her from him, just as if she had been a kitten; and then he flew down to the river side, and I followed him, and shewed him where we had found your hat; and explained to him how it was not our fault, for we had both been very civil and given you no disturbance at all, which you know Madam was true. So, close to the place where we found your hat we saw the print of your little shoe in the bank; and when my master saw it he grew quite distracted, crying out that he had murdered you, and that he would revenge you upon a wretch not fit to live (meaning himself, Madam), and so he would have leaped into the river; but by this time one of the servants he brought with him came up, and we forced him back to the house. Then he grew more quiet; and called for Mary, and gave her his purse with all his money, and bid her tell every thing about you, Madam; how you had behaved, and what you had said. So she told him, crying all the while, for she repented from her heart that ever she consented to have any hand in the business. And sometimes he would start away and gnash his teeth, and dash his head against the wall; and sometimes he would bid her go on, that he might run distracted at once and forget all. So she told him that you had written to one Mrs Douglas, in hopes that when you were dead he would take pity on you, (repeating your very words, Madam). Then he asked to see the letter, and he carried it into your room. And there we heard him groaning and speaking to himself, and throwing himself against the walls; and we thought it best to let him come to himself a little and not disturb him. So by and by he called for pen and ink, and I carried them to him, thinking if he wanted to write it was a sign he was growing more calm. Then he continued writing for some time, though now and again we heard him restless as before. At last he opened the door, and called me, "Robert," says he, quite calm and composed like, "if you deliver this packet as directed, you will earn three hundred pounds. But be sure to deliver it with your own hand." I was going to ask him something more about it, for I did not just know what he meant about the £300; but he pushed me out, and shut himself into the room. Then I bethought myself that there was something strange like in his look, and that he was pale, and somehow not like himself. So I went to the kitchen to consult with the rest what we had best do. So I had scarcely got there when I heard a pistol go off, and we all ran and burst open the door, and there we saw my master, Madam, laid out upon Miss Montreville's bed, and the pistol still in his hand; though he was stone dead, Madam, for I suppose the ball had gone right through his heart.'

Laura, dreadfully shocked, and no longer able to listen to this horrible relation, hastened out of the room, leaving Mrs Douglas to hear what yet remained to be told of the history of a man of pleasure!!! The servant proceeded to tell that he and his companions had conveyed their master's body to head-quarters, had seen it buried with military honours, and then had sailed in the first ship for Britain. That remembering the charge to deliver the packet with his own hand, he had come down to Scotland on purpose to execute his trust; and hoped that Mrs Douglas would fulfil his master's promise. He then delivered the packet, which Mrs Douglas opening in his presence, found to contain a bill for £300 in favour of Robert Lewson, not payable without her signature; the two letters which Laura had written during her exile; and the following lines, rendered almost illegible by the convulsive startings of the hand which traced them.

'The angel whom I have murdered, was an angel still. "The

destroyer came," but found her not. It was her last wish that you should know her innocence. None can attest it like me. She was purer than heaven's own light. She loved you. There is another, too, whom she protests that she loved to the last – but it was me alone whom she loved with passion. In the anguish of her soul she called it "idolatry;" and the words of agony are true. But I, like a base fool, cast her love away for the heartless toyings of a wanton! And shall I, who might have been so blest, live now to bear the gnawings of this viper – this hell never to be escaped?

'She has said that she must go to the grave laden with shame; that her name is degraded through me. Once more, then, I charge you, proclaim her innocence. Let no envious tongue presume to stain that name. Let it be accounted holy. I will save what she loved better than life, though I have persecuted her – driven her to death – forced her to hide in the cold waters all that was loveliest in woman. She says that she will meet you in heaven, – and it must be true, for falsehood was a stranger to her lips. Then tell her that he who was her murderer, was her avenger too. It is said that self-destruction is the last – worst crime. In others it may be so. In me it is but justice; for every law condemns the murderer to die. He who destroyed that angel should die a thousand deaths. Justice shall be speedy.

'VILLIERS HARGRAVE.'

Mrs Douglas had no sooner read the contents of her packet, than she hastened to communicate them to Laura. The horror inspired by Hargrave's letter, and the dreadful destiny of the writer, did not render her insensible to the pleasure of being empowered to clear, beyond a doubt, the fame of her young friend. Laura was, however, for the present, in no state to share her joy. She could only weep; and, trembling, pray that she might be enabled to guard against the first beginnings of that self-indulgence, whose end is destruction!

Mrs Douglas at last found means to rouse her by naming De Courcy, and reminding her of his right to immediate information of this happy change in her situation. Laura, as superior to coquetry as to any other species of despicable cruelty, instantly sat down to communicate the news to her lover. To her plain unvarnished tale, she added copies of the letters which attested her innocence, with Lewson's account of the names and addresses of those persons who had been employed to carry her from England.

Evening was drawing on before Laura had finished her task; and, desirous to recruit her spirits before she joined the family circle, she stole abroad to breathe the reviving air of her native hills. She had crossed the little lawn, and was opening the gate, when, seeing a carriage drive quickly up, she drew back. The carriage stopped. She heard an exclamation of joy, and the next moment she was pressed to the heart of De Courcy.

Laura first recovered utterance. 'What happy chance,' she cried, 'has brought you here just at the moment when I am permitted to rejoice that you are come?' 'Ah, Laura,' said De Courcy, 'could I know that you were alive and in Britain, yet make no effort to find you? I was convinced that Mrs Douglas must know your retreat. I was sure that I could plead so that no human heart could resist my entreaties. And now I have found thee, I will never leave thee but with life.'

The little shrubbery walk which led round the lawn to the parsonage was not half a quarter of a mile in length, yet it was an hour before the lovers reached the house; and before Laura presented De Courcy to her friends she had promised that in one week she would reward his tried affection; and had settled, that after they had spent a few days in delightful solitude at Glenalbert, she would accompany him to Norwood.

Laura has now been for some years a wife; and the same qualities which made her youth respectable, endear her to the happy partner of her maturer life. She still finds daily exercise for her characteristic virtue; since even amidst the purest worldly bliss self-denial is necessary. But the tranquil current of domestic happiness affords no materials for narrative. The joys that spring from chastened affection, tempered desires, useful employment, and devout meditation, must be felt – they cannot be described.

THE END.

Belinda

Maria Edgeworth

Introduced by Eva Figes

Like her contemporary, Jane Austen, Maria Edgeworth concealed beneath a seemingly effortless lightness of touch and humour, an awareness of the poignancy and sadness of everyday domestic existence.

Written in 1811, this is the story of Belinda and the two men who court her.

Around this conventional literary cliché, Maria Edgeworth has woven an extraordinarily complex and powerful narrative, so that a romantic comedy of manners becomes, in her hands, a rich and subtle counterpoint of themes – love, fidelity, passion, cynicism and the position of women in early nineteenth-century society – with characters all equally memorable, whether virtuous like Belinda, 'wicked' like Lady Delacour, or feckless like Vincent.

Paper £4.95   Reprint Fiction/Mothers of the Novel
0 86358 074 2   May/June 1986